Tehano

"Comanche Brave," W.S. Soule folder (CN 00081), the Center for American History, The University of Texas at Austin.

Tehano

A Novel by Allen Wier

SOUTHERN METHODIST
UNIVERSITY PRESS
Dallas

Requests for permission to reproduce material from this work should be sent to:
Rights and Permissions
Southern Methodist University Press
PO Box 750415
Dallas, Texas 75275-0415

Cover photograph: "Tom Bird and John James Haynes, both of Blanco County, Texas; taken in studio, 1868." From the collection of Lawrence T. Jones III. The cover design is a fictional creation from an original ambrotype case and an albumen print carte de visite.

Jacket and text design by Tom Dawson.

Lightning arrester illustration on dedication page by Donnie Wier.

Library of Congress Cataloging-in-Publication Data
    Wier, Allen, 1946-
        Tehano : a novel / by Allen Wier. — 1st ed.
            p. cm.
        ISBN 0-87074-506-9 (alk. paper)
            1. Texas—Fiction. I. Title.

    PS3573.I355T44 2006
    813'.54—dc22

                                                                    2005057536

Printed in the United States of America on acid-free paper

10   9   8   7   6   5   4   3   2   1

For my son, Wesley,
who rides with me always.

Also by Allen Wier

FICTION

Blanco
Things About to Disappear
Departing as Air
A Place for Outlaws

EDITED WORKS

Voicelust: Eight Contemporary Writers on Style
Walking on Water and Other Stories

Contents

Witnesses

GIDEON JONES, a westering young traveler, journal-keeper, and self-taught undertaker.

DORSEY MURPHY, an Indiana farm girl who becomes Blood Arrow.

KNOBBY COTTON, a third-generation slave who escapes with Elizabeth to Texas.

ELIZABETH, a house-slave who becomes Knobby's wife.

ETIENNE, a Cajun trapper who encounters Knobby and Elizabeth in the swamp-lands of South Louisiana.

TWO TALKS, WAHATEWI, a charismatic Comanche warrior with strong medicine.

ALEXANDER WESLEY SPEER, a young New Yorker who runs off and joins the Confederate Army.

CHARLES WESLEY SPEER, Alexander's identical twin, who fights in the Union Army.

ORTEN TRAINER, an opportunist and ne'er-do-well who takes Alexander Speer's name before redeeming himself.

LAURA ETTA MURPHY, a Civil War widow who marries Orten-as-Alexander Speer.

RUDOLPH HERMANN, a German immigrant captured by Comanches who call him **YELLOW RUDOLPH**.

PRETTY, EL PERDIDO, a ruthless Comanchero leader who discovers his Comanche past.

CONSUELA PALOMITA DELGADO, a Mexican peasant who, with her husband Miguel, adopts the Indian baby who grows up to be Pretty.

PORTIS "EYE" GOAR, an uneducated, unscrupulous, but capable cow-handler and rowdy.

MARY THURSTON, an Illinois farmwife who escapes a Comanche raid only to suffer a debasingly dire fate.

JON W. MANCHIP, a Welsh adventurer and amateur practitioner in physic who owns the town of Alhambra.

MRS. CARTER, a classically trained pianist who is Mr. Manchip's barkeep and companion.

Who is the true Tehano? The one whose face is as pale as the moon?
The one with wooly hair and the face of night? The one who puts his bottom in
a blue bag and carries a long knife? The one in the Dutchman tribe?
The brown farmer who talks Mexicano and paws the dry dirt of the
uninhabited regions? If we knew who the Tehano was, we would kill him.
But the Tehano takes different faces as the lizard takes different colors.

Ekasari, Red Dog, Comanche warrior and
civil chief, at Medicine Lodge, 1866

*Tehano or Tehanno from the Spanish tejano (or, feminine, tejana),
a Texan of Mexican descent. After Native Americans, the tejanos were
the earliest inhabitants of Texas, and tejano or tehano or tehanno
became the Comanche term for Texan.*

Prologue: A Cloud of Witnesses

Wherefore seeing we are compassed about with so great a cloud of witnesses,
let us lay aside every weight, and the sin which doth so easily beset us,
and let us run with patience the race that is set before us.

Hebrews 12:1

The Tale and the Journey Begin Together

Just before Portis "Eye" Goar died, he asked Gideon Jones—the itinerant drummer of lightning rods, self-taught undertaker, and fledgling journalist—to reattach his trigger finger. As a hole in his lung filled up with blood, Eye gurgled his last request that he not have to use a stump in gunfights down in Hades. Knobby Cotton—a runaway slave who'd saved Eye's life once in New Orleans and who'd ridden with him all over Texas and half of Mexico—had outdrawn Eye and fired the bullet through his chest. Knobby shot Eye with a Colt's Army six-shooter selected and purchased for the Negro by Eye himself back in Galveston in the winter of 1862.

After Gideon washed Eye's body with Castile's soap in a clear creek, he straightened Eye's limbs and packed cedar sap into the small hole in his chest that came out larger through his back. Gideon emptied the organs and filled them and other body cavities with cedar chips. The sap smoothed over the wound and the wood chips gave off a scent to mask the odors of putrefaction. Years later, an army doctor would show Gideon how to drain a body's blood and pump in a preserving solution of oils and chemicals, but, at the time, he worked on outward appearances using what natural cosmetics were close at hand. He split Eye's shirt up the back so it fit easily about his swollen torso. There would be no parlor viewing, not even any wooden box for Eye, but Gideon strove to restore the look of life. He told himself he was serving the departed, but in truth it was Gideon Jones' vanity that demanded perfection. He worried that the toe he had substituted for Eye's missing finger might be a makeshift readily apparent, but a skillful arrangement of the shirt cuff over the skin where he had affixed toe to finger bone proved to be all that was required. Gideon had traded for Indian warpaints he lightened with cornmeal and applied to cold cheeks to bring back color. Later, during an epidemic, he used warpaint to conceal the yellow tint of the pox, but there's no need to go into detail here about mud pastes, cornmeal, and tree sap for hiding stitched-up, rent skin and filling in wounds, or about how cactus thorns make passable pins for reattachments, or how evaporated gyp water leaves a useful powder for firming flesh, and alkali water (owing to the mineral salts) helps preserve against sun and heat. If you're like most folks, you don't really care to know the gross tricks of a primitive and provincial undertaker.

In all his years as a frontier mortician Gideon Jones' most challenging restoration was the left arm of Alexander Wesley Speer that Orten Trainer gave up to Alexander's twin brother, Charles Wesley, who brought it to Gideon for preparation and to fashion for it a long, narrow coffin. (Without its lid, the little coffin resembled one of the boxes the Germans affix under windowsills in New Braunfels for flowers.)

Orten and Alexander had been friends, had fought side by side in the great war, and both of them had lost their left arms. Gideon had heard differing accounts of Orten's wound and amputation, mostly exaggerated tales of heroism in the field, though he later learned that a duel of honor before the war had cost Ort the arm. Alexander's arm had been a payment for heroism. It was shot off above the elbow during the battle of Franklin, Tennessee, where Confederate blood ran like rainwater down the pike. For more than a year, Orten carried Alexander's arm in a long leather pouch, like an Indian's arrow quiver. Over time, in spite of Ort's keeping it well oiled, Alexander's dead flesh had drawn up and the skin was wrinkled as a prune, hard as a prune pit. The dead flesh had tightened, pulled back from the fingernails, so that they looked as long as claws. Skin tightening on a corpse—flesh drawing the scalp tight beneath the hair, pulling the skin back from fingernails and toenails—is why some who have seen exhumed remains believe hair and nails continue to grow after a body dies. Alexander's shriveled limb was as black as the skin of the former slave Knobby Cotton.

Gideon had heard plenty of stories about wagonloads of arms and legs and worse in the recent long national carnage, so he was not so much surprised to discover that the limb Ort carried was not Ort's own as he was curious to know whether *Ort* knew this, especially since Gideon recalled times he had observed Orten slip the arm from its long pouch to pet and rub away ghostly aches, phantom pains. Much later, Gideon learned that Orten Trainer had taken Alexander's papers and his name after Alexander was shot and killed by a Yankee lieutenant days after the war's windup. To complete the ruse and make his escape and to keep at least part of his promise to bury Alexander in Texas soil, Ort had switched their amputated arms so he could masquerade as Alexander Speer.

Gideon pictured that curious pair before Alexander was killed: one-armed companions, each with his severed limb across his back like an implement, part of his tack and outfit. Gideon pictured Ort and Alexander on a moonlit night taking from long carrying cases their hardened arms and strumming them as strange instruments in a duet, an exorcism of demonic pains, soundless tunes rising with the smoke of their campfire.

But such fancy gets us far ahead in the tale and jumbles up the names of witnesses whose testimonies have not yet been given.

Most folks are hooked on the here and now. This yarn takes a reader to the there and then: a some-time-ago place on the Southwestern Frontier where Gideon Jones and more than a handful of others lived out their last years. Some even managed a tolerable death. An interval of more than a century may have dimmed the glow of their earthly lives, but time's passage hasn't erased memory's portraiture of those here recalled, though their earthly bodies have long departed.

An aspiring journalist, Gideon Jones kept a haphazard record, impressions and recollections of his westward journey, describing the landscapes he passed through and saving the acts, words, and thoughts of those whose bodies he preserved. Gideon presented necromancy turned inside out, preserved with the undertaker's paints and the writer's pen the spirit of the living to call back the past. What he managed to arrest with words testifies not only to his descriptive eye but also to his vision, the range of which may be suggested by the numerous excerpts from Gideon Jones' Journal included in this story of the frontier he traversed.

Like countless others who have suffered the emptiness of unrequited love, Gideon longed most to bring back the joyful anticipation of his first few weeks in the company of Dorsey Murphy. An Indiana farm girl led by fate to cross Gideon's path on the Western frontier, Dorsey mistook Gideon for the desert nomad she had long dreamt of, but an Indian warrior rode into her life and Gideon's, altering their hearts forever.

The love of two former slaves is also recorded here, along with their love of freedom. Knobby Cotton escaped those who would own him with the plantation house-slave Elizabeth, Knobby's intended, and slogged through swampland and desert to make a life with her, though the steadfastness of his affections was tested by a dusky octoroon named Oralia.

The cloud of witnesses that surrounded Gideon Jones included a long-suffering immigrant from Deutschland, Rudolph Hermann, who eventually found a home in the new American frontier but not with the people he had expected. Rudolph truly loved only two people in his life: his young bride, Ottilie, who died before they reached America, and a Comanche boy sent into the world by the midwife who secretly delivered him. Rescued and loved by Rudolph Hermann, this baby was adopted by Mexican peasants, was stolen back by Indians, escaped to be schooled by Mexican priests, and grew to become the Comanchero leader El Perdido. Feared by the ruthless Comanchero traders he oversaw and respected by the Indians, Pretty moved freely between the cultures that were clashing on the high plains of Texas.

When the heroes and villains Gideon Jones described in his journal came together on the Texas frontier, the war that had divided the nation was largely over, but even those who had been far from the bloody battles remained affected in ways large and small. Were one able to ask the settlers, ex-soldiers, cow-handlers, drummers, gamblers, shootists, whores, and preachers their reasons for going west, they would have told different tales. But the pioneers' different accounts would pretty much boil down to the want of new beginnings. Whether they were aware of it or not, they all sought redemption, maybe even salvation.

Out west, these adventurers ran into tribes of Indians, invaders who had beat them there by countless years. The Indians were as varied a group as the pioneers and just as hard to figure. The diversity of the animating forces coexisting, though seldom peaceably, in that unsettled frontier to which they were drawn cannot be exaggerated.

By the time the guns of civil war erupted over Fort Sumter in the East, the plains tribes had all but lost the more protracted Indian wars in the West. Those bands not devoured by the "invisible killing spirits"—the epidemics—of the white skins, had been almost annihilated by constant cavalry attacks. The Indian way of life was being snuffed out. But when the "Blue-Bottom" soldiers were recalled from frontier fighting to civil war in the East, plains Indians flared back to life as quick and deadly as a prairie grass fire. The Indians who reclaimed Texas were the Comanches—Numunuu, or "Our People," as they called one another. The Comanches burned with a vengeance.

Brutal as the Eastern battles of civil war were, they were no more savage than the Indian wars. Forted up, Western settlers fed on fear and hatred. With mining camps abandoned, stage stations burned out, telegraph lines pulled down, the vast territories between Fort Leavenworth and the Rockies again became the unapproachable dominion of plains Indians. In Texas, where no competent troops remained to resist them, Comanches drove back the entire frontier close to two hundred miles. During the four years of the Civil War, twenty years of settlement were abandoned to Comanche terror.

The Comanches seemed (they felt this, too) to have sprung up from the land itself, land they held sway over for only a few generations. During their time of strength, the Comanches crossed paths with many other peoples in the American Southwest. Met, but not melded. Having no single, unifying story, Americans use the figure of a melting pot and brag about their differences. The conceit of a crucible works better, a crucible in which the temperature does not quite reach the melting or fusing point, but gets hot enough to cause calcination, or reduction.

In the decade immediately following the Civil War, the Texas frontier was the bloody scene of final combat between Comanches and those they called Tehanos. Unlike the war that had recently concluded at Appomattox, the bloodshed in Texas was not for the endurance of a nation, but for the life of a people. Fate brought those whose stories are here recalled to the Texas frontier during this death-struggle, and love kept some of them there. Love managed to flower alongside violence, though on the frontier love took longer. Several witnesses must be called in order to unspool the fine thread that binds hearts together. Before love, came hate. All of them on that frontier, willingly or not, experienced the last violent thrusts of an inevitable clash that would decide who survived, Numunuu, Tehano, or Norteamericano. The stakes could not have been higher.

Who's to say who knows another best—the mother who births him, the brother who grows up with him, the medicine man who names his totem, the lover who holds him, the friends who share his sins, the priest who listens to his confessions, the shootist who fires a bullet into his heart, the undertaker who fixes his final smile, or the mourners who stand over his mound? In some lands, one who rescues a life is, thereafter, responsible for it. Do all breasts not rise and fall with the world's one breathing? Are we not answerable for all those we know, accountable for their stories as well as our own? The undertaker Gideon Jones could not restore a soul, but each body, each visage he restored had been shaped by a story. The stories of these pioneers were separate before they were joined. The lives limned here did not run like railway cars straight down a track from origin to destination. They meandered like rivers, twisting back upon themselves and changing the landscape they cut through before they came roiling together. Whether you use the figure of melting pot or of crucible, the nature of this story means that there are different voices to conjure up from different times and different places. Time and space are as twisty as a den of rattlers. Following this tale will be like keeping up with the pea a gypsy hides beneath one of three walnut shells he maneuvers simultaneously on a tabletop. This story is spun not to con, but to entertain. Its only magic lies in poor words—divers descriptions based on memory and guesses, a few good oaths, every now and then an incantation, some conversations that echo yet.

Gideon Jones: The Way West

His Treaty with Chief Bones
(June 1865)

His first day in the true wilderness, miles beyond the protection of civilization, Gideon Jones passed hour after hour traversing a wide undulating ocean of prairie where nothing altered his view. Late into the afternoon, and still he espied no landmark, nothing by which he could gauge his progress. Anxious with anticipation—of desert heat and savage beasts and even-more-savage natives—he resisted feelings of panic, a kind of reverse claustrophobia brought on by the boundless grass and sky that made him feel forgotten by even the Lord above. His oxen and he seemed the only sentient creatures in the universe. But the Creator must have taken Gideon's fear as prayer, for He placed on the distant horizon two dark spots. Gideon turned his wagon directly toward the two tiny shapes. Slowly, steadily they became larger: two stationary humps—not the appearance of an Indian raiding party, he convinced himself. Now the humps appeared shaggy on top—maybe he was approaching two buffaloes. He cleared his Hawken's barrel of dried mud and grass. He was not sure how to dress a buffalo, but he figured he'd skin the hide to save it for cold weather and hack off and roast cuts of the meat until he learned by taste the ones to keep. By the time the unmoving shapes had become a solitary pair of trees, his mouth watered for buffalo steak. When at last he drew beneath their limbs, the horizon was streaked purple and orange. Of a sudden, the trees cried out. Shrieking black leaves lifted—a shimmering cloud of birds—rose clear of the treetops, then sank back into the limbs.

Beneath the raucous feathered trees, his oxen, tired as they were, moved faster, and he saw the pool they had smelled for miles. The water's edge was packed mud bearing animal prints. Beneath the pale-barked trees lay leaves serrated like the blades of knives. Scattered about were hundreds of bones and flat rocks with brown-red streaks he knew, from his stint in a Baltimore asylum, as bloodstains.

He pulled hard against the reins but couldn't slow the team. If this was bad water, his oxen were goners. He knelt at the pool's edge. The mud and bent grass were also stained red. His knee sank in the earth as he cupped a handful of warm water to his nose, wondering what poison water smells like. In the middle of the pool, as deep as their bellies, his oxen stirred brown clouds of water. He swallowed, tasted grass. Grit settled on his tongue and caught between his teeth. He would have to filter the water through his shirttail into his keg and canteen. When the animals had drunk their fill, he managed to get them out of the water and the sucking mud. He unhitched them and, with two lengths of rawhide, hobbled them in tall grass beyond the trees.

"Left Ox, you watch out for Right Ox." The beast lifted its muzzle and showed him what looked to be a questioning frown. "Well, you *are* your brother's keeper. You too, Right Ox. You look after Left as well." Right Ox loudly pulled grass, snorted, and ignored him.

He found enough deadwood under the trees to build a fire, and he boiled a pinch of coffee. There is no twilight out on the frontier. By the time his water boiled, the heavens were full dark, poked through with stars. Closer above, roosting in the trees, the scores of birds ignored his fire. After a while came the loud fall of rain, rain he soon discovered to be the steady droppings of the birds. Of necessity a beast of burden, he took up the yoke of his wagon and pulled it from beneath the birds' sudden storm. Not ready to give in to sleep, he gathered four fallen sticks, bound them together, and set the ends ablaze. Holding the burning fagot above his head, he explored one side of the watering hole. Bleached bones littered the ground and reflected his flickering light as scattered shards of the moon. There were hoofprints he guessed to be buffalo and other prints resembling a dog's, yet larger. In a sudden breeze the sputter of his torch darkened and tilted the earth, and thinking the ground sloped up, he stepped hard only to stumble forward over the same flatness.

When the breeze expired, a flare of light illuminated something he saw for an instant as an ivory harp discarded by a careless angel. He knelt closer to what were the perfect curved bones of a human ribcage disappearing into tall grass. Before he could make any deductions, he parted the grass and stared down at a skull that stared back at him.

He lowered his fagot. The skull lay cushioned in grass, the ribs sunk like the beached prow of a boat into the earth. He, or she, white or black or red, someone small if not young, grimaced in the jerking light, arms and legs stretched out restlessly into grass and dirt, the prairie reclaiming one of its own. He walked back toward the coals of his cookfire, a dying star come to earth a hundred yards away. He collected his pot and tin cup, rehitched his oxen, and brought the wagon alongside his new comrade.

"Right Ox, Left Ox," the words came from deep in his chest and were as breathy as the beasts' mastication. "Come meet a gathering of empty bones."

The bones were mostly intact—one hand was unconnected at the wrist but had not wandered far. One finger was missing altogether but might have been lost long before this place. Gideon wondered why the wild beasts that had frequented this killing ground had not disturbed the skeleton (male—an Indian chief, he decided). Perhaps the sand had hidden it, then, recently, been blown away. It was as if the earth had secreted away these earthly remains that Gideon might discover them and pay them homage. He wondered how long this fellow had waited for his arrival. Out here, sun and wind might rapidly reduce a corpse to bones.

It did not take long to unearth and load the skeleton into his wagonbed. The teeth were uneven and ground down to stubs. Maybe they were the teeth of one who'd hankered as much as Gideon after sweets. The skull revealed no cut marks, so he reckoned his new friend had died with his scalp undisturbed. Gideon's kinship with oxen thus expanded to include the chief in their little prairie family. He speculated whether his hospitality to a skeleton came natural because his own origins were not fully known to him. Orphaned, he had ended up in the Baltimore asylum where he toiled for months and where he grew comfortable with the charms of the dead, preparing many of them for their final journey. No doubt solitude helped incline him toward the mortuary arts. After he came to learn the pleasures of reading and of writing, Gideon marked how he saw undertaking and journal writing as companionable occupations. The first preserves the corporeal, and the second preserves the cerebral.

The fear of savages that had dominated his thoughts at the beginning of his journey had been diminished by day after uneventful day, miles and miles of nobody but himself. Now, this bloodstained ground and the chief's bare bones resurrected that anxiety, and he determined to reclaim the cautiousness he had steadily abandoned. He threw onto the fire the largest fallen tree limb he could find—to build up flames to last long enough for him to sneak away with his entourage what he guessed was three to five miles. Safely moved, he once more unhitched and made fast for the night. He lay down beside his silent bedfellow and slept until the full moon waked him. All around, grass rippled in bone-colored light, seed pods bright as the foam of ocean waves he had read about but never seen. He listened to distant howls he know as coyotes, but in his imagination these sounds became the war cries of savage Indians. He piled up armfuls of dry grass he set aflame and once more put distance between himself and where he had been. At his next mooring place he crawled beneath his wagon to escape the moon's scrutiny and managed only fitful sleep, chased in his dreams by bands of horse-riding skeletons wearing feather headdresses and brandishing bloody hand-axes. Nightmares had so far been Gideon's only compensation for his dealings with the dead.

When he waked, the enormous sky was faintly light in the east—the direction he would have guessed was west, so turned about was he from all his relocations the night just past.

"Well, Chief, how did you sleep?" He examined his bony companion in the light of dawn. "Your cronies rode after my scalp all night long. No doubt you claim credit for my escape." The breeze sang a soft tune over the grass and faintly whistled through tiny gaps between the chief's teeth, giving voice to his assent. "All right, so long as you keep away savages and bad spirits, you can rest your bones in my wagonbed, see the sights with me." Gideon reaffixed the chief's hand and with knife probe and grass brush cleaned out his joints and sockets. "You could use a good washing, but you'll have to wait for the next waterhole."

After a breakfast of beans and coffee, they continued on their way. His Indian passenger was as congenial as his oxen. The wagon bumped and bounced along, and Chief Bones' skull jiggled and rattled, nodding agreement with whatever Gideon said. The skull's yellowed maw was fixed with a look of sage understanding. Having determined he had found the perfect critic, Gideon vowed he would test on the chief, his own Boswell, the effects of impressions he entered in his journal. "Chief, you're welcome to applaud, but should I read you something you don't like, keep your opinion to yourself."

Recollections of Whence He Came

Inspired by his own recent rise to literacy and by the urging of his mentor—a Welshman named Colonel Powell-Hughes who had given him a ledger of blank sheets—Gideon was a traveler with a purpose. Naturally given to close observation, he intended to fill his pages with impressions and meditations of the people and places he encountered on his westward journey. Perhaps he would post some of his writings to newspapers back East. Now that the Civil War was over Gideon figured Americans would be ready to read about anything other than the recent carnage, and if he could fashion stories that made lively reading he might be well remunerated for his efforts.

Gideon Jones' own life was the one he knew best, the one that had always interested him most. He had to go back miles and years to begin his story. His mother, with her last breathing, in 1845 or '46 or '47—he wasn't sure which—named him Gideon, hoping he might be granted the signs and revelations of that biblical judge. Perhaps he yet would be. By the time he was old enough to ask the day and place he was born, his mother was long gone. He prayed she rested in peace. Not even she, so he had been told, ever speculated about his father's identity. Knowing no relatives, he rode the orphan's circuit for a decade, stranger to stranger, then he did a stint in the Baltimore asylum until he was on his own.

His beginning might entertain with the jaunty mood of the picaresque were he not chastened by the tale. He had no gruesome accounts of cruelty, no heart-warming sagas of saintly adoptive parents. Folks had seen him for what he was, a hungry obligation to be neither completely ignored nor fully embraced. Of what was available, he got what could be spared. He began early enough as a jack-of-all-trades (master, as they say, of none). A doctor in the asylum gave Gideon his last name when the doctor had to write it on a piece of paper.

"Gideon what?"

He shrugged.

"Jones." The doctor's pen scratched paper as he spoke. "Rhymes with bones."

And Gideon Jones he became. Perhaps there was reason mixed in that rhyme, some sign of his life to come and of his profession not as journalist or correspondent but as an undertaker of men's bones.

"You look about nine years old."

"Eleven." Gideon liked the two *ones* side-by-side, the rhyme with *Heaven*.

"Ten, even if you're small-sized." And *ten* is what the doctor wrote on the paper, but Gideon felt older. He was born feeling already grown up.

For most of his time in the asylum, he tended the dying. A chore or blessing—years later it seemed to him an amalgam of both—it was not a requirement of his post so much as a duty he assumed, perhaps because the eyes of the dying beseeched him, bade him linger and listen to lost dreams, last wishes, long confessions. Having bid a soul its last good-bye, one inherits the body it leaves behind. An empty corpse houses nothing, but it is the image that matches memories in the living minds of friends and loved ones. The abodes left behind by souls who made their departure from the asylum were often decrepit from suffering and neglect. They deserved what final grace Gideon could provide. In return for the investigation of the restorative arts their earthly bodies allowed him, he attempted to become a rescuer of faces taken away, a caretaker of memory. A simple undertaker, Gideon never claimed to raise the dead, only to preserve their likeness among the living. He knew as well as anyone the limits of the mortuary arts.

Regardless of the atmosphere out of doors, in the asylum the air was heavy and moist. Scant sunlight crept down a narrow corridor to the low-ceilinged room where his charges lay locked away. Flakes off the peeling walls, green as pond scum, fell on bedsheets like mucus coughed up. Dark motes drifted the fetid air, rusty flecks from each hard-earned breath. He ministered to the hopeless. Listened to their addled prayers and lamentations. Took their hands in his and suffered their final grips—tight-curled fingers as stubborn and hard to work loose as the crusted layers of scabs. He took charge of departures, prepared the dead for the final journey. He sponged soapy water from a porcelain enamel basin, white with a red ring around the lip. Suds soaked through oily hair, turned brown as mud in matted armpits and ran down pale arms, down bony legs, and dripped onto the muslin bedsheet a watermark, the brown stain outline of the deceased.

Life in the asylum was a kind of incremental burial. Death in the asylum meant soap and water, cleansing the body of detritus. Attempting to entomb the horrors he witnessed, Gideon shoveled detachment and resisted the lure of cynicism. He was doing an apprenticeship in the shadows of fallen angels.

The first time he ever shaved, it was to draw the blade across the cooling face of a corpse. His first adornment was a silver cross on a thin chain inherited from an inmate scarcely as old as he, dead by banging her head again and again against the floor. He washed her hair, clipped out blood-glued tangles, and, though she died in July, he covered her bare skull with a thick wool cap. The first money he called his own was four silver dollars he took off the lids of twin tots, boys, on the cooling board. He washed them, got their eyes and mouths closed, and tucked them into hospital sheets he wound round each like a mummy's shroud. The twins died in August, so he folded in chunks of ice, then toted the pair down narrow stairs to lie in state in the asylum basement until the city would send a wagon to cart them off.

That's how, after bed check on a cold December night, Gideon made his getaway. Perhaps he could simply have walked out the door. Of the asylum's inmates only the mindless were kept under lock and key, but barred doors and windows fostered fear of doctors and attendants. In the asylum, as in any hospital, months felt like a lifetime. Perhaps an escape suited Gideon's fancy for adventure. He slipped down to the basement—dark and dank, odors of chemicals, hospital waste, and mold, itchy feel of cobwebs, gritty scrape of his shoes on moist brick—where he took Miss Truella Samuels in his arms. Her brain had stopped after three or four years. Her body had lived one day shy of sixteen. He was her first beau. She was the first woman he could call his own, and she was beautiful.

A poet who immortalized beauty wrote for himself the epigraph, "Here lies one whose name was writ in water." When Gideon lived in the asylum, he had not yet received the gift of reading. Perhaps his late-coming to the beauty of words explains the great value he placed on the sublime art of poetry. Not by his poor words could he claim kinship to the poet, but by his love of beauty. Gideon believed that in true beauty there was something timeless, something deathless.

Moonlight spilled down from a small, high basement window, and Miss Samuels' muslin gown glowed. Gideon took her in his arms, and they danced stiffly across the uneven brick floor. Behind a stack of lumber, he bowed appreciatively. Her dance card unfilled, he left her standing, ramrod straight, beautiful but bashful, an eternal wallflower leaned into a black corner. He spun his own cocoon of cotton shroud and lay down, inviting the cold of the grave to enter his limbs and tighten his joints.

The clang of the burial wagon bell woke him before dawn, and two sleepy Negroes lifted and carried him to the wagonbed where they laid him beside poor Miss Samuels. He held his breath until he felt the wagon move, then he slit open one eye to watch the nodding backs of two dark heads. He hoped neither turned and espied the small clouds his breathing made. Between buildings, the sun shone on his eyelids. The bell rang and three more bodies were piled on, two beside and one upon him, heavy as a tree trunk down his length—a giant had surely died the night past. They bounced over rough streets. He wiggled for relief from the weight covering him. With each breath he drew, his chest pushed against the corpse, his expanding lungs drawing in the aura that surrounded the dead.

Hailed by a friend, his conveyers argued whether to leave their cargo unattended to accept an invitation for biscuits and gravy. The smell of coffee and hot animal fat was final persuasion.

"Hey," one Charon said, "*They* ain't going nowhere." His companion laughed low and sweet as they disembarked and hurried off for a brief liberty.

Gideon metamorphosed in a heartbeat and flew away. He pictured the return of those two municipal employees—"They ain't going nowhere"—to a wagon bereft of one of its mute passengers. Though it is wholly possible his form was not missed by either man.

He walked along a trolley line and thence for miles beyond its terminus, where the tracks had risen up to meet and fuse in a steel and log bumper. Finally out of the city, he came to a church where wagons and saddle horses told him it was Sunday morning. He untied and mounted a mule that bore him on his way. When the mule wore out, Gideon sent him back toward home with a switch to his rump. Late in the day, he came to the Potomac River and soon jumped onto a railway car of the Baltimore and Ohio where it slowed for a bend of the river it followed.

The Colonel and His Library

Having journeyed a hundred-forty miles that felt like a thousand, he was in the town of Cumberland in Maryland, a dreary place, steep-sided and shadowy. The sun, dimmed by coaldust, hid behind high hills. On one side of the town was farmland, green patches on a rumpled quilt of hills, from where he looked off at the Blue Ridge, the only sight of beauty in the purlieus of Cumberland. Ere he lighted from the cars, a man walking the tracks asked if he wanted work. Hungry and weary of motion, Gideon declared no one worked harder than he. The man gave him a slip of paper and directed him to a branch railway connecting the town to the mines, nine miles distant.

If he had looked young for ten when he was registered at the asylum, his service there had earned him an older look than the eleven he calculated he was when he told the foreman at the mine he was fourteen.

His job was to carry a small bird down into limbo with him, a candle on his miner's hat sputtering giant shadows onto the rock underworld of the Cumberland mines. If his yellow bird grew still, all the miners were to drop shovel and pick, beat their arms against the dark, and hurry like moths for the light, outrunning, if they could, the gaseous humors that had felled the bright harbinger of death.

A week later, with a fistful of coins, his first pay from the mine, Gideon wandered past Cumberland's brick-front buildings. He stared at his reflection in the window glass of a mercantile store. Covered in coaldust, he appeared as black as a Negro, and where he had wiped his eyes he looked like a raccoon in reverse, his mask as pale as his face was dark. From within the store, a musical voice spoke. A bearded man dressed like a mayor, or at least the preacher of a big church, looked down at Gideon, the man's eyes smiling even as his mouth turned down.

"We've mines in Glamorgan, foul graves for living men," he said.

"In where?"

"Land of the Cymry." The man shook Gideon's black hand as if it were washed clean. "Wales," he said to Gideon's silence.

"Like in Jonah?"

"No, lad, but just as far out in the wide ocean." The man introduced himself as Colonel Luellen Powell-Hughes, a Methodist from South Wales, and said Wales was a country like England and on the same island.

When Gideon asked if he sold soap, the colonel called forth a Chinaman named Win Shu, who led Gideon to a pump and bucket behind the store and gave him soap and a towel. The Chinaman neither smiled nor spoke. He refused Gideon's coins and with a small hand broom brushed layers of coaldust off his clothes.

Colonel Powell-Hughes took Gideon to supper at the St. Nicholas Inn, where, after they had roast chicken and potatoes, he tasted, for the first time, cake and pie and chocolate squares as dark as coaldust. The colonel named the chocolate "bittersweet," and it tasted like what Gideon thought angels might eat in Heaven. These desserts were the beginning of a lifelong addiction. More than once in the years to come, Gideon would ride a rough mount all day for a taste of something sweet. Many a night he'd lie on his blanket bereft of sleep by his longing for the least sample of the confectioner's art.

The colonel ran the mercantile store for the pleasure of being part of the community, but his real business was in warehousing and distribution. He had connections in shipping and freighting and often bought low, but added no more than a reasonable markup. Business was strong. "In fact," he said, "Win Shu and I are overworked. We could use a reliable employee, and you need to see the light of day." The selfsame evening, the kindly Colonel Powell-Hughes hired Gideon, vowing to train him to be chief clerk of the mercantile store.

So Gideon might keep records, the colonel taught him to read, to print, and to figure sums. He spent the next few years in the colonel's tutelage. With an ignorant silver pocket watch that seldom knew the right hour, the colonel showed him how to tell the time, though the colonel seldom operated on a set schedule. The door to his mercantile store was never locked.

"When the first customer comes in, we're open," he said. "When we want our supper, we're closed." With this timeless sense of his days, Gideon served the colonel in any way he asked and benefited from the colonel's instruction and his example. His musical Welsh voice woke Gideon each day and lived in his memory as sweet as any morning songbird. Win Shu brought Gideon breakfast and supper. Nights, he slept undisturbed in a solitary space in back of the store.

The colonel read aloud from his Bible the Book of Judges, wherein the angel of God appears to Gideon's namesake. God empowered that Gideon to deliver the Israelites from the oppression of the Midianites. Not once, but twice, Gideon asked God for a sign, and twice God revealed His will in the signs of the fleece. Gideon Jones wondered yet if his mother, ere she named him, knew the story of the biblical Gideon's victories and of the seventy sons begotten by him from many wives and concubines. If she knew the story, Gideon wondered who told it to her, since he doubted she could read even her own name. He felt sure he was the first of his line to learn words and figures. At the beginning of his studies, he sought companionship more than knowledge and studied hard just to please the colonel. Gideon recalled the colonel's singsong reading as another might recall his mother's voice. Before long the sparks of truth and beauty kindled flames in Gideon's mind and heart, and he read for the pleasure of going wherever words led him.

On Sunday afternoons, Win Shu served tea in the colonel's brick house. The colonel had Gideon read out loud, first from the Scriptures, then Mr. Shakespeare, then the newspapers, then the colonel questioned him. Gideon liked the Old Testament—something about laws and harsh punishment, portents and prophesies, appealed to him and rang true to his brief experiences of life. The colonel embraced the New Testament, Christ's parables and the message of love and possibility.

Of Mr. Shakespeare's works, the colonel loved the sonnets best. Of the plays, the colonel and Gideon both preferred the tragedies. "Englishman or not, the bard has no peer," the colonel said. Politics aside, he praised *Macbeth* for its sense of Scotland and for what he called its uncluttered plot. "Macbeth and his lady image Adam and Eve, with the same disastrous fall for the man who follows temptation into sin."

For news of the times, the colonel favored the New York *Herald* and the Boston *Transcript*, but Gideon liked *Frank Leslie's Illustrated Newspaper*. He reveled in stories out of Nevada about the Comstock Lode and the high life in Virginia City, where there were over one hundred saloons, eight theaters, six variety houses, and many other entertainment establishments such as dance halls. Customers could see, the stories reported, a female performer wearing nothing but a filmy gown. To Win Shu, Gideon confessed that he stared all the way to Nevada hoping to espy such beauty. Virginia City was thick with robbers and shootists, savage Indians were a constant threat, and all the men and some women wore Colt's revolvers. The colonel said prospectors, gamblers, and speculators—all who risked their future to chance or fancy—came more often to ruin than to riches.

He read Gideon a cautionary story about hundreds of businessmen bankrupted in New York by railroad and real estate speculation.

The colonel noted how Gideon squinted and twisted up his face, struggling to read. He had Gideon fitted with gold-framed spectacles that brought the words up close and clear. Then he made rapid progress learning much about this old world. Because of his ignorance, the world was new to him. He burned lamp oil late every night, reading on his narrow bed in the store. His new spectacles flashed yellow light on the dim walls and ceiling as he traveled far in his imagination.

In addition to his Bible, newspapers, and magazines such as *Harper's, Littell's Living Age*, the *Atlantic*, and the *Continental Monthly*, the colonel had a large library to which he gave Gideon access. There he read many books. Among his favorites were *The Life of St. Theresa of Avila*, Emanuel Swedenborg's *Heaven and Its Wonders*, Mary Shelley's *Frankenstein*, and the 1842 edition of the thirteen-volume *Encyclopaedia Americana*. Winter skies dark with rain clouds and coaldust made the glow of his lamp a welcome sun to sit beneath, and he spent many an afternoon in Cumberland not there at all but traipsing wherever books transported him. There are those who disparage a life spent too much in the world of books, and Gideon supposed they might be justified. But for someone such as he, on his own until he met the colonel, the people who lived inside those books were family and friends he could join whenever he desired.

During the third year of their lessons, the colonel attempted to expand Gideon's range by introducing Greek and Latin to his understanding. Confronted with Ovid and Virgil, Gideon felt a dunce. On the page their words always looked like poems, and in the colonel's melodious voice they sounded holy, but Gideon struggled with their wit and shades of meaning. In the years since, those holy poems had often surprised him by coming back the way a bird's song not consciously bidden sometimes echoes and brings back a morning's sun.

The colonel said now that Gideon could read he could go on learning as much as he'd a mind to. In the winter of 1860, he read about the shoemakers' strike in Massachusetts. The newspapers called it a rebellion, a workers' revolution. But most of what he read in the newspapers was about another kind of rebellion in the Southern states, about slavery and the upcoming election. The Democrats split at their convention and didn't nominate anyone. The Constitutional Union party nominated John Bell. The Republicans, Abe Lincoln, whom Gideon admired for being, like himself, a self-schooled man. The Democrat party met again and put up Stephen Douglas. The Southern Democrats followed with John Breckinridge and a proslavery platform. Some speculated war. Gideon told the colonel that with the Democrats divided Lincoln would carry the day. The colonel said that was true and war would come quick behind. In November, Lincoln was elected president with a solid majority in the electoral vote, but not in the popular vote. For some time to come, Gideon studied war.

With the war came the demand for flour and sugar, muslin and wool, shoe leather, iron skillets, and tin plates. When men in blue knocked on their door, there for business with Colonel Powell-Hughes, Gideon felt shamed he was not wearing a uniform, and his desire to join with others burned in his chest. He approached the colonel, told him he'd decided to enlist. The colonel stared so long beyond him, Gideon started to repeat himself when the colonel interrupted. "Aye, son. I had hoped you might be less predictable, but it wasn't fair of me to hope so."

"I can tote my share."

"More, son. More. But you don't deserve a portion of this madness. Though the bloodshed may go on long enough yet that you'll get your share. Stay here. Grow your mind along with your body. Some battleground waits for you—bide your time."

For the next three years Gideon heeded the colonel's advice. Except for the fever pitch of supply and demand and the terrible news they read on Sundays, the fighting kept from their door. The colonel hated the news they read. He'd had his fill of fighting while he was still a young man. He'd come to this country the first time as an enemy. A cornet in the British Army, he survived crushing defeat at the Battle of New Orleans and returned home in time to be sent to fight in the Battle of Waterloo. Eventually, he returned to America as a businessman.

Late in the long national conflict, Congress passed a new Internal Revenue Act increasing levies and introducing a second income tax. Colonel Powell-Hughes talked about returning to Wales. In '64, Lincoln was reelected, defeating General McClellan. The colonel fulfilled military contracts but refused new orders. The last day of the year, he called Gideon to him and offered to take him to Wales as his hireling.

"You're nearly full a man, old enough to make your way. Come with me and see another side of the world."

But Gideon told him he could not abide to be so long afloat with no land in sight. He told the colonel before he saw another side of the world, he had to take a look at this side. Win Shu poured three glasses of brandy, and they drank a solemn toast to what the colonel called "the end of uncertainty."

Colonel Powell-Hughes negotiated to sell the mercantile company and, by March, divested himself of all his other holdings. Gideon's best employment so far, his only book-learning, and the closest thing he'd known to a family, were thus terminated. He was given his next month's pay with a double eagle bonus. He made a secret decision to enlist, if he hadn't missed his chance. Some said the war's windup was coming soon, but he'd heard such talk before. The colonel made Gideon a gift of the old silver watch he had always admired, in spite of the fact that it always ran either fast or slow.

"This is the perfect timepiece," the colonel said. "Since it's always fast or slow, you know you'll be early or late so you never have to worry about being on time."

The colonel also gave Gideon his choice of any one of the books from the library. He took the concluding volume (XIII, VIS.–ZWI.) of the *Americana*. No one, he reasoned, could know about everything, and—young as he was—he was mighty curious how things end up. Also, with the final volume came the appendix, where the book started all over again, A to Z, with knowledge left out or recently learned. So, volume XIII gave him endings as well as some new beginnings. And, finally, Colonel Powell-Hughes gave him a ledger, a thick leather-bound book of pages blank as a cloudless sky.

"On the frontier, do not forget the frontier of thought. Fill the empty spaces. Ere this civil war concludes, your accounts of the wilderness may help feed the hunger for news of westward expansion. Wordsworth tells us the mind develops through experiences of the senses and through reflection and contemplation. Take down your immediate impressions so, later, your mind matured in repose may successfully express sensation and opinion."

At that moment Gideon obtained a new occupation—one of several he would learn. Journalist, he became—and editor, too: as no one was paying him for his words, no one but he was looking down to see what his racing hand had written.

Westering

From Cumberland to Wheeling the cars stopped only to take on water and wood, and Gideon saw not a soul about the darkly forested countryside. By and by he spied a wide, mud-brown river the conductor confirmed was the Ohio. Wheeling was much like Cumberland, coal-dark and dreary. Gideon asked the first Union officer he saw how he could join up. The soldier shook his head and said, "Go home to your mama." A fellow down at the docks said a body could sign up with a bonus in Cincinnati, and he sold Gideon passage on the next steamboat. Gideon waited long into the night for the *Arthur St. Clair*. Downriver to Cincinnati filled forty hours. He would not often be able to afford such speed and luxury. To guard against his impulses, he remained outside and away from the boat's saloon, where numerous card games might lure him into losses. He made his place down on the boiler deck in the open air forward of the smokestacks, somewhat protected from the elements by the Texas deck above him, the largest deck of the sternwheeler.

On and along the river was more human traffic than he'd seen since his days in Baltimore. The *Arthur St. Clair* passed forest, farm, and town. Coal flats drifted down from Pittsburgh. They passed boats, rafts, and barges, some pitched with tents and burning cookfires on decks crowded with soldiers. It was early April, damp and still cold.

Finally, behind the river's levee, Cincinnati spread into rising hills. Coaldust had followed him from Cumberland and cast the bustling city into near-dark by three in the afternoon. Commerce huffed and puffed like the steamboats that crowded the levee.

His second day in Cincinnati, a Tuesday, he set out to join the Union troops. He asked a lieutenant leaned against a brick wall reading a newspaper if he knew any recruiting place thereabouts. The soldier handed Gideon the Cincinnati *Commercial*, and he read of Lee's surrender at Appomattox. Gideon felt compelled to recall the time, the weather, and the brick wall beside him, so he might better preserve the memory of the moment he received news of the historic event. By his ignorant silver watch, it was nine past ten, but (though clouds obscured the sun) his growling stomach guaranteed it was sometime past midday, which was how he recorded it in his journal.

Safe inside Colonel Powell-Hughes' mercantile store in Cumberland, Gideon had been absent from the war. He was too late for it in Wheeling, but he'd been sure he'd catch up to it in Cincinnati. Now it had ended before he could join it. But he still felt he was chasing something, though now he wasn't sure what he was trying to overtake. Whatever it was, it was somewhere else. Maybe he was still being driven by his need to belong to something or someone. He did not know where his wandering would take him, but, like many others afoot at the time, he felt the pull of the Western frontier. Also like many others, he had no clear idea of how much capital would be required for a journey of the distance and duration he envisioned.

🕮

Less than a week after he landed in Cincinnati, the sixteenth of April, news of President Lincoln's assassination two days earlier reached Gideon. He was eating a plate of eggs and beans, scooting a bean around trying to get it on his spoon, when church bells broke out ringing. Though his watch read 3:00, the sun had already risen. As it was Easter Sunday, he guessed the bells rang so for resurrection. He was thinking what a godly town Cincinnati is, where every bell rings so on Easter morning, was vaguely thinking he might wash up and find a church to visit, when a woman at a table beside his began to weep. Hat in his hand, he offered his concern, and the lady's husband told him the heartbreaking news. Gideon did not compare himself to one as great as Lincoln, but he felt a kinship with the man's humble origins. The president was a bright example for many. It seemed important to discover and record every detail of the tragedy, and what the woman and her husband did not know Gideon sought from others. He read every word in the *Commercial* for days running. The shooting was in the president's box over the stage of Ford's Theatre just after 10:00 the night of Good Friday. Mr. Lincoln lingered all night before he died on Saturday morning at 7:22. Gideon consulted his inaccurate watch once more—high noon—when he learned the time of the president's wounding and the time of his passing. The bullet had entered the back of his head and lodged near his right eye. They carried him to the home of William Peterson, and Mrs. Lincoln went into the room just once and was taken away grief-struck. Gideon was glad the president's wife had been with him. It was believed he never regained consciousness.

At first, Gideon read, everyone thought the gunshot was part of the world upon the stage. As one who frequently wholly entered the fictive world, he wished Mr. Lincoln might have been so alive in the play that the bullet would have passed through empty space in his skull and done no damage to his absent brain that might then have returned to bid him rise from his deathbed.

Grief fell like a steady rain upon the entire city, and men went about their business with a purposeful, almost angry determination, as if they were bound to keep at it no matter the news. This communal melancholy produced a somber sense of brotherhood, and more than one dispute was quietly settled and sealed with a grim handshake. First this war had pitted them—countrymen, friends, and, even, family—against one another and, now, this, too, they had to bear.

Gideon sensed a painful new energy afoot and wanted to be on the move with it. He made no conscious decision, he did not think of any alternative. The direction he would go was manifest—like everyone else who had no home or family to go back to, he would go west. He had no direction more persuasive than forward. Feeling sorrowful, he cast a thought to Colonel Powell-Hughes, home by now in Wales, and to Win Shu, gone wherever a Chinaman who can't get back to China goes. In Cincinnati, lonely for the company of the colonel or Win Shu, Gideon noted those without family are beholden to no one and free to choose all their associations. Thus, feelings of liberation and anticipation crowded out his sentimental longings.

The prices in Cincinnati were high. Lest he deplete his modest funds on sweets and newspapers, he vowed to outfit himself and be on his way soon rather than later. He headed to the wagon lots to see what conveyance he could afford. He was not the only creature in a hurry. Droves of hogs, not knowing they rushed to the slaughterhouse, snorted through the streets. At a run to escape their head-long advance, Gideon hastened across the red clay road and collided with a lath-boned, white-haired, red-faced man who, when Gideon offered his hand in apology, smiled rather than cursed.

"Phineas Thomas Atkins, inventor and manufacturer." Mr. Atkins worked Gideon's hand up and down as if it were a pump. Gideon dusted off the inventor and begged to buy him a draught of something cool to cut the thick red dust. Mr. Atkins immediately forgave him and later confessed he had been surprised when such a lowly-looking pup as Gideon made a kind apology, and with serious and gentlemanly speech.

Phineas T. Atkins was inventing a way to transmit messages without wires by sending beams of light through tubes. In the meantime, he manufactured the Atkins Lightning Bolt Arrester and Protector for the safe transmission and ground-ing of electrical charges. He convinced Gideon the Southwestern frontier, with its legendary electrical storms, was a vast, untapped market for the grounding device. Gideon claimed he was small for his age (he'd upped it to twenty-three in the telling) and wise beyond his years, to boot, and he convinced Mr. Atkins to hire him as a sales representative. The manufacturer gave Gideon three dozen rods on consignment—each with a sharp copper tip, a blue glass ball, and a wind-direc-tion arrow fashioned from iron and isinglass. They wrapped them in straw and laid them in a crate for the journey.

Gideon could have packed his worldly goods on a decent horse for thirty dollars, but the lightning arresters necessitated a wagon. In his volume of the *Americana*, he read: **WAGONS**—*According to Moses, Egypt was the country* *where wagons were first used. The Chinese call the inventor Hiene-Yuene. The Greeks attributed the invention to Erichthonius, fourth king of Athens, and say that he used them in consequence of lameness. Wagons with two wheels may have been the first constructed; but Homer mentions four-wheeled wagons, the invention of which was ascribed to the Phrygians.*

Whoever the ingenious man who first conceived of an axis and applied it to the wheel, the streets and wagon lots of Cincinnati did him homage, crowded as they were with the vehicles. A farmer's wagon was going for sixty-five to seventy-five dollars and another sixty to ninety each for a pair of American mules, well broken.

In order to outfit his only employee (who pledged to take no commission until his supplies were paid for), Phineas T. Atkins, Gideon's second benefactor, bought him a wagon, fifty pounds of flour, twenty pounds of bacon, a poke of dried beans, and three pounds each of coffee, sugar, and salt. Mr. Atkins said he'd add thirty dollars to the thirty Gideon had to his name to buy a pair of horses, or if Gideon could come up with an extra ten apiece he could get Mexican mules. He took Mr. Atkins' thirty dollars and said he'd ruminate a while on the decision. *Wagons*, the *Americana* went on to say, *are drawn by men or beasts, or propelled by machinery. In ancient times a galley was propelled through the city of Athens by internal wheel-work, and locomotive wagons have been perfected using steam and wind. One Simon Stevin, of Bruges, built a sailing wagon that, on level ground, carried twenty-eight persons across fourteen Dutch leagues in two hours. Even kites,* Gideon read, *have been used to propel wagons.*

Well and good, he thought, so long as you didn't need to travel on a windless day. He settled on oxen, pocketing the savings from such economical locomotive power as insurance against unexpected needs during the journey before him. He hesitated over the expense of an extra pair of reading glasses, but finally parted with the money, knowing this insurance against the loss of reading his encyclopedia and maintaining his journal was a worthwhile investment. Of assets, he reasoned, he was in short supply, while time to spend he had in excess. He possessed in unspent years immeasurable riches, a gift of youth.

Thus outfitted, wagon loaded, belly full of beans, he waited at the wagon lot for Mr. Atkins to bid him farewell. Gideon's silver watch was having a fast morning or Phineas was late. He finally approached in a loping gait, carrying a parting gift wrapped in oilcloth. As a kind of afterthought he had bought Gideon a single-barreled Hawken rifle and a canister containing a couple pounds of powder, caps, and bullets.

"You can supplement your supplies from the plentiful game in the West." Phineas acted as though the twenty-six dollars spent on the rifle was a savings in beans and bacon. "Besides," these were his final words to Gideon ere he creaked off down the westward road, "where you're going I've heard a man may be judged by the gun he packs. I'd hate for the only drummer of Phineas T. Atkins' lightning arresters to be lightweighted because he carries no artillery."

Gideon added the Hawken to his provisions and solemnly shook his employer's hand. Having missed the great war, Gideon accepted the weapon as a sign of the covenant between himself and whatever just causes remained for which a man might risk his life. He was determined to find something as valuable as his soul. Neither he nor Mr. Atkins mentioned the wild Indians, highway robbers, and cutthroat shootists against whom the weapon might soon be required.

Succumbs to a Painted Cat

Gideon Jones left Cincinnati in his loaded farmer's wagon with a twenty-two-dollar yoke of oxen and the last eight dollars in Phineas Atkins' purse added to eighteen dollars remaining in Gideon's pouch. It wasn't so, but he felt quite rich. He crossed the river to Covington, Kentucky, on a crowded ferryboat.

His were strong oxen, and on a good day he made fifteen to sixteen miles. This was May, the days warming, the nights still brisk. His future was as bright as a new gold piece. In no hurry, he plumbed the track along the Ohio River through Kentucky's beautiful wilderness. Negroes planted corn in fields, and Gideon wondered if they were slaves. Droves of hogs again crowded him off the road. A stagecoach passed him by, and he later caught it stopped at an inn where he had a fine meal of cornbread, bacon, and coffee, settling for a baked sweet potato to satisfy his hankering for cake or pie.

Nearly every hill around Lexington was ornamented with a costly-looking house. It was a quiet, shady town, and Gideon thought if he lived there he would boast of the agreeably stocked sweetshops and bakeries. At one such bakery he bought a wedge of chocolate cake he devoured as he rode through the town. He passed a beautiful white house, the Sycamore Inn, with a wide porch on all sides, where two women sat drinking what he guessed was tea, and he wished he had the money to spend just one night in lodgings so lovely and genteel. He waited beside an old Kentuckian, both their poor wagons ox-drawn, while a train of railway cars for Frankfort and Louisville rushed across their path. The cars moved so fast they seemed to be sitting still, and Gideon saw clearly the figure of a beautiful woman in a window of one of the cars. He felt a momentary longing for the speed and comfort of a rail car, and recalled the even greater speed and comfort of a steamboat. Perhaps he should have waited until he reached St. Louis or Independence to outfit himself. Unencumbered, he could have ridden the rails and rivers. But his guardian angel, Phineas Atkins, had alighted in Cincinnati. Besides, Gideon reasoned, as the starting point for westward wagon trains, Independence would likely charge the high prices of high demand. Much may be missed by the traveler who rushes through the scenery at twenty miles an hour. Also, he wanted the better roads and convenience of villages and towns while he schooled himself in his wagon and team. He didn't want anyone on a westward train to judge him incapable of the trek. Free from the timetables of railway carriages and steamboats, he was seeing everything for the first time and might want to linger. So he made his steady way through Louisville to Evansville, where he crossed the Wabash into Illinois and followed the sun toward St. Louis. In his *Americana*, he read: **WABASH**, *a river of Indiana, waters the middle and western part of the state, and flows into the Ohio thirty miles above Cumberland river. It is upwards of 500 miles long, and affords good steam-boat navigation, for most of the year, 150 miles, to Vincennes, and for smaller boats 250 miles farther, to Ouiatan. Very small boats ascend to within eight miles of the Maumee. It receives several large rivers, and meanders through a valley of remarkable fertility.* If all the rivers and valleys and mountains he was to cross were to have names beginning with VIS through ZWI, he speculated he should become a geography expert ere he reached the West, though he should be delayed by time spent reading.

There was plentiful grass and not much mud, it having been a dry spring. Beginning with his Baltimore church mule and again with his team of oxen, he had discovered he had a way with animals—perhaps because he preferred their company to the company of most men. Save for stops at sweetshops, he was inclined to camp outside of towns and villages, studying his encyclopedia and, later, the celestial lights above. Daytime, he stopped at general stores and drygoods emporia and made vain efforts to peddle Mr. Atkins' lightning arresters. By St. Louis, he'd not lightened his load much, though he sold sufficient lightning rods to a store in New Albany to send Mr. Atkins a token payment.

A citizen who directed him to the post office said St. Louis was home to over a hundred thousand souls. He didn't doubt it. He got lost four times before he found the post office building, where a wall calendar told him his journey had carried him into the month of June. He penned a letter to his employer expressing his conviction the sale of lightning arresters would improve once he left civilized regions and plied their trade in the geography of extreme weather.

Having posted his letter, he found a wagon yard, paid for hay and water, and, toting his journal under his arm, left his oxen chewing contentedly. He planned to come back to sleep in the wagon. After a supper of bakery cake, he walked the noisy, bricked streets of St. Louis looking in the dark windows of saddleries and drygoods stores. Dirty and unshaven, their uniforms stained and torn, soldiers, some with ragged bandages, leaned against buildings. The hubbub passed them by as if they were beggars. Now and then an officer walked past smartly, but even the officers had a haggard, faraway look.

He passed a brick hotel two stories high and, next, a brick-front dance hall with double doors, each bearing a dozen glazed panes of glass bright with light. Gold letters on a white sign proclaimed: Gold's Opera House. Piano notes squirted from between the heavy doors as a man left and two entered. He bent forward to peer through the glass. All inside was afire, so many lamps he couldn't tell where one stopped and another began, wicks high and dancing bright with piano *plinks* vibrating the cool glass against his forehead. Something damp touched his neck, stopped, touched again. He jerked back and bumped a man who had a woman's painted lips and whose teeth gave back gold light.

"Well?" The man's white waistcoat, pantaloons, and high hat pulsed in the dark street. Ruffles flowered down his shirt front and around his coat cuffs. Speechless, Gideon stepped back. The dandy pulled open the door. Men with pink-shaved faces lined a brass-fitted bar, and their dark eyes stared at Gideon from a long mirror above glittering colored bottles. He leaned in to glimpse a large painting, the much-larger-than-life likeness of a reclining woman, her pale skin bared from the dimples of her knees all the way up to her milky throat, her pursed lips red as the lips of the man holding the door open. Tipping his hat, his soft sleeve brushing along the top of Gideon's hand, the man disappeared into the smoky brightness as an angel might enter a sunlit cloud.

A boy thrust into Gideon's face a broadsheet advertising bargains in military materiel. On the back of the paper was a poem, "Our Star-Spangled Trial is O'er," by Mrs. Ursilla Gresham, the last lines of which he scribbled in his journal: "For every Rebel sent wailing to his grave / A door's been opened for a tortured slave." He gave the advertisement back, and the boy dealt it to another passer-by without looking up.

Gideon stopped before a foaming glass of beer painted on a window. A cool draught was a reward he felt worthy of, though he'd not soon forget Gold's Opera House, lamplit Heaven. Here, louvered doors swung into a low room near as dark as the street. At a crowded bar he gulped a warm beer, breathed familiar smells: kerosene, tobacco, sweat, hay, manure. Dust floated in greenish light out-lining brass spittoons against table legs. The dress was homespun cotton shirts and pantaloons, home-tanned vests, and big-brimmed hats. Only the boots—fancy-stitched and high—were store-bought. Here, the women of evil name and fame were not as scrubbed-clean as the gents at the opera house. The pinkest skin here was the barkeep's bald head.

A girl who looked no older than eleven or twelve sat on a tabletop, a fellow with long gray hair dealing monte around her. She held a toddy in one hand, a cigar in the other. Her hair was cut short, like a boy's, and her skirts bunched up around her waist. Her naked legs—crossed at the knees on the tabletop—didn't look like a boy's legs. She put the cigar to her lips and slowly pushed it into her mouth, slid it in all the way to the red-hot tip. She pulled the cigar out again. When she started pushing the cigar back into her mouth, Gideon put his face down in his beer.

When he looked up his eyes met the beautiful face he had seen speed past in the railway car. Dark-haired and dark-eyed, she rose, smiling at him as she swayed through the crowd toward him. As she drew near, he saw she was older than the woman on the train. She looked about the age he imagined his mother would be had his mother lived to see this night. She pushed close enough their knees touched. Even later, when he depicted the moment in his journal, his face burned. But he reasoned any reader he might ever have would likely be a stranger to him, and he pledged himself not just to the facts but, as near as he could come, to the truth of what he would record.

"Buy me a drink, you pretty Texan," this gilded beauty said. Gideon knew "Texan" was her appellation for every man, yet he felt taller and stronger. Her black-smudged eyebrows humped up, and her reddened lips widened to reveal one missing tooth. Her fingers slid over the worn flannel seat of his pants. He nod-ded to the bald barkeep, who brought her a toddy. When he got no change back, he'd learned a painted cat's drink costs a lot more than a beer.

"Call me Kitty." Saying nothing else, she led him outside and to the back of the building, where she rattled the last of four doors. A man came out pulling snug his suspenders. The room was dark, but Kitty lit neither lamp nor candle. Shapes, white and floating, became a mattress, a bowl and pitcher. In the near-dark room, sounds amplified: whish-whish-whush of the bouquet of arms and legs and garments Kitty was, clink of his belt buckle, swuck and shiss of sponge and rag, the water cool where she washed him, ceramic tink of pitcher in bowl, creak of a floorboard. Kitty's buttons, collar to waist and lower, were eyes winking, then a flower scent and whiteness and warmth of flesh as she lay back, dragging him over her like a coverlet. He was grateful neither of them seemed expected to say a word. For his money he got a sponge bath and flashing pleasure he longed for again just moments after it ended. His quick effusion over, his pants were still bunched over his longboats where she'd pushed them down to wash him. She said he could stay and sleep until the knob rattled, which it did soon enough, the kind of lightning arrester Kitty offered outselling those of copper and glass construction he was peddling.

Kitty's price had seemed high, but in retrospect (considering the bath and the half-hour's rest on mattress ticking) was as fair an exchange as he would get for months to come. He resolved to spend his lodging money, whenever possible, on silent, beautiful women. Women, he decided, *all* women, would make up his special study of beauty. He felt sure the kind of beauty celebrated by the poets could be contained for him in one vessel only—surely one woman's beauty waited to cast its spell over him. All he had to do was to find her.

The wagonyard smelled as strong but not as sweet as Kitty's crib, the wagonbed harder and colder than Kitty's. One can pay to sleep in a fine hotel bed in St. Louis, yet dream he lies on a wagonbed or the cold ground, and, of course, the bed may be hard yet the dream soft and fine.

He was not long out of St. Louis before the hundred thousand souls of the city, their carriages, draught wagons, and rail cars, their houses and brick buildings, their gas lights and piano notes, seemed more dream than memory, though he still recalled Kitty's smile and the warmth of her hand through his trousers. Here was woodland quiet, evenings lit by stars, and an infrequent farmhouse lantern. Other travelers were few and separated by hours—sometimes days. The landscape passed with little alteration, and he traversed many miles lost in his *Encyclopaedia Americana*. One day he looked up and beheld a great tree he could not name. He entered in his journal this description: "Tall as a St. Louis building, black bark deeply furrowed in rows as a fresh-ploughed field, leaves as big as my hand."

He made frequent stops to rest his oxen, prolonging these pauses with rigorous exertions of his arms and legs to revest muscle and mind. He felt close enough to the frontier to watch for Indians, but he was not sure what to watch for—feathers, smoke, flaming arrows? He'd been told, "Before you see a savage, you'll hear his heart-stopping war cry and the thunder of his pony's hooves." By then, he'd heard, it's too late.

When he made an evening fire he cooked sufficient beans, bacon, or biscuits to put something by for midday. Thence, when he grew hungry, he pulled up and ate his fill of such store. Ere long, trees grew as scarce as people, so for shelter from the sun he banqueted beneath his wagon. Often, before moving on, he dozed on a soft bed of grass.

St. Louis to Independence

The westward road from St. Louis was well-used, firm, and dry. Gideon set out behind the Butterfield Stage—it danced away down the road, bobbing and darting quick as a hummingbird. All the way to San Francisco, the advertisements bragged, in twenty-one days. Fine for those with $150.00 for the fare and more for meals, for those not entrusted with the frontier's sole supply of the Atkins Lightning Bolt Arrester and Protector, for those willing to be beaten and stirred like batter, for those in a hurry, for those whose time was not their own as his was.

He followed the Missouri River to Jefferson City, the state's capital, where he enjoyed a night's rest in a room he let over a bakery. In days and weeks to come, he would recall with olfactory pangs of nostalgia the rising scents of cakes and cookies, more rousing than any cock's crow.

His next stopover was in Sedalia, where a schoolteacher pointed out Gideon had missed storm season, then offered him less than he owed Phineas for half-a-dozen rods. The teacher planned to use them to attract electrical energy for scientific experiments, so Gideon took the offer, figuring to account Phineas' loss to a scientific and educational discount.

He reached Independence the first of July, the same day the Butterfield Stage he had followed out of St. Louis was to arrive in San Francisco. Travelers in Independence were mostly on their way farther west. They weighed the hardships of a western crossing against the abundant riches claimed for Washington Territory. The talk was of wagons, weather, water, wild Indians, and of the war just ended to free the slaves.

Knobby Cotton: Out of Ashes

Born in a Slave Cabin
(June 1842)

With the exception of a Comanche warrior, no horseman I ever saw was
the equal of Knobby Cotton. Darker than a Comanche, darker than his wife
Elizabeth, Knobby is the darkest person I have ever seen—not just brown but
pure black. He's not <u>shiny</u> black like wet ink, but <u>thick</u> black like charred coals.
He's as dark as a moonless night, but his mind trails sparks like a shooting star.

—from *Gideon Jones' Journal*

From the time of his birth in a Mississippi slave cabin, Knobby Cotton had been
lanky as a child's drawing of a stick man. When the midwife handed him to his
mother, Hester, for the first time, she looked at her baby—her skinny only baby—
and said, "Child you're all arms and legs." But what most folks saw were his stick-
out ears, his stick-up shoulders, his jut-out elbows, his jut-up knees, the balls of
his heels on his long feet. "Knobby is what you are, born the last day of June—my
knobby little June bug." Hester named him Samuel, after her daddy, but everybody always called him Knobby.

Nighttime, when she got back from the field, Hester made hoecakes and
syrup, sometimes fixed dumplings, boiled rice, or baked yams in the ashes, and,
after they had eaten, Grandfather Samuel told stories about Africa, about the wise
turtle and the wily spider, and about the snake, Damballa, revered by some as a
god. Grandfather said Damballa was no god, but that his legend was still good.
After Grandfather's stories, Knobby's mother rocked him in the rocking chair

Grandfather Samuel had made the month before Knobby was born, and she sang
to him:

> The master's child's born rich and free,
> You're God's skinny gift to me
> In this poor slave cabin home.
> My knobby little colored child.

Grandfather Samuel, before he got old, had hunted down lost cattle for
Noble Plantation with as much determination as our Lord and Savior sought His
lost sheep. In those olden days many plantation owners in Alabama, Mississippi,
and Louisiana made their living from cattle and kept their slaves on horseback
working as cow-keepers.

When cotton displaced cows on Noble Plantation, as it did over most of the
South, the master put his slaves in the fields. Knobby's daddy, William, outpicked
every slave on Noble Plantation. He outpicked every slave in Marion County, Mississippi, every season for as long as memory, and earned his family a last name.

When Knobby was born, William was in his prime. He might have gotten his
son beside him in the fields and made a first-rate picker out of him had William
not died of a fever the first winter after the boy was born. They buried William in
the slave cemetery close by Grandfather Samuel's wife, Sara, who had been at rest
for years, both her hands torn off by the saw teeth of the cotton gin, all the cotton
crimson when she bled to death.

With Sara and William buried, only Grandfather Samuel and Hester and Knobby
were left in the cabin, so the master sectioned off the room with a plank wall and
moved in a slave named Hamp and his wife Rachel and their children Fanny and
Rose and Lily.

One night Hester's corn shuck mattress chattered loud enough to wake everyone in the cabin, Hamp climbing heavily onto the space where William had lain
before he died.

Grandfather Samuel spoke the slave's name: "Hamp." He didn't say it loud
and he didn't say it soft. It sounded like bones gnawed between his teeth when he
said it, and the fire that had gone to coals jumped up bright on Rachel, Fanny,
Rose, and Lily peering around the partition, four round faces stacked on top of
one another like four skillets hung on the wall.

And before the flare of the fire dimmed again it brightened the blade of Hester's cooking knife Grandfather Samuel held in his big fist and pointed as a finger at Hamp.

"I am the minister of God even to thee, Hamp, for good. But if thou do that which is evil, be afraid, for I bear not the sword in vain. I am the minister of God, a revenger to *execute* wrath upon him that do evil."

"No, Conjure Man, don't put no curse on me. I got all these children and this woman in bed with me, and I just natural looking for more room for my rest." Hamp was on his knees on Hester's mattress, his hands up as if to ward off blows from Grandfather Samuel, so afraid was he of the conjurer's power.

"Ye are of your father the devil, and the lusts of your father ye will do."

Ever after that night Hester built her fire on the left side of the mud fireplace and Rachel built hers on the right side. They took care not to let their fires touch, and no words passed between the two families.

Because they had small, quick fingers, many of the women and children were the best pickers, but Knobby always dragged home a mostly empty basket, his long fingers pricked bloody by the hard cotton pods. Master Noble encouraged Knobby's gift with livestock and took him out of the fields, where the master said Knobby was of little use. He was put to work feeding the animals, milking the cows, and mucking out the stalls. He grew tall and strong, the muscles beneath his dark skin rolling like the muscles of the horses he tended. In spite of his big-knuckled, long-fingered hands, Knobby was no picker. He was a throwback to Grandfather Samuel, the cow-keeper and drover.

"Yes sir, Grandson, your way is with the livestock, especially horses. I will pass along to you their secret language."

While he was still so small Grandfather had to lift him onto a pony's back, Knobby rode every horse in the stable. About the only toy the boy ever had was a length of rope he twirled and threw. He roped gate posts, hens, hogs, cattle, other children, and, eventually, horses. But before he ever put a rope on a horse, he learned to talk to them. He watched their eyes and their ears as Grandfather Samuel taught him, and he learned to know what was in a horse's heart.

Under Grandfather Samuel's tutelage, Knobby trained all the new horses on the plantation. Grandfather taught Knobby never to break a horse. Grandfather hated the word.

"Same way a master tells the overseer to gain control of a Negro slave—break him, break his will. Now, Knobby, sometimes you *can* make a creature do your bidding by force of might—a horse or a man. But if you treat a horse or a man with respect, he will do your will because he wants to. Our Lord and Savior gave us free will in the garden. He could have made us love Him, could have made us do right, from the start. Look how big His stick is—be easy for God to break man. Harder to love us into Heaven."

When Knobby was fourteen, he left the crowded slave cabin and took to sleeping in the stables with his horse friends, and it wasn't long before he was the one buying horses for the master. Knobby selected and trained the big jumper the master bought for his daughter, and Knobby trained the thoroughbreds the master bought after he got interested in racing stock. Knobby trained, fed, doctored, shoed, washed, and brushed the horses, and he cleaned out their stalls. He *listened* to the horses, too, and learned what they had to teach. He learned to think like a horse. He wanted to think like a man—even as well as any white man. At night in the stables, while the horses stood sleeping, Knobby dug up his hidden candle and practiced the writing and figures Grandfather Samuel taught, but more than anything Knobby learned horses and Scripture.

"From the Gospel of John, chapter one, verse one: 'In the beginning was the Word, and the Word was with God, and the Word was God,'" his grandfather said. "God's word is the only truth. John, chapter 8, verse 32: 'And ye shall know the truth, and the truth shall make you free.' God will empower the Negro," Grandfather Samuel told his students. "And His truth will deliver us just as it delivered the Israelites."

Slave Courting

One day, Knobby was pushing a wheelbarrow of dung he had shoveled from the horse stalls when a house-slave, tall, with rich, coffee-colored skin, blocked his way between the barn wall and wooden fence. He knew her as a quiet, determined girl who had come regularly to Grandfather Samuel's Sunday School. Now she was a young woman lean and supple as a thoroughbred. She stared at him. Her eyes moved slow up the length of his legs and arms and took a long rest in his eyes. House-slaves often assumed a haughty air, as if they had acquired some kind of grace by learning white customs and courtesies. This woman had an ironic air, as if house manners were just a silly game she played with children.

Knobby imagined her dropping her handkerchief and then laughing at the man who stooped to pick it up.

"I'm Elizabeth, so you will know who reminded you of your manners to step aside and let womenfolk go first."

Knobby smiled and stepped aside far enough to let her pass, but not so far he didn't smell the soap in her hair and feel the starch in her dress as it brushed against him. He felt the heat of her as she walked close, and he watched her walk away without once looking back until she disappeared up the steps and into the big house. In Sunday School she could read most any word Grandfather Samuel pointed to, and she could print out her name, ELIZABETH, because she had been a playmate for the master's daughter and had been present when the mistress gave lessons.

Knobby had come on up to being a grown man. When he wasn't studying horses or the Scriptures or writing, he concentrated on the study of women: how one woman hummed when she walked, how one swayed when she worked, how one eyed the treetops and carried her chin high as if she balanced a weight on her head, while another watched the ground as if she were searching for some lost thing and let her chin bounce along on her breastbone. When they saw him, quick and strong, most all the women on the plantation had smiles for Knobby.

All but one, Elizabeth, whose smile he sought the most. He preened and pranced, doing the ritual courtship dance of plantation slaves, who, needing a master's permission for romance, mocked the game of wooing even as they played it with all their hearts.

"Miss Elizabeth, might I walk beside you on Sunday afternoons so the wagon of my heart can be pulled next to yours?"

"Mr. Cotton, do you expect the road is broad enough for both our wagons to ride so?"

"Kind miss, I will keep two of my wheels in the brambles and the briars to make room on the road to pull my wagon alongside yours."

"I have no objection to a gentleman such as yourself drawing near so long as you be careful not to let your wheels roll up against mine. Other gentlemen have made sweet words, but their wagons hauled deceitful hearts."

Though Knobby saw Elizabeth whenever she came with the master's daughter down to the stables, or when she left the big house on an errand for Mistress Mary, it was sometimes days between times he got to talk to her. The next chance he had to woo Elizabeth, she surprised him with a forthright question.

"Mr. Cotton, I'm sturdy built and way tall for a lady—near as tall as you. If you were in the woods to fell a tree and you spied a slender tree easier to chop than a thicker, taller tree sure to take more effort, which tree would you cut to carry home?"

"Miss Elizabeth, easier is rarely better. My recent walks with you to the chapel have been the most pleasant steps of my long personal journey. In all my life, up hills and through forests, none of God's creatures has been as pleasing to my sight as you. You and I are sturdy young trees. Hewn and dovetailed, we would be stronger than we are with separate roots. Would you build a mighty house with me?"

"Knobby Cotton, I've been walking the lonely road, and I'm still ten miles away. Will you bring me home?"

So Knobby kissed Elizabeth the first time, and then he kissed her nine times more, a kiss for every mile he had to bring her home.

Vaqueros in New Orleans

Field-slaves were glad to escape the watchful eyes of the master and his family, who more closely watched the house-slaves and Knobby. Still, the field-slaves resented Knobby's lighter chores, his being in the stable and out of the weather. But, before dawn, when the caller blew his cow horn in the quarters, the field-slaves' lives were a little easier because they didn't have to tend to the livestock before they got to the crop. And when the sun set and the horn blew "quit," they didn't have to tend the animals before they could eat and rest. Also, in spite of themselves, the other slaves were proud a colored boy had such a way with horses that the master took the boy with him to New Orleans to horse-trade.

On one such trip in hot and humid October, a young drover, Portis Goar, was in New Orleans to sell a herd of Texas cattle. This Goar had in his drove about sixty head he and a Mexican vaquero were working into pens when the herd spooked. The Mexican went down, and Goar was in trouble. Knobby rode into the melee and turned the stampeding cattle, saving Goar from the trampling that killed the Mexican. Not realizing Knobby was a slave, Goar asked to buy his savior a drink, an offer the hero politely declined. Goar found a half full bottle of whisky in his saddlebags. Since Knobby kept forbearing the bottle, the drover drank for both of them. "Whew boy, I come close." The drover's voice and one eyeball twitched. Goar rubbed his nicked arms and bruised leg and took another pull. As the whisky went down, he grew increasingly grateful to Knobby.

Portis Goar rode a short, ugly horse he called a mustang. "They're all over the west of Texas, there for the taking." He told Knobby how the vaqueros would find a herd of wild mustangs and throw up a fence shaped like a funnel into a box pen they built with a gate across the top of the funnel. They'd get behind the herd and separate two or three hundred and drive them into the corral. They kept the best and turned the rest loose. He slapped dust from the thick neck of his chestnut mare. "This mean-looking Dolores will tote me as far as the day is long." He showed Knobby his stock saddle, a leather-covered wooden tree with big sheepskin-lined skirts and a big saddlehorn on a fork he'd cut from a cotton-wood. Knobby admired how soft a ride the sheepskin gave and how it kept Goar's saddle blanket from slipping.

"I've seen darkie drovers in Texas. Mexican or darkie don't matter. What matters is how a man sits a horse. Big, strong fella who rides like you won't have no trouble. Hell, I got to replace me poor Juan here, if you want a job."

"Thank you, Mr. Goar. I will keep Texas in mind."

"I got a gang of vaqueros in San Antone. We'll head down to the *brazada* the Mexicans call El Desierto Muerto, but it ain't dead a bit—plenty of Comanche Indians, Mexican rancheros, wild mustangs, wild longhorns, mesquite, live oak, and your pick of cactus—all a man can chew."

"Yes sir, all a man can chew."

"Just ask anyone in San Antone, 'Where's Eye?'" Goar pointed to his jumpy eyeball. "We got a herd picked out at a rancho up above Agualeguas. Once we get them dogies across the Rio Grande we'll run them day and night, run them like all possessed so the cussed critters will be too wore out to be ornery. Then we'll drive them to market. Shreveport's paying best dollar right now."

Knobby looked over his shoulder at his master talking to another gentleman. Knobby had never before been talked to as if he were a free man. He didn't want this vaquero, Portis Goar, to know he was a slave. Before the master came to fetch him, Knobby managed to get free of Goar.

On the ride back to Mississippi, Knobby asked about Texas. The master said it was a dangerous country. He said slaves in Mississippi were better off than free men in Texas. Knobby said, "Yes, Master," but he wondered how he was better off than Portis Goar, whose invitation to have a drink Knobby could not accept for fear of his master.

After Knobby and the master returned from New Orleans, plantation time went by in its standstill way. Any other life seemed far off, but not so far Knobby didn't think on the life of a vaquero in a dangerous place where there was all a man could chew and where what counted most was what Knobby did best. Biding his time, Knobby dreamt of freedom and earning his keep as a horseman and cow-handler in Texas. For Knobby, the words *freedom* and *Texas* had come to mean near the same thing, a dream postponed until he could make Elizabeth his wife and find a scheme to get them both away to Texas.

If he approved of a match, the master of Noble Plantation would let a slave take a mate. On Noble, slave weddings were usually held on the gallery of the big house. Samuel would read the Scriptures, the bride and groom would jump over a broomstick, and there would be a slice of white cake for every slave. Later, in the quarters, there would be music and dancing into the night, the bedtime horn silent.

The master's daughter was seventeen now and was engaged to marry the coming spring. She had outgrown her need for a playmate long ago, and soon she would leave Noble Plantation to live at her husband's family place in Claiborne County. Once the master's daughter was married and Elizabeth was free of all the wedding work, Knobby planned to ask permission to marry her.

But before the master's daughter's wedding, the war came, and first the daughter's intended, and then the master, too, went away to fight the Yankees. Before he left, the master addressed all of his slaves and told them secession was necessary to prevent the United States from maintaining its authority not by law but by force of might. "We did not make this quarrel, but we must respond to those who would dictate to us from their different station what sort of life we in Mississippi are to lead."

"My, my," Grandfather Samuel said to Knobby. "Sound familiar? Someone of a different station telling others what kind of life they can have."

Grandfather Samuel had been captured by slave raiders in West Africa when he was twelve. He kept his memories of Africa alive by telling stories. The oldest slave in the quarters and the only one who had been born in Africa, Grandfather was revered by all the slaves. Sure-handed and strong as a man half his age, he thatched the roofs of the slave cabins, and he made the calabash drums for Sunday afternoon singing. He had his own Bible, and he had the *Watt's Hymnal*, with the song words everybody learned. His first master, Leonard Viress up in Delaware, had taught Grandfather Samuel (who was then called John) to read and to write his name. When Master Viress learned his slave had gotten hold of a Bible and was reading Scriptures on his own, he was furious. He attempted to cut off Grandfather Samuel's thumb and first finger, but Grandfather stood up his full height and aimed his eyes down at Leonard Viress and said *You will have to take my life to take my thumb.* Master Viress settled for burning Grandfather's Bible and wetting the ashes down to a paste he made Grandfather eat while the master kept a gun pointed up at his slave.

"From the day those long-haired, red-faced slavers had put me down in the dank hold of their ship, my life had become ashes. Time passed slowly in the dark hold, on dark water, under dark skies, everything gray and dead, gone to ashes. What waited for me after my dark ocean passage? The ashes of lonely mud hearths in slave cabins. Every breath I took, every bite I chewed, tasted of ashes. When I learned to read there was a small flame amongst the ashes, and I would not let my master extinguish the light. So it was my Savior turned to ashes, too. The Word manifested itself in ashes, and I took ashes for my nourishment, my first communion, take, and eat, my body and my blood. Slave, you are ashes to ashes. On the slave's tongue, the taste of cremated hope, the bitter residue of nigger combustion."

Grandfather's second owner was Judah Grivot, a rice planter in Louisiana.

"There I learned the true nature of a tyrant, learned to ignore the earthly sting of the whip. I spent my days from dawn to dusk standing in muddy water, breathing rising swamp stink, squint-eyed against the sun, mindful of water moccasins. My feet festered with swamp water poison and ground itch, my legs burned with chigger bites, I ached all night long. I first loved a woman there, but vowed I would not be a slave husband, would not be a slave father."

Grivot had been shot and killed in a duel. His childless widow inherited the plantation and all the slaves, sold everything and moved away. Grandfather was taken to a slave pen in New Orleans and put on the auction block.

"The first Master Noble asked, 'What can you do?' I said I could ride a horse and herd cattle. I did not want another rice planter buying me. Master Noble did not look inside my mouth or even lift my shirt to see if I bore the whipping scars of obstinacy." Grandfather did bear the scars of the whip. He considered scars badges of honor, and in the cabin he proudly went shirtless.

"I took to horses as an angel to his harp. I learned headstall, bit, and reins. Lassos did what I told them. I learned horse language."

When the first Master Noble died and his son took over, Grandfather Samuel persuaded the young master if he spared the whip his slaves would work harder. Grandfather let the slaves believe he had cast a spell over young Master Noble to make him end their floggings. Grandfather's knowledge of herbs and healings brought slaves to his cabin late at night. He had stopped the floggings. He ministered to their needs, and they called him Conjure Man.

"Down in the swamp I learned the hoo-doo conjure ways, and then I put those dark spirits in the service of our Savior, Lord Jesus."

Slaves on Noble Plantation were treated better than most slaves. They had ample cornmeal and syrup, even meat, and those who wanted could plant gardens by their cabins. They were given plenty of tallow candles for light. Their cabins had wooden floors, windows with wooden shutters, and partitions to separate different families who lived in the same cabin. The master gave them passes to visit other plantations, and he built the chapel where Samuel read Scriptures and the slaves sang hymns and on Sunday afternoons had their school. Thanksgiving, Christmas, Easter, and the Fourth of July they were given days off and treats of coffee, bread, cake, and roasted hens and pigs. For cotton picked beyond his quota, a slave on Noble Plantation got a cash bonus. Buying or selling, the master kept slave families together. Only the master, not the overseer, was allowed to use the whip. Master did not flog unless he had a runaway, and he didn't have many runaways. But the best-treated slave is not free. Grandfather told Knobby never to trust any white person, and he chuckled when he told Knobby about the slave cook over in Natchez who poisoned the food and kept her master ill and away from his whip for weeks. Hester took exception to poisoning the slave owner's little children, but Grandfather said, "Little white boys and girls grow up to be white men and women who own slaves."

"Remember the Israelites, Knobby. We're biding our time, lying in wait, till the Lord raises us up to smite our white enemy and free ourselves. Thus saith our Lord, Grandson: 'I will deliver thee out of the hand of the wicked, and I will redeem thee out of the hand of the terrible.'"

On Noble Plantation, Grandfather, too, had fallen in love.

"I did not want to see my wife flogged. I did not want to love a family and risk being sold apart. But young Master Noble promised me he would not separate his slave families. My love was strong, so I married and made children. My daily prayer begs Jesus to help Master Noble keep his promise and, so far, Jesus has answered my prayers. But a life of ashes is habited to wreckage and ruin, and my fears have never had a moment's repose."

Separated by War

When the master went off to fight in the War of Northern Aggression, he left Knobby in charge of all the livestock on Noble Plantation. Months passed, and still the war went on. Knobby took good care of the animals, but he had Elizabeth and Texas on his mind. Then the master came home for a short spell to look after his affairs. Money was short and there was little need for field hands with the blockade hurting cotton so. The master sold most of his slaves, including Elizabeth, to a slave trader who chained her with others in his wagon he was taking to the auction block in New Orleans. Knobby could not bear to see her sold away. He begged the master to sell him with her, but the master said he could not give up Knobby.

"Were you and the girl united in holy matrimony, I would not separate you. But while I have to be away I'm relying on you and Samuel. If the trader sells your gal to someone close by, you have leave to visit. The mistress will write a pass. But with the blockade stopping cotton, few around here could afford her. I scarce know why the trader bought, except the prices I asked were so low."

After the master went back to the war, Knobby told his mama and grandfather good-bye. Hester wept and begged him not to go, but Grandfather Samuel hugged him and said, "Fly, June bug. I have prayed you would one day be free, but I never asked to live to see the day. Our Lord has blessed me. You, Grandson, are the spark our Lord sent me to kindle. I have taught you all I know. I have husbanded your smoldering heat. Burn bright, Grandson."

Knobby told the mistress a lie. He said the master had ordered him to take six of the horses to town to sell them. Standing before her with her eyeballs darting from side to side judging his words, Knobby silently prayed, *Dear Jesus please let her believe me—if it's not a sin to ask You to have her believe a lie—and let me get away safely to New Orleans and let me find Elizabeth and let her be all right and help us, Dear Lord, escape this slave life, if it be Thy will, Amen.*

"Why, Knobby, he didn't tell me a thing about selling any horses."

"No ma'am, he didn't want to fret you any. He told me to get a good return and bring the money direct to you." *Please, Dear Lord, please.*

So the mistress wrote a letter for him to carry, saying he was doing his master's business and any assistance rendered to the slave Knobby Cotton was assistance rendered to Noble Plantation.

Knobby sold all but two of the horses. He found suitable homes for them, and he got good return. He hid the money in a canvas sack he tied around his waist beneath his trousers. Leading a mount for Elizabeth, he rode to New Orleans after her, covering the ninety or so miles in just two days. The horses understood his urgency, and they ran for him with all their will. He didn't figure any white folks could have made New Orleans as fast. As he rode, the sack tugged at his waist, and he wondered if the sale of four horses had brought enough to buy one Negro woman. He kept alert for pickets and patrols, Union or Confederate—he didn't know which to expect. He knew the Federals, under General Butler, had control of New Orleans, but he wasn't sure how they would treat a slave on the loose, even one who was about his master's business.

As he neared the city, he saw mounted soldiers—blue uniforms, so he guessed them Union. The soldiers were resting their horses. Sitting on logs, they smoked and drank from canteens. He was near enough to hear their speech, though he couldn't make out the words. He moved away, keeping himself and his horses downwind of the soldiers' mounts. In a thicket from which he could hear the patrol, he waited until dark, when the men finally remounted and moved slowly through the woods. Within half an hour he was safely in the city.

Knobby talked to enough colored folks to learn New Orleans was in an uproar. General Butler had gotten rid of the mayor, and members of the city council had resigned rather than take an oath of allegiance to the United States. Butler had run the white preachers out of town for upholding slavery in their sermons, and he'd shut down the white newspapers for printing stuff he didn't like. The prisons down at Forts Jackson and St. Philip were full of white folks who had provoked Butler by waving secesh flags and harassing his officers.

"Us niggers is safe here," one old man told him. "Swear you a free man and you is. There is contrabands all over town."

Another said, "General Phelps sends Yankee soldiers a-tromping all round to help slaves escape they masters and come live at Carrollton where they feed all us cousins, feed any colored folks who ain't no longer slaves. Word is they gone get up colored soldiers for the Union, set up tents for all the contrabands."

Knobby told them about the man who had bought the slaves from Noble Plantation. Another cousin said the man might be Mr. D. D. Bohanan, who was in thick with General Butler's brother, Andrew, who could sell you a piece of paper, a permit from the general, to do just about anything. Andrew had lots of Confederate friends, especially rich planters. Bohanan did plenty of Andrew's dirty work, and word was he ran much of the city's illegal slave trade. Most times Bohanan idled around at the fairgrounds.

At the fairgrounds race track, Knobby talked to an old stablehand who had seen Bohanan with a wagonload of colored girls. Might be one of them was Knobby's Elizabeth.

Early the next morning, the stablehand pointed out Bohanan with two other men watching a little sorrel mare exercise. He was a stout man, big without being tall, heavy yet not fat. He looked Knobby up and down, slow as he might rove his eyes over a horse to buy.

"What kinda big nigger boy we got here, riding up and throwing such a big shadow over me?" He laughed without showing his teeth. He wore a brown linen suit wrinkled and creased as if it had not ever been pressed. Down the front of his white shirt were orange splotches like grease stains, and Knobby imagined a feast of pork or beef the night before. Bohanan shook his large head when Knobby introduced himself and showed Bohanan the paper the mistress had written. Knobby described Elizabeth and said his mistress wanted her slave back to Noble Plantation to run her kitchen.

"You haven't already sold her, have you, sir?"

"Why, slaving ain't lawful in occupied territory. I wouldn't do nothing unlawful. Might be I heard about this gal, though. I might even know if her and some other house niggers are somewhere put up. But, boy, you know I couldn't sell no slave to a slave, even if slaving was legal." A dewlap of pale flesh swayed beneath Bohanan's chin and jaws.

"Mr. Bohanan, sir, wartime is different. Master is away fighting Yankees and Mistress can't leave Noble lands. Mistress sent a commission for you, sir." From his shirtpocket Knobby took a portion of the money he had secreted there from his canvas sack.

"I can't trust this paper you say she wrote. You know any white man in New Orleans to vouch for you?"

"No, sir, I'm just newly here at my mistress' bidding, as she wrote on the paper with the money she gave me."

Bohanan took the money. He wore a ring on every finger, wore both gold and silver, some bearing stones that glittered in the morning sun. He said he would hold the funds while he waited for an answer to a message he would send to Noble Plantation to make sure Knobby wasn't a runaway. "You mighty proper-talking for a nigger. But I sure can't picture selling a slave to another slave."

"Sir, I thought inside Union lines all slaves are free."

Bohanan stared at Knobby for a long minute, then gave his head a shake, grinned. "A rumor spread by a abolitionist general up to Camp Parapet, one of them who want to enforce the unnatural system of amalgamation. General Butler is in charge in New Orleans, and General Butler sends runaways back to their masters. You may think you can strut free as you please, but these days you can't trust nobody. New Orleans is filled up with contrabands getting jobs other niggers want. Any free black might turn you in to save his job. Plenty of Union soldiers have their own slaves. Some, like Phelps, are ranting abolitionists. Confederate sympathizers are so mad at General Butler they call him 'the Beast.' After Order Number Twenty-eight, there are men who don't hold with slaving who would buy you just to spite the Yankee dictator."

One of the men with Bohanan said, "With the town under blockade there ain't many slaves. I hear tell some men are making better money now than when there was open auctions. No competition, steeper prices."

Bohanan scowled at the man and turned back to Knobby. "Your only chance of seeing your woman again and not getting sent back to Noble is to put down some security with someone like me." Bohanan held up Knobby's letter and money. "Which you've wisely done. 'Course, if it's just a woman you want, they got plenty up at Camp Parapet sitting around ripe for company in cane huts." Bohanan opened his wide mouth and laughed, his spittle spraying from gaps in his surprisingly small and badly stained teeth. He addressed the man who had spoken to Knobby, "Ain't it so, A. J.?" Bohanan laughed some more. "A. J. here has scratched his itch up there a time or two, ain't you, A. J.?" He turned back to Knobby, his voice soft and menacing. "But if it's one particular gal, it may take some doing. Trust and patience, boy, trust and patience."

Bohanan didn't forcibly hold Knobby, but he wasn't about to let Knobby wander off. Veiled threats about Elizabeth's welfare were sufficient to keep Knobby close. "I got to see a man in Algiers about a racehorse. Might be, after my track business, we could check on your gal."

After they led the sorrel back to the paddock, Bohanan mounted the horse Knobby had brought for Elizabeth. With the man, A. J., doubling behind Knobby, they rode to a landing where a ferry boat took them, still on horseback, to the west side of the Mississippi River. A man on the bank waved his arms like a madman. When the ferry docked in a cloud of mosquitoes Knobby realized the man had been swatting the bugs, not waving. This man was waiting for Bohanan and, following his orders, led him and Knobby to a plank shed two or three miles away.

"Inside," Bohanan said.

Inside the shed were two wooden chairs at a table that held a bowl and a pitcher of water, but no Elizabeth or anyone else.

"Your letter says your master puts great store in you for a horseman."

"Folks say I ride passable, sir."

"I'm going to give you a chance to work some horse magic this very night." With that, Bohanan left Knobby in the shed and padlocked the door from without.

The door was hinged on the inside and Knobby could have gotten out easily. But he didn't know whether Bohanan had left a guard behind and, besides, Bohanan was the one man who could take him to Elizabeth. Knobby didn't feel much protection from the Federal troops, and he didn't plan on being shot for a runaway by some angry secessionist.

Rides a Big Black Devil

In the afternoon, Bohanan came with the man called A. J. and got Knobby to go with him to a stable just outside town. Bohanan gave him a cotton poke of biscuits, ham, and apples. While they rode, Knobby ate and Bohanan talked. There were rumors, he said, about a stud horse that was going on the auction block. This horse's owner had a reputation for raising fast horses. "You heard of Gladiator? No, course not. Well, this stud is some of his horseflesh." Bohanan had been told the new stallion was magnificent, but he was said to be so impossible to handle he had never even been greenbroke.

When Bohanan, A. J., and Knobby reached the stable, four men had ropes on the horse and still couldn't get him out of his stall.

"Look at the big devil," Bohanan said, clearly both hating and admiring the horse's brute power and wild spirit.

"I wager, sir, I can ride him smooth."

"What can a nigger offer to wager?"

"You'll win all you put down on me against the horse. You can get double odds or better against me. You keep all the winnings. All I want is to take Elizabeth back to my mistress. And you keep the commission I gave you from my mistress."

The slaver grinned. "I suspect you want this gal for you, not for your mistress. You darkies rut like beasts. But why should I believe you can ride Satan himself?"

"Master trusts me with all the horses of Noble Plantation. You can double, triple any amount you risk. If I lose, you can lay claim to me and my master's two horses. On top of that, if I lose you can put me under a whip and take back your losses in blood." *Heavenly Father, grant me the strength, make me quick, whisper in the ear of this horse, Your creature, that he might understand too, and let me ride him true if it be Thy will.*

Who knows what moves the mind of a slave trader—money sure, but beyond profit, what? Maybe Bohanan saw a way to make a circus show to guarantee him reward, in cash and in cruelty, both attendants to power. He conferred with the stallion's owner, and a sideshow was arranged. Bets were open, but admission would be charged just to watch the spectacle.

By dark, a ring of cotton bales enclosed the dirt center of a large barn lighted with sputtering torches. Packed behind the bales was a crowd of watchers, every one of whom had paid to stand in the muggy, close, dimly lit place to see "a big black nigger ride a big black devil," as Bohanan had loudly advertised the exhibition.

When Knobby was about to enter the ring, the slaver grabbed his shoulder from behind.

"Wait, boy. This is going to be a show. You strip, first. Bareback and naked, black flesh to black flesh, brute to brute." Torchlight flickered on Bohanan's teeth.

"No, sir. I'm a horseman not a tent show animal."

"How bad you want to see your nigger gal?"

When Knobby removed his clothes he tried to keep the sack containing the rest of the money hidden, but Bohanan picked up his trousers and shook the sack free. He grinned, hefting the money. "More's the deposit, more's the trust. Right, boy?" It was futile to argue. Knobby nodded and entered the hot and dusty ring where the wild horse waited.

Beneath his bare feet the ground tingled, and dust hovered as alive as dry grass under a lightning sky just before the rain sizzles down. He danced over the hornet-humming, charged, dirt floor. The crowd of white men laughed and hollered—yelling, mostly, encouragement for the horse and vulgar jokes about Knobby's nakedness. He got in front of the horse and looked the animal right in the face. Torchlight shined off the tense muscles of the stallion and glowed red in the horse's eyes. Knobby watched the animal's ears. Knobby whispered horse words and with his body's movements told the horse he would not hurt him. But this horse had been so mistreated he did not trust Knobby, and there was precious little time for Knobby to earn his trust.

Slowly, long arms out, Knobby moved toward the horse as a swimmer walks from shallow water toward a deep pool he knows is over his head. The close, fetid air pressed against Knobby's naked body, warm and heavy as muddy water.

Talking *hunh, un-hunh,* chest-deep guttural horse-talk all the time, his unblinking eyes staring into the horse's flame-red eyes, Knobby got his hands on the horse's neck where scabs told Knobby's fingers how the horse had been chained and how he had broken free. *Un-hunh, easy, black boy, easy. You a slave just like me.*

Taking care to stay where the horse could see him with both eyes at once, Knobby slowly rubbed the animal's neck and kept talking low and steady. Under his fingers the horse's muscles twitched and rippled.

The stallion wanted to listen and understand, but he flinched when someone in the torchlit barn said, "Hey, nekkid boy, this is a horse, not some high yeller gal you can sweet-talk." The crowd yelled and whistled. The horse's eyes widened, and he jerked from Knobby's touch.

Unable to ease the horse the way he'd like to, Knobby got a hold deep in the wiry mane and, like the monkey many in the crowd were calling him, swung up from the horse's neck and onto his back as from under a thick limb up onto a giant tree's trunk. *Please, Lord, please.* He stroked the horse and whispered horse assurances.

Too surprised to move, the horse stood frozen. Against Knobby's bare skin, warm horse fur, damp with sweat. Then the animal took four mincing steps forward. He stopped, snorted, shook his head like someone waking from a deep sleep. Behind Knobby, someone in the milling and shouting crowd whacked the stallion across the backs of his legs with a board.

Knobby had both hands buried in the horse's mane, horsehair wrapped like twine around his fingers. Beneath Knobby's chest, the crest of the mane was bristly and pliant as a thick rope. He pressed his knees into the spaces he found between the animal's ribs. A muscle in the horse's back jerked beneath Knobby's naked scrotum and rippled beneath his forgotten cock and his inner thighs. He had his feet up against the points of the horse's hips, his long toes digging for purchase. Almost equal to his fear for Elizabeth, for himself, was his sorrow that he was forced to ride a horse who, in his terror and anger, wanted nothing more than Knobby off his back.

The first time the horse bucked, Knobby's toes grappled in horsehair to keep his bottom from leaving the horse's back, but he went so high his cock swung up and slapped his belly before he smacked back onto the horse. He got his knobby heels into the depressions the horse's flanks made and put his face into the mane, gaining another hold with his teeth clamping mane. This time the horse reared, walking on his two hind legs for so long Knobby was sure he would slide down the horse's back. Knobby's fingers burned and his teeth ached, but he held on.

The instant the stallion's front hooves hit the dirt, his back legs kicked up, once, so high the cheeks of Knobby's bare butt spanked both sides of the horse's spine, and Knobby's balls shot sharp cramping pains up into his stomach. The animal whirled, the dark earth rushed up, and when Knobby hit, legs outstretched in a sitting position, his teeth hurt up into his ears and above his eyes. He sat. The ground tipped up against the tin roof that wiggled in the torchlight, and the horse was high up there against the barn rafters.

If the horse had attacked him then, the horse would have won. But the animal stood and snorted and stared at this other blackness he had gotten out from under. Knobby got back on his feet even though he could not see them, could not feel them nor the ground beneath them, and then he was again on the horse's back, his toes in the animal's brisket, one big hand holding mane, the other grasping a long ear. *June bug, June bug,* Knobby's mama sang, *hold tight June bug, hold tight.* And Knobby got all of his June bug toes into the stallion's hair, and June bug hung on. Round and round they galloped, jerked and stopped, reared and bucked, and Knobby kept his bug mouth sucking on horseflesh and listened to his June bug wings buzz, vibrating in the swirling dust. The horse popped his tail like a slaver's whip, stinging Knobby's skin and almost switching him off. But June bug hung on.

Round and round they trotted, then round and round they walked, until Bohanan came out with a stiff riding crop and stopped the horse as if he were the one who was riding it. Some men got a hackamore over the horse's head, and Knobby slid down off his back. *Oh thank You, Jesus.* And, *I'm sorry, good horse, I'm sorry.*

Bohanan had taken off his wrinkled suitcoat, and his shirt was luminous in the torchlit barn. He turned to address the close crowd of men, the shirt tight across his back where his pink skin showed through in the sweat-shape of an animal pelt nailed up to dry.

"Nigger rides like a ape swings vines, tight as a tick on a hound," Bohanan said to the head-shaking crowd. "Lookahere." He grabbed a burning torch off a post and jerked it close to Knobby's skin, shaking stinging drops of fire onto Knobby's stomach and the tops of his thighs. Knobby was shiny with sweat and the yellow light looked liquid running over his muscles. Bohanan slapped the inside of Knobby's thigh with the riding crop. With a finger that spouted a small flame where a diamond ring rekindled the sputtering torch, Bohanan pointed at Knobby's crotch. His cock had mysteriously grown thick and turgid and swayed and danced away from his body. Some of the men hooted, and some turned their faces away. To Knobby, Bohanan said, "Guess you getting ready for the unbroke gal I got roped and tied for you. I ought to charge admission for that show, too."

Knobby was glad to be so exhausted. He was too spent to respond to the man's vulgar insults or he would have surely gotten himself killed then and there.

Bohanan collected his share of the admissions and his winnings from wagers. The poor horse was led away, another slave off to his pen. Bohanan threw Knobby's clothes at him and turned him over to an old man he called Pea, who took Knobby back to the shed room where he'd spent the afternoon.

"I tell you, boy, you're a mighty determined rider." Pea brought Knobby a towel and filled the pitcher by the bowl with clean water. While Knobby washed horse sweat and his sweat, horse blood and his blood, off his hands and chest, Pea brought a plate of beans and rice, a glass jar warm with thick black coffee. Knobby's hands and feet were cut and scratched, his flesh stung where the hot torch oil had splattered, his muscles burned, his back was stiff and sore, his balls ached.

Pea said he was sorry to lock up so good a horseman, nigger or not, and he left Knobby there to finish cleaning and feeding himself in the dark.

Alone in the stuffy hot room, Knobby wondered how long he would have to wait to see if Bohanan would keep his end of their bargain. After he scraped clean the tin plate of beans and rice and drank all the strong coffee, Knobby waited. Then Pea was there with a lantern, waking him, and Knobby cursed himself for falling asleep. "Come on, boy, Bohanan done told me to wait till after midnight, then to move you quick and quiet-like."

Pea extinguished the lantern and led Knobby in the moonless night down a grassy alleyway between warehouses and sheds to a small brick building. Pea put a big key to the padlock.

"This here is a old freight clerk's office. The inspector's desk is still in there." Pea got the door unlocked and pushed against the heavy wood, scraping white arcs on the dirty plank floor. "You got to shed them clothes again, boy. Bohanan's orders."

"Why?"

"I reckon it pleases him somewise. Maybe he figures a nekkid nigger ain't likely to run. You won't want no clothes no way for the black bucking mare waiting for you. In you go."

Anger blazed up in Knobby and he turned to grab Pea, but the door was already closed again, and the key rattled in the lock. Pea's voice came through the door, "I'll be back at sunup."

Naked, barefoot-silent, Knobby stepped into the dark room. Neither oil lamp nor candle guided his way. The emanation, the aura of another body—cloud, fog, steam, exhalation—drifted against his naked front. Part of the darkness before him moved. Warmth and stirred air enveloped him. He was afraid to say her name, terrified that as soon as he breathed "Elizabeth?" a harsh laugh would rebuke him for putting any trust in a white man's agreement. In the muggy dark, a bittersweet scent crept just beyond his recognition the way his memories sometimes teased him before they revealed themselves. Footsteps pattered, light and anxious as scattering leaves.

"Manfolk, don't hurt me," said the darkness in words he either heard or understood without hearing.

"Elizabeth."

"Not Knobby. Not my Knobby. Can't be."

He walked into her the way a sleepy man walks into the foot of his own bed, and all up and down the length of him his skin was shocked awake by her skin, both of them prickly with sweat. He knew her with all his tip ends—toes, fingers, tongue, and nose—at once he felt her breasts against his chest, his encircling arms against the washboard of her ribs, her thigh between his thighs, her pubic hair coarse against his skin, his bare hands gripping the swell of her damp buttocks. He inhaled damp earth and salt smell, odor of broken gourds.

Knobby and Elizabeth had loved one another for nearly two years, but they had not yet known one another's bodies. Knobby could have slipped around Noble Plantation after dark without stirring up the dogs, but Elizabeth went hard by Grandfather Samuel's Scriptures. For her grit, Knobby held her high, but he sometimes wished she'd fall just a little. Now, as they embraced in their nakedness, he was overwhelmed with wants and fears, as Adam must have been before the shadow of God's mysterious dark side fell over the garden after human flesh's first sin.

"Oh, Baby, Baby." Knobby kissed Elizabeth's eye, the side of her nose, her trembling chin.

"Knobby Cotton." She held him around the waist and squeezed him tight. His ribs and back were so sore from the bucking stallion, her touch hurt him.

"We've got to get out now, right now."

"Where can we go?"

"To Texas where there's all a man can chew and where what I do best is what matters."

"The Good Lord's put me in the way of a lunatic."

"In mysterious ways He works, Elizabeth." *Lord, I pray I'm talking true.*

Pulling Elizabeth by the hand, Knobby found the wall. He was momentarily glad of the darkness so Elizabeth could not see his cock that swayed out before his body like some stiff, curved divining rod. With one extended hand feeling the rough board wall, he walked blind to a corner and continued around the room's perimeter. Just before he felt it, he saw the faintly lighter dark shape of a small window. Not even latched. He opened the window and filled the space, squeezing through the eye of a needle. The instant his bare feet touched grass, his mama whispered — Hester's high birdsong voice clear as if she were in the room — "Quick as a wink" — and just that quick he pulled Elizabeth through behind him. Knobby considered looking for the horses he had brought, *any* horses, but if he found horses he would also find men.

Into the Swamp

So a man and a woman, dark-skinned and naked, whose recent ancestors had run down the beaches of West Africa, ran that night down a narrow passageway between warehouses, and then across a wide field that seemed to the runners endless, and then into sucking mud alongside slow-moving water. They entered the water almost without sound. The water's warmth surprised them, offered no relief from the muggy heat. They moved with the water, moved steadily and without speech, Elizabeth at rest in the crook of Knobby's arm held above the water, keeping dry the sack with what was left of the biscuits, ham, and apples Bohanan had given him the day before. Knobby relaxed in the water's current, letting it carry them along. All the world was shades of black. Beneath the starless and impossibly tall sky and beyond the moving darkness they were in, were the dark shapes of trees and of an occasional barn or house. The shoreline was here and there dotted with a yellow light, then of a sudden went ragged and wild with the fur of cypress, willow, and mossy oak, and no more lights burned.

After they had been a long time in the darker dark of swampy forest primeval, at the first faint delineation of light to the east, Knobby got them to a muddy wallow neither fully land nor fully water.

"I wish we had a big sack of pepper," he told Elizabeth, "but if they get after us the hounds will have almost as hard a time tracking over all this water as if we peppered their noses."

"I don't want dogs after me, Knobby. Didn't ask for this run-off-and-hide."

"It'll be all right, girl." He started to say the Lord would watch over them, but he didn't.

"It's already *not* all right."

51

Glad he had left the Lord out of it, Knobby smeared his body and Elizabeth's with mud to shield them from gnats and mosquitoes. Against the mud, he patted leaves and moss to hide them in the forest. In this protective coloring they clung all the hours of daylight to the low forked limb of a live oak like patient larvae in a cocoon. Well after nightfall, they flew fast and far away.

For the next two days and nights they portioned out biscuits and ham and bites of apple, and they drank pooled rainwater. Every step of the way Elizabeth complained. They moved by night. Working against the north star, Knobby kept them walking mostly west with wide circles around marshland and distant buildings. It was hard to judge, but he hoped they'd gotten thirty or forty miles from New Orleans.

"You call this free, Knobby Cotton? I'd be pleased to take myself back to Noble Plantation or some such proper house."

"You can't. You'll get caught and sold in New Orleans. Pretty as you are, a white man might buy you as his fancy lady. We're going to Texas to live free."

"I'm too black for pretty, and, last time I heard, Texas was a slave state same as Mississippi."

"It's not the same, not the same as any other place." Knobby put his arms around her, but she would have none of it.

"Don't be kissing on me with me all dipped in mud batter to fry in the sun. You can kiss on me when I'm good and ready. When I've had a bath and something sweeter-smelling than swamp gas is coming off my skin."

Elizabeth went into a long pout. She grudged Knobby every move she made, but she made them all the same—she didn't have much choice.

Like birds they lived on blackberries and hid in trees and watched and listened for signs of other people. When they came to a bayou or a marshy place they drank, and Knobby patched their mud coverings that dried and flaked off as they walked.

After two more nights, Knobby and Elizabeth both shaky with hunger, Knobby woke to a distant hacking, like a woodpecker's drilling. He leaned over to shake Elizabeth awake, but her eyes were open wide, staring straight up at nothing.

"Come on," he said. But Elizabeth lay motionless, eyes fixed. The hacking grew louder. He bent and lifted her to a sitting position. She acted paralyzed. "Elizabeth?"

Finally, she blinked, licked her lips, spoke in a husky whisper, "Knobby, I was frozen solid, couldn't move, couldn't make speech. I feel awful streaked."

"You've reason to be scared. You'd be a fool not to be."

"I'm ridden by a ghost. Someone whispered my name this morning, and it wasn't you. He's sitting on my chest right now, pressing so heavy I can't hardly draw breath."

Knobby sighed. He hated these superstitions. "Let me help you up." She took his hand, and he felt her arm tremble. She was wobbly. He was amazed her imagination could so affect her body. He got her to her feet, and she fell against him.

"My legs are soft like mud. I've got no stand up in me."

"My legs don't work so well either—nobody walks well on an empty stomach."

"Knobby, we've got to put red pepper by the window, keep this old ghost off me."

He laughed in spite of himself. "I'm so hungry, if we had any red pepper I'd eat it. Besides, if we *had* pepper, we don't have any window." Elizabeth looked around as if she were just remembering she was no longer on Noble Plantation. She squeezed his arm, and he released her. She stood on her own.

"Depends how you look on it. We've got no window or we've got windows all around."

Elizabeth was shed of whatever ghost had waylaid her. She stayed close as Knobby led the way through the forest. Ahead was a wide swath of low growth, bunches of tall grass, bushes and vines, saplings leaning in the light breeze. In the distance scattered amongst the greenery were indistinct shapes black against the bright morning haze. Knobby and Elizabeth reached the edge of a cornfield, squatted and stared. The moving black shapes were colored people swinging long blades. Two dark men worked with a team of mules, with rope and tackle, pulling against an enormous stump. Knobby crept from the cover of the woods out into the far field that was being cleared. Elizabeth grimaced and closed tight her eyes. He wondered if she was praying. *If she is, Jesus, me too. Me, I'm praying, and if she's not it's just because she's scared and tired and hungry. Be with us both, please, Lord.* Knobby headed toward a young Negro beneath a broad-brimmed straw hat who was swinging a short, straight blade. Nowhere in the area did Knobby see a white man. Which of the slaves was the overseer? The hacking closest stopped. The solitary Negro stood stock-still, his unblinking eyes on Knobby. As he hurried to the man, Knobby wondered what he was about to say.

"Brother, I need your help."

The man straightened to his full height, nearly as tall as Knobby, and gracefully pushed the point of his blade into the earth until it stuck up as a stalk. Where the blade entered the ground, links of rust-colored chain coiled like a snake around the man's bare foot, stretched between iron bands locked around the man's badly scabbed ankles. The man glanced toward the team of mules. One of the muleteers stood back from the work, pointing and calling out instructions. By his stance, the overseer. The young Negro pointed to a pile of brush he had made, a mound as high as a horse, and Knobby stepped over against the mound, hidden from the overseer.

The leg irons let Knobby speak plain.

"My woman waits for me in the woods. We're runaways off of a Mississippi plantation. We've come these past five days from New Orleans. We're starved and lost."

Still the man did not speak, and Knobby wondered if he had handed over his life and Elizabeth's to an idiot. The man dropped to his knees and swept away grass and stems, smoothed the ground by their feet. He poked a hole with his finger and pointed to himself and to Knobby. With a short twig he drew a hump, the mound of brush that hid them from the overseer. He pointed to the sun overhead and drew a circle in the dirt, then described an arc from the sun and wrote a "W" with his twig. Knobby looked up, looked beyond the brightness across the field. "West?"

The man drew a southerly line he marked with a "4" and intersected with a wiggly line.

"A river, bayou—a bayou. Four miles?"

The mute nodded and stood, his speech ended. He pointed to the woods from which Knobby had come, and then the man picked up his blade and swung it so it flashed in the sun, flashed so the overseer could see him chopping. Shush-thunk, shush-thunk, the blade spoke.

It was hard for Knobby to judge when he and Elizabeth had walked four miles. Once or twice he lost the sun in the thick overgrowth of cypresses that dripped with Spanish moss. Eventually, the trees ended before the grassy mound of a levee. Knobby wanted to go up the levee to see what he could see, but he made himself wait for twilight.

A crow's caw made Knobby jump, and Elizabeth giggled. Mosquitoes buzzed above them, following them up the grassy incline of the levee. On the other side was a bayou purple in the last light of day. Beyond the water were more cypresses.

Atop the levee was enough night breeze to give them relief from the mosquitoes, and they both dozed.

An owl's hoot woke Knobby. A slice of moon low in the sky threw a swath of light across the bayou like a lavender kerchief floating there. The same lavender light was adrift in Elizabeth's eyes. When the owl hooted closer Knobby sat up. Two black figures loped toward them, running in an easy crouch down the crown of the levee, a melody of clinking grew louder. One of the men was the mute from the field, his chains making the music. The other man had gray in his close-cropped hair. He handed Knobby a cotton sack and said, "Brother and sister, my name is Joseph Thomas. I speak for the slaves at Martin Plantation. Here is poor food, all we can spare."

"I'm Knobby Cotton, and this is Elizabeth."

Joseph Thomas shook Knobby's hand, touched Elizabeth on the arm. "Calvin says you are come from New Orleans. You were safer there than here. The partisan rangers are all about. They have a militia camp at New Iberia, in addition to Camp Pratt at Opelousas." The faint moonlight fell on a square of paper the man held, a crude map. "You must stay south of New Iberia and watch for the bands of militia—the Terrebonne Rangers are the worst. Most of the fighting is in Lafourche, here," the man's finger came down on the map as a dark bolt from God, "south and west of New Orleans. The Union has the Opelousas Railroad all the way from Algiers through Thibodaux to Berwick City. Union troops will protect you, get you back to New Orleans."

"No. We are bound for Texas. There's a man in New Orleans after us. He's in with General Butler's brother."

"The Yankees have taken over the cane plantations from Berwick Bay up past Donaldsonville. They're paying contrabands to work as freed slaves, protected by the provost guards. One of our slaves ran away—he's there now making ten dollars a month."

"I'm no field hand." Joseph's eyes rose from the map. "I mean no disrespect. I'm bound for Texas or Mexico, where a colored horseman can earn his keep."

"I take no offense. I learn all I can to help all my colored brothers. Take the food and the map. It is little to eat for a man your size, too big to hide away. Know this, too: gunboats are reputed to be in Berwick Bay, here, and on up the Atchafalaya. We hear all kinds of war rumors, can't know what to believe. I don't know what you'll find in the Gulf this far west—gunboats, maybe. The rangers are after Cajun deserters and other white conscripts. Rangers shoot any Negro on sight. Many hide in the swamp, but God made the swamp large enough for multitudes.

Go south, keep to the coast. If you make Vermilionville, you'll have grass plains on west to Niblett's Bluff at the Sabine." The man's finger aimed off the map's edge, but the word *Sabine* gave Knobby hope.

Joseph handed Knobby another paper. It said the Negroes in possession of this document were former slaves of the Pugh Plantation, their freedom having been purchased by Mr. James Washington of—here the words ended. Joseph penciled in *Galveston, Texas.* He wrote a date at the top of the paper and gave it to Knobby. "Depends on who stops you, this may or may not work. Most of the rangers can't read, so any writing works on them if writing works at all."

"Who's James Washington?"

Calvin grinned and Joseph said, "I made him up. Named him after George Washington. There *is* a Pugh Plantation, though. You say you're on your way to Galveston to work for Mr. Washington. Galveston is about the only town I know in Texas."

"Why don't you come with us, Joseph—the both of you?" It was the first time Elizabeth had spoken, and her soft words startled Knobby.

Joseph smiled, his teeth brown but straight. He took Elizabeth's hand. "Bless you, daughter, you and your man here. The spirit of God's children in bondage will walk with you every hard step of your way. Others count on me where I am, so I'm where God wants me. And Calvin has a promise to keep here."

"What promise?" Knobby said, then wished he had not.

But Calvin grinned and motioned with his hands. Joseph made hand signals back, then he spoke, "Our master, Mr. Albert Martin, wanted to lie with Calvin's wife. When she refused, the master gave her one hundred lashes. When she still refused, he gave one hundred more. The fourth day, she died under the lash. When the master came to Ginny's burying, Calvin struck him. He shot Calvin through the neck. Master Martin cow-hided Calvin with a carriage harness and doused his wounds, even the bullet hole, with saltwater. Master put Calvin in a well and boarded him over. Kept him there a month, lowering him cornbread and water. But he works as ten in the fields, so Master needs him. Keeps him in irons. I remind him vengeance is the Lord's, but Calvin has vowed to be the Lord's instrument to cut off Albert Martin's head." Joseph reached for Knobby's hand, held Elizabeth with his other hand, nodded to Calvin, who joined in the circle. "Let us pray Lord Jesus will guide and direct Knobby and Elizabeth on their journey."

"May He guide and direct Calvin's hand swinging a sharp blade," Elizabeth said.

Calvin and Knobby both looked at Joseph, who nodded and said, "Amen."

An Uncommon Duet

Before Colonel Luellen Powell-Hughes took me in and schooled me I was as
uneducated as any slave, but I was not without original ideas and the capacity
to learn. I cannot but believe any man or woman, dark-skinned or light, slave or
free, will respond somehow in kind to opportunity or favor given.

—from *Gideon Jones' Journal*

Knobby and Elizabeth followed Joseph's map, walking at night south and west
except two times when they saw armed men on horses and circled wide around.
Joseph's bag of yams and hoecakes lasted one day. The second morning they were
hungry, and Elizabeth was despondent.

Knobby saw in the tops of distant trees a blue different from the sky and knew
that blue as rising woodsmoke. Woodsmoke was cooked food. Knobby zigzagged
them closer to the smoke. At a narrow bayou they tried to quiet their stomachs by
filling them with water. Mid-afternoon they hid in a thicket out of sight of a bats-
and-boards shack—its brick chimney sending up the smoke Knobby had spotted.
So close were they to the shack, night breezes brought the smell of bacon and
the slap of a slammed door, followed by the yawp of a hound off after some scent.
When the hound bayed again, Knobby let out his breath because the howls were
growing distant.

"Knobby, we've got to acknowledge the corn. We're in a fix. I'm so almighty
hungry I'll soon give out." It was the first Elizabeth had spoken all day.

"I know. I have to reason this out." *Lord, help me provide, show me what to
do.*

"You reason like all creation." She slipped off but soon came back with her
arms full of brown pine needles she spread on the ground thick and soft, where she
lay down. "You reason, Knobby." She put her head down and soon was asleep.

Knobby lay beside Elizabeth. He had to close his eyes. Soldiers, a farmer,
anyone might come along, might kill them while they slept. But even if someone
killed them, he had to sleep. *Dear Lord,* he thought, *watch over*—and it was *that
quick* dawn, and he was back awake, unkilled all night, still alive in a world of danger. In her sleep, Elizabeth resisted him less, her cheek nestling inside his arm.
Mosquito bites covered her forehead, and mud streaked her nose and cheeks. Her
arms were laced with tiny cuts from twigs and thorns. *Damn everything to Hell,*
Knobby thought. *I will get her safe to Texas, or farther to Mexico, or all the way
to California.*

Knobby left Elizabeth sleeping and crept close enough to the farm shack to see a gray-headed, bony man hitch an even bonier mule to a harness. The legs of the man's overalls were rusty with clay. The man shouldered shovel and axe, put on a straw hat with a brim so frayed it looked fringed, then plodded in heavy-looking brogans after the mule he was driving toward a field of parched-looking corn. The baying hound of the night just past lay in the dirt before the house, a brown lump so motionless Knobby would have taken it for a rock had he not seen the animal walk three circles before dropping to the earth. From inside the house came singing, a woman's voice so pure and strong it was all Knobby could do not to join in when she sang:

> All my trust on Thee is stayed,
> All my help from Thee I bring.
> Cover my defenseless head
> With the shadow of Thy wing.

All morning Knobby waited from his spying place, and all morning the voice from inside the house serenaded him. His stomach growled so he feared the woman would hear it over her own singing. He should have waked Elizabeth to tell her where he was going, but she had looked like a sleeping child and he could not bring himself to disturb her rest. He hoped if she waked to find him gone she would know he was coming back for her soon and she would keep herself hidden inside the thicket.

The sun was almost overhead when the singer finally came outside, a woman too young-looking to be the wife of the skinny old man who had traipsed off behind the mule. The woman wore a bonnet and carried a basket and a bucket. She hummed as she walked toward the field where the man and his mule had become two small, dark shapes that leaned forward as if into a strong wind, inched forward from right to left.

The woman stopped humming, cocked her head, turned back, and said, "Grover, you worthless hound, come on with me."

There was a long moment in which nothing whatsoever happened, then the dog slowly pushed himself up, his front legs pushing up step by step while his behind didn't budge. Then he pulled himself forward and the stiff hind legs came along. Once he was up on all fours, the dog stretched, his back dipping down until his belly disappeared in the grass. Then he was off behind the woman, the tip of his upcurled tail dancing merrily above the tall grass beyond the dirt yard.

Good dog, Knobby thought, almost out loud. *Get on out of here with your nose and your growl and bark and most especially with your bite.*

Keeping the board house between himself and the woman, Knobby walked slowly, in a half-crouch, toward the door. When the woman stopped and switched her basket and bucket from one hand to the other, Knobby stopped, too. His heart beat so his chest ached, and he was dizzy enough he thought he might fall down. The woman went on without looking back, and he ran the rest of the way to her house. His hand on the wood latch, he held his breath. He had to force the door to move on its leather hinges. The boards scraped loudly against the packed dirt floor. From the doorway, he could not see the woman behind the house. He bent under the low door frame and stepped in. Heat rose up his naked body so sudden he took it first for fear, then he joined the heat to the woman's cookstove. The room was dark and smoky, the ceiling not much above his head. A lingering smell of bacon made his stomach buckle. His bare feet so quick and light they barely touched the ground, he ran to a crude pine cabinet and opened it. *Forgive me, Lord, now I'm a thief, help me not get caught.* He grabbed a feedsack dress and a worn pair of overalls. On the warm stovetop he found a stack of corn dodgers and one sweet potato. He had a moment's guilt—this potato was the woman's lunch. Then he dropped it and the bread onto the folded square of the dress he carried on top of the overalls. Three eggs sat in a basket on a rough-hewn table, and he dropped them onto the dress and folded it over the food. One small window in the room—it had no glass, but a leather-hinged solid pine shutter someone had swung open—looked out on the field where the man and mule still leaned into the space before them. The hound sat beside the woman's basket. Where was *she?*

Knobby whirled, ran through the door, and almost collided with the woman, who was coming back in.

A foot apart, they stood and stared at one another. This close, she didn't look so young. Her face, in spite of the bonnet, was sun-browned and wrinkled, her lips scabbed and cracked. In her dark hair, threads of silver shone in the sun bright as a knife's freshly honed edge. She wore a feedsack dress like the one Knobby had just stolen. Her mud-stained feet were bare. She didn't move a muscle, but her eyes got bigger, from the inside out, the dark pupils opening up like a flower bud in the sun. Her head was tipped back so her eyes looked up at Knobby's.

What a sight I must be, Knobby thought. He held the bundle of stolen clothes and food down below his waist, covering his nakedness as well as possible. Patches of mud and an occasional leaf still stuck to his skin and hair and he felt dried streaks of mud around his eyes and mouth. *Were there still wild Indians around here,* he thought, *she'd like as not take me for a heathen savage in warpaint. If she screams—oh, if she screams.*

"Mistress." He held his finger to his lips. "Mistress, please." *Oh, please, Lord Jesus.*

Her eyes pulsed and her lips twitched, but still she did not scream.

"Mistress, I'll not tell you a lie. I've had a difficult time of late. My woman and I haven't eaten since day before yesterday. We are freed slaves, but highwaymen stole all of our clothes. They took our freedom papers. They whipped my woman and were going to sell us back to being slaves. We slipped away in the dark and have been running and hiding since."

The woman looked around, as if she were trying to figure where she was. She made a croaking in her throat.

"Mistress, my nakedness shames me, and it shames my woman, as well." Knobby let the overalls unfold from his hand, and he held them against his stomach. He tried to stand with his naked legs behind the unfolded legs of the overalls. "I heard your pretty song this morning, your song, *Jesus, Lover of my soul.* Mistress, you and I sing to the same Lord. He's Master of us all. He gave you a voice pretty as a bird, pretty as any one of His singing birds."

"We got no money for slaves to do our chores." The woman's voice had gone husky. "I know you all to pieces for a runaway. My man wouldn't hold with helping no runaways." She looked over her shoulder as if her husband might be coming up behind her. "He wouldn't hold with nothing might bring down militia patrols on us. They call theirselves prairie rangers but they're just prairie bandits. They come checking right regular, hunting Cajuns and niggers alike, scooting all round after trouble."

Knobby looked over *his* shoulder, too, stared back through the dim room and out the bright square of the window that framed the small, dark shapes of the man and the mule. They still moved from right to left, their give-and-take as unchanging as some ocean wave God might have misplaced when He made the world, one perpetual tide God had breathed in motion in a small field of dying corn far from any sea.

Knobby wasn't sure how long he and the woman stared at one another. It couldn't have been as long as it seemed. Her lips trembled as if she were about to cry out, and before she could utter a sound, with no idea why he was doing it, softly Knobby began to sing:

Jesus, Lover of my soul,
Let me to Thy bosom fly,
While the nearer waters roll,
While the tempest still is high.

The woman tilted her head sideways, the way a bird on a limb will tilt its head, and as if she had no control over her lips and tongue and throat and lungs, she joined Knobby in singing:

Hide me, O my Savior, hide,
Till the storm of life is past.
Safe into the haven guide.
O receive my soul at last.

They both stopped, chests heaving. The woman pulled her bonnet off her head, bunched it up in her fist. "You get off this place, you hear? Run fast and don't never come back."

Thank you, Lord, thank you. Knobby took a step past the woman, so close he smelled the mingled odors of their frightened bodies, eased past her sideways so he wouldn't turn his naked backside to her. He was about to run when she touched his upper arm.

"Here." The woman thrust her wadded bonnet into his hand and squinted up. "It's a hot sun." He took the bonnet, and she said, angry-sounding, "For your woman."

Knobby glanced toward the man tiny in the far field.

And for the first time, the woman smiled, spreading her badly cracked lips to reveal small brown-stained teeth. Her sudden wide smile gave her an addled look. "Huh," she rasped. "He won't miss no bonnet. He never pays me no mind."

"If you please, Mistress, one thing more?"

The woman neither shook her head nor nodded—she simply waited, one eyebrow arched.

"How close to the Gulf are we, Mistress?"

The woman gave an involuntary smile, little more than a muscle twitch. "This place ain't got no name. You done passed Labadieville. It's back a good piece to Thibodaux and a hard way across the marsh to New Iberia. I ain't never been to the Gulf."

Knobby had never heard of Labadieville, and it wasn't on Joseph's map.

After all these miles of walking, Knobby had decided there was precious little on Joseph's map.

"How far to Texas, Mistress?" *What matters*, Portis Goar said, *is how a man sits a horse.*

The woman shook her head. "You got to cross the marshland and some days later the Sabine River. And I wager Sabine ain't near as pretty as it sounds. And I wager it's a lifetime of walking from this place."

A heartbeat later, Knobby raced through the woods, flesh stung by limbs and pinecones, the spontaneous duet in the clearing already a strange dream he could not clearly remember.

Two Talks: Child of the People

The Birth Lodge
(Big Cold Moon 1844–Sleet Moon 1845)

Perhaps because they are a people threatened on all sides, Comanches
treasure their children. I know firsthand they steal away white women and
children to make them their own. They bathe their children in streams
and rub buffalo fat on their skin. They fuss over them and call them
by pet names. I'm told a Comanche never strikes a son or daughter.
Babes are carried wherever their mothers go, and older children run wild
like packs of dogs and appear rambunctiously happy.

—from Gideon Jones' Journal

Crooked Nose moved his head about, hanging the yellow moon on different limbs
of a large hackberry tree. No warrior blood had been spilled on this ground, so no
ghosts rose with the rising moon. Full moon and clear, cold sky after two sleeps
of dark clouds, hackberry near the birth lodge—good signs. Soon, the medicine
woman, Melon Breasts Woman, would cut the umbilical cord and hang it over a
limb in the hackberry. Moon-silvered, the cord would glisten red and drip warm
blood onto frozen ground. Talking water of Arrowhead River chattered *tu-in-èh-
pua, tu-in-e`h-pua*. The signs reassured Crooked Nose he had strong medicine as
he sought the meaning of a troubling vision twice dreamed. For two sleeps past,
clouds had hidden the moon, yet no rain had fallen. For two sleeps as dark and
heavy as the buffalo robe that covered him, alone in his *kahni*, Crooked Nose had
had the same visitor. Brother Coyote had slipped silently into Crooked Nose's
sleep carrying a Numunuu baby as he would carry his own mewling pup, loose
skin at the back of the baby's neck in Coyote's mouth. Crooked Nose stirred the
banked fire with a cedar branch, dropped sweet smelling cedar onto the coals and

welcomed Brother Coyote. Crooked Nose offered venison and water, but Coyote would not put down his burden to eat or drink. Flames leapt and light shined on Coyote's fur. His black lips curled back in a grin or silent snarl. Coyote lifted a paw and steadied the swinging baby. A red flame flared between the baby's fat thighs. Now Crooked Nose knew his wife, Morning Star, would bear a son.

"Thank you, Brother Coyote, for this vision. My son will know you as his brother. From you he will take strength. From you he will get courage and cunning."

Coyote laughed his nervous, shrill laugh. Then Mother Moon came into the tipi and cast the boy baby's shadow on the earthen floor. The baby's cry rose through the smoke vent to become the shriek of a bird high in the sky. The baby kicked his legs and jerked his arms, but shadow legs and shadow arms lay dark and still on moonlit dirt. Then the shadow baby's cry burrowed deep into the earth to become the voice of a prairie dog in its burrow. Shadow arms and legs writhed over the ground like snakes, while the baby in Coyote's sharp grip hung motionless. Then Mother Moon went away, and took the shadow baby with her. The fire burned low. Coyote stood at the moving edge of light. The baby grabbed Coyote's ear and swung up onto his back. Coyote reared and circled the fire on his hind legs, upright as a man. He tried to shake the baby from his back, but the boy held fast. Still bearing the child, Coyote raced out into the night, fur flattening down the ridge of his back. The only sounds in the dark tipi were Brother Coyote's running footpads and, far away, water talking to rock. Crooked Nose could not return to sleep.

Before Father in Heaven looked over the hills, Melon Breasts Woman yipped and whined as a hungry pup. She fussed at the younger women, instructing them how to dig the hole for the afterbirth and the hole for steam-bathing. The women drove cedar stakes through soft dirt into hard caliche—stakes for Morning Star to pull against while she pushed her firstborn into the world. Father in Heaven threw his light over the earth and the jabbering and pounding stopped. Then Melon Breasts Woman came for Morning Star.

For all one sun, all one sleep, Melon Breasts Woman kept a fire going in the birth lodge. For all one sun, all one sleep, she tended to Morning Star. Though Melon Breasts Woman had helped many new ones find the path to this world, she had never brought life of her own blood. Her womb was an empty vessel, a hollow gourd.

Crooked Nose's mother, Deer Drinking, had died bringing him forth, and Melon Breasts Woman had been there to purify the birth lodge with burning sage. The sweet singe was Crooked Nose's first memory. Melon Breasts Woman had bathed him and wrapped him in soft deerskin and put him on his cradle board. The medicine woman had stayed to bathe Deer Drinking's body, to close her eyes with clay, and paint her face red for the grave. Because Deer Drinking died bringing life, special pleasures awaited her in the Happy Hunting Land. Deer Drinking's sister, Other Foot, gave her finest long dress, soft yellow buckskin with fringed arms and fringed hem and with beaded eagle's wings spread over Deer Drinking's milk-swollen tattooed breasts. The women bound Deer Drinking's head to her knees and wrapped her in a blanket given by Melon Breasts Woman herself. They put Deer Drinking high in a rock crevice to face Father in Heaven each morning as he rose.

This night, in the birth lodge, Morning Star pushed against her pain as a mountain pushes a heavy boulder, so slow even Eye of the Eagle, who sees farther than anyone, would not see the boulder move, before, finally, it tipped, turned, and burst into the world, showing other rocks how to jump free of the mountain, hurtling as fast as a charging buffalo.

Crooked Nose kept out of sight. To look upon the birth lodge, to see the women, would weaken his medicine. He waited for news of a son.

Morning Star was sixteen winters, and this was her first time to bring life. She'd been pushing at the pain since Father Sun was high overhead. Morning Star was small, but her belly had waxed round and full as Mother Moon, whose light filtered through twigs and brush near the opening of the small lodge where Morning Star's sister, Persimmon, fourteen winters and Crooked Nose's number-two wife, stood trembling. Persimmon was there because she was supposed to be, but Melon Breasts Woman needed no help. A *puhakut*, Melon Breasts Woman called on the spirit of a *pa`mouetz*. A powerful healer, the beaver swims down from his lodge and passes through a tiny opening into the world. Melon Breasts Woman clasped her hands together below her breasts and wiggled her wrists back and forth, undulating her double fist down her belly, down between her thighs imitating the beaver's journey. The baby's black hair, shining-wet beaver fur, pressed at the entrance to the world. Melon Breasts Woman pushed and pulled Morning Star's tender skin away from the baby's head. She kneaded skin with the same strong motions she used to separate a buffalo's hide from its flesh. Slowly, Morning Star's skin stretched. Melon Breasts Woman slipped her twisted, knowing fingers inside and pulled as she gently turned the baby's head.

Morning Star gripped the stakes in the ground but made no sound. Her bare feet dug small trenches in the dirt. She let out a deep breath, and her body bucked softly, giving up the baby.

Melon Breast Woman's *puha* brought the spirit of the beaver that brought Morning Star's baby down the river of birth. Mouth closed and eyes open, the baby stared fiercely at Melon Breasts Woman. Even as one hand took up a flint knife to cut the cord, her other hand found the reason for Morning Star's size. A second baby followed the first, as rocks follow rocks down a cliff.

"*Miar*, " Melon Breasts Woman said. She nodded to the opening and said it again, "*Miar*." So Persimmon pulled the hide flap aside and left, cold air coming behind her into the *kahni*. Melon Breasts Woman cut the cord and knotted it close to the first baby's belly. There was no witness as she helped the second baby into the world. The same baby, but this time his eyes were tightly closed, mouth suddenly twisted and wailing loudly.

Morning Star was tired, her breath shallow and rapid. Melon Breasts Woman cut and tied the second baby's cord. She poked fingers in four nostrils, two mouths. The first son did not make a sound. The second son stopped crying and sucked at a finger. With a doeskin tanned soft as a flower petal, she wiped both tiny bodies all over, then rubbed them with buffalo fat warmed by the fire. The first son she wrapped in her own buffalo robe. The same son born again, she placed in the deerskin blanket prepared by Morning Star.

She hid her bundled buffalo robe between the lodge wall and her medicine pouches and put the second-born child in his mother's arms. She stepped to the doorway and called Red Dog, the baby's grandfather, who waited outside to learn of the birth first from Melon Breasts Woman, then to carry the news to Crooked Nose.

When Crooked Nose had known just twelve winters, his father, Sleepwalker, was killed by Tonkawas, and Red Dog took the boy into his tipi. Under the same tipi hides, Crooked Nose and his adopted sister, Morning Star, had grown close. Even before Crooked Nose went on his vision quest, Morning Star told her father one day she was going to take her best cookpot and put it on a fire in a new tipi she would build for her new brother and herself. Crooked Nose became a strong warrior. He brought more ponies to Red Dog's tipi than any other young man in the camp could offer for Morning Star. Since his daughter was not Crooked Nose's blood sister, Red Dog had been glad to accept his adopted son's proposal. Now, just two winters after the wedding, there was again great joy in Red Dog's tipi.

"Tell your daughter's husband he now has a close friend," Melon Breasts Woman said.

Red Dog's teeth shone like chips of moon, and he breathed small smoke signals of celebration. He hurried off to report the news: *On this night is born a mighty hunter-warrior.*

An Unknown Brother

While Red Dog and Persimmon were away from the birth lodge, Melon Breasts Woman worked quickly. Some of the afterbirth she ate, the rest she put in the hole made for it. She carried the first son and slipped into the scrub oak. Half a mile from the birth lodge, she hid the baby between two large boulders of pink granite. The baby held his dark eyes on her.

For all the winters she had served as a midwife, Melon Breasts Woman remembered each baby she had helped into this world. A healthy birth was cause for celebration, especially a boy baby, who would grow into a hunter and warrior to bring his people meat and glory. This was the midwife's first twin birth. Most men would not risk the bad medicine of identical twins. Twin girls made a double unhappiness for a family and were always destroyed. When both babes were boys, some fathers destroyed only the weaker son.

Melon Breasts Woman knew no spirit wiser or more benevolent than Wolf, the creator being. Wolf and She Wolf had many pups, and some were as alike as these twin babes. She Wolf had a teat for each pup, as did her younger sister, Coyote. Melon Breasts Woman had two breasts, heavy and full since she could remember.

After she'd quit bleeding with the moon, Melon Breasts Woman had become a shaman. For many winters warriors had sought her help. Though she no longer bled, she still made milk when she helped a birth. The instant her fingers felt Morning Star's second baby, she had known she would keep the silent firstborn babe as her own secret son. Already her breasts dripped.

She climbed a slab of limestone forced out of the earth by the root of a hackberry tree, reached into the rough leaves, and draped the second son's birth cord over a bumpy limb. There was not a second hackberry tree and, besides, she couldn't risk someone seeing the other cord. She held the cord in both hands and waited to know what she should do. Coyote's song came to her from the other side of Arrowhead River. Melon Breasts Woman waded across the running water. With the help of Mother Moon she found a gap in the bluffs that rose beyond the river, and she climbed the crevice to a flat ledge where only a little needle grass and prickly pear grew.

"For you, Brother Coyote," she said. "May your spirit taste his son's strength."

She swung the slippery cord over her head and let it fly. She listened to hear the cord strike rock or brush, but there was only the soft talking of the river below. Tall cypress trees hid most of the camp from sight, but two tipis rose along the river's edge. In the moonlight, smoke streamed from the tips of the twin tipis white as milk flowing from two breasts. Without a sound, Melon Breasts Woman made her way back. As she stepped into the cold river, Brother Coyote howled once more, closer than before, and she knew he had accepted her gift.

Brother Coyote was satisfied and so was Melon Breasts Woman. This was a winter without hunger in a good camp. During the Moon of Falling Leaves the band had followed where Raven flew and had found a large herd of buffalo. Now they had all the hides and dried buffalo they needed for the winter. The river flowed strong, and the bluffs beyond protected the tipis from blue northers. This far into the hills, the spirits of the cold winds were not strong.

For many sleeps after the birthing, Melon Breasts Woman would not let Morning Star get up. Morning Star complained—she was strong again—but Melon Breasts Woman said to wait. This gave her time to make a hidden lodge for the secret son, time to nurse him, and build his strength. While she tended Morning Star no one questioned Melon Breasts Woman's movements—a *puhakut* has many secrets. Once Morning Star returned to Crooked Nose's tipi, it would not be as easy for Melon Breasts Woman to leave camp so often without someone wondering where she was going. Soon, Crooked Nose would ask Red Dog to have the naming ceremony for his grandson. Melon Breasts Woman would nurse her secret son until the naming.

A warrior who gave a name gave some of his power with the name. Some men, afraid they didn't have enough strong medicine, refused to give a name. Red Dog wouldn't refuse. Though he had seen many winters, his medicine was still powerful. He always divided stolen ponies among his men, and many warriors had become rich riding with him. Red Dog had fought the Tonks, the Lipans, the Mexicanos, and the Tehanos. Following Father in Heaven to his resting place in the hills, Red Dog had once led raiding parties onto the windswept Llano Estacado where the Antelope band ranged, a fierce band known by other Numunuu as Sun Shades on Their Backs band, for their buffalo-hide parasols. Red Dog and his Honey Eaters rode the war trail with Antelope raiders, and he became a brother to the Antelope war chief, Sure Enough Hungry. Red Dog led a mixed war party of Honey Eaters and Antelope beyond Stinking Buffalo River, called Rio Grande by the Tehanos and Rio del Norte by the Mexicanos whose ponies and scalps Red Dog and Sure Enough Hungry brought back to Comancheria.

The headman of his family encampment, Red Dog had been a wise civil chief of the Honey Eaters band many times in winters past. He smoked with the old wise ones in the tipi of the Fathers of the People, and he wore the buffalo robe painted with the rays of Father Sun to symbolize membership in the Honey Eaters council. Even young war chiefs listened close to the words of Red Dog, who, it was widely known, had grown old without growing weak. Of all Honey Eaters peace chiefs, only Red Dog was still, as well, a war chief. He had led a war party against a band of Tonks when Crooked Nose got his marriage-gift ponies. In the last Time of the Dark Fur, Red Dog's arrows had felled more buffalo than any other hunter's. Of all the Honey Eaters, there was none Crooked Nose would rather have name his son.

A Dream Vision Interpreted

A small fire burned between Red Dog and Crooked Nose, who sat facing one another in Red Dog's tipi. Crooked Nose, grinning so broadly he could barely shape words, had just asked his father to bestow a name on their new best friend. Red Dog smiled. He and his son were enjoying the happy silence they shared, and Red Dog would take the time to make his acceptance words as proud as the occasion. Smoke rose between the two men as unrestrained as love.

Tiny red rivers branched from the black pupils into the whites of Red Dog's eyes. His nose was a thick wedge, the beaten blade of a hand ax. His lips, rubbed with buffalo fat, shined in the firelight. Red Dog's cheeks and forehead bore the deep cracks of a dry river bottom. Two long queues of hair down each side of his head had been greased with buffalo fat and clamped with silver rings at intervals. A strip of otter skin was fastened by thongs at the end to hang down even farther. Woven into his dark hair were the shorn locks of Numunuu widows hacked off in grief when their husbands were killed. Bands of white rabbit fur ringed the long, bunched hair. Beads and small shells were fastened to the hair that was parted down the center, the part painted yellow. A scalp lock went to the back, decorated at the top with a downy painted-yellow eagle feather and a skunk's foot. The skunk had more power to cure wounds than even the mighty bear. Only a shaman had powerful enough *puha* to carry the skunk's secrets. Skunk claws rested on Red Dog's forehead, which appeared broader than it was because his eyebrows were plucked bare. He wore an ear-lock on the left side with a buckskin braid going down beside the ear-lock. A silver button was affixed to the left of the part. Both men wore buffalo robes opened in front to the fire. Light on Red Dog's chest danced twisted trails where scars from old wounds were embroidered with tattoos.

Finally, Red Dog spoke: "My heart runs fast with joy, as Arrowhead River runs beside us now with talking water. I will be as glad to name this young friend and to teach him the true way to live as Raven is to answer our prayers and show us where the buffalo graze."

"Thank you, my father. I too am filled with joy because I have a new close friend and because you will become his guardian as you became mine when my father went to hunt in the Good Hunting Land." Then Crooked Nose described his twice-dreamed vision of Coyote bringing the boy baby and the shadow baby.

"Your dream," Red Dog said, "is a powerful vision." Red Dog offered spicewood leaves from a deerskin pouch. Crooked Nose declined and waited while Red Dog chewed the leaves. Red Dog was reckoning the meaning of the signs Brother Coyote had brought.

Red Dog spoke as if he were alone, saying his thoughts as they came to him: "Brother Coyote has brought us a warrior baby who carries both light and darkness. His dark parts move backward even as he moves forward." Red Dog spat the chewed spicewood leaves on his robe. Their sweet odor rose with the firesmoke. "It is so with all men. The other side of courage is fear. No warrior has true courage until he faces fear. A sealed heart and a sealed mind can never fill with truth. The strong warrior has many hearts and many minds." Red Dog stopped to spit again, on the earth near the fire and on Crooked Nose's robe. Crooked Nose picked from his robe the wet bits of leaves and rubbed them between his hands. He held his hands close and breathed in the spice smell. The two men sat a long while in pungent silence.

Red Dog's voice took on the rhythms of oratory: "The strong warrior burns with the power of Father Sun, yet knows the patience of Mother Earth. The thoughts of such a one soar with the eagle even as they glide through grass with the snake. One who is of two spirits and two places at once knows what is above and what is below him—what lies behind and what lies ahead. When his enemy looks up for him, he disappears into the rocks. When his enemy looks down for him, he vanishes into the clouds. He sees in the dark with the eyes of Mother Moon. He knows how the deer and the elk feel speed, and no one can outrun him. He knows how the beaver and the bear and the skunk cure wounds, and he heals the afflictions of those who follow him. He has the courage of the wolf and the cunning of the coyote. Like the thunderbird, he startles his enemies as the lightning, and he sweeps over them as the wind."

Red Dog leaned forward over the fire and spoke again in a hoarse whisper: "Such a one must be careful and wise in the use of his medicine. His ability to change spirits—the way the lizard of many colors alters his shade to become a green leaf or a brown limb—must never lead him into false minds and hearts. If he becomes foolish and desires to know the whimsical ways of the crow, he could become trapped in those malicious feathers and be destined to cry out harsh songs over fields of grass where he used to hunt."

"Your words are for me as a fresh-killed buffalo to a hungry one."

"And I am as glad to say these words as the hungry one is to eat. The Numunuu need strong wise ones for the many suns of war to come."

"When you speak in the council of the Honey Eaters, tell the other council members Crooked Nose has a new best friend who will never follow the white man's road. Tell them we will make sorrow in the Tehano camp, and if they stay long beneath our sky their scalps will decorate our lodges."

Red Dog reached over the fire and put his hand on Crooked Nose's shoulder. "I will carry your words to the council," he said.

Red Dog took out his straight pipe made of a deer's tibia. The bowl was fashioned from the joint end and wrapped with sinew. He packed into the narrow pipe bowl pinches of good tobacco traded from New Mexico Comancheros.

In spite of his happiness over the successful birth, Crooked Nose had been uneasy about his dream-vision. Red Dog had shown him how foolish he had been. He should have recognized the strong medicine Brother Coyote had brought. Red Dog was right; fear is the prelude to courage. Now, his fear for his son behind him, Crooked Nose felt the baby's *puha*.

The two men passed the pipe to seal their pleasure and their love. Red Dog touched Crooked Nose's ears and grinned, "Listen with both ears at the naming to hear how your son is to be called and how Brother Coyote brought the name when he visited your sleep."

Naming Ceremony

Everyone in the band gathered by the running river. Crooked Nose could now show his pride in public, before all his people. Morning Star held their son, her eyes like the shining bits of the night sky that were her namesake. Melon Breasts

Woman stared into some faraway place. Corn Eater, a shaman who was keeper of the medicine bundle, sent smoke up toward our Father in Heaven and down toward Mother Earth and to each of the four winds. Corn Eater prayed for the son of Crooked Nose. He took the infant from Morning Star and carried him around the fire giving everyone a good look at this strong new one. The baby held his arms high and curled his toes.

A small shadow stepped on the baby's ankle, and Crooked Nose looked up. Near the top of a leafless sycamore, two redtail hawks darted, jabbing their beaks together—kissing or fighting, Crooked Nose couldn't tell. Only he and Melon Breasts Woman were watching the hawks. The shadow flickered on the ground as the hawks soared above the river, beaks still parrying. They wheeled and stopped, suspended motionless. Each had his beak in the same tiny quail.

Crooked Nose looked to see if Melon Breasts Woman also watched the struggling hawks, but she was gone. Why would she leave the naming ceremony of a baby she had helped birth?

Red Dog walked from his place beside Crooked Nose and Morning Star to give the name he had chosen. He stepped close and whispered into Corn Eater's ear, pulled back and whispered into Corn Eater's other ear. Corn Eater held the baby high to symbolize the hopes and prayers of Crooked Nose and Morning Star for this infant to grow to become a great warrior.

Then Corn Eater spoke the name given by Red Dog: "Two Talks."

Skin tightened behind Crooked Nose's neck, and his backbone wiggled inside him. This name was like no other. In his tipi, Red Dog had touched both of Crooked Nose's ears, now he'd whispered twice to Corn Eater. The double name Brother Coyote brought. Twice Coyote had come, the same dream for two sleeps, a dream of a dream. Two Talks—the name of one who can see from behind and before, who can speak from above and from below, from here and from there. As running rivers talk to rocks and shaking trees talk to the wind, Two Talks, son of Crooked Nose, would speak for himself and for all the Numunuu.

A Secret Journey

In the small brush arbor she had fashioned for Two Talks' identical twin, Melon Breasts Woman knelt and lifted the sleeping baby. She carried him silently through the woods to a place downriver from the camp where Arrowhead River poured over a wide rock ledge. From the tall grass she pulled a raft of logs she had laced together with buffalo sinews. A warrior's short bow of seasoned bois d'arc formed the spine for a buffalo hide cover she had stretched tightly over the logs. Sealed with wood sap and camouflaged with brush and grass, the little vessel would shelter the baby on his journey. Guardian spirits would protect him. Melon Breasts Woman prayed to the spirit of the river to carry the raft safely and to Father Sun to shine down to keep the baby warm and to Brother Coyote to run along beside the river and keep the babe from harm.

Melon Breasts Woman lifted the young one above her head and, with the roar of the waterfall swallowing the sound of her voice, declared his Numunuu name, Goes Downstream. She put her secret son on a cradle board stuffed with dry moss and fastened the board to the raft. On the raft she fastened four gifts of magic: a bear claw, a deer's antler point, a flat rock (one side the color of the moon, one side the color of the night), and a small piece of mirror she had gotten in trade with a Kiowa woman. She held the mirror shard near the baby's face and spoke close to his ear.

"Keep this bright piece of the world watching you. Look into it as into smooth water, and you will see your brother, Two Talks, looking back. You will always know him by this looking, but he will not know the name of his longing for you— his gone-away half." On the mirror's surface, Goes Downstream's eyes were bright and sure above the oval of fog his breathing made. "You entered the world before your brother so you must go first to mark a trail beyond your birthing place."

Melon Breasts Woman relinquished the raft to the river. Carried away on the strong current, the vessel with the passenger it bore became a small distant shape. When it was about to disappear, she turned away, unable to watch her secret son out of sight.

Horse Kin

In the brief season of their strong medicine, countless Comanche
warriors felt their lives merge with the lives of countless ponies.
Since the first Comanche climbed onto a horse's back, no horsemen have
been their equal. More than once I heard it told that after a Mexican has
ridden a horse all day a Texan can get another day out of it, but a Comanche
can take the same spent horse and ride it the rest of the week.

—from *Gideon Jones' Journal*

For Two Talks, memory began with the horse. Horse sweat and horse dung were the first scents he knew. After horse, Two Talks smelled mother's milk and deerhide. He smelled cedar smoke, singed buffalo, damp dog fur, urine, and dung. Dirt and weed itch stung his nose. Two Talks' ears first heard horse snort and horse stamp, then Morning Star's chest vibrating with song, her belly snarling against his ear. He heard fire popping, the yipping of children and puppies running loose through camp, Grandfather Red Dog's rock-rumble words, his father Crooked Nose's high-up-in-the-sky laughter, without-pausing river-talking, and, later, the separate voices of Hawk, Eagle, Owl, Turkey, and Crow. Two Talks' eyes first recognized horsebreath clouds, a mare's tail trailing in wind, a hoofprint as faintly visible in limestone dust as a pale moon in noon sky. Two Talks' first felt thing was horse beneath him — warm and churning between his legs — muscles rippling over bones like Arrowhead River's undulating currents over limestone. The body and thoughts of horse entered Two Talks' body, merged with his life.

Like family, horse, wild horse, and personal special horse waited, and Two Talks was born to ride them. As soon as Two Talks was off his cradle board, Red Dog pulled him up onto White Rump, and the wind sang its rushing-past songs.

Red Dog was in charge of instructing Two Talks and, when necessary, disciplining him. But just as Red Dog never had to strike his pony he never struck his grandson.

Visiting the Antelope

Two Talks had seen ten sticks of winters when what was left of their small camp followed Little Apples across the Water Colored by Clay to the home of the Antelope band high on the mesa land, the Llano Estacado the whites called the Staked Plain, a great grassy plateau where in bygone Yellow Grass Times many in their band had wandered to hunt buffalo. Two winters past they had ridden across this grassland for three suns, and then Little Apples had led them up onto a high place where he'd made a greasewood fire and used a buffalo robe to hold back and let go the talking smoke. Grandfather Red Dog's old eyes had been the first to see a faraway talking smoke say: We — wait — six — hills — after — bad — water — come — dance — war — dance — with — Antelope — brothers. Our Father in Heaven was halfway across the sky before they passed an alkali lake and found a hunting camp of the Antelope.

The Antelope hunt chief, a warrior named Stands in the River, welcomed his Honey Eaters brothers. A white stone pipe was passed, and many words were spoken. Stands in the River knew the warrior Sure Enough Hungry, who now met with the elders and spoke strongly, for one so old, in council meetings. Sure Enough Hungry was too old now to go with the hunt party. There were many buffalo this Moon of Yellow Grass, plenty to feed all Numunuu brothers. Red Dog said he would speak with his old, close friend, Sure Enough Hungry. Crooked Nose got up a Honey Eaters' hunting party to join the Antelope hunters. Stands in the River sent a rider to guide the rest of the Honey Eaters to the main Antelope camp, just two sleeps' ride toward where Our Father in Heaven rests each evening.

The old Antelope war chief Sure Enough Hungry greeted Red Dog like a lost brother. The two old chiefs introduced the warriors from their respective bands. The stone pipe was passed again. The Antelope had remained aloof from all the white council meetings.

"We make no treaties with the *taivos*, no treaties with the Tehanos. The Antelope are not like the woman-chief, Pays No Attention to Happenings, and his Honey Eaters who live like cows in the white man's reservation pens," said River Walker, a nephew of Sure Enough Hungry and a war chief with great prestige among the Antelope.

"You speak true, my friend," Red Dog said. "Not all Honey Eaters are afraid to dance the war dance. We have left the hills we used to roam and have come in search of Numunuu who refuse to walk the white man's road. The Great White Father in Washington Land said we could have all our Comanche land, but he forgot to tell the Tehanos. Pays No Attention to Happenings says the *taivos* are as many as all the leaves on all the trees in Green Grass Time. He says we must walk the white man's road or be trampled under by *taivo* wagons. He says we should live in the airless boxes they give us, take the stinging blankets and the white flour, put our children's bottoms in bags and learn *taivo* talk The Tehanos and *taivos* have made our women cry. We can make sorrow in their houses, too. I am as old as a big cedar, but it is still a good day to die."

Many others spoke. They all said they did not want *taivo* settlements in Comanche land. They did not want *taivo* schools or medicine lodges. Reservation Indians grew sickly and weak. Many of them got the white man's evil spirits inside them and died. Others drank the white man's crazy water and were good for nothing. The white man's road was for the white man, and when the Numunuu tried to walk it they lost their way.

"We do not need to learn to farm as other tribes have," River Walker said. "We are Numunuu and Our People eat buffalo. If the white man would stop killing the buffalo there would be plenty to eat forever, as there was before the white man came."

As if they had been listening to River Walker's words, two young men sent by Stands in the River rode into the camp on ponies laden with buffalo meat still warm. The riders told of a herd so large it might have come running out of the long-ago time of the old ones who tell fine lying-tales. There would be feasting and storytelling and singing until early in the morning. The whole camp followed the two riders back to the huge herd and completed the hunt. Our Father in Heaven smiled down on the union of these hunting parties of the Antelope and the Honey Eaters. Our Father in Heaven showed his pleasure in this Numunuu brotherhood by sending his largest herd of buffalo so Numunuu from the two bands might eat and grow strong together.

For a while, they did. The small differences between the two bands were more the effect of geography and climate than they were based on any different ways of viewing the world. The Honey Eaters learned to fashion sunshades, but they continued to use lighter colors than the Antelope, neither group understanding that the Antelope band's preference for warmer, dark colors was influenced by the icy winters on the high, windswept Staked Plain. On the Llano Estacado there were few dogwood or mulberry trees, so many Antelope arrows were made of ash. In the Time of Green Grass, Crooked Nose took Two Talks and several other men of the Honey Eaters band back down to their old haunts and returned with enough dogwood and mulberry to outfit many hunt and war parties with straight, true arrows.

Trading with the Blue-Bottoms

Red Dog continued instructing Two Talks in the ways of a Numunuu warrior. Horsemanship training never stopped. Red Dog had seen many winters, so he was more comfortable on a large saddle with a buffalo bone saddle tree, thickly padded with hides. He had explained to Two Talks how the women had to sew hide wet over the bone so it dries tight. Two Talks' smaller war saddle had no bone frame, just a light hide pad, and the stirrup straps were short and narrow. Two Talks' rig added little weight to a pony's burden. Red Dog showed him how to tie a horsehair war bridle with half-hitches around White Rump's jaw. A horsehide thong went around the pony's neck, and Red Dog taught Two Talks to loop this thong around his wrist and hang his body over either side, shielding himself as he shot arrows from beneath the horse's neck. On a long journey, Two Talks would wrap his wrist with the neck loop to be sure he wouldn't fall if he ate from his pemmican bag or slept as he rode.

Squinting against the sun and wind had already traced lines across Two Talks' forehead and around his eyes. His lids were always half closed against dust, giving him a perpetually sleepy look. Etched in his beardless skin were faint lines down each side of his broad nose to the corners of his mouth. As he grew older these lines would deepen, giving him a permanent scowl, though among his own people his skin creased with laughter more often than with frowns.

Fully grown, Two Talks would be no more than five-and-a-half feet tall, muscular and heavy-chested. He already had the short, bandy legs and long arms of his tribe. He was only nine winters old when he first rode after the buffalo, learning to hug his knees against the racing pony so his arms were free to shoot arrows at the stampeding beasts. Soon, he would have his own war pony. Soon, he would seek his medicine vision.

Many times Grandfather Red Dog had ridden to the old *taivo* trading post at Comanche Peak, west of Blue Water River, which the *taivos* call the Brazos. After the post was abandoned, Red Dog met the wagons of the Comancheros at the trade camp called the Yellow Houses and at other remote places. Now, he was headed down to Camp Cooper and the Indian agency near the Clear Fork Reservation and the village of Pays No Attention to Happenings, to see if he could scare up a horse-race wager with some of the *taivo* Long Knives. Pays No Attention to Happenings was a civil chief of one of the reservation groups of the Honey Eaters band. Red Dog's lips curled as a snarling dog's do. He said, "Pays No Attention to Happenings is a near-dead one. He has forgotten the war trail and grows fat walking the *taivo* road. Worse, he makes all his people follow him on the wrong path." Red Dog was taking Two Talks with him to the agency. "We may have to act as if we are reservation Numunuu," he told Two Talks. "Can you tremble like a cold one and act frightened of the Blue-Bottoms? We will win many wagers and leave Pays No Attention to Happenings and his *taivo* fathers crying in their lodges."

"Won't the *taivo* kill us with their long knives or the guns that speak many times?"

"They won't spill blood on the reservation. But we must keep our eyes open for Tehanos. The Tehano tribe does not respect hospitality to guests of the village."

Two Talks had never seen a Blue-Bottomed *taivo*, nor had he seen any of the hated Tehanos. He'd been told *taivos* snarled and barked, and would bite you if you let them. But the iron sticks they ate with made their teeth soft, so their bite was weak.

They both rode Red Dog's fastest pony, the ugly White Rump, whose left ear had been bitten off and whose other ear Grandfather had split with his hunting knife. "Always notch a war pony's ear so your hand will know him in the dark," Red Dog said. White Rump was a red-ear mustang, a prized kind of pinto that gave his rider great medicine. He bore a brown shield on his chest and brown blotches on his flanks, knees, and ankles. His hooves were striped. He had a lot of white around his eyes, and his ears were a deep brown that was almost red. The short scrubby-looking horse had flat ribs and a long back, a muscular, if bony, all-white rump. His legs were no thicker than a deer's. His head looked too big for his body, and where his mane didn't stick up like a porcupine, it lay flat on both sides of his neck. His left eye, below the notched ear, always stared up, and when he walked he leaned to the side of the bad eye. His large, dark other eye showed his intelligence. "Such an ugly one usually has some special gift. Father in Heaven likes to make it so. It is his joke on creatures who have only outside beauty. You must look close." Red Dog had seen how the little horse carried his tail high. Red Dog had looked into the one good eye and had seen the speed White Rump hid inside. "No arrow flies as fast as this one runs."

Bearing the old man and the boy, White Rump meandered back and forth crossing open country. They saw no signs of the Tehanos. Had they been riding the war trail, Red Dog would have painted on White Rump's fur many hand prints for the scalps he had taken, many hoof prints for the ponies he had stolen. For this trip, he'd removed the one brown and two yellow *taivo* scalps that usually adorned the pony's shabby mane but left the eagle's feathers and the red-and-yellow-painted rocks tied there. Tilting first this way then another, as a butterfly drifts from flower to flower, they ambled along.

They killed a deer and took the tongue and haunches, left the rest for Brother Coyote, whose big mouth they had heard the last two sleeps. They ate their fill of real meat now because Red Dog said it was not good to be hungry in a Blue-Bottom camp or a reservation village where the food was unfit to eat. It was not good to be hungry, either, when you made a wager.

"Hunger makes a poor trader," Red Dog told Two Talks.

The agency buildings were made from skinned trees grown close together to make a forest around the lodge. Wagon dust stung Two Talks' eyes. Red Dog held his nose. "Tehano and Blue-Bottom alike stink." Two Talks sniffed: the rancid smells of a hunting ground many sleeps after the kill, of soured milk and urine and dead fish caught in dried up pools. Two Talks wondered why the *taivo* did not move their camp away from the foul odors.

Screams made Red Dog jump, and White Rump chopped sideways. Two Long Knife soldier men were tied to a post. They had their bottoms in the blue bags with leggings the *taivos* called pants. They had taken their top bags off. One had the *taivo* skin the color of new wood when bark is peeled away, but the other's back was as black as warpaint. Red Dog had told Two Talks of the *tutaivo*, saying the black white-men belong to the *taivo*, who paint their *tutaivo* slaves black so they can spot them when they try to run away. Another soldier man struck the tied-up soldier men's bare backs with a long strap. Two Talks thought he should not look on this, but many *taivos* were watching. Blood striped the men's backs, and the pale one was whimpering like a pup.

From inside one of the low-walled lodges a baby wailed. A dust devil rose in the midst of the compound, and the largest man Two Talks had ever seen came out of the swirling dirt. The enormous man had fur around his mouth. He had put his top and bottom in the blue *taivo* bags and he wore blue leggings, and a *taivo* robe. Though the day was fiery, the *taivo* covered their bodies all over. Only their pale hands and ears stuck out. The giant saw Two Talks and Red Dog, and his upper lip lifted and rolled back the way a horse's lips curl back when he shows his big teeth.

"*Aho*," Red Dog said. "*Buenos días?*"

The giant's mouth made a smile, but his eyes hated Two Talks' eyes. "Kettle Belly," he said, and a short, heavy near-Numunuu, one of the Lipan, the ones the *taivo* call Apache, got up from a four-legs seat and came over.

"*Aho*. How are you my friend?"

Two Talks looked at his grandfather, amazed to hear him address an Apache as "friend." Red Dog and Kettle Belly talked a mix of Numunuu talk and silent hands talk. Red Dog told Kettle Belly he and his grandson were here to trade the yellow metals the whites prized and to wager White Hump against the fastest Long Knife horse. Kettle Belly said there was one horse in the camp who could run with a Numunuu pony, but the Blue-Bottoms had no good riders unless he, Kettle Belly, or one of the other Apache scouts raced for them. Grandfather Red Dog smiled and asked Kettle Belly why he hung about the soldier camp. He said the Long Knives promised him beef and stewed peaches and molasses. Red Dog shook his head. Two Talks wondered what molasses was.

Kettle Belly spoke *taivo* talk to the giant, whose name he said was Sar-jun, then Sar-jun barked at a blue robe who handed a long-handled bowl up to Red Dog. Grandfather put his mouth to the water. Two Talks took the bowl and drank. The *taivo* water tasted like the dead smell in this place. Sar-jun pulled off one of the brown bear's hands he wore over his hands and held the hot bowl in his big, pale fingers.

Red Dog held up a pouch and took out the flat metal pieces, and they shone as many small suns in his palm. "Gold," Red Dog said. The soldier men stared at the yellow metals like thirsty ones who saw water. *Taivos* prized gold above even horses. Red Dog had found two bags of the gold three winters ago where a wagon and team of horses had been carried away by a big rain. The bones of the horses had been still tied to the wagon and the ground was slowly swallowing everything. There had been no bones of men, nothing left in the wagon but the two bags of metals.

The Sar-jun held his pale hand to his mouth, his fingers gripped his throat as he said, "*Poisa-paa*. Don't let the officers see we're giving you crazy water." His mouth made the smile shape again, and he went away.

"Crazy water—whisky," Grandfather said.

One of the soldiers brought out the stinging blankets, and Grandfather shook his head. The soldier hand-talked and hurried to one of the long lodges.

"A squaw man," Red Dog told Two Talks. "He wants to sell me his Cherokee wife, for forever or just for now." The Numunuu did not call their women "squaw," and they did not have any squaw men in their bands as most other tribes did. To have a Numunuu wife, a man—white or Indian—first had to become a Numunuu. The squaw man came back with a girl who had seen thirteen or fourteen winters. She was half a head taller than Two Talks. Barefoot, she wore a long red *taivo* woman dress. "Cherokee women appear much as white women."

"In the tipi any woman is the same," Two Talks said. "I prefer horses."

Red Dog smiled. He'd seen Sits by the Rock slipping in and out of the woods with Two Talks and knew the older girl had been showing Two Talks new ways to use his penis. Sits by the Rock was not comely, but she was a dedicated teacher. Red Dog laughed. He knew the boy had no other experience with women. "You prefer horses? You prefer to put your pizzle in a horse?"

Two Talks laughed at himself, embarrassed but willing to be bested by his grandfather. They laughed together, and the soldier men nodded. This made Two Talks and Grandfather laugh more because the *taivo* didn't know what they were laughing at.

The squaw man frowned. He thought they weren't convinced of the worthiness of the barter he offered. He pulled open the Cherokee girl's blouse and squeezed her breasts. He jerked her *taivo* skirt up and held it bunched about her small waist. He pushed his fist between her thighs and worked a finger up into her. In the shining black hair between the girl's brown thighs the white squaw man's hand looked like a rabbit jumping.

He said, "Best fuck you ever had." He worked fingers in and out, white rabbit jumping. "One gold piece each."

Big-as-a-mountain Sar-jun returned leading a big-as-a-mountain black horse. Beside the horse walked a small Blue-Bottom whose face was as white as the cranes that eat the worms from the backs of buffaloes. The little man ruffled and fluffed himself as a bird does. With a kerchief bigger than his shirt, he wiped sweat off of his face. Sar-jun handed a round vessel to Red Dog, who tipped his head back and drank. He handed the vessel to Two Talks and whispered, "Make appearance to drink deep, but take only a taste." The crazy water left its stinger in Two Talks' tongue.

Sar-jun and Red Dog and Two Talks passed the whisky back and forth. Under his breath Red Dog told Two Talks, "Drink little and laugh much. Be as silly as the backward ones." To make Two Talks grin and laugh, Red Dog teased him about the Cherokee girl. Soon, Two Talks was leaning over laughing and Sar-jun was smiling the *taivo* smile that looked like Brother Coyote snarling.

Kettle Belly asked Red Dog, "How much gold do you have?"

Red Dog emptied the metals from his pouch so he could count them. He wagered White Rump could outrun the fastest *taivo* horse, even this big-as-a-mountain, dark-as-the-night one. When Red Dog offered to let his grandson ride for the race, all the *taivo* wagered against them. Many side gambles were made. The squaw man put his Cherokee girl up against White Rump. Red Dog shrugged at this—what did he want with a skinny Cherokee girl?—but Two Talks watched the girl out of the corner of his eye, so Red Dog grinned and nodded.

The big black soldier-horse shined in the sun like the hair in the Cherokee girl's crotch. Metal glistened between his big horse teeth and metal glinted when he lifted his hooves. His neck and legs were long, his rump muscles twisted like tree roots. The pale little Blue-Bottom rider mounted the big black from the left side, and Two Talks looked at Grandfather Red Dog, who grinned and said, "*Taivos* mount from the wrong side."

Metal thorns on the heels of the Blue-Bottom's boots rattled and the soldier's saddle clinked with hooks and rings. The little white man struck the big black horse with a leather stick, and the race was on. Astride a horse, Two Talks—squat, bandy-legged, and long-armed, like all Numunuu riders—became a thing of beauty. Like the centaur of Greek legends he had never heard, Two Talks seemed to grow from the waist up out of the body of White Rump. When Two Talks raced the shaggy mustang against the big-as-a-mountain horse, it was Two Talks running on his own four legs. What was in Two Talks' heart was in White Rump's heart. As they surged in front of the big black, as their spirits merged and filled with the joy of running-free, Two Talks and White Rump were sad for the black horse. With the fury of the blows he had taken from Sar-jun, the little white man struck the black horse, and hate moved into the black horse's legs. He struck the ground with the white-man's metal under his hooves, running against Mother Earth, making sparks on rock.

After the race, the big horse shook all over. The soldier's stick struck the horse's neck, and, behind the stirrups, the soldier's spurs made bloody gashes.

Before they left Camp Cooper with the big horse and the Cherokee girl and the other things they had won, Red Dog invited Kettle Belly to come with them and ride the true trail of the Honey Eaters band, but Kettle Belly said he would wait on the molasses. Red Dog had a look of small grief on his face as he turned away from the near-Numunuu.

So the soldier-horse could get his strength back, the light-as-bird-feathers Cherokee girl sat his back and Two Talks again rode with Grandfather on White Rump. The spoiled-milk smell of the soldier camp blew from Two Talks' nose, and he breathed the scent of cedar and grass and warm dust. Soon he smelled smoky mesquite trees, and they crossed an orange field of sunflowers. At the waterhole known as Onion Water, they stopped to refill their buffalo-stomach water bags. Two Talks told the black horse, "Your new name is Black Mountain."

Red Dog told the Cherokee girl, Small Nose, to mash mesquite beans and mix them with mud to make a poultice for Black Mountain's cuts. Two Talks told Black Mountain, "You may never be as fast as my pinto *puku*, but you can pull a heavy travois and serve the Numunuu in your own way." The horse jerked his head down but stood still in the spell of Two Talks' voice and let Small Nose smear salve over his wounds.

Red Dog drank from a jug of crazy water they'd won. "It is a good day to be an old man. I would not want to be young with so many *taivo* coming. The good thing is you will be able to die young in honorable warfare, not like Kettle Belly who is already dead. The *taivo* are as many as the buffalo once were. Did you hear the cries of their young ones? The white ones have as many children as fingers on both hands while we have only one or two in a tipi." The old man pulled up tufts of grass and piled them thick for a place to lie. Small Nose drank from the waterhole, and then she stared at herself in the pool, making her face into a face of fear and then a face of anger and then a face of surprise. She laughed, and her floating face laughed, too.

Two Talks lay down, but sleep did not come. To outrun the snow-faced man on the big horse had not been difficult, yet he and Grandfather carried new possessions: the strong horse, Black Mountain, with his heavy *taivo* saddle, the Cherokee girl, who would be adopted as a member of the Antelope band or made a slave for Morning Star or for someone who had only one wife, jugs of the burning crazy water that made Red Dog talk long and then sleep with loud snores, the green beans the *taivo* grind into dirt to make the hot black water, two of the stinging blankets, the small kettles the soldier men drink from, the brown bear's hands Sar-jun wore over his hands, moist and hard-twisted tobacco, and, wrapped in its own stiff hide pouch, one of the short guns the *taivo* tie to their blue leggings. Surely the one who won so many fine goods was ready to seek his medicine vision and to have his own war pony.

Little fires burned in the sky, Grandfather snored, and, far off, Wolf howled back. Red Dog had tied a length of rawhide around Small Nose's ankle and looped it about his wrist. Two Talks unwrapped the leather strip. Red Dog, who could hear in his sleep a leaf touch grass and could rise more silently, did not wake from his crazy-water sleep. Two Talks vowed never to fall under the spell of the *taivo* whisky medicine. Red Dog snored on, smacking his lips like one whose teeth have gone soft. Two Talks lay back into his shape in the grass and tugged the line.

The girl was a small, dark shape above him putting out the little fires in the sky. She did not giggle as Sits by the Rock had. When he put his hand on her breast, he felt this one's heart beating. Sits by the Rock was big and soft as a spread buffalo robe. This one was small and hard, and his hands touched each other behind her back. Small Nose did something Sits by the Rock had never done—this one put her soft mouth over his and shared his breathing. In the night—more even than in the day—Small Nose was not the same as Sits by the Rock.

Gideon Jones: An Unposted Letter

To Colonel Luellen Powell-Hughes

4 July 1865

Dear Colonel Powell-Hughes,

Had I your address in Wales I would post you this letter, but though you may never read my words I'm sending you my thoughts. You above all others taught me how to see. You opened my eyes to the world of books. Without the near-decade I spent in your service under your tutelage and basking in your beneficence, I would see the world much more darkly.

Be assured I am making good use of the volume of the *Encyclopaedia Americana* and the empty ledger you gave me. The entry on **WRITING** includes the observation that *because in the earliest ages, almost all knowledge is concentrated in the caste of priests, it is easily explainable that the art of writing is considered, in the earliest periods of history, as something sacred, and believed to have been brought by the gods to men, or to have proceeded from immediate inspiration.* My desire to convey in writing my westering experiences, imparts in me a reverential attitude toward the blank pages of the ledger and, moreso, toward those words, poor though they may be, with which I attempt to express what I see.

I picture you and Win Shu sitting beside me, cross-legged, on the opened pages of a giant version of Edward William Lane's translation of the *Arabian Nights*, the room-sized book our magic carpet carrying us over mountains and oceans to drift above gilded minarets. Illuminated by the pale glow of a waning Eastern moon in the crescent shape of an Arab scimitar, we are transported—as the sultan was—by Scheherazade's nightly tales, the book taking us on flights of fancy. Many's the day during my current journey I have wished for a magic carpet to carry me the great distances I have slowly traversed behind my team of loyal oxen.

I am spending Independence Day in Independence, Missouri, celebrating with slices of cherry and blueberry pie, my patriotic teeth red, white, and blue. I am at the nation's edge, on the verge of the western frontier, in a place called Kansastown. Three or four miles hence is Westport Landing, a settlement on a rocky ledge overlooking the junction of the Kansas and Missouri Rivers. Riverboats bring supplies for schooner wagons with Osnaburg covers like great white sails that set out from here to cross the wide prairie sea of grass. The landing is full of nomads—farm families, wagonmasters, soldiers of fortune, tinkers, and peddlers, a few peaceable Indians, and immigrants from worlds away. I've seen a man in a white turban and heard a Scot's brogue like yours. There are burly Irishmen and inscrutable Chinamen not nearly as friendly as Win Shu. I met two Germans who already speak English and are more educated than our American settlers. I admire all these travelers, each chasing some dream of advancement or adventure. I may throw in with one of these groups if there is a wagon train with space for me. Many say it is too soon after the war to travel safe—on account of tribes of wild Indians on the rampage since the soldiers were sent back East. Others say it is too late in the season—on account of early snows in the mountain passes that must be crossed after (if?) one escapes Indian attack and the fiery Great Desert. Add to these fears broken wagons, wide rivers, tainted waterholes, armed robbers, grizzly bears, wolves, mountain lions, poisonous serpents, and you can see why I might long for the company and protection of other pilgrims.

I hope you crossed your ocean safely and are back in those rugged hills you described to me. I picture the treeless moors as your words painted them, divided by low rock walls, white and yellow with sheep and wild mustard. I wager there are no walls yet built, no grazing sheep where I am going, but (if I'm fortunate) I may see a herd of wild buffalo.

I daily browse the *Encyclopaedia Americana*, and in the journal you gave me I am writing down impressions as I go, then shaping more detailed accounts as I have the leisure to fill in thoughts and recollect scenes. This writing has made me admire men of letters all the more—Shakespeare's reputation has nothing to fear from me. Your silver pocket watch is regularly in my palm. What better gift than a timepiece set not to the hours of this place but to some unknown, unearthly schedule of the spheres? I celebrate the freedom of each ticking moment.

Always your servant and grateful friend,

Gideon Jones

Rudolph Hermann: Immigrant Lessons

Hin Nach Texas

(*born*, March 1828–*immigrates to Texas*, May 1844)

If poems and tales can be believed, bold knights battle with gods
and dragons under Germany's somber skies, eerie dwarfs inhabit cloud-capped
mountains, fairies drift through dark forests, and talking bears lurk in dark
bowers waiting to devour children. By the time I met him, Rudolph was
at least forty, his hair as gray as sage brush, yet German fairy-tale mischief
still shone in his bespeckled, blinking eyes when he told a tale.

—from *Gideon Jones' Journal*

Rudolph Hermann was raised on poems and romances, but he grew up not
believing. In the harsh winters of poverty, Rudolph, third-born of nine children,
breathed his father's despair and his mother's anger. Frau Hermann sewed linens
for other families, but her own bedclothes were seldom washed. Rudolph's
mother was not unloving, just preoccupied, like the old lady who lived in the
shoe. Herr Hermann worked in the village bakery, so there was usually bread on
the table, though there was seldom enough, and there was seldom any money in
Herr Hermann's pocket. The man smelled of yeast and was white-bearded with
flour dust. His nights and the little money he made he spent at the *Wirtshaus*.
His children, children of a baker, had to make do with oven cakes—potatoes split
open, roasted on the stove, and topped with bacon drippings.

They lived from hand to mouth on potatoes, oatmeal gruel, black bread,
and soup. A herring suspended by a string over the kitchen table swam the dim
kitchen air night and day so the children could rub their potatoes with fish taste.
Herr Hermann's stocking drawer smelled of pencil shavings. Frau Hermann had

no sympathy for dreamers. She scowled, told their children, "He has big raisins in his head." She searched her husband's pockets for gulden and found wadded papers, poems slanted drunkenly down the pages. When the beer flowed so did Herr Hermann's tears. He recited old ballads, quoted Eschenbach, Novalis, Der Guotaere. Frau Hermann frowned. "He is *ein Schafskopf*," she said. "He would carry water in a sieve."

Herr Hermann stumbled home in the dark, his mind fogged by regret and drink and fumbling for a line of verse he knew would bring the release of tears. Frau Hermann snored in a chair, and Rudolph and his brothers and sisters haunted the kitchen, where there were still coals in the stove, though there was nothing to eat. Wind whined and snow spat against the windowpane. The herring strung up over the table slowly turned, twisting like a hanged man.

If Rudolph was off somewhere with his face in a book, there was one less mouth to feed at the crowded table, and when the boy ran away, no one came after him.

By spring, sixteen, tall and skinny and always hungry, Rudolph ended up in Bremen, where the habits of reading and writing he had inherited from his father got him hired to teach at a country school. Then he met Ottilie, the older sister of his worst student, a dark, introverted boy named Kaspar. Ottilie ached for a better life, and she saw Rudolph as someone who might help her escape her dreary lot helping her aged mother empty chamber pots at a country inn. Ottilie took Rudolph to Bremerhaven, where the ships unloaded. They prowled the wharf together. She introduced Rudolph to a sailor friend, Jakob Dosch, who had made the voyage to America and back on the *Assurance*, a brigantine owned by Radeleff and Company.

"An old tramp cargo ship converted to haul immigrants," Jakob said. "Well built, but she leaks a bit. She's solid, but slow. Two masts. The foremast is square-rigged, and she's got a fore and aft mainsail with square main topsails." Rudolph refused to be impressed by Jakob's sailor talk.

"It's all *Wurst* to me," Rudolph said.

Jakob had been to New Orleans and to Texas. "New Orleans is crowded and hot. There are Creole and Negro women. New Orleans is better than Germany, but Texas is like no other place. From the Texas coast you look north and west and see forever. No one tells you what to do, wild horses are free for the taking, there are Indians to fight, gold is easy to find, and the women go undressed with any man who wants."

"Whoever lies also steals," Ottilie said.

"It's the truth," Jakob said.

Rudolph knew his Latin and read a little Greek. In a Bremen bookshop he found copies, in English, of James Fenimore Cooper's *Notions of the Americans*, and Ralph Waldo Emerson's *Essays, First Series*, and bought both to learn the language. In the same shop he read a pamphlet about immigration to Texas. He told Ottilie what he had learned about Texas, and she embraced immigration to a new land as the surest way to a new and better life. Rudolph's teacher's salary and the pittance Ottilie's mother gave her would never provide a ship's fare. Rudolph was despondent, but Ottilie was determined. She was three years older than Rudolph, and she was sure she knew more about the world than he did—him with his face always in a book.

Ottilie earned Rudolph's devotion by teaching him what she knew of the world. He had never kissed, except his mother's pasty cheek. Ottilie showed him the joys of lips. When she wasn't kissing him, she was talking to him, teaching the teacher what he had not learned in school. She believed in the rewards of hard work. "Who diligently does his work, his soup always tastes good."

She asked her sailor friend Jakob to speak with Louis DeSaussier, the French-American ship's master of the *Assurance*. DeSaussier agreed to take on Rudolph as a ship's boy for the voyage to New Orleans so long as Rudolph agreed to serve on the voyage *back*, as well. Ottilie pleaded with Rudolph until he lied to the ship's master and said he would return.

Ottilie and Rudolph married at the inn, and after several steins of beer the proprietor gave the couple that night's lodging for a wedding gift. Rudolph and his bride slipped away, just as he had escaped his family, in the dark of night just before dawn.

The *Assurance* had her anchor lines out four days and nights, taking on stores and victuals. On board, Ottilie had to remain below decks most of the time. Rudolph's duties as ship's boy meant doing every menial chore he was told. Caulkers worked. Pitch and tar burned Rudolph's eyes and nose. The stern end of the hold was empty except for huge ballast stones and salt-shit-smelling bilge water that coated his trousers from the knees down.

The ship's carpenter, replacing rotted boards near the stern, kept Rudolph busy carrying planking. The carpenter's hammer echoed in the damp, empty chamber. He stopped hammering to wipe his cheek with his sleeve. "Don't worry, boy. Most of her's good oak beams, well seasoned. If she takes on water it's the caulkers' come up short. Then you'll join the poor settlers with a turn on the pumps."

By the 8th of May the repairs and revictualing were completed. Emigrants arrived on covered riverboats from Bremen. Wooden crates packed with their necessaries were swung over into the hold to join the ship's store of salt pork, corned beef, peas, beans, rice, sauerkraut, potatoes, flour, and plums. There were casks of drinking water, kegs of pickled herring for seasickness, and a supply of medical needs—quinine, Glauber's salt, sodium sulphate.

On the 10th of May, with the ringing of a bell, ship's master Mr. DeSaussier assembled the crew and all the emigrants on deck. He introduced Captain Hendrie, an orange-bearded, pot-bellied Yankee from Massachusetts. Captain Hendrie called on Reverend Weser, an emigrant Lutheran minister, to say a prayer and lead them in a hymn. The sun was shining. Shining, too, were the cheeks of emigrants, some already green from the sway of the deck. The *Assurance* leaned with the weight of passengers crowding the rail for a farewell look at the fatherland. Only the ship's crew would see German soil again.

"Haul up anchor. Heave-ho. Hoist a sheet."

Rudolph ran the deck, climbed up, climbed down, coiled rope.

"Clear the harbor."

Ships' masts darkened the horizon behind, a forest of winter trees. Sails rattled, waves beat tarred wood, the shoreline slowly shrank. The *Assurance* rode low, heavy with the weight of so many dreams, so much longing, so much fear.

The first nights at sea were the darkest nights. Down in the dark cabin, the air stale and smelly, straw whispered secrets beneath Rudolph's long, restless legs. Against him, Ottilie's body was heavy with sleep and slippery with sweat, and beneath everything the roll and the sway reminded him how far they were from solid ground. Babes cried. Rudolph longed for a cup of wine or a pipe to relax him, but wine was doled out small, and no flame, not even a whale-oil lantern, was allowed below deck. A fire at sea—there's a hellish thought.

Rudolph found a guidebook someone had left on the main deck. He opened it and read the title page.

THE STAR OF TEXAS
or
GOOD ADVICE FOR THE RICH LIFE IN TEXAS
Being
THE IMMIGRANT'S GUIDE TO THE REPUBLIC

The Result of Enquiry, Investigation, Observation, and Travel
In That Beautiful Land
With a Map and the New Constitution of Texas

BY AN IMMIGRANT
Late of the United States

Hail, the Prairieland of Riches!
Golden grasses, Azure skies, Rivers flowing
Home of Freedom, Peace and Beauty
Where Man will Reap the Dreams He's sowing.

With an Introduction by the Rev. Josiah Horn of Joplin, Mo.

New York:
Published by R. B. Bausch
And sold by George A. Marrs and Co., 79 Wall St.
Hubert Whitlow and Co., 233 Pearl St.
and by the booksellers generally

Rudolph opened the guidebook at random and mouthed the English words: —*one brace holster guns (percussion locks); 2–8 lbs. powder in flat canisters; good split and ribbed percussion caps, tin cases; bullets, bullet screw, ladle, lead; friction matches in tin container; powder-flask; oil-cloth gun cover; superior spy-glass (9 inches long) and leather carry case with shoulder strap; sailor's sheath-knife with belt; axe, hatchet, whetstone.* He tucked the book in his shirt.

Work began in fog and ended in darkness and rain. Rudolph's hands and shoulders were raw and sore from wet rope and rough boards. Peas and beans bloated the immigrants' stomachs. Every other one seasick. Slop jars filled and spilled. Men, women, and children lay in the smells their bodies made and wished for sleep. Water was strictly rationed, and nobody washed till it rained. According to the immigrant guidebook: *Sea-sickness is not at all dangerous, and there are few cases of death occurring. Rather, it has wholesome bodily effects by purging the stomach and eliminating disorders of the lungs, liver, and other organs. Sea-sickness passes after the first three or four days followed by an increased appetite. At this time a dash of quinine before supper or a herring with vinegar and pepper and a glass of red wine will strengthen the stomach.*

Captain Hendrie stood at the rudder, braced against the sternpost, steam rising from a tin cup between his hands. He and Rudolph stood in silence, staring at the green chop of the North Atlantic. Captain Hendrie's orange beard glowed like embers in the night: the man nodded, coals shifting. The bolt to the captain's door shot, *bam*—Rudolph imagined the report of a holster gun, hammer hitting percussion cap—and Captain Hendrie disappeared into his cabin.

The boatswain's whistle was a lost bird crying out in a fable. *Good Advice for the Rich Life in Texas* began with arrival in Texas. Not mentioned were gales stirring up the bottom of the ocean until the ship sailed vertically through waves and wind equally wet and foaming. *Strike topmasts.* Rudolph held to the taffrail. He couldn't tell sky from sea—both gray-green, both icy and salt-stinging, both howling mad. Sails were down, but the wind chased the masts. Vomit, seaspray, and rain soaked the upper deck. Not mentioned in the guidebook was the look on Mr. DeSaussier's face capping the climax of terror.

On the 12th of June, storm-battered, they laid up. Not mentioned in the immigrant's advice book were repairs at sea. Not mentioned was bilging, the godawful and endless sound of water coming in through the hull. Not mentioned, the blood rushing to Rudolph's brain and pounding with the pounding of the pumps, blisters on top of blisters from the pump handle, the fearful pumping of his heart and lungs.

After three days of repairs they were days off-course. Low on water, all portions were halved. Not mentioned in the immigrant guidebook: rancid pork, weevils in the flour, tongue-swelling thirst, and surly sailors.

At dawn on the 16th of June, the *Assurance* hailed a five-masted clipper, the *Emma*, biggest ship afloat. Out of Antwerp a full three weeks behind the *Assurance*, the *Emma* sent over one barrel of water, half a keg of wine, a little corned beef, and enough bad news from home—trouble for the Ministry of the Reich—to worry all the settlers about ones left in Deutschland. Riots and maybe war behind. The wide ocean and maybe Texas ahead.

The bilious fever was not mentioned in the guidebook. After ten days of seasickness and dehydration, Ottilie took the fever. She called for her mother and did not recognize Rudolph when he mopped her forehead with a rag. Men, women, and children all burning, packed into plank rooms in steerage. No porthole: air to breathe had to come down the steps from the upper deck. The fever-struck lay on rough sailcloth-covered straw mattresses, on bunks stacked close, four on top of one another, locked in the smells of tar, sweat, excrement, and the black vomit, not mentioned. To escape the close foul air, Rudolph carried Ottilie up onto the foredeck, where she died without knowing his face. He noted the date, July 23rd, his Ottilie gone and Texas still nowhere in sight.

Five putrefying corpses sacked in sailcloth lined the foredeck, shrouds weighted at the feet with ballast stones. On the lee side of the ship a sailor called Little Joe held the end of a narrow plank balanced on the gunwale, one end out over the sea. On this makeshift bier lay a sixth corpse. The burial bag, open at the head, revealed Ottilie's face, the color of the winding cloth. Rudolph braced himself against the bulwark and stared at whitecaps on green swells. Captain Hendrie nodded to Reverend Weser, who began a funeral hymn, "In *Himmel* it is *wunderschön*." Rudolph lurched to the rail and vomited overboard. With a chop of his palm, Captain Hendrie stopped Reverend Weser. The captain reached into his coat and brought forth a pouch. Sprinkling dark tobacco over the body, he said hoarsely, "Dust to dust." A nod, and the quartermaster, Mr. Keene, produced a big curved needle and sewed the bag closed. Little Joe lifted the end of the board, and Ottilie's weighted winding sheet slid off and dropped into the sea with barely a splash.

"Our Father," Little Joe said, saying the prayer to end the service as if he were relaying a mate's order. Captain Hendrie pulled Rudolph from the parapet, dabbed at the vomit on Rudolph's shirt. Little Joe and Mr. Keene were already lifting another body onto the plank.

North of Hispanola, late afternoon on the 8th of August, they sighted Watling's Island, where Columbus landed, off to the northwest. Caulkers and pumps at work in the hold. Rudolph tied and untied knots high in the rigging on the mizzenmast to avoid a turn on the pumps, to avoid standing thigh-deep in choler and black bile—the humors of despair, to avoid breathing the aqueous, foul-smelling darkness.

Two days later they were becalmed on the tip of Haiti. Worse, even, than the unmentioned storms, seven days and nights of dead calm. The sea tightened with rigor mortis. The sky petrified and stopped breathing. A week of nights so dark and still Rudolph bit his arm to know he was not locked deep in an enormous shard of obsidian, to know he was not already dead and buried. Captain Hendrie dropped a longboat to the island for firewood.

The men returned with news of a schooner on the other side of the island, her anchor lines out. She was flying no colors, and her nameplate was blackened over with tar. They saw no sailors, and the natives ignored their questions. Captain Hendrie took this news with a scowl and disappeared into his cabin. Some of the sailors wanted to take the longboat to see what was about. The immigrants worried she was a pirate outfit, but a sailor sneered, *"What would she want with us, an immigrant ship?"*

Finally, Captain Hendrie found enough wind to get them around the island. He gave Rudolph the telescope and sent him up to the crow's nest. Even in such light breezes the topmasts leaned and swayed like trees in a gale. His eye to the glass, Rudolph lost where he was. All blue blur, then whiteness he thought was sandy shore but was only sailcloth close up. Brown lines he took for strands of his own hair became, as he turned the glass for focus, the schooner's masts. Captain Hendrie tacked into a thimbleful of breeze and brought island greenery between the schooner and Rudolph. When he found the schooner again, distance had diminished her. Lifeless, for all Rudolph could tell.

The crew grumbled. Rations were low. Haiti had little more than firewood to offer. Now there was fuel, but little to cook.

At anchor off the island of Cuba, loading water barrels into a longboat. Not mentioned in the handbook, how heavy the empty wooden barrels were, heavier still when the longboat returned. Not mentioned, clouds of mosquitoes. The men brought back a little coffee, plenty of sugarcane. Rudolph cut sections of the cane and sucked the sweet juice, a stub of cane in his mouth like a fat green cigar.

The next morning, Rudolph woke to a sudden wailing down in the hold. Frau Lindheimer delivered a smidge of a baby girl. Herr Lindheimer and Herr

Schleuning took the first dipper of Cuban water and christened the baby, Johanna Galveston Lindheimer, born the 23rd of August. Three men of a Westphalian singing society sang: "*Gott ist die Liebe,* bless our children, safely complete our journey. *Hin nach Texas.*" Everyone sucked sticks of sugarcane. They talked of birds and flowers, freedom and hope. They hugged and they smiled. Even those whose loved ones were buried in the ocean, even they sang along. But not Rudolph. He silently shook his head, then he went down to the lower deck to look for rats to kill.

Just when Rudolph reached the lower deck, he heard the faint cry from the crow's nest, "Gulf of Mexico." He joined the other immigrants crawling like ants up into the sunlight with the ship's crew. So many of them gathered at the rails, he feared the ship might list. In the far distance rain squalls darkened the horizon, but the *Assurance* had sunshine and steady winds. Those distant storm clouds, a sailor told Rudolph, hid the Keys of Florida.

In America: New Orleans

Two days later as sunrise bronzed the Gulf the *Assurance* entered the mouth of the Mississippi at Pass a L'Outre. Larger ships dropped anchor to transport cargo to small steamers for the trip upriver to New Orleans.

Mr. DeSaussier laughed at the other masters. "Cap-tain Hen-drie, he know thees re-verre, ev-ree move she make. He weel make her run back-ward, by Christ."

On both sides of the wide river people walked and rode along the levee, an earthen wall built up a good ten feet above river level. Between Fort Jackson and Fort St. Philip, Captain Hendrie told the immigrants to get rid of their worn clothing and smelly bedding. Freshly bathed and wearing the best clothes they had left, the pilgrims came up from steerage with combed hair and shining faces and threw their ragged clothes and bedding overboard. When a torn shirt hit the water they cheered as if the hardships of the past and the deprivations of the journey were being shed, too. Negroes along the levee waded into the brown water and swam out into the currents to grab dresses and trousers. Upriver, yellow bunches of ripe fruit, dropped overboard by banana boats, bobbed like big many-fingered hands. A lazy sun peeked through fog rising off the water, then retreated again, abandoning the river and the ship to gray sky. Light curved down a broad arc of the river, a wharf lined with boats, and, beyond the wharf, a row of buildings. In a cloud break, Louisiana light dazzled: the row of buildings flared up the way a stick flames when laid on embers. Clouds closed again, curtaining the city with shadow. Mr. DeSaussier pointed to the sloping land between the levee and the river where rough barges were grounded among pale green willows. "See, boy, on the *batture*, flatboats from up re-verre." Most of the barges were crowded with cattle, horses, mules.

Captain Hendrie took the *Assurance* past merchant ships to land adjacent to a steamship. Rudolph counted nineteen boats, the flags of the United States, Spain, France, Holland, England, Russia, Sweden, Denmark, Germany. Stacked on the levee were bales and bales of cotton, roping and bagging bleached by the sun. All down the wharves were piles of lumber, old fishing nets, barrels and crates, the detritus of furs and hides.

Rudolph told Mr. DeSaussier he was bound for Texas and asked for his pay. The ship's master laughed. "Cap-tain Hendrie gave or-derre to pay Rudolph nothing till he re-turn to Bremerhaven." From his pocket Mr. DeSaussier gave Rudolph a handful of coins, a French five-franc and several Spanish piasters. "Get you something to eat. Be back at noon for unlading. Nine day, cast off again."

Rudolph's canvas sack bounced against his back. On the wooden gangplank his shoes echoed over water. Then, after so long, motionless footing. He stood a few minutes, unsure of what to do next. His legs swayed, the soft dance of the sea hard to forget. He had never seen such a mix of humanity, never heard so many different tongues. He was starved.

For as far as Rudolph could see down the New Orleans wharf and three tiers deep were warehouses and sheds, oyster houses, drinking shops. Boat clerks with their paper books discharged freight from the merchant ships. "Heave-yeo-up," hollered a drayman lifting a beam onto a wagon. Sailors in clean shirts and tarred hats stepped smartly. Mercantile house clerks accepted consignments in corn, flour, tobacco, whisky, molasses, pork. One said, "Boat of lead from Galena." An inspector pierced the side of a barrel of pork with a hollow tube and withdrew a sample. Shirtless Negro men, muscles purple and shining as eggplants, laughed and lifted huge wooden boxes, swung bulging burlap sacks, loaded them onto wagons. Flatboat men with long, shaggy hair carried pelts up the *batture*. Wiry men in leather leggings—the vaqueros Rudolph had read about—waved floppy-brimmed hats, whistled and shouted at cattle they herded into holding pens. Boatmen sat in circles on the ground playing cards, or leaned, dozing, against buildings. Indians with animal skins over their heads, knives at their waists, held out copper-colored hands for coins. They were not as tall as the picture book Indians, and they did not have feathers for hair. Men in frock coats with felt collars and cuffs stood talking beside wagons and stalls, sometimes stopping to yell at a dock worker or kick a resting Negro. Boys no older than six or seven ran barefoot among the crowds and snatched oranges from crates, bananas from the ground. Rudolph grabbed a boy by his shirt and took two ripe bananas from him. The boy jerked free, ran a few steps away, and picked up a rock. He cocked his arm, then threw the rock at a team of mules hitched to a heavy freight wagon. Whips smacked the air, and teamsters' curses rose to meet the cries of gulls and pelicans.

Rudolph shoved a banana into his mouth and let himself be carried along in the throng. Pitch and tar burned his eyes. Roasting coffee beans scented the sticky air, and the salt-smell of fried pork singed his nose and throat. He climbed over an iron railing that surrounded the Place d'Armes, an open field opposite the wharf. A group of settlers sat on the grass listening to a boy play a guitar. Standing behind pyramids of West Indies fruits, dark-skinned fruiterers hawked oranges, mangoes, pineapples, and cocoa. Old men in white trousers and bright shirts offered big green parrots, little red monkeys, and ladies' lap dogs for sale. Hucksters cried out. Wooden show boxes tied around their necks displayed gold watches that sparked when the sun came from behind clouds. Rudolph stopped to look in a show box of shining knives bigger than any sailor's sheath-knife he'd ever seen.

"Got money, boy?" From his pocket Rudolph pulled a handful of Rhine gulden and the French five-franc and piasters Mr. DeSaussier had given him. The knife vendor reached for the five-franc, but Rudolph's fingers closed on the money. The blade man licked his lips. "Bowie knife, boy. Fourteen-inch blade, three inches wide at the base. Feel the heft." Rudolph pushed past the vendor, who said, "I got Arkansas toothpicks, cheaper."

Rudolph crossed Canal Street, all around him big drays and heavy carts, little Creole ponies hurrying smart hansom cabs over the pavement. Hungry, he followed a well-dressed man into an inn, a crowded room shuttered and smoky that smelled almost as strong as the lower decks of the *Assurance*. Two black dogs prowled the floor for scraps, a red monkey sat on a stool eating a piece of chocolate cake, and parrots bright green as limes perched on pegs along one wall. Leaned against the wall were shovels and pick axes. Men wearing white suits, silk shirts, gold pins and rings—merchants and planters and clerks—crowded the tables talking loudly and banging their fists so the room was filled with the constant clatter of cups bouncing in saucers. Rudolph got a sausage from a bowl and asked a yellow-eyed man behind a counter for a cup of coffee. Oily rainbows shone on the sausage skin and floated on the surface of the thick, black coffee. Rudolph put a piaster on the counter. The yellow-eyed man took it, returned no change. Rudolph had no idea what the rate of exchange was, but guessed he'd been robbed. He sat in an empty chair at the end of a long plank table, ignored by several men busy talking.

"Don't touch molasses."

"Sour is it?"

"Hides are better."

"I knocked hides down at fifteen cents. Beeves are next to nothing. Wish Texas annexation would pass. Tanners about starving."

"Don't touch soap. It's nearly nothing."

"Lost a thousand on rope, but beeswax is quick."

"Sugar," said a red-faced man just walking up.

"Rum," said one tapping his teeth with a spoon. "Drink up. Polk'll beat Clay, Birney hasn't a prayer. Polk will bring Texas in." Glasses raised. Chuckles all around.

"Flaxseed and feathers, fifty-four forty or fight," the red-faced man said.

"Sold fifty hogsheads of medium tobacco," said one with a dirty collar.

"Try hay and beer."

"Beer's flat as my wife," said a fat bald-headed man with a big gold breast-pin.

"The hay's musty," said another.

"Butter's running down," said Dirty Collar.

"Captain," Breast-Pin said, "I'll go you shingles for vinegar. You take the staves."

Captain—tall, a feather in his hat, which he wore tilted low—laughed. "Vinegar's rising, let me have a brandy first."

"Wheat."

"Candles."

"Twine."

"Lead."

"Deerskins."

"Cattle and cotton." Everyone laughed.

"Texas annexation will pass. Another slave state *and* war with Mexico. Business will be better," Breast-Pin said. All nodded or wagged their heads. A moment's quiet. Then a parrot squawked, *Land o' cotton, Land o' cotton,* and everyone laughed again.

Rudolph left the frenzy of the café, crossed Canal Street, stepped over a narrow ditch full of standing water peppered with tiny black bugs. The indolent sun slowly warmed wrought iron and stucco, wood and dirt. Late morning now, and huge flowering magnolia trees shone waxy in the heat. Scent of the big white flowers and other scents Rudolph's nose had never smelled, of orange japonica, of rouge-red camellia, of purple bougainvillaea. Behind this sweet sting of blooms, the oily wharf smells of pitch pine and dead fish, ripe and rotten fruits and vegetables, manure, mud, and wet rope resonated—a persistent bass chorus of odors. Rudolph had never been so hungry.

Noon, and the fog burned off. The river reflected the sun like a wide mirror, and steam rose from low moss-covered rooftops. An enormous Negress appeared in an open doorway, filling the space. Her elbows rested on her hips as on pillows. Behind her, leaves narrow and pointed as knifeblades. She held out her arm, something white in her hand: a bird, a white dove. Rudolph walked close enough to touch the woman's ebony arms before he realized the dove was a feathery tear of bread. He took the bread, so warm in his hand it felt alive. *Danke schön*. Light-headed, he brought it to his face and breathed in the smell, his father's bakery smell. In Rudolph's mouth the bread took on the weight of the wet, heavy air, leavened breathing.

Meets Portis "Eye" Goar

In a windowless saloon close by the wharf, a room long and narrow, dimly lighted by oil lamps on the wall behind a plank bar, Rudolph spent a piaster on a cocktail and got several Prussian silver groschen in change. The barkeep poured brandy in a glass, added a drop of water, stirred in sugar. The first sip coated Rudolph's tongue with an itchy sweater of sweetness. At a table by the door a whore sat between two boatmen, both her hands busy, one in each man's lap.

Light slanted across bottles and glasses—the door opening. Rudolph was surprised to hear rain pelting the street. A man came in, an oilcloth slicker slapping against his legs. Rudolph recalled storms at sea. "Goddamn this New Orleans weather," the man said. "Pouring down and the sun still shining."

"Devil's beating his wife," the barkeeper said.

The man smelled like a wet dog. Rainwater off his slicker pooled on the packed-earth floor. A brass spittoon with no shine left sat beside the man's boots, which were huge with mud. His left hand was brown as the plank it rested upon and bore the dark whorl of a scar round as a knothole. The first finger ended in a brown stub at the first knuckle. The others ended with splayed, horn-thick nails. Under the wide end of each nail was a curve of pitch black. The long barrel of a military pistol poked out from beneath the slicker. The heavy gun clattered down upon the bar, and the man rested his right hand on the butt. With a motion as natural as scratching an itch, the man reached behind the bar and came up with a full bottle of rum. One eye fixed and unmoving, the other jumpy as a flea, the man held the cork in his teeth and drew off the bottle. He spat the cork into the spittoon and put the moving eye on Rudolph. The man tilted the bottle and splattered the plank bar for the seconds it took for the barkeep to position an empty glass under the fall of rum.

Rudolph placed the last of his piasters alongside the foot-long pistol barrel and, trying to hide any trace of an accent, offered to buy the man a drink.

"If you ain't the tallest Dutchman I ever saw." The man lifted his hand from the pistol long enough to give Rudolph's a rough shake. "Portis Goar, from Texas. I answer to Eye, or, just Goar." The man's jumpy eye and his several scars made him appear older than Rudolph judged he was. Eye told anyone who cared to listen that he had been working a wrecker's boat scavenging the Texas coast from Galveston Inlet to Aransas Inlet. Threat of war with Mexico cut down on shipping, then a spell of calm weather cut down on storms, so he took a job of work as an enforcer for a broker in land grants, but that got "near about unpleasant." A dispute over property rights nearly cost him his life, but he only paid half a finger—his upper lip surprised him and grew back. All he figured he had left was to become a drover. "Texas beeves drove to New Orleans ain't worth but a dollar or two a head."

"It's a fact money's a problem," the whore said.

"Not having any makes me feel downright mean," Eye said.

"How mean?" the whore said.

"Mean enough to do what I do." Eye looked at Rudolph and shook his head. "Damn fool immigrants." He held out his glass and the barkeep filled it again.

"How bad can it be over there for you folks to keep coming, full of questions as children?" he asked Rudolph, who only shrugged. "Load after load, I meet them at the Galveston dock with Mexican handcarts. They pile the carts high with trunks of Sunday clothes, as if there'll be anyplace fit to wear them, and farm tools, as if anything'll grow in the wild-horse desert I'm leading them to. They get a labor of land and a sixty-by-ninety-foot town lot—a red square of dirt. Other colonies, Austin's, Dewitt's, Burnet's, give a league of land and a two-acre town lot.

I get my pay all the same." Eye turned and faced the whore. The shadow of his hatbrim hid his expression, but she felt his jumpy eye moving all over her. "But I'm not so mean I don't hate my part. What's the expression in books? *An exercise in futility*. Sure, I tell them about the country. Land on fire. It burns. Wind rises with the sun and blows hot all day. Locusts buzz the noise of blood rushing in your ear. Land as far as you can see red and crusty as a scab. Everything that grows has thorns—mesquite, prickly pear, Spanish dagger. Everything that breathes, stings—ants, tarantulas, centipedes, scorpions, and snakes—every kind of snake from every kind of nightmare. 'Cept there won't be no water moccasins like near the Gulf. No more mosquitoes neither—not enough water. Prairie snakes fast as a horse at trot, rattlers slower and more deadly. I tell them all about it. 'It's a country of parasites you're walking a month to.' Bot-flies lay eggs on horses, bore into stomachs, and turn into worms. Gadflies lay eggs in old tick wounds and in a day and a half hatch maggots. What grows? Besides hardship and misery? 'Well, there's corn.' I tell them, 'You'll have cornbread for breakfast and coffee made from roasted corn. For lunch, corn mush with your cornbread, and supper's the same, another cup of corn coffee, sometimes a jackrabbit all bone and muscle, sometimes prairie dog, and when you're hungry enough, prickly pear. Sure,' I tell them, 'you'll scatter them seeds, you'll plant corn, melons, beans, peas, and everything but some of the corn will burn up and you'll wish it would, too. Set out orange and apple trees, they wither and die.'"

Eye took a pull on his rum, and Rudolph filled his mouth with the sweet brandy cocktail.

"I tell them, but you think it does any good? 'Listen,' I tell them, 'cattle die of thirst. You'll share alkali water with your plow horse or mule till everything burns up in the fields and you start thinking about horsemeat, mule steak.'"

The bartender topped off Eye's drink. The man nodded and went on.

"The Widow Krueger—Indians killed her man, rode off with her daughter, left her one son. Son went off his head in the heat, wandered around and fell into a den of rattlers. *That* coily nightmare. I was at the burying. Hot gust of wind come up and blew Widow Krueger's hat in the boy's grave. It plopped down on his blanket—no trees, no wood for a box. Then she went hatless in the sun, hoping for her brains to fry. Think on it." Eye looked around the barroom as if to gauge the effect of his tale on his listeners. "But these people persist in their foolishness. The Lord's supposed to watch over idiots and children. Add immigrants. They cut loose the only slaves in the colony. They made up to the Mexicans and talked about irrigation. Herr Lindheimer shot a tough old deer and they invited the freed slaves and the Mexicans and a couple of starving old Indians. Thanksgiving—like them other pilgrims."

For the first time all afternoon, the whore smiled, and her hands lay still in the laps of the men she sat between.

"A crazy idea—could have been anyone's, they'd all been too long in the sun—to have a wedding party, marry everyone to this new life." Eye smiled. "I reminded them married life's Hell." He winked at the whore. "No flour or sugar for a wedding cake, the women got three of their round hat boxes. Biggest box on bottom, middle-sized box next, then that air little one atop. For icing, they spread cornmeal mush over all and set him out in the sun to bake hard as adobe. Old Man Waldeck produced a jar of powdered arsenic carried all the way from Germany to kill weeds and rats. Ain't no weeds and rats surviving here in the new land, so they put the poison to different use, mixing a spit-paste to whiten up the icing. Better not lick the bowl nor stick a finger in for a taste. Way they all wasted most of the day making the cake, put me in mind of them people in the Bible melting down all their gold to make a cow idol."

Rudolph wanted another brandy, but he hated to interrupt. Besides, he wasn't sure he had enough money.

"Finally, a reason to open them trunks for fancy duds and keepsakes they'd toted across the ocean. Late afternoon and hot as the hinges of Hell, they set the wedding cake out in the dusty street and promenaded in embroidered shirts with stand-up collars, wool frock coats, round felt hats from outta them cake-shaped boxes. Their faces, red as the desert, stuck out of white collars above black coats. They looked like buzzards circling. Indians saw the cake sitting out in the road, war danced all around it. Freed slaves laughed. Mexicans called it a fandango. Ole sun went down sudden into the barren land, heat underfoot all night. Hot winds died down like a burned-out fire. Mexican guitars and Injin drums stirred the still night air and it throbbed with heat like coals. All night they grinning to beat the band—Mexicans strummed songs about love, yesterday's slaves crazy-danced, Indians did story pantomimes, and every Dutchman sang German beer hall songs to the fiery taste of mescal." Eye stared at the swallow left at the bottom of his glass as if he wondered where all his drink had gone. "Them people, they hang onto their foolishness like a comet to its tail." Eye shook his head and polished off the dregs of rum in his glass. "And what for? Next day, the wedding party's over, the sun hot as ever. No honeymoon out there. Next day, wool coats and felt hats packed back in trunks, put away with all their shivaree. Next day, the hollow wedding cake was still baking in the sun, so many layers of hot air, a graven image of sweetness poison to eat."

He leaned close to Rudolph. "How 'bout you, Dutchman, you want to be a farmer in some Texas colony?"

"I am German—not from the Netherlands."

"You people call it Dutchland, don't you?"

"Deutschland."

"So you aim to make your fortune without planting corn?"

"*Ja*, I need geld."

Eye lowered his voice and asked who Rudolph's ship's master was. They drank up the rest of his piasters, then Eye put a gold piece on the plank. After a couple more brandy cocktails, Rudolph's English got better. The two men sitting with the whore left, and she joined Eye and Rudolph at the bar. Eye bought her a drink, but said, "Not tonight, sweetheart. We got to go make our fortune."

The afternoon thunderstorms had stopped. There was no twilight. Darkness just fell, a black curtain. Yellow snakes slithered down the streets—oil lights reflecting on wet bricks.

Eye had no more plan than theft and violence. He said the ship's master would be carrying plenty of money. By midnight he and Rudolph lay in wait on the wharf. A half-moon had risen over the Mississippi, casting before them the dim shadow of a mast that looked like a gallows frame. The river lapped peacefully against wooden pilings, and on the planks above, sleeping immigrants snored, their bodies darkening the moon-silvered wharf like so much strewn cargo. Eye nodded toward a cab stopped at the end of the dock.

His back to them, a man closed the cab door, a woman momentarily visible inside. Beneath a rattle of horses' hooves and wooden wheels Rudolph and Eye slipped up behind the man, grabbed his arms, and walked him away from the wharf. Eye pressed his pistol barrel against a swell of flesh above the man's belt. Rudolph grabbed for the man's face and gripped a thick beard—this was not Mr. DeSaussier.

"Fools," the bearded man said. "Nothing on me but a few bank bills. I'm not carrying real money at four in the morning."

Eye slammed him against a building, pushed the pistol against his jaw. The man's wiry beard whispered against the barrel.

"I'll take you to my office and give you gold if you'll let me go."

Rudolph pulled from the man's wallet a sheaf of bills issued by a New Orleans bank. "Enough," Eye said, "for a day of drinking, not much more."

They looked for a cab or a horse, but the streets were deserted. By the time they'd walked to the man's office in a shed near the wharf, rooftops and trees were outlined against pale light. The man took a ring of keys and opened a heavy padlock. Inside, he bent to light a lamp, but Eye pushed the man's hand from the globe.

"Think we let you show light?" Eye brought the gun back to strike the man, who squeezed his eyes shut and clenched his jaw. Eye didn't hit him.

"Just in here." The man opened his eyes and blinked as if he might weep. He reached into the drawer of a library table. Rudolph was thinking the drawer held no gold when the table scraped across the plank floor and a blade sharp and cold as ice stung Rudolph's side, freezing, then burning. His ribs vibrated, his chest and both arms suddenly weak. *Nein*, he thought, *I am stabbed to death.* A sharp crack, and the man groaned. Another crack, flint sparking stone, the butt of Eye's pistol against the man's teeth and jawbone, then the whump of the man's head hitting the floor.

Eye knelt over Rudolph, the jumpy eye peering down. Rudolph's pantaloons were wet down one side. Two bright blue bees spun just above his nose, flew backward and brightened into the yellow spew of a match. Eye's face glistened, his moving eye on Rudolph, the other eye fixed on darkness. Rudolph looked down: a leather handle nested in a blood-soaked wad of his cotton shirt. From the list of essentials, *Good Advice for the Rich Life in Texas: sharp sheath knife.* Rudolph felt an urgent need for a bowel movement. The match went out. Eye struck another and held it up under the globe. He turned down the wick, the light low. On his back, the man rasped bubbles in blood that ran from his nose and mouth into his beard. His split upper lip flapped like coattails with each wheezing breath. A gold tooth glinted on the floor. Rudolph took the pistol, put the barrel to the man's head, and cocked the hammer.

"Too loud," Eye said.

Rudolph's hand trembled. Surprised at his anger, he lowered the hammer. He reached for the knife in his side, but, again, Eye stopped him.

"Pull the plug, you'll bleed like a stuck pig. Rest up. Likely, he had no gold to start."

Rudolph smelled himself—sweat and urine. He was suddenly sick but was afraid if he vomited, his insides, cut loose by the knife, would come out of his mouth. Blood pooled in the seat of his pants, and his crotch was cold, soaked with urine.

"This is all we got time for," Eye said. He pulled a stack of bank bills from an envelope and held it close to the lamp. In his other hand were a few gold coins. "A gold eagle, couple of quarter eagles."

"Have you *ein*—a knife?"

"I got nothing. Let's get gone."

There had to be something—anything sharp, pointed, or heavy enough. No man had a right to kill another because he had need of money. Rudolph found a handkerchief in the man's breast pocket and forced it down the man's throat. His wiry beard pricked Rudolph's palm. The man wheezed and blood splattered his bare neck below the beard. Rudolph held his side, keeping the knife in place while his other hand scrabbled like a crab along the floor and found the man's face. His free hand squeezed the man's bloody nostrils closed.

"No time for that," Eye said.

Air whistled in and out around the handkerchief in the man's mouth the way winter came through the kitchen window in Germany.

"*Stirbt, Gott* damn you."

Eye pressed down on the stuffed mouth and sealed the purple lips. The stub of Eye's cut-off finger pressed into the man's cheek where his beard ended. It looked as if the finger was inches deep in flesh. The body began to buck, the man's boot heels banging against the floor—loud enough, Eye said later, to wake the dead.

Sunup, they rode double on Eye's Mexican mare, Dolores. Rudolph had to hold his feet up or they dragged in the grass. Pursued by no one, they loped down the levee. Clean wash hung bright on the limbs of a dead oak behind a board house. When Eye jerked a white petticoat from a limb, Rudolph ached too much to ask why. Miles downriver, Eye signaled a southbound steamer with the petticoat flag. While they waited in the willows for a lighter, Eye unwound the leather wrapping of the knife grip protruding from Rudolph's side. Every twist, the German bit his lip. Eye backed the pommel off. Beneath the leather, the heart of the hilt, a shape of wood in his palm. He worked off the cross guard.

"Hold tight." Eye got a flat bottle from his saddlebags and put it to Rudolph's mouth. Rum scalded his lips where he had bitten them. Men in the lighter shouted and threw ropes. Eye wrapped the wound tight with strips of clean petticoat. He wouldn't leave Delores, and with a shirt over the mare's eyes stepped her onto the barge. When they reached the steamer, he rigged a rope harness and with the help of the captain swung the horse aboard. Some stolen bank notes satisfied the captain, and they got under way. Sabine City, six hours. Galveston, thirty-six hours. Matagorda, sixty hours. A dark line of thunderheads awaited them.

Lightning flashed, rain poured down, thunder shook the deck. Eye offered

Rudolph the last swig of rum. He shook his head, and Eye finished the bottle and tossed it into the spray. Rudolph reached into his pocket and brought his fist back out. He opened his palm for Eye to see. In the eerie green light of the storm, the only bright shining thing was the gold tooth in Rudolph's hand.

Eye laid Rudolph on a tabletop in the captain's quarters and held a lamp close to Rudolph's blood-soaked side. "Don't seem to be leaking none." The captain stepped in followed by a short man in a dress shirt with no collar. "Goddamn if it ain't Gerald," Eye said. "Dutchman, this here is Gerald Madden, who runs a livery stable in Galveston. He brought my Dolores through the colic two year ago. I prefer a good horse doctor over most people doctors. Plenty of folks get knifed in Galveston, so Gerald's well practiced in mending punctures."

Gerald's hand was cool and soft on Rudolph's forehead. The horse doctor leaned close. "I make no promises." His gray moustache was a wooly caterpillar above his pink lips. "Worming a horse is a far cry from probing and stitching, but you don't have much choice. Unless I get this blade from between your ribs, infection will set in and you'll die. There's a good chance infection's already started, and you'll die even after what I'm gonna put you through. Either way, I apologize." To the captain he said, "Get whatever liquor you got, whatever burns the most. Eye, turn up the lamp. And captain, I need my bag from below deck."

A wet rag covered Rudolph's face. It smelled like a mix of brandy and coal oil, and he gagged. Ottilie smiled down at him, a gray moustache above her lips.

"You've been gone so long I wondered if you were coming back," Gerald said. "I pulled the blade out. Sewed off a blood vessel, packed you. The rest is up to you."

Eye's scruffy face appeared next to Gerald's. "Gerald says you're only the second man he's operated on. If you live, you'll even up his doctoring record."

When the steamer reached Galveston, Eye laid him in a handcart and rolled him beyond docks and the bright sand to a small house where Gerald Madden said he'd look in on him. In darkness and in light, in and out of dreams, the days of Rudolph's recuperation were as wave-tossed and lonely as the journey over the ocean from Germany. He was clear-headed enough from time to time to realize he was on a cot in a windowless room. On the nearest wall was a painting of a river running through a narrow valley surrounded by mountains, dark and brooding, that reminded Rudolph of Germany. But the rest of the landscape was brighter than any place he had ever seen. The painting shimmered so that Rudolph imagined the sun had sunk in the river and rested on its muddy bottom, sending up the light. He slept fitfully, waking to the river of light, then drifting off again. An old Negro, his black face frosted with a close-cropped beard, brought in a tin bowl of soup and carried away the porcelain bedpan. Rudolph lost all track of time. Then one day he got up and walked stiffly around the room. Gerald said eight days had passed. Stitch by stitch he snipped knots from Rudolph's side and pulled out the black threads that had tattooed the pale skin. A day later, Eye visited.

"I got a job of work to do, and it's gonna keep me tied up a spell. Since you're too mean to die, I'll leave you to your ownself, for now. You best get inland, away from the miasmas of the coast. It's mostly whores and thieves here in Galveston." Eye winked. "The Dutch society can point you to New Braunfels, like as not the best of the German colonies."

Back on the Immigrant Road

The Mainz Society recommended immigrants go by schooner down the coast to Carlshafen and from there by wagon to the colony being settled by Prince Solms. Rudolph was determined to stay on solid ground. He hired a Mexican to transport him by ox-drawn wagon, slower but cheaper than a muleteer. They followed Buffalo Bayou to Houston and took a muddy trail to La Grange and the Nacogdoches Road to New Braunfels. The twelfth of September, after three weeks and two hundred miles, Rudolph's side aching less, they crossed a running stream bordered by live oaks and passed neat log cabins with small enclosures of farmland. At the confluence of the Guadalupe River and Comal Creek, they had arrived at New Braunfels.

Above a hilltop fort named Sophienburg after Prince Solms' fiancee flew the imperial Austrian colors. A settler said, "*Nein, nein.* These officers, they forget to bring a Deutsche flag."

"*Viele Köchinnen verderben den Brei,*" Rudolph said.

The wide main street was crowded with newly painted houses, most with porches and gardens. Men in short German jackets nailed the framing for other houses. In the town center, a stonemason set white squares of limestone for a building. Stores displayed signs in German, but more signs were in English, as if these immigrants were taking hold of the outstretched hand Texas offered. At the marketplace, the flag of the Republic of Texas was hoisted.

An innkeeper had a room and work for Rudolph: furniture to repair, water to haul, firewood to cut and split, windows to reglaze, shingles to replace, foodstuff to purchase and stock. Matthias Verlag, a carpenter, agreed to take on Rudolph as an apprentice when he was free from work at the inn. Rudolph liked the smell of oak and cedar, the feel of sawdust on his hands. He saw more in the grain of a board than he had ever suspected lurked there, and Herr Verlag praised Rudolph's knowing hands. Each morning he swept up sawdust his new oak headboard—hewn and planed in Herr Verlag's shop—shed under Rudolph's tossing and turning. What kept him awake nights was not the sounds of the bucking body he had smothered in New Orleans, but Ottilie's face as white as her shroud on the pitching deck of the *Assurance*. The innkeeper and the carpenter each paid him a small wage. The room provided for him had freshly plastered walls decorated with panels of blue stenciling. His lodging and meals provided, Rudolph's savings grew. He wanted for nothing, save close companionship.

A Marker for Ottilie

In November, an itinerant stonecutter, Manuel Joaquin Tablada, passed through New Braunfels. With Tablada's guidance, Rudolph purchased from the local mortuary a pink-granite, winged cherub. Tablada chiseled into the stone:

Ottilie Hermann

1825–1844

Nach uberstand'nen schweren Leiden
Bin ich versetzt in hohen Freuden

The stonecutter spoke Spanish and some English but no German. He said, "*¿Que quiere decir eso?*" Rudolph translated the inscription: "After suffering I have overcome/ To get great joys in my future home." The stonecutter's only son, José Arcadio, serving under Santa Anna, had been killed in the siege of the Alamo. Señor Tablada said he hoped Rudolph might find joy in Texas, and Rudolph realized the old man thought Texas was the future home, the Heaven referred to in the inscription.

Rudolph secured a choice town lot where he might one day build a house. On the lot grew an ancient live oak, its limbs spread wide and curved close to the ground, then lifted at the ends, reaching for Heaven. Beneath these arms he set Ottilie's marker.

Some time after the stonecutter's visit, Herr Verlag asked Rudolph if he was still going back to Braunschweig. "*Nein*, I will stay here where my Ottilie is."

In December he purchased from Hugo von Husen, a Prussian staying at the inn, a .607 caliber Dreyse—von Husen called it *das Zündnadelgewehr*—a single-shot percussion lock rifle adopted by the Prussian army. He showed Rudolph how to operate the breech-loading action, a slide system, allowing the rifle to be quickly loaded, aimed, and fired. Rudolph hit the first target his instructor named, a cedar limb high up a limestone outcropping, and von Husen said Rudolph was a sharpshooter.

Finds Baby Moises

In the days to come, Rudolph tramped along the Guadalupe River with the *Zündnadelgewehr*, and deer, rabbit, and wild turkey began to appear on the inn's menu. Happy to have the game Rudolph shot, the innkeeper loaned him a horse so he could forage farther from town. A clear, cold day in January, he crossed the Guadalupe where it ran barely up to the horse's hocks and rode north. For supper he roasted a rabbit over a mesquite fire beneath a limestone bluff beside the Blanco River. Avoiding a nearby settlement, he sat close to the fire enjoying his solitude. Struggling with English and the flickering firelight, he read the macabre stories of Edgar Allan Poe in *Tales of the Grotesque and Arabesque*.

The Blanco was bounded along the south side by bluffs pockmarked with small caves where nighthawks nested. More elevated and rugged than New Braunfels, this was the loveliest area Rudolph had seen in Texas. *Ottilie*, he thought, *if you were with me still, we'd make a home on this Blanco River*.

By noon the next day, he had ridden several miles north and was off his horse following a gobbling into the brush. He cupped hand to mouth and imitated the gobble-gobble. A flock strutted through the brown grass, and he shot two before they scattered. Between tree trunks, moving water flashed silver. He gave up on the other turkeys, went back for the mare, and walked her to the river he figured was the Pedernales, a good fifteen miles north of the Blanco. Something dark moved on the water, and he wondered if there were beaver in Texas. But it was no animal. He waded close, and his breath caught, but not from the cold water. What moved on the river was a covered cradle on a raft—a tiny floating Conestoga wagon made of wood and hide. Wrapped in fur, an infant was held inside. Splashing icy water, Rudolph carried the cradle and baby to shore.

This was an Indian child, or Mexican, this Moses, not many days old. Beneath ·

wet black hair, the baby's dark eyes looked up solemnly. The tips of its tiny wet eyelashes were matted into points like dark thorns. Rudolph pulled the naked baby from its fur cover, and curly tree moss spilled out. On his knees, he rubbed the small arms and legs that were deep purple. Along lines of bone—at elbows, knees, and down both shins—the purple flesh had a whitened, frosted look as if the skeleton were working toward the light. The body was rigid, like the porcelain dolls of little girls in Braunschweig. Rudolph put his ear against the narrow chest, bare and cold as the plucked breasts of the wild turkeys hanging from his saddle. The infant's heart beat faintly—a slow and distant drum. Under its nose some liquid had dried clear and shiny. The full lips were dark, bluer than the rest of the face. The baby's arms, bent at the elbows and outstretched like a doll's, swayed up and down when Rudolph lifted it, and he half-expected the infant to laugh and reach for him. Inside one tiny elbow was a dark line of mud Rudolph wiped away with a fingertip.

He spread his fur blanket on the grass and laid the baby there. A boy baby, its penis lay like the tip of a tongue below a knot of scabbed flesh that protruded from a belly as round as the small head. Against the black fur, tiny fingers spread. The baby's hands were distant blue-white stars. Rudolph opened the front of his greatcoat and shirt, and against his warm chest he held the icy little body. He wrapped his coat over the baby swaddled inside his wool shirt and studied the raft. An arched length of wood, most like the lath slat in a chair back, curved over the raft and supported a stiff animal hide roof. Sticky tree sap smeared over the raft's wood bottom sealed out water. Hanging by rawhide strips from the roof were decorations or amulets—a large animal claw, a polished rock, the tip of an antler, and a shard of mirror that twisted and turned, giving the sky to the river and the river to the sky.

A breeze tugged at the feathery dark tips of cedars that lined a rock outcropping. The susurrations of rushing water, of breeze in treetops, flickers of light and shadow surrounded Rudolph and the child, making them the still, silent center of the universe. In the infant's round open face and serious eyes Rudolph saw the face of some ancient Greek philosopher gazing up at the heavens, prying into the secrets of the universe. The face he saw was out of a heavy book with thin pages of small black letters interrupted by richly colored illustrations—a history book, or a Bible his father had read from. Beneath a deep blue sky, a wise-looking old man in flowing robes sat on bare ground. Scrolls of papyrus lay scattered around him, and sketched in the dirt before him were triangles and numbers and strange-looking symbols. Behind the man's domed head was a white domed building supported by white columns. He held an instrument of wood and brass, some measuring device. The other hand reached for the dark skies and all the knowledge held there.

Snug inside the greatcoat, the baby rode against Rudolph's chest as he had seen many a Tonkawa Indian babe in New Braunfels strapped to its mother. If he dropped the tiny body he feared the round head might crack open and spill out stars and letters and numbers and symbols. He tied the raft-cradle to his saddle and rode steadily into the evening, stopping only to water the mare. Still in the saddle, he ate a cold supper and wondered whether to try to feed bread or cheese to the infant. Rudolph dozed in the saddle, surprised each time he startled awake to feel the baby inside his shirt. He dreamed he was sleeping with Ottilie, and their child lay between them in the bed. In the dream he felt a father's overwhelming worry, the fear for life so vulnerable.

When he reached New Braunfels it was still dark, but to the east, trees and houses stood out against the lightening sky. He carried the baby to his room, built up a fire from the coals in the stove, and, leaving the baby wrapped in a feather quilt on his bed, fetched the bathing tub. "*Ja, Moises*, I will be right back."

The inn's kitchen was cloudy with steam and odors of meat roasting, potatoes frying, bread rising in the oven.

"*Guten Morgen*, Herr Hermann. *Wie geht es ihnen?*"

"*Guten Morgen*, Fraulein. I am well, *danke. Und ihnen?*" He gave the innkeeper's wife the turkeys and asked for a cup of warm milk.

She happily took the birds and set milk to heat on the stove. By the time the kettle whistled, the milk was warm. In his room, Rudolph emptied the steaming kettle into cold water in the tub. He put warm milk to the dark mouth, but the baby would not drink. He dipped the corner of his bed linens into the milk, then slipped the sodden cloth between the baby's lips. He squeezed the material so milk dribbled onto the tiny tongue. The babe sucked the cloth. Over and over, in the manner of dipping a quill into an inkwell, he dipped the corner of the sheet into the cup and then lay the wet cloth between the infant's lips. The milk slowly went down in the cup. The babe stopped sucking and looked up. "*Guten Morgen*, little one," Rudolph said.

He dipped his arm into the tub, testing the heat, then eased the baby in and soaped the wrinkled neck and smooth back. He worked suds between each tiny finger, each tiny toe. The eyes were deepset and slanted, the lashes thick and dark. The shape of Rudolph's finger was dark behind the pink, translucent skin and cartilage of a small ear. He held the body up in the water, and the legs swung down and moved as if the baby were walking. The soap-slick skin slipped in Rudolph's hands, and the body bobbed, momentarily immersed, shifting light and water moving the baby's lips in silent speech neither Indian nor English nor German—a language of bubbles and ripples. The purple-brown skin was taking on a rosy sheen at the knees, elbows, chin. The frosted opalescence of milk glass or porcelain that had looked to Rudolph like a white skeleton beneath its flesh was darkening. Now the little body was quickening, its fingers growing red and rising out of the copper tub as tiny flames, fire on water.

Rudolph rubbed his finger across the baby's upper gums, and a hardened gel of mucus let go and floated away. Rudolph moved folds of loose skin back from the bald pale end of the penis, smaller than his little finger. The dark hole in the penis was a worm's mouth, mysterious as a tiny third eye. He laved water between the thighs, then lifted the infant out. Water ran down shining skin, luminescent in lamplight. He patted the baby dry with a hand towel and laid him under the bedcovers. Overcome by exhaustion, Rudolph lay down beside the babe and was immediately asleep, dreaming he and his Ottilie watched the boy crawl, then walk, then ride a horse, and shoot an arrow. A strong boy, he climbed a twisted oak, eyes flashing among green leaves, the tree shaking with the boy's laughing. Rudolph and the boy talked about the Nile River and Phoenician traders and Roman conquerors. They opened a thick book to a picture labeled, in English, *An Early Star Gazer*. Still dreaming, Rudolph thought, *This is my first dream in English.* The baby's face was on the body of an old man in long robes, drawings in the dirt before him and white scrolls scattered about, his eyes lifted to the heavens. Beneath the picture, Rudolph read: *Like curious children, early people wondered if far-off heavenly bodies had the power to affect the destiny of man. The Greeks named five of the stars which moved in the sky, calling them planets, the Greek word for wanderers. Six hundred years before the birth of Christ, Thales, one of the seven wise men of ancient Greece, drew maps of the heavens.*

Rudolph woke rested and refreshed. He nestled the baby in a feather pillow and carried him to the innkeeper's wife. He told her how the drifting raft had borne the nearly frozen infant, an Indian Moses who had survived in his basket in the bullrushes. When she saw the small brown body and how Rudolph had bathed it so clean, she wept and put the baby against her shoulder, where he coughed and spat up. A Catholic from Cologne, she crossed herself. "We must baptize him for the sake of his soul, and find a wet nurse for the sake of his body."

The Blessed Wild Horse

The story Rudolph Hermann told me about the Indian babe he called
<u>Moises</u> was further proof of the interconnectedness of each life in the
wide universe. When Consuela Delgado needed an outlet for her grief,
the babe needed her nursing mother's affection. Rudolph followed behind for
the babe's sweet sake, hovering nearby like a Comanche's guardian spirit.

—from *Gideon Jones' Journal*

Consuela Palomita Delgado hurried down the wide dirt street of the unfamiliar
town. West of the *jacales* where Los Mexicanos lived, the grim German men and
the Mexicanos they hired chopped and dragged cedar bushes and twisted oaks,
clearing lots. January sun flashed on the blades of axes, machetes, and two-man
saws. Stonemasons stacked rocks into low walls, growling teamsters drove wagons
piled high with yellow boards. Women in long coats swung buckets of milk, butter,
eggs. Washerwomen hung linens on rope lines. Consuela carried willow baskets
stacked inside one another—smallest on top, largest on bottom—baskets she had
woven during long hours while her husband, Miguel, had chased a band of wild
mustangs in the rocky hills west of where the busy street turned back into needle
grass, yucca, cedar, and scrub oak. Miguel was one of the *remuderos* for a large
Mexican hacienda. For the past three years he had been trying to catch a herd of
wild mustangs led by a cunning gray stallion. January was a slow time at Hacienda
del Caballito. El Patrón, the owner, had let Miguel follow this herd, and Miguel
had persuaded his wife to accompany him.

The days since her *niño*, Ignacio, had been stillborn ran together like one
terrible night of unspeakable dreams, a night of waking soaked with sweat afraid
to sleep again. Miguel thought if he took her away from their *jacal* on the big
Hacienda del Caballito, traveled beyond the village of Montclova and out of
Nuevo León, even out of Mexico, she might escape the darkness and return to
him. He had started giving her long looks again, lifting his eyebrows and winking
as if he had dust in one eye. Consuela knew he expected her to comfort him in the
way men always want women to comfort them. He talked silly, as men do when
they are afraid to say what they want. "Miguel, *el siente pelota por* Consuela,"
Miguel said, as if they were not lying beneath the same blanket. *Que parada.* He
wanted *ponerse las botas* to take advantage. She would turn away from him and

go to sleep, but Miguel would be pleased with her backside, so she faced him and drew up her knees, two strong gateposts. Fortunately, whenever Miguel followed the tracks of *un caballo* bronco, especially *el gris*, whom he had sought for so long, there was little room in his head or heart for any other thing and soon he was snoring, dreaming not of his wife but of *el gris*.

Miguel liked to pretend God's will was no more than luck. To believe in luck—unless one were guileless and knew no better—was to ignore God's plan. Not to believe in luck was easy. What was difficult was to understand why God would take back a life He had promised. Consuela believed God was more arbitrary than luck. Part of her asked forgiveness for questioning His holy motives. Part of her defiantly thought only El Diablo would act so cowardly as to take her baby's breath. She had not attended Mass or made her confession these three weeks since Ignacio had come to her without life. One of the padres from Monterrey who visited the church in Montclova had come to see her.

"You did not come to the Mass," the padre said.

"No."

"Trust God. You are not too old, you will have other *ninos*. You will be happy again. *Con el tiempo* your heart will stop hurting."

"My whole body hurts."

"I warn you, do not test God. *¿Comprende usted?*"

But she did not understand. If she should not put God to a test, why was it all right for Him to put her to a test? When the padre told her she should pray, she knelt and closed her eyes: "*No me falta nada*," she prayed. So, when Miguel asked her to come away with him, she gave him a hard stare to be sure he knew she would not lower her knees to comfort him, no matter where he spread the blanket. "*Importa poco*," she said and climbed into the cart.

The day Consuela and Miguel arrived in New Braunfels Miguel met a Señor Urbina, who had so many sons he no longer had to work. Señor Urbina told Miguel about a *jacal* abandoned because it was too close to the river in flood time. Miguel and Consuela would be gone back to Nuevo León before the rainy season, so they could safely stay in this *jacal*. Señor Urbina said that, in fair exchange for two of los broncos, his youngest son, Domingo, would help Miguel catch this herd and the gray devil who led them.

Miguel fixed a leak in the roof of the *jacal*, and Consuela moved in the few belongings they had brought from home. Then the women visited. Maria Lavalla

Urbina dragged one leg because a cart had run over her. Maria Ledon never stopped grinning. Catalina Pachuca was short and fat. Catalina's sister Reina bragged about the German storekeeper who had asked permission to call on her. Maria Contreras was an old widow. Aurora Asbaje had a daughter, Estrella, who held to her mother's skirt. Delores received them outside in the yard, where there were only some big stumps on which to sit. Consuela stood. *"Aplatose por favor."*

Maria Urbina, Maria Ledon, Catalina, Reina, and Aurora—all of them except the child, Estrella, who chewed her fingers—preened and screeched like jaybirds in one tree. *"Las mujeres son muy música,"* said the Maria-who-was-a-widow, chewing her toothless gums between words. The women ground corn they had brought while they jabbered about the Germans, about other *mujeres*, about their children, and their men who were mostly gone nowadays all the way to Indianola or Galveston where the Germans kept arriving with *dinero* they paid to carters and to be shown easy things like where to find limestone for building houses, though a *jacal* was faster and easier.

The Mexicano women told Consuela that before so many Germans came and named this place New Braunfels a padre used to ride from San Antonio once a month to say the Mass and hear confession. Now, there was Father Martin. He spoke both the German and the English words, and, of course, the Latin words God and the angels used and priests know so they can say the Mass, but Father Martin did not know many Mexicano words.

Consuela nodded to show she was listening, but she gave little in return. She had her grief to keep her company, and the defiance she nurtured in her heart toward God seeped into her feelings for everyone else.

Sunday morning, right after Father Martin celebrated the Mass, Consuela walked out of the little church just as Catalina Pachuca asked Aurora Asbaje if she still bore milk.

Aurora giggled. *"No queda ni una gota de leche,"* she said.

Consuela could not ignore the fact that she overheard Catalina Pachuca and Aurora Asbaje on the holy day of Epiphany. Consuela pictured her husband Miguel's face if she were to tell him God had called her to nurse the child of some German *mujer*. He would make the frown he made when he worked to unknot one of his ropes pulled tight by the anger of some *caballo* who didn't want to be taken from the ones he loved—Miguel's left eye squinted, his mouth twisted down on the right. The tip of his tongue swelled out like a red sore between his lips. Her simple husband thought the stillbirth of his son was the same as when a mare's foal came out dead. Men understood blood and wailing only, not the silences that follow. For men, important things, pleasures or pains, have to be wet or loud. Miguel was worried because her tears had not flowed. Consuela knew he would not understand a sadness that lived deeper inside than the eyes.

Father Martin gave Consuela directions and told her to go rápido to the inn where the hungry baby was. She asked no questions. One should not question a priest any more than one should question God. Bigger at least than five or six *jacales*, the inn rose two floors above a stone-paved porch. From four upper windows linens hung like the speechless tongues of ghosts. Back home, in Nuevo León, Consuela washed bed covers and clothes in Rio Salado, spread them over low mesquite limbs to dry, dresses she had sewn for Ignacio had been blue and yellow like blossoms on the thorny mesquites, not this indifferent German white. She had come with Miguel to this place of hills to catch *el gris*, but soon she would return to Montclova. She wondered where the German place was, the home these Germans had left with no intention to return, and she wondered why they had left and why this woman did not nurse her own child. She took from beneath her collar the small wooden cross on its leather thong and kissed it even as she wondered, again, why God would send her a child and then take it back. Would the innkeeper be angry if a Mexicano came to his wide front door? The door opened and a woman pale as the stone walls, her hair even whiter though her face was not old, smiled at Consuela.

"*Guten Tag*—I mean, *Buenas días.*"

"*Buenas días.*"

"Please to *schnell*, rápido."

Consuela followed the woman, La Patrona, the landlady for the inn, through a room with a fireplace higher than a man's head and down a long hall where the tallest, skinniest man Consuela had ever seen appeared. This man's hair was yellow and glowed as a halo.

"*Guten Tag*, Herr Hermann," La Patrona said.

He did not speak. He gripped his hat so tightly he bent flat its brim. Like a saint's long robe, his coat covered him from his neck to his shoes. La Patrona and the tall man led Consuela to a small close room with a scent that took Consuela back to the church in Montclova where sweet-smelling smoke rose from the padres' swinging censers.

When she saw the baby, her breath stopped. Sunlight from the one window shone above a bed, shone there as the star of Bethlehem had shone over Jesu's manger behind another inn.

The *niño* had black hair, dark skin. "*Es* Mexicano?"

"Indianern."

Consuela had been wrong to think La Patrona would not suckle her own baby.

The tall man bowed his yellow head as if he were praying. Consuela picked up the baby and looked into eyes she recognized. She wondered if her breasts would still flow. She opened her *camisa* and the man turned his face away.

"He never cries, this baby," La Patrona said.

The baby's mouth on her nipple was cold then warm, pricked like sewing needles, and the instant the baby's tiny biting gums touched her flesh, Consuela *knew* she was in the midst of *un milagro de Dios*. This was *her own baby*, her Ignacio, sent back to her after being in Heaven. "*No es el Indio, es* Mexicano."

La Patrona of the inn told Consuela the tall sunburnt man (La Patrona named him Ru-dolph Her-mann) had rescued the baby from a river where he had found it afloat on some kind of Indianern raft and had ridden all night with the infant wrapped inside his shirt and saved the child from freezing. The man's yellow hair and burnt skin glowed with heavenly light like an angel, Ignacio's guardian angel who had returned him.

"The baby's *namen* is Moises," the angel said.

Consuela had expected him to speak the Latin words God and angels use, but she guessed angels could speak any words they wanted. He had followed Ignacio's soul to Limbo and brought it back. He had taken Ignacio's small box from the ground and coaxed his infant soul back into the still-perfect body.

With long, pale fingers the angel showed Consuela trinkets he'd nestled in the folds of a blue and yellow quilt in a cedar-smelling cradle he'd made for Moises with the help of one of the town's carpenters. Consuela smiled. An angel could make what he wanted without the help of any carpenter. She fingered the trinkets: a smooth stone, a sharp mirror shard, a piece of antler and a claw, and she wondered if the angel had brought these things from Heaven. Were there deer and beasts with claws in Heaven?

La Patrona told Consuela that before Herr Hermann could have any *kinder* of his own, his beloved bride had died on one of the big boats the Germans rode to Texas. Consuela looked up into the angel's eyes. They were the changing colors of storm clouds, gray then green then gray again, and they showed a sadness without tears that lived much deeper inside than the eyes, a sadness she didn't think any heavenly being purely angel could feel. Maybe this angel, in a faint copy of Cristo, had been made partly into a man.

🪶

For five days Consuela stayed at the inn nursing and caring for Ignacio, and for all those days he never cried out. He watched everything around him. A baby who never cried could only be a miracle of God.

The day of Ignacio's christening, Father Martin baptized the baby and christened him Moses Ignacio Delgado. The priest spoke the Latin words of Heaven and the coughing, dry words of the Germans. Then he read from an English Bible, from the Book of Saint Mark:

> And He took a child, and set him in the midst of them: and when He had taken him in His arms, He said unto them, Whosoever shall receive one of such children in my name, receiveth me; and whosoever shall receive me, receiveth not me, but Him that sent me.

And from *la epístola* to the Hebrews:

> Be not forgetful to entertain strangers: for thereby some have entertained angels unawares.

It was left for Consuela's simple, good Miguel to speak the Mexicano words:

"*Por* Dios, " Miguel said softly, almost a prayer, then, louder, "*Le salvo la vida.*"

Consuela knew the priest thought Miguel meant God had saved her life, but Miguel meant her *niño*, little Ignacio, had saved her life. Of course, both amounted to the same. As if God wanted to be sure Consuela realized He had performed *un milagro*. He also arranged for Miguel to capture the bronco mustang.

"Wife of mine, the gray may be of El Diablo. He is cunning, but he is also of the angels, so strong is his devotion to his herd." Miguel's eyes were bigger than the eyes of the excited Domingo, Señor Urbina's twelve-year-old son who had helped capture the gray and his herd. Miguel put his hand in her back and pushed. "Come to los corrales at Señor Urbina's. Come see."

Consuela cradled Moses Ignacio in her rebozo. Domingo ran ahead, saying, "*Aquí tenemos seis caballos. Aquí tenemos ocho caballos.*" At one corral he beamed and said, "*Este caballo negro es el mío y el pinto es de mi padre. Todo los ostros son para ustedes.*"

"*El gris*, he runs circles around the others," Miguel said. "He had only to desert those he leads and he would have been free." Miguel spread his arms. "He could run *para siempre* if he wanted."

She laughed, happy with Miguel and the Urbina boy, able, now that Ignacio had returned, to be happy with herself. She was so happy she felt as if she were happy for the first time. One of the horses snorted, and as wind ripples water, the animal's muscles rippled its brown hide. Tonight, Miguel would get the comfort she had denied him these past weeks. At the thought of it, she reached for Miguel's arm. "*Con permiso.*" She held onto her husband.

"*Sí, sí.*" Miguel told of the box canyon the *muchacho* knew of and how they tricked the gray into thinking he had led them away from his herd when they were separating him from the other horses.

"Then, Señora," the Urbina boy's voice trembled, "we drove the herd into a canyon that has as the way out no path except the way in."

"By all that's holy, I hated to rope him," Miguel said.

"Then why did you? You had the rest of the herd, why did you capture him, too?"

Miguel cocked his head. "Why, Consuela, that's how it is between men and horses. They are given four legs to run from us, and we are given *reata* and cañon walls and *muy esquemas* to catch them. It will be this way until men have caught all of God's wild horses, and then the lives of men will be poorer than they are now."

While Consuela nursed Ignacio back to health, her husband and *el gris* kept each other happy. Training the horse, Miguel clucked low in his throat, stroked the gray as a lover, and called him lover's names: *novio* and *querido*. Consuela sometimes found herself staring past the corral where dust devils spun up into the blue sky, but Ignacio's dark eyes never left the whirling, bucking, prancing, snorting dance of man and horse. By the time Miguel had broken the stallion to saddle, Ignacio was strong enough for the long ride back to Mexico.

Rudolph Hermann asked permission to come with them to Hacienda del Caballito so he might be near enough to watch Moises grow up. Consuela told her husband they could not refuse a man at least part angel. Miguel told the angel-man that he, Miguel Delgado, would petition El Patrón, who owned their *jacal* and the land around it farther than eyes could see, for permission for the angel-man to live on the hacienda.

And so they set out: Miguel rode the still skittish gray who sidled and halfheartedly bucked, only to have Miguel fuss sweetly and stroke his neck and turn him to keep him on point. Consuela drove a small Mexicano cart pulled by a strong, docile mule. Ignacio was nestled in the cradle secured by one of Miguel's many ropes. Consuela looked back at Ignacio and, behind their cart, at the angel-man in an open farmer's wagon, a big rifle on the footboard. The angel-man picked up the coiled *reata* Miguel had given him and held it high in a salute. Consuela waved back, noting how the ring of rope shone in the sun like a halo above the angel-man's yellow hair.

The angel-man's farmer's wagon rode low, and its wheels made deep ruts under the weight of a pink granite gravestone. The dirt of New Braunfels still clung to the stone's base beneath carved German words Consuela could not read and the name she recognized of the angel-man's earthly wife, Ottilie. The top of the stone had been chiseled into an angel, its wings white now with the dust of the trail. A half-dozen of the best horses out of the newly captured herd, barely greenbroke, brought up the rear of the train. The morning sun cast westward the elongated shadow of the granite angel that topped Ottilie's gravestone, so the dark shape of one wing lay like a blanket over the back of Consuela's cart and kept the sun out of the eyes of the babe, who lay on his back and watched every tree and rock that passed.

Alexander and Charles Wesley: Brother against Brother

Alike but Different
(born, 1846–alarms of war, 1862)

Colonel Powell-Hughes told me the beginning words of everyone's
story are the seeds containing his story's end. From what I have learned about
Charles Wesley Speer and his twin brother Alexander Wesley, they were conceived and born out of disparity. Can such differences be reconciled?
Can two solitudes ever truly greet one another?

—from *Gideon Jones' Journal*

Wesley and Wesley. To all appearances, outwardly, they were the same. Identical
twins born out of a union of disparate halves. Their parents, Samuel Titus Speer
and Mary Ophelia Lupton, might have originated the notion that opposites attract.
Tall and dark-complected, Samuel Speer was like an afternoon shadow stretched
out beside Mary, who was small and fair. They never saw much of anything eye to
eye. Black were Samuel's hair, his bushy brows, his deepset eyes, his beard—black
the suits of clothing he always wore. But his dark demeanor was a counterfeit
appearance created out of his secret shyness. When the sun shone on Samuel's
black beard, Mary saw whiskers there as red as strands of bright red sewing thread.
And for all his hard words, his hand gave only gentleness.

Samuel's passion was for vicarious adventure as he experienced it in the accounts of pirates, brigands, duelists, soldiers, and outlaws, accounts he had been
devouring since he was a boy. After he read Alexander Forbes' book, *California*,
about the possibilities of that new land, Samuel became devoted to expansionist
politics. After he read *Sketches and Eccentricities of Col. David Crockett*, Samuel
talked about the frontier as if he were an old Indian fighter. He read everything he
could find about the Republic of Texas, and whenever he appeared to be on the los-

ing side of an argument with Mary he made a fist and solemnly said, "Remember the Alamo." What Samuel called history, Mary thought of as the gossip of violence. On one thing they did agree: they wanted a house full of children.

They married in the First Methodist Church of New York City on May 11, 1837, the day after the New York banks stopped all payments in specie. It secretly pleased them both that their wedding ceremony was one calm moment in the midst of the city's financial panic. The speculation in Western land that followed the failure of hundreds of banks fueled Samuel's already burning interest in Texas, and as years passed his speculative talk fueled the imaginations of his twin sons.

Samuel bought property in Murray Hill, a neighborhood just being developed, where, he assured Mary, the abundant sunshine and the excellent drainage afforded by the elevated land would provide a felicitous site on which to build their home.

In the large brick house in Murray Hill, Mary gave birth to four girls in a row, each one as fair of hair and complexion and as pretty as their mother was. The day she told Samuel she was pregnant for the sixth time (there had been one miscarriage), he was sitting in the kitchen pulling at his dark beard and poring over newspaper accounts of President Polk's having sent General Taylor to lead troops against the Mexican army. While he read, he wheedled raw cookie dough from Anna, the maid.

"We are all equal in the eyes of God. Yet you support the expansionist Democrats, who want to bring in more slave states," Mary said.

"Mama, why can't you and the damned Whigs see war with Mexico has nothing to do with extending slavery?"

Anna flung cookie dough on a hot baking sheet and shook her head. "Don't get him started again, Mrs. Speer."

"I've got news for you, Samuel, that *might* be as exciting as the wild frontier. I'm going to have your son this fall, and I don't want him fighting in a Democrat war."

For just a moment Samuel was speechless. Then he was back in his traces: "Girls don't have the glory of going to war."

Mary held up the latest Poe, *The Raven and Other Poems,* she had forgotten she had carried into the kitchen tucked under her arm. "My son will sooner be a poet than a soldier."

"Any son of mine who didn't seek glory where he could find it, and I'd know you for a harlot, Mama, cause I'd be sure my blood wasn't running in his veins. But I won't be surprised if you birth another daughter."

"This one *is* a boy, and he'll vote the Liberty ticket and fight slavery—if we haven't abolished it by the time he grows up."

"Throw his vote away on the likes of that has-been, Birney? You see why women aren't allowed to vote? If this boy thinks like you do, I hope he is another girl."

For their daughters' names they'd agreed on virtues: Faith, Hope, Charity, and Prudence. For a son, Samuel insisted on "Alexander," after Alexander the Great, king of Macedonia and conqueror of Greece, the Persian Empire, and Egypt. Mary favored something godly and wanted "Wesley," after her grandfather, John Wesley Lupton, whose father had been a devotee of John Wesley, founder of the Methodist Church.

Mary struggled through a long labor, finally bringing forth Samuel's first son before the sun rose on the same day, Samuel liked to point out, the Oregon Treaty was signed with Great Britain, making Washington, Oregon, Idaho, and part of Montana undisputed United States territory. Grandmother Speer got Alexander's birth cord cut and tied, cleaned mucus from his crying mouth, and had him washed off and wrapped up. The whole time Mary had been carrying, they'd heard only one heartbeat. Before Grandmother could wonder out loud why a smallish baby like Alexander had made Mary so big, here came another.

When the fifth child turned out to be the long-hoped-for son, his name, Alexander Wesley, was waiting. When this first son turned out to be two sons at once, Samuel immediately produced "Charlemagne," Charles the Great, king of the Franks, crowned emperor of the Romans. Mary would not be outdone and, so, declared "Wesley" a strong enough middle name to be used twice.

A year later, Alexander and Charles Wesley (Mama had declared "Charlemagne" too unwieldy for everyday use, and in retaliation Papa had dropped the "Wesley" from Alexander whenever he addressed his older son) began their birthday with breakfast in matching high chairs. Samuel stared at the boys, the white china cup of coffee he held against his unkempt beard looking like a piece of fruit hanging in a dark bushy bower. Morning sounds came through open windows: bird songs and dog barks and, now and then, horses' hooves and carriage wheels passing smartly by. From the kitchen stove came the snap and flicker of fire, the hiss of a green log, the scent of woodsmoke beneath the suety smell of ham grease glazing the china plates and over all the faint scent and warmth of kerosene lamps that maid Anna lighted every morning when she arrived before dawn.

A knock sent Anna to the back door, but no one was there. Clunk and creak of wood and leather made her look to the street. All she saw was a wooden van reined in at the curb. On the exposed driver's seat was a large wood box with a glass window.

"Madam."

Anna looked down and the face of a dwarf looked up at her like a rising moon. He held out a thin carved box with a gold clasp on the side. When she took the box he nodded and she opened it like a book. Staring back at her was a miniature likeness of the miniature man.

"I am Jarvis VanWyck, Professor of Daguerreotypy, one of the world's finest disciples of the sun. I am willing to preserve forever the likenesses of the newest members of this household."

"How do you know about them?" Anna said.

The dwarf winked, grinned, tapped his disproportionately big skull. He told Anna, "Little people know lots of things." And he told her he'd been there when the ship *Sachem* arrived from Siam with Chang and Eng, joined at the breast-bone, the very same twins Mr. Barnum had exhibited at his American Museum. Then he showed Anna other daguerreotypes he'd made—a goldfish, a soldier in a fancy uniform, a bride and groom—in velvet-lined boxes that opened like paper dolls cut and unfolded once. The goldfish appeared enlarged, distorted by the curved glass bowl, its mouth round as an O, the face of a trapped thing. The soldier was resplendent with medals that reflected light as spots on his chest. The bride and groom faced one another, duplicate figures hinged where they were mounted in the same display case that joined them like the Siamese twins, like the matched wings of a butterfly. The dwarf held up a brown bottle that he said contained an accelerating buff that was his secret mixture and that resulted in images as lifelike as those reflected in any fine-looking glass. The man reeked of sulphur and other chemicals that reminded Anna of cleaning day. He offered a five-dollar daguerreotype for two dollars. Anna said "no," of course. Two dollars, a week's wages for a working man. Stubborn, she again said "no." Later, Mary told Samuel it was shame they couldn't go back and reverse Anna's decision. Then they'd have a likeness to document the twins' first birthday. Samuel remarked he needed no such keepsake or image to preserve the births that were, in his words, *indelibly etched*, in his mind and on his heart.

Twins the boys were, peas alike in a pod they were not. From their birth they displayed their differences. A pugnacious and ostentatious infant, Alexander seemed to know he was named for a world conqueror. Samuel made no secret of the pride he took in his older son's loud cries and in the way the infant furiously waved his tiny red fists.

"I tell you, Mama, Alexander will live up to his name."

Mary tried not to show she favored the younger Wesley, her lastborn child. Of course she loved them both, but she felt more in tune with Charles Wesley. She knew Samuel interpreted Charles Wesley's more thoughtful demeanor as docility, possibly even weakness, but she privately celebrated the boy's silences and steady stares as indications of patience and wisdom. She marked Genesis, where the Lord tells Rebekah:

Two nations *are* in thy womb,
and two manner of people shall be separated from thy bowels;
and *the one* people shall be stronger than *the other* people;
and the elder shall serve the younger.

Mary worried that Alexander the Conqueror's first victim would be his brother. He was always trying to dominate Charles Wesley. The first time she put them together in a crib, Alexander kicked Charles Wesley in the head. Later, when the twins were older, Samuel's main concession to equal treatment was to whip both when either was suspected of mischief. That was not equal treatment, though, since Alexander was nearly always the guilty party. Charles Wesley never complained. He enjoyed getting credit for sinfulness he aspired to but, somehow, fell short of. As they grew up, Alexander told Charles Wesley he was a scaredy cat so many times Charles believed he must be one. In appearance only were they mirror images. Alexander slept with his right arm crossed over his left, while Charles Wesley crossed left arm over right. Alexander bore a small birthmark on the back of his left thigh, the mark resembling a tiny flag waving. The same flag unfurled in the opposite direction on Charles Wesley's right thigh. Hot bathwater turned both banners flaming red, while the boys slapped at each other, splashing water against the wall where, over time, it made a stain like a low, dark cloud.

By the time the twins were two, Mexico had recognized Texas as part of the United States, ceding to the U.S. thousands of square miles of territory—what would one day become the states of New Mexico, Arizona, Utah, Nevada, California, and parts of Colorado and Wyoming. When they were too young to understand, Samuel read to his sons newspaper accounts of General Zachary Taylor's occupation of Matamoros and of his victory at Buena Vista. Now, he told them with glee, Taylor was the Whig nominee for president. In July Mary attended a women's convention in Seneca Falls where she spoke in favor of giving women property rights—rights soon granted by the New York legislature. In November Samuel celebrated General Taylor's election and chided Mary for supporting Van Buren.

"It's a good thing you can't vote," Samuel said.

When President Taylor died, the twins were not just walking and talking, they were running and arguing. Alexander, in every way conceivable, distanced himself from Charles Wesley, even preferring the company of one or more of his sisters. In the fall, Mary attended another women's rights convention in Worcester, Massachusetts, where she advocated giving women the vote and total equality in divorce proceedings. When Mary brought home a copy of Mrs. Stowe's best-selling novel, *Uncle Tom's Cabin, or Life among the Lowly,* she provoked an argument with Samuel that raged between them for years, as it raged between regions of the nation.

"It figures some woman would write such a distorted tale," Samuel said.

"Papa, how can you ignore the horrors of enslavement?"

"This book is sentimental, maudlin, melodramatic, exaggerated female tripe. A collection of less-than-half-truths."

"If it's even half-true it's too true."

From beneath the bristly cover of his dark brows, with probing eyes and outrageous proslavery declarations, Samuel ambushed abolitionist friends. He loved to argue. Had they lived in Tidewater Virginia or the Mississippi Delta, Samuel would have been unable to prevent abolitionist slogans from escaping his lips. He had never talked to a Negro, never even stood close to one. His heart was as soft as his talk was hard. But he so romanticized the frontier, especially the slave-state of Texas, he could not admit even to himself that slavery was anything more than an economic issue. The Texas of Samuel's imagination was peopled with Indians, Mexicans, and Texans: vaqueros working cattle, Rangers fighting Comanches, desperate shootists engaged in duels, and handsome gamblers with scandalous pasts. Oh, what he would give to fight Mexicans and Indians in Texas. The next best thing would be for his son Alexander to be a frontiersman. He seemed already to have conceded Charles Wesley was no hero-to-be.

Alexander mimicked Samuel's enthusiasm for masculine adventure, and it was clear his aim was to please his father. The gifts he asked for were toy soldiers and fighting ships. Grant Samuel this: every tin soldier, every frigate and corvette he gave to Alexander, he always gave an identical one to Charles Wesley. But

Charles left his warriors and warships in their boxes, where Alexander found and appropriated them. The elder twin needed the reserves since most of his lead infantrymen had at least one arm shot off.

The twins shared a large room on the third floor of the brick house directly above their parents' bedroom. One night—the boys were about ten at the time—Samuel and Mary had sent their sons to bed and retired to their room, where Samuel sat in the wingback chair reading while Mary brushed her hair. Shouts and loud bumps overhead sent them rushing upstairs. Alexander was standing up in his bed, screaming, "Kill it. Kill it." Charles Wesley held a writhing green snake.

Samuel, who was none too fond of snakes, stopped in the doorway. "What has transpired here, Alexander?" he said, as if only Alexander could be counted on to narrate the incident.

"When I pulled back my covers, this fine fellow fell out onto the floor," Charles Wesley said. He held up the snake for emphasis, and Alexander leaned back against the wall, standing now on his pillow. "Alexander put him in my bed, I'm sure of it. He was hanging back to see me climb in bed."

"Kill it, Papa," Alexander said.

"I'll take it outside," Charles Wesley said.

"Not in the house yard, son. The back meadow." Samuel stepped far aside the doorway to let Charles Wesley pass with the serpent.

Mary leveled her gaze on Alexander, who clambered down from atop his bed and said, "It must have crawled up from the garden,"

"Up three flights of stairs?" Mama asked.

"No harm done," Samuel said. "A boy's prank." He turned and went downstairs.

Mama waited in the boys' room until Charles Wesley returned. She bade him use the bowl and pitcher to wash both hands. "Were you frightened?"

"Of a garter snake? I took him far into the grass."

"It only startled me when you threw him at me," Alexander said.

"He fell from the covers, as you know," Charles Wesley said.

"Not another word. Sleep now, both of you."

The next day Mary questioned her daughters. Alexander was guilty of the incident, but she knew he was too fearful of snakes to have captured one himself. Finally, after her mother promised confidentiality, Prudence confessed that Alexander had promised her his Jumping Jack, her favorite toy of his, if she could catch a frog or a snake for him. She put the garter snake in one of maid Anna's laundry bags, and Alexander had only to unknot the bag and put it under Charles Wesley's covers where the snake could crawl out.

"I'm not a tell-tale," Prudence said. "I only told because Alexander kept his Jumping Jack. He said the joke didn't work so I didn't get paid."

Mary shook her head at her daughter, but kept her confidence. What Samuel dismissed as a manly prank she saw as the act of a cowering bully, and she kept a close eye on her oldest son. For several days after Charles Wesley had released the snake, Mary observed from an upstairs window Alexander walking in the high grass of the meadow on one of the pairs of wooden stilts the children played with. He struggled to manipulate the stilts while carrying with him the long-handled garden hoe.

Mary and Samuel disagreed often about how to raise and discipline their sons. Mary did her best not to argue in the presence of the boys, but Samuel had no such scruples. In fact, it seemed to Mary that he spoke against her prohibitions in front of Alexander so that he might appear to be the boys' champion. When his sons were no more than twelve, Samuel began giving them sips of beer and whisky. Against Mary's fears that strong spirits would stunt the boys' growth, Samuel laughed out loud. "Whisky," he said, "is especially beneficial to the humor of blood and will develop their sanguine, ruddy aspects." Mary shook her head. Logic was useless against such medieval notions. A couple of years later, she pointed out that the boys seemed to have developed a taste for liquor. Rather than show concern, her husband named this inclination "manly precociousness."

Samuel arranged lessons for Alexander in horsemanship. Mary insisted Charles Wesley get lessons as well. Twice a week they were instructed in riding and in the care and grooming of their mounts. Much to Samuel's surprise (and Mary's delight) the reports from their trainer consistently praised Charles Wesley's abilities over Alexander's as a horseman, and Charles Wesley was the one who stayed at the stables brushing both sorrel mares. Mary pointed out to her husband that Charles Wesley's obvious affection for the beasts and his gentle hand won their devotion over Alexander's reliance on boot heel and riding crop.

A Civil War

In spite of a middle-aged man's love of military glory, Samuel was secretly glad the twins were too young for duty when war finally broke out. In June of 1862, when it became obvious McClellan's peninsular campaign would not succeed, Lincoln issued a call for three hundred thousand more volunteers. That month the family celebrated the boys' sixteenth birthday with a croquet game. Throughout the game Charles Wesley's dark green ball haunted Alexander's mustard yellow one, rolling gently against it and giving Charles Wesley the right to smack his brother's ball far into the bushes. But Charles Wesley always chose instead to take aim at some other player.

"Even in this damn game I can't get shed of you," Alexander said. "I'm going to volunteer to join the Rebs to stop you from shadowing me."

"You boys are too young, and I'm too old. Glory missed. But if I could fight, I would join the Confederates in this fight against Northern aggression."

"You would not," Mary said. "This is illegal rebellion against the law and the moral right." And to the boys: "Your father is a curmudgeon—and a romantic to boot."

In July, when President Lincoln signed a measure passed by Congress to authorize calling up men between eighteen and forty-five for nine months in the militia, Samuel was fearful. He was convinced Congress would pass an all-out conscription act. Though the boys were too young to be conscripts—to "see the elephant" as the newspapers put it—Samuel fretted. In August Lincoln ordered a draft of three hundred thousand militia, but the draft was not acted upon. Samuel was not the only New Yorker resistant to the draft. The first service many New York soldiers saw was to control the draft riots in the city. Mary and Samuel kept all the children safe in Murray Hill and read about the riots in the newspaper. Some journalists and politicians argued the war would soon be over and no more men would be needed, but still others claimed now was when the need was crucial. By the end of the year, the Federal forces seemed poised to strike the South with a mortal blow. The president's Emancipation Proclamation on New Year's Day stirred resentment that led to Democrat victories in the fall elections. The new year began with heavy storms and an apparent lull in military action. Generals seemed reluctant to begin any major offensives during such bad weather, but most New Yorkers felt major battles would be coming with the spring thaw.

Before light, the morning of March 15, 1863, Charles Wesley waked to the creak of Alexander's bed. Already dressed, Alexander bent to pull on a sock, and his shirt tightened across his back. "Going to see a girl I met, lives in Brooklyn. Be back late," he said.

"There's no girl in Brooklyn." He suspected Alexander was off to join the Confederates as he had talked about for years. Charles Wesley knew his brother's motives were to make Papa proud and to free himself of the twin brother, who could not help but be his shadow.

"There's a girl somewhere, though. Weddings and war are going on down south while we sit with tutors and go round and round in a riding ring."

"We're New Yorkers, part of the Union."

"I was born for the West and wide distances. You are part of this city's close spaces." Alexander waved his arm toward the window. "Do you think it amused God to make us in one another's image on the outside, while he fashioned our minds and hearts so different?"

"You came more from Papa, and I from Mama."

"A mama's boy you are."

"Aren't you afraid, going off to war?"

"I told you, I'm going to see a girl in Brooklyn."

"You're off to somewhere farther away than Brooklyn," Charles Wesley said. Alexander smiled, and Charles Wesley felt a flush of connection if not love. "Now I know why you've been saving all the money Papa has given you this past year. And your birthday money, too." Alexander gave Charles Wesley a carefree, devil-ish grin and the younger twin felt regret for the brothers they might have been to one another. He believed he saw through Papa's braggadocio, too. He was sure the old man did not want Alexander out of his sight. And, now, Charles Wesley hated to watch his brother leave. He knew Alexander was off to the war and adventure and glory and he thought, *Alexander looks just how I would look if I were bold and brave.*

Alexander stood to go. "I'll watch for you in Yankee blue. And I'll meet you down in Hades."

Charles Wesley nodded. His throat was too knotted up for speech. Alexander carried his boots, and his stockinged feet made no sound going down the stairs. Charles Wesley lay on his back and stared at the window until it began to fill with faint light. Drizzle streaked the panes of glass illuminated by a gray and cloudy sky. At breakfast, Papa asked Charles Wesley where his brother had gone.

"After some girl."

Samuel winked at Mama, who did not smile. "Takes after his Papa," she said. "Sixteen and already up to no good."

Mama stared long at Charles Wesley, who met her gaze without blinking. She shook her head. A tear shone on her cheek, but she said nothing.

Long after midnight, when Alexander still had not come home, Charles Wesley heard their papa through the bedroom wall.

"Beware the Ides of March," he said. "Beware the Ides of March."

Alexander Rides a Boxcar South

Alexander Wesley slept sitting up in a boxcar so crowded with men those not lucky enough to be against one of the four sides had to lean against one another. As packed as the rail car was, Alexander felt he had more room than ever before, could breathe air Charles Wesley wasn't also breathing. Cold blew in through the open car doors, but with the doors shut the air grew thick with body heat and gamy odors. Fetid as the close bodies were, none of them was Charles Wesley, so Alexander reveled in his freedom. Nobody on this train knew he had a twin brother. For the rest of the war, Alexander Wesley Speer was an only child.

Everywhere were soldiers, volunteers from Maine, New Hampshire, New York, and Philadelphia. Some were decked out in splendid uniforms, but most looked as if they'd just stepped down from a farm wagon. Most had already been mustered into the service of the United States, though many volunteers climbed on board without benefit of papers. The whole railroad was boxcars of soldiers and Alexander had seen no lists or records. The cars stopped often to take on more men. They were shoved onto side tracks while newcomers loaded their horses, then the fitful journey resumed. Alexander felt as if he'd joined some great herd of beasts moving haphazardly southward, milling and squirming and churning, growing in number and momentum. Everyone assumed he was one of them, a volunteer for the Union cause. He introduced himself as Alex West, an alias close enough to the sound of the truth he was not likely to be caught off guard—a name that pleased him in its secret containment of his ultimate destination.

At the Susquehanna River there was no rail bridge. The cars were rolled onto a great railroad ferry, iron-hulled and side-wheeled, the *Maryland*. They crossed the river, wide and smooth, the water gold-plated by a setting sun. Through tons of wood and iron—car floor and walls and wheels, railroad ties and track, mighty ferry hull and deck—the gentle sway of the river bobbed men's heads as if they were cork fishing floats. Alexander sensed some meaning in the constant motion of the river, the mimic motions of ferry, rail cars, and men, but what the meaning was he couldn't say.

The river crossing—about a mile—didn't take long, but on the other side they waited and waited before they were pulled back onto solid ground. Now, the railbed swayed near as much as the river. The going was slow and the iron wheels screeched, keening long into the night, as if reluctant to bear them toward the fields of battle.

Alexander waked with a start, surprised he had slept. Charles Wesley breathed deeply against him. His arm had drifted in sleep and now lay across Alexander's chest. In the darkness, he pushed away his brother's arm, reached across the elbow's bend to where muscle and bone no longer Charles Wesley became the body of a man called Jenks. Without waking, Jenks coughed, and the arm slid back across Alexander's chest. He moved the arm again, got to his feet, and, holding the swaying side of the car, made his way over legs and feet to the opened doors. Cold air splashed over him. Trees were the blackest shapes against a black sky knife-pricked with the bright sting of stars. Alexander breathed deeply, taking the cold into his lungs. On his own for the first time since Charles Wesley had grabbed his ankle as they swam down the birth canal, he felt more alive than he ever had.

Truly alone for the first time since birth, he acknowledged the fear that had dogged him since he could remember. He was afraid of being afraid. He—not Charles Wesley—was the family coward. To divert attention from himself, he had almost daily found ways to call Charles Wesley's courage into question. "Scaredy cat," he'd said over and over, more often and the louder for his secret knowledge that he was the frightened one. Now, miles from home, as he opened his top buttons and let the blowing air fill his shirt and chill his skin, the warmth and weight of his twin's arm lingered there. Getting away from Charles Wesley was as impossible as escaping his own self.

The cars entered a wide curve, leaning into the rails, and Alexander had to resist the pulling force of the threshold, gateway to darkness. In the curve, he saw the locomotive ahead, its gray breath of smoke long and furry as the tail of some beast. Boxcar after boxcar followed, a gray shape in each doorway, himself repeating himself for as far back as he could see.

At dawn, the cars slowed as they crept up a long slope. Men stirred, and Alexander moved from the doorway to let one after another relieve himself. He returned to his space beside Jenks, who looked at him and laughed.

"Hey, look who run off and joined a minstrel show."

"Nigger-face," someone said.

Alexander wiped his cheek, leaving a smear of dark soot on his sleeve. With the tail of his shirt he wiped his face clean and thought, *I'm traveling in disguise.*

As soon as he made his way down south, Alexander hoped to find a company of Texas cavalry. Already he was planning his first military action—the liberation of a Yankee mount from the horsecars for service in the Confederate Cavalry. A boy from Bradford, Vermont—his name was Benjamin, but there was already a Benjamin in his group who had signed with the First Vermont Volunteers so they called this one Bradford—had slept sitting up beside Alexander. When Bradford woke up he claimed he was assured of the cavalry because he had brought his horse, a sleek chestnut mare he had loaded with other soldiers' mounts two cars back. Alexander said he was set for the cavalry, too, by dint of his horsemanship, and the two shook hands. Bradford said he felt certain they would ride side by side, comrades in arms.

In Baltimore the cars stopped, and colored men brought buckets of water. Jenks said it was seecesh water laden with poisons. A man called Tiny, big as a bear, held a dipperful.

"I'd sooner die of poison than of thirst. We're on our way to war, so soon's good as late." Tiny drank the dipper down. "If this be death, death tastes good."

Most were so thirsty they took several draughts. Alexander asked one of the colored men where to buy whisky. The man's words ran together with his tongue and spittle. "A pine doll" Alexander finally translated as "a pint for a dollar." Bradford allowed as how he'd never tasted spirits. Alexander gave the Negro five dollars and told him to bring two pints of high quality and keep a dollar for himself.

"I've been spoiled by my papa's aged whisky," Alexander said.

"I was never allowed the smallest sip," Bradford said. The boy shook his head.

He's amazed, Alexander thought, *at my worldliness*. "My mama disapproved, but every Christmas and New Year's and on my sixteenth birthday Papa poured me enough for his toasts," Alexander said.

"You've seen the old darkie and your money for the last time," Jenks said.

"He's got to come back. He's carrying Bradford's first taste of strong corn."

A slow hour passed, and Alexander and Bradford decided Jenks was right. Alexander was just dozing off when someone jerked his leg. A dark shape crouched over him.

"Here you is, general." The old colored man stood a bottle between Alexander's legs. "Better than two a them little bottles, I got a uncommon steep bottle from the doggery-keeper: he say it gone tetotaciously ex-fluncticate you." What language was this darkie growling?

The colored man smiled, proud-like, wrinkles at his eyes turned up, eyebrows and hair like tufts of cotton against his skin. This was as close as Alexander had ever been to a Negro. All light in the dim boxcar seemed collected in the neck of the whisky bottle illuminating the dark hand. Creased, leathery skin the color of strong coffee lightened as if by cream poured into a palm, the undersides of fingers caramel- or coffee-colored. Fat fingers ended in yellow nails, long and sharp-pointed as claws. The wrinkled, dark hand, large and in motion, seemed covert, shy, reluctant to reveal the skin's horizon where dark met light: a cloudy, misty, foggy line that reminded Alexander of the coloration in fur and feathers, of birds' eggs and of rocks, of the striation where wind or water has worn away earth. Before Alexander could think what to say next, the old Negro saluted him and crawled crablike over legs to the open door and disappeared.

Was the darkie—and others like him—the cause of this long war, the reason all these men were piled in a boxcar like cordwood? He was dark as a beast and his talk was closer to grunts and growls than human speech. *What*, Alexander wondered, *does the life of such a creature have to do with my life?*

After his first slug, Bradford judged whisky overrated. One morning soon, he might think differently. His head would be too large for the Yankee cap some aunt had sewn him, and his chestnut mare and Alexander would be gone. *Charles Wesley*, Alexander thought, *would never steal a horse, not even as an act of war.*

They waited three hours before a corporal passed along shouting for everyone to climb out and walk to the Washington Depot. Alexander rode behind Bradford on the boy's mare, Alice, and Alexander vowed never to be infantry, but he kept this to himself—the infantry hated the cavalry. As he'd already heard many times over: "Whoever heard of a dead cavalryman?"—which meant, of course, to impugn the valor of horse soldiers. The use of strong talk to cover fear was something Alexander had learned from his papa.

The cars for Washington, first late, then slow. By morning, the bottle of whisky—not good whisky, either—was empty and Bradford was snoring loudly. They'd spent the night stopping and starting, mostly sitting still in the dark. Alexander figured they were no more than ten or twelve miles out of Baltimore. They slowly passed army tents, row after row of pointed roofs bright and clean in the sun as sheets hung out to dry, everything too fresh and new-looking to have to do with the business of war. Troops, a mass of blue, filled a clearing beside the tracks— men singing hymns, the first outward sign all morning it was the Sabbath. The cars rolled by so slow the men on board were able to join in singing "Come Holy Spirit, Heavenly Dove." Alexander marked well the familiar words:

And shall we then forever live
At this poor dying rate?
Our love so faint, so cold to Thee,
And Thine to us so great.

He marked, too, soldiers guarding the rails. He'd have to keep to the woods once he left these Yankees. For miles they passed hillsides of tents. March winds puffed canvas into the domes of minarets, the rail car a swaying magic carpet Alexander rode into a fictional landscape conjured up by Scheherazade—tales Papa had read out loud, tales Charles Wesley always liked more than Alexander did.

By the time the cars halted in Washington, Alexander's head was stuffy, his stomach sour from the whisky, but he was in better shape than poor Bradford, who was so dizzy Alexander had to help him walk. They were marched to the Soldiers' Rest, a barnlike dining hall where they were fed a meal of stringy salt pork, stale bread, and something passed off as coffee, though it looked and tasted like muddy water. After they ate they waited a good two hours before they were marched to a place called Camp Chase, an endless tent city spread out beside the Potomac. Here they were issued tent cloth and blankets. Two men buttoned these shelter cloths together, stretched them over a horizontal pole supported at each end by muskets, fixed bayonets stabbed into the earth. Alexander tented up with Bradford.

The nation's capital was astir—teamsters shouting, mules braying. The mud and dust of transit filled the air, the roads abused by heavy army wagons. Never had Alexander seen such confusion. The Capitol Building had been turned into a hospital, its unfinished dome still surrounded by scaffolding as if the workmen had heard the call to arms and put down hammers and trowels to pick up muskets and bayonets, or, deadlier, the knives and saws of surgeons. Everywhere were men with one arm or none, with bandaged stumps and carved wooden legs, with canes and crutches, men wrapped round with bandaging who moved stiff as Egyptian mummies. It was as if the dead and near-dead had risen to limp and jerk about in a macabre minuet ignored by those with two good legs. Two dimensions co-existed, world of the dead and world of the living, one crowded dance floor with two kinds of music.

The unfinished national monument to President Washington was a brick tower rising above the trees, abandoned as the tower of Babel when its builders felt God's fury and scattered in fear. If Papa were here, he'd have something to say about the sorry condition of the nation's capital.

Now there was nothing but waiting. Every day they heard their officers were going to assemble them for the beginning of drills. Alexander had to make his move soon, before the companies were organized, before names were recorded or checked, lists made. Yet, every day he found some reason to put off leaving. Maimed men at the hospital made him imagine sword blade or lead ball taking off an arm or a leg, and his heart beat so fast and high up in his throat he feared he might choke on his pulsing life.

The next morning, before he had time to change his mind, Alexander told Bradford he was going to the hospital to look for a friend from home. No one went to the hospitals if he hadn't been ordered there, so he knew Bradford wouldn't offer to come along. Likely, Bradford thought Alexander daft. Alexander was disappointed when the boy offered him the chestnut to ride—now he wouldn't have the thrill of stealing the mare from her livery. If Alexander admitted it, Bradford's trust made him feel guilty, too. But not so guilty he didn't take the horse.

Alexander stopped at the hospital just long enough to stuff a wad of blood-stained bandage beneath his shirt. Behind the cover of a hedge, he cut away wool from his left shin and wrapped the healthy, unblemished leg in the bandage he had stolen, displaying the bloodstains on the rag.

He crossed the Long Bridge, a half-mile at most, into Virginia, walking Alice a good distance behind a blue battery of artillery, its cannon wagons rumbling ominously over the bridge. He could hardly believe he was in Virginia, in *the Confederacy*, though it felt much the same as the city behind him. *Where exactly*, he wondered, *does the fighting begin?*

A captain on a tall roan rode up, his hand extended, and Alexander's heart beat wildly.

"Son, tell me your injuries came on the farm you're returning to—you're too young to have a battle wound."

Alexander told the captain he was from New York and had been shot in drills by another in his company of volunteers. "Shot right here in the capital before I've seen any real fighting."

"It happens. A blessing if it keeps you from worse." A streak of gray ran through the captain's dark widow's peak of hair, and eyes the blue-black of a musket barrel stared at Alexander. "From New York, too." The captain shook his head, dark eyes ashine with tears. "No older than the eldest of my sons. Pray God neither of them ever sees this bridge."

"The doctors told me the brisk air would do me good, away from vile hospital humors."

The captain stared at the bloodstained bandage wrapped around Alexander's leg.

"It doesn't hurt, sir," Alexander told him. "Not anymore."

The captain nodded and reached out and squeezed Alexander's shoulder. The captain, Matthew Kistler, rode slow alongside Alexander and talked about his sons, Todd and Mordecai, and his wife, Lucretia, who he said "is not a strong woman." There were tears in his eyes, again, when he asked Alexander about *his* family.

"I've got sisters only." Alexander was liberating himself further from the yoke of twin brotherhood. Before he had to think of more to say, he was interrupted by a loud report of iron striking iron, the prolonged cracking of heavy timbers. Men in the artillery battery were shouting and someone was screaming. The stolen mare and the captain's horse bumped shoulders and jerked their heads up and down. Alice snorted and sidled into the middle of the road before Alexander could rein her in. Captain Kistler rode off to the artillery soldiers, dismounted, and disappeared into a melee of bodies and voices. Shortly, four men emerged carrying a bucking, jerking blanket between them, a fifth man upon the blanket, writhing and moaning, holding his arm and side where blood soaked his blue tunic. They got him onto a wagonbed, and all disappeared in a red cloud of dust.

Matthew Kistler rejoined Alexander. "Cannon trunnion bounced and broke the cap square, cracked the carriage cheek, and caught the man's arm. Looks bad enough to keep him from loading cannon or lifting a rifle, not so bad he's likely to lose the arm. Lucky both ways."

Not even Papa wept as often as Captain Kistler. Those tears gave Alexander his strongest-yet foreboding about the glories of war, an intimation he brushed aside lest it turn into more fear. Alexander gnawed the inside of his cheek and tried not to drop the reins, slippery in his hands.

He and Kistler soon reached an enormous encampment identified by the captain as Fort Albany, where he'd been for two weeks expecting daily to be given new men, to be returned to the front. He invited Alexander to visit with him at his tent. Alexander realized he reminded Captain Kistler of his sons and made him not so lonely, but Alexander worried about questions he might not be able to answer, so he said he'd best head back to the hospital.

So he did, for a short ways, and then he turned off the road, eased Alice through a wood and down a long hillside, following the setting sun. He kept cover between himself and the hundreds, maybe thousands, of soldiers at Fort Albany. When he no longer saw tents, he swung south again, moving into twilight, keeping an eye out for campfires or farmhouse candles.

Alexander expected roadblocks, guards and questions, demands for mysterious military papers. He continually rehearsed in his head a tale sufficiently vague and convoluted yet sprinkled with enough detail to give it the hard ring of truth. After several days, he'd not had the necessity of testing his thespian talents. He kept to the woods and old trails. Sometimes the trees were so thick about him he couldn't keep the sun in sight to know he was staying south. He was scared every minute he was awake. When he slept, he slept fitfully, often in the saddle because he was afraid to stop moving.

At a place called Carter's Store—not a store at all, just a couple of run-down cabins where a creek came close to the trail—a woman so covered with dirt he couldn't say whether she was white or Negro gave him some squirrel stew and something like thin pancakes. She never told him her name. She said a Yankee general was coming their way with a heap of soldiers, going to join more Yankees near Fredericksburg. General Lee was between them and Richmond. Sparks were gonna fly.

"Hie on home, child, lest you get caught up in the fight." She wrapped him up a mess of those gritty pancakes and gave him a jug of water from the creek beside.

And so it went for the next couple of weeks. Folks fed him when they could, farm women and Negroes mostly, the men gone, of course. Some of these folks thought him too young for the fight, though he'd seen plenty in uniform with smoother faces. He felt an urge to confide in these helpful strangers, to tell them he was off to join the Rebels, but he kept his counsel, made up stories as needed to explain his bandaged leg.

Twice he dodged soldiers, small patrols in Federal blues. If it wasn't hunger it was fear making him light-headed all the time. Once, he was dozing in the saddle—Alice had found a narrow road where the walking was easier than in the woods—and someone coughed. He opened his eyes. Close by, men were talking. And there they were, a Union patrol, just ahead, going the same direction he was down this same old road. He eased up on the reins and stroked Alice's neck, praying she wouldn't snort or nicker or stamp her foot. He leaned down to muffle the drum-beat of his heart against her mane. When the soldiers diminished into a spot of blue and brown, he got down, legs shaking, and led Alice back into the woods, where he hid in a grove of trees until sunset before going on under cover of the dark.

The first week in May, he finally arrived in Richmond. Leading Alice across the James River bridge, he espied ahead of him a crowd of men wearing yellowish-brown shirts and an assortment of brown and blue trousers. Most wore rawhide leggings and wide-brimmed hats.

"What soldiers are you?" he asked.

"We're *Chubs*, Texans," came the yell.

Here's my destiny, he thought, and with the fear and innocence of a little boy he fell in beside a man ten years and many battles older than he—Silas Nunner, he learned, from Alleyton, Texas, near the Colorado River. Every state's troops, Silas told him, had names. Texans were "Chubs." Arkansas boys were "Joshes." The names ringing in Alexander's ears and heating up his chest were *Colorado River* and *Texas*.

The Texans were just arrived to help defend Richmond against a Federal cavalry attack expected under General Stoneman. Alexander asked if he could join them. Silas Nunner asked a captain named Foster, whose face was shadowed beneath the brim of a dust-colored hat.

"Sure. Come on along," the captain said. His lips did not move when he spoke.

They were headed to the hotels. This would be the first night in many that any of them had slept under a roof.

Word was Hood's Texas Brigade was headed their way, back from the Blackwater to join General Lee's army. Soon as they'd seen some sights and had a drink or three, Silas Nunner said, he'd take Alexander to the regimental colonel to sign him up and get him "right smart of a set of Confederate grays," and a cap, belt, and sword. In spite of his fear of battle, Alexander longed to feel the weight of a sword swinging from his waist.

Once they claimed a room in the three-story brick Dillard House and stacked their raggedy outfits on the beds, Silas Nunner said they had to go "reconnoiter vice," and he took Alexander to the lamplit Capitol Square, where prostitutes promenaded in satin and feathers, and men rode slowly by in open carriages and hacks whistling and gesturing lewdly. Silas grinned and winked. "I'd be more'n glad to let one of these lost gals lure me to her chamber of sin and demoralize me, 'cept I'm fearful of the clap and the pox she might give out in change. But I don't see the risk in gazing at them, all gaudy with nature's decorations."

A boy not more than twelve or thirteen paraded by in a tan frock coat, his long blond hair pulled back behind his ears, from which dangled bright silver earrings. He stopped and faced Alexander, let his coat open, and, leering at Alexander, cupped his bulging crotch. Silas grinned and shook his head. Soon, the boy was leaning on the arm of an officer. As the two walked off, the officer's hand moved down the back of the boy's coat and rubbed circles on his bottom.

Alexander did not admit he had never before known that a man might woo and embrace another man. He tried to think what such wooing led to and felt so confused and almost scared he put those thoughts out of his mind and suggested to Silas they find themselves a barroom that served good whisky.

In a dram house across from a soldiers' hospital they sipped whiskies at a polished wooden bar. A civilian with only one arm was talking quietly but insistently to the barkeep, who appeared to pay little attention. In the mirror, the civilian's shining blue eyes caught Alexander's stare. The one-armed man nodded, a flame of hair flaring above his forehead, and was at their side without having walked there, it seemed. He gave a short bow, and Alexander tensed. Was this another of those who would couple with his own sex? Silas Nunner did not seem alarmed.

"Lieutenants? Captains?" And before Alexander could say "privates" the redhead said, "I introduce myself as Orten Trainer, artist of the sun and deeply appreciative citizen of the Confederacy. May I buy you cavalrymen a whisky?"

The inconsistency would occur to Alexander later, that Orten Trainer could identify Alexander and Silas as being in the cavalry but not note they wore no insignia of rank.

"What is an artist of the sun?" Silas asked.

"A professor of natural sciences, I specialize in ferrography, capturing human likenesses to preserve them eternally." Orten Trainer curled down his mouth and told Silas, "You probably know the ferrograph as a tintype—though I use no tin in the process—a miniature likeness of remarkable fidelity to reality that I am able to capture on sheet iron." He held up close to Silas' face the lapel of his coat, on which was affixed an oval pin, like a small brooch, bearing the tiny and solemn visage of John Breckinridge. "If you're not a National Democrat, I've got John Bell as well."

Back home, Mama had several daguerreotypes and a whole album of *cartes de visite*—paper calling cards—each one bearing a photograph of the guest who left it behind, and a few special cards Papa had bought of New York actresses, pugilists, circus riders, and military heroes. Alexander had heard of tintypes, but these were the first he had actually seen. He thought them fascinating, but Silas seemed uninterested.

"Who wants a resemblance? I want the real view," he said. "You can't hear the cannon or smell the powder in a cavalryman's portrait."

"My artistry is not of resemblance, nor even portraiture which often tells the flatterer's lie. My camera captures reality, seizes and holds the moment. As for hearing and smelling, I wager what appeals to one sense may stir the others to life," Orten Trainer said. "Whenever I hear the tune 'Old Zip Coon' it takes me back to Florida and the time I fought the Seminoles. There was a fiddler with us who could not lay off 'Old Zip Coon.' We hied through the swamp with that song in our heads, and it still conjures up heat and damp and powder and shot so real I duck and flinch. If I fix your face and send it home, I'm convinced your voice will fill your mother's ears, lonesome for the words of her son."

Soon Orten—"friends cut it down to Ort"—was telling Alexander and Silas all about his service in the Federal troops during the Second Seminole War. "Deep dark in Southern swamp the moss keeps out the sky and you can't tell mud from water. Whole world's the color of coffee and just as warm. Dark side of the moon, boys, underside of human life."

Silas Nunner stared at Ort. "You don't hardly seem old enough—"

"Dark side of the moon. Darkness over all the land."

The barkeep brought their drinks, and Ort declared someone had stolen his clip of bills. "Oh, Richmond," he said, "you've become the domicile of plunderers and pickpockets. Boys, the apprentice thieves in this city can steal the buttons off your coat as they bid you God's blessing." Flush with Samuel's money, Alexander paid for the whiskies and for yet another round. "Where were we, boys?" Ort asked.

"Dark side of the moon," Silas Nunner said.

"Nightmare swamp," Ort said. "Seminole drums and my heart beating counterpoint. Thick vines and tree snakes filled the boughs above me and before me the deadly abyss—swamp water roiling with water vipers, black and bottomless quicksand sucking under anything it touched. I crept out on a rough-barked log. Got halfway out on the downed tree when one end lifted up out of the blackness hissing and roaring as a dragon, rows of teeth long and sharp as harpoons, the log's other end swinging like a poleax. Gentlemen, I was astride the back of a Florida alligator, a prehistoric beast still surviving in those godless swamplands, a creature so terrible Ole Satan himself fears to let one loose in Hades."

"What did you do?" Alexander asked.

"I pulled down a thick vine and wrapped it as a noose around the savage reptile's enormous snout, and then I rode the bucking beast across to dry land. Fortunately, I still had two good arms at the time." Ort said he fought, hand to hand, with the great Seminole warrior and chief, Osceola, neither able to deal the other a mortal blow, so evenly matched were they in fighting strength and passion.

Silas said he'd had about all the terror he could take for one night. He leaned close to Alexander's ear and whispered that Orten Trainer was a lying wag if he'd ever known one. Alexander saw truth in Silas' accusation, but Ort's musical speech intoning tall tales, his red hair dancing, were hypnotic, and Alexander liked his yarns, fact or fancy. Silas saluted and lurched out of the bar to make the long walk back to the Dillard House.

Alexander reluctantly followed Silas to their hotel room, but he made a drunken pledge to visit Ort's boarding room and see the camera with which he made likenesses.

Just before sunup the next day, Silas Nunner left Alexander in line at the surgeons' tent. Two weeks earlier, a wounded soldier brought unconscious to the same Confederate surgeon had been undressed for treatment and discovered to be a female, the wife of another volunteer. This woman's unmasking had led to stricter checkups. Now all recruits had to strip.

The line of naked men moved slowly. Alexander waited his turn directly behind a boy named Miller, short and slightly built, who didn't look much more than twelve. It took perhaps another quarter of an hour before Alexander followed the Miller boy into the sunwarmed tent. Over Miller's tow head, Alexander watched the surgeon, a fat old doctor named Leander Whitfield, frown and jerk his arm toward the boy, who cried out and bobbed his head.

"Is it stiff all the time?" Old Dr. Whitfield's voice loud in the tent, certainly audible far outside.

"No sir," Miller said, the backs of his ears and neck red as a rooster's comb.

Dr. Whitfield's arm jerked again followed by the slap of flesh against flesh. "Only if you play with it?" the doctor said. Then he felt the back of Miller's head. "Yer skull's about as hard. Fine for the service." Miller hurried from the tent, his head bowed against the laughter that followed. Dr. Whitfield announced to all in earshot, "They won't send *him* back as a female who got past me." The doctor examined Alexander, nodded, declared him fit for war, and ushered him out of the tent. Behind him, Alexander heard the doctor exclaim, "Godamighty, man, you didn't have to bring your own club. The army'll give you a gun."

Officially inspected and then uniformed, Alexander joined the Texan Chubs to defend against Northern Aggression. Undyed, his Confederate government-issued "grays" were almost white.

"Hey, we can't let you go to the lines already wearing your shroud. We got to get you set up." Silas produced a dye he said was made mostly from walnut shells. Soon Alexander's trousers and overshirt were the yellowish-brown that had earned the nickname "butternuts" for Confederate soldiers everywhere. He wished Papa could see him like this, before he ran and hid from battle. Now that he had his butternuts, he would ask Orten Trainer to make a tintype of him he could send home to make Papa proud.

Silas Nunner brought news that Orten Trainer had left his boarding house in the night without paying. Silas took too much pleasure in the way the one-armed man's skulduggery had proved him right in his judgment of character. Alexander said he would stand for the bill, and he bade Silas direct him to the establishment. The narrow, two-story house was cramped but appeared clean, at least in the foyer, where the landlord came out to meet Alexander, who said that he had been sent by Orten Trainer to settle for his lodging.

For two weeks Alexander tromped around Richmond watching for Orten and waiting for orders. Every day brought new rumors about where the Chubs would be sent. Most spent their time drinking, gambling, and whoring. Emmet Jenks had a deck of cards bearing the likenesses of Jeff Davis and Generals Lee, Beauregard, Jackson, and J. E. Johnston. All the Queens had the face of Mrs. Jefferson Davis. The playing cards reminded Alexander of what Ort had said about his tintypes. When Jenks wasn't playing euchre, keno, or poker, he was haunting a chuck-a-luck board where he sang to the dice. Richmond was full of saloons, dram houses, and bawdy houses, but Alexander was more drawn to the plentiful horse races at which he won several wagers.

One morning on the steps of the Dillard House, a voice singing his name, "Captain Alexander Speer, Colonel Speer?" stirred Alexander from a daze of waiting. Red hair tipped with orange by the rising sun behind him, Orten Trainer grinned at Alexander, who shook his hand. "Ort, where have you been these past days and what are you up to so early in the morning?"

"Well, general, I have been away securing ferrography supplies. As soon as I returned I resolved to seek you out." As he said these words, Orten wrapped his only arm around Alexander's shoulders and drew him so close the one-armed man's rough-stubbled chin scraped against Alexander's just shaven cheek. He thought of the boy with long hair and earrings he had seen walk away with the officer and momentarily wondered if Orten might be afflicted with such perversity. But Ort immediately released him, slapped him on the back, and laughed deeply as men laugh so Alexander relaxed that concern.

He laughed and made way for Orten in the hotel doorway. "Seek *me* out?

I've been watching for you all over town," Alexander said. He was glad to see the man and hear his musical speech. They made their way down the street to the first dram house they could find. Alexander was mesmerized by the rhythms of Orten's words, by the deftness with which he managed bottle and cup one-hand-edly, and by a tongue of his bright red hair fallen down over his forehead to lick at his equally red eyebrows.

Alexander was in the capital of the Confederacy, yet he still had not found the war. There were signs of it—men in uniform, artillery rolling up and down the streets, a hospital of wounded—but nothing had happened yet to prove him a coward. The Capitol grounds where the Confederate congress met was as pretty and as quiet as a city park. Alexander and Silas Nunner sat on benches and watched pigeons strut on the lawn, drink from soothing sounding fountains, and perch on the marble shoulders of Henry Clay. Night after night, Alexander slept in a hotel bed and heard not cannon and gunfire but carriage wheels and women's laughter. He was supposed to be near the fighting, but, so far, Richmond did not seem much different from New York.

The seventeenth of May they were ordered to the cars, but rode only a couple miles north to Camp Lee, where they were joined by men who had survived prison at Camp Butler in Illinois. All of them, every man in Richmond with two good legs it seemed, were on their way to the Army of Tennessee. Many like Alexander had long anticipated their first experience in battle: now they knew they would soon see the elephant.

News from the Front

Early June, a letter was hand-delivered to the Speers' door, the envelope creased and bearing a streak of mud most like a bloodstain. Samuel's coal-speck eyes hurried down the sheet, then he read out loud:

> —arrived in Richmond and was walking across the James River Bridge
> when I came to a crowd of men just arrived to help defend the city against
> an expected Federal cavalry attack. I asked them what soldiers they were,
> and they yelled out they were Texans. I asked them could I join them, and
> one named Silas Nunner said to come along with him. Now, Silas and I

are squared away in a hotel called the Dillard House. Rumor has Hood's Texas Brigade is headed back from the Blackwater to join General Lee's army. Tomorrow, Silas is going to take me to the regimental colonel to sign up and get me some Confederate grays and a sword. So, Papa, by the time you get this I will have joined the Texian Cavalry to defend against Northern aggression. If this letter reaches you, tell Mama and my sisters I love them. It is hard to get a letter posted from here to <u>Yankee-land.</u> Now, Papa, To arms! To arms!

I remain—

Your Faithful Son, Alex Speer

"To defend against Northern aggression," one of Samuel's favorite clichés, haunted him in his favorite son's handwriting. He handed the letter to Mary. Her lips trembling, she read the note again, silently. Then she said, "He has no word for his only brother, his identical twin. He has shortened his name to 'Alex' and dropped 'Wesley' altogether." Mary wiped away tears, but rather than blame Samuel, whose talk of Texas and the noble South had doubtless fired their elder son's imagination, she took her husband in her arms and gave comfort as she could.

A week later, when Charles Wesley announced he had enlisted with Company B of the New York Volunteers, Mary was the one uttering clichés. "A house divided," she said, and then she slowly shook her head. Samuel's mouth opened, and his beard moved up and down, but no words came out.

He retreated to his study and after a while called for Charles Wesley. When his quieter son sat down across from him, Samuel took from his desk a walnut box containing one Harper's Ferry Dragoon pistol. A .58 caliber percussion model that fired the standard 500 gram minié ball, the Model 1855 was issued in pairs. The pistol was cradled in maroon velvet beside an empty pistol-shaped space aiming the opposite direction inside the box. Samuel removed the weapon and handed it to Charles Wesley.

"Make it your mission to find the rightful owner of the match to this horse pistol, the brother of the one I am giving you."

"You already gave the other to Alexander?"

"I knew him for an adventurer."

Charles Wesley nodded. He did not voice his thought that Papa had counted on Alexander's courage leading him off to war, and that he must be surprised that his second son would soon be in uniform, though of a different color. He wondered if the possibility that the two pistols might be fired at one another had ever occurred to Papa.

Charles Wesley Joins the New York Volunteers

Charles Wesley's first day in the war was a perfect day for patriotism—mid-June but springlike—red, white, and blue of brick buildings, cottony clouds, and distant sky. He rode horseback with the rest of the volunteer company down Broadway. Mama and Papa had been among those who lined both sides of the street and marched along with them. Many onlookers cheered them on, but mamas and papas held handkerchiefs to their eyes, and Charles Wesley's papa wept louder than his mama. The company was undrilled and many of its mounts had recently been pulling a plow. The volunteers wore a mixture of gray, brown, and blue uniforms sewn at home by mothers and aunts and sweethearts.

Between the quiet tears and loud cheers of loved ones and well-wishers, horseshoes clanged against brick, musket barrels clinked against haversack buckles. The afternoon sun swam beside the recruits and flashed off squares of window glass. Charles Wesley saw something familiar—Alexander wearing a dark blue uniform like Charles Wesley's sewn by their maid, Anna, riding right at him on a matching sorrel mare. Charles Wesley took a second look: just himself, riding towards himself in a slant of glass, disappearing into himself as he passed—an image he followed through his time in the war: Alexander riding away from him, receding into the future.

Company B, New York Volunteers off to war, the air rent with *huzzas*. Colonels and majors were commissioned by the governor, but other officers were elected. Veterans included a banker who had served in the Illinois militia and fought Sauk Indians in Wisconsin in the Black Hawk War. Jameson Hall—his father an alderman—was elected first lieutenant after he bought beer for all the company. Charles Wesley was made an officer, though barely, as second lieutenant, and he knew Papa's name and money had secured his rank. A regular army sergeant, Leo Farnham, was on loan to train the volunteers, and Sergeant Farnham had been chosen to accept the company flag. Color-bearers would be chosen later. To bear the colors was a high honor, but it brought severe risk—in battle the color guard was a primary target. Charles Wesley was elected from among the officers to march forward with Sergeant Farnham to accept the colors. The ceremony was held at the City Hall Park, where the company dismounted and formed wavy lines in front of a platform decorated with red, white, and blue bunting. Several aldermen sat on the platform with Mrs. Bettina Indira Woodbury and five maids of honor from the Brooklyn Ladies' Auxiliary there to present the battle flag the auxiliary had sewn. A substantial-looking wooden lectern had been placed front and center of the platform.

Mrs. Woodbury and her court appeared more formidable than Company B. The ladies wore identical scarlet dresses and matching scarlet shoes. Blue satin sashes adorned with white stars swathed their ample bosoms. A single red rose rested behind the right ear of each maid of honor. A silver tiara peeked up from Mrs. Woodbury's swirl of red hair. Sunlight through tree limbs made an openwork pattern, shadow mesh and light cast over everyone assembled as if they were all caught there in an enormous net. A diamond of sunlight shone on Mrs. Woodbury's bosom, two shadow lines crossed her face, a wiggling dark "X" Charles Wesley would think of later as crosshairs in a sharpshooter's gunsight marking a spot between her eyes.

Company B's bugler, who was making a transition from mouth harp to horn, stepped out from the rows of uniformed soldiers and made a call resembling the cry of migrating ducks. When the quacking ceased, Mrs. Woodbury stood, raising her heart behind the shadow X. Her bosom expanded as she approached the lectern. Her feet seemed barely to touch the platform. Her belt was cinched tight. From the waist up she swelled until it seemed she might float, lighter than air, her feet together swaying back and forth like the pendulum in a clock. The inflated spheres of her scarlet-clad breasts, her puffed-out pink cheeks, her bulging blue eyes were all as round and bulging-tight as a cluster of silk balloons. In one hand she carried the flag folded into a blue triangle. In the other hand she held what looked like a roasted turkey drumstick. One of the frock-coated aldermen—a short man whose nose was at the same level as Mrs. Woodbury's bosom—stood and struck a match he held to Mrs. Woodbury's drumstick. Black smoke billowed up, and the smell of coal oil drifted into the crowd. Holding her torch aloft, Mrs. Woodbury struck a determined pose as she paused for the exposures of sunshine artists' cameras. The flaming torch she held beside her face left several lightning-colored ghosts of Mrs. Bettina Indira Woodbury floating in Charles Wesley's vision—fat fairy or overweight angel, her image repeated itself in the shadows of trees as she spoke:

"From his lofty aerie the eagle of American freedom has heard the fanatic cries of rebellion. In the more savage hinterlands of our republic those who would shackle the ideals of liberty have taken up arms in violent treason and betrayal.

The bright red in this flag is the blood spilled by the heroes of '76. You are the sure sharp talons of the eagle of American freedom. You carry the hopes and dreams of us who must remain behind." Mrs. Woodbury's torch began to sputter, more smoke than fire rising beside her flaming hair. Her eyes rolled up toward the failing flambeau, and a gust of wind sent a swath of oily smoke into her face. It was impossible to know whether the tears she blinked away were precipitated by the acrid cloud or by the burning fervor of her words: "Carry high, with our high hopes, this banner made by weaker female hands and preserve and protect these noble colors as you would preserve and protect our womanhood. For whenever and wherever Columbia is threatened, Columbia's daughters are in peril." The lectern swayed forward, then Mrs. Woodbury gripped its edge and pulled back as a coachman might rein in a runaway team. For a breathless instant Charles Wesley thought she would topple over the edge of the platform right into his lap, but she regained her balance, and, all the time keeping the smoking torch aloft, continued: "And when this flag unfurls on the field of battle let it be a beacon shining our trust and love upon each one of you. And let this flag inspire you with the confidence of God's aid and protection, for when a nation ordained by God and dedicated to godly principles is unlawfully rebelled against, that is a rebellion against God. Accept, then, this standard and march beneath it into the conflict with the certainty that you strike with God's might, for God's right."

Mrs. Woodbury's voice quavered. The torch, rather than simply burning out, continued to spew streamers of smoke like a magician's cuff spewing endless black silk handkerchiefs. She stood with eyes lowered and waited for one tear to work its way onto her quivering jaw, where it jiggled bright in sunlight. There was a moment in which the men of Company B and their well-wishers seemed unsure what to do next—pray? cheer?—when Sergeant Farnham rose and walked forward. Charles Wesley hurried to accompany the sergeant up onto the raised stage.

Facing the crowd, those on the platform also faced the afternoon sun, partially shrouded by the torch smoke hovering just overhead that seemed to Charles Wesley to prefigure the smoke of battles yet to be faced. In the audience, Mama nodded and raised a fist. Papa dabbed again at his eyes with a white handkerchief, then waved it high. Sergeant Farnham brought his feet together with a hollow clunk and bowed smartly as he took the flag from Mrs. Woodbury. He turned and saluted Charles Wesley and, handing him the flag, nodded toward the lectern. For weeks, Charles Wesley had dreaded his fear the first time he would face enemy fire. He was lucky he had not been told he would have to address the crowd. No doubt this was why he had been elected to accept the flag.

Gripping the podium to steady his nerves, he nodded to those assembled on the platform. "Mrs. Woodbury." Charles Wesley nodded. "Ladies of the Auxiliary." He nodded again. "Citizens of the great city of New York." A final nod. "We accept this beautiful flag out of the hands of these beautiful ladies with pride and honor. May God favor us in the din and smoke of battle." Here Sergeant Farnham gave the slightest hint of a smile and a few volunteers giggled. Mrs. Woodbury took this opportunity to hand the torch to one of her maids of honor seated behind her. Charles Wesley continued, "Favor us each time we draw saber or raise musket for the Union, now and forever." He took the flag and let the colors unfold over the front of the platform. He faced the wavy rows of young men who, like him, knew nothing about soldiering. "Men of Company B," he said in a voice not much louder than a whisper yet audible to everyone in City Hall Park, "may this standard guide us through the conflict and lead us safely home." He wished he had the courage of his brother, Alexander. He wished he anticipated the glory of the battlefield. But he felt only a strong sense of duty to his country and an abiding fear that when the time came to start the ball he would reveal himself as a coward. His hands gripped the flag and trembled so that the banner stirred as from a breeze.

The torch was nearly spent. Only a wispy gray trail drifted from it as it was passed from one maid of honor to the next and on down the line of seated aldermen until the last in line stood and cheered and hurled the darkened torch over his shoulder, high into the air behind him.

"Huzza. Huzza. Huzza. Huzza."

Alexander Partners with Orten Trainer

I've known men who look East (toward schools, churches, and hospitals)
and men who look West (toward empty prairie, unclimbed mountains,
and uncharted waters). Orten Trainer was a third kind of man.
He paid little attention to a compass. The direction Ort always looked was
away. You may know someone like Ort, one who always finds the fault
of his every misfortune but never finds it in a looking glass. Orten made
such a practice of dodging blame, he perfected the habit even as he
perfected himself. He had to change his name to change his nature.

—from *Gideon Jones' Journal*

Fueled by repeated failures, Orten Trainer was an optimist. When Ort's crops came in short and poorly it was because of drouth or flood, bad soil or poor seed, worms or grasshoppers. When the weather or nature went against him, Ort just naturally went someplace else where he'd heard the weather was perfect, the soil was rich, the seed was prime, and there were no worms or grasshoppers. Ort began this habit of moving on when, at age fourteen, he left Virginia one rainy March morning to escape six days a week of hard work on his daddy's farm and one day a week on a hard bench in a Quaker meetinghouse. He headed north first, to Washington, where he met some young Federal troopers who were just back from Florida, where they'd fought the Indian chief, Osceola, in the windup of the Second Seminole War. Ort heard so many tales about fighting Indians in Florida that he told a few himself and began to believe he had been there. From Washington he meandered south to Richmond, where he mucked out stalls at a livery house, unloaded wagons for a mercantile company, peeled potatoes and washed dishes for a room in a crowded boardinghouse, spread sawdust and carried jugs and casks back and forth across a dram house floor. Town jobs didn't work out for Ort: bosses were unfair, other workers were lazy, boardinghouses were unreasonably expensive, dram houses were dens of iniquity.

Next, he took up women, a calling for which he had talent, if you'll agree musical speech and an eye for unnoticed beauty are talents. He also had a good nose for the smell of money. His first wife had inherited a drygoods company, and she kept Orten better than he had ever been kept until she found him in bed with a neighbor who inevitably became his second wife. The second Mrs. Trainer had few resources beyond her lovely and youthful appearance. After this disappointing second marriage, Orten sought emotional and financial stability. He thought he'd found both in a lady several years his senior, the widow of a cotton exporter. Unfortunately, before Orten could persuade her to marry him, her son challenged Ort to a duel.

Orten proclaimed dueling both uncivilized and unnecessary. Devoted to his challenger's mother as he was, Orten declared he would sooner give up the widow than risk fatally wounding the offspring of one he loved so. To demonstrate his convictions, Orten left Richmond before first light one Monday in May, riding a gift horse the widow had given him, his intention to ride south to Petersburg for an extended visit. But the widow's son overtook Orten near where Grindall Creek enters the James River. There, weapons in hand, the widow's son and three who rode with him convincingly pressed his case for a duel.

Orten got confused about how many paces he was to step off before he turned and fired. He explained to the man's double that was why he fired early, before the widow's son had turned to face him. Orten overshot his mark—"I, of course, aimed to miss"—and the widow's son wounded Orten high in the left arm. "In light of my error it is God's good grace that has run our course to such a just conclusion." Though the widow's son and his second had unkind words for Orten, the young duelist had emerged from the contest unmarked, having preserved his mother's honor. He grudgingly bade Orten, wounded as he was, to keep moving south. In great discomfort, bleeding heavily, he continued toward Petersburg afoot, the widow's son having disputed ownership of the horse. A peddler gave Orten a wagon ride to a Dr. Trammel's house in Petersburg. The doctor, squinting through inadequate spectacles, dug lead from Orten's arm in a prolonged and painful surgery. Under the doctor's nearsighted ministrations, the wound festered and gangrene set in. Trammel muffled Ort's complaints with a rag soaked in ether, and when Ort regained consciousness the doctor's Negro houseboy was changing the dressing over a raw stump where the old butcher had sawed off Orten's left arm and sewn down a ragged flap of skin.

The cut off arm throbbed, as it had when the bullet ripped through muscle, tendon, and bone. The pain was so raw he reached in the dark to assuage the piercing aches and clutched his twisted bed covers, startled to rediscover the absence of the arm. How could something no longer part of him still hurt him so? When he could stand the torment no longer, he got up in the dark and, hands outstretched like a somnambulist, went to the old wardrobe where he kept his worldly goods. There, leaned up in the corner like a rifle or a fishing pole or a walking cane was the limb. The skin, exposed to the elements, was dry and leathery. The moment Orten gripped the dead flesh, his pain diminished. He lit a lamp. The arm was dusty and lint-specked, the skin shriveled and dark as a prune. The fingernails looked to have grown since the arm had been amputated. He wiped the hand with a soft rag, polished each long fingernail. A druggist had sold him a bottle of sweet oil to help preserve the dried skin. The oil contained scent of peppermint and offered the added benefit of keeping Ort's room smelling tangy.

He took the amputated limb to a seamstress who drew a pattern and sewed a length of brown canvas into a scabbard for the arm. For waterproofing, she soaked the canvas in a mix of melted white wax and spirits of turpentine and hung it out to dry. She reinforced the canvas with leather ends, and sewed on a carrying strap. The bag was as fine a thing as Ort had ever owned.

When the War between the States broke out Ort was thirty-nine years old, one-armed, untrained, unemployed, and back in Richmond Town. He scraped up enough funds to place and win a wager on a horse race when the sure winner pulled up lame. Mr. Hazel T. Brown of Charleston, South Carolina, was the unlucky loser, and it turned out Brown had insufficient funds to cover his bet. In lieu of a worthless IOU, Ort had accepted a large camera, glass plates, and chemicals Brown possessed. It had been Hazel Brown's artistic calling to make a visual record of war. He had intended to follow right into battle the Rebel infantry company made up of his Charleston college teachers and classmates and there to capture daguerreotype views of their victories. He had tearfully given over his equipment to Ort.

Having had no luck peddling the camera, Ort visited a portrait studio to learn if there was anything useful about owning the equipment of daguerreotypy. The proprietor, who introduced himself as Professor Smith, answered Ort's inquiries by saying, "The daguerreotype belongs now to history." He showed Ort several card photographs and talked at length about the paper on which they were printed, about bromides, iodides, toning dishes, and baths. If Ort was interested in field work, taking views of the landscape rather than studio portraits, he might want to investigate ferrotypes—exposures made on the more durable stock of thin iron sheets. Ort returned to the studio as an apprentice at half-wages. Once he learned how to operate the camera he slipped away with enough paper and chemicals to get started making card photographs himself.

But the word "durable" stayed with Ort, and he conceived the business scheme of making ferrotype likenesses of Mother and Sister and Wife and Child that a soldier might carry with him through the vicissitudes of camp life. All Ort lacked were sufficient capital and a likely location to get started. Then chance intervened when he met young Alexander Speer, recently arrived in Virginia with pockets jingling from New York. When Ort learned Alexander had gladly paid Ort's hotel bill, a grateful Ort joined his benefactor and the youth's comrade, Private Silas Nunner of the Texas Cavalry (dismounted).

Early one morning Orten was awakened by loud knocking. He stood a little unsteadily on account of the copious amount of brandy he had taken for his health the night before. Shaking his head, which felt large and fuzzy, he invited Alexander in. In the orange light that flared against the uncurtained window, the camera stood staring like a waterbird on one leg, an avian Cyclops. A wooden box, the camera had a lid on front that lifted to reveal a tube that looked like the barrel of a mighty gun. The box rested on an iron shaft that could be raised or lowered with a little turning wheel. The back of the camera was a hinged glass square that framed the view. Above this glass was affixed an open box of shelves on which Ort kept jars of the chemicals he used in his sophistry of freezing time. Tacked around the back of the shelves was a generous amount of black material that looked like canvas but felt slickened as oilcloth. Ort's only hand lifted and held back the tenting as if it were a curtain rising on the stage of some great drama.

"Can we make a tin picture now?" Alexander asked.

His enthusiasm reminded Ort of a drawing he'd seen in a book: a boy lifting a flap of the sky and peeking up at the sun, moon, and stars, at all the celestial wonders awaiting him.

Ort bowed, inviting Alexander Speer to step with him under the canopy, to kneel close and squint down the tunnel of light through the lens that put the North Pole at South and made you see things differently. Alexander said it reminded him of a sideshow act his papa had taken him to see, a man slamming saber blades through a box out of which his assistant's head and arms protruded. .

"After we go have some breakfast to steady my view, you can be the professor of ferrography, if there's sun enough through these high windows."

"Me?"

"I suffer the need of two arms. I'll guide you as I sit for you. I'll pose you first, teach you the process."

"Imagine the pride on my papa's face when he receives my portrait in the uniform of the Confederacy," Alexander said.

After the youth bought them both a breakfast of ham and biscuits and a draught of ale to ease the pounding in Ort's head, they returned to his studio, a makeshift in the boardinghouse room. Alexander stared into the camera glass.

"The bed looks turned over. The whole view is upside down."

"A trick of the equipment. I have grown so accustomed to viewing men on their heads, I hardly believe it when I see them walking on their feet. First, always instruct your subject to gaze without blinking at some fixed thing."

In the glass, Alexander was made small and balanced on his head. Orten explained each step in the process. After he had made several exposures of Alexander, Orten sat for the youth. Posed stiffly, Ort held out his only hand so that a tamed blue bird painted on the oilcloth backdrop might appear to sit fearlessly on his extended finger

Ort told Alexander to keep his eye unblinking and focused, so he would see what the camera saw. "Coat the glass plate with that cloudy concoction in the tall bottle. Be sure it flows to all four corners. Then drop the tent and dip the coated plate into that cake pan. I filled it with silver nitrate earlier. It takes four minutes for the chemicals to bond. I'll time you. As soon as my lips quit moving, take out the glass slide and put in the plate holder, then lift the slide and count seconds: one, two, three, four—"

"How long does it take?"

"Six to ten seconds. Then you'll cover the lens and bring down the slide. Easy, yet with authority."

Alexander nodded. While he stared into the lens, holding his face so still as to mimic a corpse, Orten wondered whether light might burn onto the surface of Alexander's unblinking eye on the other side of the lens the visage of his new mentor in the art of replication and, when the image maker knew his craft, deception. "Five, six, seven, eight—"

"Done." Ort said as he stood. "Now, if we could afford a darkroom, we'd transport the plate holder there. Leave it under the tenting, and I'll complete the process. I will repair later to your hotel with our results."

Late that same afternoon, Orten met Alexander at the Dillard House with a bottle of brandy, two tin cups, and the miniature resemblance of himself to prove Alexander's tintype artistry. While Alexander stared at the likeness he had made of Ort—who was frozen in time, gazing steadily at the dead-looking, yet upright, bird on his finger—Ort declared he'd never seen a man as gifted with a sight as Alexander. "A born ferrotype artist," Ort said. "You bedazzle me with the way you took so natural to the operation of my camera. Gift of God. You're one for uncommon talents." Ort drained his cup and let the alcohol burn behind his eyes until tears wetted his cheek. "Alex, you come natural to unnatural capacities, and it is your duty to share your natural gift of God."

"Duty?"

"Alex, is your mother alive and well?" Orten lifted the flap of hair back onto his head.

"I pray so, Ort."

"If I had your Godgiven gift and, mark this Alex, if my mother could be reached by any earthly mail, I'd post her my smiling living visage." The red lappet of Ort's hair was loose again.

By week's end Alexander had posted his likeness home, where, he confessed, he'd like to post himself. By then, Ort had persuaded him how much comfort they could offer the mothers and wives and children of the Confederacy. He explained how a tintype could be made on most any blackened surface—paper, leather, oilcloth, glass—but that sheet iron was best. "It cuts easily with tin shears, but it is very durable. Durability in wartime unlocks the door to our success."

"Something is not right here, Orten."

"You mistrust my word?"

"Here is the wrong." Alexander held up the tintype of Ort he had been study-ing. "If I am such an artist, why in the likeness I made does the bird sit on your missing arm, yet your other arm is lost?"

Orten laughed loudly, shaking his head and wagging his tongue of hair. Still chuckling, he took Alexander by the elbow and led him to the bar, where they both appeared in a beveled mirror behind a row of bottled spirits. "With which arm do I hold you in the looking glass? The ferrotype gives back a reversed image, mirrors what it sees."

By suppertime, Ort had persuaded Alexander to partner with him in ferro-graph artistry. Soon after Alexander handed over investment funds, the man set up a wagon offering tintype likenesses for soldiers to mail home. SEND YURE SELF HOME TO MOMA read the sign Ort one-handedly painted and nailed above a windowless shack, the construction of which he had supervised, built atop the foundation of a freight wagon purchased with the last of Alexander's most recent envelope of his papa's money. They rode this gypsy contraption over to a charred lot where a dram house between two others had recently burned down. On a street crowded with Reb soldiers and businesses of iniquity, they set up shop. Because his missing arm might bring in some sympathy customers, Ort posted himself outside where he called to passersby.

Orten, Alexander surmised, was more impressed with his purse, which was fatter than most recruits' because of his father's largesse, than with his skills as a tintype operator. But he had nothing better to do with his time and money, and he thought he might actually get good return on his investment. Instead of the wooden daguerreotype cases in which most portrait-makers mounted their tintypes, Ort fashioned paper envelopes with a cutout in which the picture was visible. These could be cheaply made and easily posted home, where they would fit into family albums.

Following news of Reb victories Ort's brightly painted portrait wagon, to which he attached a tent gallery, attracted lines of soldiers, homesick boys every one, willing to shell out a few coins to send a likeness home to Mother. Ort sold the tintypes for one dollar and told Alexander all but a nickel was their profit. He hoped to buy a four-tube camera or, if they could amass the funds to invest in a new nine-tube model, they could, with four moves of the glass, get as many as thirty-six likenesses on one whole-sized plate.

"That is a count I find dear indeed, Alex. Thirty-six dollars made on one plate."

Apparently, Ort was not the only professor of the sunshine arts who could count. Soon other traveling portrait galleries were set up around the camp and competition lowered the prices and shortened the lines. When news from the front slowed and the waiting stretched on, the lines of subjects dwindled. Adding to Ort's business woes was an increasing difficulty in securing sheet iron and chemicals. Paper was in such short supply some newspapers were being printed on wallpaper. Money got so tight, Ort started biting his nails and picked up the habit of running his damp fingers through his red hair.

The portrait partnership ended one warm and humid evening when Orten and his painted van and all the business capital disappeared. Silas Nunner, who'd declined Ort's offer to take advantage of the investment opportunity, was angrier than Alexander, who missed Ort's singsong stories more than he missed the money lost. Silas opined that was because the funds were not hard-earned by Alexander but had been doled out by Papa Speer. Alexander laughed and suggested Silas' anger might be eased if he let Papa Speer buy him a glass of bitters.

Orten holed up in Petersburg until he had eaten and drunk all the profits of fer-rotype art. Civilian life had become risky business—especially for Ort, who feared his Southern way of talking would make travel to the North dangerous. Thirteen dollars a month soldier's pay did not attract him, but military protection and an enlistment bounty did, so he returned to Richmond, where he volunteered for the ranks of the Confederacy. The South needed men with two good arms but would take men with one, and he was put into the Army of Tennessee.

Once Private Orten Trainer had spent his enlistment bounty, the Army of Tennessee began to be a real disappointment—rank and promotion were based on wealth and politics, officers didn't know how to lead, food and equipment were substandard. He persuaded his comrades he was a natural soldier, then had the unnatural bad luck (due to the disgraceful quality of army weaponry) of a jammed gun forcing him to retreat from his first action.

Ort was on the horns of a dilemma—speculating how he could remain in an army that offered little real opportunity for a man of his talents, or how he could arrange to be discharged of his military obligation—when Private Alexander Speer showed up again, still in the service of the Texas Cavalry (dismounted), now joined to the Army of Tennessee. The boy had a heart as forgiving as Ort's smile. The way he clung to Alexander made folks say, if it weren't for Ort's fiery red hair, they'd appear to be brothers, though there was the age difference of some twenty years.

"I have no brother, I have sisters only," Alexander said.

Ort smelled something fishy about this boy, soon figured what he smelled was the odor of money. Since he liked that smell above all others, he managed to mollify Alexander as to the confusion during which he'd unintentionally taken more than his share of their ferrotype profits. He was surprised how little effort it took to gain Alexander's forgiveness and to enjoy the boy's trust once again. Alexander was as disingenuous as any man Ort had ever met.

He figured one day there'd be a just reward for the man who took under his wing the only son of a wealthy New York family. He did not recognize the real reason he wanted Alexander's confidence and companionship. Alexander was the first person who had ever treated Ort as a friend. Unable to admit how much he liked the way Alexander's kindness made him feel, Ort winked at himself in mirrors and said, "Mr. Trainer, you sly Reynard. If you are patient, more opportunities for admission to the henhouse will be revealed through this naive Alex Speer."

Gideon Jones: At the Frontier's Edge

Anticipates an Arduous and Dangerous Journey
(July 1865)

Hard by Independence, just north of Kansastown, was Missouri's famed Westport Landing, jumping-off point for the Western frontier. When Gideon learned a late-leaving wagon train was to depart the immigrant road to California by the fifth of July, he signed on, figuring the security of protection from wild Indians and whatever other difficulties lay in the uncivilized territory ahead would be worth the fee he negotiated down by arguing he was just one man with no family. He gave his age as twenty-five, figuring if he added five years he would add weight to his words if not his frame. The wagon master, a Major Joshua Benson, gave the first of many squint-eyed scowls making it clear the major neither believed nor liked anything Gideon said.

Westport Landing, where the Kansas River emptied into the Missouri, was full of people with time on their hands—settlers and Major Benson's men all waiting for him to tell them it was time to roll, wainwrights and farriers resting up between sweaty work with the train's wagons and horses and mules, storekeepers who were supplying most of the train's necessaries, riverboat men who were supplying the general stores, and the usual idlers who hang around railroad depots and boat landings and wagon ports just to see and hear all the coming and going. And, of course, there were sporting girls and gamblers of all stripes, and a brigade of preachers sniffing the air for the scent of wayward souls they might save. Gideon ate many a slice of pie, drank many a foamy beer. He listened to talk about the westward trail, and he asked questions. During the war troops west of the Mississippi had been sent east, leaving most frontier forts unmanned. Indians moved back into their old territories. Without soldiers to protect them, white settlers hadn't fared well against Indians.

"A whole boodle of whites up and run off, skedaddled back East. Most all of Texas is afeared," a musky-smelling man in buckskins said, his tongue twisting his words around a knot of tobacco. With a good number of thirsty men, he leaned against the bar of a saloon the owner had recently reopened. He had not closed for fear of cannonade but for the dear cost of spirits during the war and the absence of able-bodied drinking men gone East to fight. A canvas banner over the bar proclaimed the saloon's new name in fresh black paint: PROSPERITY HOUSE.

A preacher who stood in the saloon doorway but would not enter such a den of iniquity held high his Bible. "The gospel is mightier than the gun. My mission is to reclaim the savage wanderers of the plains from their bloody and godless ways."

The saloon's bartender shook his head. "Pastor, I don't doubt you'd cast your lot amongst redskins to offer spiritual aid, but that way ain't open yet. No Indian's going to give an ear to 'Thou shalt not steal,' nor 'Thou shalt not kill,' nor 'Love thy neighbor.' Least not till they improve themselves—put seed to ground and labor for food and cover. They got no crop nor house nor barn store to lose—but the white man's goods is there for the taking. And whooping in and stealing's a lot lighter than following a plow all day in the hot sun." The bartender grinned. "Lighter, too, than hefting a heavy keg of beer to dole out a nickel at a time."

According to the bartender, only a few brave or foolish souls had made attempts to cross the great desert all during the war.

"I closed down in '62, didn't reopen till just this March. Before the war, I couldn't stop drawing beers long as it took to catch my breath. Then it run to a trickle. The few who risked the trace during the war paid with blood bad as any back-east soldier."

"Hell, if all the tall tales is true, Indians done killed more settlers than I killed deer in all my life," the buckskinned man said.

"You a Indian lover?" someone wanted to know.

The man answered by spitting his wad of chew on the dirt floor toward the end of the bar where the question had come from.

"You might not talk so big if some red buck cut out your tongue," the barkeep said.

"Or hung your greasy scalp on his pole," said a man Gideon had seen earlier through the window of a restaurant. The man had cut up a platter of eggs till it was like yellow soup and then he'd mopped it up with bread.

"That ain't all the red bastards cuts off," a boy in faded overalls said. Then he squinted his eyes and twisted his mouth—giving his face a look Gideon could one moment name as angry and another as salacious. "Any of you fellers ever known a gal what was taken off by red Indians?" He answered his own question. "Well, *I* have." He let that sink in a minute. "My sister, is who." The man who had cut up his eggs stared at his shoes. The barkeep turned to get a bottle of bitters—*McBryan*, Gideon squinted to read on the label. "They cut off both her titties. Now, she's flat as you or me."

The doubter, the man in buckskins, grinned and said, "Comelier than you, I'll wager."

The other men laughed, relieved, and took long pulls from their drinks.

Yellow Birds

On his westering journey, Gideon had noted that whether alone on an empty wagon road or in a crowded settlement like Westport Landing, sunup was usually a peaceful time. At dawn children were still in bed and most men and women were too sleepy to be loud or troublesome. Gideon especially enjoyed the free morning music of nature's avian orchestra. At Westport Landing bright yellow-and-black flocks of goldfinches woke him with their random songs, a clear and breathy kind of whistling. His *Americana*'s entry, **YELLOW BIRD, or AMERICAN GOLDFINCH**, explained that *the female and young are of a brown olive color* but that in spring and summer *the males put off their humble winter-dress, and now, appearing in their temporary golden livery, are heard tuning their lively songs as if in concert.* The encyclopedia also said of the yellow bird that *Its migrations are very desultory, and probably do not proceed very far, its progress being apparently governed principally by the scarcity or abundance of food.* Nature often taught the Maker's simplest lessons. As he observed the migratory settlers camped around him who were waking up to meager breakfasts measured out against their stores of foodstuffs and the long journey that lay ahead, Gideon could not keep from feeling anxious about the weeks and months of difficulties that surely awaited the wagon train he had signed onto.

Talk of Indians

If attacked by Indians, western settlers who escaped with their lives lost their planting season and had to fort up at some frontier stage stop or at some deserted outpost. During the war, the line of westward settlement drew back eastward a hundred miles or more. Now, territorial regiments calling themselves Union troops were forming to fight Indians. Blood flowed on both sides. Everyone said it was too soon to travel the trail, too risky to make the crossing. And everyone agreed Major Benson and anybody foolish or desperate enough to sign on with him were crazy. *So*, Gideon thought, *I have signed onto a crazy wagon train.*

A former Union lieutenant said, "Now the South has been defeated, the settlers expect Washington to put a stop to the Indian attacks. But Washington's more worried about policing the Rebs. The 'Indian problem,' as politicians like to call it, is a long way out of sight of Washington, and anything out of sight is out of them politicians' little minds." According to the ex-officer, the only current military action against Indians was directed against the Dakotas and Northern Cheyenne, who attacked anyone crossing the range of the northern herds, country those tribes considered their private buffalo hunting ground.

Major Benson preached protection. He wore the dark-blue wool trousers of the Union Army with the reinforced seat and legs of the cavalry. His train was to be shepherded by ex-soldiers and army scouts, many of whom had ridden with Colonel Pfeiffer in New Mexico when he wiped out the Navahos. Major Benson claimed several wagons of settlers from earlier trains were to join him from stockades along the way. Most of these were supposedly waiting at Fort Laramie to throw in with the wagon master for the rest of the way to the Territory of Washington.

Gideon's was the eighth and final wagon to join Benson at Independence—a small train compared to ones that had taken the Oregon Trail before the war. In the late '40s, it had not been uncommon for fifty or more wagons to set out from Westport Landing. Gideon's fellow travelers were farm families from Wisconsin, Illinois, Indiana, and Ohio. Some of the men had already been mustered out of the Union Army, some had been wounded and quit the war early, some had been too old or too young to fight. Many of those who did fight returned home to farms gone to ruin while they were away. Some were restless after four years marching and sleeping on different plots of grass or mud.

For a farmer from Ohio or Indiana the victorious end of the war inspired a sort of vicarious feeling of might, and to a settler holed up in Kansastown watching his money slip away month by month, the time seemed right to take a chance against wild Indians and other dangers and, God willing, make the Territory of Washington in time to claim land, get winterized, and have crops planted the next spring. The settlers who weren't swapping tales and bets in Kansastown's saloons were resupplying and readying outfits for the crossings—the Great Desert and the Rocky Mountains. Everyone wanted to leave right after Independence Day, a kind of double party with plenty of speechifying and patriotism and lots of wishes "good-bye" and "good fortune" for the settlers.

Packing Their Necessaries

Major Benson found Gideon washing down a bowl of blackberry cobbler with a schooner of warm beer. The wagon master gave Gideon a flinty stare and a list of necessaries for the journey. Gideon took the paper, finished his beer before he read the list. He'd come this far—what more did Benson think he needed? Gideon felt sufficiently supplied as to his meager needs of arms and ammunition—he had the Hawken, powder, caps, and bullets as yet unfired. The cooking articles struck him as family outfitting, more than he would have use of. Other listed items—herbs and medicines, campstool, needles, pins, thread, thimble, scissors, shaving mirror and razor, tin wash basin, Castile's soap—seemed the fancies of a dandy. Gideon trusted little any man who shaved while on the move. Besides, his light beard would pass as road dust for a week. Had he money for a spyglass with leather case and shoulder strap, an oilcloth tent floor and bedding cover, shoe leather, pegs and lasts, a patent leather drinking cup, then he would not have had to tote three dozen of Atkins Lightning Bolt Arresters and Protectors to peddle, and he could have spent his money on the Butterfield Stage.

For his wagon, Gideon bought a spare king bolt, linchpins, iron rings, and staples. Also rosin and tallow, melted together, for greasing the wheels. Had he money for a spare axletree and ox-bows, he would've tied those under his wagon. A tin lantern and oil were too dear. He got sperm candles he hoped to husband by sharing light cast from wagons better equipped than his. No one owns a ray of light once it leaves his lantern.

Wagon boxes were fitted out with hasps along the side holding bowed strips of ash over which was stretched new Osnaburg or canvas white as sugar. The undersides of the wagons were black, all the seams tarred for river crossings. Everyone but Gideon had plows and shovels and wooden chicken coops packed with biddies strapped to the wagons' rears. And everyone else's wagon led a milk cow or two along, tied by the horns with enough rope to let them graze when the wagons stopped.

Hiram Thurston's wagon had four little apple tree saplings, root-balled and burlapped, tipped with tiny buds nonetheless, and tied down one side of its bed.

Once, as Hiram Thurston was pouring water over the wrapped roots, Major Benson shook his head and said, "Them trees will never cross the desert—won't no one on my train waste water on such foolishness once we leave the green country. Heat don't kill them, duststorms or hail will. And if they make it to the passes mountain snows will freeze them."

You can bet Thurston heard the wagon master, though he gave no indication. He'd been worried about the trees since leaving. But they were all Mrs. Thurston had asked. He'd told her there are apple trees in Washington, but the quiver in her jaw, her eyes dancing, made the trees not so much a request as a demand. In return for giving up her home and the few pieces of furniture and pretties she'd managed to get hold of, for putting up with six months of fear wondering every moment whether the cries of Indians would be the prelude to torture and death, six months of worry over the children's irritability and mischief and illnesses, six months of cooking outdoors, bouncing up and down hour after hour, breathing dust and insects, suffering the sun and wind and lightning and hail and dust and snow, all the other reasons not to move on—wolves and bears and rattlesnakes, broken axles, bad water or no water at all—in return for all that and more, four little ole apple trees didn't seem much to lay claim to.

"I got to give Mary her due," Hiram told Gideon. "She says these four little trees will pollinate until she's got a hillside of white blooms—a apple-blossom mountain, she says."

"Maybe they'll make the trip." Gideon tried to sound encouraging. Hiram squinted one eye and gave his head a shake.

"Womenfolks is touchous, have twitchy ways. Mary's pa died not long before we left the farm. He was way proud he once met John Chapman—the one folks has taken to calling Johnny Appleseed?—met him in a orchard in Indiana. Place he died."

"Mrs. Thurston's pa?"

"John Chapman. In '45 he got the pneumonie in Indiana, died in a orchard, according to Mary's pa. The Miltons, Mary's family name, they all said John Chapman was a healer, he had the sight. Mary raised up these saplings from seeds her pa gave her, seeds he said Chapman gave him. Come Hell or high water, I'm toting them with us."

Mrs. Thurston's infant son, James, wailed and Mrs. Morgan's two boys chased each other around the wagons firing stick-guns at the Pitchers' boy. Mongrels ran about barking, tails curled above their backs. Even they knew it was time to move on. Most folks had a lot of misery to leave behind—the graves of dead children, bad crops and debts, snow and ice. The long war ended, a soldier could leave behind fighting and hardship, could leave a burned-out homeplace, could try to leave the memory of limbs and corpses swelling in the sun like a field of squashes and melons Satan had planted on his farm in Hades. A man leaving all that behind him and with six hundred forty acres somewhere in front of him is willing to shove aside what he hears about sudden prairie storms, dangerous river crossings, the parched Great Desert, deadly serpents, and bands of murderous Indians.

Two Talks: Many Moons of Weeping

Remembers Joining the Antelope
(The Moon of Grass Turning Brown 1856)

I studied the Comanches as hard as I had studied my Virgil and Ovid with
Colonel Powell-Hughes. It was clear to me the United States government could
not stop its citizens from entering the Comanches' hunting range. And the only
other way there could be peace between bellicose plains tribes and land-hungry
whites was for the Unites States government to overwhelm the Indians by
force of might. As far as I can tell, no peace treaty ever changed a thing.

—from *Gideon Jones' Journal*

The People had no silent talking that a marking-stick could make lie down on
the white man's paper to sleep until a tongue woke it and breathed it back to life.
All Numunuu talking is living words—they come one after the other from the
mouth of a Numunuu as his arrows come from his bow. The power of the arrow
is the power of the Numunuu, because the Numunuu and his bow are one. The
power of the living words is the power of the Numunuu, because the Numunuu
and his words are the same. Numunuu talking does not hibernate as a bear. Like
burning embers, Numunuu words must be breathed or they die out. The white
man's marking-stick talk is unfaithful. It will rise from the paper when any tongue
wakes it.

Before blood moons rose and Two Talks led a raiding party of Antelopes on
the war trail, before Two Talks became a great Numunuu war chief, during the
Moon of Grass Turning Brown, he stood in a council meeting of the Antelope
and told of the road he had walked as a youth in a Honey Eaters band of the
Numunuu, near the end of their time of strength. He told why he left the Honey
Eaters' road to walk with the Antelope. He told why the Antelope should study the

footprints of the Honey Eaters, who now made a deep cowpath walking the same circle inside the reservation pen. Two Talks said the Antelope should dance the war dance and paint their faces black and hang so many Tehano scalps on their scalp poles they would shade all the lodges of the Antelope from the sun.

To keep this true talking from dying, Antelope men who were in the council meeting that day breathed Two Talks' living words into other ears. Later, white men listened to those who kept Two Talks' Numunuu talking alive in their hearts, and these whites tried to echo Two Talks with marking-stick words on the white man's paper, words without story-pictures. On the white man's paper where there is no living talking, Two Talks' words slept long.

The marking-stick words are black slanting shadows of Two Talks' living talking. How to bring back Two Talks' voice to breathe life into these still shadows? Be still, be still and silent, be silent and listen, listen well.

Council Meeting Oratory

I was born by the light of Mother Moon in the shadow of the oak and the hackberry. I was born during the time of Big Cold Moon just before Sleet Moon. The first singing I heard was Arrowhead River. I was born hungry for buffalo blood, pecans, and sweet persimmons. I was born to the aromas of horse sweat, mother's milk, and cedar smoke. I did not know the white man's scent. Like one of Brother Coyote's red pups, all I wanted was to live and die between the timbers and the prairie. But the Tehanos wanted the thick grass of my birthing place as snakes want eggs in a sparrow's nest.

In the first time of new grass following my birth, my grandfather Red Dog was one of the camp headmen who represented the Penatekas band and journeyed to the council at Comanche Peak to hear what words the new Great Father of the whites had to speak. My grandfather Red Dog brought with him other Honey Eaters, but none of the Antelope band from the north came. Some said the Antelope band showed bravery by staying away, but grandfather said the Antelopes showed disdain, which is sometimes better than bravery. The white talkers put their marks to many promises, saying they would give the Honey Eaters many presents. They would build trading posts and send smiths to put the steel shoes on the Honey Eaters' ponies and keep their guns speaking right. The white talkers also said no white would enter the Honey Eaters' land without per-mission in white man's writing from the new Great Father in Washington Land. Red Dog spoke words at the council asking if the Great Father could see this far from Washington Land to know if a white entered Our People's territory without his words in marks. Red Dog said this prom-ise would be broken before all the marks on the paper were made. The Honey Eaters had to promise to stay away from the Tehano ranchos, to give up all *taivo* captives and all captured horses, and to buy guns and crazy water only at the new trading posts. Red Dog said neither side could keep these pledges, and he would not put his hand to the marking-stick, but many chiefs of the Honey Eaters band did.

For the next two times of yellow grass, the Honey Eaters found many buffalo to kill. For all Honey Eaters those were dark-fur times of much to eat, of laughter and the telling of stories. Meat hung heavy in our lodges for two times of cold moons. Even when the snow flew and ice stiffened the sides of our tipis we were warmed by tales of past battles the Honey Eaters had won. When the time of green grass came again many young warriors sought their *puha* and the warpath they should ride, the enemy they should challenge.

Our camp heads who had marked the promise paper talked against the warriors who wanted to attack the Tehanos. These council talkers led our raiders south to cross Stinking Buffalo, the river the Tehanos call the Rio Grande, where they took many Mexican horses and brought back Mexican women to work in the camp and Mexican children to adopt or to trade to other bands or tribes. A young Honey Eaters man said we should take all the territory below Stinking Buffalo River, and Red Dog said we could, but it was better to let the Mexicans work hard raising all these horses for us so we could take them when we wanted.

When I had passed my third Big Cold Moon, a gray bitch appeared one morning at the tipi of my father, Crooked Nose. From that day on, the cur trotted at my side and would not let me out of her sight. My moth-er, Morning Star, wanted to send the dog away. "No, my wife," Crooked Nose told my mother. "Brother Coyote sent the dog to watch over our new son." My grandfather agreed the gray bitch was a strong good sign.

It was a time of green grass when many whites crossed our land. They came so many together we let them pass—we had not put our mark on the promise paper, and these whites did not hold up any words from the Great Father in Washington Land, but they had many guns that spoke fast. Some of these whites were from the tribe of the Dutch Men, whose words sound like antlers clattering. Before these, many from the Tehano tribe came. We watched them pass from a distance. After dust from their passing lay down to rest, our homeland seemed quieter than ever before. We hoped each dust that rested was the end of the white ones. But it was not.

Many whites died in their wagons from sickness spirits that ride with them, and their *taivo* brothers did not bury them but left their bodies behind in the grass. Invisible white killing spirits hid near these dead bodies, and when Honey Eaters warriors took the steel knives from the belts of these dead ones or the metal fasteners from their coats, sickness spirits got on the hands of these men and rode them back to their camp. The whites left behind their sickness spirits in the waterholes of the Honey Eaters band, and when we drank the water we drank the spirits. The invisible spirits hid in hats and blouses the whites dropped from their wagons, and when our women and children picked up these hats and blouses and put them on, they put on the killing spirits.

The spirits of the white disease found all the camps of the Honey Eaters and overpowered the guarding spirits of lodge after lodge. The Ones You Can't Fight Because They Won't Show Themselves brought hot skin and killing cramps.

The gray dog sent by Brother Coyote to protect me growled at our tipi door and would not let me walk about the camp. When the first one of our band died from the *taivo* sickness, Grandfather Red Dog said each family should go away and make separate camp. This would confuse the killing spirits, and they would have trouble finding all the Honey Eaters. Some in our band did not want to separate. They were afraid of the white man's strong bad medicine, and in their fear many families slept together in the same lodge. The stronger-than-a-buffalo sickness from the whites hid in the belly of one child in this lodge, and as the child slept between his mother and father the invisible spirits got into their arms and legs. After three more sleeps, the quieter-than-a-rock sickness had got into the arms and legs and heads and bellies of each Numunuu in this lodge and cooked and squeezed them every one to death from the inside.

This was the Summer of the Most Sorrows in the camps of the Honey Eaters. To keep the invisible spirits from the whites from getting into them, children ran from their dying parents. Sometimes the sickness spirits still found these small ones. Sometimes these small ones got away, but if they were not old enough to find food, they starved to death. Many Honey Eaters died, some where they hid in their lodges, some where they had fled or been abandoned in the woods. We passed the winter wailing for our dead brothers and our dead children.

When green grass time came again, the murderous *taivo* spirits went away. The gray dog sent from Brother Coyote also went away. The disease from the whites had killed more of the Honey Eaters band than all the white guns that had come before them.

Following the Summer of the Most Sorrows, there was another council with the whites who talked for Our Father in Washington Land. Few Honey Eaters were left alive to go to this council. Grandfather Red Dog went, but he still would not put his hand to the marking-stick. Grandfather wondered if the killing spirits from the whites had inhabited the promise paper at the council at Comanche Peak and gotten on all the Honey Eaters' hands that had touched the paper. This time the Great Father in Washington Land wanted Our People to promise to stay north of the River of Wild Hogs the Tehanos call the Llano. Many of the surviving Honey Eaters had become near-dead. The terrible invisible spirits had weakened those they had not killed, and these near-dead Honey Eaters took the gifts from the Great Father in Washington Land and touched the marking-stick.

This same time of yellow grass, Grandfather went to another council, a small one with the white tribe from Dutch Land at the place the white tribe called Treaty Hill. The Dutch Land talkers did not have many more of the English words than the Honey Eaters. They used the Mexican talk and hand talk. The Dutch Land talkers gave every Honey Eater who marked the promise paper a heavy pouch of *ohapuhiwi*. They said we could trade the gold for fine goods at any Dutch Lander trading post. Grandfather did not make a mark, but the Dutch Landers gave him a pouch of the sacred metals anyway. Grandfather Red Dog gave the clinking bag to me. He said the Numunuu who stayed around the white trading lodges had been the first to be killed by the invisible spirits. He thought the longer you stayed near the whites, especially if you ate their food or drank their water, the easier it was for their invisible warrior spirits to sneak inside you and weaken and maybe kill you. I asked Grandfather if the gold metals might be so heavy because the killing spirits also hid inside. We buried the pouch of metals deep and then cleansed our bodies in the waters of Arrowhead River.

Because of the invisible spirits, Grandfather hated the whites more than ever. For the *taivos* to use the Ones You Can't Fight Because They Won't Show Themselves was cowardly. "A brave one does not hide from a fight," Grandfather said.

By the time the Moon of Recently Green Leaves passed, Grandfather had killed a Tehano for every finger on his two hands. Ten sticks of Tehanos. Ten sticks of scalps hung from his pole: four scalps were the color of a high sun, two were the color of a buffalo robe, two were the color of the bitch-dog Coyote sent to protect me, and two were the color of dried blood. Grandfather wore new treasures in his hair. He borrowed many wives in our camp. Grandfather had seen forty sticks of Big Cold Moons, but he grew young instead of old. I thought he would soon be as young as I. I thought he would get so young I would carry him around the camp on a cradle board as he had once carried me.

When I was nine sticks old, Major Neighbors of the Blue-Bottoms sent talking to all the members of the Honey Eaters band who had survived the Summer of the Most Sorrows. Major Neighbors was one Blue-Bottom Grandfather Red Dog said we could trust. Major Neighbors had always done the ways of doing he had talked. A Blue-Bottom from the soldiers' lodge brought the talking from Major Neighbors. This talking made Grandfather sad. Major Neighbors wanted all Honey Eaters to live on a reservation on the Clear Fork of the Brazos River. Grandfather had thought Major Neighbors walked the same road the Numunuu walked.

"I was wrong to think so," Grandfather said. "If a fish looks up from a river and tells the Numunuu where the river goes underground and where it comes up again—and his words are true—the Numunuu think he is not like other fish who never tell us the truth. And if the fish says how pretty we walk, we begin to think the fish can jump out of the river and walk beside us on our road. But a fish, even if he says true things, must spend his suns and his sleeps in the river with his own kind. The Tehanos and the Numunuu do not breathe the same way."

Ten sticks plus two of warriors remained in our band—four sticks in the third or fourth age group. They met to decide what talk they would send to Major Neighbors. Corn Eater was now in the third age group.

He no longer kept the medicine bag—he had passed it on to his son, Ten Buffalo—but Corn Eater's words in the council tipi still stung: "We Honey Eaters will never overcome our losses from the Summer of the Most Sorrows. We must take the white man's road. We must eat his meat and speak his words. Major Neighbors will bring us beef to eat and build medicine lodges for our children. Only the white medicine lodges have the *puha* to keep the killing spirits out of our children. Major Neighbors will build teaching lodges where our children will learn the white man's talk and the white man's walk. The Great Father in Washington Land has more whites than the night has stars. No matter how many whites we kill, the Great Father sends more. Our *puha* is not as strong as the white man's invisible killing spirits. The Tehanos have taken our hunting land for as far as the eye can see. Let us say good-bye to the ways of Our People and take the *taivo* gifts. Let us be pleasing to the eye of the Great Father in Washington Land so he will remember us and be good to our children."

A long quiet followed Corn Eater's words. He had said what many believed, what all feared might be true. My father, Crooked Nose, said he wondered if the Great Father in Washington Land would be good to the children of pups who hurried after a free teat. "He who would eat the honey must bear the bee's stinger."

Then Grandfather Red Dog spoke. "I am—like the Honey Eaters band itself—in the fourth age group. We have fought many brave battles with the whites, especially the hated Tehanos. The Honey Eaters who eluded the invisible *taivo* sickness spirits in the Summer of the Most Sorrows are few. Our names are no longer on the trembling lips of every white. But we do not have to spend our last cold moons in the airless houses of the Tehanos. Our teeth grow soft, but we can die chewing buffalo meat we have killed honorably, instead of chewing the meat of a cow brought to us by a white father. If the Honey Eaters have grown so weak we would walk to the Clear Fork Reservation of Major Neighbors to let the Blue-Bottoms enclose us as they fence cattle and sheep, then I will no longer call myself a member of the Honey Eaters band. I cannot speak the names of reservation Honey Eaters. They are dead to me. I will cross the Water Colored by Clay—in *taivo* talk, the Red River—and live among my brothers of the Antelope band, the Ones Who Wear Sunshades on Their Backs. The Antelope will welcome me and any who walk with me, and Numunuu ways they still follow will keep us from becoming near-dead. My son, my grandson, and I will dance the war dance with my Antelope brother Sure Enough Hungry. We will kill many Tehanos and take many horses. I do not want my son and my grandson to have to grow old in a Tehano animal pen. Our People have long said 'brave ones die young.' I am past my time of dying—let it come while I am still strong to draw a bow against the Tehano."

And so two ways of seeing were spoken, and two different paths were taken. Those Honey Eaters who went to live on the Clear Fork Reservation were no longer of Our People—they were dead to us. When one of Our People dies, we no longer speak his name. So I cannot say the names of those who joined the *taivos'* sheep in their fold. The men in our band were more than the arrows in a full quiver and many gave up their names. Of the old, wise ones, all became dead to us except Grandfather Red Dog. Ten Buffalo looked on his father's face for the last time. Then he moved his lodge, his wives and children, and all of his horses beside our lodges, and he brought with him the medicine bag. Our encampment was small, and we had more women and children than warriors, but we had a full quiver of horses and many Mexican mules when we took down our camp on the Arrowhead River the Tehanos call the Pedernales. Our women loaded our travois and we followed Little Apples, because the owl had hooted to Little Apples in the sunlight and told him he had asked the hawk, because of his speed, to fly from his home in the cedar hills to where trees are afraid to grow and tell Sure Enough Hungry his Honey Eaters brothers were coming to smoke the large walnut pipe with him and to join him on the war trail. The owl told Little Apples to listen each sun-coming-up and he would hoot him which way we should go.

I remember this trip as my time of leaving childhood. We left under the Moon of Grass Turning Brown, and red and yellow leaves fell like the bright tears of Our Father in Heaven, who shone down and warmed us on our way. I left behind the familiar white hills and clear rivers and the twisted-and-always-green trees of my growing up. Now I will take up my bow against the Tehanos. When next I ride through the Honey Eaters country of my young and learning days, I will not be near the tipis of my home camp. I will be on an Antelope war party raiding the Tehanos. And if the Great Father in Washington Land casts his eye on us, his lips will tremble, and maybe he will be fearful to send all of his many whites. But if one day he sends more whites than stars in the night sky to fight us, then it will be a good day to die.

The Blue-Bottoms Attack

In the tipi of Crooked Nose there was little buffalo meat left, but this was during the Moon of Recently Green Leaves, so Two Talks and his family ate their fill anyway. The tipi was hung with pouches of fresh-picked berries, and onions from the river's edge floated in a horn bowl of water. A small herd of buffalo had been spotted just one sun's ride from this large camp where Two Talks and other former Honey Eaters now lived with their new Antelope brothers beside a water with no name that ran down from the Water Colored by Clay. In the yellow grass days to come, huge herds of buffalo, heavy with fat and thick fur for the winter, would darken the grass for as far as Two Talks could see. When the yellow grass days came, Two Talks would kill a buffalo by himself. Now, the down was on the cottonwoods. This was the time to ride the war trail, and Two Talks wished he already had his *puha* so he might prove himself in a raiding party against the Tehanos.

Crooked Nose's tipi—near the brush arbor lodge of the Antelope warrior Sure Enough Hungry—was surrounded by more Numunuu lodges than Two Talks had ever seen in one encampment. He was Antelope, now. It was his turn to join other boys his age, boys soon to be warriors, guarding the herd—nine hundred horses, including twenty-five of the big *taivo* horses without spots Antelope raiders had taken from Blue-Bottoms.

For the past several nights the Cherokee girl, Small Nose, had slipped from his father's tipi and crawled beneath Two Talks' robe in the brush arbor where he now slept by himself. She had thrashed and bucked against him until Father in Heaven reddened the sky. Soon Two Talks would find his special totem and become a warrior and capture enough ponies to purchase Small Nose or an Antelope girl to be his wife and sew buffalo hides for Two Talks' own tipi or cut willow limbs for a brush arbor lodge. He would sit in his lodge and recount his victories on the warpath. But this night he was proud to stay up and guard the horses while even the camp curs were sleeping.

Two Talks spotted White Rump in the quiet herd and the rangy old mustang came over and nuzzled his arm, the horse's warm tongue taking in the salt-taste of dried sweat. White Rump was a pale shape of light in the darkness, as if a spirit ghost floated beside Two Talks. A steady, low breeze stirred the grass and sent a ripple down the horse's back. "You beautiful, ugly one," Two Talks said, and the horse shook his head, his bright eye a star hung low in the heavens.

By the time Two Talks began telling White Rump the third version of how he would prepare for his upcoming vigil to seek his personal *puha*, Father in Heaven approached, orange above hills to the east. "I will fast for four suns," Two Talks told White Rump. "I will smoke sumac leaves and pray and open my flesh so blood and pain may keep my thoughts focused and my heart pure." White Rump's one good ear rose like a distant mountain peak dark against the light that came before Father in Heaven stood up above the edge of the earth. Then White Rump's split purple ear twitched, and Two Talks heard a lonely bleating from high above—and he looked up for a goose. By the time his heart beat once more, Two Talks remembered the goose cry was not a song of this green grass time, yet again there came a far-off goose call. He put his ear to the ground and heard horse weight like thunder, and he remembered from Old Camp Cooper the flash of sound from the kissing lips of a Blue-Bottom playing the yellow pipe the Long Knives call bugle that speaks like the goose.

Two Talks leapt from the rock ledge onto White Rump's warm back, and the pinto ran as the goose flies. Tipis and lodges bobbed up and down rushing toward them, goose calls now strung together like running water. The slap and clink of leather and metal echoed with the honk of bugle. Now the snort of horsebreath and wheeze of Blue-Bottom breathing beat warm against his back. The band's huge herd ran with him, and all around him ponies scattered like brown leaves blowing over the grass and between the tipis and lodges. Two Talks' voice caught in his throat, and his warning came out like the bleating cry of the bugle that chased him. Numunuu were slow to rise from their heavy sleeps. His voice finally worked. "*Taivo*," he said.

Everywhere, dogs barked, and one dog, run over by a stampeding horse, yelped and yelped. A cookpot clanged over and over, bounced and rolled between horses' hooves. Like moles out of the earth men with wild ungreased hair and no warpaint poked heads out of tipis. *Taivo* rifles barked louder than the frenzied dogs. Numunuu hurried out of every tipi and lodge, women carrying and chasing children, men notching arrows to bows.

By the time Two Talks reached the tipi of his father, Crooked Nose was putting Morning Star and Persimmon on the back of a horse to carry them to safety. Then Crooked Nose tossed Two Talks a bow and a quiver of arrows.

In front of their tipi, Red Dog knelt, arrows leaving his bow as hornets from an angry nest. A *taivo* horse screamed and collapsed and rolled in a cloud of dust, blood running from Red Dog's arrow in the animal's neck. The old warrior hurried over to the Blue-Bottom rider whose leg was caught beneath the horse. Red Dog smashed a rock on the man's skull and brought his knife across the man's forehead. "*Aieee,*" Grandfather said as he jerked up and peeled back the scalp, hacked it loose. Red Dog sliced the bucking horse's throat to still the beast so he could crouch behind him. *Taivo* bullets ripped holes through the hide tipi and sunk into lodgepoles and into the dead horse and into the earth itself.

Sighs and groans rose over the campground and filled the spaces between lodges as smoke rose and drifted over coals. Blue-Bottoms on big horses made a wide wall of brown and blue thundering across the camp. They threw torches setting fire to tipis and thatched lodges, burning hide bags of dried meat, mesquite flour, fresh berries. Crooked Nose seized a rifle from a dead Blue-Bottom's grip and fired into the *taivos.* By the time he emptied the rifle he'd hit three Blue-Bottoms and two of their horses.

In the midst of dust and smoke and the cries and moans of Numunuu and horses and dogs, Two Talks stood tall and still as a tree. He fitted an arrow to the bow his father had tossed up. Against his fingertips beeswaxed buffalo ligament drew strength like the long muscle in his leg when he crouched for a jump. He looked down the straight shaft of the arrow. Dust-colored faces of charging *taivos* stilled, and Two Talks knew he was seeing through the eyes of the arrow. The tense ligament leapt from his fingers and sent flying the fast arrow and it seemed to jump into the shoulder of a Blue-Bottom just when its buzzard feathers brushed Two Talks' fingertips.

While Two Talks was fitting another arrow to his bow, a Blue-Bottom leaned from his saddle and pulled Small Nose up with him. Two Talks loosed an arrow at the man's mouth, but the *taivo* held Small Nose in front of himself as a shield. Two Talks' arrow pierced her throat. Her eyes opened wide, but she did not cry out. From deep in his chest a growl came out of Two Talks' throat like the howl of a wolf. The *taivo* horse chopped sideways, then reared. In the moment of the animal's confusion in the din of yells and rifle reports and hoofbeats, Two Talks caught the horse's tail and pulled himself up behind the Blue-Bottom. Two Talks was too close for the Blue-Bottom to use his rifle. The horse labored under the weight of three bodies. The Blue-Bottom swung his rifle like a club, but Two Talks knocked it away. He grabbed for the *taivo,* who thrust Small Nose between them, the arrow bobbing in her neck. Rifle shots behind them were forest twigs snapping. The moans of Numunuu whirled together as the whine of the plains wind. The Blue-Bottom reached for a pistol, and let the horse's reins drop. The leather hit the ground and the galloping horse stepped on the end of one strap, jerking its head down into its churning legs. The horse pitched headfirst into the ground. Thrown forward, Two Talks wrapped his arms around the *taivo* as a bear squeezes the trunk of a tree. Hurtling through the air, Two Talks groped for Small Nose, but she was gone. He landed on top of the *taivo*, who slammed hard into the short grass. The earth trembled like the skin of a struck drum, and he felt like the drum club. When the earth stilled, the tremor moved inside his head and shook every one of his teeth. One hand gripped the furry chin of the *taivo* and the other grabbed a clump of hair above the high forehead. He jerked both his hands against one another as if he were throwing a buffalo calf. He felt the give of muscle and then the snap and let-go of bone. Bonepoints broke the skin of the Blue-Bottom's neck the way pale wood pierces bark when a limb splinters. A white knob of bone rose from warm pooling blood. Two Talks sliced the scalp off the front of the Blue-Bottom's head and stood, one foot planted in the middle of the man's broad back, calling Coyote with a wail of blood fury. The *taivo*'s big boots dug two smooth places in the grass, spasms moving his legs back and forth as if he were trying to walk down into the earth. The big horse, only stunned, had gotten to its feet and was now grazing, its yellow teeth loudly pulling loose the tough grass.

Two Talks ran to Small Nose, who lay on her back as if she had stretched out for a nap. A large bullet hole in her chest oozed black blood. Her mouth rested in a straight line, her countenance unfrowning. Gray clouds had come to rest in her eyes. Two Talks lifted her and found the smaller hole where the bullet had entered her back. His arrow had gone through the side of her neck. Cradling the back of her head in his palm, he pulled her up into his arms and held her close. He cut her skin where it held his arrow and lifted out the shaft. Using the same barbed arrowhead that dripped the Cherokee girl's blood, he opened the flesh of his right hand. He held his bleeding hand against her neck so his blood mixed with hers. He gripped the bloody arrow shaft and left his blood with hers there, too. This arrow he would save to kill a *taivo* chief.

Two Talks picked up the reins of the still grazing *taivo* horse. He put his moccasin in the stepping place *taivos* hang from each side of their horses and swung himself into the wide seat of the saddle. How did the Blue-Bottom ride in a saddle so stiff and heavy you could not feel the horse warm beneath you, could not know the tightening and stretching out of hide and flesh? Two Talks' feet did not reach the stepping places where the Blue-Bottoms held their feet when they rode. He squeezed his knees and leaned, and the big horse turned easily. He brought both heels softly against the horse's sides and the willing animal galloped back toward the center of the camp. Two Talks had arrows yet to spend, but the Long Knives were already gone. Like a wind full of lightning and hail they had swept over the camp. Dead dogs lay twisted over upended cookpots. The bodies of women and children gaped red, gored by bullets as a knife digs the red fruit from a melon. A young man lay on his face making a deep red mud of the settling clouds of dust. Quail Song knelt over the body of her husband, her head thrown back, her knotted throat moving up and down with her keening song. Without interrupting her grief wail, she took from his belt her husband's knife and hacked off the fingers of her left hand. Babes on cradle boards bled where their tiny corpses had been slung: into the ashes of cookfires, into piles of blackberries strewn from rent and charred hide bags, into the thorns of yucca and wild roses. Worse were the near-dead. Lance Shaker, who carried the medicine bag for the Antelope, as Ten Buffalo carried it for the former Honey Eaters who had joined the band, stared at the white curve of his intestine that poked through the hole where a bullet had passed, his own innards slowing the painful flow of blood that would let him die. White Rose, a big, sweet girl Two Talks had played with as a child, screamed and thrashed against her mother and sister, who tried to hold her still, her swollen belly soaked dark with the blood of the babe she would now deliver dead.

Two Talks, Crooked Nose, and Sure Enough Hungry rode a circle around the camp on both sides of the river. The riverbank held the deep, slick trails of wagons weighted with the bigger-than-a-man *taivo* cannon guns that had made dry ponds in the spaces where tipis had stood. With his looking reed, Sure Enough Hungry saw a red dust cloud at the place where the sky lies on top of the grass. Sure Enough Hungry handed the looking reed to Crooked Nose and shook his head. "The *taivo* Father in Washington Land has emptied the pockets of his greatcoat and spilled all of his Blue-Bottoms onto our path. Never before have I seen such a big dust of Blue-Bottoms," Sure Enough Hungry said.

"Can we catch them, my friend?" Two Talks asked.

"We might. Just as you might leap after a rattlesnake bites you once and then land in the den where all the rattlesnakes of the world wait. Better to kill them one at a time and cut off their rattles until you wear so many the other snakes hear you coming and shake their rattles in fear and give away their hiding places."

"My arrow knows the taste of blood now," Two Talks said.

Keening Songs

The three returned to camp where the women tended the wounded and dying. Fifty-six of the Antelope band had been killed, most of them women and children. Though they had been surprised at dawn, the Antelope warriors had put their arrows into many Blue-Bottoms. As always, the *taivo* raiders left behind their wounded and dead where they fell. The Antelope women alternately treated the wounds and washed the dead bodies of their children, their sisters, and their friends, and exorcized their horror and anger by mutilating the Blue-Bottom corpses and harrowing those *taivos* so unlucky their wounds had not been immediately fatal. These unfortunates were slowly skinned alive. They were made to suffer for as long as possible so their screams and weeping might salve the wounded bodies and the wounded hearts of this still mighty Antelope band of the Numunuu.

While the Antelope women performed rites of torture and treated the wounded Numunuu, the warriors and older boys gathered to make plans for moving the camp from this place of ghosts and to talk of the war trail they would ride against the *taivos*. Grandfather Red Dog was the only man from the fourth age group. Most of those so old took themselves off to die, but Red Dog seemed to grow young again like a tree struck by lightning or broken by wind that sends a new green shoot up out of its charred or broken places.

"Like the old dog for whom I'm named, I've had many good hunts. I do not want to become so fond of sleeping by the fire that I die as pitifully as an Apache farmer, wrapped in his blankets with no blood scent in his nostrils. But like the heart of the bitch whose litter has been eaten by a mountain lion, my angry heart will not rest until I have tracked and killed that same cougar. I demand a good day to die, not this day of tears. I demand that my strong pup, Crooked Nose, and his pup, Two Talks, have that same good day to die."

Sure Enough Hungry stood up, and he took Two Talks by the arm. "I have not known the joy of a close good friend—my children are all daughters. One sister buries the other. We know many moons of weeping. I claim the shared fathering of our young ones soon to be men. Our women have wounds to wash, bodies to stand in the rocks. While they bind our hurts, we must seek the war road against the Tehanos, against all *taivos*." Sure Enough Hungry nodded at the big warrior who carried the medicine bag of all the Honey Eaters who had joined the Antelope band. "With the death of our medicine man whose name we no longer speak, my new friend will now carry the medicine bag for our band."

"Our friend, Coyote, shakes us in his teeth. I seek healing medicines to make Antelope wounds quickly scar over, medicines to make our rent places grow back stronger for having been torn apart," said Ten Buffalo.

Two Talks walked to the burial place Morning Star and Persimmon had prepared for Small Nose. She was not born Numunuu and had not been adopted or married into the People, but she had become Numunuu in her way of dying, and they buried her as one of Our People, wrapped in beaded doeskin, standing in a hole in a rock cliff facing where Our Father in Heaven gets up every morning. Two Talks rolled a rock over Small Nose's grave, and a crow lighted on the hairy limb of a cottonwood and called out to Two Talks.

"Crow, what do you want with me?"

Knobby Cotton: Escape to Waterland

A Perilous Route to Freedom
(September–November 1862)

Excitement in Louisiana. We understand the bodies of four Negroes, the property of prominent families in Galveston, have been found in Rouge Bayou in Terrebonne Parish by some men who were attracted to the place by a clan of buzzards. The bodies were found floating close to the surface, held by forked limbs that to all appearance had been put over them for the cause of keeping the corpses to the bottom. Their necks were printed by rope and their abdomens opened up and the innards removed, leaving little doubt the bodies were put in the bayou in hopes an alligator or other carnivore would dispose of them. The men who found the bodies are accused of the killing. Our informant declares these men innocent, and says once they are questioned by the authorities they will be released, so we shall omit their names. [news story copied from the *Seguin Mercury*, Seguin, Texas]

—from *Gideon Jones' Journal*

"Knobby, I've been out of my mind with worry. I waked up and you'd gone off. Afeared to move, I scrunched here in these sticker bushes all morning."

Knobby didn't say a word, just opened up the farm woman's bonnet, weighted now with eggs and sweet potato and cornbread. Elizabeth put her face close to the food, smelling it like a hound. They ate the eggs raw, sucking out the deep orange yolks and licking the slick insides of the shells. They broke the sweet potato in half and each ate half of a half, saving the rest with the cornbread. Then Elizabeth stuck her finger in her mouth, poked at the bonnet with her moistened fingertip inside and then sucked the finger, eating cornbread crumbs.

They came out of the woods and into soft grass that squished when they walked. Where there was no grass, water filled the space. In one of these watery clearings they washed off in order to put on their borrowed clothes. Though Elizabeth had been naked before him for more than two days of running, she walked shyly away to the other side of the pool to wash off the mud. The farm woman's feedsack dress was snug on Elizabeth, but she smiled as proud-looking as a white lady in a plantation-ball gown. She loosened the shoulder straps of the overalls Knobby had squeezed into, let them out as far as they would go, and still the legs hung no lower than the middle of his calves. He gave a little dance, splashing water, and Elizabeth pulled on the sun-bleached pale blue bonnet and tied it under her chin. She bowed at the waist and he bowed back, and they both laughed out loud for the first time since Noble Plantation.

They kept in the grass, walking crouched, always north and west, sun-slant through the whispering blades a beacon they followed. Twice they spotted cabins or sheds—board huts built up on wooden legs—and they circled wide away.

They followed a narrow channel of water where it cut through the grass and, judged against the sun, ran southwest, widening as it flowed. A hawk gliding overhead dropped from the sky like something killed. It dimpled the water's surface and rose again. A fish flashed silver, caught in the bird's talons. "I wish I had a fishing pole, Elizabeth. Ole hawk's got a fish supper, and all we've got is half a yam and some cornbread."

"Let's us eat what we've got, Knobby. I'm starved to death."

"We might as well carry it inside us as outside."

Elizabeth stepped onto the shorter grass, and it sank and she slid away from him.

"Knobby, it's moving. The earth is moving."

He jumped after her, grabbing her hand, and they held onto one another, the grass beneath them drifting slowly toward the edge of the lake. *Dear God, don't let us drown.*

"Knobby, are we in some dream? I never walked on moving ground before."

His foot went right through the grass, right through the sod beneath, of a sudden plunged into water. His wiggling toes and kicking foot felt nothing solid. Writhing-snake, spider-web, dark-night terror raced up his leg into his groin and iced up his belly and chest. He came out of the grass the way the hawk had come off the lake, and his sunken shin and foot came free, shiny with black mud. The half a sweet potato shot from the overalls' pocket like cannonball from barrel, rocketed a good twenty feet over the marsh, and plopped into the water. Close to tears, Knobby searched for a ripple where the potato had sunk.

"Look what I've done, Elizabeth. Look what I've done."

"Still got the bread."

Water bubbled up in the hole Knobby's leg left behind, the smell of a struck match rising from the floating grass. They ate the cornbread except for one small piece Knobby hid deep in his pocket, something to give Elizabeth in the morning. At least they weren't going to die of thirst.

Several times the grass underfoot moved, and they learned to recognize the greener grass on the floating islands and to keep to firmer footing. Elizabeth stopped where the marsh grass gave way to a wide, watery pothole and held to his shoulder. Her finger to her lips, she nodded to the edge of the pool, where a turtle the size of a big skillet sat in the sun. Mossy green, his head bobbed, mouth open like a singing bird, a red blotch on each side of his head. Knobby knelt silently and drew Elizabeth down beside him. "Unwind some twine off your feedsack dress," he said.

"What're you going to do?"

"Unravel."

Knobby drew the square of saved cornbread from his pocket and looped the end of the thick thread Elizabeth gave him. He wrapped the bread with several loops of thread, making a kind of net to hold the bread. He gave Elizabeth a *stay-close* tug and a nod, and they duck-walked to where the turtle sunned himself. Knobby pitched the bread onto the grass beside the turtle, but he didn't take notice. Knobby tried again, but the turtle didn't even twitch. Elizabeth pinched Knobby's arm. She took the line and flipped the bread onto the water, where it floated past the turtle. Turtle took a look. Elizabeth gave a twitch, turtle scrabbled after. Inch by inch, Elizabeth twitched the sinking bread closer. Turtle followed. Knobby got between the turtle and the pothole. When Elizabeth had Ole Turtle in the grass, she let him catch the bread. Time he bit down, Knobby pounced and grabbed his shell. Ole Turtle's head jerked sideways, snapping. Hissed like a snake, only louder. Knobby held the shell on the sides where neither the hissing beak nor the clawing feet could get to him, and in a blink Ole Turtle jerked head and tail and all four feet in under his hard cover.

"I've got him, Elizabeth, or he's got me. I don't know which. This damn country doesn't have any rocks or limbs lying about for a man to use for hitting or clubbing."

"I'm about hungry enough to eat him live," Elizabeth said with no trace of a smile. Knobby swung the turtle down and brought his knee up hard, like he was breaking a limb, and he cracked the yellow bottom of the shell. Turtle's head and feet all came out at once and Knobby dropped him on his back. Dodging the hissing, snapping mouth and the clawing feet, Knobby brought his bare heel down again and again, crushing the bottom of the shell.

"Where's your little toe?" In spite of himself, Knobby counted his toes. Elizabeth chuckled down deep in her chest, sounded like Grandfather Samuel storytelling.

Knobby gutted and dressed the turtle with his bare hands, tossing entrails into the water and rinsing away blood and yellow balls of fat. What he wouldn't give for a knife, and for a match and firewood. Elizabeth chewed the raw flesh with her eyes closed, chewed fast and swallowed fast. They ate all the meat Knobby could pull loose. For the first time in days his stomach felt full, and he lay back and tried to empty his mind.

When the wide sky pinkened with sunset, they rose and continued west across the wide marsh. Knobby carried the turtle's top shell at his side like a stiff-brimmed hat.

"What're you going to do with it?"

"We can dip up water to drink."

"Knobby Cotton, just because I'm hungry enough to eat raw turtle doesn't mean I've got to drink from its nasty shell. My own hands will do me just fine."

Still, Knobby toted the shell.

"Woods ahead," he said. "We won't have to sleep lying in this wetness."

"Good, I don't want to get as water-wrinkled all over as my wet feet are."

The channel they had followed all afternoon widened into a bayou separating them from the trees. They looked across at willows and oaks and tall cypress. The bayou was freckled with rings and kissing smacks filled the air as fish dimpled the surface feeding on swarming insects.

"I ain't swimming this snaky-looking water, especially not in the devil's darkness."

"Elizabeth, we've got to cross."

"I've put up with enough. About time I rethink falling in love with you, Knobby Cotton. God himself would have trouble getting me out in swamp water." Even as she railed at Knobby, Elizabeth was walking steadily toward the bayou. At the edge Knobby took her hand and together they squished down into the soft bottom. A few inches down the muck was firm enough to walk on. Every few steps Elizabeth stopped and looked Knobby in the eyes and said there was no way she would ever cross this wide water. Even in the middle the bayou was only chest-deep. Elizabeth waved her hands, swatting at mosquitoes thick beneath the brim of her bonnet. Knobby breathed in a mouthful, felt them catch in his throat, dry and prickly. He breathed them out and they continued jerking and humming, tiny winged Jonahs out of Knobby's whale-mouth. He fanned them away with the turtle shell, and Elizabeth shook her head, but she didn't complain when he fanned air up under her bonnet. From the woods on the other side tree frogs filled the night with hollow clicking songs—ghosts beating sticks against limbs. Knobby slapped at mosquitoes, and his hand slid down his arm slick with blood. Elizabeth was on her knees laving mud on her exposed skin.

"No moon to see by, we can't walk these black woods," she said. "Must be a whole army of water moccasins and lizards and who knows what other crawly critters live in those swampy woods. But sleeping *here* we'd just feed the gallnippers."

They found an open swale of short grass between the bayou and the trees where marsh breezes kept most of the mosquitoes away. Knobby drew Elizabeth against him and softly kissed her lips, surprised she did not resist. Beneath her touchous ways there was some slight give. Soft, her lips. The taste of mud and a faint sulphur smell. His thigh pressed between her legs, warm through her dress and his overalls, and a different kind of emptiness pulled at his belly—not the tugging of starved for food, but the pure hunger of desire. He moved his hand up the side of Elizabeth's thigh, over her hip, down to her waist, over her washboard ribcage to nest in the feathery hair of her armpit. He pressed his lips to hers again and drew his hand forward to cup and hold her breast. He rose on an elbow and looked down at her closed eyes. Her lips were still, slightly parted, her breath soft and steady. She was deep asleep, the bonnet still on her head. Knobby put the backs of his fingers against her throat and felt life pulsing there. He kissed her chin and snuggled against her, and all the stars went out like extinguished lamps.

A Swamp Dweller

An animal from the woods, dark and small, a weasel—no, a wild pig, bigger even, poked hard at Knobby's swollen foot. *Po, yi*, the creature said, *Po, yi*.

"*Po, yi, Negre.*"

Knobby sat up, his mind struggling to reconcile the wild pig of his dream with the short, wiry old man who looked down at him from a gray cloud from which poked the long barrel of a gun. The man jerked his chin toward Elizabeth, who stirred, restless in her sleep, but had not waked up. Knobby rubbed her shoulder, wondering what he had gotten them into now.

"What is it, Knobby?"

"*Mais*, what is it, I want to know this, me, too," the man said.

"Oh Knobby, it's a old ghost who's been riding me. Get off, Ghost, get off, please."

"He's no ghost, Elizabeth." Knobby rubbed Elizabeth's shaking shoulders and spoke to the odd-talking man. "We are travelers, sir, just passing through on our way to Texas." *Jesus, help me know what to say.* Knobby stood up into a swirl of early morning fog.

"Texas? *Non, non.* I don't believe."

Knobby started talking faster than he could think what he was going to say. The man was small, not much over five feet tall, his skin as weathered and dark as a leather bridle. His long nose hooked down over the middle of his lips. His cheeks sunk in on both sides as if he were sucking on a bone, trying to get the marrow out. His stubble beard was grizzled, black and silver, as was his hair that looked to have been hacked unevenly with an ax. He wore brogans weighted with black mud, moss or fungus covering the toes. His brown twill britches were patched with hide at the knees and covered halfway down his thighs by a long shirt with many bulging flap pockets lining its front. One eye squinted—the man still aimed the gun at Knobby—but with his open eye he was listening. Knobby heard the story he was telling as if *he* were his listener, and he added to the story as his listening ears demanded. "I work all the stables for Noble Plantation, sir. My master freed me and made me a hired man. While he is off fighting in the war, he has sent me to Texas to buy horses so he will be well set-up after the war is ended."

"*Non.* Me, I think no man come to this marshland to find Texas, no, and no man bring a woman out here. I read about some slaves uprise down to Tabadieville, down near Thibodaux. Me, I think you runaway slaves, you."

"I'm a freedman. Highwaymen fell upon us and robbed me of my master's money. We ran in the dark and got ourselves lost."

Elizabeth reached two fingers inside her dress and removed the paper the slave Joseph had given them. "Here. This paper says we're free."

The man studied the paper, neither speaking nor moving his lips. Knobby could not tell whether the man could read.

"We were trying to find the road but were afraid soldiers might shoot us," Elizabeth said.

"*Non*, no soldier boys. This is Monsieur Etienne's trapline. No war comes here."

"Who is this Monsieur Etienne?" Knobby said.

"*Moi*, I am Monsieur Etienne." He lowered the gun. "Who are you, *Negre?*"

Knobby stuck to his story. Monsieur Etienne grinned at everything Knobby said. But the strange-talking little trapper did not care about runaway slaves or the war between the Americains and Confederates.

"Here is Acadienne, me and this country, from the *bois*"—Etienne pointed to the woods—"to *la fourche*"—he spread his first two fingers into a fork—"*des grosse bayou*"—Etienne spread his arms wide—"as far south as Pointe Chevreuil, this is the trapline of Etienne, yes."

"If it's not too much trouble, Mr. Etienne, could you point us in the direction of the Sabine Pass and Texas?"

"It's a long, long way, *Negre*, take you two, three week, *if* you know how you go. You go north, maybe you run into soldier boys. *Aux vases*, all the swamps is safe. War don't come here, no."

"Will you show us the way to go?"

"Maybe I do, maybe I don't. You hungry, no, you woman and you?" He gave them strips of dried meat. "*Boeuf*. Better and more we eat later, yes."

Etienne led them through the fog to a long dugout boat he called a "pee-roe," made of a single huge cypress log, with carved prow in front and back. There were no seats in the long, narrow pirogue. It was piled with heavy spring traps. Another long-barreled musket, like the one Etienne carried, lay beside the traps, and, next to the musket, a knife with a blade long enough Knobby would call it a short sword. Etienne pitched Knobby's turtle shell into the grass. He had Knobby sit in the front of the pirogue, Elizabeth in the middle beside the traps. The narrow boat wobbled when they climbed in, but even with their added weight did not ride low in the water. Etienne pushed off and stood in the back, where he wielded a long pushpole, poling them through the shallow water.

When Elizabeth sat, the feedsack dress tightened across her hips and rode up above her knees. Knobby could lose himself in the stretched places of the poor dress. He imagined how Elizabeth looked to a man alone in this swampland where Knobby figured there were few women. He wanted a blanket to throw over her, to cover her better than the feedsack dress with the unraveling hem, to hide her from the man's hawk eyes. Knobby had never before felt jealousy. Maybe it was a sign of freedom. Maybe it was not possible for a slave who owned nothing to feel jealous. But did his jealousy mean he was thinking of Elizabeth as a thing he owned, as the master had owned them both?

Beneath tall cypress and scrub oak thick with Spanish moss Etienne pointed out other inhabitants of his marshland, *terre bonne*, he called it. He showed them the heads of otter pups sticking up like small stumps from the fog-shrouded water.

A serpentine movement across the bayou made Elizabeth tremble for fear of a snake. Etienne said it was a mink, prized for its pelt. "Look up, there." High in a cedar, a marsh hawk watched them with yellow-circled eyes. Lining the water's edge were bushes Etienne named *roseaux*, and impaled on the purple thorns of the *roseaux* stems were small snakes and lizards Etienne said the black-beaked butcherbird had hung out to cure. "Come the winter, when the snake and lizard hide away, the butcherbird eat his dried kill, him." When the grass grew thick across the narrow path of water Etienne hacked it away with the sword he called a cane blade. Mosquitoes rose like smoke from the cut brush and Etienne gave Elizabeth and Knobby a salve to rub on their skin. "*Le m'decin.*" The oily paste smelled faintly of polecat, but it not only soothed the itch and sting of bites but also kept away the mosquitoes hovering like low, black clouds over the bayou.

They came suddenly into a large clearing, and Knobby and Elizabeth blinked at a bright streak of orange where the sun was about to rise. "Lac à La Hache—" Etienne said, chopping his hand down like the axe the lake was shaped like. With a finger to his lips he pointed up, where a cluster of dark specks slowly became an angled line of birds. "*Canard noir,*" Etienne said. Knobby stared blankly. "*Poule d'eau.* Good to eat, him." The ducks circled the lake, getting closer as they flew— gray ducks, brown ducks, black ducks, ducks with bright green heads. "*Dos-gris,*" Etienne said to himself or to the musket he lifted toward the sky. Though Knobby knew it was coming, the explosion made him jump, the muzzle flare as orange as the streak of dawn. The boom came back from the water's surface like a wave slapping the side of the pirogue, and a brown duck dropped like a leaf suddenly become a rock. Before the gunshot stopped ringing, Etienne laid the fired musket in the boat, and raised and shot the second gun. This time one of the green-headed ducks hit the water, wings splashing in a brief flurry. Etienne poled them out into the lake. He reached the green-headed duck first, its wings still now. But when Etienne touched the duck it came to life and thrashed in his hand. He grabbed its head with his other hand and twisted the neck with a soft *snap*. The brown duck was fatter than the green-head. "*Pa-pere* and *ma-mere*, drake and hen."

Etienne plucked the ducks, saving the feathers and down in a cotton bag he pulled from one of the many pockets of his shirt. Knobby had not seen the sheath at Etienne's ankle from which he slipped a narrow-bladed knife, slit open the ducks, and pulled constricted entrails from the carcasses. In the cool fog, steam rose from the glistening offal in Etienne's hand before he flung it out onto the water, where it disappeared in a furor of brown bubbles. He rinsed his hands, wrapped the cleaned ducks in wet blades of grass, and laid them in the bottom of the pirogue.

He showed them mounds of mud and grass that rose from the floating grass islands—muskrat homes. Along the edges of Ax Lake he showed them wild rice growing. He poled them through the grass, the floating islands pushed away by the flush points of the pirogue. Etienne pushed the set of his pole and the pirogue wouldn't budge. Etienne hopped out onto the firm grass. *"Trainerant,"* he named the grassy passageway over which they dragged the boat until they came to a pothole and it led to another pothole, forming a watery trail through the grass. Mullet swarmed at the surface of these watery holes, and tiny shrimp fed in duck-weed around the edges. He lifted cane sticks Knobby thought were growing and revealed the anchor to a steel trap that held a muskrat, pink-white flesh showing through the fur where it had pulled against the trap's teeth. The animal hissed and bared its teeth. Etienne lifted a heavy stick from the pirogue and with one prac-ticed motion crushed the furred skull. By the time he opened the trap, humming blue-green flies covered the animal's wound.

They left the string of small lakes and entered another dark bayou amongst cypresses and mossy oaks, the bottom of the pirogue piled with muskrat, rabbits, and a fox. These traps Etienne had not rebaited, but had collected and added to the pile in the boat. "You look strong, *Negre. Mais,* I hold in my head, me, all the trails and traplines from way up *de arc des* Fausse Riviere, down to L'anse Atchafa-laya, and all the way west to Lac Calcasieu. Next after Calcasieu the Bayou Negre he finds Sabine Pass. I think, me, with these ways I keep in my head and with my pirogue, I bait you to help me."

"What help do you need?"

"Me, I show you. First, we eat, us, yes?"

Etienne poled over to a *roseaux* bush where a dark blue strip of cloth marked a limb. He lifted the thick twine of a trotline and gave an upward tug, nodded, and knelt in the boat, pulling up the line, working the pirogue diagonally across the bayou. Some of the hooks were bare, the bait stolen by something that had dodged the hook. The catch was mostly catfish, eight- to ten-pounders judging by their thunk in the bottom of the pirogue, a couple of perch Etienne seemed to prize, a copper-colored fish he called buffalo fish, and one long sharp-toothed creature Elizabeth thought was an alligator. Etienne said he almost was. He was alligator gar and he grew near as big as a gator. The next to last hook was bare, but when they got to the last hook closest to the bank, the line was jerking hard. Knobby reached for it, thinking this would be the biggest fish of all. Etienne stopped him and slid his pushpole down and lifted the line. A green fish's head was on the hook, but the rest of the fish disappeared into the wide-hinged mouth of a huge gray snake. Impossibly, the snake, four or five inches in diameter, was swallowing the fish that bulged from inside the snake's body at least two inches wider on both sides. Knobby picked up the cane knife and would have chopped the snake in half, but Etienne stopped him again. "Cotton mouth is hungry, too. Perch, he dead already and fill with venom. To kill the snake, it make you feel safer, but me, I feel safer to let him live so I remember how many he is out here with me." He cut up the gar, about three feet long, and used gar meat and muskrat entrails to re-bait all the hooks but the one at which the moccasin still dined.

By the time Etienne poled them down the bayou to his treehouse—a small plank box built high among three enormous cypresses—the fog had burned off and the sun beamed through the dense foliage. A weathered plank shack suddenly appeared between tree trunks, and Etienne tied up the pirogue to a cypress tree. He unloaded his traps and the day's catch, then turned the boat upside down. He took a coiled rope from a hollow tree and with the authority of repetition tossed it up against his shack where two pegs hooked a wide loop and the rope unfurled as a climbing ladder.

The shack was maybe ten feet by ten feet, the board floor covered with deer-skins. Two windows hung with burlap let in air but not insects. Etienne lighted a candle and took two iron pots from a shelf. He put Elizabeth to work chopping cloves of garlic big as Knobby's knuckles, red peppers, and pungent wild onions. The candle threw a nimbus of light around Elizabeth and cast her head's dark shape large on the board wall. The sound of her chopping and the scent of burning wax comforted Knobby with security, a sense of civilization.

Outside, Etienne tossed Knobby a knife and one of the muskrats from his traps. Knobby watched him gut and dress three muskrats in the time it took him to imitate and get one critter cleaned. Knobby held up the pink-white body, mangled by his untrained hands. Etienne laughed. "*Mais*, I don't care, me, no."

Sitting on a short curved bench, Etienne used a heavy knifeblade with no handle to scrape pearlescent flesh from the underside of a pelt. The meat gave up the hide with a wet kissing noise. Up and back Etienne deftly drew the blade—no wasted motion. Finished, he fitted the pelt over a wooden stretcher. He took longer with the fox. When the hides were stretched, he nodded to Knobby to help him gather them up. Knobby followed him to a shed thirty yards away. Knobby's nose told him why the shed was distanced from the house. The small rancid-smelling building was warm, and more hides dangled from its ceiling. Etienne hung the stretchers from bent nails and built up a fire from coals still glowing red in a castiron stove in the room.

"The furs they dry, N*egre*, a month, yes."

Knobby was pleased to show he knew how to gut and skin a catfish. They put the fillets over a fire outside. The two plucked and cleaned ducks Etienne surrounded with wild rice in an iron pot. The pot he buried in coals. He added Elizabeth's pile of chopped garlic, peppers, and onions to a stewpot he'd loaded with chunks of rabbit, muskrat, and venison, and put it to simmer on a small stove inside his house. The fish was ready first, and Elizabeth burned her fingers she was in such a hurry to get the meat to her mouth. Bowls full of the spicy stew followed. When Etienne finally dug the pot out of the coals, the duck flesh had swelled and come off the bones. The tender meat was smoky and sweet, and Knobby sucked the bones and gnawed them to slivers. When they had eaten their fill and more, Etienne poured cups full from a crock of whisky. The master had never allowed his slaves to have strong drink, so Knobby had never tasted spirits. Brown as the bayou water, the whisky was innocent-looking. On his tongue the first sip pricked all the places the garlic, peppers, and onions had missed, and it flamed up behind his face, warming his cheeks and stinging his eyes to tears. The heat spread into his chest and heated his stomach. Elizabeth drank her cup down without coming up for air, no tears in her eyes.

Etienne nodded toward a mattress lying on the floor, gray moss stuffing leaking from a tear in one side. They even had pillows, cotton sacks stuffed with the feathers and down of ducks. Etienne took what looked to Knobby like a long fishnet and strung it across the room from the ceiling beams. When Etienne blew out the candle, the room filled with the sparks of frog peeps flung through the deep silence of swamp as stars are flung through dark and empty heavens. Etienne crawled up into the net and it curved with his weight and hung in the dark cabin like a crescent moon.

Knobby wondered what Etienne had done with his muskets. He wondered how far they were from the nearest soldiers and if those soldiers were Federal or Rebel.

As if the man had heard Knobby's thoughts across the dark space, Etienne spoke, his voice low as if he were giving a benediction. "N*egre*, you can't trick Monsieur Etienne any sooner than you can catch the weasel asleep. You remember the weasel if you think on slaying Etienne while he sleeps."

Darkness surrounded them, cast like a wide black net for as far as Knobby could imagine: the dark of night and tree shadow and water, and that outer dark held the inner dark of snakes and alligators and swamp-men like this Etienne and maybe soldiers and all the ghosts Elizabeth could conjure. Lying down on a soft bed in the center of so much darkness, his hunger sated for the first time in days, the whisky burn made Knobby feel he glowed, gave off light the way Etienne's candle had. Whenever he was close to a white man he felt like running, but where could they run? And why? He didn't feel fully free, but he didn't feel like a slave anymore, either. He wondered if the swamp man held them captive, or, strange as it sounded describing a white man, if he was their friend. The last thoughts in Knobby's head were: *no white person can be trusted. Jesus, all the Bible drawings paint You white, but Grandfather said You're as black as any man who goes to You in prayer.*

Elizabeth's hand shaking his shoulder was warm and damp, and he pretended to be asleep to prolong the feel of her skin on his. He smelled coffee and opened his eyes.

"I woke up by myself, Knobby, no ghost riding me. No one whispered my name, and I wasn't frozen stiff. I feel good again like I thought I might not ever."

"You needed food so your stomach could relax. I'm glad the ghost is gone."

After a breakfast of coffee and figs and the rest of the stew, Etienne made an offer. His traps needed rebuilding. Parts had to be robbed from ruined traps, rust had to be scraped off and oil to be rubbed in, teeth needed sharpening, ropes needed replacing—a week's job, maybe less if they worked hard. With the refurbished traps, Etienne could run a new trapline. There were channels he wanted to follow, trails he wanted to bait farther west, toward the Sabine. If they helped, Etienne would get them closer to Texas.

Etienne Keeps His Word

In Acadian French and broken English, Knobby learned steel spring, trigger pan, jaw post, clamp and catch, wing arm, anchor rope and knot. Elizabeth scraped rust, filed jaws of teeth, rubbed on oil that smelled like Etienne's mosquito salve and repellent. By day, they knew the songs of hammers and files, of close-by larks and ricebirds and of faraway geese, by night, the harsher music of rasps and cold chisels, of close-by frogs and owls, of alligators.

When she wasn't scraping steel Elizabeth was cutting frog legs to fry, boiling crabs Etienne showed her how to season, rinsing blackberries he brought her. Bent over the bow of a trap, Knobby heard Elizabeth and Etienne murmur up in the treehouse, doing cooking chores. Each time the murmuring or the clunk of wooden spoon against crockery stopped, Knobby argued with himself about jealousy.

Etienne served a sweet blackberry wine with their supper. At bedtime, he poured the whisky Knobby had come to look forward to. When all but two traps had been made new, the candle-flame floating on top of whisky in his bedtime cup, Knobby said, "Mr. Etienne, even the good Lord rested after six days."

"You say, you, like priest? Ho. *Mais*, you right, yes. You woman, she sleep?"

Elizabeth sat in her chair, hands folded in her lap, both eyes closed. Knobby carried her from the table and laid her on the mattress. He drank the rest of the whisky in Elizabeth's cup, then lay down beside her.

The rope ladder groaned and trap jaws clanked, clanked again, and Knobby opened his eyes. The burlap window screens were squares of gray morning light. Heat steamed from two cups of coffee on the table beside a plate of cold venison. Elizabeth's sun bonnet lay on the seat of her chair atop a pair of cotton britches and a long-sleeved yoke shirt. Beside the chair, a worn pair of brogans sat, toes curled up stiffly.

"Elizabeth, her, she can fit my clothes I think. But you, Knobby, I don't think so. I sewed you some water shoes, see do they go on your feet." The shoes looked like two square-scaled fish, their soles thick yet pliant. "Alligator skin. Scare off the snakes, no?"

Knobby pulled on one shoe. It was plenty wide, but his toes poked the end.

"*Piquer*." Etienne cut a wide hole in the toe of each shoe. Elizabeth did better, needing only to wear the shoes awhile to stretch them into comfort.

All morning Etienne poled them away from the sun, guiding the pirogue with his trailing foot, his movements easy as the swish of marsh breeze through grass. Elizabeth asked about a bird with wide purple wings and crest-feathers silver in the sun. Etienne said he was *beau*, the night heron the Americains call grosbeak, a blessing of the marsh, a good talisman.

Midday, they passed two alligators sunning on the mud banks and Knobby lifted one foot and shook his new alligator shoe at them. The reptiles did not recognize the former life of the shoe. The gators lay heavy and oblivious as logs.

Late afternoon, Etienne poled them across a lake to Atchafalaya Bay on the Gulf. Elizabeth trailed fingers in water, brought them to her lips. "Salty. Stings."

"The Gulf, her bite, she is a healing sting. The gator, he trudge down here in springtime to soak him, salty water get off him leeches. See, along the edgewater sand crane take him walk."

"The Gulf of Mexico," Knobby said, "The Gulf of Mexico, amen."

The Gulf was wide and smooth, like an empty blue china platter God had set down. They pulled the pirogue onto the marshy beach. Etienne told them to gather wood, then he waded into the ocean. Gray-green clouds billowed. Breezes came off the water, and the waves grew stronger. Knobby and Elizabeth sat by their stack of wood and watched Etienne's dark shape bent against rows of white crests rolling steadily in.

"Looks just like he's out in the field, picking cotton," Elizabeth said.

"Think on wide water. Our forebears caught like animals and shipped across an ocean so wide they couldn't see land on any side—brought from Africa where they lived free," Knobby said.

"I don't know any of my grandfolks. Don't know when they were brought over, don't know where to and don't know where from."

"Grandfather Samuel told me night after night. Had me promise my children would know the slavers who packed him in with others in a ship's hold, no light for days on end, a nightmare of urine and vomit. Took him to the West Indies, swapped him for molasses and tobacco. A West Indies slaver took him on to Virginia. Human beings traded for another man's sweet tooth, his after-supper pipe."

Etienne waved and called. Knobby waded out. Waves pushed him toward land then pulled him toward the open sea. Etienne dragged a big sack. Knobby took one side of the bag and they pulled it to shore. Etienne dumped out a pile of bumpy rocks. He slipped the edge of his knife against one of the rocks he said was an oyster, and it opened pearly white, containing a brown lump Etienne sucked into his mouth. Knobby held a raw oyster in his mouth like something hot. On his tongue it jiggled, firm yet liquid, like a raw egg yolk. He bit down, and warm juice filled his mouth, tasted like the Gulf smelled, salty and grassy. He chewed a satisfying resistance inside the tender bite, as if God had put a bit of gristle there to remind him he'd been cast out of the garden.

Etienne took flint from one of his many pockets and sparked a wad of fine, dry grass into flame. The wood burned quickly down to coals in which they nestled handfuls of unopened oysters. The first pangs of hunger sated by eating them raw, they later sat back and enjoyed coffee and roasted oysters while clouds darkened and moved toward them. The tide was going out. Heat lightning pulsed along the horizon. Closer, a curve of pearly green light glowed over the water and brightened the sky so much Knobby thought he could read if he had a book. Light moved along the shoreline as if the crescent moon had sunk underwater to light up the ocean floor. Etienne smiled. "Glowfishes. Sometime you see dem when the tide she is go out. The old ones call they bright schools Jonah's Lantern, from dat whale where he live, no?" The underwater cloud of fish-light rocked back and forth and drifted away with the tide. The waves beat harder, the grass shushed in the wind, the coals fell into ashes and, then, hissed with the first fat drops of rain.

From beneath the overturned pirogue, Knobby could not see the Gulf for the pour of rain. Etienne lay on his back and snored, one hand holding a tin cup on the sand out beyond the overhang of the boat, rain pinging and filling the cup.

"I don't think I can sleep up under here, Knobby, all close and hidey-hole feeling," Elizabeth said. Knobby drew her against him and hummed, "Jesus, Lover of My Soul," the hymn he had sung in the strange, brief meeting with the farm woman just weeks ago, yet as distant-seeming as childhood. As far away as Grandfather Samuel when he was young and lived a free life on the other side of the ocean. As distant-seeming as the war going on all over the land north of this wide gulf. If he faced Africa, way over the water, he was turning his back on Noble Plantation and on the soldiers shooting at one another.

"Elizabeth," he spoke her name so quietly he wasn't sure if he'd said it out loud or only thought it. The rain had let up some, but it still drummed steadily and resonated inside the hollowed-out cypress. "Sweet dreams, Elizabeth." Her closed eyes didn't flicker, but her lips rested in a small smile, and he was content not to repeat himself.

Saltwater Wedding

Knobby lay on his back, blinked open his eyes. White birds like bits of clouds floated in a blue sky. Seagulls, Etienne had named the white birds. They sent high-pitched cries—cree-cree—across the ocean, just as crows, familiar to Knobby, blessed fields with their caw-caw. Bright white in the wide sky, seagulls seemed prissy, mere decorations hung over the ocean, while black crows were vital, a natural element of fields and forests. *Seagulls and crows*, he thought, *like white people and Negroes.* The blue sky almost made Knobby doubt his memory of the night before, the steady drumbeat of rain against the pirogue they had slept beneath. Where was the boat? Where were Etienne and Elizabeth? Knobby got to his feet, looked all up and down the strip of marsh grass where land became ocean. Three shapes from reclined bodies remained pressed down in the sparse grass, his own the darkest, the dampest of the three.

"Knobby." Elizabeth's voice coming out of the ocean, coming toward him with the waves, tide coming in. "Monsieur Etienne's gone. Come see."

A shallow trench showed where Etienne had dragged the pirogue across the sand and soft grass back to the bay. At the edge of the bay was a dark humped shape—a crouching man? Larger than Etienne, the crouching man held a long-barreled gun, had a head of shaggy red hair. Elizabeth was halfway to the man who did not move. When Knobby ran closer, the crouched man became two canvas bags stacked on top of one another. One of Etienne's two muskets leaned against them, something red-furred on top as if a dog had climbed there and curled up to sleep.

Elizabeth lifted the mound of fur, and it unfurled like a red flag. A vest of fox fur, the fox Etienne had trapped their first day together sewn to others. Knobby backed into the vest, more a sleeveless coat, it hung so long. Down the front, leather loops held buttons that were some animal's claws.

The first canvas pack held a full water bag, strips of dried beef, packages of venison and smoked sausage. In a small pouch were several gold coins and some State of Louisiana scrip. From the bottom pack Knobby took powder and shot for the musket, a flint and stone, a narrow-bladed fillet knife. Two long lengths of twine were wrapped around a short piece of bone, a fish hook tied to each line. An oilskin pouch held the stinking salve for keeping away mosquitoes. The grass- and bloodstained blade of Etienne's cane knife was bright-edged where it had been recently sharpened with a whetstone he had also left. At the bottom, nestled in two clean cotton shirts, was a crock of the dark whisky Etienne had produced each night at his cabin.

"Thank you, Lord, for these Thy gifts," Knobby prayed out loud.

"Thank the little swamp man."

Elizabeth placed the items in a ring around her, knelt in the center, and ran her hand down the heavy musket barrel, passing her fingers over metal as a lover touches flesh. Her voice sang out over the white-capped waves as a crow cries out over white cotton rows. She clapped her hands, slapped the water bag, and sang, "Water to drink," crossed her arms, slapped her shoulders, "meat to eat," she slapped beef strips, then shot and gunpowder, "powder and balls to shoot," slapped her knees, "flint and stone to cook and warm," right hand to left knee, left hand to right shoulder, singing on, "money to spend on what we want." She danced juba, the dance she had learned back on Noble Plantation, where they danced in a wide clapping circle. Elizabeth danced and chanted the names and uses of things they now owned. She sang in juba the way someone learning a new tongue sounds out the names of all she knows. Shaping by naming her world, Elizabeth blessed each thing she touched and made it real.

She finished her incantation and looked long at Knobby. They stared at the wide ocean, then they looked down the strand of sandy soil where waves lapped marsh grass, then they looked back at the bay at willows and cypress. For the first time since Etienne had found them asleep on his trapline, they were alone. When they had run from New Orleans into the swamps, they had been alone as only interlopers can be, aliens in someone else's place. Now, alone again, they felt more in solitude than alone. The gifts left by Etienne were their first shared possessions, and this place, too, they felt belonged to them, for a little while at least. They were not yet safely escaped, not fully free, but they shared a sense of what freedom feels like.

Elizabeth ran into the waves, ran far out. Neck deep in the Gulf, she took off her feedsack dress and tossed it toward shore. Knobby kicked off his alligator hide shoes and ran in after her, the water cold. She said, "I'm rebaptizing myself, making everything clean and new." He leaned against the water's push and pull, his feet unsteady on the bottom. "I'm washing off mud, washing off swamp. Washing off New Orleans, washing off slavery." He thought of all the mud they had yet to walk through, but he laughed just the same. He pulled off the farmer's overalls and the waves carried them after Elizabeth's dress. He dove into a foaming wave and paddled toward Elizabeth, who laughed like a child. "Person needs baptizing again and again, Knobby. Plenty of baptizing to get through this life to the next."

Naked, as they had entered the forest weeks ago, they came out of the waves and stood and let sun and wind dry them, frosting their edges—their brown noses and chins, elbows and knees, forearms and shins—with a glaze of salt. White-capped as the waves breaking against their ankles, they clung to one another and kissed as if for the first time. The sun was warm, but the wind was chill. Elizabeth's breasts were cool, full drinking gourds he pressed his lips into. Back in Mississippi on Noble Plantation slaves had married by jumping over a broomstick. Having no broomstick, they stuck Etienne's cane blade up in the sand and jumped over it, marrying one another before God and His seagulls. They stood side by side, and Elizabeth said words of Scripture she had saved for this moment:

I'm black, but comely, you daughters of Jerusalem,
like the tents of Ke-dar, like the curtains of Solomon.
Don't look on me, because I'm black, because the sun looked on me—

"Amen," Knobby said.

Elizabeth lay on the sand, her damp hair bushy in the salty wind, her body brown as molasses. Knobby lowered himself on top of her and their toes twisted together against the clean grit of sand. And while the sun looked upon them, they joined their bodies and made one living flesh. *Coupling*, Knobby thought, *this is what coupling means*, and he lost himself in giving and taking.

Wholly spent, skin sweat-stuck to skin, they uncorked Etienne's crock and took long, deep draughts of the spirits, their bodies so inflamed they gulped whisky like air.

Knobby and Elizabeth spent eighteen days walking the rest of the way to Texas. They passed through saltwater and fresh, through mud, marsh grass, and pine woods, through daylight, moonlight, and no light. They put on the shoes Etienne had given them and turned inland. They dodged alligator holes and stood frozen when water moccasins swam past. They veered wide of board huts up on stilts like spindly-legged gray waterbirds feeding in shallow water. They lay together in their blankets, and Knobby learned Elizabeth's soft indentations, her bony protrusions.

He counted the pores in her forehead and cheek, the tiny dark hairs that gathered into eyebrows and then grew sparse again. If her eyes and her lips most often took him in, they were not the only parts of her face he celebrated. He ran his finger along the curves of her ear. Sunlight turned her translucent brown flesh as red as a stained-glass angel's heart Knobby had seen in the window of a church in New Orleans, a church bigger than the house at Noble Plantation. He loved Elizabeth's wide nose and long ears, all cartilage—hard like bone and soft like flesh—springy with gristle, alive as a green switch. She flared her nostrils like a spirited filly. And if he loved her long fingers moving over his body, he loved as well her cracked and grass-stained nails, her darkly lined palms pale tan as sand and just as gritty. Her long hair whipped his bare back and stung like a horsetail. Knobby learned Elizabeth's parts, loved them democratically, committed her body to memory. Daylight or dark he knew every surface. *Heavenly Father, Thou hast blessed me.*

For days they watched on the horizon the distant gray shape of what they guessed was a gunboat. Then one morning it was not there anymore.

"I miss the ship," Elizabeth said. "I had made it up to be our guardian angel."

The boat's absence worried them. When night came, Knobby left their flint and stone packed away, and they made a cold camp wrapped up together in Knobby's warm fox fur vest.

Before dawn, Knobby scouted ahead, alone, working his way north to take advantage of the cover of brush and trees. In tree-shadowed forest, he climbed an ancient live oak draped dark with moss and, from his high perch, sighted a clearing and in the clearing a saltworks.

Negroes made small and jerky by Knobby's vantage point fed fires beneath giant castiron pots and fogged the air with medicinal-smelling steam. Saltier than the Gulf, the salt steam stung Knobby's eyes and nose, burned his throat. The early light turned lavender a white-suited, white-bearded white man barking orders at a huge Negro whose bullwhip cracked like a bolt of lightning over the bare backs of Negro men who shoveled salt over the ground to dry in the coming day's sun. Streaks of dawn through the treetops turned the salted earth phosphorescent purple. Men shouted, fires and the big overseer's bullwhip popped, and wagon teams creaked and clanged hauling salt to the terminus of a railroad track at the north end of the clearing. Beside the railbed, crystalline blocks of salt had been stacked into massive columns like the pure white mansion of a white planter's dream. Rays of first sunlight flared gold against the capstones of this heavenly plantation Negro laborers were building but were not allowed to enter. By shouts and the whip they were continually sent back to the fiery cauldrons and the iron shovels of Hell.

Beside Knobby in the tree, Grandfather Samuel read aloud: *And the Lord said, I have surely seen the affliction of my people in Egypt, and I've heard their cry by reason of their taskmasters, for I know their sorrows. And I am come down to deliver them out of the hand of the Egyptians, and to bring them up out of that land unto a good land and a large, unto a land flowing with milk and honey—*

Knobby and Elizabeth made their way south, away from the saltworks, back to the Gulf, where Knobby combined their goods into one pack and floated it on a crude two-log raft. All day they waded and swam the raft against the waves, going miles wide of the saltworks.

All their days of westering, Knobby did not once dare to fire the musket, though he was tempted by flights of geese and other birds he could not name and by an occasional deer. Elizabeth became proficient with the line and hook. They feasted on fish, crabs, and oysters. The dried beef strips lasted the whole trip. In a stand of stunted pines they shared the dregs of the whisky Etienne had left them, recorked the empty crock, and later hurled it into the Gulf like shipwreck survivors tossing out a message in a bottle, only their bottle contained no message. Their prayer was: *Let no one find any record of our passage.*

Above the grass plains between Vermilionville and Niblett's Bluff the sky was low, cloud-weighted, and gray. Cool breezes whispered in Knobby's ear that winter was hurrying after. Elizabeth looked up at the somber sky. She squeezed Knobby's hand. "Husband, back on Noble Plantation the field hands is picking the cotton, their days darker and longer than ours."

Knobby thought of his mama, Hester, whom he knew he would never see again. He could not let his mind or heart rest on that thought. Even leaving slavery for freedom, there were people and places, memories, he wished he could bring with him.

Elizabeth, guessing his thoughts, said, "Your mama and granddaddy both have a little happiness can't no one take away from them now, because they can see you running free."

Border Crossing

The Charon at Sabine Pass wouldn't take Etienne's Louisiana scrip, but he was happy to ferry them across for one of the gold coins. Over the whine of windlass and the creak and moan of block and tackle, the ferryman warned Knobby it was illegal for Negroes to immigrate to Texas and offered plenty of free advice.

"I don't have the scantist idea if you be slave or free. The only colors I care about are gold and silver. But if some other one was to catch you, he'd like as not sell you for a slave unless you have a man to go you a bond before the law."

Knobby was glad he had not mentioned the forged papers of freedom he carried.

"Like as not, you're a slave off the island whose master lit out for the mainland when Commander Renshaw gave everybody time to skedaddle."

Knobby neither affirmed nor denied he was a slave on some mission of his master.

The ferryman squinted up at Knobby. "You ain't dressed fit to be someone's city slave. You're no black jayhawker?" Knobby shook his head. "I figured not. Not with a gal along with you. Any Mexican sees her, he'll carry her off to Mexico with him. I don't know why Mexicans crave darkie gals so. Ain't their own gals dark enough?"

The ferryman was full of talk for such a brief river crossing: A gang of jayhawkers and runaway slaves had been plying the area, foraging and burning, making their own savage war. Federal gunboats had fired on Indianola the day before. The ferryman had heard that after Renshaw's Yankees had captured Galveston they'd also taken Corpus Christi. He opined there were draft dodgers up in the Big Thicket and skirmishers and bandits of every stripe everywhere about. Added to the misery in these parts was the yellow fever that had been raging at Sabine City. He said if Knobby heard a German accent that man was his friend because all Germans were nigger lovers. "But anyone might kill for a musket in a second. You hang on tight to it."

The ferryman wanted to shut down the ferry and drive a wagon up to Shreveport to bring back victuals made scarce by the blockade. He showed them a yellowed Shreveport *Semi-Weekly News* advertising coffee, flour, shoes, cloth, buttons. The paper listed the following prices:

Plain Cotton Dress	$200
Wool Coat and Vest	$ 90
Boot Blacking (per box)	$100
Cotton Figured Shirt	$ 10
Soap (one cake)	$ 6
Whisky (per gallon)	$ 65

Treasury agents in Louisiana were poorly paid. For a fee, the ferryman said, they'd issue a trade permit for anything. There was money to be made. "Ever time I go to shut down the ferry, here comes Lieutenant Dowlin from the Texas Artillery riding in with a patrol from the earthworks yonder, the last bend you can eye upriver—they're proud to call such Fort Griffin." The ferryman spat a wad of something brown into the even browner river, laughed, and shook his big, shaggy head. The lieutenant had threatened to put him in irons and haul him off to a prison camp up near Hempstead. "Lieutenant's got them shiny chicken guts on his sleeve. That little bit of gold braid, an he's bucking to be a hero leading a mob of Irish bastards off the wharves at Galveston. I reckon the lieutenant would make a better fist at preaching than he does at soldiering. Says my ferry's a war necessary, for transport of troops. I ain't seen no troops all summer except them Irish recruits. They kindly overproud of a half a dozen cannons guarding a shifting sandbank."

Galveston Island had surrendered to Federal gunboats just weeks ago in October. After they rode the ferry across Sabine Pass, Knobby and Elizabeth kept along the Gulf, hiding in the mud flats whenever they spotted a horseman. The ferryman's saying freed Negroes could not enter Texas worried Knobby. But here they were, legal or not.

White and pink shells lay partially buried in mud or sand, more shells than they had seen in Louisiana. Elizabeth picked up two large ones. Five spikes ran across each shell. She curled her fingers down into the pearly openings and wore the shells like gloves. Her dark wrists now ended in pink fists with spiked knuckles. Knobby had once had a dream in which a Negro overseer had big fists spiked like these shells. In the dream, the overseer hit Knobby in the face over and over. Knobby woke with cuts around his eyes and over his nose.

Cranes and other waterbirds did a steady business down the shoreline, feeding in the wet sand. Where the ocean ended in marsh grass and stands of pine, herds of small deer bounded past, and, as Knobby and Elizabeth walked by, a cloud of geese rose out of the wet grass and settled again as if someone had fluffed up a bedsheet and let it billow back down.

The afternoon of the fifth day Knobby spotted a herd of horses, and he grinned and motioned for Elizabeth to walk quiet. The horses were spread out grazing. When they got within a few hundred yards of the herd, one of the horses lifted his head and looked at them. He whickered and the other horses gathered close. The herd trotted a couple hundred yards away, and the animals looked back at Knobby and Elizabeth. "Come on," Knobby said, and he and Elizabeth crept after the horses. The herd waited until Knobby and Elizabeth were within a couple hundred yards, then they trotted off again, whinnying and whirling about. For about an hour Knobby and Elizabeth followed the wild horses, then stopped to rest.

"Knobby, look."

There was water on both sides and, far ahead, beyond what looked like low rock walls, was more water. Except for the grass and mud flats behind them, they were surrounded by water.

"We've run way out to the tip of a finger of land. Unless we can find some way to cross the water, we'll have to go back the way we came," Knobby said. Hoofbeats made them both turn, looking for the wild horses. Galloping toward them was not the herd of wild horses but a knot of men on horseback. There was nowhere to run.

The horsemen quickly got close enough for Knobby and Elizabeth to see their dark blue uniforms. A boy with a man's voice asked them to identify themselves. Knobby told the soldiers he and Elizabeth were returning to Galveston from New Orleans. Making up the story as he told it, Knobby said Rebel soldiers had stopped the cars and lined up all the Negroes on the railbed, said they were being taken to Port Neches to help build Fort Grigsby. Knobby said he and Elizabeth got away from the Rebels and were trying to get home.

The boy, a Lieutenant Estes, saluted Knobby and asked all about the Rebs and Fort Grigsby, questions Knobby answered with just enough details to maintain the lieutenant's interest. He said Commander Renshaw might want to question them. The lieutenant did not ask to see any papers. He told them they were at Bolivar Point and took them to a longboat.

The boatman, who also wore a Federal uniform, pointed out Fort Point ahead of them and, just inside the bay, Pelican Spit and, beyond it, Pelican Island. The shore was flat and bare of trees or notable landmarks of any kind except a tall lighthouse barely visible in the distance.

Two Talks: Walking with Crow

Seeks His Totem
(Leveling toward Cold Moon 1858–Big Cold Moon 1858)

Like most whites, I was slow to realize Comanche religion is not just
another version of white religion. As far as I know, the only beliefs we share
are that a great flood once destroyed the earth and that there is an afterlife.
Comanches have no notion of one all-powerful god. Father Sun and Mother
Moon and Mother Earth are too distant and vague to bestow power on
individuals. Comanches seek guardian spirits who reside among them.
A warrior must have a special spirit to guide him. Comanche horses and dogs,
domesticated, have no supernatural powers and must be watched over like
their owners. Braves pray to the deer for quickness, to the bear or skunk for
healing powers, to the eagle for strength—especially in war—and to the wolf
for wisdom and ferocity. The wolf's younger brother, the coyote, is powerful
but dangerously mischievous, as is the cunning but capricious crow.

—from *Gideon Jones' Journal*

Only three moons had come and gone since Small Nose had passed on to the
Good Hunting Land of the Dead, and Two Talks still missed her every sun. He
longed to ride the war trail against the Blue-Bottoms who had killed her, but first he
had to find his *puha*. He was afraid he might look for his sign in the wrong place,
or might incorrectly interpret the vision the spirit world sent. When the time drew
near for Two Talks' vigil, he was visited by Crow in a dream. Crow was known by
all Numunuu as a trickster, powerful but deceitful, and many Numunuu feared
the treachery of the crafty bird. In the dream, Crow told Two Talks to come out of
his warm tipi to ride to Crow's lodge so they might parlay about a great war party
Two Talks was to lead against all Tehanos and Norteamericanos and Blue-Bottom
soldiers.

"Leave camp with Our Father in Heaven riding on your arrow arm, and ride until Our Father sits on your bow arm. Where a river no longer runs, I will question you. If you answer truly, I will guide you to a place Our Father never lights. You must pass a long night doing battle in this dark world. Then I will lead you to shining light, and you will see me as I am." Crow's black eyes and yellow beak were the only moving things among all the mountains in the darkness of the dream. "When my feathers are as white as the hair of the old ones, you will know the other side of Crow, who may become your guiding spirit." Crow nestled his yellow beak beneath his feathers, closed his eyes, and disappeared. Two Talks waked from the dream world as Our Father in Heaven was beginning his journey across the heavens.

Two Talks found Crooked Nose still wrapped in his buffalo robe. Morning Star and Persimmon slept on each side of his father, Persimmon's leg thrown over Crooked Nose's knees so her bare foot came out from beneath the fur and rested on the hump that was Morning Star's shape. Two Talks woke his father and whispered how he'd had a dream vision. Without speaking, Crooked Nose pulled himself from between his sleeping wives.

"Let us confer with Red Dog."

Grandfather Red Dog sipped from a buffalo horn cup in which a sassafras root floated. He offered his son and grandson cups of the root tea. It was not polite to blurt out his business so soon, but Two Talks was with his father and grandfather, and once he got a steaming cup of tea he could wait no longer.

"It is time for me to seek my medicine vision," Two Talks said.

"It is good," Red Dog said. His lips made a wide smile. "My eyes look upon a strong young one who has passed ten and two sticks of winters and who rides as the wind passes. Only your father frees arrows faster and truer." Crooked Nose nodded and Red Dog said, "But my eyes cannot see into your heart, Grandson. Are you sure you are ready for the vigil?"

"Grandfather, truly I am *not* sure, but I feel it is so. This sleep just past, Crow spoke to me in my dream and said it was time for my vigil."

"To acknowledge your uncertainty is the sign of growing wisdom," Red Dog said. He stared into steam rising from the horn cup and slurped tea. Then he looked directly into Two Talks' eyes. "But it is foolhardy to listen to Crow."

"Does Crow not have powerful medicine?"

"There is none stronger, but there is none I trust less," Crooked Nose said. Then he said to Red Dog, "Perhaps I should give the Eagle Dance for Two Talks so he can gain power from the shaman, Ten Buffalo?"

Red Dog's voice sounded far away. "Ten Buffalo has carried the medicine bag well since our band parted ways with his father. But Two Talks has been called by Our Great Father to receive stronger medicine than Ten Buffalo can give."

"My father is still not too old to speak with a warrior's wisdom. I agree, we will not offer the Eagle Dance. But what of the call of Crow in Two Talks' dream?" Crooked Nose asked.

"Of all the spirits, Crow and Coyote have the least compassion," Grandfather said. "But Coyote is a close relative of the Numunuu and favors us. Crow's mighty medicine carries great risk."

"Crow said he would come to me during my vigil to parlay about a war trail I must ride against the Tehanos and the Blue-Bottoms," Two Talks said.

"Such a war chief could take us back to our moons of strong medicine, but, in spite of the sweetness of Crow's words—because he speaks like honey—be cautious," Red Dog said.

"A worthless rock requires only a sparking-flint to kindle light. Crow's call to me may be a trial, a test of my willingness to risk much in order to gain much."

"Your words reveal a decision already made. If you would trade with Crow you need preparation. I will help you, though I am troubled by Crow's visit. We must go to Ten Buffalo so he can open the medicine bag for you. I have made strong medicine in my time, but I grow old. Your father will give you what medicine he can, but you must have fresh, strong medicine if you are going to parlay with such an untrustworthy spirit as Crow," Red Dog said.

They found Ten Buffalo bathing in the creek. He came out of the water naked, muscles across his stomach twisting, his skin darkening as thunderheads twist and darken before a rain. He had two scars, one long and moon-pale down his leg—from a Lipan lance, one jagged oval like a pinecone on his belly—left by a Tehano musket ball. Ten Buffalo was only six winters older than Two Talks, but his body bore the marks of bravery and prestige most men could not claim in a lifetime.

Ten Buffalo squatted by the stream, water dripping off him into the grass, steam rising from him into the cold air. The whole time Two Talks told his dream, Ten Buffalo did not move.

"It's good you came to me. Your old grandfather's medicine has not soured with age as my father's did, but Red Dog is past his time of most strength. Your father is a mighty hunter, but your dream says the Great Spirit may make Crow your guardian. You'll need the power of the medicine bag to undertake a vigil with Crow's spirit mediating."

Two Talks did not like the wounding words Ten Buffalo spoke about Grandfather Red Dog. Now, more than ever, all Numunuu men had to be able to ride the war trail against the Tehanos and the Blue-Bottoms. Grandfather's bones ached as much as those who used to sit in the elders' smoke lodge that was no longer respected, but Grandfather rarely joined any of the old men's societies. He was not ready to change from a warrior to a kindly one, to one who is made the butt of men's jokes and must laugh at himself while women and children laugh at him. Many of the old ones ended their lives themselves, rather than becoming useless and scorned. Two Talks knew his grandfather secretly chewed tree fungus for his toothaches and rubbed buffalo fat on sore muscles. But Two Talks knew Grandfather would gladly aggravate the pains of old age to ride the war trail one last time, no matter how badly he suffered. Grandfather's teeth had grown soft, but the old warrior had not grown soft with them. Most old men were ignored at the council because they spoke against war. Some old ones—like Ten Buffalo's father, Corn Eater—turned bitter and became sorcerers who used their medicine to jealously cast spells against the younger men. Grandfather had remained young and had escaped the contempt heaped on many old ones. Grandfather was the one Two Talks most wanted to help him prepare for his vigil, but he was also glad to have his father's and Ten Buffalo's medicine.

Prepares for the Vision Quest

At a remove from the camp Two Talks constructed a sweat lodge, weaving willow limbs and covering them with wet clay as Ten Buffalo instructed. The hides Ten Buffalo gave Two Talks to stretch over the wood frame were smoke-blackened and smelled of old tales. He built up a hot fire in the center of the small lodge, lugged big rocks in, and put them in the fire. Ten Buffalo, Crooked Nose, and Red Dog entered the lodge and sat with Two Talks around the heated rocks. Naked except for their breechcloths, none wore paint. All decoration was removed from their hair. Two Talks' hair was chopped off straight at shoulder length, not yet long enough to be bunched into queues. Ten Buffalo carried a full skin of water and a pouch from the medicine bag. He dipped a pronghorn's tail into the water bag and slapped the hot rocks with it. Steam rose as if from inside the rocks. Fireglow shone over Grandfather Red Dog's chest, narrow and sunken as a young boy's. His skin bore the tattooed outline of an old battle scar coiled like a twisted rope around one sagging nipple and down to his belly.

Crooked Nose and then Red Dog invoked the spirits to cleanse and purify this boy to prepare him to find his medicine and walk the way of a Numunuu warrior. Then they left the sweat lodge. Alone with Two Talks, Ten Buffalo opened his pouch and withdrew dried grasses and sticks he threw on the fire. They stuck to the white-hot rocks and pungent smoke rose, scenting the steam when Ten Buffalo swatted the rocks with his water-laden pronghorn brush. Ten Buffalo took from his pouch a skunk's tail and passed it over Two Talks' ears and eyes, and down his throat, chest, and belly.

"Mighty healing spirit of Skunk, purifying and restorative power, cure and cleanse this soon-to-be warrior of any unseen sickness. Purify every crevice or hollowed-out place inside his flesh or bones where a bad spirit might hide a sickness or a fear. Smooth any barb or spur in his body a bad spirit might hold onto, and in the grip of any false or mischievous spirit make Two Talks slippery as an eel. Heat his blood so it will melt any cold doubt or dread." Ten Buffalo took the dried head of a coyote, and with his hand inside the fur held the head up like a puppet, its mouth open, fangs bared. "Brother Coyote, close relative of the Numunuu, many winters ago you brought this boy to Our People in your own teeth. Do not desert this your human pup who goes to match wits with the wily unknowable spirit of Crow." Ten Buffalo brought the coyote's face close to Two Talks' face. Firelight gave life to the empty eye sockets, and saliva and blood appeared to glisten on the ivory fangs. Ten Buffalo pressed the fangs around Two Talks' wrist, pressed them into skin where Two Talks' wrist-heart drummed. "Know your pup by your own teeth marks, Coyote, and share your cleverness so he can be equal to Crow's guises."

Two Talks sweated a pool onto the packed earth. Ten Buffalo gave Two Talks willow bark to chew—purgative and laxative, it knotted his stomach until he had to empty his bowels. Last night, he had supped on wild onions, plums, and venison. He would eat no more until his vigil was over. Ten Buffalo gave him a small hide pouch of spicewood to chew, sumac leaves to smoke. This smoke would sharpen his senses and aid him in his search for a true vision.

"Remember, Two Talks," Ten Buffalo said, "you will soon be a warrior, but still no more than a man. Be mindful: the spirits of Mother Earth, of Our Father in Heaven, of Mother Moon and the small fires in the sky, of wind and rain and thunder and lightning, of all the rocks and trees, and of the strong animals, are mightier than man." With those words, Ten Buffalo left Two Talks alone before the coals of the sweat lodge fire.

When Our Father in Heaven lay down behind the western mountains and his fingertips turned the short grass red as the low flames of a fire over all the land, Two Talks emerged from the sweat lodge. His legs trembled from being folded beneath him all day. Now, Our Father in Heaven was going to rest, and the air outside the sweat lodge blew cool. Two Talks' sweat-soaked skin puckered up bumpy as a buzzard's flesh after the feathers are plucked for arrows.

When Two Talks came out of the hot, dark willow hut into the chill of winter sunset, Grandfather Red Dog's dark shape waited. "The night you came forth from Morning Star's womb, Coyote came to Crooked Nose in a strong vision," Red Dog said. "Melon Breasts Woman, who brought you into this life, said she hung your afterbirth on the limb of a hackberry near the birth lodge—another good birth omen. You must not accept ordinary power, for the spirit world knows you speak with the wisdom of one who knows the moment before and the moment after. The spirits will be benevolent."

Two Talks wanted to ask Grandfather in which direction he should ride and how would he know the place where he should make his vigil, but he knew he had to find such answers on his own now.

He was slipping his hide saddle onto the broad back of Black Mountain, the stallion he had won from the Blue-Bottoms in the race at Old Camp Cooper, when Grandfather walked up leading White Rump by his horsehair bridle.

"My old war pony asked if he could carry my grandson on this journey that will last the rest of his life. This horse is an ugly one, but he still runs fast. This may be his last trail before he carries me off to my dying place." Two Talks' chest burned with happiness and with pride. Grandfather gave Black Mountain a pat on the rump. "This big black one is strong, but White Rump knows all the paths in our land."

"*Haa*, White Rump is my friend," Two Talks said. The mustang snorted and nodded his big, bony head up and down, his fixed left eye stared up at the purple twilight sky. Seeking worthy words to leave with his grandfather, Two Talks said, "As Ten Buffalo instructed me, I will be mindful that I am only a man and not as powerful as any spirit."

"Those words do not reflect the thoughts of the grandson of Red Dog. No Numunuu warrior grovels before a man or a spirit. Ten Buffalo sometimes feels a greater weight than the medicine bag holds. It is often so with those who are close to power. They begin to believe in the power instead of themselves. Medicine alone is a flame with no wood to burn. It is the destiny of all spirits to aid the Numunuu. Our Father in Heaven warms us because it pleases Him to do so. A bear or a wolf or a beaver or an eagle or the thunder or a tree or a rock shares strength because it pleases it to do so, as it pleased Red Dog to name his grandson and teach him how to ride the Numunuu trails. The benevolence of the spirit world is as the benevolence of the human world—that is to say, it is a selfish benevolence because of the pleasure in watching a flame one sparks burn hot. As you seek the one who will empower you, respect the spirits you encounter but do not fear them, not even Crow. Your gift from birth has been the gift of seeing twice with one look. Your thoughts and your heart can know the two truths of any one thing. Such knowing is a kind of shape-changing. I think Crow sought you because you are the only one who can give flesh to the truth of his spirit. If anyone can follow Crow without being lost in his feathers—recall how they change in the sun, now black, now blue, now green, now black again—my grandson can."

"Thank you, Grandfather. Your words are as an echo. They give me back something so familiar I might have spoken it myself long ago, before memory, and now it returns to me on the air. I will respect any spirit if it touches me, but I will fear nothing."

Red Dog helped his grandson paint his face and gave him precious paints to take with him.

"My grandson, these are your warpaints now. Take the ocher, white, yellow, and blue to use them freely. The vermillion is as hard to find as a red bird among the brown. I gave to Comanchero traders at the Yellow House trading place many furs for the red paint."

"Soon, I will be ready to wear black, Grandfather."

"Perhaps I will paint my face black for the warpath one more time and ride with my warrior grandson. I am still strong enough to wear the color of death." Red Dog nodded at the marks he had made over his grandson's nose and across his cheeks. "After you have your vision, you will have your own paint scheme. You will paint up for the return ride to our camp to display your joy and your strength."

Wearing only breechclout, leggings, and moccasins, carrying no weapon but his small-bladed hunting knife, taking with him no food, Two Talks mounted the scrawny little horse. Besides the knife, all he carried were the small bags of colored paints from Grandfather, a buffalo robe, a bone pipe in the pouch of spicewood and sumac leaves Ten Buffalo had given him to smoke, and flint and stone to strike fire for his pipe. Even his water bag was empty. He would be gone at least four days and four nights. He would have to find water for himself and for White Rump. He breathed deeply. *Today, then. Perhaps it is best the day has chosen me instead of the other way around.*

Grandfather Red Dog held his fist against his jaw where his teeth hurt most of the time and he walked through the crunching winter grass with a hitch, as a lame horse lopes, the age in his bones drawing him toward the cold earth. The old man's bones hurt less in green-grass times. Two Talks pictured his grandfather's grin when he told the other men in the camp, "Your Numunuu brother, Two Talks, goes now to talk with the spirits that they may show him where to find his *puha*. Soon, we will have a new warrior-hunter in our band."

Two Talks gave White Rump his head, and the mustang found an easy gait and carried them through the darkness. The old horse headed south, in the direction of Arrowhead River, near whose banks Two Talks had been birthed when his family still called themselves members of the Honey Eaters band and rode the southern reaches of Comanche land. They would not ride all the way to Arrowhead River, as it was many suns away, but Two Talks was glad to be moving back toward his beginnings. A sky spirit had struck a fire to warm the high heavens and a big log in the fire had shifted, flinging fire sparks into the darkness above. One spark was trailed by a streak as red and furry as a fox's tail. Surely this was a strong sign. Only the sound of White Rump's hooves in the grass—a regular whispered drumbeat—interrupted the silence of the world.

A Taivo Story-Picture

By the time Mother Moon climbed completely above the western mountains, White Rump was swimming Two Talks across the Blue Water River the *taivos* call the Brazos. Two Talks filled his water bag. A buck drinking at the river lifted his head into the light of Mother Moon, and his antlers looked to be made of the silver the *taivos* prize next to gold. The buck stared long at Two Talks, but did not bolt. The light of Mother Moon shone on water dripping silver from the buck's chin, giving him the beard of a mountain goat. Hungry, Two Talks saw himself killing and roasting the deer. Then a brown she-bear lunged out of the shadows and reared up on her hind legs. She stood as tall and dark as a drunk, unpredictable Karankawa who eats his enemy. Was the buck with silver antlers a sign? Did the she-bear rear up to speak to Two Talks? A deer sign was not as strong as a bear sign. One whose guardian spirit was a buck might be fleet of foot but easily spooked. A bear sign would be strong but difficult to keep because bears are easily offended. Were the spirits telling him to take the bear for his totem? He remembered Grandfather's advice, *You must not accept ordinary power*, and he sat his horse and smoked his bone pipe until the buck leapt into the woods with a flick of his white tail and the bear dropped to all fours and lumbered into the dark.

Two Talks and White Rump were still racing south when Our Father in Heaven got up in the east and cast his light on the low wind-bent shapes of oak trees, their twisted arms wearing dark winter leaves. Closer to the earth grew the sharp blades of *mumutsi* the *taivos* call Spanish bayonet and short grass that bristles like fur over the dry skin of sand that rides the eternal plains wind stinging the eyes and noses of the Numunuu, causing grinding noises between their teeth. On the western horizon, stars outlined a prickly pear cactus, but when White Rump brought Two Talks close they were not stars but sun-sparked thorns, spikes holding the light of Father Sun. All around him: light-tipped brightness, scents of sand and sage and sweat, shapes of grass and cactus and oak trees. All around him: homeland of Our People. But beyond the windspread shape of oaks rose an unfamiliar shape, a shape not with the earth and wind as one thing, a shape Two Talks recognized as a *taivo* lodge made from lying down trees on top of one another to make a closed pen. No smoke rose from the lodge, no horses nor cattle nor sheep nor chickens moved outside the lodge. No dogs howled. Two Talks fitted an arrow to his bowstring. He walked White Rump close. Flat boards were put over the window openings and over the closed door.

"Yee, yee, yee," he cried. He kneed White Rump, and the horse loped around the cabin. "Yee, yee, yee," he cried again. No *taivo* shrieked or fired a gun. Two Talks rode up close, coiled the end of White Rump's rawhide neck loop around a board fixed across the door, and backed the horse. Wood creaked and the board pulled free. He got off the horse, leaned against the door until it scraped inward, and stepped into the *taivo* lodge.

Opening the door stirred dust in the slanting light. Bits of sand rode a breeze into the cabin and sparked in the sun like stars at night. His nose brought him the bad odor of all whites: human and animal droppings mixed with the dead fish and urine odor of genitals and the sour smells of spoiled milk and rancid meat-fats. In the low-ceilinged lodge dimly lit by the bright shape of the doorway he saw the raised frame lashed over with rope—like a drying rack for jerked buffalo meat—on which the *taivo* spread their blankets to sleep. Another raised frame was planked over. At Old Camp Cooper, Two Talks had seen *taivo* women setting out their strange food on such raised planks. Two of the *taivo* sitting frames stood alone by the planked-over frame. On the earth before the *taivos*' little lodge-for-fire built of stacked up rocks was a big *taivo* black metal pot. There was a big see-through-it pottery of the sour cucumbers the *taivo* eat, and there was a big rope-bag of their white cornmeal Two Talks reached his hand into. The white cornmeal had short brown worms in it, but it was cool and soft, soft as Morning Star's best tanned deerskin. Two Talks smoothed the soft meal over his arm, dusting his skin moon-white. Maybe the cornmeal would be good for warpaint. On the packed earth lay one of the *taivos'* open hide pouches fat with the squares of skin whites call paper—a sleeping place for *taivo* writing without story-pictures. The writing looked like dead ants scattered on the thin white skins. Two Talks did not know how to make the marks talk, but he knew the white skins could be used to roll up tobacco in for smoking without a pipe. The cornmeal had turned into gray mud on his sweaty arm, so he scraped it off and left the heavy bag on the lodge floor. The *taivo* stink was making his head hurt. How did they sleep penned in by the hard walls of tree trunks smeared with mud? Nothing was worth taking from this place except the pouch of word skins to use for rolling tobacco.

Just as he was leaving the cabin, Two Talks spotted a story-picture fastened to the wall above the sleeping frame. He pulled the corners loose where the story-picture was stuck with iron thorns into a layer of mud between two logs and carried the big paper outside, where he could see it better in the sunlight and where he could breathe without tasting the foul stink.

Two Talks stared at the story-picture and wondered if it belonged to the *taivos* or if they had taken it from Indians. It was much like the story-pictures Gray Robe used to make in the Honey Eaters band, but Gray Robe marked his likenesses on the smooth shoulder blade of a cow. This drawing showed a warrior with long dark hair and wearing only his breechclout. Men from some band who all wore long, loose robes were torturing the warrior. They had him tied to a timber as high as a tipi pole, his arms stretched on a cross-timber, and someone had thrust his lance into the warrior's side. The wounded warrior had a nose the shape of an axe-blade. His skin was dark brown, but he had *taivo* face fur. He must be in a warrior society like one of the secret societies of the Rope Heads, the Kiowa warriors who don't pluck their face hairs. Why would *taivo* have on the wall of their lodge a picture-story of a bearded Numunuu warrior? Was it medicine to protect them? He wrapped the picture-story around his right shin over his deerhide legging and tied three rawhide strips around to hold it in place. Perhaps the holder of the medicine bag, Ten Buffalo, could explain why a warrior's image with face fur waited for Two Talks in a deserted lodge of the whites.

Listens to Crow

Two Talks' moccasins were still damp from crossing Blue Water River when cold winds came leading gray-green clouds, darkening the sky. This was the first strong wind since brown grass days. By nightfall this wind's icy breath would freeze the land. The spirits were sending this cold wind as a sign. Two Talks whispered into White Rump's upraised purple ear. The horse stopped still. Nearby, Coyote called—unusual in the middle of the day, but this was no ordinary day.

Two Talks slid down and spoke to the cloud-darkened sky, "Coyote, my ears are open to your voice."

Coyote howled again and, leading White Rump, Two Talks followed the sound down a narrow rocky draw. He lost all sense of time. He felt shaky with hunger, and when he flushed a covey of quail the thought of eating the birds entered his head, but he would have to be near death before he would eat a bird or a fish. Such food made you as nervous-acting as the quail or perch you ate. Eventually, the escarpment he traversed brought him to a rough chaparral of mesquite trees, prickly pear, and greasewood. He picked his way up a barren limestone ledge and found a dry creekbed where he rested and listened again for the voice of Coyote. He looked up as if waking from a dream. Mother Moon hung from the highest limb of a cottonwood tree. When had Our Father in Heaven gone to bed? Had Two Talks slept? He listened a long while for Coyote's yowl, but Coyote was no longer speaking. If one is to hear the voice of the great spirits one must stay alert. Two Talks sat in the cracked dirt of the creekbed, where water had not run since last spring's rains. He remembered Crow's instructions: *Where a river no longer runs, I will question you.* He took out his hunting knife and made a cut across the fingers of one hand. The sting should help him stay alert, but he felt almost asleep, his head light and his eyelids heavy.

Two Talks sat on the highest limb in the cottonwood tree, the same limb from which Mother Moon hung like a big white fruit. A limb smaller than a child's finger held Mother Moon and Two Talks, yet the limb did not break, and neither did it bow down. He hunkered there, his toes gripping bark, his knees squeezed against his chest, his arms around his knees on which his chin rested. He looked down where he lay sleeping on his back. He saw himself wake and open his eyes, and then he went blind and was no longer high in the cottonwood tree but lay flat on the cold ground. His eyes were open wide but he saw only blackness.

"Caw," Crow said. Then in a voice as hoarse and creaky as his call—caw, the sound stretched into Numunuu words—Crow spoke to him: "I have thrown off my warm robe and opened the flap of my tipi, left my young and comely wives who had just brought me sweet corn to eat, and flown through the cold and dark to bring my good friend a story."

"Of all spirits, you are the most deceitful. I will not hear your story."

"I came to you while you slept and let you share sight with me from high in the cottonwood tree so you would know I see truly. Now we are in your dream as deep as death. Unless you listen, you will never wake. Women who love you will slash their flesh and their wails will pierce your dreams for all sleeps to come. The hearts of your father and grandfather will be heavy for countless moons. They will bury you high in the rocks and you will dream on even as worms inhabit your body and buzzards tear your flesh. And I will pull off your scalp to make you a hairless one so you won't be allowed into the Happy Hunting Land. Denied entry to the afterlife, your spirit will wander forever with the Little Men in your waking dream."

"Speak, then, Crow. I will listen, but only so you will release me."

"You have heard it said I am a flying sorcerer, but I say to you those were words for cowards. Only the Numunuu are strong enough for Crow's medicine, and from all the brave Numunuu I have chosen you to receive my power. Do you know the source of my medicine?"

"No more than I know why Our Father in Heaven has a greater light than Mother Moon, why he casts more warmth than do the small fires of the night sky."

"Crow is the only spirit who moves freely from this world into the world hereafter and back again. I carry the wisdom of the world hereafter, the knowledge of things never seen or known in this world. In this world I am called malevolent, but in the afterworld where brave ones go I am known as the most benevolent of all spirits."

"No one has ever returned from the perfect valley to this world of the life-before."

"If no one has ever returned from the other world, how would the Numunuu know about the other world? How do all Numunuu, no matter where they roam, know of the Good Hunting Land? Because the first Crow, grandfather of grandfather of grandfather Crow, flew back from the other world to this world many many winters ago to visit the dreams of the first Numunuu so they would know and tell their children, who would tell their children in turn, of the world after this world."

Two Talks was a captive in his dream, so he could not but listen.

"When Our People's enemies, the Lipan, whom the *taivos* call Apaches, tried to live where the Numunuu followed the buffalo, Our People rode the war trail against them. Numunuu warriors found the Lipan camps and took their horses, took the useful women and children, killed and scalped the men, scalped the Lipans to keep them out of the afterworld. I can tell you, my friend, I have seen few Lipan warriors in the afterworld, and those I have seen there bear the mutilations of Numunuu courage. In the afterworld there are many buffalo and there are mostly only Numunuu to hunt them. I have not seen a single Tehano in the other world."

"If Tehanos ride in the afterworld, it is not the Good Hunting Land." In the total darkness, Crow's yellow beak curled open in a slight but satisfied-looking smile. When the yellow curve disappeared, Two Talks knew Crow had tucked his beak back under his wing of night darkness. The dark that filled Two Talks' sight was Crow's feathers.

"I just flew from the Good Hunting Land. My memory is strong. There is no longer room in this world for the Numunuu and all the other tribes crowding in: the Tehanos, the Norteamericanos, even the Rope Heads the *taivos* call Kiowa, and who, while not Numunuu, have long been tolerated by Our People—even they use up Numunuu space and eat Numunuu buffalo."

"Though you are Crow, all your words, so far, are true words."

"The *taivo* and the Tehano warriors are not as strong as the Numunuu, but they are as many as the buffalo who darkened the grass in the old time. The *taivo* lodges are as full with children as a Numunuu warrior's quiver is full of arrows when he departs on a war trail. For each *taivo* warrior you kill, many others come to take his place."

"Then we must make more arrows, Crow. What else is there for the Numunuu to do?"

"I have flown all the way from the other world to see if Two Talks is the Numunuu for whom his dead friends wait—one of great *puha*, a great warrior to lead the Numunuu on their last war trail."

"But I have not yet ridden on the hunt or the war trail."

"You are entering a time of purification. You must perfect yourself in the skills of tracking and killing. You must *become* the warrior for whom the Numunuu wait. After you have come into your full strength, when the time is right, you must find all the Numunuu lodges and speak to them of Crow's vision. Tell all the bands they have wandered from the Numunuu road. Tell them Crow wants them to enter a time of purification so they will be ready when you bind them together with the powerful thongs of the spirit world."

"Who am I, Crow, to bind together all bands of Numunuu?"

"Who are you to question Crow, who has chosen you? Hear Crow's words."

"I hear you, Crow, but what will make all the Numunuu hear me?"

"I will put my words on your tongue. I will give you the breath to make the dead walk upright again. You will gather all the Numunuu into one great lodge

and tell all the People to dance—as the Kiowas and the Dakotas and the Cheyenne do—the sacred sun dance. After purification and preparation, you and your
men—the last Numunuu war party in this world—must kill as many of those
who are not Numunuu as you can and then you and your men must take all
your best horses, take your women and children and gather them into a great
new Numunuu camp. This entire camp must take down its tipis, load up its travois—no man, woman, or child, no dog, horse, or buffalo, no arrow, cradle board,
shirt, or cooking pot, no Numunuu thing may be left behind. I will show you
where the hidden trail passes into the other world, the place the spirits of the brave
find to enter the Good Hunting Land. You must guide this last Numunuu band
to the secret place. You must stay at the entrance way until every Numunuu has
left this ruined world. This is my great gift: this last band of the Numunuu will not
have to die. The People still living in this last time will pass directly to the Good
Hunting Valley. Of the Numunuu, only you and your shadow will remain in this
world. With strength I will give you, you will push a mountain onto the trail and
seal up forever the way into the hereafter world, so none who are not-Numunuu
can ever follow."

"And what of me, left alone in a world all not-Numunuu?"

"Yours will be the glory of the last Numunuu to die a warrior's death. When
your spirit enters the afterworld, all of the People will greet you. If the *taivo* find
the opening, they will make an endless line into the other world. They will make
it their world, just as they have made this world theirs, and then the Numunuu in
the afterworld will be forced onto the white man's road and into his pens with his
cattle and hogs for time without end."

"How can I be sure there is no trick hidden in your story, Crow?" The sound
of Two Talks' own voice woke him. Small clouds of his question drifted on the
cold air.

In the dry dust of the riverbed his outlined shape lay, and like a tiny lance in
his chest, one downy green-blue-black feather was stuck. Beneath his breechclout,
girded to his thigh, was a small yellow-and-blue beaded pouch to carry his magic
sign. In this pouch Two Talks secreted away the feather Crow had left behind—a
pledge of strong medicine.

Wrestles His Shadow

A vigil seeking *puha* lasts four days, one for each of the directions of the earth.
Crow had come to Two Talks on the first day of his solitude. In the dry riverbed

he chewed the stiff, cold sumac leaves from Ten Buffalo, and bitterness filled his mouth. He gave most of the water in his bag to White Rump, saving a swallow for himself.

The creekbed narrowed, and the way grew steep. Wild onions scented the air, mixing with something rank and raw. A huge blue rock rested in the creekbed. Up close, the rock was not a rock but the bloated body of a Blue-Bottom soldier who had yellow hair. With one stroke, Two Talks cut the scalp lock. His stomach knotted, then he was on his knees spewing forth the sumac leaves and whatever else remained in him from the day before. In his hand small white worms crawled the scalp. The soldier's body was swollen and crawled with flies. Two Talks threw down the scalp and, pulling the horse behind, he ran. He searched the shadows for anyone who might have seen him, Two Talks, a Numunuu warrior, scalping a dead Blue-Bottom and running from maggots he would eat if he were hungry enough.

Voices whispered all around, as if the grass and trees were telling secrets. Whispers stung Two Talks' bare shoulders and back. Sleet was coming down faster and faster. In the fading light he hurried toward a shadowed overhang in the cliffside, a space high enough to get White Rump in out of the sleet, the entrance to a cave. He would rest only a moment. But he must have slept, because he was awakened by a warrior who looked like himself—the warrior with face fur from the picture-story—and the warrior attacked him without a word. They rolled in the dirt, and sharp rocks pressed Two Talks' back. With fists of stone the warrior hit Two Talks. "Are you Numunuu?" Two Talks asked. The warrior said, "I am Shadow." When Two Talks woke, he was tired and sore, and his leg was wounded by the shadow warrior.

In the gray light of the cave's entrance White Rump stood stamping his hooves. Two Talks felt his way deeper into the cave. The opening narrowed, and he crawled on hands and knees until the passageway ended at a rock wall. He felt above him where a narrow space rose high. He craned his neck up toward a small circle of light, like an eye far above him. The vertical opening was not much bigger around than Two Talks' body, the edges rough enough to climb. It was like being inside one of the tall smoke passages the *taivos* build on top of their rock lodges-for-fire. Numunuu warriors often climbed onto the roofs of *taivo* lodges and down their smoke paths to get inside while the whites slept at night.

As he climbed the narrow opening, the bright eye above grew larger. He stopped to rest, pressing himself against the rock, sweat stinging his eyes. He felt as though he climbed for many days until he reached his hand up out of the earth into cold. Was he about to enter the afterworld, the Good Hunting Land? How could it be so cold? He pulled himself up through the hole and stood in a world all cold brightness. His moccasins rested on ice crusted over snow. The air was snowflakes drifting, falling like puffs of smoke-talk words.

Two Talks looked up to the white needles of a pine tree where a white bird perched. "My true friend," said the bird in the voice of Crow. "You have fought with your shadow all night, and he did not prevail against you, neither you against him."

"In the cave I dreamt such a struggle with one who looked as I look."

"If you can fight yourself to a standstill, you are ready to be a mighty Numunuu warrior, ready to take Crow as your guiding spirit and totem."

"You sound like Crow. Are you covered with snow to make your blackness white?"

Crow's yellow beak curved in a smile. He spread white wings and dropped with the flakes of snow to a limb at eye level with Two Talks. "Of all Numunuu, you alone have seen Crow like this. This is my other way of being." Crow beat his wings and ruffled white feathers from his neck to his tail. No snow flew to reveal black feathers. "When next your shadow comes to you, you must begin to gather your war party from many bands and tribes." Then the white Crow took flight, merging with the flying snow.

Two Talks walked to the edge of this white world. He was high above a valley crossed by an ice-glazed creek. He walked around the edge seeking a way down, but the only way back was the way he had come. He swung his feet back into the dark hole, and a small white feather floated up from the top of one moccasin. Two Talks rubbed the feather to get the snow off, but it was white through and through. He put it in his medicine pouch with the black feather and crawled back down into the earth.

White Rump had gone from the outer cave to graze on short winter grass glazed with ice. The sleet had let up, and toward the mountains the sun was bright behind the clouds. Though he had neither eaten nor rested, Two Talks felt strong. He leapt onto the old war pony's back and rode after the brightness.

Killing the Bull Buffalo

They have no set mealtimes but eat whenever they are hungry. When meat is plentiful they gorge themselves, likely accounting for the paunches so many develop. When a buffalo is butchered, women and children beg for raw innards, relishing guts and brains and guzzling hot blood while smoke rises off it. Buffalo meat is either speared on long sticks stuck up over a fire or boiled in castiron pots. Having noted how Comanches fail to wash their cookware, I ate only the roasted meat, charred outside yet bloody within. Compared to beef, buffalo is leaner and tougher and has a sweet and somewhat nutty flavor.

—from *Gideon Jones' Journal*

Two Talks had found his *puha*. Crow, powerful and wily, was to be Two Talks' guiding spirit, his totem. He felt as if he carried a huge bees' nest—inside was the most and the sweetest honey but he had to be careful not to be stung. He nudged White Rump. The old mustang stretched out, reaching his muzzle into the sun, and at once they were galloping, the grass all brown blur beneath. This was part of being Crow, this flying low, Two Talks knew. Like Crow gliding first one direction and then another down the brown rockface of a canyon or over tall grass jeweled with dark seeds, Two Talks leaned left and then right, flying wherever he wanted. Horse riding, Crow gliding, the same. The back of his breechclout and the back of his hair trailed behind him, wind-lifted, weightless, the feeling Crow knew as tail feathers rising on warm currents of air.

"*Yie, yee, yie—aaiiieeee.*" Two Talks let loose a warrior's cry. All around him the wind parted the grass, lifted dirt into red clouds. Into the wind he spoke: "Out of my way grass and earth, out of my way grasshoppers and grubs, out of my way jackrabbits and prairie dogs and rattlers, out of my way deer and buffalo, out of my way Lipans, and *taivos*, and Tehanos–out of my way all creatures so unlucky to be other than Numunuu." His chest beat like a ceremonial drum warning the world a Comanche war party was being born, set free over the land as Crow flies free and powerful. When he was ready, after he had prepared himself, Two Talks, Numunuu warrior under the sign of Crow, would lead the mightiest war party ever. *Out of my way all you others.* White Rump loped through the grass that whispered loud at their passing, spreading word to all the grasses ahead: "A Numunuu warrior and his fast pony are coming." Our Father in Heaven was close to the tops of the mountains when a dark shape crossed the sky—Crow leading, showing Two Talks the path to take. Crow turned, flew a circle far ahead. Two Talks pulled up, and White Rump stood stock-still. Two Talks put his palm on the side of the horse's neck. Beneath where the crow circled, a single buffalo rose from the grass like a dark boulder. This was during Big Cold Moon, long after the dark-fur-time when the buffaloes had put on their winter fat and fur, yet there the beast was, alone in all this grass. Crow was affirming Two Talks' *puha*. He wished he had his bow and arrows, or, even better, a long lance, so he might kill the buffalo in the more difficult and courageous way. If there were trees near, he could find a straight limb to lash his short knife to. But he saw no dark shape of tree. He saw no shapes but the brown hump he knew was buffalo and the pointed mountains, many sleeps' ride away, where Our Father in Heaven sat waiting to see how the Numunuu hunter with no bow and arrows and no lance would kill this buffalo.

"You," Two Talks said to the sun, "stay right where you are. Don't go to sleep as early as you usually do. Stay to light the way of this new Numunuu warrior." He reached behind his back and touched his sheathed knife. "Open your eyes, blade, to see the space between bone. Open your nose to smell hot blood. Open your ears to hear the drumbeat of heart. Open your mouth to bite deep. You, Crow," he said, "fly away now. I do not need any help to kill this buffalo. White Rump, ride close."

He didn't have to press his knees to goad White Rump. Once more, they were flying low. When the bull with wide horns saw them coming he leaned away so sharply Two Talks was afraid the beast might fall down. But the buffalo did not fall. For so large a creature, heavy as a boulder, the buffalo was quick. He turned as suddenly as a wild pony and ran as fast as a jackrabbit. Even high on White Rump's back, Two Talks felt the thunder of the bull's hooves. White Rump kept about two horse lengths from the buffalo—far enough that if the bull turned to butt or gore the horse would have enough space to whirl out of reach. The buffalo huffed and snorted. His thundering hooves stirred a dust cloud. White Rump ran the bull a long distance. Eventually, they approached a mud wallow where a frozen waterhole reflected silver and purple in the late afternoon light.

"Let's turn him."

White Rump galloped closer and the buffalo veered away. The mustang turned and turned, flying a circle as Crow had done. Two Talks leaned in, turning the circle tighter and tighter. The bull's breath exploded—great wheezes and snorts—and his eyes widened and rolled back until Two Talks thought he might see into the animal's skull. The buffalo kept trying to run straight, but White Rump was always ahead of him. Closer and closer they sped as the circle tightened. The buffalo slowed to a trot and raised his head, tossing his horns in Two Talks' direction. Long strands of the beast's spittle shone in the sun as ropes of silver he slung into the grass. Two Talks said, "*Hakahpu* buffalo? *Ke? Haa.*" White Rump ran at the buffalo only to jump away at the last moment when the bull tried to gore the horse. Four times the buffalo made a long run, and each time the horse outran him. Again and again Two Talks herded the bull into a running circle. He wondered if the buffalo would still run past the sun's setting and its rising again. On the racing horse's back, leaning toward the buffalo, Two Talks felt as if he were a cloud between lightning and thunder.

The buffalo stumbled, and Two Talks urged White Rump close, but the buffalo got his feet under him quickly. Two Talks held the neck loop and pulled his far leg over the racing mustang to ride with both feet toeing the single stirrup on the side of the thundering buffalo. The next time buffalo stumbled, the wily White Rump angled up behind him so close one of the buffalo's rear hooves struck the horse in the shoulder, just missing Two Talks' knee. Buffalo hoof against horseflesh, skin slapped, hoof sparking bone—snap: Two Talks sprang light and quick, as Crow from a breaking twig leaps to a lower limb. The buffalo almost ran out from under him. He landed on the buffalo's rump and grabbed with both hands thick fistfuls of fur. Tall grass whipped against his legs with the noise of a knifeblade drawn fast back and forth against a sharpening stone. Grassblades cut his knees and thighs above his leggings. His legs were too short to fully straddle the buffalo. He kicked off one moccasin to hold fur with his toes, but the other moccasin was too tight to shed. For two long gulps of air he hung on, storing up strength. White Rump continued to run beside the buffalo, forcing him to keep running a circle. There could be no pony with a stronger heart than this one. The buffalo lunged from side to side and shook himself, trying to get the weight off his back. He jerked back his head and one horn caught Two Talks under his ear. The horn point rent flesh down his jaw, ripped a seam down his neck and bumped quickly over his ribs to his stomach before he could push himself away. Blood ran down his side, onto his thigh, and onto the buffalo's back. Warm blood soaked the fur slippery between his fingers. With his left hand he grabbed for the horn and missed, almost falling into the rushing-by loud-clattering grass. He grabbed for the horn again and caught hold. Hard and smooth as an icicle, the horn was warm in his grip. The bull jerked his head down, and the horn Two Talks held tight pulled his whole body forward on the animal's back. His toes slipped where his own blood still flowed. Holding the horn with his left hand, he reached back with his right for the knife. The buffalo lurched then burst with speed, and Two Talks' body rose, strung out above the buffalo's back like a streamer decorating the head of a horse racing into a battle.

His knife's blade was no longer than his foot. He hoped it would be long enough to stab through fur and fat. He brought his arm down hard, aiming for the space behind the short rib where a hunter's arrow, if shot true, could find a path all the way through, wounding the buffalo mortally. His first thrust hit bone and jarred him from his hand up his arm to his shoulder and into his jaw. He almost dropped the knife. He stabbed again and the knife sank deep, but the animal beneath him did not slow. He twisted the blade and pushed so hard the handle and half of his hand sank into buffalo flesh. He stabbed and stabbed, cutting away a flap of fur so he could plunge the knife deeper beneath the hide. Blood spurted, a hot and hard spray stinging his fist. He rotated the blade and pressed it deeper against the hot force of blood. His fist was fully inside the buffalo, and blood painted his arm to his elbow. His hand and arm followed the knife's blade, tunneling through flesh and blood so deep he thought the point must come out the other side. White Rump rushed past, and Two Talks realized the buffalo had slowed down.

Brown grass they careened through was streaked with blood, Numunuu blood and buffalo blood. "Thus it has always been, thus it should always be, Buffalo, our blood mixing on the plains," Two Talks said. The buffalo turned his head, as if to better hear the voice on his back. Grass lunged up, the bull toppling forward on his knees and chest. Streaks of light bloodied the sky, and Two Talks looked up to see Our Father in Heaven slip behind the arrowhead peak of a distant mountain. "Our Father in Heaven delayed his rest to watch this Numunuu hunter make his kill." He lay a long while atop the blood-soaked fur, the bull beneath him twitching and jerking in his death dance. When the buffalo lay still, Two Talks rose and almost fell, his head was so high above him, so weightless. His body burned from neck to belly where the point of the horn had ripped. His arms and legs ached. Grassblades stung him where he stood. His face, chest, both hands, and one arm and foot were red with blood and bits of buffalo gore. He was almost fully a man. He had found his *puha*, and now he was blooded in the hunt. All that remained was to be blooded in war. As many ways as he hurt, Two Talks had never felt better. His chest filled with heat, tightened with love and admiration for the buffalo who had died with so much strength and courage. He put his sore arms around White Rump's neck, leaving red blotches of blood on the white fur. He inspected the pony's shoulder where the buffalo had kicked him. The skin was cut and the flesh bruised, but bone under Two Talks' fingers felt undamaged. He would return to the mud wallow and make a paste for the horse's wound. He gave White Rump all the water left in the bag. Weary as he was, he worked happily under the darkening twilight sky. He cut open the bull's thick fur robe. Morning Star or Persimmon would tan this hide for him and its wide shape of blood would be a good memory. Using both the handle and the blade of the knife, Two Talks hacked at the buffalo's skull and reached in for the raw brains, rewarding himself with delicacies he had earned. After eating the brains, gray and softly wrinkled, he pried the skinned carcass open and located the liver. He cut free a purple strip of the smoking organ and sucked it into his mouth. The warm meat was tender, streaked with the salty juices of the gall bladder. Morning Star had always celebrated a good hunt by bringing him warm salt-tasting liver and links of chewy gut to strip between his teeth.

While he butchered the buffalo, Two Talks frequently looked up at White Rump's split red ear. It would twitch at the first sign of danger. When he'd eaten his fill of the tastiest organs and drunk from his cupped hands plenty of warm blood, he made a paste of buffalo blood and dirt and packed his long horn wound. He quartered the carcass and cut away as much meat as White Rump could carry, wrapped it in the buffalo hide, and tied it over the mustang. The stomach he saved for a large water bag. He left the big heart of the strong beast so the buffalo spirit would replenish the animal and send many more buffalo throughout Numunuu land. After the spirit of the horse, the spirit of the buffalo was closest to the spirit of Our People.

Near-black streaks of blood marked the grass all the way back to the mud wallow where Two Talks had first seen the buffalo. He had run the beast a long way. He did not have to scoop out much mud to find water. Gritty, cloudy, and cold, the water smelled strongly of the insides of the earth, but it satisfied the thirst of man and horse. He rinsed the buffalo stomach, knotted the gut at its end, and filled it till it bulged. He walked White Rump to the top of a swell. From here, the horse could see and hear and smell for a long distance around them. He removed the horsehair bridle and affixed it to the thong around White Rump's neck, making a lead long enough to tie to his ankle yet give the mustang free movement of his head. After a short, restorative nap, he would begin the long walk back. He could not wait to tell Grandfather Red Dog and others of his vigil and hunt. From the darkness where he had left the purpled bones and heart of the buffalo, Coyote howled two times.

The distance back was much longer, since he was walking and leading a heavy-laden horse, than it had been on the back of a low-flying crow. Two Talks did not like to walk over the earth, but this journey he did not mind. White Rump carried enough buffalo meat to feed many lodges. To arrive overdue, after much worry in Crooked Nose's tipi, would make for a greater celebration.

Returns to Camp a Man

Near the end of the third sun since he'd slain the buffalo, Two Talks went down into the arroyo where the creek talked loud. Close to the water his moccasins sucked and kissed mud. Soon, he spotted the tops of the tipis at the edge of the camp. The tipis' shadows were long teeth in the face of the bluff where Our Father in Heaven flared on the rock. In the red light Two Talks took out the small pouches of paint and the brush with the chewed willowtip, and he used the last of the water in the buffalo stomach bag to mix white, red, and a little yellow. Behind a big rock near the bank was a still pool of water edged with ice. Here he knelt and bent over his reflection and painted white clouds over his forehead. On each cheek he used the precious vermillion to outline two crows' beaks he filled in with yellow ocher. To reflect the two natures of Crow revealed to him, as well as his own doubled name, he bisected his face from hairline to chin with a white line. For the warpath, he would paint one side black. He made the two crows' beaks on each side of White Rump's blood-speckled neck. A camp mongrel must have caught their scent on the breeze—the dog yapped and howled a welcome Two Talks hurried to acknowledge.

After the children who reached to touch him, the first of the People to greet him was Sure Enough Hungry, who had led several successful raids against the *taivos*. "My young warrior brother has returned." He embraced Two Talks. Out of the corner of his eye, Two Talks saw his father, Crooked Nose. Sure Enough Hungry addressed the gathering crowd, "Did I not say this one would be a mighty warrior who will have great magic against the enemies of the Antelope band?"

Now the men came up to clap Two Talks' shoulder or take him in a warm embrace. Crooked Nose and Red Dog stood to the side, smiling and watching their offspring receive his due glory. Morning Star and Persimmon got the meat off White Rump and cut it into thin strips that soon sizzled over a big cook fire. All present, especially the young boys, wanted a taste of the soon-to-be-a-mighty-warrior's first kill so some of his strong *puha* might enter their bodies.

Mother Moon was high in the cold sky before Two Talks had finished reciting the story of his kill. Most of what happened on his vigil was private. Grandfather Red Dog, who had named him and helped him prepare for his vision, and Ten Buffalo, who carried the medicine bag, were the only ones to whom Two Talks would speak about his encounter with Crow, though all could see the crows' beaks painted on his cheeks and on White Rump's neck, and they knew the powerful and cunning Crow had become Two Talks' medicine guide for life. After he had told for the third time how he leapt onto the running buffalo's back with nothing but a hunting knife and rode the bull to his death, he was allowed to leave the fire gathering and sit before Grandfather Red Dog in Crooked Nose's tipi.

Two Talks recounted all that had happened and all of Crow's words. Grandfather was most surprised by Crow's appearance in white feathers. "I have never seen a white crow. Birds' feathers do not grow white with age. Crow may have painted himself with the white paint of ghosts. Or he may be covered all over with caliche dust, or powdered with snow, or he may be hiding himself with a small cloud. If the lizard can change color to disappear, Crow could manage it easily. In spite of his strong medicine to guide you, you must always beware Crow's tricks."

"Grandfather, Crow's last words for me were these: 'When next your shadow comes to you, you must start gathering all the Numunuu for battle.' What can Crow have meant by these words? Our Father in Heaven always casts my dark shape upon the ground, so how can my shadow come to me?"

"Remember the vision your father was given at your birth. Brother Coyote slipped into Crooked Nose's sleep carrying a Numunuu baby as he would carry his own pup. This boy baby was you, and Coyote was watching over you. Your father offered Coyote food and water, but Coyote would not put down his burden to eat or drink. Father in Heaven lighted up the night and came down into the tipi and cast the boy baby's shadow on the cold earthen floor. The baby's cry rushed up through the smoke vent to become the shriek of a bird high in the sky. The bird was Crow, destined to be your life guide, the source of your main medicine. The baby kicked his legs and jerked his arms, but the shadow baby did not move. Then Father Sun went away, and took the shadow baby with him. The shadow baby is a missing part of you, some knowing or memory or different life you will recognize when it returns. This is why Crow appeared to you as the familiar black crow and as the unknown white crow. The baby who still hung from Coyote's jaws reached up and grabbed Coyote's ear and swung up onto his back. Coyote reared onto his hind legs and circled the fire, upright as a man. Coyote tried to shake the baby from his back, but the baby held fast. Coyote dropped the baby and raced back into the night. This foretold how you would kill the buffalo by riding on his back."

Two Talks unrolled the picture story he had taken from the *taivo* lodge and showed Grandfather how the warrior's face, except for the beard, mirrored Two Talks' own face.

"I have heard the reservation Indians talk of the white man's spirits, the single Spirit Father the *taivos* call God. The black robe missionaries named him 'He's Us.' I have long wondered how the *taivos* can see the many spirits who fill the world—all the animals, all the plants, all the rocks and rivers and winds and stars—and say there is only one Great Spirit. I asked the black robes if this He's Us was the Great Spirit for all peoples, why he had never come into the lodges of the Numunuu. The black robes said I had not recognized He's Us when he came.

Yet I seek my visions with my eyes open, and the *taivos* turn their faces toward the ground and close their eyes as in sleep," Grandfather Red Dog said.

Two Talks shook his head. "One who is prepared to receive a spirit's vision must open both eyes wide and look everywhere about."

"From the reservation Indians I learned the pale skins wait on this one, He's Us, who is a spirit their One Father sent long ago and will send back, like an echo, to bring the white men strong medicine. All white men keep their eyes shut and wait for this one called He's Us to return from the world after this world to show them the way to the Life After. Now, Crow says *he* has been to the Life After and returned, as he says Two Talks must do. Perhaps the *taivos* should keep watch for one with darker skin than they. Perhaps Two Talks is the He's Us who will go like a prayer and return like an echo from the world that follows this one," Grandfather said.

"I still do not understand how my shadow was carried away if just yesterday it walked beside White Rump's shadow over the grass."

"Was the shadow beside you yesterday a small shadow crawling on four legs?"

"No, Grandfather."

"The shadow running away from you in your father's vision was such a shadow. I think perhaps all Numunuu have many shadows. For each sun, a different shadow."

"Where do all my shadows from days gone by stay?"

"I think they may wait in the Life After to make one dark, strong shadow. The medicine woman who helped Morning Star birth you, she whose name I cannot speak because she is dead, could help untie this knot, but we will have to wait until you lead us through the secret opening into the Good Hunting Land to ask her. Before she died, this medicine woman spoke to me of your other half being carried away by water. I thought it was woman talk, talk of what comes out of woman parts during birth and other woman rites. Maybe Coyote or Crow tricked her into sending your birth shadow away?"

"What if my birth shadow, whatever part of me or of my memory Crow means, never comes back? What if he comes, but I do not recognize him?"

"Your *puha* is strong. The spirits favor Our People and they favor you among Our People. Both tricksters, Coyote and Crow, are united to guide you. When the time is near for you to lead this last Numunuu attack, your birth shadow will reappear." Red Dog put his hand on his grandson's shoulder. "When your shadow rejoins you, you will be reunited with the dark Crow part of you to lead Our People in these dark times. Like all Numunuu before me, I have hunted the buffalo and ridden the war trail. For us, I think there are no other trails. After a good death, there is the other world. I do not fear our death rattle if we can make our going out noise one great war cry. To follow the white man's trail is to be the living dead. After such death, there is no other death, no other world. Let the Numunuu enter the afterworld on our best war ponies, with our faces painted black, with bows and lances in our arms. To keep not-Numunuu spirits out of the other world, *ho*, would make it a good day to die."

Knobby Cotton: Holed Up in Skyhouse

Directed to a Place of Strumpets
(November–December 1862)

Before the Civil War, Galveston, though smaller, was as cosmopolitan as New Orleans, New York, or Boston. At Galveston wharves ships unloaded Parisian silk and ladies' apparel, Dutch chocolate and cheese, finely crafted German guns and tools. Jewels, cosmetics, medicines, sugar, salt, coffee, powder and lead were unloaded from New Orleans or from the North. Restaurants served iced drinks, good liquors, wine and champagne. In Galveston you could daily feast on fresh oysters, red fish, turtle, pheasant, duck, quail, lamb, venison, and beef. Just imagining the quince and berry pies, the delicate pastries, makes my sweet tooth ache. I regret I never journeyed that far south.

—from *Gideon Jones' Journal*

Knobby saw ships' masts before he saw the buildings of Galveston. The Yankee longboat carried Knobby and Elizabeth past two merchant ships that looked abandoned.

The wharves were crowded with U.S. Marines, but only a few stevedores pushed handcarts. Their boat tied up at Kuhn's Wharf beside a Union gunship. Knobby and Elizabeth were taken past the three-story Hendley Building—on top of which Marines with spyglasses looked down at them from a watchtower—four blocks to Post Office Street and the Customs House, above which flew the flag of the United States. They waited in a bare room for over an hour. A lieutenant who never identified himself led them outside to the back of the building, where they were met by a man introduced to them as an attorney, Mr. William Pitt Ballinger.

Knobby didn't know what else to do, so he showed Mr. Ballinger the freedom paper. The attorney studied the document for only a moment, one eyebrow raised, the paper fluttering in the steady Gulf breeze. His eyes moved quickly over the worn clothes Etienne had given Knobby and Elizabeth. Knobby still wore the big vest fashioned from fox fur but now it was salt-stiffened, mud-stained, and ragged.

"These are bleak times. Galveston is in the hands of the enemy but is not deemed worth fighting for. Our misfortune may, however, be your good fortune," the white attorney said.

"We have few resources and cannot compensate you, sir, but will you be kind enough to advise me about our legal status?" Knobby asked.

"Well, well. Outward appearances to the contrary, you're mighty well spoken. Quite a few of the men who hire me forget to pay. I suppose I can offer advice to someone who has the gumption to ask it for free." Ballinger waved Knobby and Elizabeth over to a row of hogsheads. He extended an arm, offering them seats on the plank top of a crate as if they were in his law office. They sat, and he leaned against a hogshead opposite. He rubbed his jaw. "Before we gave up to the enemy we were under Texas law requiring individual legislative approval for any free Negro to immigrate here. We were also under ordinance of the City of Galveston requiring that a bond be posted by a man respected before the law who would take responsibility for a free Negro's good conduct. Before Commander Renshaw's arrival, the law and ordinance were enforced with little consistency. Galveston has always been a sophisticated city, more persuaded by individuals and their talents than by statute. But under the flag that now flies over our Customs House you and this gal are curious cargo indeed, Knobby Cotton."

Elizabeth began to weep. "Knobby, what are we going to do? Where are we going to light?"

Knobby gritted his teeth. He knew Elizabeth had been long-suffering, but increasingly he wished she were more silent in her suffering.

"I do not believe free Negroes and slaves together do well," Ballinger said. "Free Negroes harbor runaways and often encourage in slaves habits of idleness or dissipation. But many citizens have fled this Union occupation and taken their slaves with them. Free Negroes all skedaddled north—can't blame them. I can count the free Negroes in Galveston on one hand. One is a fine fiddler, an instructor of dance. Another is the best barber in the city. There's Major Carey who runs a livery stable. The last is Leatherwood, proprietor of a pleasure palace that, with others like it, is a libel on the town but less of a nuisance than the burlesques of the histrionic art appearing at the Galveston Theater before the war. I might add, even in these times of Union occupation when penury and depression are epidemic and nine of ten shopkeepers are closed for want of business, Leatherwood's temple of hedonism prospers."

"And this Leatherwood is a freedman?" Knobby asked.

"More free, under this occupation by the enemy, than I." Ballinger wrote a note to Leatherwood introducing Knobby Cotton and his wife, Elizabeth, as travelers caught in the vicissitudes of war. He wrote that Mr. Cotton, contrary to his appearance, seemed to be a man of uncommon intelligence, and the attorney offered his services further in this matter if he were needed. With the note, he gave Knobby directions to a short street—or did he mean Short Street?—that lay at the edge of a neighborhood Ballinger called Smokey Row, his lip twisting into a scowl when he named it.

Ballinger sent them north, back toward the bay from which they had come. They crossed Market and Mechanic Streets and came to The Strand, a wide avenue of packed white sand and shells that sparkled in the afternoon sun. They had to stand aside for a man with a water cart working his way down the wide avenue wetting down the sand. Ballinger's directions sent them down the watered and shining sand in search of a cross street numbered 27. The Strand was lined with mercantile stores, drygoods emporiums, hotels, restaurants, barrooms, billiard rooms, and livery stables. Many of the buildings were brick and nearly all had ornate iron storefronts. For all the appearance of prosperity, many of the stores were closed up. They walked past houses painted as bright white as the dazzling sand streets. Several of the houses, most of the new-looking ones, were raised four or five feet on brick or wooden piers so the first floors were about at eye level. These piers were covered with lattice and beautified by the big leaves of fig and pomegranate trees. Oleanders fifteen to twenty feet tall grew around the houses. Though it was almost December, a few white and pink flowers bloomed in beds and flower boxes.

Knobby was surprised to see a tall, skinny Negro no more than sixteen or eighteen, black in all the bright whiteness, boldly standing on a corner with his hands in his pockets whistling a song, "Pop Goes the Weasel," that Knobby had heard bands play at dance parties back on Noble Plantation. Knobby and Elizabeth stopped, and Knobby asked the boy if he knew the way to Leatherwood's house. The whistler took one hand from the pocket of a long frock coat that had been fashioned from a crimson blanket and pointed down the street in the direction Knobby and Elizabeth were headed. "The backside of Smokey Row," the boy said. Then he bowed and took Knobby's hand and pumped it several times and started whistling again.

They had walked a long distance from the Customs House. The buildings and houses on these streets were not as grand as those closer to the bay. The door to a tavern opened and two Marines staggered out. Leaning together, they meandered down the street and disappeared inside another door. In this part of the town many houses needed painting or a broken window repaired. Knobby wondered if Elizabeth noticed the women lolling around on porches and talking in the sandy side yards. The plinking of pianos came from more than one doorway along with bursts of muffled male laughter. A man leaned against a wooden pier beneath a house and cleaned his teeth with a knifeblade. He stared at Knobby and Elizabeth when they passed and interrupted the cleaning of his teeth long enough to cut a wedge of tobacco and shove it into his mouth.

They came to the house where they had been told they would find Leatherwood. The windows were painted lavender by the setting sun, and the hardware on the closed front door shone like gold. Nearly all the houses Knobby had seen were white or a once-white gray, but Leatherwood's two-story house—save its high brick piers, rose-colored shutters, and silver-shining tin roof—was as blue as the deep-blue sky.

A mule team snorted and pawed in the side yard, so Knobby and Elizabeth followed the sounds to find a freight wagon two Negro boys were unloading of wooden barrels they bore up wood steps through double doors at the back of the house. Elizabeth headed toward the same back entrance, but Knobby took her elbow in his hand and steered her back to the front.

"We're off the plantation. Let's at least *act* free."

She stopped at the elevated front porch and nodded toward a hanging sign painted pretty as letters in a book. The sign, a plank hung sideways like a railroad depot sign, was painted with a cloud and across the cloud, in gold letters: S K Y H O U S E. Tiny gold wings decorated the first S and the E at the end. Floor-to-ceiling windows all around the first floor were shuttered with pink louvers propped out from the bottom like pouting upper lips. Knobby and Elizabeth ascended to the porch. The front door held an oval of rose-colored glass, and roses were etched into the glass itself. Beside the door was a knocker in the shape of a bird. Knobby lifted the bird's brass wing, sunwarmed, and let it strike the plate. Almost immediately, the door opened.

Knobby saw no one in the dark entry of the house. Then the brown face of a midget or a boy, Knobby couldn't tell which, emerged about waist-high looking up at him.

"We're not open till full dark." The midget's voice was clear and sweet. "Please return then."

"We've been sent to see Leatherwood."

The midget seemed to see Elizabeth for the first time. He looked back over his shoulder into the dark recesses of the house then nodded the barely perceptible nod of a bidder at a horse auction. The little man stepped back, opened the door, and gave a bow so slight Knobby wondered if he had only imagined it. "Please come in and be seated. Mr. Leatherwood will be down directly."

They stepped onto softness, rose-colored carpet cushioning their steps into a long, dim room. The only light came from the bottoms of the tall, narrow windows where the shutters were propped out with rods.

"Please excuse me." By the time the midget had spoken he had vanished.

A white piano perched at the end of the room like a huge bird about to take flight, its upright lid like a bird's lifted wing. Against the walls sat more sofas than the mistress had had on Noble Plantation, sofas puffy in pink and wine, sofas with polished wood feet and scrolled arms, as curvy as the piano. Knobby and Elizabeth, in their mud- and salt-stained clothes, sank onto pink velvet cushions that filled the spaces between their thighs and between the two of them like the buoyancy of the ocean floating and caressing them.

Behind the piano—in the back of the house where Knobby had seen the boys unloading barrels—dishes or glassware clinked and voices rose and fell. Overhead, footsteps rapped as if a gang of woodpeckers was at work on the upstairs floors.

Golden light spilled over their shoulders, and they turned to see a Negro girl about Elizabeth's age step down off a stool from which she had lighted a wall sconce. The girl smiled and nodded, her black hair lacquered-looking in the oil light, her face hidden in shadow.

Elizabeth neither spoke nor moved, and Knobby attempted to follow the lamplighter with his eyes only, keeping his head fixed. She moved with the easy grace of habit, dipping down off the stool at the same time as she scooted it forward to the next sconce, rising on one foot on the stool, her long taper extended in one arm as her other arm tilted back the glass chimney just far enough for wick and taper to meet, the single flame brightening then separating then glowing as the girl tilted down the chimney and dipped back to the ground to move on to the next until the room filled with small suns.

Within that radiance appeared a figure, the room's light now a nimbus describing the dark shape the way gold outlines robed saints in Bible drawings. Words came from the light-surrounded darkness in the way Grandfather's Bible testified that a voice had once spoken from within a burning bush.

"Mr. Cotton, Knobby Cotton." This voice was not the rumble of thunder but the wafting of smoke.

"You know my name?"

"I have been waiting for you."

Knobby smelled smoke on the man's whispery words. Before Knobby saw the extended arm, long fingers (each with its own jeweled ring) wrapped firmly around his hand.

"I am that Leatherwood you were sent to find." The disembodied voice belonged to the hand gripping Knobby's, and the voice was close. Knobby held out Ballinger's note of introduction, but Leatherwood shook his head. Knobby wondered how the man could already have intelligence of their arrival.

Now the light fell whole on Leatherwood. Knobby averted his eyes from the scarred face, but the fingers clasped his hand more firmly, so Knobby looked full at the man: clouded eyes gave back the flames of the wall sconces. Like gemstones protruding from burnished rock, those eyes flared within a raccoon's mask of dark skin. Outside the mask the flesh was as pink as a white infant's. The forehead appeared high, because no brows interrupted the upward curve from eyes to grizzled hair, and what hair there was ran in crooked furrows like some withered crop in a season of drouth. The sleeves of the man's white ruffled shirt were rolled to his elbows, exposing hairless forearms mottled pink and black as his face. Leatherwood looked as much fair as dark. Ash gray though his hair was, his form showed none of the frailty of age. He stood tall, legs spread, black wool knee britches tucked into polished black boots just below his knees. Still grasping Knobby's hand, Leatherwood gave to Elizabeth his other hand—rings on all these fingers, also.

"Woman, how are you called?"

"Elizabeth." When Leatherwood took her hand Elizabeth rose from the sofa and bowed slightly, a white lady at the opening chords of a reel. "Mr. Leatherwood." In these surroundings, as elegant as Noble House, Elizabeth was acting like a house-slave again. Her obeisance made Knobby distrust this Leatherwood.

"Please—titles sound false on us people of color. I am 'Leatherwood,' and I hope you are 'Elizabeth' and 'Knobby.' You are both welcome here. There is lodging for you, bathwater, clean clothes, warm food. After you've been tended to, we'll talk. Oralia," he said, his voice rising, tremulous, as steam warbles from a teapot.

A woman in a simple white smock walked in, no shoes on her stockinged feet. Like the lion in Grandfather Samuel's African tales, the woman moved in a way both stealthy and fearless, her shape beneath the smock shifting like lion muscle. She looked too ferocious and too beautiful to be an actual living thing. Her deep brown skin had the luster of hand-polished wood. Her nose and lips rose in lines so straight they looked fashioned by one perfect tap of a chisel. Her cheeks held the soft swell of a glassblower's breath. Her neck was fashioned with the soft rings a potter's encircling fingers make in wet clay. So large and black were her pupils it seemed she had no whites in the eyes, and when she met Knobby's stare her face showed absolutely no emotion.

"Oralia, take our guests up."

Without a word, Oralia gave first Elizabeth and then Knobby an inclination of her head, then turned and led them up the narrow carpeted stairs. In spite of her silence, Oralia's manner seemed to Knobby to invite intimacy. She ascended the stairs as if she could see behind her, pausing with each step until Knobby was sure he would press against her, but she rose at the last possible moment, taking the next step so that their bodies remained tantalizingly close yet just far enough apart they did not touch. Did he imagine that the whispering he followed was made by the woman's silk-stockinged legs beneath her white dress? He breathed in the perfume that trailed Oralia, the sweet smell of a gardenia but with some peppery spice mixed in. Behind him Elizabeth climbed heavily, and he hoped his inflamed passion did not give off a scent she could recognize.

Leatherwood's Mysterious Past

The boyish midget—*my name is Denis, and I am thirty-three years old*—who had opened the door at Skyhouse brought them clean clothes: a muslin smock for Elizabeth, a flannel shirt and striped woolen pants for Knobby. One of the Skyhouse girls, Belinda, put her bare foot next to Elizabeth's. Belinda's toenails were painted red while Elizabeth's were cracked and grass-stained. Belinda gave Elizabeth a pair of satin shoes that matched the rose carpet. Knobby thought she might wear those shoes to bed.

They did not see Mr. Leatherwood again for two days. They spent their time soaking in hot baths, sleeping as late as the Skyhouse girls, and eating. In an enormous kitchen a cook named Christine spoke German and served them "coffee, sure enough"—meaning it wasn't ground corn or peas or tree bark like some islanders had to drink because of the blockade—with all the sugar they could spoon. Every afternoon Christine served up feasts the likes of which Knobby had never seen, not even during holidays at Noble Plantation. There were tureens of oxtail soup, curried sausages, leg of mutton with caper sauce, venison with port wine sauce, platters of fried eggs, bowls of green peas, mashed potatoes, cabbage, and squash. Christine always outdid herself with dessert: rum omelettes, brandy-peach and jelly pastries, bread and rice puddings, pecan and persimmon and mince pies. Since the girls would have champagne all evening they had milk or tea at dinner, but Knobby was offered brown porter, pale or red ale. He and Elizabeth were offered claret and champagne cider.

Knobby and Elizabeth made love without the earthy smells of grass and swamp gas, but on the soft feather mattress with piano music and shrieks and laughter and boot-stomping coming from other rooms. The atmosphere in Skyhouse made Knobby feel sinful lying with his own wife, and what confused him was the laughter of adventuresses in adjoining rooms somehow increasing his pleasure. He remembered the Scriptures, how Jesus ate and drank with publicans and sinners, how He forgave the sinful woman who washed His feet with her tears and the Samaritan woman who'd had five husbands when she met Him at the well. Maybe a brothel was just the right place to recover from a three-month trek dodging murderous strangers through swamplands.

Knobby had heard stories about New Orleans brothels, but, of course, he had never been inside one. And he had never imagined *black* sporting women. Slave men didn't go to whorehouses, and why would a white man pay to lie with a Negro girl when slave girls were his for the taking? Belinda said Skyhouse always had one or two black girls, even when the Confederates controlled Galveston, but she couldn't remember seeing a Negro customer.

"Before the war, Leatherwood come to Texas from New Orleans, with a woman called Blind Fanny. Some say Blind Fanny's his mother. Some say she's his wife. Others say she's a conjure woman. She's for sure old as Methuselah. Leatherwood took such fright of the ocean, he wouldn't get on no ship again, not even to go upriver to escape the war," Belinda said.

In New Orleans, Leatherwood had been manservant to some rich man's only son, had followed the boy around town, one bar to the next, out to horse races, back to gambling rooms, waited for his charge, and always got him safely home to his rich daddy.

"Leatherwood waited for the white boy in fancy whorehouses where madams stuffed their bosoms fat with money. I think rich white folks like to use us colored cousins for jobs like that—manservants and valets and maids—because it don't actual count when we see their sinful secrets. Leatherwood saw them special French-talking yellow gals—you know, them white colored girls—how they cost more than a good racehorse and was fed and combed better, too. That gave Leatherwood some money ideas. Rich white boy went off to be a Reb officer—took

Leatherwood with him to keep his care in the army, but the cousin wasn't about to be no camp follower now he had money plans. He slipped off and drug old Blind Fanny to Galveston on horseback. Leatherwood showed around a letter from the rich man in New Orleans saying Leatherwood was a Negro to be counted on, saying nothing passed his lips. Then Leatherwood hired to the Winters Plantation where they kept cotton-field slaves." Belinda closed the door and lowered her voice. "Mr. Winters had this mulatta gal, some say he paid four thousand dollars for her, but Missus Winters she wouldn't let the gal dark her door. Mr. Winters keeping her locked in a cabin. He gave Leatherwood white wages, said he and Blind Fanny could live in the big house, not in no slave quarters. Mr. Winters put Blind Fanny in a chair by a window and pulled back the drapes like she could see. Soon, Leatherwood be Mr. Winters' private man, all the time hearing his whispers." Belinda raised her eyebrows. "Slaves in the quarters said Leatherwood was a conjure man, he moved invisible between the big house and the mulatta gal's cabin. He carried a big trunk back and forth, some say it was full of trouble to spill out. Come Christmas, the big house caught on fire and burned about to the ground. The trunk had been opened up. Everyone got safe outside but the Winters' little son, Reuben. Leatherwood ran smack back into the burning house. In a upstairs window he saw the child in the flames like Shadrach. Leatherwood carried Reuben out of the fiery furnace, his own hair and coat aflame, his eyebrows burnt off. Blind Fanny was failing in her years, and when Leatherwood came out of the collapsing house, his arms and legs flaming, his hair sending up black smoke like a chimley, Fanny fell out dead, sprawled in a chinaberry bush." The narration of Fanny's death seemed to have taken Belinda's breath and speech. She eased down into a chair.

"Then what?" Knobby said.

Belinda looked up, smiling as if she were seeing them for the first time. She offered Elizabeth, then Knobby, a praline and took one of the sugary candies for herself.

"Tell the rest," Elizabeth said.

Belinda shook her head slowly, not in denial, but in affirmation of just how good her story was, how a body could not be rushed. She chewed and swallowed the praline and then, in her own time, went on. "The graveyard on the Winters Plantation has a black iron fence around the family graves. Granite headstones carved with pretty words. Down below are slaves' graves with wooden crosses if they have markers at all. But one colored lies amidst all the white Winters, and you like as not guessed *Fanny* is the name carved on the stone." Belinda shook her head. "There's more. Mr. Winters, he buried Blind Fanny in the family plot, and he settled a sum of money on Leatherwood. Standing there over Blind Fanny's fresh-filled grave, in plain view of the preacher and everyone, Mr. Winters said, 'Leatherwood, what more can I do to repay the debt of my son's life against Fanny's?' Leatherwood spoke out, laid a claim to the mulatta gal, spoke her name when no one knew she had a name: *Grant me Oralia. Let me serve as her bondsman and protect her that she might accompany me and care for me in my aging.* Everone said, *Oralia—that her name.* They say that's when Mr. Winters' face got froze up—twisted like it is. But he had to give what he public vowed, Mrs. Winters beside him in her black dress staring like a crow. He wrote the bond papers that selfsame day and settled on Leatherwood the mulatta, Oralia, and two mules and a wagon heavy-loaded with food and clothes and gifts from Mrs. Winters and all the daughters and Reuben, too, who was still such a sprout he give Leatherwood a child's wooden sailing ship and it floated perfect. Always struck me funny, since Leatherwood's fright of riding on the water kept him in Texas and brought him to the Winters. What brought him here, too, bondsman to all us girls black and white, to you two also, it seem."

Knobby did not ask what he wanted to know: whether Oralia took customers. Quietly prowling Skyhouse on a Sunday afternoon, he espied her leaving a room at the top of the stairs and glimpsed a man in a chair wearing a blue suit or a Federal uniform. Leatherwood, or a Union officer? When Knobby returned to his and Elizabeth's room the door was partly opened, and he stood just outside. Sitting on the edge of the bed with Elizabeth was Skyhouse's other Negro girl—called Little Bit—wearing a shiny red shift that came just to the tops of her thighs. Little Bit was a small girl but big in places a Skyhouse customer likes big. Her skin was the color of strong tea. Her red-brown hair looked ironed-flat and hung straight as a curtain down her back. Elizabeth giggled and turned her head before the dressing table mirror. Knobby stopped still: Elizabeth had yellow hair.

"And sure it's a man's world, girl, a *white* man's world. So *we* girls got to take *our* pleasure where we can." Little Bit lifted what looked like a fluffy white cat from her lap. Elizabeth pulled off her yellow hair and took the cat—*not a cat, a wig.* She arranged the white wig over her head so it fell in long, ropelike curls making her look like book drawings Knobby had seen of men in old-timey France and England. Little Bit handed her a white bundle with straps like saddle cinches hanging down. Little Bit tilted her head back giggling, and Elizabeth bent over unfurling the bundle that became a garment she stepped into, a lacy white costume that covered her only from the bottoms of her breasts to just above her belly.

Little Bit gently spanked the side of Elizabeth's thigh, slapping Knobby's breath away. Just as he backed silently from the door, the midget said, "Mr. Cotton. You have a caller."

Elizabeth looked up. Her eyes stared right at him, but he couldn't tell if she had seen him. He took the first few steps downstairs two at a time. A man with skin so white he looked faintly blue waited. The man wore a black derby hat, a black frock coat too large for him, a brown cravat, white dress shirt, and brown Nankeen trousers. In a heavy German accent he introduced himself as Ernst Reinbach, an admirer of Herr Leatherwood. Would Herr Cotton be so kind as to join him and some associates that evening at a saloon near the wharves, the Neptune?

The Union Loyal Liberation Front

In Texas it is widely held if civil war had not come the Mexicans
and Germans would have been the downfall of slavery in the state.
The Mexicans by fraternization and intermarriage, the Germans
by their liberal thinking and political action.

—from *Gideon Jones' Journal*

The Neptune smelled like the stables on Noble Plantation—straw, dirt, dung, and sweat—with the sweet odors of tobacco and whisky stirred in. Straw was spread on the brick floor to soak up mud and horse dung from boots and brogans. Yellow kerosene light reflected off the castiron handle of a hissing, smoking woodstove. A spittoon squatted at one end of an iron footrail that ran the length of the bar, the spittoon giving back the faint shine of lamplight.

Herr Reinbach was from Fredericksburg, a German settlement at the edge of Texas' western frontier. He bade Knobby and four other colored cousins who had accepted his offer of a free drink to join him at a table opposite the bar. The wiry little German described himself as a recent immigrant from Deutschland, formerly a member of the Adelsverein, which he explained was the German Emigration Company, an organization he and some other German men had formed to protect the interests of German immigrants in Texas.

"In Texas, Deutsch must sound like Dutch," he said. "They call us Dutchmen." He smiled with his lips but not with his eyes. "We maybe should wear wooden shoes." He told them he had accompanied Prince Solms Braunfels to Texas back in '44. Following a disagreement of principle, Reinbach had left New Braunfels and moved farther west to Fredericksburg. Most recently, he had become active in the Union Loyal League, which had fomented sympathy for the Union by urging Texans to dodge the draft until companies of Texas militia took over Fredericksburg and declared martial law. "Comal County is majority German. The only county in Texas that voted Union."

Reinbach gave the barkeep a wave, and the fellow slow-waltzed his way from behind the bar and the woodstove with five empty glasses and a bottle of something darker-looking than whisky. Knobby sipped the raw syrupy-tasting spirits and wondered why Leatherwood had arranged this meeting.

"Enjoy the rum, gentlemen. A blockade runner risked the lives of his sailors to bring it past Union gunboats." The German cleared his throat. "The secessionists gave everyone six days to take the oath of loyalty to the South, so I removed myself to Galveston. I seek brave men to go with me to Mexico to aid the cause of freedom and be safe from Confederate tyranny."

At the bar was a man in a U.S. Marine's uniform. Two white girls bent over some civilians at a table against the back wall. The snap of cards was the only sound in the room. Knobby wondered what the other patrons thought, seeing five Negroes in the saloon.

With the support of the Federal authorities in Galveston, Herr Reinbach was recruiting men for a unit similar to the Texas United States Volunteers that Judge Davis had organized in occupied New Orleans. Every man who joined the Union Loyal Liberation Front was promised a new outfit—horse and saddle, rifle and shot, a pair of store-bought boots.

"Each of us deserves a uniform of distinction—a dark capelet, gold braid and epaulette, red tunic, leather crossbelt, and a sharp *curtein* on our sash." Reinbach stared over his rum as if he were looking into a shop window displaying military regalia. He set his glass down. "But, of course, uniforms and insignia would compromise free movement. The United States cannot blockade an international river, so the Rio Grande escapes the Union blockade. Supplies pour across the river like water through a hole in a dike. French and British merchants in Mexico exchange muskets, shot, shell, food, clothing for Texas cotton. Even Yankee shippers trade, indirectly supplying the Confederate Army. Our Union Loyal Liberation Front will stop up the hole with as many fingers as possible."

"Freedmen ain't legal in Texas. You got a fix for us?" asked the Negro Reinbach introduced as Herr Columbus.

"Right now you are under the protection of the United States military. When the Liberation Front is active—when you ride the border—you will be in defiance of the laws of Texas. We will support your freedom with our weapons and, if necessary, our lives. At other times, when it suits our purposes to pose as citizens of the Confederacy, I will post the necessary bond for the behavior of each free Negro who rides for me."

"You going to be our new master, and you on the run from the loyalty oath?" Herr Columbus tilted his head and light reflected on his spectacles as if a gold coin were pressed over each of his eyes.

"I will provide the money, but each bond will be posted by a citizen respected by Texas authorities. There are men who have pledged me such service in secrecy," Reinbach said.

"Is your outfit part of the Union Army?" a heavy, thick-necked Negro opposite Knobby asked. The man had been introduced as Herr Flood.

"The Liberation Front has the blessing of the Union, the blessing I am told of Herr Lincoln. Even the governor of Texas, Herr Houston, saw secession as the contemptuous defiance by a few planters of the patriotic Texas majority. After the liberation, every man will receive a section of land for his contribution to our national cause. First liberate the land, then you may inherit the land."

"What about my wife—what happens to her while I'm off liberating?" the one called Flood asked.

"I will arrange Gulf passage to Matamoros." The German picked up his glass, set it back down without drinking. The one wearing spectacles, Herr Columbus, drained his glass and left. Reinbach raised his voice. "Negroes and whites are equal in the Liberation Front. Citizens of Mexico, also." Herr Columbus loudly closed the door behind him, but the German went on, "Civilized nations observe us. We must become the instrument of freedom. The doctrine of slavery is dying on battle-fields in Virginia and Tennessee. The evil those doctrines spawned, hatred's corpse, must be buried deep. Texas must rise from the dark shadow of this mound."

One of the men in the card game hooted and another said, "Shut up and deal."

"What's the pay?" Knobby asked.

Reinbach frowned. "Pay is your bond posted so you are a free Negro in Texas. And for every recruit: a horse, a gun and ammunition, good boots, all he can eat, and safe passage for his family. We fight for the harvest of a free nation."

"But what's the wages?" asked Herr Flood.

"Enlisted men get twenty dollars a month—and a salvage percent of contraband intercepted before it reaches the Confederates."

Flood drained his rum and smacked down the empty glass. "Less than cotton jammer wages. But there's no cotton to load. Where do I mark?"

"Here is my sergeant, now." Coming through the door, beneath the brim of a weather-beaten dark-stained hat, was a cloud of cigarette smoke. A face as ruined as the hat emerged from behind the smoke. One eye pulsed—its coal-dark pupil moving side to side, then up and down—the other eye held so still it looked painted on. The man grinned, a cigarette at the corner of his mouth twitched, and a thin scar along his upper lip widened and stretched, sugar white above red-chapped and brown-scabbed lips. Not a face to forget, the face of Portis Goar, the drover Knobby had saved from a trampling two years back in New Orleans. In a hand that bore a dark, round scar like a knothole between his thumb and the dark stub of a missing first finger, the sergeant held a quill pen.

Sergeant Goar unrolled an enlistment document and uncorked a clay crock of ink. The Negro, Flood, made a shaky "X" on the paper.

Knobby signed his name. "You don't remember me?"

Goar fixed his good eye on Knobby. Behind cigarette smoke the other eye darted back and forth like a rat terrier. The face tightened, then brightened. A puff of smoke came with each word out of the man's mouth, like Indian smoke signals Knobby had heard about. "Sure, the darkie horseman. New Orleans, the time old Juan went down for keeps." Now Goar spoke to everyone in the barroom, "Boys, this darkie," he squinted at the paper on the bar, "Knobby Cotton," the sergeant's hand clamped down on Knobby's shoulder, the man's grip reminding Knobby of the time a mule had bitten his arm, "he sits a horse better than I do, even with me being about as good a vaquero as they is." Goar lowered his voice. "So, you finally figure to ride the devil's trail through El Desierto Muerto, where Colonel Colt makes every man equal."

"You told me Texas is where there's 'all a man can chew.'" When Knobby repeated Goar's expression, the man grinned again.

Though Flood, John Johnson, and Knobby were the only recruits he'd collected, Herr Reinbach seemed pleased. "The Confederates have a new commander of the military department of Texas, Brigadier General John Bankhead Magruder—the man struts like a rooster and puffs like a windstorm, dangerously sure of himself. The first thing he did was send a warning to the mayor, giving time for civilians to get off the island. The Rebels are coming soon. We want to relocate to San Antonio before Christmas." He told Sergeant Goar to tend to the needs of the new men, shook hands all around, and excused himself. John Johnson left a couple of minutes behind Reinbach. Flood had another glass of rum, then he left, too. Knobby stood against the bar, alone with Sergeant Goar. Goar tossed the burning stub of his cigarette onto the floor. "This calls for something better than the rum the Dutchman set you up." Goar lifted off of the enlistment paper an unopened bottle labeled "McBryan," and the coiling paper corner struck his hand like a snake. He banged the bottle until the barkeep brought clean glasses. "We'll have us a drink or three of these bitters, then we got to arrange to get your plunder together, a good hoss and tack, all your necessaries."

"What was he meaning by salvage percent?" Knobby asked.

"The Dutchman figures the Feds to buy the foreign goods we keep away from Johnny Reb. We'll be running our own private horse-blockade. Me, I figure the Rebs got a bigger need, they'll pay the most. We'll charge a pass-through fee, kindly a army tax. For the right pay, we let goods slide through an spare ourselves hauling stuff back to the border for the Union or having to cart it out to one of the Comanchero trading places."

"Is a Comanchero some kind of Comanche?" Knobby said.

"No, but they're about as mean. Comancheros are traders, most out of New Mexico. Most are Mexican or half-breed Indian. They don't give a damn what side you're on so long as your money's good. A Comanchero will sell anything or anyone if the price is right. Indians give Comancheros safe passage on account of they tote guns and whisky. Comanches sell white captives to them. The meanest honcho of all Comancheros is the hombre known as Pretty." Portis "Eye" Goar paused and looked down. Knobby looked, too, and saw his black toes where Etienne had cut open the front of the alligator hide shoes. Eye did not say anything direct about the shoes, and he didn't laugh at them either. "Tomorrow, we'll go to Greenleve's and get your boots and riding outfit." They downed their drinks and said goodnight.

Leatherwood Makes an Offer

Yellow light shone down from between the slats of the tall shutters, so Skyhouse appeared to be surrounded by stacks of gold coins. Knobby hurried up the back steps. Piano chords he had been unconsciously listening to became louder, and light spilled over him. He stared at the unfamiliar striped pants he now wore and wondered who he was. Leatherwood stood in the opened door, flames from the kitchen stove licking up behind his ears as if he burned yet from the Winters Plantation fire. "Do come in. It is time we have our talk."

Leatherwood's ringed fingers threw a gaudy rainbow on the ceiling and down the wall. Scarred pink skin puckered on the back of the hand that held the inside of Knobby's elbow and guided him. The workings of veins, finger bones, and knuckle joints beneath stretched the pink skin tight, so the fingers kneading Knobby's arm resembled the harrowing teeth of a gin jerking clouds of cotton into long tendons of fiber. The midget Denis bent over the piano playing "Listen to the Mockingbird." The parlor behind Knobby was before him in the mirror over the bar. More customers than girls occupied the front room. Most wore suitcoats. A couple were in shirtsleeves, suspenders crossed over broad backs like ropes binding shipping crates or bales of cotton. In the mirror, Little Bit sat on the lap of a man on one of the courting seats, one high-heeled shoe dangling off a stockinged heel. Cigar smoke and perfume burned Knobby's throat. Oralia came down the stairs in sync with the piano trills of the Mockingbird.

"You had a satisfactory meeting with Reinbach." It was not a question, and Leatherwood did not wait for an answer. "He will have documents drawn up—showing a bond posted making someone responsible before the law for your behavior." The red jewel on Leatherwood's pointing finger glistened like a bead of blood. Involuntarily, Knobby touched his pocket where he felt the paper the slave, Joseph Thomas, had given him, the counterfeit declaration that he was a freedman. "You need a convincing history, Knobby. I have great expectations for you and your lovely Elizabeth."

Oralia came up with a silver tray. "Some Madeira, Mr. Cotton?" Her somnolent words rose and wandered sleepily, brushing, then prodding Knobby's ears as a sleepwalker's extended fingers feel their way around corners and down long corridors.

Leatherwood's speech twisted and burned, pungent as woodsmoke. "Does it surprise you to be drinking fine Madeira in times like these? We are a cosmopolitan city. Even with the blockade, *because* of the blockade, a great deal of money is being made. We people of color can always benefit from such times because money is the equalizer of all men."

The nutty-tasting wine warmed the space behind Knobby's eyes. Oralia refilled his glass.

Denis was playing "Lorena." Leatherwood's tongue, gray over pink like the insides of seashells, slid from between his lips and dipped into the wine, then retreated back inside his mouth. He nodded at the large white piano. "Before the war, in one year alone, twenty-three grand pianos were purchased in this island city. You've been in our kitchen. This evening a white man brought me tea, raisins, two kits of mackerel, several bottles of port and Madeira, and coffee-sure-enough. Tokens of appreciation." Oralia refilled Knobby's glass. Leatherwood's high voice whirred, insistent, like the warning of the rattlesnakes Knobby had been told were all over the island. "Leave a rattler be," everyone advised. Blood sluggish and heavy with wine, his tongue swollen-feeling, Knobby held to the bar as to the rail at sea. He pictured twenty-three pianos flying off ships and perching on the roofs of twenty-three houses, every one playing a different tune. Elizabeth's name in Leatherwood's voice brought Knobby out of his reverie. "Elizabeth is welcome to remain here. Our girls are fond of her, and she seems content. Why let her risk travel to Matamoros? I can arrange her safety here with Commander Renshaw."

"What kind of position would she have at Skyhouse?" Knobby asked.

"Christine needs help in the kitchen, and here, serving drinks and the like. People of color must help one another. She would repay me in the ways I have mentioned." Knobby drank another glass of the Madeira and stared at an embroidered buttonhole in Leatherwood's fancy frock coat. The man droned on: "Reinbach is an idealistic fool, not unlike our former Governor Houston—Reinbach can take the risks while we reap the reward—my good fortune is also yours—difference between a nigger slave and you—officers Union or Confederate—words and money—no longer a slave but not yet free—indenture—investment—feudal times again—protection—oath made in blood—what Elizabeth wants—lovely Elizabeth—" In the mirror as in a tunnel of yellow light in which Leatherwood and Oralia curved on either side, Elizabeth—hair brushed and shining, satin dress matching her new shoes—appeared and disappeared carrying a silver tray of drinks. She came and went with piano songs: "Sweet Evelina," "Lily Dale," "Katie Darling," "Annie Laurie," "Juanita," "Leila Is Gone." The time between songs grew longer until Knobby forgot to hear the piano the way one forgets a conversation after long silences. Leatherwood said goodnight. The parlor grew darker around its edges. Oralia kept Knobby's glass full and rested her hand, damp and cool, on his arm. Long into the night her warm words breathed against his ear: "Elizabeth has more to learn—fly higher than she can fly—she likes it here—her own room—new pleasures—gold coin—opium—her shepherd—return on your flock—recompense the cunning—"

Chasing Two Rabbits

Knobby opened his eyes to bright sun, his bedcovers twisted around his chest and between his legs. He lifted his head, and the room spun around. Blue spots danced in front of his eyes. Blonde Elizabeth sat at the dressing table in a long shimmery robe bright green as spring leaves.

"Finally," she spoke to the mirror. "You decided to come back from the dead?"

Tobacco and whisky and a hint of roses, a small cloud of smells, encircled his head. Perfumes and dusting powder, scents of flower garden and candy store. Had one of the girls given Elizabeth bottled drops of rose? Or had Oralia left fragrance on his arm? Elizabeth patted the wig, pulled the blonde hair this way and that. Holding the green robe close at the neck with one hand and close at the waist with her other hand, she left the room without another word.

Knobby stood, naked, before the washstand. His eyes stared at him, red around the edges. His beard showed in patches on his chin and cheeks. The corner of his mouth was discolored, ashy-looking as a bruise, but when he rinsed his face the mark came off red on the towel. One hand against the wall to steady the still swaying room, he stood over the pot and relieved himself.

When Elizabeth returned she smirked and traded him a cup of steaming coffee for the chamber pot she set out in the hall. Knobby drank the coffee down like medicine. Elizabeth handed him an apple. "Belinda says this makes a man's breath bearable, even kissable."

Knobby bit into the apple and juice ran down his chin. He was still chewing the first bite when Elizabeth opened the green robe. She wobbled on high French heels over to the bed. Lines of light ran up her stocking-whitened thighs and glinted on clasps hooking the silk to her lacy outfit. Above her crotch, tight, close coils of hair shone like black embroidery. She straddled him and took his rising cock in her fingers, brushing and pulling it against layered folds of her flesh the way someone dabs and pokes a brush to get paint into crevices. She moved and touched him in new ways, and he wondered, *Who has taught her these things? Little Bit? Belinda?* He imagined Oralia instructing her, and his body bucked. Elizabeth's eyes widened, squeezed shut. She rested her newly blonde head on his chest, and he studied the white lace against her round chocolate nipples, how they looked like cookies the mistress at Noble Plantation offered on a doily when she served tea. Knobby imagined Elizabeth going upstairs with a Galveston businessman. Unbidden came the image of Oralia leading him up those same stairs.

Knobby remembered a tale Grandfather Samuel had told him, an old African tale about *loomba* and *doky ndoomba*. "You have heard you cannot catch two rabbits, for when you chase one, the other will get away," Grandfather said. "But hunters in Africa lure a hare out of his way by fashioning a devil woman of straw. Her hollow form is wrapped in cloth of red and purple. On her straw face are painted eyes of black and lips of red, and bits of colored rock tied to her skirts make bright music in the breeze. Before the hunter sets the devil woman in the hare's path, he puts a drop of honey on her mouth and rings her breasts and skirt with birdlime." Knobby asked Grandfather what birdlime was, and Grandfather's nose wrinkled and lips twisted up. "Child, it's the sticky stuff you spread on tree limbs to catch birds when they land. Birdlime cleaves stronger than river mud, freezes you against it tight as ice." Then Grandfather smiled and went on with his story. "Silly ole *loomba*, hopping along, spies the bright shine of devil woman. He greets her, but she just keeps shining, doesn't say a word. 'Speak to me, girl,' *loomba* says, but her red lips are sealed. *Loomba*, angry, grabs her pretty shape, and birdlime fastens his hand on *doky ndoomba*. Next, *loomba* grabs *doky ndoomba* with his other hand, and birdlime holds that hand tight. 'I'm going to kick loose if you don't let go,' he says. But everybody knows a devil woman is deaf to all desires but her own. The hare—so strong and quick—kicks with one foot and then the other, and before you know it, he's trapped, joined up with evil forever. But he's not done. He squeals hare words for help, and one of his friends comes running. 'Pull me loose, friend,' the first hare says. His friend laughs at his predicament, but he grabs hold and tugs. 'Push against this silent woman,' says the first hare. By and by, both hares are stuck in birdlime, and the hunter can take his time skinning their hides and eating them up."

Beneath closed lids, Elizabeth's eyes moved in a dream. Knobby eased himself out from beneath her. She lay on her side, blonde wig coppery against dark skin, long legs in stockings and lace, wearing the rose satin shoes in bed. She looked like she belonged in Skyhouse, available for anyone who could pay the price. Knobby hoped they had not escaped Noble Plantation just to be snared in a different kind of bondage. The obvious pleasure Elizabeth took from the finery of Skyhouse irritated him. In fact, it made him feel morally superior to her and, then, he wondered if his true feeling was fear he would never be able to provide her with such riches. Maybe he was guilty of the same kind of infatuation. He could not keep from comparing Elizabeth, rough-hewn and homespun, to the sophisticated and exotic Oralia. Even if he wanted to, he knew he would not be able to get Oralia out of his mind. But he did not want to. Even if he didn't act on his lust, he liked keeping it alive, building it up in his imagination the way you build up a fire just to see the logs burn. Even now, watching Elizabeth sleep, it was Oralia who flickered like a candle in his mind. He hoped he hadn't led Elizabeth all the difficult way to Texas only to get them both caught in birdlime Leatherwood had spread across their path.

Purchases His Outfit

Elizabeth did not want to leave Skyhouse and her new friends and new clothes and new foods for another difficult and dangerous journey. For two days they had argued. Early the morning before she was to take Herr Reinbach's steamer to Matamoros, she sat up in bed in the total silence of Skyhouse and shook Knobby so violently, whispered his name so urgently, he woke thinking the house was on fire.

"Knobby. Knobby Cotton, what do you mean to do? After weeks in Etienne's swamps we've got a room of our own and food in the larder and you join a white man's gun gang?"

"It's an army, and there are at least three Negro soldiers."

"Any Negro generals?"

"This is a chance to fight for the Union against slavery." The quaver in his voice and knot in his throat surprised Knobby. Elizabeth set her lips and stared straight ahead. He took her hand, limp, in his. "Elizabeth, I'm no house servant. I can't do anything in a whorehouse, and I sure don't want you doing anything in one."

"Since when are you a soldier?"

"I'm a horse handler. I intend to get us into cattle country where a Negro man can be a man if he is a horseman. You're going to ride safely on an armed Union boat down to Matamoros. Herr Reinbach made arrangements. You'll have a nice place to stay down there."

"What do I want with Mexico? Why do I want to go where I don't know the talk?"

"You can't stay here alone."

"Leatherwood calls me welcome."

"We jumped the broomstick together—you're my wife. Doesn't that mean anything?"

"Husband and wife cleave to one another, not you go riding off in a gun gang and send me alone to Mexico. Bad enough I was a slave, when I got sold away I had to leave my family and the only place I ever knew. Then you come and got me and we had to run off into the water. Etienne was a godsend, and alone together in his water world, we weren't slaves anymore. Since we walked back onto the earth, it's all different." She flopped facedown on the bed and refused to talk anymore.

He left her sulking in bed and put on the flannel shirt and striped wool pants

Leatherwood had given him. Eye had promised to come take Knobby to purchase his outfit for the liberation front. He determined he would get some new clothes and return this shirt and pants to Leatherwood. Wondering if he was a fool to expect a white man to show up for a colored, he sat on the porch of Skyhouse to wait for Eye. Not ten minutes after Knobby sat down, Eye came whistling around the corner. He spied Knobby and held up a fistful of cash.

"First, we get you boots and a hat, then a few necessaries till you'll have right smart of an outfit." The first couple of mercantile stores they went to were closed up, windows boarded over. "Back when the Yankees finally invaded and General Hebert gave the orders to evacuate, everybody drug all their wares off to Houston or Liberty. They laid planks over the railroad bridge and drove cattle and horses across. The cotton presses all shut down. Governor Lubbock wanted the town burnt out and all the cisterns broke up, so the Yankees couldn't occupy it. Would have been a damn waste. As is, ain't one store in ten still doing business, but grog shops. Now this General Magruder says the Rebs are coming back, I figure everybody will leave but the convent nuns and the hard cases. You notice nary a church bell rung Sunday?"

Greenleve, Block and Company—*wholesale drygoods, furnishings, notions, boots, shoes and hats*—was still doing business. The salesman who met them at the door addressed Eye.

"Help you with something, sir?"

"As you can see," Knobby said, "I am the one in need of new clothing."

"Hat to boots, we going to do him up right smart. Ain't skimping none neither." Eye grinned at Knobby and said, "I don't hold much with Reinbach's coveting a uniform so much. Seems to me a right smart man gets him on a uniform and soon enough the fancy blouse is doing his thinking. Most times, military stripes turn right fair men into asses."

"Vaquero, sergeant, and, now, philosopher. Eye, you do not disappoint," Knobby said.

The salesman stared at Knobby. "You don't talk like a nigger." He nodded at Eye. "He talks more like a nigger than you do."

"Our money's doing the talking for the both of us. You savvy that?" Eye asked. The salesman nodded and led them to a stack of wide-brimmed hats. Eye bought Knobby a sombrero of light gray felt and a big blue paisley wipe to tie around his neck. He got a pair of tall decent-if-not-fancy boots. Eight dollars the pair, the boots had high French heels, red tops, and lone stars tooled on the sides. The store-bought boots pinched some, but Eye said once they got wore in the heels would slip smooth so Knobby wouldn't blister, and he'd never wear anything else.

"Damned if you don't look the man, now, Knob. I allow you look true enough to walk in the Tremont House and take a room, rub against the big dogs."

The Union Loyal Liberation Front bought Knobby a wool blanket, an India rubber groundcloth, a rain slicker, a tin cup, an iron spoon. Eye unfolded the blanket and laid it on top of the sheet of India rubber and rolled the two together so the rubber was on the outside.

"There's your bedroll, Knob, tight against the weather."

Eye said Knobby also had to have some chaps—buckskin armor against cactus and thorny brush. The storekeeper offered Knobby a canteen, but Eye said they had good corked gourds for water. Their next stop was at a gunsmith's, in a place called Brick Front Store.

"Herr Reinbach says the gun makes the shootist. Strong gun, strong man."

The gunsmith had got hold of a cache of Confederate guns when the Rebs lost control of Galveston. He offered a good selection, but the prices were dear. He had a couple of English five-shooters—a Bentley and a Tranter—a Remington Navy Model with the octagonal barrel, a Whitneyville Walker, a couple of the lighter Colt's Dragoons, and one Colt's Army Model, all .44 caliber. He had two Colt's .36 caliber six-shooters, and he had a Le Mat grapeshot revolver.

"Lookahere," the gunsmith said in a raspy voice, "This Le Mat is the over and under beauty General Beauregard carries, what he used at Corinth." He handed the revolver to Eye, who handed it to Knobby. "Cylinder has chambers for eight .44-caliber cartridges. This lower barrel fires a .60-caliber shot charge. Nine shots without reloading."

Knobby hefted the Le Mat, heavy as a musket, then looked to Eye, who shook his head at the grapeshot revolver, looked down the barrel of the Colt's Army single-action six-shooter.

"Not bad rifled," Eye said. "No pits neither. Looks well took care of."

Knobby hefted the big Walker.

"Percussion," said the gunsmith. "Solid gun. Nine-inch barrel, octagonal. Goes fifteen-and-a-half-inches and weighs four-an-a-half pounds."

Eye shook his head. "Too heavy."

Knobby picked up one of the dragoons. "This is lighter."

"See here," Eye said. He pointed to the trigger spur. "On your dragoon or the Navy Model you got to holster it butt forwards, use a twist around draw. This Colt's Army Model has a rear angled spur so it sets your holster butt backwards. You draw and cock regular."

Knobby opened and turned the chamber of the Colt's Army .44. The smooth wood stock held a dark stain of sweat—the sweat of some Rebel cavalryman fighting to keep his slaves. *Gun,* Knobby thought, *you are about to change sides.*

Eye picked out a used cartridge belt and a slotted open-toed scabbard, the leather worn enough to flex and swivel easily. Just over a foot long and weighing two to three pounds, the revolver was larger and heavier than Knobby had expected, but it had good balance and felt natural in his hand. The pistol's sleekness put him in mind of a racing horse, mane and tail flying.

Next, the gunsmith tried to sell Knobby an army rifle musket. "The Enfield and Springfield have been tested, tried and true, throughout the war. The Springfield is a .58 caliber. The Enfield is a .577, but you can use the same bullet, standard minié ball, in either one. I like the heavier Enfield, if you're not afoot."

"A man afoot ain't no man at all," Eye said. "A musketoon tears flesh at both ends. Ain't you got no Henrys?"

"This gentleman knows his shoulder arms," the gunsmith said and turned to Knobby. "You could do no better than a Henry rifle." The man lowered his voice and glanced around as if he were about to reveal a secret. "As rare and as prized as the Henry rifle is, I do happen to have one—and just one." He looked Knobby in the eyes, "The Henry rifle is a new model—a .44 caliber, sixteen-shot repeater. A damn good shooter with plenty of shots in reserve. I bought one off a Federal officer after they occupied the island. This weapon would retail for at least sixty dollars. They're hard to come by. I could easy get a hundred and a quarter, but I'll let it go for one-ten."

"Ain't you telling a windy," Eye said. "More like forty-five dollars, new. This ain't new, not by a jugful."

Eye and the gunsmith haggled back and forth until they settled on seventy-eight dollars.

From the gunsmith's, Eye and Knobby walked several blocks to a livery stable run by a Negro called Major Carey. The six-shooter rubbed Knobby's hip in a reassuring way. The Henry on his shoulder made a shadow like a pointing finger he stepped into every step he took. They passed white-painted board houses and a brick building Eye said was a hospital. They came to a wagon yard crowded with two-wheeled Mexican handcarts. Beside the wagon yard was an empty lot, a large livery barn, and a corral full of small, skittish horses. Not as dark as Knobby, Major Carey was yellow-toned. He shook hands with Eye, and stared at Knobby as hard as the drygoods salesman had, probably wondering why Eye was horse shopping with a Negro, or what another Negro was doing in Galveston these days.

"Gentlemen, business couldn't be worse. I have nowhere on the mainland to drive my stock to. I'm at your mercy—come steal some of my horses."

Knobby was tempted to say the liveryman didn't talk like a nigger, but he held his tongue. The stables held American and Spanish horses starting at one hundred dollars without tack, Mexican horses from twenty-five dollars, and, out in the corral, mustangs for ten dollars up.

Eye said, "Forget them American and pure Spanish horses. The general will go sixty, maybe seventy, for mount and tack. Mexican horses make out fine grazing—no grain to buy."

"Mexican horse," said Major Carey, "is the same as a mustang only better because he's been bred and raised on a ranch. Tough as a mustang but more manageable."

Knobby needed Eye's opinion about guns, not about horses. He studied the Mexican horses in the stalls, then he listened to what the mustangs out in the corral were saying. The mustangs had short backs, long pasterns. They were bloody at the mouth where they'd been bit broken—and not long ago. He'd like to shove a metal bar in this Major Carey's mouth, see how quick he turned and stopped. None of the Mexican horses or the mustangs would go fourteen hands. He'd get more horse for the money with the cheaper mustang. A near-wild animal was keener, might outlast a ranch-bred mount. The mustangs were mostly paints, singular and picturesque, but Knobby mistrusted their gaudiness. All the well-bred horses he'd known on Noble Plantation had been dark solid colors. One mustang mare, barely broke, was solid black. Even in the small corral she kept her distance from other horses. She appeared fast, and none of her motions were labored. She eyed Knobby with cautious curiosity more than fear or anger.

Appraising him with one eye squinted, one brow lifted, the black liveryman interrupted Knobby's deliberations. "If it's long-lasting you're after, I can let you have a fine mule—reasonable."

"I'm not buying a pack animal," Knobby said.

"Only good mule is a dead mule." Eye grinned as if he'd made the best joke in Texas.

Two bays looked pretty good, and Knobby spotted a sorrel that might go over fourteen hands, showed no blood at the mouth, and looked hardy. He pointed out the sorrel, and Major Carey took a coiled rope from a nail in the gatepost, made a big loop in the rope, and swung it backhanded above his head. The excited horses ran circles in the enclosure. When the sorrel came around, Carey rolled the loop out, but the animal dodged and the rope collapsed. It took four tosses before the sorrel ran into the loop. The rest of the mustangs ran and snorted, kicking up dust. None of Carey's horses liked the man.

Knobby took off his scabbard, handed Eye his pistol and rifle. Major Carey got a halter on the sorrel without much fuss, and the horse took blanket and saddle with a defeated look in his eyes. Before he mounted, Knobby ran his hand down the horse's neck, down each leg. "*Huh*, pumpkin, *huh*—easy now," Knobby said. The joints were sound, strong. The animal tolerated Knobby's touch, didn't shy. In the lot adjacent to the corral Knobby walked, then trotted the sorrel. This one wanted to please, hadn't been broken, had sense if no training. But Knobby kept looking at the black mare. She reminded him of the big black devil he'd ridden in New Orleans. Smaller, of course. She had mustang legs—deer's legs—and moved as quick. Her body was not as long as the other mustangs', but she had the same roach back ahead of the coupling. Knobby unsaddled the sorrel and put him back in the corral.

When Knobby pointed to the black, Major Carey said, "I was thinking you know horseflesh. Now I have my doubts." Knobby grinned and took the lariat. The liveryman shook his head. "The black is a snide horse, like some black folks."

Knobby slid the end of the lariat into a small loop. Talking to the black and watching her perky ears and big eyes, Knobby swung the loop once and pitched it over the horse's head.

"Well, I'll be." Major Carey looked at Eye, who leaned against the gatepost. Only the pulsing of his one eye betrayed he was not asleep. He watched without comment.

Knobby expected the black to shy, but she did not. She let him slip the bridle on, and she accepted the bit, though her mouth was raw. "Sorry, girl. We'll salve your lips, and you won't bite metal ever again," Knobby told her. Her side was marked with rowel cuts where some wrangler had spurred her. Knobby rubbed her neck. He took the saddle blanket and, talking softly all the time, moved it back and forth across her back. When he tightened the cinch, she puffed out her stomach remembering the earlier horse-breaker. Knobby waited until she inhaled, then cinched the saddle tight. He mounted. She didn't budge. She waited until he had her outside the corral, then she arched her back and left the ground all at once. Knobby was ready. He went up and came down with her. His new hat went up higher and came down in the sand. "Ha. You're surprised I'm still here. I think we can be friends," he said. The mare answered by stepping on Knobby's new sombrero.

Eye sauntered over and picked up the hat, beat it against his thigh, knocking dust out. He dangled the hat by two rawhide thongs. "Forgot to tighten your bonnet strings. Got it wore in proper, right fast."

Next, the horse showed her speed. Before Knobby had her out of the lot, she was at full gallop. She took off down a side street, and he let her run for blocks. Then she whirled and ran most of the way back. Suddenly, she charged the brick wall of a drygoods building. Knobby checked her, and she stopped so quick a lesser rider would have sailed over her laid-back ears.

Major Carey came running down the street, Eye strolling a ways behind. Knobby turned the mare and trotted her back to Eye, who stood grinning. "Damn, if I don't wager this black could give my Dolores a run."

The liveryman caught up to them. "You want her, you can have her for thirty-five."

"Thirty-five? Why she wasn't hardly greenbroke before Knob here did the trick. I wager she still ain't done."

"She's got some pluck. I can take twenty-five."

"I don't allow you will. I reckon none but Knobby can ride her, and he might buy elsewhere."

"You buy a saddle and tack, too?"

"Not this saddle," Knobby said. "It's so long it'll bring kidney sores on her. And no bit."

"It's a good plains saddle. I gave sixty dollars for that saddle."

Eye snorted. "With what horse underneath for sixty dollars?"

Back at the livery, Knobby found a hackamore with plenty of life left in it. He looked over the sale saddles. He was used to hornless Eastern rigs. Eye pointed out a heavy Mexican-style saddle with a *mochila* covering he said he favored. Most of the used stock saddles were handmade with sheepskin or goatskin covering the saddle tree. One had a rawhide seat. Knobby picked it up. Lighter than the Mexican-style, it didn't weigh more than twelve or fourteen pounds, had a smaller horn, and had a hide seat stitched onto the tree. Leather covered the fork, and there were leather outer skirts behind the cantle and leather-lined sidebars. The wooden stirrups were wide enough for Knobby's big feet.

"I like this one, if it sits okay."

"That's a Texas saddle. It's a changed up Mexican-style with littler rings," Eye said.

Knobby picked a thick saddle blanket to pad the black's sores and swung the lightweight Texas saddle on. It had one cinch in the middle, what Eye called a "center-fire rig." He said Knobby might want to double-rig it later, especially if he ever worked cattle with a short rope.

Major Carey said he was getting the little end of the horn, but if they were paying in gold or in Mills money he'd take fifty dollars for the black mare, the bridle and bit, and the Texas saddle.

"What's Mills money?" Knobby asked.

"R. and D. G. Mills and Company is the biggest bank in Texas. Robert Mills is likely the richest man in all Texas, too. Mills money's good as gold," Carey said.

After they settled on the black, Eye told Knobby, "Set your horse once more." Knobby swung up onto the black, which stood calmly. "Now, swing your holster around." Eye loosened the scabbard and put Knobby's new six-shooter on his left hip. "Swung over like this, she rides butt forwards and you can grab her with a cross draw." Knobby reached across his stomach and drew the pistol. He practiced the cross draw a couple of times, then he swung down off the black and slid the holster back to his right side. "One more thing. Check your cylinder regular. Keep it loaded—five in the chamber and the firing pin on empty. Do it the same time every day. I load up last thing at night, after I get in my bedroll. 'Never forget' is my nighttime prayer. I make sure I have five full cylinders, and I say my prayer no matter how wore out I am," Eye said.

"I'll remember."

Eye paid Carey extra to stall the mare and rub salve on the spur cuts. Knobby planned to get to know her, work with her until the Liberation Front left for San Antonio. He whispered he would be back soon, told her since she was as black as him he would call her Darkie. She twitched her ears and nuzzled his hand with her nose soft but for the prickle of her long whiskers.

Eye had to go back to the Neptune Saloon for a smile of old bourbon and to sign up some more recruits. "Before I tote the signup sheet to the general, we've got to sally forth to one more stop. There's a last bit of fixins you want." He took Knobby to the Ahrens Rope Factory, where he had a man cut thirty-five feet of half-inch manila hemp from a huge roll. "I know how good a roper you are. Your outfit ain't full up without a first-rate lariat. This ain't out of the general's poke. Ever foot's on me." Eye bought petrolatum and paraffin and told Knobby to mix them half-and-half for conditioning and waterproofing the hemp.

Knobby carried his new treasures up to Skyhouse. He wanted to spread the new fixins out on the bed and show them to Elizabeth, but she was not in the room. He folded up the shirt and pants Leatherwood had loaned him. On the muslin bedcover his metal cup and spoon, his pistol and rifle glinted in sunlight through the window. He put his hand on each, silently counting juba, hard metal cool to his touch. He brought the new tin cup to his lips and pictured himself drinking coffee, or, better, whisky like the Cajun Etienne had, by a campfire out on El Desierto Muerto. He fitted the sombrero on his head, tilted it back, tilted it forward. He wished there were a looking glass in the room.

He opened the cylinder of the Colt's and slipped in five cartridges, eased the firing pin down on the empty chamber as Eye had instructed so he wouldn't accidentally shoot himself or his horse as he rode. He cinched the scabbard on his right hip and practiced drawing. Then he put it on his left hip, butt forward, and practiced drawing across his belly. Eye had said the cross draw was best for a man on horseback. His first few tries Knobby had trouble grabbing the pistol without looking down at it. In the days before the war, when there had been dancing parties on Noble Plantation, his mama had laughed about the white men who danced looking down at their feet. She had danced with him in the little slave cabin, humming their music under her breath. *Mama*, he thought, *I wish you could see me now. I can step lively, and I will dance to make you proud.* A dancer who had to look down might get laughed at, a gunfighter might get shot. Eye had told him fast draws were for dime novels. In a real drawdown, steady aim and nerves won the fight. Knobby worked on pulling the .44 smooth and steady. He visualized another gun firing at him and concentrated on gripping the pistol without trembling. Alone in his room, Knobby did not get much faster on the draw, but he got more reliable. He practiced all afternoon. The good Lord steadied his hand. He aimed true and shot straight. That day in his room Knobby killed the nameless slave raiders who brought Grandfather Samuel from West Africa. Knobby gunned down Leonard Viress III, the master's son in Delaware who made Grandfather burn his Bible and eat the ashes. Knobby shot Grandfather's next master, Judah Grivot, the rice planter, shot dead the first time years ago. Knobby shot the slave, Hamp, who crawled onto the shuck mattress of Knobby's mama. He shot D. D. Bohanan and his man A. J. who made Knobby ride the black devil in New Orleans. And, finally, he killed the master of the plantation in Louisiana who murdered his slave Calvin's wife because she would not lie with him and had since kept Calvin in chains.

When Elizabeth came in, she sat on the edge of the bed and slipped two cartridges from the belt that held Knobby's scabbard. She rolled the bullets back and forth in her palm, the brass cases clicking against one another. She gave him long looks that made him turn away. He tied a slip-loop in the end of his stiff, new rope, the same way he had rigged his horse ropes back on Noble Plantation. Eye had called the slip-loop a honda. It was full dark when Knobby went outside and stretched the rope between a tree and one of the porch posts of Skyhouse. He left the rope tightly tied to get any kinks out. Just before he crawled into the soft bed with Elizabeth, he remembered Eye's nighttime prayer and checked the cylinder of the new six-shooter.

Sends Elizabeth to Mexico

Herr Reinbach's steamer to Matamoros turned out to be a rickety old steam packet, freshly painted up to make it look seaworthy. The morning was wet and gray, and a cold wind was blowing out to sea. Eye called it a blue norther, visible as a line of cloud dark purple as a bruise and so straight it looked drawn with a knife. Knobby had second thoughts about putting Elizabeth at sea in such weather, though she seemed resigned to going. When Reinbach yelled into the wind that there would be a guard of Union soldiers on board and a Federal gunboat to escort the steamer, Knobby got easier in his mind. Had Elizabeth smiled, he would have felt fine.

Besides Elizabeth, eight women and five children were getting in the long-boats to the steamer. Flood's wife and children were the only other Negroes. Knobby guessed John Johnson, the other Negro recruit, had no family. Knobby carried Elizabeth through the shallows out to the pitching boat. Breaking waves were so big he had to turn his back against them and spread his legs to keep from being knocked down. Elizabeth stared straight ahead and spoke barely loud enough for him to hear her over the ocean spray and the slapping waves. "I don't think I will ever lay eyes on you again, Knobby Cotton."

"You'll lay more than eyes on me, I promise. Here," he took his new paisley wipe from around his neck and dabbed the tear shine off her face. He tied the bandana around her neck and leaned to kiss her. The boat rose and dipped, and Knobby's kiss landed on the top button of her blouse. An old sailor in the lighter cursed, and the men at oars leaned back, their jaws tight, eyes squinted against the cold wind. The boat rocked through the chop and moved off. Elizabeth's shape appeared and disappeared in clouds of seaspray between green ocean and gray sky.

Orders to Mount and Ride

The norther, stinging cold, howled across the island and played itself out. Two days after Elizabeth left, the winds died down, clouds came in from the Gulf, and a steady drizzle set in. Knobby moved out of Skyhouse and slept at the livery stable with Darkie. He worked with the mare, practiced his shooting, and waited for orders.

Christmas week, Herr Reinbach sent word for the Liberation Front to slip out of Galveston. He warned that at least one regiment of Confederate Cavalry was active east of town. Well after midnight the day after Christmas, the newly recruited soldiers of the Union Loyal Liberation Front walked their horses out of town, west toward the middle of the island. Eye pointed to three large trees close together where he said the pirate Jean Laffite had buried a treasure chest before he left Galveston for the last time. They passed a Federal picket at Eagle Grove, at the island side of the railroad bridge. Some of the men wanted to lay planks over the rails on the bridge and walk the horses across to Virginia Point on the mainland, but Eye said they'd come smack against a Confederate guard on the other side. Instead, they rode on west past fruit farms and small clusters of horses, cattle, and sheep. Eye guided them to a small lake where they filled their water gourds. "This is the only sweetwater lake I know of on all Galveston Island. Everything else is salt-fouled." They moved through empty mud flats and grass too coarse for grazing. "Nothing much grows this far down the island. Dove weed and goat weed, sea oats near the dunes." Dunes rose twelve to fifteen feet, darker shapes of black than the night sky. The horses broke sand dollars and snail shells under their hooves. Mosquitoes and sand flies buzzed around the heads of men and horses alike, and Eye doled out strong-smelling shark oil they rubbed on their necks and faces and between their horses' ears. Eye warned everyone to listen for rattlers. "Likeways, don't ride over no gators—they're in here thick as fiddlers in Hell." At the water's edge Eye pointed to a purple blob trailing long rootlike tentacles. "Watch the jellyfish. He'll sting you bad, Knob." Eye dismounted and knelt in the shallow waves and picked up a ball of something black. Knobby wondered how Eye had spotted the dab of blackness on the dark shore. "See here." Eye got his rain slicker from his bedroll and stuck his finger through a hole in the slicker the size of the .44s in Knobby's cartridge belt. He stretched the slicker tight over his boot top and smeared a pinch of the black ball over the hole. "Karankawas used this tar to waterproof their canoes. It'll dry as a good patch on any tear." He pinched off another piece of the tar and put it in his mouth. He grinned, chewing, the tar a wad of black between his teeth. "It's not bad for a chaw when you got no tobacco, or when you can't risk the flame of a smoke." Behind a dune overgrown with tall sea oats the men paused to eat hard rolls and sip the fresh water from the lake. When everyone had eaten, Eye snugged his hat down and rode Dolores into the water. "Stay close," said the fog and mist from where Eye had disappeared.

"Don't make no unnecessary noise to give away what the fog's going to hide." Knobby nudged Darkie with his knees and followed the voice into the water. "There's a reef out here, somewhere underneath. This is where the Karankawas waded back and forth from the island to the shore even before pirates landed here." Eye had brought, tied to his saddle, a long cross brace from a broken ladder at the livery stable, and he stuck it down in the water. "Shallow all the way." Nine men on horseback, each carrying all his gear, no packhorses or mules on leads, they moved slowly with faint noises of leather creaking and water lapping against horses' legs, and these sounds were carried away in the strong breeze.

Water rose over Knobby's boots and filled them, the weight anchoring him to Darkie, to the earth itself. He thought of the water moccasins in Etienne's swamp and was glad this was saltwater. Knobby was surprised the ocean felt warmer than the air. The mare moved as steadily as the waves, a surging, rocking rhythm that made Knobby feel as though they were rushing across the water and, at the same time, as though they were standing still, cocooned in fog and thick salt air, lulled by the smells of salt and fish, the buffeting of the breeze. The men around him were shapes of darkness bobbing as small boats drifting away. So dreamlike was the passage that when the mare's sway became a sudden leaning up and pumping through sand and silt, Knobby wondered if he had slept most of the way across. Then his legs out of warm water were cold in the breeze that hummed again in the grass. To the east, the fog grew gray with the coming morning, but to the west, where they headed, dark night continued.

He was in Texas now for sure, no longer protected on an occupied island. But no Rebel soldiers took shape in the fog. For more than an hour they walked their horses through marsh grass and mud flats. As they moved farther inland the fog grew thinner, and Knobby made out the men and horses close around him. They were as raw-looking as the gray coastal horizon. Knobby, big Flood, and John Johnson were the only Negroes. Knobby had met the rest of the nine, but recalled only names: a fair-haired smiling boy named Dwight, one they called Irish Pat, and the German Rudolph Hermann who was older than the rest of them. Rudolph called Knobby "Herr Cotton" and shook his hand as if they were longtime associates easy with one another's company. This Rudolph was tall, a little stooped—Knobby figured from bending down to look people in the eye or from dipping his head under doorways and roofs. Yellow-gray hair and gold-rimmed glasses made Rudolph seem wise in the way Grandfather Samuel had been wise. Knobby could not picture the quiet Rudolph shooting Reb soldiers or dodging Indian arrows. Of the other three, one who rode a paint horse had long black hair braided down the middle of his back. Had this one, who they called Swede, not been so fair-skinned, Knobby would have thought him an Indian. The other two were nameless to Knobby—one he thought of as Stiff Leg because he walked with one leg always locked at the knee, and the other as Skinny, because he was.

Eye had cautioned Knobby against the impression of appearances. "I wouldn't sally forth in so dangerous a country if most of these men hadn't already proved their spunk. We'll fare tolerable well. Some more rascals are waiting to join us in San Antone."

They kept a close watch for Confederate Cavalry patrols, for Union troops coming in off the Gulf, for bandits and renegades. Eye said they didn't have to worry about Indians, yet. The land was timberless, low and marshy, and they moved steadily through the thinning fog. Knobby hoped the weather out on the Gulf was better, and he prayed Elizabeth's steamer plied easy seas all the way to Matamoros. Eye had said the fog was a lucky break. Knobby asked how the sergeant knew his way through the grayness.

"Follow the breeze. I mark it against my left cheek today, blowing warm and wet from the Gulf. Long as I keep the feeling against my left cheek, we're moving steady west, a mite northwest. If there's not enough wind to feel, spy the grass tops. No stir there, look to how clouds drift off."

The black mare got better every mile. Knobby spoke softly in her ear, "Come on Darkie, strong Darkie, sweet Darkie." He knew they were friends for life.

Eye remarked late in the day, "No quit in her, is there."

That night they hobbled the horses and made a cold camp of cornbread and jerked beef. Eye rigged a mosquito bar across two saddles, and the men slept in a row up under the bar serenaded by the bellows of bullfrogs. A few mosquitoes found their way inside the netting, but mostly the men were spared. The smell of shark oil mixed with body odors. Mosquitoes outside the netting hummed furiously, and Knobby wondered if he would be able to sleep. He heard a clicking—Eye saying his prayers, checking his pistol cylinder—then Knobby knew he had fallen asleep because he was in a dinghy on the Gulf and Elizabeth's face and hands, green as the ocean, rose toward the surface, and she screamed, *Lord Jesus, Lord Jesus,* and Knobby woke to the high-pitched voice of John Johnson calling out in his sleep, *Lord Jesus.* Knobby reached and touched the man's coiled ebony hair that was wet with sweat and gently shook him awake.

All morning they moved through fog and grassy marsh, the same as the day before. Eye trotted Dolores up beside Darkie and spat. "Crawfish land." Near noon, the sun began to burn through the fog. They rode from gray clouds of fog into bright silver pools of light and back into gray. Pine scent put Mississippi all around, and Knobby's mother Hester's face shone darkly in shafts of sunlight. Above tall pines, blue sky again, the sun bright, the air cold. Out of pines and into prairie grass and back into pines, all afternoon.

Rudolph Hermann rode reading a book he rested against his saddle pommel and sometimes said sentences out loud, sometimes in Spanish: *Que sera, sera,* sometimes in English: *What must be, must be,* but more often in German: *Was sein muss, muss sein.* The German words sounded to Knobby like the wintry clatter and click of frozen tree limbs against one another. A regular mockingbird, Rudolph talked whatever language he read or heard.

They passed south of some log houses on a distant bluff scattered with live oak and pine and two enormous magnolia trees by themselves on top. Eye named the bluff the town of New Washington, but to Knobby it was more Mississippi. How could he miss a place where he was a slave? That he missed his mama and Grandfather Samuel did not surprise him. It did not surprise him that he missed other cousins on the plantation, too. He even missed ole Brandywine, the master's big gray jumper. What did surprise him was how he yearned for the call of birds from the moss-draped oaks around the white-painted stables, the sweet mix of oat dust and dung on a warm morning, even the fresh-turned fields and the cotton plants, their brown pods swelling to burst open white and fluffy as fresh-baked biscuits. He missed the sleeping breathing sounds of folks crowded together on their poor ticks in the quiet dark when they had the whole night away from the fields or the wagons or the gin or the house kitchen, safe from the overseer or from some white stranger who might show up on any day and buy someone they loved and take him away forever. He breathed pine scent deep. The sun flashed between the magnolias on the bluff. When it flashed again, then again, he realized someone was swinging metal—a scythe-blade or some such tool. He wondered if a slave labored on the bluff, and he raised his arm in greeting. The answer returned was the rapid-fire attack of a woodpecker on a hollow trunk.

Now they were out of the wet marshland, to cover up hoofbeat and hoofprint Sergeant Goar instructed the men to shoe their horses with moccasin-like wraps of hide and to tie hide bags under the horses' tails so they couldn't be trailed by their droppings. "It's a Comanche trick," Eye told Knobby. "Their ain't no end of a horse a Comanche don't consider."

Late afternoon, they stopped at a double-hewed log house that sufficed as general store and tavern with a steam mill attached. The miller had ground no meal for days and was glad to serve them whisky and sweet potatoes. He did not ask their business, and when Stiff Leg inquired about army patrols the miller shook his head. Before dark, they crossed the tracks of a railroad Sergeant Goar said connected Harrisburg with Richmond. Not far beyond the railbed prairie ended, and they rode into timber and canebreaks as sudden as crossing a border drawn on a map. "We're near to the Brazos. Private Cotton, you scout ahead with me."

Herr Reinbach was the only one Knobby had heard use military rank in the Union Loyal Liberation Front. It took a second before he realized *he* was Private Cotton. He and Eye walked their horses in afternoon shadows of sycamores, oaks, locusts, and hackberries for three or four miles to the bank of the river. The water was up close to the bank and clouded with mud from recent rains, but the current was not strong. Downriver they came to a cleared area where hoofprints diced up the mud. Eye hunkered down and put his hand to the ashes of a dead fire.

"Stone cold." Eye walked to the river's edge, spread wide his arms. "*Los Brazos de Dios*, Mexican for 'the arms of God,' and I reckon she's long enough even for His arms."

Lord God, Knobby prayed, *protect me in those arms.*

On both sides of the river, here about a hundred yards across, were tied two dugout log canoes. "Knobby, ride back yonder and get the others. We'll ride these boats across and swim the horses beside us. Camp on the other side."

They crossed the river and made camp in a pecan grove near a patch of grazing grass. With a hand ax, Eye cut stakes about five feet long and pounded them a foot or so down into the soft black earth—a stake every eight to ten feet—making a ring. He tied his lariat to Knobby's and two others he borrowed and ran the rope from stake to stake, making a corral for the horses. Each man, before he loosed his horse in this enclosure, removed the hide wraps from his horse's hooves and the bag from beneath its tail. The bags they emptied of dung.

Flood shot two long-eared rabbits he called mule rabbits and skinned them slick as you please. Rudolph said the big rabbits were called jack hares in Texas. Eye cut two spits of green hickory and skewered each hare. Flood made a fire with fallen limbs, and they boiled coffee. When the pecan coals were red-gray, Eye laid the meat directly on top. The sizzling meatsmoke on top of the coffee smell made Knobby shake with hunger. Eye turned over each hare, searing the meat on all sides. Then he stuck each spit up in the ground and the men pulled off meat in strips, licking their burned fingertips. The rabbit, blacked on the outside, pink and juicy inside, was better than a Christmas feast on Noble Plantation, better even than the lamb tenderloin, curried sausages, and venison with port wine sauce served in Leatherwood's whorehouse kitchen.

The men spread their bedrolls around the fading glow of the cookfire, their saddles at their heads as pillows. Eye rolled a bedtime smoke, picked up a long twig and stuck it in the coals, lifted the burning twig to tobacco. The red tip of the cigarette moved up and down and Knobby heard a pistol cylinder click as Eye performed his bedtime ritual. Knobby rolled up his rain slicker to cushion his neck. He stretched out with his six-shooter in its scabbard still tied to his hip. The youth, Dwight, stepped over Knobby's legs, then squatted down, interrupting Knobby's prayers so he had to start over. Up close, Dwight did not look so young. Chewing his words and a rabbit bone that stuck out of his mouth, he said, "Now we've crossed the Brazos, we've got to add Comanches to our 'look-out-fors.'" Dwight's hand closed on the handle of Knobby's revolver, and their eyes met. He gave Knobby his ready smile and slipped the pistol from the scabbard and put it down through the space between the forks of Knobby's saddle. "Under here it stays dry and handy. No one can get to it without waking you."

"I thank you for good advice," Knobby said.

Dwight's smile flared with the fire. When the flame went down, shadows cast the young man's face into a frown. He stared past Knobby into the darkness and speaking mostly to himself said, "Lest we forget the poet's tale," and then in a lilt between singing and praying he recited: *"The Assyrian came down like the wolf on the fold. And the sheen of their spears was like stars on the sea. And the eyes of the sleepers waxed deadly and chill."* Then he slapped Knobby's empty scabbard, laughed once, and crawled between his blankets. No sooner had Dwight rested his head against his saddle than he was softly snoring.

West of the Brazos they crossed uneven sandy land marked with clumps of oaks. The same good eye Flood had used spying and shooting the jack hares brought warning of riders to the south. Eye holed them up under a live oak, its limbs curving close to the ground like protecting arms hiding them. Here they drank from the same clear spring that fed the giant oak, watered their horses, and filled their canteens. Eye rolled and smoked a cigarette. Some of the men alighted and napped on the grass, but Knobby was too full of this new country to sleep.

They crossed the Colorado, having stopped for directions at a cabin where a man Eye called a "charcoal burner" said the river was no more than eight miles distant, they would enter the timber in another five miles. This man, his teeth black, his face and clothes filthy, stared at Knobby and Flood and asked if Eye was a nigger hunter. "Right many runaways hereabouts. Nigger stealers is doing lively. A coffle of niggers was led through here a fortnight come yesterday. A boss man asked could they water the soots, unchained them right here."

"That so?" Eye turned to Knobby and loud and clear said, "Mr. Cotton, this dumb shit charcoal burner has acted the damn dog, but we shouldn't linger here, so I ask you not to shoot him all to pieces." The man's mud-smeared face went ashen, and he turned and ran into the cabin closing the door behind him. Irish Pat suggested they wedge a log against the door and burn the cabin down, but Eye said to save their matches for meat worth roasting.

When they reached the Colorado River, Darkie plunged right in. The water was no higher than Knobby's saddle skirts, and the nimble little horse picked her way up the steep bank on the other side. West of the Colorado the land was higher and drier, covered with short mesquite grass the horses liked. Where there were no twisted scrub oaks, there were bright green mesquite bushes, and, along creeks Eye said ran dry most summers, limestone outcroppings shone white in the sun. North of Salado they found the road to San Antonio, sand so loose their horses sank up to their pastern joints. This looked like desert to Knobby, nothing but mesquite bushes and prickly pear cactus, but Eye said they would not see real desert until after San Antone.

Gideon Jones: An Unposted Letter

To Win Shu

8 July 1865

Dear Win Shu,

I speculate where you may be, if you remained in Cumberland or if you are westering like me. At Westport Landing, I saw some Chinese bound for California where I'm told there are full cities of Chinamen. A man in Kansastown called all Chinese people Johns or Johnnie. I wonder why. I don't picture you among your countrymen, but somewhere making your own way.

I wish I could sip again your strong green tea. You added much to my education. The colonel spoke to me of many things, but <u>you</u> listened to me. Your silences are eloquent. I thought hard for words to make you nod or lift your brow. I asked a question, you answered with another question. Your questions took me places I had never been before. Perhaps you would lift your brow, ask me one more question.

Two days past I listened to a teamster describe snow so deep it covered the roof of a prospector's cabin in Nevada. Snow covered everything except the cabin's smoking stovepipe. He said it gave the appearance of a hole in the white world, a hole sending up smoke from the infernos of Hell. Talk of so much snow reminded me how you hate the cold, and I penned a verse that may amuse you.

Where does a Chinaman go
When it snows?
Only the Chinaman
Knows.

I wonder where you've gone, old friend? I hope you are in a warm place where birds always sing.

Your former clerk and companion,

Gideon Jones

Alexander and Charles Wesley: Wake Me for the Shooting

Alexander Sees the Elephant
(June 1863–May 1864)

I believed I'd missed a mighty adventure because the great war ended
before I could get in it. After I met some veterans, I wasn't so sure. The ones
I talked to weren't bragging any. Charles Wesley Speer told me that while
he was soldiering he felt far away from the war, especially during battles.
Only since he'd gotten out, he said, had he begun to feel it.

—from *Gideon Jones' Journal*

Alexander Wesley, true to his dreams, was in the Texas Cavalry, but, in spite of his
determination not to, he became a foot soldier. Every man in the Texas brigade
felt the same way. "A Texan don't walk a foot, if he can help it," Alexander heard
chanted out step by step and month by month as the Texans walked all the way
to Atlanta and then all the way to Tennessee. In Texas they had organized as
mounted cavalry, then had been dismounted. The main thing about soldiering,
Silas Nunner pointed out, is that "it don't turn out the way you expected."

Alexander and Silas Nunner and the rest of the Texans outfit had orders to
take the rail cars to join General Bragg's Army of Tennessee. The hospitals were
emptied. Those too sick to walk would follow once they got upright. The Texans
left the cars at Wartrace, Tennessee, where they found General Bragg and made
camp. Major General Pat Cleburne put them in his division. They moved camp
to Tullahoma and combined seven weary Texas regiments into two. When they
weren't walking through thick woods or down some mud road, they were cutting
and dragging trees and digging clay to build breastworks, or they were cooking up
rations to carry with a fresh forty rounds of ammunition and all their other necessaries. Baggage wagons? Just something else Alexander learned was not always

part of soldiering. They carried their baggage—skillet handles fit down into gun barrels, meat (when they had meat) came along on bayonets, blankets were rolled full of other items and tied across shoulders. And plenty of men in the dismounted cavalry ended up walking barefoot. They were a motley lot. They wore homespun uniforms, stolen shirts, Confederate caps, and big-brim hats. They carried Enfield rifles, Mississippi rifles, old U.S. muskets with percussion locks, even buck and ball double-barrel shotguns.

Alexander "seen the elephant" for the first time in the thick woods near Chickamauga Creek, where they'd been ordered to stay put. Close by, Union troops who were dug in behind log works fired on them until dark. Exposed as they were, the Texans were ordered not to return fire. In the trees and brush the moonless sky was as dark as blindness. Under this cover of darkness they moved off through the woods, bullets whining and howling around them like a wind-storm. Alexander thought to run, as he'd always feared he would, but in the dark who could tell which way to bolt? He could hear the war going on out there in the dark, but he couldn't see a thing. The next day began with cannonading that shook the ground, white smoke like clouds come low to earth. Ahead of them, distant Rebel yells and Yankee hurrahs. All day they moved about in the woods, sometimes firing, sometimes being fired at, but mostly just moving and stopping, moving and stopping, then waiting to move again. A full day in the war, and Alexander had yet to see the face of a single enemy.

Come dark again, Alexander slept in a ditch, short naps late into the night, waking to artillery fire or distant yells only to rest his face against cool dirt to sleep again. A waking nightmare. He dreamt their whole army was ordered to charge the Union troops. Minié balls whistled all around, the air was endless noise—pop of musket fire and roar of cannon, rattle and scrape of steel bayonets, thump of rifle butts, and crack of bone. He was running up a hill and the ground went soft and uneven, slid beneath his feet. He looked down at a Yankee soldier on whose swollen face he was standing, and the face was his own, was his brother's identical face. *Alexander*, Charles Wesley called. *Alexander*. All around him soldiers walked over bodies as if they were fallen logs, and then Alexander realized he was wide awake. He looked around to see if anyone else had heard Charles Wesley cry out. Could others hear what he dreamt? If anyone heard, he gave no sign. Like as not, each had his own nightmare. The shooting had mostly stopped, though it rang in his ears for hours. And as he had all of his life he heard his twin brother call out, *Alexander*. If Charles Wesley followed him even into battle, pulled at him and dragged him back even in the midst of this Hades, was there anywhere Alexander might escape his brother, the supplanter? *He wants to be there when I turn and run, to see me cowardly so he can tell Papa.*

The shooting died down, and they were ordered to re-form lines and put out a picket. No order to stack arms. Those who didn't sleep standing up lay down where they stood, with no tents, no supper. In the dark, a wounded soldier cried out for just one drop of water, yet Alexander was so exhausted he fell immediately to sleep. Come daylight, he remembered no dreams.

They stayed put for more than a week and never set up tents. Alexander was assigned to help Ordnance pick up weapons from dead soldiers—the first time he saw an enemy's face. His detail took watches, rings, money, and letters from the pockets of the dead. They took food from the dead men's knapsacks—Alexander ate around the blood-soaked parts of a pound cake. He pulled shoes off dead men's feet. He pried a corporal's fingers from his Enfield, and the man's bloated body lifted and its fixed eyes stared straight at Alexander. He dropped the rifle, and the body dropped back down, the accusing stare fastened on Heaven.

Wintering

After Chickamauga they pulled back to Chattanooga, where they fought at Missionary Ridge, and at Ringgold Gap, and then they fell back to winter at Dalton, Georgia. Alexander still had not turned and run from battle, but every time he fired and reloaded he had to force himself to rise and fire again. He was sure he would yet disgrace himself.

Mail from home equaled foraged food in lifting the spirits. Letters from wives and girlfriends were read over and over and were shared with chums. Paper was hard to come by, and ink was even more dear, yet men labored over letters to loved ones. He began several letters to Papa, but the only one he ever finished was the one he had sent from Richmond when he'd first joined the Chubs. Though he always pictured his brother still home in New York, Alexander guessed by now Charles Wesley was in Yankee uniform. Alexander knew he should write to tell Papa he was now in a Texas regiment in the Army of Tennessee, to tell Mama he was alive, to tell his sisters he thought of them—though he seldom did. But when he tried to write about camp life he hated how dreary it sounded, and when he tried to tell Papa about the Texas Cavalry (dismounted), he grew angry with Papa's foolish romantic notions. Angry with himself, angry that he'd tried to take Papa's notions as his own to cover his cowardice, Alexander ripped up or burned his letters. Also, he worried about mailing a letter that told where he was. He feared, somehow, Charles Wesley might come and find him. *If Charles Wesley finds me, he will know I am the scaredy cat I named him so many times.*

To pass the time of waiting they sometimes had drill. More often they pitched a tolerable baseball Silas Nunner made by wrapping a big walnut with strips of cotton and binding it with rawhide he'd soaked to draw it tight. Emmet Jenks put his jacknife to work on a fence rail bat until it fit smooth in your hand. When it was too cold or too wet for baseball, they shot marbles inside someone's tent. Newspapers were hard to come by unless someone got one off a Yankee. They were passed around until the ink got rubbed away—"Have the words been completely read off of this one yet?" was Ort's regular question. There were plenty of Bibles in camp and a few good books. Alexander managed to borrow a Shakespeare, and Scott's *Ivanhoe* he reread with a knot in his throat remembering Papa's reading it out loud. Charles Wesley had insisted on being Ivanhoe and Alexander had socked him in the stomach only to have Mama send him to the kitchen for dinner. Mama never knew he liked eating in the kitchen with maid Anna better than sitting next to Charles Wesley at the long dinner table.

With makeshift sets and props, the young warriors put on skits—satire grown out of suffering burlesqued the quartermaster, the surgeons, the paymaster, and the farmer's daughter comic romances.

Come Christmas, Alexander and Silas Nunner had a break from cornbread and the sticky blue beef the commissary handed out. Alexander foraged a piglet from a farm, and while it roasted they cut off chunks of pork and fried them, added water and crumbled up cornbread for a Christmas "cush" to hold them till the pig was done enough to eat. More than one fire had some kind of Christmas meal on the flames. Alexander guessed every pig, cow, and chicken that belonged to a farm nearby was either roasting under these pines or was under lock and key inside a farmhouse. Ole General Cleburne sent around a barrel of whisky for Christmas cheer, but it was typical Confederate whisky—mean as a skunk and about as smelly. Some of the boys had foraged a mess of eggs, so they whipped up a nog, and the whisky went down a little easier, but it was not so smooth Alexander Wesley didn't yearn for some of the fine spirits his papa let his boys have at Christmastime and other special occasions.

Over at Emmet Jenks' cookfire, Jenks had got out his fiddle and someone played a flute. Strains of "Home, Sweet Home" drifted with pungent smoke into the pines and drew a crowd. Several voices soon harmonized on "Annie Laurie," and then "Lilly Dale," and "Her Bright Eyes Haunt Me Still." As the nog went down, the singing got worse but sounded better.

Just when Silas judged their oinker ready to eat, Orten Trainer's red hair appeared above the tent roof, his face hidden by canvas. Ort offered a story about lassoing a pelican to cook during the Seminole wars in Florida. "I roped him in flight and flew him like a kite till he was wore out. When we wrung his neck, a bucket full of fish fell from his bill pouch and flopped around trying to swim in the sand. We dined on grilled pelican stuffed with sea trout." Even Silas Nunner laughed and didn't protest when Alexander invited Ort to join in their feast.

No Christmas roast or turkey Papa ever carved tasted better to Alexander than that roasted piglet. Christmas night, he lay beneath his blanket and held beneath his nose fingers that still gave off the sweet smoked-pork smell. A steady fall of sleet ticked the tent and faintly, from Jenks' campfire, came the murmur of voices and the bone click of dice—a soldier's lullaby.

Skirmishing and Waiting and Skirmishing

They remained entrenched along a ridge near Dalton until spring, skirmishing all around them: at Buzzard Roost, at Rocky Face Gap, at Snake Creek Gap. One night in May they pulled back to prepared defenses at Resaca, the beginning of months of calculated retreats, grudgingly giving ground to Sherman and keeping the Army of Tennessee in fighting shape. They fought at Resaca and near Pickett's Mill. In early June it rained so hard Alexander waited for lightning strikes to see where to shoot. Everyone in camp had an army of lice on him. When they weren't fighting they sat around and cracked graybacks, picking at the lice like dogs after fleas.

Late June the rains eased up and the roads began to dry out, but skirmishes and battles continued. They fought near Pine Mountain and at Kennesaw Mountain. General Johnston got nicknamed "Retreatin' Johnston," but his army was still in good shape. Then Johnston got replaced with General Hood, and Alexander feared the worst. The worst came and kept on coming. In Atlanta, Silas Nunner took a ball of grapeshot in his head and was dead before he hit the ground. Early on, with every skirmish or battle, every exchange of fire, Alexander had figured he was bound to get hit. After a while, he felt sure no shot would ever find his flesh.

Alexander held Silas Nunner's arms when they swung his body onto a pile of bodies on a wagon. But two years' slogging knee-deep in blood had persuaded Alexander if you got killed it didn't mean you could lay down your musket—just that after you died you marched quieter, you no longer got hungry, and you could see through the woods at night. Silas was cold as a wagon tire, but he still marched with Alexander every hurtful step. Together they marched across Georgia and on up Alabama to the Tennessee River. They marched barefoot with empty stomachs, and they fought without position or support. In their long march they passed the graves of men they'd buried months earlier.

In north Alabama, Alexander, Orten Trainer, and Silas Nunner's ghost sat on a rock ledge and shared a tin cup of rusty-tasting water.

"Now I've seen the monkey dance a few times, I don't mind if I never see him dance again," Silas said in Alexander's ear.

"Don't be all sulky and glum," Alexander said.

"I ain't kicked against nothing," Ort said.

"I was talking to Silas."

Ort shook his head. "It's a waste of breath, talking to a gone coon. Silas is a ghost, long past answering you. I wish the big bugs would quit backing and filling and make up their minds. All the starting and stopping makes me feel more all-overish than facing the mongrel Yankee army."

Below them, men crossed the Tennessee River on pontoons. From Alexander's vantage point, the men appeared to step off the bank and walk on water to the other side. He didn't doubt it one bit. The miraculous had become commonplace. He passed the cup.

They went through Tuscumbia and Florence, camped near Rawhide, Alabama. The regimental commander said they were going into Tennessee, going after the enemy into his territory. Hood vowed they wouldn't risk a bad fight but would take the Union forces on whenever there were like numbers and good ground. Alexander didn't believe a word of it—he'd seen thousands of good men die because Hood wanted to look better than General Johnston.

"Hood's brave with other men's lives," Orten said. "I vow I'll not die in Hood's vain name, not for Johnston, neither. They both fashion futures on the deep foundation of our bones."

Ort was right about Hood. But Johnston didn't put on airs. More than once, Alexander had seen Johnston knee deep in blood alongside his men. Alexander had yet to lay eyes on the headstrong Hood. If Hood was brave, then bravery was willful and determined ignorance.

The Bloody Franklin Pike

What does it mean when a rooster crows at midnight? Tuesday morning, dark and cold in Columbia, Tennessee, Alexander was on picket. The town clock struck the hours from one A.M. until five. By mid-morning, the regiment had crossed the Duck River and was marching toward Spring Hill. Many marched barefoot on the frozen road, the gravel brown with bloodstains. Word was skirmishes waited up ahead at Spring Hill, but by the time Alexander got there it was afternoon and, except for some sharpshooters and distant artillery, he didn't hear any fighting. By dark all shooting had stopped. In the middle of the night a barrage of artillery waked him. Word was, Hood had let the Yankee general, Schofield, slip his army up the pike toward Nashville, and Hood was shelling an empty road.

At first light Alexander and his part of the Army of Tennessee were marching right up the pike toward Franklin. In spite of himself, Alexander marched the cadence the drummers beat. Federal troops were reported in a defensive line between Hood and Franklin. Alexander and the Texas Chubs passed pots and pans and broken-down wagons the Yankees had cast off. More dead and wounded lay along the pike than he would have thought possible from the skirmishing he had heard the day before. Everyone said they had Billy Blue on the run, and they hurried after the expected rout. Alexander and Orten and the rest got to Franklin before noon Wednesday. They waited hours for the opening of the ball. Finally, around four in the afternoon, Hood made his move coming out of the hills in a deadly frontal attack.

A distant voice gave the order to "fix bayonets," and Alexander wondered if it was a Union or Confederate order. All around him steel clattered against steel, so he anchored his blade to barrel end, and then there was quiet, a pause while soldiers all over the field silently prayed, remembered parents and girlfriends, tried to slow their pounding hearts. During this quiet moment Charles Wesley spoke his name again, *Alexander*—and Alexander's prayer before battle was to damn his brother for tugging at him still and could they please just start the dance. Then Alexander's own voice, almost as far away as the bayonet order, joined the unearthly Rebel yell, an animalistic yowl he thought might never cease, an almost involuntary scream that unleashed a fury in him. The savage merger of brain and body when he joined this orgiastic cry was what he imagined the plains Indians of Papa's books and tales must have felt when they gave vent to blood lust with their famous war whoops as they thundered down on a train of the white man's wagons.

Thunder shook the earth and the sky rained balls, hailed canister and grape. Before Alexander the ranks were mown like so much grass, and behind him some-one—was it Silas Nunner's voice?—continually urged, "Aim low. Aim low." Alexander fired into smoke white as clouds. He fired, fell flat, and tore open another cartridge with his teeth. With the taste of spilled powder on his lips, he rolled on his back to reload, jamming home the charge. He rose and fired, fell flat, tore open a cartridge with his teeth, rolled on his back, reloaded, rose, and fired. He did it again. Again. All around him, men did the same, their faces warpainted with gray powder. The frenzy of the first few minutes gave way to numb, almost workaday, repetition. He was having a dream in which he was storm-tossed on a boat, hanging on in the midst of stinging sleet and salt spray, tying with sore and aching hands a knot on which his life depended. Each time he got the knot tied it came undone.

Minié balls and cannonballs shrieked and moaned and boomed. The screeching music never paused, but now its din came from far away. Where was Silas Nunner gone to? Alexander didn't know any of the faces around him. Now he was in some still, quiet place in the midst of Armageddon. Invisible inside a cloud, he took his time reloading, got to one knee and gazed about for a particular Yankee, took aim, then squeezed the trigger with lustful slowness. On his back, ramrod in his hand, he looked up past myriad low-flying pieces of lead through a gash in the cloud of smoke and glimpsed the winter-blue sky, or was it the blue regimental flag he had noticed for days? He had a bird's-eye view from high above the carnage looking down on himself and the others all over the field as so many wiggling worms.

After noon, the Confederates carried the advance. Union lines almost broke, then they came back strong on the interior lines. "Close up, boys," some popinjay said. Troops fought hand to hand astride the pike. Few took the time to reload and shoot. Some thrust bayonets. Most simply swung their rifles as bludgeons.

Alexander was not thirty yards from the breastworks, in front of a cotton gin. Behind him and on his left, as much as he could tell in the smoke and dust, Rebs were jabbing and swinging muskets into wave after endless wave of Union troops. Rebel support on the right was pulling back, leaving Alexander and his comrades in a crossfire. Blood ran off the pike in an awful stream and pooled around his frozen feet. A minié ball whistled by. Hood had betrayed them all.

Of a sudden, Orten Trainer stood right beside Alexander. They looked at one another, and both stopped fighting to smile in recognition. Alexander felt a profound desire to touch Ort's face, when a Union cap and coat got in the way. Alexander jerked on his trigger, but nothing happened—he had not reloaded. His nose tingled—the end of the Billy's rifle barrel was so close. The Yankee squeezed shut one eye, as if he need aim from only inches away, then lurched like a dance partner into Alexander's arms, clubbed from behind by the butt of Orten Trainer's Enfield. Alexander stepped back from the stunned Yankee's embrace, and the man jerked up straight, struck in the face with a Confederate ball. The struck man's smile, his teeth dazzling white inside his beard of spilled powder, was a gory red-ringed tunnel through which, momentarily, Alexander saw one brass button on a fallen officer's tunic. *As soon as this body falls out of my way*, Alexander thought, *I will reload and shoot another enemy*. The dead Union soldier hit his knees, and behind him Ort winked and knelt to fire.

Alexander went to raise his rifle, but his left arm didn't come. Two minié balls had hit above his elbow, taking his left arm off below the shoulder. The arm, his own arm, hit the earth like a tree limb. The fingers moved in the grass as if they were trying to crawl under cover. His right leg stung, then burned like a hot poker. He dropped to his knees, grabbed his shot-off arm, and crawled behind an ice-crusted elderberry bush. He pressed his severed arm against spurting blood and bone splinters, pushed the arm back in place, stanching somewhat the glut of blood. Ort knelt close, ripped a Union shirt, tied off Alexander's bleeding stump. Ort pressed the shot-off arm against Alexander's ribs.

"Alex, safeguard this lost limb. Let no one persuade you to give it up." Ort spoke slowly and musically as always, as if they were alone in a Richmond dram house and not here on the quaking, bloodstained ground. He reloaded both their rifles and got Alexander to his feet. "Go. Armistice for you." His hand pressed into the small of Alexander's back.

Far below him, Alexander's boots moved—at first he thought the feet were Ort's. The earth tipped away, then tilted back. Alexander turned in time to see Ort disappear into a cloud of smoke and icy dust.

"Orten," he said. "Orten?" Cannon boom answered, then a distant voice, not Ort's singing speech, someone's plea for water—*just one drop of water please God*. Reeling and swaying like a drunk, Alexander stumbled along with no idea what direction he was going. There were so many dead Confederate soldiers lying on the ground, he had to step on top of some. "I'm sorry, forgive me," he said to glazed eyes and locked grimaces. Once he left the pike, frozen grass held so much blood he slipped in it and fell twice. His uniform was spotted all over with other men's blood. Minié balls and grapeshot whizzed and zinged like hornets, but nothing touched him. He had not turned and run, had not ever run. He gripped his own shot-off arm and marveled he felt little pain. He was almost glad of the wound—after all, he had gotten through his fear to the other side, and all there was on the other side was endless walking. He was someone walking, someone wounded, not a coward, just someone walking. For the next long part of his lifetime he walked, and walking he dreamt a dream of walking.

He waked in a moving ambulance. Every bounce on the muddy road sent pains up his leg and down the place where his left arm should have been. A bushy gray beard pressed close.

"Someone got your arm tied off good, son. The bleeding is slowed, and you're come through safe. This will help." The gray-bearded man jabbed Alexander's left shoulder, and the gray whiskers and red face above him went away. The wagon cover receded, the bouncing wagonbed and creaking wheels went silent, and everything got dark and silent and kind of floaty and went swimming altogether away.

In Pap Willie's Care

Alexander opened his eyes. The swaying wagon cover had become a church ceiling with wooden crosses nailed to the rafters. He looked down the walls until he saw his legs on the floor near the altar. All around him on the floor and lying on pews were wounded Confederates. The same man from the wagon brought him water and checked his stump. The gray-bearded, bald-headed man said he was a Confederate nurse. He said his name was William Frank but Alexander could call him "Willie" or "Pap Willie" like everybody else did. Pap Willie told Alexander they were in a makeshift brigade hospital. What was left of the Army of Tennessee had followed the Union forces up toward Nashville. Major General Cleburne had been killed in the battle at Franklin, the same day Alexander had lost his arm.

"Pat Cleburne," Alexander heard himself rasp, "was worth a dozen of General Hood."

A field surgeon neatened up Alexander some, sawed off splintered bone at his left shoulder, trimmed fat, and sewed over the bony stump a flap of skin tight as a drum. He asked about his leg, and the surgeon lifted his eyebrows, said he must've overlooked it. Then he cut away the trousers and wiped off dried blood. Light shone through a hole in Alexander's calf.

"Guess you can keep this one." The doctor slapped Alexander's leg. "Looka-here." He stuck a long metal rod in one side of the leg and it came out the other. "You look like you got a Indian arrow through you. Clean as a whistle, missed all the important stuff."

Clean as a whistle or not, the leg throbbed like Hell, hurt much worse than the stump of his shot-off arm. When the too-cheerful sawbones gave Alexander's calf a final slap, the pangs stabbed all the way up to his teeth.

It took him nearly two hours to find his left arm and hand in one of the piles of arms and hands and legs and feet beneath the church windows. Twice, he claimed limbs that looked like his own, only to see a gold ring on one hand and too much hair growing down the other forearm. When he finally gripped his lost arm, he felt through the torn-off sleeve still covering the hard flesh the warm hold of his living fingers, felt in his dead arm feelings he had always felt there. He drained out all the blood left in his severed arm, then washed the arm in icy water from a cistern. He held the left arm down with one knee and used his right hand to clean blood and dirt from the lines in the stiff left palm and from beneath the fingernails. He soaked the arm in brine. Once the flesh was cured, he wrapped the arm in a shelter cloth, and holding it steady between his thighs he bound it tight with rawhide strips. He was already learning to make better use of his remaining right arm and hand.

The nurse, Pap Willie, brought Alexander a whole deerhide to wrap around his shot-off arm. The hide, tanned and soft, had been a gift to the nurse from an Alabama boy grateful for morphine dreams. Pap Willie shook his head, his beard pointing south in the cold wind. "There's a line of ambulances unbroken from Carter House at Franklin south to Thompson Station, at least eight miles. Eight miles of pain and misery. I bet you could line up the corpses end to end and circle around the world a time or two, maybe stretch the dead right up to the moon and tether old Luna tight with a chain of blood."

"There's dead aplenty," the field surgeon said.

The surgeon put Alexander in charge of two wagons collecting bodies from the battleground. He drove one wagon and directed men who lifted and carried. Two days had passed since the fighting, yet they found a man still alive. Knocked unconscious by a wound to his head, he had lain out so long with no shoes on his feet, he was partway frozen, his flesh blackened from the feet up. The surgeon took off both the man's legs above the knees. Alexander and the soldiers stacked wagonloads of bodies like cordwood across the back wall of the church hospital. When they swung a frozen body into place on top of another, the corpses clicked together like dice.

Fifteen days Alexander stayed in Franklin listening to rumors and trying to mend. Rumor was, the Army of Tennessee had been completely defeated. It was no rumor the Confederates had been unable to break the Federal line. The Yankees pulled north across the Harpeth River, and the Confederates moved behind them, going on to Nashville. Confederate surgeons and patients got transfers back to Columbia. Alexander couldn't help hoping the Yankees got Hood, since the bastard had killed more Rebs than any Billy Blue.

The wounded who couldn't walk were loaded on ambulances to be moved south. Alexander's leg had gotten red and swollen. Pap Willie said Alexander had a secondary infection, the erysipelas, St. Anthony's Fire. Alexander bit a piece of wood every bouncing mile until Pap Willie gave him morphine, and then all his hurt places, all his sharp edges, curled soft like leaves or birdfeathers or fishtails, and the bouncing ambulance turned as slippery smooth as a boat riding soft swells.

In Columbia Pap Willie lanced Alexander's leg and scraped out the infection, worse pain by far than the shot had caused. He waited to see if he would get to keep the leg, and he listened to more rumors. Six days after he arrived in Columbia the army train came through town—a long staggering line of Rebs, beaten and hurting, filing slowly south. When the Texan troops finally passed by, the boys held up for Alexander. He strapped his left arm over his shoulder and, leaning on a freshly made crutch, followed Silas Nunner's shade into a quiet huddle of friends. It was three days until Christmas.

Alexander looked for Orten Trainer's red hair among the Texans and asked after him. Ort's was one of many missing faces. No one had seen him since the fighting at Franklin. A pink-faced boy who didn't look old enough to shave took Alexander's one elbow and supported him. The boy was with the Chubs, but Alexander had never seen him before. Alexander described Ort and asked the boy if he'd seen him.

"Is he your brother or some kin?"

"I don't have a brother. He's a friend."

"I been looking for my brother since we got separated months ago up in Knoxville. You seen my brother—my spitting image only a mite older? And taller, too, a mite?" the boy said.

Alexander shook his head. Then he spotted Ran Smith from Shreveport, on the Red River in Louisiana but near enough to the Texas border that Ran had ended up with the Texan Chubs.

"I seen Ort scoot across the pike ahead of me," Ran told Alexander. "He knocked them Billy Blues into a cocked hat, I say he did. But they was thick as fleas on a hound, and I ain't seen Ort since that hard hour."

Alexander nodded. Ort was either marching somewhere in this same long line or was in a hospital tent or was a Yankee prisoner or was one of the dead in Pap Willie's chain of blood that reached the moon.

In the faces remaining was a weariness deeper than sadness or suffering. Wordless men nodded or touched Alexander's one hand or patted him on the right shoulder. After only a mile or two it was clear his leg wouldn't go along. The Texas boys held up again, determined to find him a wagon or a horse, but no luck. Then they took him up a purse.

Captain Foster himself gave Alexander the money and told him, "To Hell with Hood and this suicide. Stay here with the ambulances. Before the Union troops catch up, hire yourself a ride to somewhere safe. You deserve it, son. You're a war hero. And you spend it ever bit, cause we sure won't get to. We'll meet you later, in Texas."

Alexander felt guilty taking the money, but he was far from any bank that might honor a draft on Papa's New York account. The captain wrote out a wounded furlough and wiped the paper against Alexander's bandage that was seeping blood. "Let them study this furlough close, son, see can they find anything wrong with it."

By midnight Columbia was all but deserted. Two surgeons and Pap Willie had remained with those wounded not yet able to walk or die. One of the doctors had asked every officer who passed to send more ambulances, but none had come. Most said the Union troops would be through by morning, and everyone left behind would be taken captive. Alexander waited at the Columbia depot, but no cars were rolling. He had the wounded furlough and near two hundred dollars from the Texas troops, so he paid a tow-headed boy to find a wagon and get him somewhere out of town.

The boy, maybe twelve years old, didn't talk much, but he knew the country around Columbia. "There's a big old farm down to Sandy Hook," he said. Then he drove the wagon for miles before he spoke again. "It's way off the pike tucked between the ridges. No menfolks left there but a granddaddy and a little boy. I wager you can work off a few meals on the Purcell place."

The Purcell Place

That night Alexander slept in a hayloft on a farm between Sandy Hook and Mount Joy. The pounding in his leg receded into a dull ache, but beside him in the hay the length of space where his left arm should have lain tingled and burned the way lightning simmers in the heavens heating up to strike. Repeatedly, he fingered with his right hand his left stump, unable still to convince himself his arm and hand and fingers were in a deerhide bundle leaned against the barn wall. Finally, he got the bundle, unwrapped the severed arm, and rubbed the yellowed leathery flesh the way he had seen Orten stroke his dead arm, until the tingling went away.

Mrs. Purcell, big enough to block out the light coming through the barn door, waked Alexander with grits, biscuits, and molasses. He had tasted grits during the winter at Dalton, and he didn't like them. But when he dripped some of the molasses off his biscuits into the grits, the sweet mush tasted kind of like oatmeal. Mrs. Purcell leaned against a post watching him eat and talking the way someone talks when she hasn't had anyone new to listen to her for a long time. Her lips were brown with tobacco juice the color of the molasses in his grits and nearly put him off molasses for good. Every few sentences Mrs. Purcell turned her head sideways to spit into the hay. Every time she spat she hit the same spot in the hay, the brown stain slowly spreading into the shape of a hand with all five fingers spread, or of a Christmas star fallen into the hay of the manger. Alexander guessed he thought of the manger because he felt blessed and safe here in a warm, dry barn with only the animal sounds of snorting, chewing, tail-swishing, and stamping hooves.

"Mr. Purcell, my man Lemuel, skinniest man you ever seen, mighty funny, Lem rail-skinny and me, well," Mrs. Purcell wrapped her arms around her ample belly and gave herself a hug, "I'm built up right solid. It appears unlikely, but there's times opposites draw tight, and Lem said I carry myself good. He marched off with a herd of Tennessee volunteers in the war's first week, fool just couldn't wait, and died with Confederate troops down to Shiloh. Both my older boys followed on. Jerome, big like his mama, died of the measles in Virginia, so big and strong you wouldn't hardly judge he'd take sick and die—they sent the body back, though, and he weren't so big as when he left, seemed to have shrunk-in a mite—he's buried on yonder hillside with a granite stone freighted all the way from Nashville. And Josiah, my middle boy, is with 'Pap' Price's Confederates. His last letter come from Arkansas but said they was headed out to Missouri. Lord, he's the onliest one left can come back home alive. My daughter, Sissy, she'd have her own family started by now, her gone on seventeen, but the Searcy boy she was promised to got right off killed—Tom Searcy was the firstborn of Mason and Louise Searcy who have a homeplace above the Wiley farm what joins our land up yonder behind the barn. Tom was killed same as Lem at Shiloh. Onliest male child left home in these parts is my babe, Caleb—don't let him bother you none—pray the Lord this killing ends before his time comes to soldier, pray it's over no mind who wins, cain't neither side win with so much losing. Lem's daddy, Old Jack, he's the one has held this place up. We're ever one proud to hide you away. I hope any other mother would treat my boy Josiah the same out west in Arkansas or Missouri or wherever he is on God's green earth. I apologize for keeping you in the barn, but we can keep you hid easier out here in case any Yankee patrols come by. Where was you raised up at? Who's your people?"

"Just my ma and pa and me, ma'am, a place out Texas way. I don't imagine you'd know any of our family." By Mrs. Purcell's expression he could tell he had not given an entirely satisfactory answer, but it was all she or anyone around here was going to get out of him. He didn't say so, but Alexander worried about Confederate patrols nearly as much as Federals, unsure if the wounded furlough Captain Foster had fixed up for him would save him from being charged a deserter. But, apparently, the boys in butternut had given up Tennessee to the Federals.

Caleb, who was eight, brought Mrs. Purcell's soup and cornbread to Alexander every day and asked so many questions about the war and how it felt to have your arm shot away that Alexander feigned sleep so he wouldn't have to think up answers. When Sissy brought the soup, he was wide awake.

He had not known many girls, but none of the few he had known was anything like Sissy. She was almost as tall as he was, but her form was shapely. The way her cotton shifts lay up against the hollows of her and pulled tight over the swells of her fired his imagination. She stepped from sunlight into barn shadows, her face wavy behind steam from the bowl of soup she carried. She stepped lightly, her bare feet whispering against the straw, dark brown compared to her cornsilk skin. On her bosom, striped by sunlight between barn boards, lay a twist of hay Alexander took for a fallen lock of her hair until he reached and took it in his hand.

Sissy's speech was softer than Mrs. Purcell's, more musical. But, like her mother, Sissy dipped and chewed, her full pink lips dark with tobacco juice. Though she seemed more demure than the city girls Alexander had known in New York, she had ways that seemed almost immodest. In his thoughts, he defended this in her by how close to the fighting she had lived and the ways war had touched her. But even as he made excuses for her immodesty, it made his pulse race and his palms sweat.

"Captain Speer, I hope this day finds you growing strong," she said. He had not said he was *not* a captain. Her tobacco-darkened tongue slid over her teeth, licking away the brown juice.

One day, after Alexander had been hiding out in the Purcell barn for a couple of weeks, Sissy stepped halfway through the opened barn door. Sunlight behind her illuminated her white skirt and the white bloomers underneath, so the darker shapes of her legs appeared before him just as images had developed on Orten Trainer's tintypes. Sissy's honey-brown eyes met and held his, and Alexander felt sure she knew she was exposing her shape to him.

"Captain Speer, you know my intended died in the cause."

He nodded, his throat too tight for speech.

Sissy swatted her arms back and forth, brushing the sides of her skirt. "I didn't put off my mourning till just last month. I put off my mourning, and right then you showed up."

"My good fortune."

"You don't talk like around these parts," Sissy said.

"No, ma'am, I'm not from Tennessee."

"You don't even talk Southern, do you?"

"I'm from Gotham." Why hadn't he told her what he'd told her mama, that he was from out in Texas? Least he should do is keep his story the same. But it was harder to lie to Sissy than to Mrs. Purcell, who seemed to expect lies. "New York City."

"I declare. Are you Union in the guise of a Rebel?"

"No, ma'am. My papa always had Texas in his heart, and I got set on being a Confederate cavalryman. My papa never did hold with abolitionists, either."

Sissy came and knelt beside him on the straw. She took his hand and rubbed her thumb across his palm. "You've not been raised up working a farm."

Alexander shook his head. He couldn't deny it.

Sissy rubbed his hand again, then let it go, and stared at the barn wall. "My intended was the oldest of his pappy's boys. Their farm is just up the creek from here and would have passed on to him." She looked Alexander in the eye. "Thomas was seventeen when he went away and made a die of it. He was just a private. May I ask how old you are?"

He added on a few years. "Twenty-one." The lie came out easy enough. He didn't confess he was just a private. He wished she would rub his hand some more.

"Old as you are, most likely you already have a family, a wife up in New York?"

"No wife. Just my parents. After the war's windup, I'm bound for Texas."

"I've heard tell Texas is a perilous place."

Alexander involuntarily touched his stump. "Not so perilous as Tennessee a few weeks ago."

"I reckon twenty-one is old enough for about anything. And you being city-raised and a captain, you like as not have seasoning even beyond your years."

"After these four years of war, there aren't many truly young men left."

"Nor time nor reason left for spooning in the proper ways. Before the war, I'd of felt bound to lay ever approach to courtship before my parents. Now, my pap's dead along with Tom Searcy who had asked for my hand. I might have give him the mitten if I had known you were going to mosey onto our farm. With Pap gone sucker, I reckon Old Jack will have to stand in for giving me away. Mama worries I might not make a good marriage."

"Forgive my boldness when I say you'll have many suitors calling."

Sissy smiled and worked her tongue inside her mouth. Her chin tightened, and brown juice lined her lips. "You talk like a book, captain."

From outside the barn Mrs. Purcell said, "Sis-sy. Sis-sy."

Sissy turned and spat, then she buffed her mouth with the back of her hand and giggled, her golden eyes narrowing. "Sissy's my nickname." She leaned forward and touched his shoulder just above the stump. "My given name's Celeste."

From that moment on, Alexander addressed her as Celeste. When Mrs. Purcell was around, Celeste acted shy and faraway, but alone with Alexander she behaved as if they had known one another forever. He didn't know what to make of her. He'd never talked with so outspoken a woman. Then again, he'd talked with few women save his mother and sisters.

Alexander tried to think of excuses for spending time alone with Celeste. He dreamed he drew her close, and she came willingly. As he was about to press his lips to hers, she grinned and a knot of tobacco distended her cheek, brown spittle running from the corners of her mouth. Right then he opened his eyes and stared up at the dark loft. He regretted not having kissed Celeste in the dream, but he was glad his first taste of Celeste, even in a dream, was not the taste of chewed tobacco. Awake, he hoped to kiss her when she was not dipping.

The Purcells were not rich, but they weren't poor. They had their farmland, a good matched team and a decent wagon, a milk cow, and some chickens. Mrs. Purcell had canned fruits and vegetables left from last spring, there was a crib full of corn for meal, and she managed to trade eggs and extra milk for whatever was available and affordable in town. Often all she got was beans, but sometimes there was bacon, sometimes flour, and once in a great while, sugar. There had been no coffee and no tobacco for Old Jack this whole year. But Mrs. Purcell's food tasted a far sight better than what Alexander had gotten in the Army of Tennessee, and he slowly regained his strength and even put back on some weight.

As he was able, Alexander helped Old Jack repair tack and tools. Mending harnesses and filing scythe blades were hard work with one arm, but, compared to soldiering, Alexander liked feeling like a farmer. For him, the war ended on the frozen Columbia Pike in Franklin. If Texas was anything like being in the cavalry, it was going to be a big disappointment. He could do worse than staying with Celeste, making his peace in these hills, as lovely as any place he'd yet seen. Without bullets and artillery, it would be a fine place to be. Alexander imagined himself as a beloved uncle to little Caleb, working the fields with Celeste's brother, Josiah, home safe from Arkansas.

Alexander stared down at his hand, a hand that would smell of fresh-turned earth, a hand Celeste would caress to feel the hardness from a man's labor—one good right hand that would learn how to hitch teams, hoe rows, fix fences as naturally as it turned the pages of books, picked up dessert spoons, wrote out bank drafts. He could become a benevolent leader in this rural area, make sure Caleb and other children had schools and opportunities—there was much Alexander could offer. The South would need men of vision. To remove, night by night, the layers of cloth covering Celeste's shape, to learn by touch her hidden parts, that alone might be worth a lifetime.

Charles Wesley in a Brothers' War

A brothers' war, some called it. Charles Wesley had heard stories of troops, in the confusion of battle, accidentally killing their own men, and he had heard stories of brothers fighting on opposite sides—a New Yorker who joined the Rebels shot and killed at Bull Run by his younger brother, a Union corporal. *And it came to pass that brother rose up against brother and slew him.*

In the beginning, Charles Wesley shaved every morning and in his mirror saw Alexander's face. Though he wore the dragoon pistol Papa had given him, along with the curved lightweight saber and the carbine he had been issued, he soon shed his knapsack, disposed of every nonessential ounce in order to spare his horse. Remounts were scarce. The men traveled light, foraging and living off the land. Charles Wesley tossed out razor and mirror and let his beard grow. Saber blade, tin cup and plate, farm ponds and bowls of soup—any surface that gave back his face—gave him his brother in disguise, and more than once he did a double take.

In October on patrol duty in Virginia, Charles Wesley finally faced his fear of battle, the opening of the ball, the dance he had so dreaded. Sergeant Farnham spotted a Confederate unit and gave a whispered order to dismount so they would not be easy targets for the Rebs' rifled muskets. They hobbled the horses and crept as quietly as possible between tall chestnut trees. At the edge of the woods, they waited. No chaplain rode with them to offer solace, but many of the men prayed openly. Charles Wesley felt such praying was cheating. He reasoned God would hear any prayer under duress as whining or begging, and he vowed to pray only when he was in a good station. He hoped God would not think him too proud. When the order came to fix bayonets, Charles Wesley's hands did not tremble, as he had feared they would, but moved with a calmness he felt come over him with the sudden silence as men hushed their praying. His mouth felt as dry as the autumn leaves overhead, a gold canopy that sheltered them. Across a grassy field where a couple of years earlier crops had been raised, the horizon moved. It took a minute of staring for Charles Wesley to realize the movement was a line of Confederate infantrymen.

"Center dress," someone said, and with the purpose and quietude of a hunter Charles Wesley stepped out from under the yellow leaves into sunlight so bright his eyes ached. From the trees behind came birdsong. For days in the saddle he had watched his horse's legs. They seemed the legs of another creature and, at the same time, his own flesh and bone—as if he were some satyr who walked on his own hooves. Now, his feet tingled as if he had jumped and landed hard from a great height, and his own legs seemed as far beneath him as his horse's legs had seemed. The patrol got almost all the way across the field before the Rebs heard or saw them. Almost at the same moment came the command to charge and the deep, hollow sounding *hurrahs* of his comrades and the clatter of small-arms fire. Shots buzzed by like bees, and he smelled clover. Clover in October. He knew he was running because grass blurred beneath his feet, but he felt as though he were idly striding across a Sunday lawn, and he worried he might trip on a croquet wicket.

Faces rose and bounced toward him twisted and red with screams, and he watched for Alexander so he would not shoot his own likeness. But shoot he did, emptying the carbine and dropping it aside to draw his dragoon pistol. He fired and reloaded. Fired and reloaded.

Charles Wesley had no idea how much time passed, but he was aware of a moment when time simply held still for a moment, a moment when men on both sides of the fight seemed to hesitate. All shooting and yelling ceased, and he heard leaves falling from limbs and softly landing in the grass. All of his comrades stepped backwards, looking all around them, their eyes open wide as if they had just been given the gift of sight. Rebs in ragtag uniforms, dirty butternut and browns and grays, came up from the tall grass and stepped from behind tree trunks. Where were they all coming from—was the very earth sprouting them?

Later, Charles Wesley would be told how he had grabbed the sleeve of the man closest to him and shouted to the rest of his outfit. He alone, he was later told, rallied the Union troops and led them into the fierce Confederate firestorm. When his courage was recounted, it seemed to Charles Wesley they must be talking about someone else. Had Alexander come into the fray? The soldier described sounded more like a man gone completely out of his head than someone overcome by courage. But at the time of the fighting he only wanted to stop the sound of the leaves falling, so he fired and reloaded.

He had no memory of how the fighting stopped. He heard no command. He heard nothing. After a chaos of noise, he was in a silence so profound it sounded the way darkness looked, and he lifted his eyes to the sky, surprised the sun still shone. All the birds had disappeared, and he wondered if they'd been shot down. Above the dust and smoke the heavens were cloudless and so blue Charles Wesley imagined that instead of gazing down sorrowfully at His creatures in mortal combat, God had been whiling away the afternoon with a brush and paint, making His sky too blue to be real.

Dead grass had been painted, too. Streaks of dull red stained the earth, and bodies lay twisted comically. In places men lay atop one another or wrapped in one another's arms as if they were dancing or were lovers caught in perversion. Severed arms and legs lay scattered as deadwood falls in a forest. Against Charles Wesley's foot rested the cheek of a Confederate who looked no older than ten or twelve, a boy who had lain down to nap in the sun. Beside this boy lay one of his gray-bearded comrades with a gory hole in his chest as if some giant had forced a spade between his ribs, pried him open, and shoveled out his heart and other innards. But the boy had no visible wound, and Charles Wesley knelt and held his hand over the blue lips to feel for breath where nothing stirred the air. Charles Wesley waited for his own face to look up from the field of corpses stiffened by death, blackened by powder, reddened by sun and by blood, slickened and shined by sweat and spit and tears. "Alexander?" he asked over the field of blank-staring faces, but no echo returned his query.

Company B had two dead, two wounded, and ten missing. The Rebs were routed, leaving behind seventeen dead. The fighting would be listed as a skirmish, but to Charles Wesley it had been all-out battle. He received slaps on his back, handshakes, *hurrahs*, and a field promotion to first lieutenant that day, but his pay remained the same, $105.50 a month. Days later, in another skirmish that felt like all-out war along the Rappahannock River, he ran and grabbed a fallen Lieutenant Young and pulled him to safety. Until Major Anderson pointed out the blood, Charles Wesley did not know he'd taken a minié ball through the top of his boot and the ball had lodged in his leg. Shot in the stomach, Lieutenant Young died that evening. For courage under fire, Charles Wesley was promoted to captain and his wages were raised to $115.50 a month. A private who took the same risks drew $14.00. Captain or private, he still waited in the rain at the medical tent to have his leg butchered and probed for the minié ball. Most men agreed they'd sooner face the Rebs than their own surgeons.

Long minutes, hours, days—for two years Charles Wesley waited to encounter his twin brother, but his likeness never charged, yelling, toward him, nor stared mutely up from the fields of the dead. But late on an afternoon near the end of November—Charles Wesley had lost track of the day's date, but he knew it was after Thanksgiving and before the first of December—his outfit was in a forced march over frozen ground. Leaves and twigs sparkled sunlight and cracked underfoot as if they were fashioned from crystal. In one moment of this icy beauty, pain bore through his arm so hot he knelt to spot the Johnny Reb who had shot him. But there had been no shot. When he went to raise his rifle, his left arm was numb. It was a week before he could heft his weapon, or any weight, with the left arm. The surgeon pronounced him sound. He understood it was Alexander wounded in the arm, and he believed, at least, his brother was not yet killed. Their twin-blooded connection still flowed beyond Alexander's escaping it. The left arm came and went after that—sometimes it fell to his side with no warning, and it might take only minutes, sometimes hours, once two full days before the feeling came back all the way to every finger on his left hand. When his arm pained him the most, he wondered if that meant he was near Alexander. But if the arm's unpredictable throb was a divining rod for his brother's presence it never pointed with certainty, and Charles Wesley could only think it meant his brother was alive and aching somewhere on God's bloodied earth.

Musters Out

The day he was discharged, Charles Wesley spent waiting. He lay awake in soft morning light easing through the canvas dog tent. He listened to the steady breathing of the three men who shared the tent with him: Jack Clay, Zachary Young,

Jephthah Dunham. They all three had grit. After months protecting the Army of the Potomac, they had spent the remainder of the war in movements around Washington, their orders to defend the capital.

What could I tell Papa about war? Charles Wesley wondered. He took out his gold watch, a gift from Mama. The face of a watch, that's the face of war. Not bugles nor drums, but watches and clocks sound the beating of war's heart. Charles Wesley's war was two years that lasted a lifetime, yet seemed no longer than a deep breath. Two years of waiting, interrupted by skirmishes that held still the hands on his watch, its face as frozen as the faces of the dead who stared up from the battleground. In the cacophony of killing, Charles Wesley could not hear time ticking, and he felt filled up—*my cup runneth over.* War was a lifetime of waiting interrupted by brief battles that lasted forever but never long enough because on the timeless killing field there was joy. Each time he was not killed Charles Wesley reasoned he had overcome his fear, and each time he was wrong. For him, every bloody dance was his first. *Fix bayonets.* Those words made his mouth dry and his chest heavy. Waiting and terror were the same. Would Papa understand if Charles Wesley told him war was waiting for war? Continual and dark fear interrupted by bright flashes of delirious joy. For two years he stared at his watch and dreaded an encounter with the enemy. Such encounters were few and infrequent, and the waiting terrified him. His terror was less of the enemy than of himself, of his performance as a man, whether he could face his fear again. But the shrieking, rattling, buzzing, booming killing times were the moments Charles Wesley felt more alive than he had ever felt. Would Papa understand if Charles Wesley told him war was more intimate than nakedness, and the pulsing moments of killing were most like the flash of pleasure a man has in bed with a woman? And then came the guilt of survival and the exhaustion and disappointment of being fully spent. Immediately after the shooting, he could not recall the joy, and it was overcome, again and again, by the waiting.

The waiting was almost over, but Charles Wesley wondered whether having been in the war he might not spend the rest of his life waiting for whatever was to happen next and in constant anticipation miss his life as he felt he had missed the war. Three weeks ago, they'd crossed Bull Run not far from the old battlefield and camped near Fairfax, Virginia. The first of June, they'd made breakfast at midnight, crossed the Long Bridge over the Potomac and marched through Washington for the grand and final review. Since then, they'd been encamped north of the city waiting to be discharged.

As he walked from his spot on the color line after roll call, heavy dew wetted his boot tips, and he left a trail of dark steps behind him in the wet grass. Back at the tent he and Clay watched Young shave, and they all waited for breakfast call. Dunham was making his usual morning visit to the sinks. Breakfast was coffee, bacon, flapjacks, and beans. There was even sugar for the coffee. The men chewed and shook their heads, what grub. With food like this they might've won the war months ago. After three years' duty Charles Wesley liked his coffee from the bottom of the pot, thick and black as the mud on his boots. The men waited through sick call, listened for the call to guard mounting. Young, who hoped to see his sweetheart by day's end, put a sweet finish on his toilet—the last of a hoarded bottle of rosewater he rubbed into his scalp. The memories that had sustained them through months and years of suffering were closer now than ever. But home was not the tug Charles Wesley felt most. It was Alexander he must find, and he knew Alexander would be inclined not north and east but south and west.

There was a paymaster in camp, but rumor was he had not brought any gold. But Papa had arranged a bank draft—Charles Wesley could get money when he needed. He'd loaned his sorrel mare to Young, who promised to take good care of her. Charles Wesley rubbed the mare between her eyes. He doubted he would ever reclaim the horse. Young's Maryland farm was just a good day's ride, and Charles Wesley would reach Texas faster if he took a rail car south to Knoxville and then west to Nashville, where he could board a Cumberland River steamboat and eventually make his way to New Orleans and thence a steamer for the coast of Texas.

Charles Wesley picked up the tin shaving mirror Young had left on the tree stump. Charles Wesley bared his teeth. Bearded and with something in the eyes, something not there before, the face in the mirror looked like the face of a wild man, all hair and beard and teeth. The face might inspire fear. Hadn't he gotten himself through two years of war? Time and again he walked upright and incautiously into battle, and the minié balls whistling by did not fell him. He wondered if Alexander had feared the furies as much and felt sure his brother had never known real terror. Each time the shooting started, Charles Wesley had been surprised how the terror left him. And each time the shooting stopped, the terror returned like a faithful cur. He reasoned that the mongrel, fear, had guarded and guided him. Unmoved by speeches about God and nation, politics and economics, bravery and masculinity, unmoved by sentiments shared for wives and sweethearts, mamas and papas, sisters and baby brothers, aunts and cousins, dogs and horses left behind, Charles Wesley went into battle naked of everything but his fear he would not perform well. Now he was certain his fear of failing was what had birthed his few moments of being unafraid and joyful, and he carried his fear inside him, lean and hungry as pride.

There would be no inspection today, no drill, no duty. Tents were struck, soft white roofs collapsing in billows like puffs of smoke all down the hillside. Loaded wagons rattled out of sight. It was half past ten before Charles Wesley lined up again to receive his discharge and service papers. He stood waiting until "roast beef," the dinner call, when he was next in line to step into Major Anderson's tent to be saluted and told good-bye with a handshake. There were rations to waste — fresh beef, fried onions, boiled hominy butter, roasted potatoes, more sweet coffee. There was hardtack pudding, too — a farewell joke.

By noon, the camp was almost empty. The last order to stack arms was called, and Charles Wesley leaned a length of oak into the pile of weapons for Ordnance. He wasn't going to give up the seven-shot Spencer rifle. For most of the two years his mare had borne him and a heavy Enfield muzzle-loader. When he got the opportunity, he had gladly given all the money he had (forty-eight dollars) for the Spencer. He might need it in Texas. And he packed away the Harper's Ferry Dragoon pistol from Papa. Charles Wesley had carried and used the pistol all through the war, and he would tote Papa's gift all the way to Texas, where he might have use for it if the tales about fast draw shootists were true and where he hoped to find Alexander bearing its mate.

Late afternoon, Major Anderson's voice broke when he bid his men godspeed. Men wept and *hurrah*ed and clasped hands. Charles Wesley walked with Clay, Dunham, and Young back to the bare tent site where their gear was stacked. Charles Wesley wondered if his friends were listening, as he was, to the distant jingling of bridles and bits, the creak of heavy-laden wagons, and the steady breeze through the treetops.

Clay, Dunham, and Young formed an impromptu line and, one by one, embraced Charles Wesley. Buttons clicked against buttons, bones cracked.

Charles Wesley did not have to be at the railroad depot in Washington until the next morning. He would sleep one more night on a flattened brown square of grass where the tent had been. He joined the few others still in camp around a single fire and cooked an abundance of last rations. When everyone had eaten his fill, the men passed around a big pot of coffee and quietly traded stories, memories of the campaign in the Carolinas. After a while, Charles Wesley left to lie down on the spot of earth where he and his tent mates had slept the night before.

Under a warm and cloudy June sky he spent this last night in the army as he had spent the past year of nights, waiting for sleep and dreading his dreams. Awake in the late night dark, he wandered the camp as he had wandered others before it. He had stepped without fail over ropes and pegs between tents scattered like shavings of the moon over the dark hills. Tonight, the tents were gone, and without their pale shapes the darkness was darker, a visible darkness. The air was damp and heavy. The minié ball lodged in his left leg burned, and he concentrated on the cool spaces between the hot aches. He was anxious to be on the way west, but he made himself wait until the sky lightened enough for him to make out black shapes he knew were trees.

A bird sang out overhead, another answered. How long since he'd heard birds sing? Maybe the whole two years. He sat up as quietly as if Clay, Dunham, and Young still slept beside him, as if the enemy still crouched just beyond a nearby picket line, and he pulled on his boots. The top of his shirt was damp, and he pictured tiny seeds of dew, perfect as jewels, resting on the nap of the cloth as he had seen them rest on wrinkled green leaves. He was light-headed from nerves and lack of sleep, but strangely rested-feeling and alert. He stood up and habitually reached for his Spencer.

The camp was deserted, no reason to walk to the sinks, so he stood beside the shape of himself in flattened grass and arched his stream into the dark. His left side hurt every time he emptied his bladder. It was a good bet the surgeon had left shrapnel there, the way he'd left the minié ball in his leg. All surgeons know is how to hack away, to cut off. He'd lain half a day in rain and mud before they'd dug the shrapnel out. Beside him, but out of reach, a man unable to roll himself over had drowned when rainwater filled the gully. All around them on the ground lay hands and feet and arms and legs, body parts pitched like scraps on a garbage pile by surgeons purple-stained with gore.

He rolled the wadded blanket inside the India rubber sheet and tied the roll over his back, right shoulder down to left side. He walked slowly, the bedroll moving in rhythm with his steps, pushing against the back of his neck, then dropping away so the air made a cool spot below his right ear. He had not been alone for two full years, and he savored the quiet and the solitude. He gazed all around him seeing the countryside as if for the first time. Ridges of hills looked like brigades of blue. Clouds exploded silently along the ridgetops like artillery hits. A long, gray, serpentine wave of fog, a Reb brigade, slipped around a hillside and disappeared into dark forest. One gray regiment separated and eddied into a slow line moving out from the cover of trees. Fine blue mists of fighting men rose from the fog below and fell from the clouds above. A few miles south, civilians all over Washington slept in their dim, quiet houses, unaware of the battle still raging. Phosphorescent light flashed—friar's lanterns or will-o'-the-wisps—the air was alive with gases, bodily humors, souls waiting in line, whole divisions of souls, the blue and the gray, finally mustering out, some bound for heavenly peace, others to continue war's endless hitch in Hell.

The sole of his right boot was worn through, and moisture seeped up to his right foot, cold and achy in the wet boot while the left remained snug and dry, though above the foot his left leg ached some from the minié ball. He wondered if the earth itself ached: its flesh bruised by minié balls and canister and grape, scarred by fires and axes, cut by bayonets and sabers, gouged by breastworks and trenches and graves, stained by so many tears and so much blood. He wondered, idly, whether the moisture that had moved into his foot carried the blood and decayed matter of other men. Had he already trod on Alexander's bones and blood?

Alexander's Last and Best Christmas

Christmas Eve night was so cold Mrs. Purcell moved Alexander from the barn into the house. There were two sleeping rooms, and Papa Jack slept in a lean-to built onto the kitchen to keep him warm from the cookstove. With her daddy and two of her brothers gone Sissy had moved in with her mama, so Mrs. Purcell put Alexander in the children's room with little Caleb. "Captain, you take Jerome's bed. It's got a right good tick."

Christmas morning was dark and windy and rain drummed against ice-rimed windows. Mrs. Purcell lifted a round castiron cover off the cooktop and pushed more wood into the stove. Orange flames licked at her hand and shadows danced on the wood ceiling until she dropped the iron cover back into place, a black patch over the stove's glowing eye.

"Sissy made melt-in-the-mouth biscuits special for you, Captain. I give a good lay for the flour, but we'll have better than cornbread for Christmas. Sissy, honey, reach to the top of the pie safe and get me the coffee I hid away."

The girl leaned into the punched-tin doors and reached one arm high. Barefoot, she rose onto the balls of her feet, her dress flattened against her backside, hitched high. Alexander looked up her body from her heels to her tightened calves and the twin dimples in the back of both her knees to the curtain of hem about halfway up her thighs. She bounced on her toes until she could grab the coffee tin, her bottom rippling like a muscled horse's rump.

Mrs. Purcell brought a pot of water to a boil. Celeste poured coffee beans into a grinder, then steadily turned the crank. Papa Jack's hand held to the small of Celeste's back as he leaned over to move his nose in and out of the smell rising from the grinder. Alexander wished the spread fingers pressed against Celeste's narrow form were his own.

After the coffee had steeped, Celeste poured first Alexander, then Papa Jack, a cupful. There was even sugar.

Papa Jack's grin was wider than Mrs. Purcell's china cup against his lips. "I tell you what, this here is more valuable than gold. We ain't got no buried money, no hid jewels. All our treasures is stored up in Heaven but for this here coffee."

Alexander wouldn't argue. He told them how, one night in Georgia, a corporal on their picket line swam to the middle of a river separating the two sides to meet a Union picket and, treading water, traded his rifle and thirty rounds of ammunition for a little pouch of coffee. Paddling splashes and the two voices carried over the surface of the river.

"Billy boy, I'll drink this coffee to your health."

"Reb, I'm going to shoot this rifle to your health."

"Just let me have a cup, first. Then I can die satisfied."

Alexander didn't know if the corporal's own rifle and bullets felled him, but he did die the next morning, his tin cup still warm from the coffee he'd been drinking when he was hit. "I reckon he died happy," said Papa Jack, his words a kind of benediction.

The rain slacked off, and for a long while the only sounds in the farmhouse kitchen were gusts rattling the door and window, flames breathing in the cookstove, and Papa Jack softly sucking coffee. Alexander ate half a dozen of Celeste's biscuits.

"I believe the captain's gaining back his strength." Celeste grinned and put another warm biscuit on his plate.

There came a flash at the window, a distant rumbling—thunder or shelling. Whichever storm, Alexander was glad he was not there. Like the ghost of Silas Nunner, who sat with the black hole in his head across the table from him, Alexander was not going to war anymore. Charles Wesley hadn't called his name since he'd lost his arm. *Now Charles Wesley will grab after me as always and grip the empty air where my arm used to be.* Soon as he thought it, Alexander relented.

The old anger against Charles Wesley did not flare as before. What if he never saw Charles Wesley again? What if he had been killed in battle? It was the first time he'd thought it all during the war. *I hope I do see Charles Wesley again,* he thought. *I'll shake hands with him, my one hand stronger than he'll expect, and I'll make peace with him.*

Alexander felt hidden and safe. The window flared again, and the panes rattled in their frame. Sleet ticked against the glass, and he wondered if sleet fell this moment wherever Charles Wesley was. Alexander hoped Charles Wesley was spending Christmas inside someplace dry and warm.

Mending

More and more, Mrs. Purcell treated Alexander as family, and she let Celeste go with him on long walks, unchaperoned.

"You need to walk the muscle back into your poorly leg."

The first time Alexander walked with Celeste, she espied a scrap of newspaper against a rock. The paper, frozen and yellowed, was still legible. His words small clouds, Alexander read:

> Several entertaining candy pullings have been featured at private gatherings in our fair city. We are blessed with citizens who recognize the need for maintaining some kind of society not in spite of but because of the current war of Union aggression. It is true the young seek out amusements and the climate of bloodshed in which all must now exist leads those of short-sighted vision to all manner of excess and evil practices. Let our substantial citizens, those who respect righteousness and civility, the church members and the leading merchants, accept their duty to offer amusements to channel the baser motives of our young men. We sadly acknowledge that even among pious young damsels there have been disturbing examples of mischief and immorality. All our citizens must wake up on this matter if we are to succeed in limiting these shameful excesses to the anticipated moods of the rough sex. Alas how...

There the fragment ended. On the reverse was an advertisement for ROBERTSON'S TONIC BITTERS and an offer of a reward for runaway slaves:

$200 REWARD
STOP THE RUNAWAY AND HORSE THIEF!

RAN AWAY and stole four horses from the undersigned in Marion County, Mississippi about the 9th of September, a Negro boy KNOBBY, aged about twenty-five years. Said Negro may have abducted a girl, ELIZABETH, or persuaded her to run away with him. Both fugitives fled New Orleans and may be headed upriver. Two of the horses were sold and have been recovered. I will give $200 for delivery to me of both Negroes and the other two horses. Fifty dollars reward will be given for the boy, KNOBBY, if he is lodged in jail so I can retrieve him, or twenty-five dollars for information as will lead to his apprehension. Said Negro is wiry but well-made, 5 feet 10 inches, and of a very dark complexion. He has a delicate foot for a Negro and speaks surprisingly well. He will tell a plausible story when interrogated. His skill is as a horseman. His back is unstriped by the whip. The girl, ELIZABETH, is large and, for a Negress, comely, with long, bushy hair. The two missing horses are a roan mare, four years old and fifteen hands high, and a sorrel gelding about the same age and size. The sorrel has a long black mane and tail.

Any information concerning said runaways will be thankfully received.
> Address,
> WM. B. NOBLE
> Marion Co., Mississippi.

"How'd this little ole piece of newspaper get all the way out here on our land?" Celeste shook her head and spat a dark stream onto the cold ground. She read aloud the last few words of the candy pulling article — "anticipated moods of the rough sex" — and she grinned at Alexander.

He figured the paper had found its way here the same way he had found his way from New York to stand in this frozen field close enough to inhale Celeste's scents of soap, tobacco, and rosewater. He dropped the paper and took her hand. She grinned at him again and shifted her jaw.

"Captain, if you've got it in mind to kiss me, I have to tell you I'm a respectable girl. I also have to tell you this chaw does not impede my lips in no way."

She was right. In spite of their peppery sting, Celeste's lips moved against his with a life and a will of their own. By the time their lips unyoked, he was short of breath, but even in the raw breeze he was warm through and through.

"Now I've been kissed."

"Captain, I hope you ain't implying I'm worldly wise?" She lowered her voice. "You have drug something out of me I didn't know lay within. I may be one of them *pious damsels* led against my nature to follow the *example of immorality* shown by one of *the rough sex*."

"Let me lead you further." Alexander pulled her against him.

"I done followed far enough for one walk." She did let him take her hand until they were back in sight of the house.

During January and late into February, small Union patrols visited the Purcell place. Alexander had gotten in the habit of taking long walks about the farm. He always checked the clothesline before he came down from the woods. When there was a patrol at the farm Mrs. Purcell (who put her own and Celeste's washed underclothes inside a pillowcase to dry since no lady's unmentionables should be visible to passersby) hung out Papa Jack's red union suit as a signal for Alexander. The Federals didn't seem interested in finding deserters. Mrs. Purcell gave them something to eat and got what news she could. Their scouts reported skirmishes as close as Franklin and Corn's Farm, Tennessee, and Tuscumbia, Alabama, but opined the war was near concluded. News of General Hood's removal cheered Alexander. What was left of the Army of Tennessee had been sent east to help General Johnston hold back Sherman.

Alexander's leg healed up, though it ached whenever he got cold. The ghost of his cut-off arm often tingled the length of space where the arm used to be and would not let him rest until he unwrapped the dried limb and stroked it. He helped Papa Jack tend the team, the milk cow, and the few chickens that had so far survived the roasting pot. If he stayed until after the last frost, he was determined to learn how to plant. He would sow what seed a one-armed farmer could.

By March, the Union patrols stopped entirely. It was as if the rest of the country, wherever there was still war going on, had lost all interest in central Tennessee and in Alexander Wesley Speer. It was clear the war was almost over, and the main talk now was how the windup would be.

Alexander managed to kiss Celeste again, risking discovery one evening when he returned to the house from the privy and found her alone in the kitchen, bent over, banking the cookstove fire. She yielded willingly enough, and this time she had rinsed her mouth out for sleeping and tasted salty-fresh. She ran her fingers up the back of his neck, and he put his mouth on hers again. Just then, Mrs. Purcell said from the bedroom, "Sissy, time you got to bed."

On a cool morning in late April, Alexander announced he was going to walk up the creek to a fish pool Papa Jack had told him about. "Maybe I'll catch supper."

"Why, Captain, that's a long piece. Your healing leg might give out," Mrs. Purcell said.

"I'll mosey up there with him," Papa Jack said.

"Papa Jack, you can't walk so far no more, and you got to drive the wagon to Mount Pleasant today. I'm bounden to see if you can swap my eggs for a mite of flour. Sissy, will you guide the captain? Papa Jack, ride Caleb with you. I got mending to do, and I stitch best with it quiet."

Papa Jack reminded Mrs. Purcell how the wagon bouncing stirred up his bowels, but she leveled a look on him that reminded Alexander of the time he had looked up the barrel of a Yankee musket. Before he could shoot, the Yankee had fallen dead from a stray ball. Mrs. Purcell didn't fall, but the silence she fired must've hit Papa Jack solid, because he didn't say another word.

Celeste put a few cornbread sticks in a cheesecloth sack, with some dried apples for a special treat. Alexander had Papa Jack's fish pole and stuffed a dozen or more crickets into an empty sock. They headed off under a morning sun already warm. A light breeze shook the tops of trees where birds darted back and forth loud with song in the bright new leaves.

They walked beside the slow running creek on soft earth edged with feathery dark green ferns. Where they climbed over a huge fallen chestnut tree, Alexander offered Celeste his hand. Once she got over the tree trunk, he kept hold. He was glad of the creek whispering over rocks, the breeze rustling limbs, and some crows caw-cawing high above, because he was all out of words.

From the crest of a hill Alexander spotted the fishing hole, a pool about half the size of the Purcell barn. He sat on a rock and unwrapped the twine from the end of the long pole. It took him several tries to work Papa Jack's hook into a cricket's back so the bug still twitched. Celeste removed her shoes and lay on her back on a slab of rock the size of a bed. She spread her arms and fingers, lifted her knees, and gripped the rock with her toes.

"I love this place. When I stretch myself out and close up my eyes, I feel the whole world's slow spin."

"It's like the Garden of Eden," Alexander said.

Celeste raised her head and looked at him, one eye squinted, one gold in the sun. She stuffed a pinch of tobacco inside her cheek, gave her head a shake, and lay back down upon the rock.

Watching Celeste, Alexander swung his line out over the water. The nearly weightless bait drifted on invisible currents of air and settled on the water closer to shore than he'd intended. He went to lift the pole again, to flip his cricket farther out, when a ring appeared around the bug, and the water puckered and made a loud kiss. The long loop of floating twine lifted taut, sunlit beads of water dripped off its length, and the pole jerked almost free of his grip.

Celeste's eyes were closed, but she was grinning. The pole bent and strummed. The line cut right then left through the water. He had to stand to land the fish. He pulled it splashing from the water, and it danced in the air like a dervish.

Celeste beamed like a child. "You got hold a one already. A good one."

He swung the fish around and, holding the bent pole against his side, grabbed at the line. Though it took him four grabs, Celeste never came to help the one-armed man. If before he had maybe loved this girl, now he knew he did.

The fish was broad and flat, shaped like Alexander's hand, only twice as long. Along the top of its back webbed fins rose like fingers. Above its pouted mouth and big, round eye it was pale orange. Behind the mouth, around its gills, it was brilliant blue. The rest of its body was green gone gray at the bottom. Beneath these colors that shifted in the light and shade, four dark vertical bands marked its side as if a sooty hand had left the black impression of fingers.

"A bream. Mighty good if a body don't mind picking around bones."

Celeste took the fish, and without saying so, by doing it slow, she showed him how to slide his hand from the head back, smoothing down the sharp fins so they couldn't prick him. While he got another cricket on the hook, she ran Papa Jack's stringer through the fish's gills and put him back in the pool tied to a green stick she shoved into the mud.

Alexander caught another almost identical bream as soon as his cricket hit the water. Celeste said, "They're layin' on their beds. You got them now."

"Their beds?"

"They hollow out places on the bottom to lay their eggs. Nesting beds." When she said "nesting beds" this time, her voice quavered. She led him around to where the sun slanted on the pool's edge and pointed at scores of small craters underwater. It looked to Alexander like a battlefield pocked by cannonballs.

In the next half hour Alexander caught six more bream, all close to a foot long, at least a pound each, and two less colorful fish Celeste called "shellcrackers."

Celeste walked out of sight behind huge rocks along the pool's upstream end. As he fixed another cricket on his hook, Alexander heard her humming. He was getting pretty quick at one-handed baiting. He cast his bait out onto the water, and Celeste spoke from the far end of the pool where she stood waist-deep in the water, "Think you can catch *me?*"

In the sun, her pale hair was silver atop her tall, slender form, and from this distance she appeared like a spoon stuck up by its handle. At least a minute passed. Alexander held his breath, didn't move. Across the pond, Celeste's head bobbed between the trees. She shook her hair like a playful pup and grinned wide, spitting a brown arc into the water's edge.

"Coming, slowpoke?"

No two-armed man could have put down his pole, pulled off his shoes, and gotten to the other side of the pond faster than Alexander. Knees high and splashing, he ran through the mud until the bottom dropped out from under him, and he was swimming side-armed. Though the midday sun was warm, the water was so cold Alexander's breath froze in his chest. Celeste leaned over toward him, giggling. His feet touched bottom, and he ran up out of the water. She disappeared into the woods. His wet trousers slapped against his legs and the brush. His cold scrotum drew up tight against him. His socked feet numbly hit the ground. Celeste's hair shone, moving like a bright sun between bushes. He leaned against a tree trunk and caught his breath. Celeste bumped against him. Her eyes took some of the blue from the sky to turn from gold to aquamarine, like copper that's been exposed to the elements.

"Up there." She lifted her chin toward the treetops. She wrapped both her arms around a rough, shaggy trunk, a bear-hug embrace, and inched her way up the tree. Her bottom wiggled, her toes pressed white where they squeezed the bark like fingers getting firm purchase. She rose above him, muscles flexing in the backs of her thighs, her skirt billowing like a rising curtain.

He climbed after, dodging bits of bark she sent down into his hair and eyes. The rough trunk left white scrapes across the stump of his missing arm. The pale bottoms of Celeste's feet disappeared into some kind of treehouse. He pushed himself up with his one arm and realized they were in a sniper's stand, a board rectangle about six feet long and three or four feet wide—the size of a small bed, or of a grave—with board sides to hide a prone body.

Celeste leaned back against the side board, her knees drawn up to her chest. Her skirt dripped onto the dry boards. Between her thighs, her underwear made a wet pouch. She crossed her arms over her breasts and pulled the top of the dress off shoulders that gleamed like smooth, brass knobs on the tops of bedposts.

She pulled down the dress top farther, exposing her breasts, and on her knees she crawled to him and peeled open his wet shirt. Her warm breasts flattened against him, her nipples poking like fingertips. Her fingers in his wet hair, she pulled his face to hers and they kissed, their mouths a mix of cold and warm, lips and tongues. She pulled the dress off over her head, and it lifted as fog. She rolled her underwear down into a rope around her ankles, soft shackles she kicked into the boughs. She helped him tug off his wet trousers, underwear, and socks. Body against body, they stretched lengthways on the planks. Celeste's legs locked around his, and she squeezed his thigh, her patch of pubic hair a discernible tingling against his skin. She rocked against his thigh as if she were astride a horse. She slid one hand over his cool belly, and his skin involuntarily rippled. She purposefully gripped his cold and shrunken cock, and it thickened in her warm fingers. She slid her hand down over his tightened full sac and opened her fingers against his buttocks. Hefting his body in her hand as if she were taking his weight, she let her legs unwrap and lay back flat.

They murmured and gasped, but neither spoke. He was now swollen so hard her fingers no longer met thumb to fingertip. She did not so much pull him to her as she held him steady and fitted herself onto him, enveloping him in her slickness and heat. She rolled over and he rolled with her, boards satisfyingly rough against his shoulders and back. Now she came down against him as a scabbard against a knife hilt, wiry hair sparking between them, pricking soft belly flesh. Her arms around his trunk as she had climbed the tree, she rocked against him. She brought her knees up along the outsides of his legs and straddled him, twisting and bucking over him, her breasts swaying hypnotically over his face. Her face twisted — half-smile, half-grimace. Mewling low, she collapsed onto his chest, muscles inside her clenching and unclenching as a spasmodic fist.

They lay still and quiet. Leaves all about their heads rattled in a light breeze, and a close-by bird twittered over and over. Celeste's lips made soft susurrations against his chest, and when her warm drool glued her mouth there he thought she had fallen asleep. He put his palm on the narrow indentation at the base of her spine, lightly stroking a patch of downy hair above the swell of her buttocks. Her lips, slippery with saliva, moved over his nipple and sucked so hard he jerked and hit his elbow against the platform. A deep manly-sounding laugh came from deep in her chest. She leaned back, her eyes meeting his, his chest cold where she peeled off him. His still firm and unspent cock slid from inside her and slapped against his belly, the air around it dry and cold, and he wanted it back in her wetness and heat.

She sat up and straddled him again, spread so firm against him the curled hairs on his chest caught water from her arrowhead of pale pubic hair, and the drops momentarily melded, clinging to her and to him alike. Between her thighs, wet cornsilk hair made a light gold seam against her flesh, as if God, when He made her, had sewn her together there. She rose on her knees, and the muscles inside her thighs lengthened and tightened, pulling apart the delicate seam of hair beneath which her flesh opened in layers like the bream's pulsing gills, burnished red to nacreous pink.

Her hands gripped his arm and the stump of his missing arm, and, as he lifted his back and pushed with his heels, she lunged forward on her knees until they rose all but their feet into the rattling leaves of the tree. Their mouths met. Their tongues fought. He exhaled into her, and his breath returned to him from out of her, and she drew the shared air back again.

When at length she lifted her face from his, his mouth felt empty and his insides cold. He reached his hand up to her face, and she seized his forearm, pressed it firm between her breasts. She reached back and found his cock, now curved stiffly up. On her knees, she held to his upraised arm, twisted it like a boat's tiller, guiding herself—up, back, over, and down onto him.

Their thrashing shook the treetop as if a wind gusted. Celeste rocked above him with a rhythm he hurried to match. When she held and squeezed the shoulder above his stump, a muscle there clenched, and his phantom limb flexed down its whole length, his lost hand, his lost fingertips rubbing against her breasts. Then she said, *Oh, oh,* and another phantom spasm, this one from somewhere low in his spine, ran the circuitry of his body and flashed from his belly up into his whimpering throat. Together they sank upon the rough deck and lay so for a long time. Alexander slid from inside Celeste, slowly slowly sliding down and then out of her. A breeze pebbled Celeste's skin with goosebumps. Alexander pulled on his almost-dry trousers.

"Well, Captain," Celeste began—these the first words between them since he'd run after her across the fishing pool—"I suppose you think I'm lower than dirt, low as a army whore."

"If there's blame to put it has to come to me. I'm older and your mama trusted me."

"Before the war I wouldn't allow not even one kiss until after Tom Searcy spoke his permanent ambitions. Now I done lost all virtue. War makes everything different."

Though he had never before felt called to make such testimony, Alexander knew if he declared his love for Celeste he could make their passion morally acceptable. He did not put such store in words of love, but he had an intuition that once spoken such words might tame ardor. He let pass the moment for his responding, and guilt washed over him. Then came questions to his thoughts, the author of which he couldn't guess. *Isn't there supposed to be blood, and her crying in pain, not the kind of crying out she's made? Has she already given all to the Searcy boy, her virtue purchased by the words I cannot speak?* Such thoughts increased his guilt, and he regretted he and Celeste couldn't be as they had been this morning at the breakfast table. He stared at beads of sweat between her breasts and on her upper lip, and instead of making words his mouth found hers again. Alexander's blood roared and against one ear there was a sudden clinking with the shaking of the tree, as if some angel had leaned down from the sky to scatter a handful of coins, wagering on this love bout in the tree boughs. Again they bucked and grunted like beasts, this second coupling more ferocious and longer-lasting than the first and to the flesh more pleasing because each knew it was solely lust and knew the other knew, too.

Spent a second time, he opened his eyes and there beside them on the planks two metal cartridge casings rolled with the rocking of the treetop like long seed pods. These had made the clinking he'd heard as heavenly coins.

Celeste picked up one of the casings and looked at Alexander.

"Cartridges. Big—maybe a number fifty-six. From up here it would be hard to miss, especially with a scope. Metal so dear, can't believe he left these behind."

"Who?"

"Reb sniper, I imagine. You ever hear rifle fire from your house?"

"Sometimes. But I thought this was just a deerstand."

"If it's a deerstand it's been used lately for a different kind of hunting."

"Pretty." Celeste had the silver shell cases over the thumb and fingers of her left hand and held out the hand as if to admire a ring. *A wedding ring*, Alexander thought. He said nothing. "Make strong sewing thimbles," she said. "No needle could prick through." She stood the cases in a row on the board. "Wait." Still naked, she shimmied down the tree. Her pale shape reappeared farther away between the trees. He had slipped into a dreamworld, had entered some aboriginal land where the war was left behind like the sniper's cartridge cases and a beautiful wood nymph had led him up into the bowers of this tree to make love.

At once Celeste was back at the base of their tree, and then she was coming up through the opening, a yellow leaf between her breasts, the cheesecloth sack in one hand. She spread cornsticks and dried apples between them, and they deliberately ate each piece one after another.

"Sissss-seeee, Sissss-seeee," came up through the treetops.

Celeste froze, a red apple tip sticking out of the corner of her mouth like a tongue licking her lips. She patted the air, indicating Alexander should get low behind the side board. Mrs. Purcell came into the clearing beneath them. Celeste slowly pulled her dress back from where it lay bunched on the big limb, but her underwear had fallen down onto the end of a lower limb and rested there like some out-of-season flower, a big magnolia blossom on this shaggy hickory.

Celeste raised her arms as if lifting a rifle to her eye, squinted down the imaginary barrel and pulled her trigger finger.

"Where are you, daughter?" Celeste's mama was talking to herself. She carried a big wad of cloth. Seen from high above, a bald spot on the top of Mrs. Purcell's head shone like a silver cartwheel. "Sissss-seeee," she said again. Then she shook her head and picked her way back through the bushes in the direction of the farmhouse.

When she was out of sight and, Alexander hoped, out of earshot, Celeste let go a snort. "I like to have died," she said. "I have to pee, and I couldn't hold my giggles and my need to go."

Alexander leaned out on the limb that held Celeste's underwear and shook the blossom free. It hit a lower limb an easy arm's reach above the ground. They climbed down and dressed, Alexander certain Mrs. Purcell would reappear any moment. Once they were clothed and had found Papa Jack's fish pole and the stringer of bream, Alexander relaxed.

Celeste had brought a tin spoon and a sharp knife, and she showed Alexander how to make an "S" cut to remove the bream's head and guts, how to use the spoon to scrape away the scales that floated at the water's edge like hundreds of sightless eyes. Once the bream were gutted and scaled and rinsed in the cool water, Celeste picked fern leaves and dunked them in the pool, then lined the cheesecloth sack with them and filled it up with the cleaned fish.

They stood a moment by the water's edge, each for different reasons reluctant to return to the farm, to the lives that waited, full of uncertainties.

They walked back down the path without holding hands. Mrs. Purcell waited before the farmhouse door. "Lord, gal, where-all did you two get to?" she asked. When Celeste went inside her mama closed the door behind them, and Alexander retreated to the barn. He could not hear Celeste's reply, but he heard the skillet clang and grease sizzle. He smelled fish frying while he busied himself with a file against the blade of a neglected adze he found in an empty barn stall.

🦋

Just at dark, horses' hooves pounded clay and a wavering voice sang, "She'll be riding six white horses when she come." Alexander peered out of the barn, afraid a Union patrol was on the prowl. Celeste stood before the house with a long cooking fork in her hand, Mrs. Purcell behind her in the doorway. The Purcell team came up the lane at a canter, and the wagon slid behind in billows of dust. Papa Jack hollered and pulled up. The horses, wet and foam-flecked, heaved to a halt. Alexander hurried out and grabbed hold of the reins at one of the horses' bits.

"Cake," Papa Jack said. "Cake."

As if they were in a skit on stage, Papa Jack and Caleb both held up packages.

"Flour," Papa Jack said.

"Sugar," said Caleb.

Together they jumped from the wagon. Papa Jack pumped Alexander's hand, and Caleb hugged his mother, who'd hurried out to meet him.

"Mama," Caleb said, "you're going to bake a cake."

"Because it is finally truly over," Papa Jack said.

"I ain't baking a cake over the Confederate states getting whipped."

"Then bake one on account of Josiah coming home soon."

News from Mount Pleasant had General Lee surrendered in Virginia two weeks ago, and Mobile surrendered ten days ago. Confederate soldiers were to be given paroles.

That night they ate fried fish, corn pone, yellow cake, and sweetened coffee. After supper, Papa Jack played "The Goose Hangs High" and "Dixie" on his mouth harp. Mrs. Purcell didn't say a word to Caleb about going to bed. The celebration lifted the cloud that had settled over Alexander and Celeste, even as it made more pressing the questions they held unspoken.

Three weeks later, a Union patrol rode up in a cloud of dust. Alexander listened from Papa Jack's lean-to room as the young Union lieutenant told Mrs. Purcell he had orders to return to Nashville. He said the Rebels were all pulled back and soldiers on both sides were being mustered out.

The way Mrs. Purcell and even old Papa Jack stared at him, Alexander wondered was it possible they knew what had happened between him and Celeste that day up in the treetop.

"I reckon you were going to tell me, soon as you got your plans fixed out?"

"Yes ma'am," was all he said, but it didn't seem to be all Mrs. Purcell wanted to hear.

Celeste wouldn't walk the path with him. It was near a week before he caught her alone.

"Captain, I'm thinking you used me for fun and don't have no permanent intentions."

"That's not true, Celeste." He took her hand that she gave up grudgingly. But when he got her up close she seemed to soften some. "What has passed between us means more to me than anything. You're someone God made special and didn't make any other like you," he said. The more he talked about how lovely and sensitive she was, the more he believed it was true. As he spoke his feelings out loud, he was discovering what they were. And when he found himself kissing Celeste again and her pressing hard against him and not stopping his hand from slipping beneath her blouse, he thought they might just drop to the grass and couple right there, so close to the house he could hear Mrs. Purcell yelling at Caleb though he couldn't make out the exact words. But Celeste pulled back and put her eyes on something just above his head.

"When you leaving?"

He didn't know whether to deny it, or take advantage of her saying it.

"When?" she asked again.

"Sooner I go, sooner I can come back for you."

She nodded. "Better not let Mama nor Papa Jack know you're sneaking off this way."

"But, Celeste, I'll come back for you. I got to get my record straight, get an honorable discharge. You don't deserve to start out with a deserter."

"I'll wait till I'm for sure you ain't coming."

Alexander couldn't think of any more words, so he kissed her again, but she didn't kiss back. All the next day Celeste avoided him, and he decided she had said all the good-byes she was going to say.

That night, after everyone was asleep, he took his knapsack from beneath Jerome's bed. His dusted tunic, his butternuts Mrs. Purcell or Sissy had washed and folded, sat atop the bag, alongside his severed left arm in its leather wrappings. Inside the knapsack were his tin plate, cup, fork and spoon, and his skillet, all washed. There was half a bar of gray soap, two sheets of paper and an envelope, a good pencil, and his "housewife" full of needles and thread. He stuck in his razor, took out the pencil and one of the two sheets of paper wondering where Celeste had found something so dear.

From the time they had found the piece of newspaper in the field, Alexander had known Celeste could read. He wrote: *I'm sorry to leave sudden-like, but think it is best this way. I am gone to get my discharge papers. I'll be back to ask permission to court Celeste.* Alexander didn't know how much money he'd need to get to Texas, but he left half of what the Chubs had collected for him with the letter, on Jerome's pillow. *This money,* he wrote, *just a token, cannot repay all I owe you. I will hire a boy in Columbia to return your horse I'm borrowing.* He would take the envelope and other sheet of paper. *I'll write you as soon as I reach Texas. I will send for Celeste.*

He decided his chances would be better in uniform with his bloodstained pass, so he quietly slipped on the clean but tattered trousers, shirt, and tunic that had lain for weeks beneath the bed. Out of habit, he shouldered his knapsack. He wondered if he'd need his cup, plate, or skillet. He picked up his left arm and gave the bare, small room a last look. Caleb lay on his back, legs splayed, skinny arms above his head—a position in which Alexander had seen many a soldier lying dead, but this boy's chest rose and fell. He hoped Caleb would never be a soldier boy. The room had no window to crawl out of, so Alexander had to go through the house to the door.

He stuck his severed arm down in one of his boots, both of which he carried to keep his steps quiet. He made it to the door without waking anybody. When he put his hand to the latch, he was surprised to feel a cheesecloth sack hanging there. Safely outside, he stepped into his boots. The sack contained the last of the yellow cake, and a note he was unable to read in the dark.

He took a bridle he had mended himself and slipped the bit into the mouth of the roan he thought was the weaker horse of the team. He led the horse a good ways from the house before he pulled himself up and rode bareback the four miles to Mount Pleasant. He thought he should save the cake for later, but he ate it while he rode, scattering crumbs like Hansel in the Grimms' tale. All the lights were out in Mount Pleasant, so he rode on to Columbia, where he found a light at the depot and reached into the cheesecloth sack for the paper on which was written, in a schoolgirl's uneven hand:

Dere Captun,

   The ink bottel is allmost dri so I will bee short. I am ancious for you agoing far out to Texus, sow daingeroust a state. I am ancious I may never see agin my dere Captun and youre hand I held to my bosom. Carey this porchun of cake and when you eate sum you will bee eatein hour wedin cake. I will ceep you saft in my hart and pray you carey me in youre hart.

Celeste Purcell

Rejoins the Army

Nobody in Columbia paid Alexander much mind. Everyone was still upset by reports Abe Lincoln had been shot. With Lincoln dead, folks thought the windup would go harder on the South. Alexander left the roan with a boy at a livery stable, after getting his solemn oath he would ride to Sandy Hook and return the horse to the Purcell farm. Alexander paid the boy in advance. Alexander was tempted to send a note to Celeste, something about wedding cake, but he did not.

Alexander took the cars north, surprised there were no soldiers about. But when they reached Spring Hill there were plenty of soldiers, most of them wearing Federal blue. Alexander was taken off the train and held for six hours while Union officers scrutinized the wounded furlough Captain Foster had given him months ago. Every time they sent him along to someone else he had to peel back the leather from his severed arm to show he wasn't carrying a rifle.

Questioned about the date of the pass, he said he had no memory. His story, and he stuck to it, went from the ambulance and a dose of morphine to waking up in a farmhouse. He'd been in and out of fever, didn't know how long he'd stayed there—his wounds had been slow to heal. Soon as he was able he'd gotten a ride to Columbia and taken the cars. He was looking for someone to tell him what to do. The Yankees gave him hardtack and weak, but real, coffee and marched him to a cross street where a store had been turned into military headquarters.

The low-ceilinged room was smoky and smelled of coal oil. Lamplight wiggled up the plank walls. A lieutenant colonel sat behind a table, writing. Alexander recognized Captain Kistler—Matthew Kistler—the Union captain whom Alexander had met his first day in the Confederacy, crossing the Long Bridge from Washington into Virginia. The colonel's dark eyes widened.

"Don't I know you, soldier?"

"We did meet once, sir, in '63."

The colonel stared, trying to remember this one-armed man with haunted-looking eyes.

"I was different." Alexander held up his wrapped arm. "I didn't have to carry my arm in a sack. I wasn't afoot, then. We rode together from the Long Bridge into Virginia to Fort Albany. A cannon broke its carriage." Still the colonel just stared. "You told me about your sons. I'm from Gotham, too." There. The colonel's eyes were wet. Now he saw the boy's face behind the hollow cheekbones and the world-weary eyes.

"A Rebel—were you, even then?"

"In my heart, I was. Though I didn't know what it meant. Don't know now, for sure—"

"Right." The colonel cut him off. His pen scratching and *tumping* on the table gave Alexander a funny feeling in his teeth. "Vernon," the colonel said, no louder than ordinary conversation, but the front door opened and a lieutenant came in.

"Yes, sir." The lieutenant saluted and took the paper from the colonel.

"Escort this wounded soldier to the cars for Nashville." The colonel stared in Alexander's direction, but Alexander knew the man was seeing something inside himself. "We've turned a generation of children into old men, and the president's body rides a slow train."

Alexander wondered about the colonel's family, his sickly wife, his sons, but did not ask. The colonel's head was turned, and the side of his face Alexander could see shone like brass in the glow of the lamp. It was apparent the colonel didn't believe Alexander's story, and it was just as apparent he didn't particularly care. He had other concerns.

The Rebs the cars carried wore patched and mismatched uniforms stained with blood, powder, and dirt. Many were shoeless, and their fixed eyes stared with the unseeing, vacant look of starvation. Their necks were bent, their shoulders hunched. The crowded cars passed slowly through Franklin, close to the pike where Alexander had stood in a hail of steel and lost his arm and his illusions, such as he had left by then. As Franklin slid by in the car window, he was mildly surprised he felt nothing. Someone toward the front of the car said, "Nashville coming up." They rolled past deserted breastworks Alexander figured were Confederate abandoned after the fighting way back in December. Then they passed the Yankee camps, and a few in blue stood and saluted the cars bearing their recent enemies soon to be their countrymen again. After the Yankee troops came a cemetery with endless rows of gravestones. The markers went by in the window the way crops in a field go by and make you try to count the rows though you know you can't keep up. The rectangular stones reminded Alexander of playing cards he'd seen a sergeant shuffle in a fancy way, making the stretched deck into an accordion he pulled apart then squeezed back tight. Beside Alexander on the seat, Silas Nunner shook his pale, ghostly head. In the car window, Charles Wesley winked.

The cars entered the Nashville depot, and a gate shut behind them. The platform was thick with soldiers, most in butternut and gray. Gated in, Alexander felt herded. Tired, dispirited men called out commands. The paper Colonel Kistler had given him and his transfer to Columbia and the wounded furlough were read, and he was pushed along from one place to another. He was hollered and whistled at, prodded along. And for the first time since the battle at Franklin, he heard Charles Wesley call his name, once, in an uncertain way, *Alexander?* He looked for a Union uniform on his brother's body. He knew Charles Wesley's voice was only in his head, but for the first time he wanted to answer back. A Union lieutenant put another brand on Alexander's paper, and he was marched to an open field behind a long warehouse near the depot, one of scores of Rebs rounded up, fenced in, and left to mill around.

They checked Alexander's papers, but no one searched him for a weapon. Once he showed them his arm was not a rifle, they were satisfied. No one had found his money. He sat on hard earth and drew his knees up, put his finger down the side of his shoe to feel the padding of Confederate bills. If the money was worth anything, it would not be for long. He should spend it, or exchange it for greenbacks if he got the chance. He rested his head on his knees and opened his eyes, for a moment or for longer. It was still light when he woke. A shadow lay across his shoes, and he looked up at a waving red pennant of hair.

"Ort? Orten Trainer?"

"Blessing from Providence, Alex. You are a blessing from Providence." Ort knelt and set down his own cut-off arm, and then he gripped Alexander's right arm with his.

Alexander lowered his voice. "I shouldn't be surprised, Ort. You must have smelled my money."

"A lot of good it'll do either of us, Alex. We're destined for the Nashville pen."

"I heard President Johnson is going to release all Confederate prisoners."

"If the prison serves hot meals, hand me a long sentence and shackle me in the mess hall."

They were given Yankee rations so plentiful Alexander felt a pang of sadness for all the hungry days and nights suffered by so many Rebs. A little food and equipment might have made the difference, but he was long past refighting even his own small battles, much less the entire conflict. The Yankee guard handing out rations nodded kindly, and Alexander nodded back and realized how easily he would be Unionized again.

Early the next morning a Union sergeant bunched them up, and they waited in front of the locked gates. The sun rose bright in the cool June morning, and the smoke of their breathing rose toward a blue sky. Word passed among them they were headed directly into prison. A clean dark blue uniform approached, and the Union sergeant came to attention. Wearing the uniform was a boy who didn't look much over fourteen, sixteen at most, but he wore the plain shoulder straps of a second lieutenant, and he carried a grown man's rifle.

"Sergeant," the lieutenant sounded as young as he looked. "Is your detail ready to be mobilized?"

"Sir, they are a dreadful ragged lot, hungry and wore out. But I guess if we take it slow they have a little march left in them."

The lieutenant leveled his rifle at the Rebels. "Get them in formation, sergeant."

The sergeant seemed bewildered by the officer. He gave a barely noticeable shrug and ordered the Confederates to fall in. Ort helped Alexander up. Men started making a wavy line, four abreast. Alexander knelt to retrieve his left arm in its carrying case. He grabbed the arm and stood just as the lieutenant passed. The boy's face blanched and his eyes enlarged. Alexander saw what was about to happen, but it happened so quickly he couldn't stop it. He felt trapped in a dream, desperate to run but unable to move. The lieutenant swung his rifle and fired without raising or aiming the gun, its stock against his thigh when he shot. Alexander's chest went hot, too heavy for him to hold up. The ball's impact spun him around a full turn, and he sat down hard. His back was hot and wet. He looked down at his chest, at a dark hole no bigger than a thumb, and he heard his mother read him the rhyme about the boy eating his Christmas pie:

He put in his thumb,
And pulled out a plum,
And said, "What a good boy am I."

The Rebs broke and made for the lieutenant. Had the sergeant not shot into the air and gotten a mob of Yankees between the lieutenant and the Rebs, they'd have killed him bare-handed.

"He swung his rifle at me."

"Weren't no rifle, you damned fool."

"Get him out of here," the sergeant said. Then he called for a medic. The sergeant handed Ort a kerchief and he wadded and pressed it into Alexander's back so hard it took Alexander's breath.

"Ort?" Alexander sounded like someone else, someone as young and unsure as the lieutenant.

"Right here, Alex, right here."

A shadow moved over the field darkening everyone but Alexander and Ort, the sun shining down on just the small space they occupied together.

Alexander, is it you? Charles Wesley asked.

"Leave me be. I'm not ready to be found."

"What is it, comrade?" Orten asked.

"Take me to Texas, Ort. I've headed there all my life. Bury me there. Take the money under the arch of my left longboat. When you get me there, write my papa."

"Alex, your hand reads easier than mine. We get to Texas, you can write your pa."

"Pledge me, Orten, don't let them send me home to Gotham. Don't let them bury me where it gets so cold. Put me on the cars south. Dig my grave in warm Texas dirt. Your oath?"

"I vow I'll get you to Texas, and I'll write your pa when you're there safe."

"There's a sheet of writing paper in my kit." *Poor Celeste*, Alexander thought. *How long will you wait for my letter? Are you planning our life together in perilous Texas?*

Was it candle-lighting already? How could dusk fall so suddenly? Alexander could barely see Ort's white teeth beneath the graying ember of his hair. How could a field of soldiers empty so quickly? Alexander peered down a cannon, a long black barrel, with Ort's face far away at the other end. The popping of a flag interrupted the quiet, though Alexander felt no wind. He was sleepy, but it couldn't already be night. He just needed to lie down on this cot and rest a moment. Bent over him with a tin cup, Ort blocked the sun and made a cool shadow. On the side of the cup was Charles Wesley's face. Alexander didn't want to be buried where Charles Wesley couldn't find him. Charles Wesley's grasp no longer held him back. The double iron gates creaked open. Charles Wesley knelt beside him, and Alexander saw his own lips move, knew the words as his lips formed them though he heard nothing: *Charles Wesley, you've a beard, now. And you're all grown up in the eyes. I'm glad you found me. I was not a coward, Charles Wesley.* He touched the stump of Alexander's amputated arm. *Some have called me a hero. Isn't it amusing?* He put his lips on the cool edge of the cup Charles Wesley held out.

Where his missing arm should be, Alexander felt the warmth of Charles Wesley's hand. He was glad his brother was here for the shooting. "Wake me when the shooting starts." Had he spoken, or only dreamt it? Pitch dark out and no sign of troop movements. No rumble of artillery, yet. If he could just be sure Charles Wesley would wake him, it would be all right to nap here in the warm dark. "Don't forget to wake me. Wake me for the shooting."

New Arm, New Name

By the time a Union medic got the blood slowed and the wound bandaged, Alexander was dead. Orten Trainer and the medic lifted Alexander onto a canvas litter. The Federals wouldn't release the body, but the sergeant let Ort ride in the ambulance. Alone with Alexander's body, Ort switched their papers and took the money from inside Alexander's shoe as he had bade him do. Ort pulled from its hide wrappings Alexander's severed arm the second lieutenant had mistaken for a rifle. Ort unstrapped the canvas bag that held his own amputated arm, lay his arm on Alexander's deerhide, rolled it up, and tied the bundle to the dead man's knapsack. Alexander's arm was longer than Ort's, but it fit with room to spare inside the ample bag. "Best I can do, Alex."

Ort and Alexander were close enough in size to match the vague descriptions in their papers. Ort was glad he'd worn his cap the day before, when the Yankees wrote everybody's mustering out documents—for the first time since he'd joined the army his papers did not list his red hair. A Union doctor took a quick look at Alexander and signed a death warrant. Ort leaned over the litter and gave the body a hug, "Good-bye, Orten Trainer. I'll keep your memory alive."

Alexander's blood marked Ort's coat. When the doctor saw the bloodstain, he called for a litter. "Let's have a look." He held Ort by his one arm. He opened the coat and showed the doctor his unblemished shirt. The doctor nodded. "So many wounds."

The medic who had driven Orten and Alexander to the hospital waved at him from the dim corridor. "Hello, Confederacy." The medic had some foreign accent Ort couldn't identify. "Your group is surely gone by now—they all been put on steamers for downriver. I have a body to pick up and carry to the cars. Help me with the coffin, and I'll ride you back to the depot."

"Is there any way I can get started somewhere today?" Orten asked.

The medic shrugged and pointed at a Union lieutenant behind a desk at the hospital's entrance. "I hope you've got some gold hid away. If you don't, you can aim to walk home." The lieutenant looked for Orten's insignia, but his coat and shirt were bare. Ort handed him Alexander's papers.

"Where are you bound for, Speer?"

"Texas. I'd rather take the cars than ride the river, if the railroad's taking any on."

The lieutenant scowled. "The cars are loaded with Union corpses. You want on a car with men you maybe killed? I wish I had you a casket to ride in."

"I don't believe I killed anyone, Lieutenant. And there are Confederate dead piled on wagons all down the Columbia Pike, corpses without the comfort of coffins."

The lieutenant's knuckles were white, his jaw clenched. A vein at the side of his forehead pulsed. He thrust Ort's papers—Alexander's papers—to the ambulance driver. "Take him to Captain Barnes. Tell the captain this Private Speer was involved in a shooting incident in which a parolee was killed." The lieutenant turned to Ort. "The captain will know what to do with you."

The medic nodded at the lieutenant, nodded at Orten, who followed him out to the ambulance. "Sorry, Confederacy. The lieutenant's brother was killed in a skirmish in Virginia, a week *after* Appomattox. He nurses anger against grief." Orten helped the medic load the coffin in the ambulance. "I'm ordered to take you to the prison, but Captain Barnes is a fair man. He will surely not punish you."

Orten did not like the risk of being sent to the Nashville Penitentiary. He liked his chances here and now with this foreign medic better than his chances in a Federal pen. When the ambulance was hidden by a row of trees, Ort climbed into the back.

The medic looked back over his shoulder for just a moment. "What are you looking for?"

"Don't want to go to the pen and leave my arm behind." *Maybe,* Ort thought, *the Yankee who shot Alex was right to think this arm's a weapon.* The medic's head was framed in the sunlit opening of the ambulance cover. Ort picked up the pouch holding Alexander's arm and eased up behind the medic. With a rueful smile at a pun—*taking up arms* went through his head—Ort hit the back of the medic's skull. The near-petrified limb made a soft whack, and the man slumped over. Ort pulled the medic inside the ambulance, stripped him to his longjohns, swapped uniforms, and took his papers, including a bill of lading for the coffin— identified as containing a Sergeant Joseph Murphy of Indiana. The corpse was ticketed for Louisville.

A knot rose, but the medic's skull didn't feel split, and his pulse was strong. Orten stuffed the medic's handkerchief in his mouth. With casket rope he tied the medic's feet together, tied his hands behind his back. Ort pushed the bound gray-clad body down a weedy slope behind a deserted brick building. "I hope you wake up no worse for the wear, Billy boy," he said.

War's Final Shot

The cars Charles Wesley rode to Chattanooga and then on to Nashville were packed with Rebels trying to get home and a scattering of men in blue. The mood was not festive, but neither was it funereal. There was little sense of animosity. Had someone from a distant land, someplace on earth where the ground had not trembled from horses' hooves and cannon and the heavy fall of bodies, had someone ignorant of the long war been suddenly put upon the rails with Charles Wesley, that person would not have guessed the many men in gray had been defeated by the few in blue. He might have guessed the blue-clad men were ministers, angels even, guiding a careworn flock of sheep to some place of promised rest. Creaking and groaning, the heavily loaded cars somnolently rolled on, as if the entire journey were up a long, steep grade.

Charles Wesley's left arm began to ache and soon it pulsed so he could barely shoulder his way through the crowded Nashville depot. Union troops and legions of surrendered Confederates packed the platform. Rebs overflowed the station building. Outside, a fenced and gated railroad yard was covered over with gray and butternut, as if with a sooty hoarfrost, though the June sun shone down. Word was, Reb prisoners were stacked like cordwood in Nashville.

Charles Wesley squeezed his throbbing arm. He couldn't decide if it was likely or unlikely he might find Alexander somewhere in this endless horde. It did seem possible Alexander might be here among so many Confederate soldiers, but the numbers made it seem unlikely Charles Wesley would spy him. There were rumors they would be released, rumors they would be shot. Charles Wesley searched for a face that matched his own, but no eyes gave back his stare.

He located a bank and withdrew money on Papa's draft. Then he found a house where meals were being served and had eggs, ham, and cornbread, steaming hot sassafras tea. He held the hot cup of tea against his left arm and got some relief from the throbbing. When the tea cooled he drank it down and got another hot cup to hold against his arm. He had not much time before he should board the steamboat on the Cumberland River. He went back to the depot and walked the fence, looking one last time for Alexander among the Rebs being sent home.

Charles Wesley spotted a familiar jawline. His hand touched the whiskers on his own face. Could it be Alexander's beardless cheek he espied? Charles Wesley glimpsed the man's face before another stepped between them. The face belonged to a one-armed man. *Of course,* Charles Wesley thought, *Alexander has lost an arm, that's been my occasional pain, his daily ache of missing flesh.* Charles Wesley hurried to the gate, keeping his eyes on the one-armed figure in the crowd.

"Alexander," he said, "Alexander Wesley Speer."

A Union sergeant near the gate stepped over. "Soldier?"

"My brother, Sergeant. I'm looking for my brother."

"Amongst the Johnnies?"

Charles Wesley nodded. "My twin. Have you seen my face on any of your prisoners?"

The sergeant stared at Charles Wesley, cocked his head as a dog does when he hears some far-off sound. The sergeant squeezed his chin in his hand and frowned.

"I saw a one-armed man. I thought for a minute — my face without the beard? We didn't, I mean, *I* didn't have the beard before the war. And he had both his arms."

"I'll open the gate. You can look." But before the sergeant closed the distance, a *snap* behind him made him turn. Muffled by all the milling men, the report was like a faraway clap of thunder, and Charles Wesley caught the sergeant's quick glance up at the bright, clear sky.

"Sergeant, wait," Charles Wesley said, but his words were lost in a din of shouts and rushing steps. Someone screamed for an ambulance. A whistle blew. A dozen or more blue uniforms sliced into the mob of brown and gray. The crowd surged like floodwater, hit the wire fence and bowed it out, clanged against the gates that angled out like the prow of a ship.

Charles Wesley didn't know whether to run the length of the fence and enter the depot from the other side, or wait to see if the sergeant came back to let him in once the melee was under control. He hurried down the fence trying to spot the one-armed man again. By the time he got to the brick depot wall, an ambulance wagon was rushing off. Armed guards blocked the entrance, and even if they could hear him over all the yelling, Charles Wesley doubted they'd let him in, now. He went back to the gate, but the sergeant had disappeared.

Charles Wesley managed to position himself by the gates when they were opened several hours after the rifle shot had rung out, and the Rebs were marched out and down toward the river, where several boats waited. The pain in his left arm had eased completely. There was no reason to think the pain had stopped for any reason other than the hot tin mugs of tea. All year the aching had come and gone without warning. Might be the rheumatism. Many men young as he complained of it after months of sleeping on the wet, cold ground. And even if the pain were some echo of a wound Alexander bore, it did not prove he had lost an entire arm.

Charles Wesley spotted a one-armed man, six inches too tall, and then another far too old. In all, five passed by who had but one arm, yet none mirrored himself. He followed the lines down to the boats and caught sight of the man he'd seen, one good arm carrying a leather scabbard like a sword. How could Charles Wesley have thought the man was Alexander? Though there was a similarity of size and shape, this one-armed man's head flamed with wild red hair.

Feeling a fool, Charles Wesley vowed he would slow his heart and go more cautiously. After two years of war, how had he lost his wits so fast? Who but a dolt would wager he had found his brother so easily out of a mob of hundreds? Charles Wesley shook his head at his folly. Aching, whether of the arm or of the heart, no more than wishing, ever made anything happen.

Orten by Any Other Name

Orten had no trouble at the depot. The Yankees didn't question whether he was who his papers said he was: Corporal August von Zuccalmaglio. Ort was glad he didn't have to say the name out loud. In one of von Zuccalmaglio's recently resoled boots—a better fit than any Confederate quartermaster had done during the war—Ort hid Alexander's papers. Ort's cup ran over with names he might call himself. The Union uniform and papers identified him as a Union medic. Alexander's papers identified him as a Reb private. He could be anyone he wanted. Orten stepped onto the cars in Nashville as a Union corporal. A few hours later he stepped off at Louisville and watched the unloading of two coffins bearing Union soldiers of the Thirteenth Indiana mistaken for Confederates in heavy rain at Cheat Mountain and shot by Ohio troops.

There to receive her husband's body was a widow Ort heard identify herself as Mrs. Laura Etta Murphy. Though there was nothing ugly about the woman, neither was she close to pretty. But the Widow Murphy had shiny, dark hair wrapped tight about her head. Ort imagined her hair unpinned swaying against the small of her back. She was thirty if she was a day, but she had the shape of one who'd never birthed a babe. So there was that, her shapelessness, but more was the way she carried her shape. She neither strutted nor posed as a demimonde does, nor did she hunker beneath her black hatbrim as a decorous widow does. Ort's eyes met hers, and she stared right back, not flirtatious so much as confident. Not wanting a name he couldn't pronounce, he buried von Zuccalmaglio and resurrected Alexander Speer, transferring him to the Union army and promoting him to corporal as he had in a letter to Samuel Speer. Ort put what he hoped was a youthful if world-weary smile on Corporal Speer's face and marched into the bivouac of the widow's eyes.

"Mrs. Murphy, begging your pardon for my intrusion into your grief. I'm Corporal Speer. I served with your brave husband. When I was put on the muster roll and offered transport home, I could think of no finer duty than to accompany Sergeant Murphy back to his home. Permit me to say I never expected so uncommon a widow at my journey's end."

She raised her hand in a sweet salute. When the coffin lid was lifted for the widow to confirm Sergeant Murphy's identity and sign papers of receipt, Corporal Speer stood at her side. They gazed at the man they'd both loved. Ort's gaze was his first, so he ran his eyes over the corpse putting to memory the aspect of his beloved sergeant: the beefy face, the bushy brown beard, and the missing ring finger. Ort took the widow's elbow and guided her to a depot bench.

"You all right, ma'am?"

"Corporal Speer, I am quite all right."

"Alex, if it pleases you."

"Alex. Do you intend to see Joseph all the way home?"

"All the way home" was across the Ohio River to a farm in Indiana, near Corydon. Orten drove the late sergeant's buckboard. From time to time, Alex leaned back and put his hand reverently on Sergeant Murphy's casket in the wagonbed. Alex and the widow talked the whole sad way from Louisville. Her talkativeness made Ort bold to ask about Sergeant Murphy's farm. Six hundred forty acres, more or less, of rich bottomland, the widow said, not without pride. Neither of her children having yet attained legal age, she reckoned she was sole inheritor.

"A mighty responsibility."

"I feel a certain dread, now I'm alone in the world."

"With your permission, ma'am, I'll stay around long enough to help you put everything in form for the future—yours and Sergeant Murphy's children's."

She turned her unblinking smile on Corporal Speer. "You have a good heart, Alex." Then she took between her hands Alexander Speer's one strong arm that held the reins to her team and rested against his good shoulder her head with its long and lovely hair. Ort didn't care what Laura Etta said so long as she kept chirping like a songbird, so long as her dark hair kept whispering against his shoulder. Her words (and his) were appropriately solemn, but her eyes were as bouncy and vigorous as the ride on the spring-supported board seat.

Laura Etta Murphy: Beds with the Devil

A One-Armed Man Holds Her Tight
(June 1865)

Out here on the edge, a marriageable woman may take as her man
a wild ruffian, a gambling rakehell, a lazy scofflaw, or worse.

—from *Gideon Jones' Journal*

It had been nearly a year, eleven hard months, since Joseph Murphy had enlisted and left Laura Etta to manage the farm. She shouldn't fault a man for going to a war he didn't choose. Nonetheless, she had resented all her husband had left her to do more than she had missed the man himself.

Laura Etta found herself writing her sister back in Pennsylvania more often than she wrote her husband. When she'd left Pennsylvania to come west with Joseph, she'd said good-bye to family and friends. Her ma and her pa had died without her near, and then she and her sister got out of the habit of corresponding. Annie stayed at home, never married. A schoolteacher, she sent long picturesque letters, and they helped fill Laura Etta's evenings after young Joe and Dorsey were asleep. When the war ended Annie wrote of coming out for a visit, once Joseph was back. Laura Etta had imagined riding with her husband to pick up her sister at the Louisville depot. She envisioned Joseph in a long army coat, resplendent with brass buttons, his hair and beard freshly combed. Instead she'd made the ride alone to pick up Joseph, not Annie, and she'd come back with a one-armed stranger beside her on the buckboard.

Like many other husbands and fathers, Joseph Murphy had come home in a box. He looked nothing at all the way Laura Etta remembered him. After Joseph left, she'd found it difficult to recall his face, and seeing the face in the coffin did not help at all. The face in the coffin was sallow and gaunt with big eyes and a long nose, a beard sparse and unkempt. And the meager body, sunken into itself, looked worn-out. Raw-boned fingers sharp as animal claws clutched an unfamil-iar-looking heavy wool coat that filled up the space in the coffin.

Laura Etta remembered her husband more the way their son Joe was: tall and strong and younger than the man in the coffin. *Could the corpse,* she wondered, *be someone else?* Maybe the army had sent Joseph to some other woman. Maybe some other widow was wondering who the fellow was in her box. Maybe Joseph was still alive. Maybe some wife wondered who the fellow was in her bed. Joe had grown his father's big hands and feet, but the rest of his body had not yet caught up. His hands and feet moved clumsily. She felt a deep pang of sympathy for this son who didn't know what was expected of him. The boy wanted to grieve for his father, but Joseph had always treated his son like a hireling. This year of his father's absence had been one of the nicest years of Joe's young life. He had worked the farm harder than ever, but he'd had the pleasure of only himself to answer to. Now, the boy didn't know what to make of Corporal Speer. This Alex-ander Speer shaped his words melodiously and as slowly as if he were slow in the head, his one arm swaying with the lilt of his talk. Laura Etta saw Joe see Corporal Speer stare at her, and she saw Joe see her, his mother, for the first time in his life, as a woman. Her daughter Dorsey, on the other hand, made it clear she disliked Corporal Speer. But Dorsey had not much liked her father. She was one of those girls who had got interested in boys sooner than she could do anything about it, especially since she lived way out on a farm, and the more she pined for a boy to be in love with, the more she withdrew from the men in her family. Laura Etta saw herself in Dorsey, in the thick hair coal black as Laura Etta's had once been and in the way the girl walked smooth and level with her chin high, as if she bal-anced a jug on her head. Dorsey was more comely than her mother. "Pretty" was more in how one carried oneself than just in features, and Dorsey carried herself with an awareness, no, an *assumption* of her beauty.

Laura Etta knew she herself was not pretty. Plain would be more the truth. She didn't have any poor features, but her only beauty was in the dark hair that shone with a washing and came down past her waist. There was the hair to display with quiet pride, and there was the other she could not but display. Though it was a sin, her pride rode in this, too. This other was her shape. Corporal Speer was not the first man to stare at her the way he stared, but Laura Etta did not put much store in the longing gazes of men. Men, she had learned, longed for many things and once they acquired them forgot how much they had wanted them. A thirty-four-year-old farmwife who had borne and birthed four babies, Laura Etta presented a figure improved by age. Flesh made into muscle by work had held off fat. Her waist had always been tiny, and she had small feet. Etta Mae was born dead, then Laura Etta had Joe, now seventeen, followed by Dorsey, fifteen. Tabitha Jo, a complete surprise, was born five months after Joseph left for the war and died of a fever four months later, before Laura Etta got news of Joseph's death. The mystery was how, right after she buried Tabitha Jo, Laura Etta had her milk dry up, yet her breasts kept their nursing fullness. Not so much large as firm, they stood up stronger now than the day she'd married Joseph. She couldn't explain the almost arrogant way they poked up or the dark pouting of her nipples, but she doubted they'd stay so forever.

Corporal Speer's eyes had moved over her the first day at the depot, and if she allowed herself to think on it she had known then how well she fit to the curve of his eyes. And if she allowed herself to think on this, too, Corporal Speer had also assayed Dorsey's shape. Laura Etta had a vague premonition of the reckoning that could come from that appraisal, the cost of which would be incalculable. Regardless of what transpired between Corporal Speer and herself, Laura Etta determined she would closely watch the ledger of her daughter's interests.

There was a part of herself Laura Etta held aside for a man, a part with only enough room (and perhaps only enough patience and energy) for one man at a time. Her son had been in that place during the past year, and before him his father had filled all her space. She wasn't sure what to expect from her children. Mothers lose daughters early but can sometimes keep sons. She had lost Tabitha Jo before she weaned her, she had already lost Dorsey to growing up, and she was losing what little hold she'd ever had on Joe. He was daily slipping away. She'd been lucky not to lose him to war. Now she'd likely lose him to drunkenness and fighting and running with other boys (all about the same) or to some girl scarcely older than his sister. Knowing this, Laura Etta began to let him go in her mind so she'd be used to his being gone when the time came. And as she let Joe go, she became more and more aware of the empty place he was leaving inside her. When she met Alexander Speer she knew he was going to fill the space. She wrote Annie about him, wrote how Alex had been a corporal in the army with Joseph but didn't tell how he was a one-armed man. Annie's reply, long in coming, said she would likely not be able to visit. She was terribly busy with the revival of her school now they'd put down the slave owners' rebellion. Annie also mentioned how a year seemed the minimum period of mourning allowed by good taste. Laura Etta felt differently. She'd worn black dresses since the letter had come making her a widow. Those few weeks of waiting for her husband's corpse was long enough in mourning for her though she was sure it was not nearly long enough for the ladies in Corydon, whose sense of timing was more like sister Annie's. She'd been dressed in black the day she met Corporal Speer, and now, a week later, the widow Murphy became Mrs. Alexander Speer.

Laura Etta knew Annie could never fathom how her sister might marry a man she had known for only a week, a stranger. But life out here was different than back in Pennsylvania. Out here, close to the frontier, Laura Etta had grown accustomed to quick decisions. Her choices were more limited than her sister's, and the stakes were higher than in the steady country back East. It is true she did not know her new husband, nor much about him, but she had not got to know her first husband for a year or more after they wed and even then not so well as she knew other folks. And she never got to know Joseph well enough to identify for certain the body he left behind.

When they signed the marriage papers Laura Etta learned two things about Alexander Speer: he could write his name pretty as you please, and his age—the age he wrote down—was thirty-nine. She calculated that against her age, which she listed as twenty-eight, a figure that looked good on the paper.

Her Second Wedding Night

The night of her marrying Alexander Speer, Laura Etta lay in her shift on the cotton tick and, with fear and curiosity, waited for her new husband the same way she had lain on the same tick waiting for Joseph Murphy almost eighteen years ago. She had been sixteen. Her hair hadn't been as long, and she hadn't learned how to wash it so shiny. Her breasts then were soft nubbins.

Her memories of Joseph Murphy naked were of his backside. Joseph had always come to her in the darkness, and his front had been a bristly warm weight covering her. She remembered his husky breathing and the muffled breath of feathers inside the tick squirming to get out of his way. Laura Etta always held her own breath, never made a sound, while Joseph labored over her, a man working with a will toward finishing. When he stopped he always gave her a pat, a man slapping a horse or a cow or a set fence post or a stacked sack of feed—a man satisfied with the job he'd done. Then he slid out and rolled, slippery, off of her and onto the floor on her side of the bed, from there to rise and walk heavily after a cool drink of water. In warm weather she'd hear him relieving himself, his stream hitting the ground outside the open bedroom window.

She'd seen Joseph Murphy's bare backside many times, as he passed through the square of moonlight the bedroom window was. Fine brown hairs covered his shoulders like daddy longlegs spiders. Sun kept a red collar around his neck, but, below, his flesh was white as fatback. He had no waist, no loin—his shoulders drifted like a snowbank down to the backs of his thighs with only the small, dark breach between his flat buttocks to give his torso any definition. Summer or winter, when Joseph came to her he worked up a sweat and a good enough thirst he had to have one last dipper before he slept. Alex was different in every way. The man never worked at anything, and she'd never seen him sweat. When Alex came to her bed, first thing he did was relight the lamp she had blown out.

"Sit up, honey." This one-armed man's voice was high and trembling. "Sit up for me so the lamplight can spill down you."

She scootched up onto her elbows, her cotton shift tight behind her neck and across her breasts. A new husband, Alexander Speer, a stranger almost, stood beside the table on which the lamp sat. Only his face was visible, lighted from the chin up. His lips and long nose sent shadows up into his red hair, hair tipped with yellow light like flames. She wondered, almost serious, if she were about to couple with the Devil, and she felt in the man's flaming hair for horns.

When Alex stepped toward her his only hand moved to his groin, and he held and lifted himself. Laura Etta's breath caught when the light darted down there. The man-thing curved up at her, stiff and swollen on the end like a knob. He let go of himself, and he twitched, jerked, vibrated like a divining rod. But what took her breath was not what he had, it was what he didn't have. The curve of his rod disappeared into a red bush of hair like a small fire built on the hillock of his behind, and no loose sack swung there, no wrinkled fist of skin drew up tight against his warmth.

His hand at her side pinched her as he pulled at her shift. She put her weight on her elbows and lifted her bottom to free the shift, and when she arched her back her incomprehensibly full breasts thrust up toward her new husband. He tugged, and her shift came up over her breasts. Cool air surrounded her breasts, then the soft shift was around her neck softly choking her, then it burned her chin, and she sucked cloth into her mouth and bit down, breathing in her own muffled sounds and the sour smell of inside her mouth. Blindfolded by her shift, she saw the bright cloud that filled her sight every time she jumped from a creek bank and plunged underwater. Unseeing she more consciously felt the man's hand and his fluttering lips, slippery with sweat and saliva, move from one breast to the other. She unclenched her teeth, and the shift flew off of her. The flaming back of Alexander's head bobbed beneath her chin. Muscles in his neck and back trembling, he jerked from one breast to the other as a hummingbird feeds—here, there, back again. His lips and tongue pulled and pushed at her. He sucked hard, his teeth pricked skin. Her hands, fingers spread, pressed into the small of the man's back. Then he was up on his knees, his only hand at his groin, holding himself there, again, and talking out loud.

"Say hello."

She wondered if he meant her, wondered: *is this Alexander Speer crazy, is he the kind of crazy who would hurt a woman?* He cast his voice off so the words didn't come from his lips, and he made the words high-pitched, mouse-squeaky, holding himself out in his fist as he trilled:

"Hello, Laura, how about a kiss?"

He let go of himself to reach and squeeze the back of her neck. He pushed her face down, and he came up off his knees, half-standing in the bed, bringing himself up to her lips.

She did what he wanted. She closed her eyes and breathed through her nose. She put her mind on making skillet bread. She went through it all: getting eggs from under the hens, pulling and kneading the cow's teats for milk, stirring in cornmeal, building up the fire. Just when she was pouring batter into the hot grease-slickened skillet, what he wanted was over—with the taste of salt and raw egg in her mouth. What was it she swallowed from no sac at all? She dried him with her gown, careful not to put her hands or mouth where his sac should be. *The war,* she thought. But she saw no scar, no sign of any wound. They had to be there for all the rest to work, and so she looked again, wondering if she was seeing wrong in the jumping lamplight. *Without them,* she thought, *no children*—and a weight lifted. *Did what she just swallowed carry no life? If it were so, oh, if it were so, there'd be one less fear.*

And he did things to her, too, things Joseph Murphy had never done. Alex's hand, his fingertips against her skin, was not the rough hand of a farmer. This new husband made her thighs tremble as if she'd put down a load after miles of toting. His tongue bumped down her ribcage, and she turned her face into the tick to muffle moans she surprised herself by making.

And when he seemed through, and she felt through, felt there couldn't be other things to do between a man and a woman, Alex did not give her a pat and go for a dipper of well water. He lay atop her and poked at her some more, and with his tongue and his teeth and his fingers he made her twitch and flinch for a long while longer, until he fell sudden into sleep like a baby resting his head on her chest, the damp tips of his hair crimson in the lamplight.

Laura Etta couldn't sleep. She lay there and listened for her children in the next room, but the little farmhouse was all over quiet. Then, she did not know why, she began to cry. Her throat clenched and unclenched, and tears trickled to the corners of her mouth, warm and salty, and she wondered if this was the crying she'd never done for Joseph Murphy even when they'd buried him in his box. She thought the crying might be because of the things she'd done this night with this man who lay sleeping on top of her like a never-grown-up child, or it might be because of the two children in the other room, both of them near grown-up and the constant wondering what lives those two had waiting for them. *Maybe even,* she thought, *I'm weeping for Annie, and the distance—not just the miles—separating us.* It made part of her mad that she didn't know if she was crying tears of sadness or tears of joy. It made some part of her mad that another part of her felt sweetly melancholy lying there crying.

Early the next morning, Laura Etta opened her eyes. A window-shape of sunlight lay over their still naked bodies and brightened the wall beside the bed. Alex's head rested on her breast. The shadow of the wood strips that held the windowpanes put a dark cross in the light on the wall, and she wondered if the cross was a sign, and if so, was it for good or against evil? Alex slept without snoring or twitching, the stump of his left arm pressed into her ribs. She lay perfectly still. The shape of light lengthened and crept across her arm to Alex's head, where it illuminated in his red hair more gray than she had noticed before.

She ran her fingers over the palm of Alex's only hand—skin smooth as the man's talk. This was not the callused hand of a farmer. Her new husband showed little interest in working Joseph Murphy's land. Sergeant Murphy had left behind a good buckboard and team and a tidy savings. The war had wound down. Summer was upon them. After her new husband poked and prodded, moving her up and down the soft tick, he talked about the Territory of Washington, where there was more than enough land for everyone. The weather there was mild, there was plentiful rain, and everything grew fast and big. Indian tribes there were friendly and, he said, worked almost for free. Laura Etta drifted into disturbed sleep, half-hearing the high-pitched drone of Alex's waking dreams.

"Where we're going," he said, "every white woman has an Indian girl to wash and clean and cook. I've seen the Seminoles down in Florida, Laura Etta, and there's no equal to Indians for strong girls. Where we're going, a woman like you won't be wasted on dirty work. Where we're going, we can come into our own."

Alex was spinning dreams. Laura Etta had sworn nothing would pry her from the farm, the first place she'd ever had of her own. But she knew she had to give up her home, give up land no one could own anyway, or give up this husband she'd taken her chances on. The children had less choice than she. They would be dragged along like the milk cow tied behind the wagon. She thought of packing up again, of having to leave behind the few pretty things she had, and she wondered why God made women give up their dreams for the dreams of men. Then she did the only thing she knew to do: she told herself they'd make a better life in the Territory of Washington. She prayed it was true, and she told her husband: *Yes, let's sell out and move on.*

Leaves the Farm Behind

After days of selling-off, giving away, and packing up, Laura Etta sat on the board of a heavily loaded wagon. She remembered Lot's wife, nameless in the Scriptures, and she did not look back. "Gee-up." She clucked the team into motion, the wooden wheels turning. Laura Etta's lips shaped the names of lands and peoples of long ago, names she sounded in her mind: Ur of the Chal-dees, Har-an, the land of Canaan, the place of Si-chem, the plain of Mo-reh, Egypt, Beth-el, the fertile plains of Jordan, the cities of Sodom and Gomorrah. The turning wheels repeated the names of the places Lot had taken his wife and two daughters, and Laura Etta wondered where she, Alexander Speer's wife, and her two children were being taken.

Gideon Jones: Meets a Prairie Angel

On the Trail of True Love
(July 1865)

Gideon stood with Mary Thurston beside her family's wagon and watched water she had just poured over the burlap-wrapped roots of her little apple trees drip through the burlap balls and make four dark spots on the bare earth. The few leaves remaining on the saplings cast dark shadows the breeze made wink like eyes on the Osnaburg cover. A wagon rattled up alongside, and the dust settled down around two women—mother and daughter they appeared—huddled together on the seat. The elder's hair was piled high on her head, a dark oval like a hornet's nest topped with a bonnet too small. The younger's long black hair was uncovered and untethered, and it lifted and jounced in the breeze with the gait of the wagon.

The older woman held the reins, and she slowed to a stop right beside the Thurston wagon. Sunlight gamboled on the girl's hair—Gideon's breath caught in his throat. He longed for her silky looking hair to spill between his fingers. He longed to know its scent. In that moment Gideon knew the desire of the wild savage, and he thought the word, *scalp*—though he would have lain down then and there and died to protect every raven strand on her lovely head—he of a sudden felt the savage's lust for a human pelt. Darker than her hair, if that be possible, were her eyes. Her look was as straightforward as the stare of a St. Louis painted vixen, yet the sun only, no rouge or lip paint, had reddened her cheeks and lips. This young woman's beauty glowed from the inside out. A tiny constellation of freckles twinkled across her nose. Her eyes held Gideon's, and she spoke to him only.

"So you do exist." She smiled and tilted her head to one side for just half a breath. Her words danced as seeds on the tips of grass stalks bob in the breeze. "They told me a lone driver had joined the train. My name is Dorsey."

His Heart Is Captured

Time surely passed—a moment, a week, a month? A crow wheeling overhead cawed sharply, and Gideon realized his mouth was open as if he were the source of that bird's raucous remark. How long before the crow's cry he'd stood speechless Gideon could not guess. The moment was outside of time, and for all he knew the crow was some witch taking shape to cast a spell over him. "A lone driver" sounded somehow grand. Immediately, he sat taller on the wagon board. Was he all that "a lone driver" implied? If ever he was, surely it was during that timeless interval on the timeless grassy sea. That moment his life changed. He was charged and marked as sure as a lone prairie tree is electrified and blackened by brightness when lightning flashes through it. The crow cawed, wheeled above them again, and veered away in the wide sky.

"You're Gideon." When Dorsey smiled at him Gideon thought he had never been smiled at before, and he knew he was Gideon more certainly than he'd ever been from his mother's naming him. Had Dorsey said, "You're Bartholomew," then Bartholomew he would have been, or even Alice or Louise or Tabitha. Had she said, "You're Crow," he would have spread his wings and flown.

And as singular as it may sound, Gideon was never to alter this first day's impression of Dorsey. At once, he felt as if he had known her all his life and that she was brand-new and perfect. An angel just shaped in Heaven, she had flown down onto the prairie and touched the ground before him as a bird comes from the sky to light on a limb. He had considered the effects of living out where civilization ends and men and women newly forge their own laws. His immediate and lasting love of Dorsey seemed at the time as certain as a law of nature, and he knew the connection he felt there beneath the widest sky and brightest sun he had ever known would last as long as his lifetime. *Even beyond death,* he thought as he recalled Mr. Shakespeare's *Romeo and Juliet* that Colonel Powell-Hughes had said was not one of his favorites owing to its stiff blank verse and the unlikeliness of its conclusion. Gideon wondered were the colonel to know Dorsey, would he find Romeo's devotion and his final act so unlikely? Beneath blue sky and bright sun Dorsey dazzled Gideon, and dazzled he would remain. He managed to get his head to nod, a nod so slight he couldn't be sure it was his head moving or only in his head that he moved.

"Is it true you bear with you human bones and haul a crate of rifles? Word is they're bound for Indian fighters you made a contract with."

"I'm no gunsmith. Bones, yes," he croaked, looking back at the Chief, plainly visible in his wagonbed. "But I'm no gunsmith."

Dorsey's mother extended her hand to Mary Thurston, speaking to her as if Gideon were not standing there at all. "Ma'am, I'm Mrs. Speer—Laura Etta. This is my daughter, Dorsey Murphy. We lost Mr. Murphy in the war. My husband, Alexander Speer, is over to Mr. Benson's with my boy, Joe. I was told to take a place by the Thurston wagon." While she spoke, Mrs. Speer stared at the saplings tied to the Thurston wagon, but she didn't ask about the trees.

"Well, you're where you belong. I'm Mary. Hiram is off somewhere worrying somebody about something. Pleased to meet you both." Then Mary Thurston, kind lady, introduced Gideon. "And this young man, Gideon Jones, has come from back East."

Gideon followed Mary Thurston's lead and extended his hand up to Mrs. Speer, who had no choice but to take it in her own. Hers was the callused hand of a farmwife, hard but not rough. Here was a woman who likely rubbed lard on her skin every night at bedtime. Gideon gazed long at Mrs. Speer, trying to see where Dorsey came from, but the older woman's face contained nothing of her daughter's. The mother's eyes seemed faded by the sun, her mouth drawn down by the bouncing of the wagon. He longed for the feel of Dorsey's hand in his and would have risked reaching out in her direction had her mother not pressed his hand tighter and used his grip to support her descent from the wagon. Only then in the comely shape of a younger woman did he recognize any inheritance Dorsey had from her mother. He averted his gaze lest Mrs. Speer read his thoughts, but she had directed her attention elsewhere.

"Dorsey, swing our wagon roundabout and come up behind."

"Yes, Mama." Dorsey smiled, for Gideon alone he was sure, and took up the reins and without once yelling at her team drove them smartly off in a wide circle.

Though all he desired was to stare at Dorsey—to drink in her smile, her dark eyes and hair, her fair, freckled skin—Gideon turned away and made himself busy moving things about in his wagonbed. He wished he had a cover to throw over Chief Bones. His hand fell upon the final volume of the *Americana*, and he opened it as some open the Holy Scriptures, letting God's breath blow the pages and God's hand guide the reader's eye to fall on some verse of destiny. The riffling sheets of the encyclopedia stopped long enough on page sixty-two for his eyes to light on **WALTZ**, to read and have stamped indelibly on his heart: *It is a mistake to suppose that the waltz music is always gay.* So portentous did the message seem, Gideon wondered whether God had caused the encyclopedia to open there to reveal His inspired word.

When Gideon looked again at Dorsey's wagon there was just the shape of her left arm held out from the front side of the wagon waving to him as she turned the wagon back toward its place in the train. Outlined by the sun, her lovely arm moved slowly up and down against the air as if the wagon were winged, and he waited, transfixed, for the wagon wheels to lift and spin brightly through air. Though the wagon did not leave the ground, Dorsey had it so quickly in place it might have flown there. The team and wagon stirred the dry road, and the late afternoon sun shone on ordinary dust, though it glittered as he imagined gold dust did when sifted from a prospector's sieve. Then Dorsey alighted from the wagon, her blue skirt fanned out, and he made haste to reach her and say something more. *What would he say?* He walked as fast as he could without breaking into a run, and he urged his brain to be fast, too. He'd say, "I bear the bones of an Indian Chief, taking him back to Indian lands for burial. The long crate in my wagonbed holds not rifles, but lightning rods." He'd say, "Even a whole crate of lightning rods could not protect me from being struck by your flashing beauty."

But he had always lacked the courage for such pretty talk. Dorsey stood by her wagon waiting, Gideon hoped, for him. He needed to say something, and right away. When he stood close enough to reach out and touch her, she smiled, spreading freckles across her nose and cheeks. He felt as if he had just driven his wagon over a great abyss—his stomach rose up into his chest. He opened his mouth to speak, and he listened to see what he would say. Perhaps she sensed how he was struggling to make his tongue and lips form words, perhaps she was just following her natural inclination to be outspoken, but Dorsey filled the silence for him.

"I wish we had thought to bring along shade for our wagon seat."

"Mary Thurston has a dream of apple blossoms in Washington Territory."

"We had apple trees in Indiana."

"My dream would be of pies and apple butter."

"One pie takes two pounds of apples. And I use lots of sugar and butter and cinnamon."

Gideon smiled at Dorsey, whose face was all shadows and brightness—hair and eyes black, and teeth and clouds white, the shape of her gilded by the sun. Their talk of apples recalled his studies with Colonel Powell-Hughes, whose knowledge of Greek and Roman times was extensive.

"In ancient Greece," Gideon said, "when a man wanted to ask a woman to be his wife, he would toss her an apple. If she caught it, her answer was yes."

Dorsey smiled and glanced again at the four saplings. "I guess we women have been reaching for apples since the Garden of Eden."

Dorsey Murphy: Good-bye to Indiana

Escaping the Farm
(July 1865)

Never have my pages seemed so barren. This day I met a dark and
lovely angel. I can find no words to fully describe this farm girl or the
charms she casts. Her beauty is so quiet it goes almost undetected as a
white hare in snow or a spotted fawn in brown leaves. Her raven hair
rises on the breeze like a bird and merges at night with the heavens.
I recall lines in Colonel Powell-Hughes' *Shakespeare* from a sonnet
to the bard's dark lady, supple words I bend to Dorsey's shape:

> I never saw a goddess walk
> My mistress, when she walks, walks on the earth,
> But, by heaven, my love is as rare
> As any she belied with false compare.

I hope these borrowed words my memory surely falsifies are not
tainted by the rejection Shakespeare's dark lady returned.

—from Gideon Jones' Journal

For Dorsey, leaving the farm was an answer to her prayers. Leaving was wishes
made on stars and pully bones come true. She had daydreamed many a young
man who would ride up and win her heart and thunder away with her, but she had
never imagined the angel of her deliverance might be a red-headed one-armed
man who got off a railroad car and won her mama's heart, a man who would step
down off the same railroad car that brought her daddy's body back from the war.

When her mama insisted Dorsey lean down into the coffin and kiss her daddy good-bye, she had brushed her lips against one stiff eyelid as a moth or butterfly kisses a windowpane and flies away. She could not believe the man in the box was anyone she had ever known. Her papa seemed to have gone away long before he left for war. She remembered the gray line of the part in his dark hair when he bent to say grace before meals and how he acted shy, almost embarrassed, around her. When she kissed the face in the coffin, the full beard pricked her cheek, and she realized she could not remember ever kissing him before, could not remember his ever kissing her. She had thought him stern, though now she would name it narrow, plodding, unimaginative. She had occasionally imagined a different husband for her mama—though not as often as she imagined someone for herself—but she had never dreamed up anybody like Alexander Speer.

The first thing she saw, of course, was what Mr. Speer did not have—his left arm. Then she saw the red hair aimed off his head in whatever direction the wind was blowing, the hair and his sly, pale blue eyes, always half winking no matter what he was saying, winking about the weather or about plain old pancakes. She noted how skinny he was—not weak-looking skinny, but mean-looking skinny. Then his Southern way of talking. Slow and singsong sly, the way Dorsey had always imagined the voice of the fox in rhymes and tales. In her mind, Mr. Speer became Reynard the Fox. Her mama was one of the hens, and Dorsey wondered why this fox had slipped into this henhouse. Dorsey didn't quite believe all he was after was her mama.

Her brother Joe didn't seem to care. After their daddy went away to fight, Joe became the man on the farm, and Dorsey knew he wasn't going to become a boy again just because their mama brought another man home. In his mind, Joe was already gone away on his own. He was just waiting for the right time for his body to take off after the rest of him.

Once Mr. Speer declared they were leaving for the Territory of Washington, Dorsey was willing to risk any snare the fox might be laying. Born on the farm, Dorsey had never been farther away than Corydon, and Corydon was not much better than being on the farm. She didn't know what to expect on the journey. Mr. Speer said they would cross the Great Desert and go over the Rocky Mountains where it snowed year long. Dorsey had a vague notion of the wonders of San Francisco, just under the Territory of Washington on a map Mr. Speer drew at the kitchen table with his one good hand. He said hundreds of families had crossed the Great Desert and more would be going, now the war was over. He said people were on their way even as he spoke.

Dreams a Desert Nomad

Dorsey's heart beat high in her neck, and she pictured a sandy space wide as a river-bank where covered wagons rolled side by side, and girls with the faces of farm girls she knew walked along in pretty dresses, bonnets and parasols keeping the sun off their skin. They camped at an oasis where a desert spring pooled up, where green grass and wildflowers were shaded by leafy green oasis trees bearing desert fruits. At the oasis, Dorsey met a man who looked like the drawing in a book her teacher, Mr. Dillard, had brought to school. Dark-eyed and mysterious, the man wore a hat like a head bandage Mr. Dillard had told them was called a turban. Men who wore these hats rode camels and were known as desert nomads. In Dorsey's dreams this desert nomad pulled her up behind him on his camel and rode her away on a sea of sand to a city of billowing tents that glowed like the sails of lantern-lit ships. She lay on pillows in her nomad's tent, and he fed her grapes like the ancient Greeks had fed their queen. Dorsey became friends with a dark-skinned girl. They bathed in a desert spring and danced under the stars with their nomads.

Even if she wasn't going to the other side of the world, at least she was leaving Indiana. In Washington Territory they'd make a nice farm on a winding river and sell apples from trees growing on green hillsides. Apple picking would be so much nicer than helping plow or cleaning up the stable, though she guessed they would have a stable in the Territory of Washington, too.

The Duerfeldts Disappear

Dorsey had a girlfriend, Binga Duerfeldt, just one farm away. Binga was a heavy, big-boned girl, maybe a little simpleminded, but she had a ready smile and sang like an angel in the Baptist church. Binga and her family had made their way west to Indiana after coming to America from Hanover in Germany. Binga's mother, Anna, spoke only German, but her father, Ernst, gave English lessons every evening to Binga and her sisters, Adelaide and Louise. He taught them what he called Roman letters, what he said was writing American. Binga taught Dorsey *Guten Morgen* and *Guten Abend*.

Binga was the only girl close to Dorsey's age who lived close enough for Dorsey to ride to see alone. Dorsey liked Binga, and didn't like her. The not-liking part sometimes made Dorsey feel guilty, but not so guilty she wasn't determined not to end up like Binga, always so satisfied with her life. Dorsey was a little jealous Binga had already crossed the ocean and lived in two countries, but Dorsey was going to do more exciting things than Binga, and they both knew it.

As soon as Mr. Speer and Mama told Dorsey and Joe they were leaving the farm, Dorsey wanted to say good-bye to Binga. Truth be told, Dorsey wanted to brag she was leaving Binga and her lesson-studying church-choir kind of life behind. So, early one Sunday morning Dorsey slipped off on her brother Joe's bay mare, so she could get to church and find Binga before services started. But Binga was not at church, nor were any of the Duerfeldts. Dorsey waited until the first hymn, and then she quietly left and rode to the Duerfeldt place. On a gray and windy morning cool as March but with spring a secret the air kept, Dorsey rode down the familiar dirt road past empty fields she didn't feel the least bit sad to leave. But she might *act* a little sad for Binga's sake. Above the Duerfeldts' front porch something white jerked like a flag in the wind. When Dorsey got within shouting distance, the white flag became Binga's bedroom curtain flapping through an upstairs window.

No one answered Dorsey's calls. No dogs barked. There were no chickens in the yard, no mules, no cow in the pen. Her steps were loud on the porch. She knew no one was home, but still she knocked and waited. Finally, she tried the door and it squeaked open as always, but it felt lighter and pulled easier than she remembered. Inside the house was colder than outside. The furniture was there, but Mrs. Duerfeldt's knickknacks were gone. A layer of dust deep enough for Dorsey to draw in with her finger covered the top of the parlor table. A square lighter than the rest of the wall showed where the gilt-framed painting of the lady who stared at a bowl of fruit used to hang. The blue china bird Mrs. Duerfeldt had brought from Germany had flown from the mantel. A castiron kettle sat on its three little legs, its wire handle curved around its belly the way Mrs. Duerfeldt always held her arms clasped over her fat middle. The long hooked runner Mrs. Duerfeldt prized had been taken up from the stairs, rows of tack holes outlining ghostly pale wood. The stairs creaked and dust cricked under Dorsey's Sunday shoes.

Upstairs, all the beds were stripped of linens and the big tick was gone from the double bed in Binga's room. Gone, too, was Binga's painting of a knight in a silver helmet kneeling beside his white horse. Dorsey struggled with the window and got it closed with a bang. The sucking wind stopped. The white curtains hung lifeless. On a small plank table by Binga's bed was a book: *Josh Billings, His Sayings,* by Henry Wheeler Shaw. Binga had printed her name across the inside cover, BinGA kARolinA duErfELdt. Picturing Binga's eyes squinted up tight printing the uneven line of letters, Dorsey felt a pang of emotion she did not understand—not sadness exactly, and not pity, but something closer to anger. She read one of Josh Billings' aphorisms: "The muel iz haf hoss and haf Jackass, and then kums tu a full stop, natur diskovering her mistake."

Dorsey took *Josh Billings, His Sayings* and carried it home with her. She opened the book often, and read the page where Binga had printed her name. Dorsey kept finding herself at her window staring in the direction of the Duerfeldt farm. Her hands on the window glass were cold and stiff as the bristly seeds on the beautybush by the porch. In winter the big bush was full of the brown seeds, but in spring it would be covered in pink flowers. Binga's mother said the beautybush was like a woman, willing to be ugly most of the time just so it could be beautiful in the spring. Binga's mother said a girl had to wait for beauty. She was full of old sayings and sad thoughts.

What did Dorsey care about a chubby German girl who didn't even tell her good-bye? Dorsey was determined never to be like sweet, simple Binga. Yet Binga's simple name crawling crookedly down the page made Dorsey's throat knot up and her breathing get tight in her chest.

Mr. Speer learned Ernst Duerfeldt had sold his place off sudden, back in February. Fritz Mueller got twenty-four of Ernst's fine Plymouth Rock chickens for next to nothing. Mueller figured the Duerfeldts had left in late March or early April.

"Just like Ernst to leave in the spring thaw. He looks for trouble if it don't find him first. He must have figured March was the best time to get his wagon stuck a hundred times before Evansville," Fritz said.

Knute Nelson shook his head. "Damn Saxony fool. Took a few hens and a rooster, the milk cow, Mrs. Duerfeldt's sewing machine, a couple pieces of furniture flat in the wagon bottom."

Knute said the Duerfeldts had gone west, though Fritz Mueller thought Ohio, where Anna Duerfeldt had a sister. Gone without a word to anybody. Ernst had always been hard to figure.

"Ask Ernst to plow a curve, you can count on him to plow straight," Mueller said.

Knute Nelson shook his head again. "The man would argue with a fence post."

On the Wagon Seat

Dorsey didn't have much time to fret over Binga's disappearance. Laura Etta drove Dorsey and Joe as if they were a matched pair of mules she had wagered on in a race. In just two days, their mother had the household packed up. It was well before dawn the May morning they left Joseph Murphy's farm that Mr. Speer had sold and started for the Pacific slopes.

As their wagon bumped along spring unfolded into summer. The whole earth was awake, and even the grass, as slow as grass is, was astir. When Dorsey and her mama were alone on the wagon box, Joe and Mr. Speer jiggling along on horseback, Laura Etta complained the journey was so much sameness the days creaked continuously into one long day. "I'm sick to death of fields and trees and rivers and ponds and sometimes flat places and sometimes hilly places and sometimes clusters of buildings, but always the same buildings, the same houses and barns and sheds and stores," Laura Etta said.

It was true their wagon bumped and lurched through the still landscape as slow as some Sunday afternoon in late summer back in Corydon, but none of it bored Dorsey. Each time they passed a sign with a town's name on it, some name she had never heard, she realized how new the country was to her, how new her own life was, and she decided she was just now beginning her life. She studied the familiar things they passed, seeing everything for the first time. Trees were no longer just green, they had separate leaves of different colors and different shapes, and they had limbs that curved up or that curved down or that had been broken off by wind or exploded off by lightning. She was seeing things she had seen before but had never recognized. She recognized things she had never seen.

Without church to mark Sundays, Dorsey had to ask Mr. Speer what day it was. He had copied the calendar on the wall of the Corydon bank onto the inside cover of Dorsey's mama's Bible—all the days and months for the rest of the year, even past Christmas to next year—little squares he'd drawn and put the numbers inside. Then, with so much newness to look at, Dorsey forgot to ask the days, and they all became one long time containing smaller times, like an envelope that holds a long message made of sentences made of words made of letters, every letter at least a moment. They crossed southern Indiana, went through Evansville, ferried across the Wabash River and took nearly forever getting to St. Louis, busy and grand beyond Dorsey's dreams. St. Louis put the days of the week back in Dorsey's head for a while.

They arrived on a Monday, the streets full of people and the music of commerce. Dorsey begged her mother to ask Mr. Speer to take a job in St. Louis so they could live on a paved street with gaslights in a two-story house with a piano. In St. Louis she would meet a rich tradesman in a blue frock coat who would marry her and take her across the ocean to London, England, and Paris, France, where they would eat strange food and drink wine and do whatever they liked. Her mother snapped at her.

"I don't want to hear such talk. Don't need to hear it."

"What talk, Mama?"

"You just never mind, Dorsey. Shut pan on the daydreams. You'd best just grow up."

Dorsey was sad to leave St. Louis with hardly any time to experience the glories it offered, but she knew there were new glories ahead, and she kept her eyes open, ready to receive wonders she knew were coming her way. Nighttime, when all the space around them stilled and quieted and the creak and squeal of their wagon echoed in her ears, she stared up at the immense sky and watched stars fall. She was like one of those quiet, bright stars, separate now, casting her own light, no longer part of the old, dark sky.

Missouri was even wider than Illinois, and hotter. Dorsey wanted to get to the Great Desert to camp in an oasis. She perked up good when they got to Independence—June 29, a Wednesday, just light enough left for her and Mama to cook up a party kind of supper using all the last special treats left from a stopover in Jefferson City.

Independence was lively though more homespun than St. Louis. Next came Kansastown, more spread out than Independence. Just north of Kansastown, they stopped at Westport Landing, where riverboats docked and wagon trains were made up. This was where Mr. Speer said they would join a wagon train of other families going to Oregon and on to the Territory of Washington.

Dorsey gazed off at the broad Missouri River where the smaller Kansas River joined it, and she felt sure this must be what the ocean looked like. She had never seen so much water. Even more amazing was the expanse of land and sky that spread out beyond the rivers, a world of space that went on as far as she could see, broken here and there by small clusters of distant trees. The river shore was crowded with paddle-wheel boats and covered wagons. Smoke rose from campfires, and birds careened and dove over the water. But what drew Dorsey, seemed to pull on her flesh as surely as if myriad fingers gripped her arms and legs and tugged, was the rolling and endless land that easily contained two rivers, several large riverboats, and countless wagons and teams.

At Westport Landing there were settler families and soldiers in uniform and sun-darkened men—Mexicans and mountain men and muleteers and French trappers and Indian traders—men who wore buckskins, men with hair long down their backs and who looked like Dorsey had expected Indians to look. When these men smiled at her their teeth flashed white, and she wondered what kissing their lips would feel like. There were real Indians, too. Indian men wore nothing but animal hides draped from their belts, muscles clenched in their naked bottoms that were as black as the skin of a Negro, so why were they called redskins? Negroes, of course, might be black as coal or not so dark as her brother Joe after a summer in the sun. The black Indians were short and wore no feather headdresses. How could she have lived so long at Corydon and not have known there were so many different people living in the same world all so alive in such different bodies? One Indian whose skin was the color of dried blood wore a deerskin blouse and deerskin leggings somehow made almost white and decorated all over with shiny porcupine needles. Just looking at these people inside their different-sized and -shaped bodies, under their hide or fur or wool or cotton clothes, made Dorsey feel, what?—not happiness exactly but more than just ordinary comfortable—what she felt was a deep, keen *satisfaction*.

Back in Corydon, people talked about Indians as if they were all one tribe, as all-alike as the girls were all-alike in the Sowers and Reapers Sunday School Class—but now Dorsey knew Indians weren't all alike. This reddish one with porcupine needles sticking off him, bright in the morning sun's rays, was different from the short, black Indians. When Dorsey asked this red Indian, in English, *What tribe are you?* Laura Etta's face turned red, too, and she demanded to know why her daughter would speak to a strange man—a heathen savage. The Indian showed no sign he had heard Dorsey or her mama's outburst.

"He's a Dakota," Joe said. "The wagon bosses call him Heavy Arse or Horse Arse because he's always sitting down. He's got a business selling settlers horses everybody knows have been stole from other settlers by other Indians."

Dorsey's mother set her jaw and stared ahead. Joe grinned, and Dorsey thought he partway admired Heavy Arse for making such easy money. She thought maybe she did, too.

Unmarriageable Men

Only one wagon master was putting together a train, and Mr. Speer signed on. The train was smaller than Dorsey had expected—only eight wagons (not counting two supply wagons for the wagon master, Major Joshua Benson, and his men), eight families so anxious to move west they were willing to go in spite of stories about Indians on the rampage with most of the soldiers from the Western forts not yet back from the war in the East. The merchants of Westport Landing, glad to see the settlers back, discounted supplies.

"Victuals are cheaper now than they will be later," Mr. Speer said.

Dorsey wished she had been more specific when she'd prayed and dreamed and wished on stars and pully bones. She wished she had wished the wagon train have at least one other girl her age. She had halfway thought they might catch up with the Duerfeldts. If Binga were here, Dorsey would whisper how the mountain men, trappers, and muleteers in their buckskins and with their long, greasy hair looked just the way Dorsey had always pictured seafaring pirates. And she wished she had wished the wagon train would have some unmarried young men. Besides Joe—who, of course, didn't count—there were three or four boys far too young and one, Amos Carter, just the right age, who was already married, with his own wagon and his plain-looking wife giving suck to a baby girl. Besides, Amos Carter seemed just as solid and dull as Dorsey's dead papa. She was not going to settle for a life of cooking and cleaning and tending children. She wanted an adventure with a desert nomad.

Nearly every one of the major's men had cast his eyes over Dorsey, especially a bearded one named Bill Sloan, and the major's top scout, a Mexican named Rafael Flores, but the major's men were dirty-looking and old—maybe as old as thirty—and they were sweaty and smelly. When these men tried to talk to her their tongues twisted up inside their mouths, but Rafael Flores said things to her that gave her a little thrill, things she hoped her mama didn't hear.

Flores was a big man who wore his hair braided down his back like a girl or an Indian. He stared at Dorsey without blinking. He was dark and mysterious, his hair and eyes were black, and his skin was the color of Joe's bay mare. Dorsey didn't know the exact meanings of the Mexican words he said, but he said them in such a way that she understood their intention.

"*Yo siento pelota por* Dorr-sey." Flores stretched her name out, said it just under his breath until it no longer sounded like a word she'd always been called by, but instead became a word shameful and delicious to hear. He rode up to her wagon and pointed at the sun, "*Hace sol,*" he said, and when he was right beside the wagon he opened his mouth and curled his tongue at her, then smacked his lips together. "*Tengo sed,*" he said. And when she handed him a dipper of water, he managed to cover her hand with his and held her hand, not the dipper, the whole time the water bobbed down his throat. His palms were hard-callused, and under the ends of his broad fingernails were black rinds of dirt. His eyes turned up at the corners as if they were smiling, and he moved so light and easy on his feet Dorsey wondered how it might be to dance with Mr. Flores.

Then, near to the day they were set to leave, an intriguing young man joined the train, a driver all by himself. Mr. Speer told Dorsey the newcomer, who'd pulled into Westport Landing hauling a wooden crate in his wagonbed, was a drummer, but he didn't seem much like the drummers Dorsey had seen back in Corydon. For one thing, drummers were old men like Mr. Speer, but the new-comer was just the perfect age whatever number of years old he was. She guessed him a few years older than she. For another thing, drummers carried suitcases full of stuff they were always trying to sell to anybody who'd listen. For a drummer, this fellow was mighty quiet. Rumor was he carried rifles in the wooden crate he hauled in his open farmer's wagon, but the first words he spoke to Dorsey, responding to the question she put to him, were "I'm no gunsmith."

Later, after Dorsey and this young man had shared the firelight and starlight of many prairie evenings, usually under her mama's watchful eye, Dorsey laughed and told him how, the first time she saw him, she was fascinated by the human skeleton that lay beside the crate in back of his wagon. What a strange companion she thought the bones made. Some on the train thought he was a doctor or a student of physiology. Gideon shook his head and said since meeting her he was a student of female charm. Dorsey said he was the charmer and that she did not believe one word of his pretty talk. But secretly, she thought him a wizard from a storybook, except wizards were too old to compare.

Alone with her chores Dorsey whispered his name, *Gideon*, sent to her right out of the Scriptures. He wasn't as tall as her brother, Joe, but he seemed to Dorsey somehow superior—smarter at least. He was long-armed and long-legged but not gangly like Joe. Gideon reminded Dorsey most of a greenbroke horse the way he moved quick-like and looked easy to spook, and the way he was always watching everything. When he did speak, "I'm no gunsmith," his voice quavered a little like cottonwood leaves in a breeze but nonetheless was steady and calming. She listened to all he said yet paid scant mind to his words or hers. She was too intent on studying him: *His dark hair is cropped short in front, but grows down the back of his neck long enough to curl up from under his ears. His face is a boy's face, open and unblemished, but the deepset eyes when he takes off the reading glasses are older and rest in a nest of lines from all the thinking he must do. His lips are thin, but his mouth is not unkind-looking. When he talks, his lips seem not to move at all, but when he smiles his lips draw back like window curtains to reveal straight, small teeth as bright as day. His hands are large for the rest of him, and his nails are not bitten back nor caked beneath with black.* She wondered why Gideon traveled alone in an open wagon. She marveled how most times when she looked back behind their wagon he was nodding along with the reins looped over his foot, the sun flashing off spectacles he wore to read and write, a thick book open in his lap—either the one he read or the one he was filling up with words. She longed to be one of Gideon's books, held so reverently, the object of all his attention.

Gideon Jones: The Territory Ahead

Their Train Rolls
(July 1865)

Early the fifth of July, after an Independence Day of pies and cakes, speechifying and patriotism, and lots of *good luck*s for one another, Gideon's train finally headed out, already needing to make up time. All the settlers had worked hard getting resupplied, making their outfits ready to cross the Great Desert and the Rocky Mountains. Most trains left no later than May. They had to cross the Rockies before the first snows. Everyone knew about the Donner Party stranded by mountain blizzards until spring and forced into cannibalism.

Major Joshua Benson was about the only man tough enough or fool enough (depends who was talking) to risk both Indians and blizzards. But he claimed enough cutoffs to shave a month off the journey. He also said his men were seasoned, so none of the usual slowdowns—bad fords, insufficient supplies, wagons in disrepair, quarrels among the immigrants, even Indian attack—would take place on his train. Gideon had understood that their armed guard of seasoned Indian fighters was to number thirty or more, but strung out along the road he counted no more than eight men who were not settlers. He looked back over his shoulder at the junction of the two rivers, gleaming like knifeblades in the sun, and he looked ahead at the dusty wagon road and the wide, cloudless sky. He reached beneath his wagon seat for his canteen and took a long swig of warm water. Almost as soon as he had corked the container, he felt thirsty again.

His wagon carried little save Chief Bones, the crate of lightning arresters, the Hawken rifle, and a few necessaries. He offered space to the Thurstons, and Hiram toted a steamer trunk to Gideon's wagon, leaving space for Mary and baby James to rest beneath the Thurston wagon cover. There were eight wagons of settlers and two supply wagons, most too heavily loaded to bear the weight of passengers, so several men, women, and children were walking to the Territory of Washington. Alexander Speer was not among the footsore.

"I'm unaccustomed to walking," he said.

The first day out, Dorsey held the reins and drove the Speer team while her mother, Laura Etta, rode under the wagon cover with a bellyache. Mr. Speer rode a small bay, bareback. Gideon was not sure why, but he was glad Dorsey didn't carry the blood of the one-armed, flame-haired Alexander Speer. On the short-legged bay, Speer's feet almost touched ground. He trotted from wagon to wagon like a little red terrier, holding his chin up stiff as if it were his pride. He kept his cut-off arm in a deerhide case slung over his shoulder or tied down to his saddle like a rifle. He wheeled the bay around to talk to Hiram Thurston a while, then trotted ahead, hailing young Amos Carter, offering unsolicited advice about one of Carter's mules Speer declared was favoring a foreleg.

Gideon was still aglow from his first look at Dorsey. As if he were one of the lightning rods he hauled, held high into Heaven's fiercest thunderstorm, a mighty bolt of Dorsey had struck him, entering his eyes, electrifying his heart, and piercing him to the bottoms of both his feet. From now on, he expected to live with this charge keeping him, body and soul, energized.

Dorsey's hair, dark as the tarred bottom of the Speer wagon, reflected the sun as bright as the Missouri River they were following. Her creamy skin dappled with freckles called to Gideon's mind holiday mugs of eggnog Win Shu had sprinkled with grated nutmeg in Colonel Luellen Powell-Hughes' brick house. Dorsey hummed and sang to the mules, and Gideon sat as still as possible, not wanting the creak of his board seat nor the slap of his reins to get between his ears and her singing. Mile after mile he followed her melody, a melody he would never stop hearing.

First Camp

They made first evening camp near a creek not far from where it entered the big river. Dorsey headed for the creek, and Gideon wanted to follow her into the tall grass, but he tended his oxen, whispered to them how she walked easy and light as a doe. Before the sun was down, she was back. Her hair, wet, was even darker, like the bark of a tree after rain. She held her head sideways and with both her hands twisted her hair like a heavy, black rope, splattering the earth with creek water. She saw him watching and laughed in the most natural way, her smile spreading across her cheeks. She was like a speckled puppy spoiling for play.

He made cold supper, hoping Mrs. Speer would invite him to sup with them, but she was bent over with stomach cramps and talking through her teeth telling Dorsey what to do to fix the meal. Busy with fire and skillets, Dorsey seemed to pay him no mind. Feeling melancholy, he walked alone a far distance out into knee-high grass. Though he'd never seen an ocean, he knew how it felt to wade far from shore and to feel the pull of strong hidden currents.

Summer nights on the plains were nights of glory. Glowworms flew over the fields like baby stars running and jumping, learning to fly up into the wide sky already filled with myriad family reunions of stars. Gideon stretched both arms and turned circles, and the stars spun dizzyingly far above. He stopped and let earth sway beneath him, and he wondered if Colonel Luellen Powell-Hughes might be standing right now under another night sky feeling beneath him the sway of another wide sea. He pulled out the watch the colonel had given him. The watch long ago lost its wits. It ran and stopped and started up again according to some unearthly schedule. The hands of the old watch were as nomadic as wagon travelers, wandering a ways, stopping, starting up again.

Using his thumbnail (something else the colonel taught him) Gideon struck a match. For the moment, the watch hands were at rest, horizontal: a quarter to three. He stood in the brief glow of the match and thought that somewhere on this capacious earth—perhaps, even, wherever the colonel was—the *true* time was a quarter to three. The match went out, and Gideon gave the watch a shake. Like rolling wagon wheels, the tiny gears inside spun and ticked time against his ear. In the dark, the true time mattered less than the ticking and the feel, solid and cool, of time in his hand. In the dark, he couldn't see the circled wagons whence he'd walked, but he knew they were there, away off before him, where he saw resting and dying stars, the campfires of his fellow travelers, adventurers all.

A Lifelong Kiss

Two more nights passed before he was able to spend time with Dorsey out of sight of Mrs. Speer. They had made an early camp in anticipation of rain from thunderheads that had built up all afternoon. Ere they had the wagon covers lashed down and everyone sweating beneath hooded India rubber rain slickers, the clouds sailed away into the darker eastern skies.

"We all look like a procession of ghosts in these rain shrouds," Dorsey said to Gideon as she walked by his wagon.

He jumped down and matched her stride, the deep grass whispering against their rubber rain skirts. She pulled down her hood and shook loose her long hair. Then she unfastened her slicker and held it like a sail above their heads where it filled with the afternoon breeze and seemed to carry them both out into the wide and empty space surrounding the circled wagon train. Behind a swell of land they rolled up their ponchos and sat to watch the sun sink orange and burning into the grass beyond. Made bold by the faint smell in the air of the rain that had skipped over them, Gideon took Dorsey's hand and was rewarded by her hand squeezing his, and he felt her pulse beating in tune with his own. He secretly pledged then and there to remain at her side wherever the winds of the prairie or the winds of fate should take her.

They did not speak about the orange and golden sky, nor how it made the grass tips glow as if the whole world were aflame. Instead of pretty talk about all the shining light that lay before them, they spoke of their early lives and the dark times they had left behind. She described her life before the war, farm chores she didn't mind and a father who was quiet but kindly before he went away to war and drifted away from her life forever like the rain clouds that had blown over the wagons that afternoon.

"The railway cars brought him home in a box like goods ordered from the mercantile store. Packed in the coffin was a stranger in a big coat that disguised anything I could recollect about him, and escorting him came a red-headed stranger with one arm and a singsong voice that still makes me think of preachers and patent medicine drummers. I don't understand what mama finds beneath his red hair to like."

Gideon dared not speak his thoughts that a widow with two near-grown children soon to leave home on their own might choose most any available man against the lonely life that waited for her on the untended farmland she had inherited.

He learned that like himself Dorsey had retreated into the worlds of books, though they had had different libraries to roam. He quietly told her of his days in the asylum, where the only girls he had known were ill of body or mind and where the only girls' hands he had held were the cold, lifeless hands of corpses. He had no memories of his blood father, only of Colonel Powell-Hughes and of Win Shu, both of whom had helped birth his mind. She had heard Chinamen eat rats and asked if it was so.

"Not Win Shu. He favored roasted duck and cooked it with brown sugar."

"Why, even I have eaten duck and goose."

"He drank green tea with whisky." That did not seem strange enough to satisfy her.

"I know the Indians won't disappoint. They're out there right now, aren't they?"

The sun was fully down. The western sky burned red and turned the grass purple as with blood. "Not tonight. Tonight there's only you and me."

"You can't see Indians until it's too late." She drew his face to hers, and their lips clung together for a moment that would last Gideon's lifetime.

Toting Water

The end of their first week out of Westport Landing one of the settlers, Angus McDonald, disregarded Major Benson's advice to unload from his wagon a maple pie safe and leave it on the trail. After McDonald conferred with his weeping wife, he said they'd not leave off the furniture. Less than an hour later, McDonald rolled over a dished-out place and broke his axle. The train lost half a day getting the wagon unloaded, the axle repaired, the wagon reloaded. Mrs. McDonald removed her linens from the pie safe and left it standing sentinel beside the trail.

Dorsey said it seemed they might wander at least as long as the Israelites.

The major stared from under the dark ledge of his brows. "If you expect to get there at all, little gal, I better be obeyed better than Moses was."

That evening, Gideon walked alone with Dorsey to the waterhole close to where the major had bade them circle up the wagons for overnight. She shook her head and without blinking told Gideon she could not abide the major. She was certain he was due to meet some man his equal in meanness who would end his life. Gideon made a joke about the major not deserving so harsh a sentence, but Dorsey's mouth was set, and he could not provoke her to smile until they had filled the water keg and he wobbled beneath its weight. She thought he was pretending weakness, and she laughed and kissed his nose. The damp spot where her lips had brushed was like a diamond on his skin. His knees had buckled, but her kiss strengthened his will to overflowing. His legs summoned sufficient power to bear his burden easily. Beneath the weight of the keg, and to prolong their privacy, he moved like a tortoise back toward the wagons.

"Don't you want to set down the water for a rest?"

"It's not heavy." He hoped his voice was not strained.

"If you go much farther without a rest, we will be within my mama's sight."

He lay the heavy cask on its side. Dorsey lifted her skirt and straddled the keg as if it were a little horse. He faced her on the same mount, and she drew his lips to hers. Against his fingers, the sleeves of her cotton dress still held the sun's warmth. Their chests pressed together. The keg sloshed beneath them, and their bodies surged like river currents swirling against one another. Gideon smelled starch and tasted in Dorsey's breath the clean smells of green grass and of camphor, but while he knew the bitter taste of camphor from medicines at the Baltimore asylum, the lips that anointed his were sweet as honey and spicy like mint. With her knees locked, Dorsey shifted back and forth and made the water keg rock and sway, and her lips and tongue swam against his. The prairie rolled for him then, and not just because they rode a wooden bronc full of swaying water. Riding thus in full darkness he could not judge how long they remained clamped together, but long before he'd had a sufficient draught to slake his thirst for Dorsey, her brother Joe whistled from close by, sent out to call her back to the world of campfires, tin plates, and stern looks.

A Dispute with the Major

The wagons weren't long out of Fort Leavenworth before Alexander Speer locked horns with Major Benson. Gideon thought Alex, as his wife called him, fancied himself a smooth talker. Nooning, they were stopped in some trees around a muddy pool. While Mrs. Speer looked to watering their team, Mr. Speer wandered off amongst the trees. He hollered for Major Benson. He'd found an arrow carved across a dead tree and crudely engraved beneath the arrow the message: CUT OF. Bark was peeled away where the second F should have been. The arrow angled away from the river, visible some miles distant as a dark curve of trees.

"Here's a shortcut, Major. The map of experience left by those who have preceded us."

"Speer, ever mother's child who has crossed the prairie has tried to leave his mark. I can't go off ever time we see a sign clove in a tree trunk or some rocks stacked up somewheres. We follow the Missouri up a good ways yet before the trail turns."

"That's miles out of the way. This cutoff likely veers directly to the Platte."

"My way may not be the shortest way, Speer, but the trail is the safest way."

"We departed Westport Landing past a safe leaving date because you offered cutoffs to save weeks."

"My cutoffs are mine. I know they're true. This here is going after a ghost, like as not."

Six or eight of the men stood gathered in the trees. The major looked at every face. With months of travel facing them and mountain snows to beat, they were all interested in shortcuts.

"Major, we hired on this train and pay your wages. You owe us protection," Speer said.

Hiram Thurston said, "We've got land to claim on the Pacific slopes, houses to build—I got apple trees to plant and tend. If we wanted safe we could stay home."

The major's eyes flashed darkness at Hiram, darker still at Speer, then stared about the circle of men lingering a moment on each face, taking some kind of measurement. When he stared at Speer it appeared the man's stump where his arm was missing flexed as a muscle. Major Benson's coal-bit eyes found Gideon's, and Benson's eyes pulsed, or so it seemed, held on longer than they had held others. Gideon half-expected the major to ask, *What about you, boy?* He remembered his Ovid: *Medio tutissimus ibis*, "You will go most safely in the middle." But the major did not ask his opinion.

"Don't be fools. This is just an Indian trick. Lead us into ambush." The major turned and walked back to the wagons.

"I reckon the major knows whereof he speaks," McDonald said. "He was right about my missus' pie safe. I vow we best take the guidance we're paying the man for."

All the men, except Speer and Hiram Thurston, followed right on Major Benson's heels. Hiram stared a moment at the arrow, then he and Speer walked together to their wagons. They shook their heads and talked in low tones. In Hiram, Speer had someone he could influence. Gideon felt sure there were more disputes to come between Mr. Alexander Speer and Major Benson.

Gideon stayed a while and studied the carved arrow, the uneven letters: CUT OF. He speculated where he would end up if he followed the direction that might decipher the trunk-carved hieroglyph, but he knew the only direction he was going to follow was the way Dorsey took.

Conversation with Mr. Speer

That afternoon they were in the hard ruts of a well-traveled route still following the Missouri. Gideon's oxen need little driving—they ambled steadily along—and he was reading his volume of the *Encyclopaedia Americana* as Chief Bones and he bounced along. He skimmed the **V**'s: **VOGLER**—*George Joseph (distinguished* *practical and theoretical musician, born at Wurzburg, in 1749),* and became interested in the tones of **VOICE** by which men and animals express their feelings and rational men convey ideas and emotions. This was a subject of inquiry well fitted to awaken the curiosity of the naturalist, physiologist, and philosopher. Gideon studied Mr. Arnott's table of articulations, in which the perpendicular line on the left is to be considered the opening of the mouth, and the line on the right is the back of the mouth, so the four divisions indicate the places where the various letters are pronounced. At the top of page fourteen Gideon read: *The effect of the sexual functions on the voice is well known; but the mode in which this effect takes place is not explained. This influence is observable even in birds, which delight us with their amorous melodies at the season of pairing; in woman, whose voice acquires its metallic tone and its fulness at the age of puberty; and particularly in man, who does not possess, till that period, the "voices" peculiar to him.* At which point he was interrupted by a melodious, almost feminine voice, asking, "What's drawing you so deep in I might think you asleep and dreaming with your eyes open?"

He looked up at Mr. Speer jiggling along beside him on the bay. Gideon had to look over the tops of his reading glasses to focus Mr. Speer, otherwise the man and the horse became a blur of blue on brown. Speer seemed to have forgotten all about his earlier dispute with the major. Certain Dorsey's stepfather would think him impertinent if in the echo of the one-armed man's peculiar singsong voice he read from the entry before him, Gideon covertly slipped a finger ahead a few pages and read from where his eyes lighted, the entry (he glanced up the page as he read out loud) on **WILL**: — *rational will, is the volition operated on by external influences, directing it to the attainment of supposed good, or the avoidance of supposed evil. This will even brutes have, as they are capable of seeking the agreeable and shunning the disagreeable; but of will in a higher sense, as influenced by the moral principle to seek what is good in itself, without reference to present pleasure or pain, brutes are not capable.*

"The moral principle," Mr. Speer said, "a gift of God."

"Denied brutes?"

"I've surveyed the human landscape. I was in the army with a Cherokee sharpshooter who taught me about the Indian nation. A savage is no brute among his kin. Where no one has morals they're not practically missed." He closed his eyes and in his curiously singsong voice, said, "God's gift to the Indian is ignorance of the moral so the Indian can be as uncommon savage as he needs to be." Mr. Speer's hand dropped to the carrying case that held his severed left arm. He moved his palm down and up the canvas. "And mind," he said, "civilized man sometimes forgets the moral law when he wanders far from the influence of civi-lization." Gideon wondered if Mr. Speer's comment about forgetting the moral law was meant for *him*, a warning where Dorsey was concerned. Gideon started to point out that Indians were not so much uncivilized as they were differently civilized, but he thought better of such a remark.

"What do you think of the shortcut—my argument with the major?" Speer asked.

Ere he carefully considered it, the proverb escaped Gideon's lips: "*Medio tutissimus ibis.*"

Mr. Speer's eyes closed again.

"You go the safest in the middle."

Speer nodded, as if to say "I know," then he gave a snort of a laugh and, eyes still shut, he scooted away on the merry bay mare, leaning left as if pulled by the weight of his missing arm, both man and horse turned-loose racy, crazy-acting as anyone Gideon remembered from the Baltimore asylum. Gideon had seen the man slide his severed and stiffened arm from the hide case he carried it in and pet and stroke the blackened limb as if it was a living part of him that still ached or itched. The man seemed to have itches, or at least the urge to scratch, all over him.

Gideon wondered if Mr. Speer did know his Ovid. Speer seemed to know, certainly thought he knew, what to expect from the prairie. More than once, he argued with Major Benson about when and where to overnight or how best to repair a broken axle or splice a whiplash. Mr. Speer was always ready to argue, but if there was work needed doing he was slow to act. He had his wife's boy, Joe, who was three or four years younger than Gideon, do all the labor. By his own admission, this was Speer's first trip west. Benson had twenty years of mountain service, buffalo hunting, and scouting for the army. He laid claim to riding under Kit Carson and, later, under Colonel Pfeiffer in the New Mexico territorials. The major called this country kin. Told the settlers which grasses to let the teams eat and where to find water when a pond was dried up or poisonous. Said he'd been in the hogans of the Navaho, the tipis of the Arapaho, and the grass house villages of the Wichita. Professed to know the sign talk of all the Indian tribes. But Speer's high, loud confidence showed how unimpressed he was with Major Benson's knowledge and experience. Speer's ways concerned Gideon only so much as the man's behavior affected Dorsey, whose life Gideon was already imagining as for-ever twined with his.

Dorsey Murphy: Beyond the Treeline

The Madness and the Joy of Space
(July 1865)

Our train made early camp late one afternoon, and I walked Dorsey
away from the wagons to observe the setting sun. It was then, with her,
I first heard the prairie songs of crickets harmonizing with whistling quail, joined
as dark fell by the lovely, lonely call of whippoorwills. The sun-streaked sky
cast Dorsey's fair skin crimson, and round about her loveliness the breeze
and wild grass calmed to a stillness I thought of as reverence.

—from *Gideon Jones' Journal*

When their wagon rolled out of Westport Landing, Wednesday morning the fifth
of July, Dorsey expected a line where trees and grass stopped and turned into miles
of desert sand, but everything pretty much stayed the same. There was even a kind
of road from the wheels of other wagons, and the train bounced along in the dirt
ruts. Dorsey was disappointed: they could have been on any road in Indiana. Her
mama was still bothered with stomach cramps, so Dorsey drove the team. When
Mama felt well enough to handle the mules, Dorsey rode the box on the Thurston wagon with Mary and her daughter, little Lucy, a quiet girl who sat taking in
every blade of grass, and baby James, one of three nursing babes on the train.

Mary Thurston was a farmwife like Dorsey's mama but not just like her. Mrs.
Thurston asked Dorsey to call her Mary, and she talked to Dorsey as if she were
grown. After weeks of sitting beside her mama, Dorsey liked listening to Mary's
different-sounding voice. Whenever Mary had to tend to Lucy or baby James or
when her husband wanted a break, Dorsey drove the Thurston team. The Thurston wagon was heavily loaded, and their milk cow came along slow, secured by a
length of rope and encouraged by Hiram's spotted fice whenever the little mon-

grel remembered to nip at the cow's hocks and yap. Mary's four little apple trees trembled against the wagon's sides and cast shadows against the cover. Dorsey liked to crawl inside the Thurston wagon to sit in the tree shadows and pretend she was on an apple farm—hers and Gideon's—in Washington Territory.

Another Dispute with the Major

Their first Sunday on the trail Major Benson stirred everybody for an early start, and Hiram Thurston balked.

"We'll not travel on Sabberday," Hiram said.

"Amen," said a gray-haired woman by the Waller wagon who held a fry pan in one hand.

"We got a late start, Thurston. We can't take Sabbath day layovers and beat mountain snows," Major Benson said.

"All who don't obey His commandments," the old Waller woman said, "will be struck down." Her grandchild came up and hid his face in her skirt that the prairie breeze wrapped around the backs of his bare legs.

"You can read Bible verses first, if you want," the major said.

Hiram nodded once and disappeared into his wagon. By now most everyone in the train had come around to see what the commotion was. Back on the seat, Hiram held a big family Bible open on his lap and read loud enough for everyone to hear:

—the seventh day is the Sabbath of the Lord thy God: in it thou shalt not
do any work, thou, nor thy son, nor thy daughter, nor thy manservant,
nor thine ox, nor thine ass, nor any of thy cattle, nor thy stranger that is
within thy gates—

"There's a world of red Indians and border ruffians out here who hasn't read the Bible," the major told the assembly. "They're most all-fired wrathy against Christian folk, and they don't know they aren't supposed to give us Jesse on the Sabbath." The major paused to let his words reach everybody. A murmur stirred the crowd as the breeze stirred the tall grass. Major Benson said, "Acknowledge the corn, men, we're across lots from the most savagerous killers there is. For the sake of your women and children, we got to pull like all creation to make it across these murderous plains. If we can't hie a considerable distance this and ever Sabbath—after we hold a short service—we're all gone coons. So I'm settling this hash. Roll with us or roll alone. Nobody's forced against his religion. But I can't give back any money. The rest of us will follow the eleventh commandment: 'God helps those who help theirselves.'"

There was consternation at Hiram's wagon and the Wallers'. Dorsey asked her mama what they were going to do.

"Mr. Speer says it's no sin to Moses if we make time best we can," Laura Etta said. Dorsey didn't see why God would care whether they parked their wagon on the prairie every Sunday, making themselves an easy target for Indian arrows, or kept rolling toward Washington Territory. The train crept along so slow it hardly seemed like they were *working*. But it bothered her how the decision was all Speer's. How could they just leave the Thurstons behind, all alone?

Then Gideon stepped forward and asked if he could read from Mr. Thurston's Bible. He patted his shirtpockets, then he plumbed his trouser pockets with both hands until he came up with his eyeglasses. Bespectacled, he had the grave look Dorsey associated with ministers in dark robes. Gazing through the thick lenses, he turned pages, hunting the section he wanted. "I read from the Book of Matthew, chapter twelve, verses ten through twelve":

And, behold, there was a man which had his hand withered. And they asked him, saying, Is it lawful to heal on the Sabbath days? that they might accuse him. And he said unto them, What man shall there be among you, that shall have one sheep, and if it fall into a pit on the Sabbath day, will he not lay hold on it, and lift it out? How much then is a man better than a sheep? Wherefore is it lawful to do well on the Sabbath days.

There was a long silence. Major Benson stared long at Gideon, his eyes squinted to a dark line. Dorsey thought the major should be pleased Gideon was mediating, but the look on the major's face was anything but pleased.

The Waller woman wrinkled her brow. "Do we do right to drive our teams on Sabberday?"

Gideon removed his eyeglasses. "What do you think, Mr. Thurston?"

Hiram smiled at Gideon and nodded to the Waller woman. "Jesus says the Sabbath is made for man, not man for the Sabbath. I reckon I'd druther go with Jesus than the Pharisees."

And so the dispute about traveling on Sabbath days was settled, but there were many other contentious disputes between Major Benson and the men who had put their eight wagons under his protection. Dorsey felt sure one of the conflicts would one day lead to a violent confrontation. She hoped Gideon would not suffer any dire consequences.

Fort Leavenworth

By the time Major Benson called a stopover at Fort Leavenworth, Dorsey had quit checking the calendar. She wondered if they would ever reach the Great Desert. They spent two nights at the fort. Dorsey thought the layover would give her a chance to visit with Gideon, but Major Benson kept all the men busy doing things to the wagons and loading new supplies. The fort was astir because the United States Congress had ordered a whole company of Negro soldiers to be signed up to protect the settlers now the Southern rebellion had been put down. Major Benson and several of his men made jokes about the Negroes and clearly resented seeing them in army uniforms, but word around the fort was that these colored men, veterans of some of the meanest fighting of the war, might make the toughest outfit in the army.

Inside the timber walls of the fort every day seemed to Dorsey muggy and cloudy. The high walls kept out sunlight and cast long shadows made darker by smoke from cookfires and by dust horses, oxen, and lines of soldiers stirred. The walls kept out the prairie breeze and kept in odors of dung, urine, and garbage. The walls kept out silent space and kept in loud commands, babies' wails, animal snorts. The fort was dark, smelly, and loud. Far above the enclosing walls a bright patch of sky undulated like the blue flag of a faraway country. Dorsey longed to travel to that empty and shining place.

From Fort Leavenworth, the train headed northwest toward the Platte River, which Major Benson planned to follow until it forked to become the South Platte and the North Platte. The train would follow the North Platte past Ogallala to Fort Laramie. Separating the two forts were over six hundred miles of prairie and desert, wind and sun—six hundred miles to cross where, Major Benson warned, rattlesnakes and wolves were plentiful, where stampeding buffalo flattened everything in their path, where water was scarce, and trees and flowers hardly existed. Miles and miles of unknown territory inhabited by hostile beasts and more hostile savages. Dorsey couldn't wait. Major Benson warned they were still at least forty days and forty nights from Fort Laramie, and then they had the Rocky Mountains to get beyond.

Dorsey's mama declared they'd already wandered longer than the Israelites, and she wondered if they would ever reach the promised land.

Feels Like Home to Her

They followed the Missouri River north for what seemed a good little ways beyond Fort Leavenworth, then Major Benson headed them due west. Late afternoon, they came of a sudden away from the occasional scattering of trees that had followed the road since they'd left the fort and rolled into a broad expanse of brightness. Brilliance everywhere, nothing dark in sight.

Dorsey looked back—east—at the treeline, just that, a line of trees behind her as far as she could see north and south like a line of clouds across the sky marking where storms ended and sunshine began. Ahead of them, endlessness. A wide sea softly swaying, its motion so slight it appeared alternately to be still as a painting, then alive and breathing as a living creature. Undulating grasslands and the undulating blue sky were all there was.

There was no sound but the wind and, then, her mama's breathless exclamation: "All this empty space makes me feel crazy. Just sky and grass and wind—nowhere to *be*, no place to keep a secret."

But Dorsey knew that wasn't true, *she* had a heart full of secrets. There was Gideon, who kept his wagon always in sight of hers and who never passed up any chance to visit when the train nooned or overnighted. There was the wide and comforting sky that made her feel somehow safe, though it unnerved others who were scared. Scared of Indians, of high rivers, of bad weather, of snakes and wolves and coyotes, of sickness, of getting lost, of running out of supplies, of running out of faith. As she left the treeline behind and rolled away from the shadows of leaves and into the wide openness of the land, Dorsey wanted to jump down and run. Here, where no trees deigned to grow and spread their limbs, Dorsey felt herself stretching tall and spreading her arms wide. She lifted her arms, her fingers opened to the sky. Never in all her dreams of the Great Desert had she pictured such a wide sea of dancing grass. Wind through the grass put music in her head as when the church choir sometimes filled the air with a held note that pushed against the roof rafters. Her heart beat strong against her ribcage, yet its pace was measured, calm, and sure. Silver-tongued rogue though he was, her new stepfather, Mr. Speer, was responsible for her being here now, and a curious affection for him filled her chest. This feeling must be why men like Mr. Lewis and Mr. Clark risked their lives and suffered daily discomforts on their arduous expeditions of exploring and mapping the wilderness. For a moment she thought every settler who had passed this way before her, every young woman who had rumbled in a wagon away from the familiarity, the safe feeling, of trees into this open and endless space, must have felt this exhilaration. But one glance at her mama, who, when she wasn't stealing fearful glances at the swells of grass, kept her eyes squeezed shut, told Dorsey not everyone felt the way she did. What memories or dreams did Laura Etta watch behind her closed lids?

"I swear, Mama, you hold yourself so tight under that sun bonnet you're like a groundhog afraid to come out of its burrow." Laura Etta didn't seem to hear Dorsey. "Look at this new land, Mama. It's more heavens than land."

Dorsey wondered the true nature of the sudden and deep connection she felt to the distant horizon, the wide sky—what was the cause of her happiness? She was still miles and weeks of hardship away from the Territory of Washington and an uncertain future. The only dream she could see clear was of the young man, Gideon, whose wagon bore his two precious books, a crate of lightning rods, and a human skeleton. What did she know of him beyond her heart's excited guesses? Irrational as it seemed she was profoundly joyful and deeply at peace, and the source of her joy was not mainly Gideon—though the prospect of being loved by him excited her heart—the source of her joy was this endless rolling plain, grass sprouting thickly and unevenly as hair on some uncouth and rowdy urchin's unkempt and bobbing head. She had never seen or fancied anything like these endless plains beneath this endless sky, so why did she feel, more than ever in her life, she was coming home?

The Turning of the Wheels

There was no longer even the suggestion of a road—no dirt ruts to follow. Dorsey's mama, her cramps having let up, was on the wagon box driving the team. Dorsey caught Gideon's bright spectacles staring over the top of his opened book. Pen in hand, he watched her. Wondering how he could write words on a bumping wagon seat, she leaned forward to wave at him, pulling the muslin dress across the small of her back, the thin material pressed around her narrow waist the way she imagined his hands holding her tight.

Mr. Speer rode along on Joe's bay. Mr. Speer had bought Joe a scrub mustang from the Indian horse-trader, Horse Arse, and Joe rode her, but he wasn't happy about it. Dorsey liked the grass better than the dirt roads the train had been taking—theirs was the next-to-last wagon and got all the dust. All that was visible of the wagons ahead were their white covers. Rolling and dipping above the tall grass, the billowing wagon covers looked to her like whitecaps rising and falling on the swells of an ocean. Dorsey had never seen a real ocean, but she had seen drawings in books, a painting at school of ships at sea, and she had sailed the world in her daydreams. Sometimes the wagons ahead disappeared entirely, as if swallowed by the grass, and for those minutes Dorsey felt as if she were the only person alive on God's whole earth. Then the wagons emerged, and she felt both disappointed and glad to have other people back in her world.

The other wagons floated along, and as Dorsey drove their wagon grass came up above their wheel hubs and whispered huskily against the wood spokes, scraping against the wagon bottom. In the grass brushing against wheels and the breeze rippling the Osnaburg wagon cover, Dorsey heard steady, labored breathing and the swish and rustle of petticoats and skirts, the sounds of some long, formal march. And on the heat-wiggly horizon she saw a lake surrounded by tall trees and meadows of flowers where picnickers spread quilts of food and set out jars of lemonade. She saw a handsome two-story house with a curving verandah crowded with laughing girls who looked just like her, while young men wearing spectacles like Gideon's descended from buggies all around the yard. As the wagon bumped along, the picnicking figures and the guests at the house party drew closer, until they turned silver in the sun and flattened out and became giant silver dollars laid sideways on the horizon. Then the huge coins winked away, and there was endlessness again. Curlews wheeled high overhead. Every now and then a crow cawed. Miles away, turkey buzzards made a dark, moving ring like black stars in the white sky. Quails Dorsey couldn't see whistled questions she couldn't decipher.

In the late afternoon heat, clouds built up, mimicking the muscular arms and shoulders of the bulging prairie. The darkening sky slowly rolled endless green swells as black as night, and thunder rumbled and echoed all around. Lightning struck as a shriek, ending with a clap that made the planet seem to tremble. Rain came in silver sheets that soaked the wagon covers and soon leaked through. Dorsey's mama spread a sheet of India rubber over their food and clothes, and that stopped the rain, but it pooled in the folds of the India rubber and in the wagonbed and soaked what dry clothes they had.

After a storm, time and again—that day and the next—wagons sank, stuck in low places, and when horses, mules, and oxen strained to pull them out, harnesses snapped, animals got loose, axletrees split. Even small streams flooded their banks and couldn't be crossed until the rain ran off and the streams went down. Then the sun came back out, and steam rose off the land as off a skillet sizzling. But, at least for a while, there were pools of water to keep the kegs full.

After the rains, the dust started up worse than ever. Between being sunburnt and breathing grit or squishing along in mud and stinging rain, Dorsey preferred rain. Now that their wagon was baked dry, the right front wheel took to barking. That's how it sounded to Dorsey, like an old dog giving one lonely bark each time the wheel went around. Dorsey leaned over to watch the wheel rim come up and go down in its endless circles. A place on the rim, an indentation or a spot of sunlight, looked like an eye. Each time the eye came up staring, the wheel gave a single bark. Creak, creak, creak, shudder bark and wobble, creak, creak, bark— over and over and over. The barking stayed with her even when they nooned and the wagon's brake was set, and it stayed with her at evening's rest and in her dreams. After four days, she asked her brother if he could stop the wheel from making the noise.

"What noise?"

For some reason it made her mad Joe hadn't even noticed the repeated noise. Her mama would say wasn't it just like a man, not to notice something that would drive a woman crazy. It also angered Dorsey when all Joe did was smear some axle grease somewhere around the wheel hub and the noise stopped. But she still could not stop listening for the bark. Now the wheels just made their usual creaking and shuddering, and she missed the bark. She even missed, almost to tears, the imaginary dog who'd done the barking. Was she being just like a woman— missing a thing that had gone away, missing it just for its having left even if it had been a nuisance when it was near to hand? Was that how she had missed her father when he went away to the war? Was that how she missed her friend Binga gone off ahead to the frontier?

Bathing in a Prairie Pond

Major Benson made everyone save ox dung to burn for cookfires. One afternoon, he spotted the tops of a line of trees and turned the wagons toward them. The trees grew all along a narrow stream, and the major had called an early stopover for men to chop and split wood and fill the water kegs. Dorsey walked upstream.

From behind her she heard the voices of the men working, their axes so distant they sounded like woodpeckers. She ran her hand over the thick, rough bark of a tree, sad so many were being cut down. These trees were big, ancient. For years they had shed their leaves and grown new ones alone on the prairie, touched by wild Indians only—if at all. Now they were felled for firewood. She remembered huge fires under castiron pots deep as she was tall, the farmers' wives back in Indiana making soap. She was glad to be far away from the heat and the steam, woodsmoke and lye stinging her eyes. Soap making, like hog butchering and crop planting—the ways farm families marked the passage of time. She had hated that about staying in one place, had hated all the years being just the same year over and over, this year's crop measured against last year's, this winter's snow compared to last year's. She liked better this moving through the landscape and the seasons.

She had no idea where she was or what the time. She felt she was all brightness and heat. Her hair lay sunwarmed on her neck, her arms were splattered with sun and leaf-shadow, her legs itched in the high grass. She followed the stream to a small pool in a grove of trees. She pressed her fingertips against rivulets of bark just to feel the rough hide of a tree. Prints in the mud around the pool looked like dogs' paws and cows' hooves. A frog hopped into the water, mud bubbles rising, rings of water following one another in ever growing circles away from the disturbance. Spiders thin and dark as strands of her hair moved swiftly across the surface, and a cloud of mosquitoes hovered over the waterline. Holding her skirt up against the backs of her thighs, she crouched and relaxed her bladder that still ached with the wagon's bumping. She reckoned herself almost a wanton, the way it thrilled her to squat here in the sunny outdoors and pee like an animal. She sniffed and tried to think how she could describe the delicate scents from inside her body—grassy and vinegary smelling. She wiggled and bounced on her heels, shaking herself clean, then stood and walked to the water's edge. One foot at a time she unlaced her shoes and pulled off her socks. Her feet sank. Slick dark mud squished up between her toes cool and slippery soft. She swatted at mosquitoes and stepped into the pool until the water was above her knees and lapped at the edges of her upheld skirt. She stood perfectly still and brown clouds of mud settled, clearing the water enough for her to see the tops of her shins. She tilted her head back, stared straight up: willowtips dipped and swayed beneath the drift of two clouds stretched long and thin. Standing so, her feet firmly anchored in the earth, Dorsey fancied she felt the actual slow turning of the planet. Without moving her feet she pulled her dress up over her head, and the breeze pressed her cotton shift against the backs of her legs. She pitched the faded chambray dress, made new for the journey, onto dry grass, and she let herself collapse slowly, first bending at the knees, then leaning forward into deeper water as an exhalation of breath. Her toes no longer touched the mud bottom. This far out in the pool, the mosquitoes left her alone. She treaded water, and bubbles rose and broke softly between her shift and her hot skin. In what shade the small trees cast, the water was cooler than Dorsey expected. Her hair fanned out on the surface. When she lifted her head, her wet hair pulled, heavy. She moved toward the center of the pool where a small, black bough with a yellow blossom stuck up out of the water. She stopped when the bough and blossom moved toward her, became the black head and yellow throat of a snake. She had seen plenty of snakes on the farm and had been terrified every time, but this snake did not frighten her. It passed close by and tiny ripples broke against her wrist. The snake appeared to be without fear and without guile. "What kind of snake are you?" she asked. "Is yours a fatal bite? Do you have knowledge with which to tempt me?" She had always, she realized now, thought of the serpent in the Garden of Eden as a male. She wondered why. At her first opportunity, she would have to reread the Scripture to see if God's word named the creature male or female. *Or,* she thought, *perhaps Gideon knows from that book he reads all the time.* The snake swam smoothly across the pool and onto the bank, where Dorsey saw he was yellow all down his underside. She knew the snake slid now over impressions her feet had left in the mud. After his head entered the grass beneath her dress, his tail was still coming out of the water. The snake was at least as long as she was tall—as alive as she and taking up a length of space equal to her own and, yet, invisible now. *In all the endless space that seems to give only of sky and grass, she wondered, how much life crawls and burrows out of my sight?*

In the embrace of water and trees, she pretended away the wide spaces, the wider world surrounding her. For a moment she forgot the wagon train and Mama and Joe and Mr. Speer. But she did not forget Gideon. Did that mean she loved him? She did love to talk with him. He said words she had never heard and read to her from the encyclopedia he carried. Yesterday he had opened the wooden crate in his wagonbed and shown her the lightning rods he carted. She'd been disappointed when he'd told her he was not a gunsmith, but these rods were better than she'd imagined. Fashioned of shining copper tubing sharp-pointed to pierce dark clouds, each rod had a turning wind arrow with feather and point all curlicue, a globe of colored glass blue as the earth spinning in the heavens. He'd recited a poem to her, spoke it from memory, about the great god Zeus throwing lightning bolts. In his spectacles, Gideon reminded her of her teacher, Mr. Dillard, who knew everything.

"You read more than any man I ever saw, except my schoolteacher back in Indiana."

"There's a world to know from books."

"The world is here," she said. She spread her arms and looked around them. The world had gotten so much wider since she'd left Indiana, and its size excited her. "It's all around us, and with your nose in that encyclopedia or writing in your journal you might miss it."

He grinned. "I always have one eye on you."

She felt her lips widen, even though she didn't want to smile and show how pleased she was. "Show me what you write in that book," she said.

"Not until I write something better. You might think me dull." *Not dull,* she thought. *But different from the boys I have known before.* If she were honest, she was not sure how she felt about a man who spent so much time reading and writing. When Mr. Dillard did it, he was at school.

She lay back in the water, closed her eyes, and let her mind float just like her body. A thought came to her that when Gideon was sleeping she could steal away his book to read what he wrote and see if she was in there. She knew it was a bad thought, and she wondered if she would do something bad like that. Another thought came to her—*maybe.* Out here she might do lots of things she would never have done back in the safe and civilized East.

Yesterday, when Dorsey had asked him to tell her more about the orphanage and asylum in Baltimore, Gideon had grown vague and quiet. She told him she had never even seen a demented person. He grinned and mentioned Major Benson and that made her laugh. She had never seen Baltimore or any back East city. But, now, she had seen St. Louis. She confessed to Gideon she had often wished she were an orphan, beholden to no one. She wished she could look into her mama's farmwife face without seeing her own face there, too. She had once told her friend Binga she wished she could be adopted by a new mother who would take her far from Indiana.

Binga had frowned. "Your problem is you keep wanting a different past."

"A different past? It's the future I dream about."

"This is the day the Lord hath made. We will rejoice and be glad in it."

"Oh Binga, why do you always preach? Can't you have an opinion without God?"

"Dorsey Murphy, you better ask forgiveness or God may strike you dead. You keep wishing to live a different life—same as wishing for a better past. Until you let go of the past, you won't ever be happy."

Dorsey wished Binga were here now, beside her in this pool of water, this wet dimple on the endless prairie. If Binga were here, Dorsey would tell her they were the only people who had ever stood under these trees, the only people who had ever bathed in this pool. She would say this was like the Garden of Eden. And she would tell Binga she had met a dealer in lightning rods, a young man she hoped might save her from an angry god.

Knobby Cotton: Where Cowards Ain't Set Out For

San Antonio de Bexar
(January–April 1863)

Eye tells me there yet stands, north of the town of San Antonio, a charred
limestone house where he himself has seen faintly visible on smoke-darkened
stones the chalked inscription: DON ANTONIO LOPEZ DE SANTA ANNA,
EL NAPOLEON DEL OESTE, MARZO 1836. I ask if he thinks the Mexican general
truly was there, and Eye says Santa Anna was "a high flung fellow" who
"traipsed considerable nearby." In Texas, I feel the breath of history still warm.

from *Gideon Jones' Journal*

From a distance, the white buildings of San Antonio shining in the winter sun
reminded Knobby of the blocks of salt he'd watched slaves haul and stack at the
saltworks in Louisiana. The riders of the Union Loyal Liberation Front came to
the San Antonio River and followed its twisting course into the outskirts of the
town. Mexican women and children stood in the dirt yards before their *jacales*,
one-story shacks made of sticks driven close together into the ground and covered
with mud to make a wall. A group of women stood in the river's edge chopping
wild tule, the reeds with which the *jacales'* roofs were thatched. As the riders
passed, the women looked up but did not wave or smile. Dogs ran at the horses'
heels yipping and barking, then ran back to their yards to sit proudly and pant,
their hanging tongues bobbing up and down. Mexicans were almost as dark as
Knobby, though their hair grew straight like flat blades of shiny black grass. After
about a mile of these stick houses, the main plaza showed above mesquite trees.
Eye led them in from the north and they came to the rear of a two-story stone
building—the Plaza House Hotel. They rode around to the front of the hotel, and
Knobby looked up at a balcony across the entire second floor. Opposite the Plaza

House sat the Cathedral San Fernando squat and square beneath its bell tower, and on the corner next to the cathedral was a hardware store. A plank building's faded sign announced an auction business. On the east side of the plaza rose a three-story store and two other buildings housing drygoods and mercantile companies. Toward Commerce Street were more stone buildings, and in the other direction, a long adobe house, closed up, bore a sign for THEISEN and DUNLAP. The rest of the plaza was lined with one-story adobe buildings and several board, adobe, and stone houses. In front of one of these, Eye dismounted and tied his horse. Knobby and the rest of the Liberation Front followed Eye through a deerskin flap hung over the house's doorway. The stone wall was four or five feet thick and opened into a dark corridor. Down this corridor they walked past several doorways until yellow light and muffled voices guided them into a room dimly lit by tallow candles and a flickering fire in the center of the packed dirt floor. Two long planks nailed to braces along the back wall made a crude saloon bar. Behind a scattering of pottery cups, bottled spirits lined the back of this board counter. There was no bartender. Eye reached for a bottle of McBryan, filled one of the pottery cups, and passed the bottle down the board. By the time it reached the last man, Eye was ready for a refill. The bottle was emptied on its way back toward Eye and another was pulled forward to take its place. All this pouring and drinking was done under the watchful eye of a big Mexican man who sat on the only barstool at one end of the counter.

Speaking Spanish, Eye ordered food for everyone, and soon a Mexican woman knelt at the fire on the floor stirring a pot and stuffing tamales wrapped in corn husks into the coals. They ate standing at the bar. The same woman who cooked the food served them with a silent smile. Knobby ate eleven tamales and two plates of beans, wiping the plate clean with the last tortilla in a basket the woman set out. When all the men had eaten their fill, Eye slid some coins down the bar. *"Hace frio."*

"Sí, Sí." The Mexican on the barstool gathered up the coins. *"Gracias."*

"De nada."

"Hace frio?" Knobby said.

Eye laughed, held the stub of his shortened first finger up in air as if he were testing the wind. "Means, *it's cold.*"

From this saloon, taking the opportunity to walk off their meals and flex their saddle weary bottoms, they led their horses to a kind of barracks—a long, low adobe building on Nacogdoches Street. Sergeant Goar told everyone to unsaddle and then bring their plunder inside. They followed the sergeant into a room with a window and a wood floor, a fireplace full of coals. Eye rented four rooms for a month, eight dollars in advance. The proprietor, a German named Sauer with spectacles pinched on the end of his nose, said the others had been here a week. They had the other six rooms, two men to a room. He didn't know the where-abouts of the men just now. He showed them a newspaper written in German reporting that General Magruder sneaked into Galveston on New Year's Day and retook the city for the Rebs.

"I reckon we got out just in time," Eye said.

"In back is the kitchen, Herr Goar. There's catfish to fry and, if it hasn't spoiled, plenty of bear meat," the German said.

"I don't hanker for bear, mostly fat and too sweet."

Two to a room, they dropped their saddles and other necessaries on their bunks. Eye intended to spend his nights in the bed of a whirligo girl called Ham-bone Hanna. Knobby shared a room with Flood. Back outside they led their horses all the way to San Pedro Creek, the western boundary of the city. On the other side of the San Pedro, in the Mexican quarters known as Chihuahua, narrow dirt streets snaked between *jacales* fenced with hedges of tall skinny cacti planted so close they grew together. Inside these enclosures were goats and an occasional hog. Smoke rose from the low mud houses carrying the smells of roasting corn and pork. White chickens darted and bobbed around like clouds come to ground. Dogs barked, chickens clucked, and children shouted and whistled. In a few min-utes Knobby was lost—the houses looked alike, the narrow streets twisted and turned. Eye stopped before one of the cactus fences and went inside. He emerged with a Mexican he introduced as Rojas. "Rojas is a first-rate *remudero*," Eye told Knobby. "A wrangler like your own self." Rojas led the men and horses through a gate into a large yard fenced with the same mudded sticks as the walls of the *jacal*. The men removed reins, bridles and bits, and turned the horses into the corral.

Eye rolled and lit a smoke. He lined the men up and handed out enough gold coin to get them all in trouble. "I reckon you're all going to be staying out with the dry cattle tonight. Try not to get in no cussfights. After midnight I don't want to leave Hanna's bed."

Dwight and Irish Pat invited Knobby to go with them to find another saloon. Hoping to learn Elizabeth was safe in Matamoros, Knobby went with Eye to the telegraph office to see if there was a message from Herr Reinbach. When there was no word from the Dutchman, Eye went off to Hambone Hanna's. At the plaza Knobby found Rudolph Hermann looking up beyond the hotel balcony at the moon. The lanky German nodded, the red tip of his cigar moving up and down. Gray puffs escaped Rudolph's mouth with each word he spoke, as if he were sending Indian smoke signals.

"For a while after Texas seceded, I couldn't get cigars. Then, any cigar would have been the best I ever tasted. Now Sergeant Goar brings me plenty, but not one lives up to my anticipation." He shook his head. "When the mouse is full, the flour tastes bitter. *Komm*, Herr Cotton."

Rudolph led Knobby to a German saloon down the street where he said their comrades waited. This place was more comfortable than the Mexican saloon they'd been to earlier. Small rugs were scattered over a tile floor, and there were tables and chairs, most of them occupied with men in suits who were drinking beer and talking loudly in the German words Knobby liked to hear. John Johnson and Irish Pat sat at a table with a half empty bottle of Old Crow before them. Dwight was tilting in a barstool like a man at sea, shining his boyish smile on two girls in calico. Knobby wondered where Flood was. One of the German patrons faced the room, his back against the bar, nodding and smiling at several men who made a semicircle around him. He stuck his hand out, forefinger extended as a pistol barrel, trigger finger jerking. "*Piff, paff, puff. Ermordet von Indianern.*" The man closed his eyes and translated his own tale: "Murdered by Indians."

Rudolph Hermann was the only one who didn't laugh. His eyes were large behind his glasses and Knobby thought his look sad. Rudolph put a coin on the plank, and the bartender slid him a crockery stein foaming with beer. Rudolph took a long draw, wiped lather from his lips, and said, "What I don't know, won't bother me so."

"It's not my business, but I can't quite figure why you joined this outfit. I mean, what does a German care about an American war?" Knobby asked.

"Herr Cotton, I am not going back to Germany. I am here now, *ja*."

"You don't seem the soldiering type."

"*Nein?* Well, you don't seem like one, either. I may not look like a killer, but I have killed a man years ago. We all have things to atone for. Maybe to fight slavery will make up for something I want to forget I did when I was a *Jüngling* like you."

The German emptied his mug and ordered another beer. Knobby could tell Rudolph had said all that he was going to say tonight.

Waiting for Reinbach's Message

Two more weeks passed without word from Reinbach about the arrival of the steam packet to Matamoros. Knobby could not get Elizabeth out of his thoughts.

He imagined catastrophe after catastrophe. Then, early on a Sunday morning, a German teamster came to Herr Sauer's barracks with a message from the Dutchman. The steamer's engine had failed and the boat grounded on a sandbar. They'd been stuck five days before a U.S. Navy warship had rescued them. Everyone, Reinbach said, was fine. The women and children were settled in good quarters and enjoying the gaiety of Matamoros. All Liberation Front patriots must be ready to leave San Antonio the moment he sent word. The ferry between Brownsville and Matamoros was running twenty-four hours a day bringing Texas cotton into Mexico for the European market and sending money and goods back for the Rebs, who were organizing a large overland caravan of supplies that would leave Brownsville for Austin by late February. Eye and his men were to intercept the train of freight wagons and confiscate all contraband. Reinbach would send to Eye code words, *Reiter fliegen*—a page torn from a German songbook, the music and lyrics for "The Broken Ring"—meaning the caravan had left Brownsville.

The first week after Reinbach's message Knobby was jumpy, expecting to leave town. But as days passed into weeks with no word, he began to wonder if he would ever get out of San Antonio de Bexar. Confederate agents freely came into and went out of San Antonio. Life in the town continued in such ordinary fashion Knobby found it hard to believe there was a war going on. The Germans in town asked Knobby and the other Negroes, Flood and John Johnson, what they thought about the Emancipation Proclamation. Knobby asked to read it, and someone handed him a newspaper but the words were all German. Rudolph Hermann put on his spectacles and translated: "I do order and declare all persons held as slaves within said designated States, and parts of States, are, and henceforward shall be free." But Hermann pointed out the proclamation pertained only to places indicated, "the people whereof shall then be in rebellion against the United States."

"So, if Unions rush in and take Santone, then they'll free us Negroes?" Flood asked.

"*Ja*. And it means you, Flood, and you Knobby, and John as well, *any* Negroes, slaves also, now can join Army of the Union—if you can get yourself to it."

"I'm not a slave, anyway," Knobby said. He finished his drink and went back to his bedroll in the barracks room, but sleep was long in coming. With Elizabeth safe in Mexico, Oralia haunted Knobby more than ever. He remembered her steady look and the way she led him up the stairs at Skyhouse, letting him step so close he felt the warmth of her body through the white dress she had worn. What had her body been saying to his? What promise had she hinted at? He wished they could have talked in private. With Elizabeth gone, he thought of riding back to Galveston to see Oralia. The time before sleep was his only time alone with her, and every night he hoped she would come to him in his dreams. But most often it was Elizabeth who found him in his sleep, and his recurring dream was of a horse running away with her and him chasing her and calling to the horse to bring her back. Tonight, the barracks room was still and warm. Oralia's gardenia scent wafted to his nose. Oralia's hips rolling firmly beneath the white dress as he followed her up the stairs filled his eyes. Oralia's legs in silk brushing together whispered into his ears. He wondered if he would ever get all the separate parts of her fitted together and in his bed.

The next day Knobby learned Rudolph was leaving San Antone, heading out for a hard day's ride north to New Braunfels, where some innkeeper he knew was so ill he might die. The gangly old German had let out his stirrup leathers so far they just cleared ground, and in high grass his feet in his stirrups left a trail. He often forgot to wear a hat and his nose was always red and peeling. His blond hair was shot through with gray and shone in the sun as gold and silver. *"Auf wiedersehen, adios, good-bye,"* Rudolph sang in his high yodeling voice, his arms and legs out in an awkward wave, and Knobby felt something like affection for the strange man.

Rojas the Remudero

After Rudolph left, Knobby passed his days with the Mexican *remudero*, Rojas. Flood and John Johnson lay around in their rooms, but the barracks reminded Knobby of slave quarters, so he went there only to sleep. Eye was still laying up with Hambone Hanna. Irish Pat had got a mongrel pup he spent hours with, and Dwight was ever after some new *Fraülein* or *señorita*. Knobby and Rojas rode the mustangs daily to keep them from turning wild again. They went over Liberation Front tack, rubbed saddle oil into leather, and made repairs as needed. Knobby recoated his hemp lariat with petrolatum and paraffin and worked the salve in, flexing the rope. Rojas slaughtered two steers and showed Knobby how to cut and stretch lengths of the beef, then to pepper the meat strips, and hang them out in the sun until they were jerked. They crossed San Pedro Creek into Chihuahua and shot targets against a limestone bluff. Knobby was a fair shot with the Colt's six-shooter. With the Henry rifle, he seldom missed the skinny neck of a gourd at forty or fifty yards, and anything Rojas tossed up Knobby hit with the shoulder gun.

After siesta time Rojas taught Knobby to drink mescal, the taste between brandy and whisky but cheaper than either. They ate chili con carne con frijoles and tamales sold from oxcarts in the plaza. Rojas said the best chili con carne was made with the dark meat of the wild turkey. Nighttimes they spent in the Mexican or German saloons breathing the odors of tobacco, damp wool, and cedar. They drank beer like it was water, then drifted up and down chilly and dusty streets waiting for something to happen. There was gambling—poker, monte, and faro—but Knobby and Rojas were among the few in San Antonio not addicted to games of chance. Weekends offered horse races they did wager on—usually wagered well because they judged horses well. They did their share of hug dancing with whirligo gals and dark señoritas, but Rojas had a wife and three children in his *jacal*, and Knobby had Elizabeth on his mind when he could clear it of Oralia, so they stopped short of joining San Antonio's sporting women in their small cribs.

One cold night Knobby and Rojas walked down Houston Street and abruptly the wind whined and groaned. Rojas made the sign of the cross and Knobby looked up to see three corpses swinging from limbs of cottonwoods that lined the street. The whining was not the wind. It was the creaking of the hangman's ropes. Knobby had never before seen a hanged white man.

"This," Rojas said, "is the work of the vigilance committee. There were twice as many strung up before the war."

For four days the dead men twisted on their ropes. Above the thick nooses around their necks their faces were swollen and bloated, and the sun turned the corpses black. Some said the hanged men were Reb deserters, but others said they were gamblers who tried to cheat a local house, and still others claimed they were Union sympathizers assassinated by a Confederate agent. The fifth day after Knobby and Rojas first saw them, the bodies and the ropes from which they had swung were gone. Knobby walked Houston Street every few nights, but he saw no more lynched men. He did witness a duel in a gambling room set up in back of a grocery house on South Alamo Street. Rojas said the gambling hall had been run before the war by the notorious desperado Bill Hart, until he was assassinated by another rascal, Bill Taylor. Someone had resurrected Hart's business in monte, chuck-a-luck, and hazard. Two toughs no more than fourteen or fifteen argued over dice. Ruffian friends tied each boy's penknife in his right hand and bound the rascals to one another, right hand to left hand, left hand to right hand. The contortions that followed were like the flips and twists of acrobatic performers in a traveling show that once stopped at Noble Plantation on its way to New Orleans. More dance than duel, the gyrations of the youths and the slashing of their small knives ended with them both bloodied and on their knees, more exhausted than hurt. Untethered, the two curs laughed, pouring from a bottle of bitters drinks for each another as well as splashes as medicine for their bleeding gashes.

A Medicine Show

If the rowdies had waited a night to duel they could have healed their wounded bodies and their tormented souls with a remarkable remedy available from a traveling physic. A single mule pulled the doctor to the plaza, his cart's ungreased wheels—a good eight feet in diameter—squeaking so loudly they woke Knobby from his newly acquired custom of a late afternoon siesta. The squeals of the cart had also waked Rojas, who came from the plaza to Knobby's room.

"*Un carro de mulas* on which someone has built a cabana with a roof as red as Hambone Hanna's hair—a mule cart like you've never seen. It waits in the plaza. The wheels of the cart are as yellow as the blossoms of the huisache tree. A red porch on the cabana sticks out like Hanna's big bosoms, and on it sits a medicine doctor in the white robes of an angel. *Vamonos.*"

Flood's hatless black head stuck up above the crowd in the plaza. He made space for Knobby and Rojas beside the cart's porch where a man stood in a white frock coat and pantaloons that shone orange and pink in the wavy flame of a torch. The broad brim of a low crowned *poblano* hat made a halo around his head. He leveled his eyes at the crowd, and everyone got quiet. "Ladies and gentlemen, señoras y señors, I humbly request a few moments of your time in order to consider a matter of singular consequence, no less than the bifunctional nature of our physical and spiritual existence." Loud words, whistles, hand claps, and foot stomps burst from the crowd as a covey of quail breaks from cover and which expired into a scattering of coughs and sighs like the birds' wingbeats. "I am Bertrand Selwyn Carroll, schooled in physic and epistemology, Doctor of Physiology and Metaphysics, come to you directly from California, having undertaken a mission of such magnitude that I journey with the authorization and under the diplomatic dispensations of the governments of both the United States and the Confederate States of America, as well as the seals of Great Britain and Indonesia. My duties have taken me to the great cities of the Americas, of Europe, England, and Asia."

As one voice, the crowd said, "Ooooh."

"Permit me to say no city on earth matches your own San Antonio de Bexar so far as regards a healthful climate, clear atmosphere, constant and rejuvenating breezes. The scheme of Nature in the formation of this region is too evident to be mistaken."

"What's he talking up?" Flood asked.

"Even those blessed to live in a city that escapes the highest concentrations of the poisonous principles of vaporous air must stand sentinel against diseases of the soul and against bodily malignancies owing to adventitious causes such as exposure to unknown contagion and the miasmata rising from putrid matter you cannot anywhere elude."

"I'd as soon listen to Dutchmens as this foreign talk," Flood said and stepped around the cart and disappeared into the crowd.

"Is there a single man, woman, or child amongst us, my brethren, who is not afflicted either of body or of spirit?" The crowd grew quiet, everyone straining to hear. "Our wretchedness surely competes with the mortal pains of the heroic souls who died yonder beyond the river at the Alamo, 'But Brother Dr. Carroll,' you say, 'there is no remedy for the afflicted soul save the heart of the tormented one.' Bless you, your clear-eyed truth. The human heart is the abode of the spirit. The head rules in earthly matters and leads us astray by reason of the brain's impressionability. Of the entire corporeality the brain is most accessible to infectious maladies through the portals of eyes, nostrils, ears, and mouth. At the body's crest and utmost limit, the brain is exposed to sun and darkness, to wind and cold, to the blows of overhanging and falling objects. This extreme position is necessitated by the brain's function as overseer of bodily mechanics. And though the overseer may wield the whip, he directs his lashes only as the owner of the estate dictates." Dr. Carroll pulled from his pocket a white handkerchief and waved it as in surrender, mopping the sweat-shine from his face. He stared right into Knobby's eyes and seemed to speak directly to him. "The heart holds true deed to all the territory of the body. The practitioners of the occult offices of the so-called science of phrenology argue the conformation of the skull, abode of the brain, is the source of character and mental capacity." Dr. Carroll jerked down a shade from a rod above the edge of the porch. On this shade was drawn a large diagram of a human head. Knobby had removed his hat, and his head was suddenly cool in the night air. The head drawn on the shade was divided into sections the way fields are fenced off on a farm, or lots laid out for a town, or plots for a graveyard, and each section was labeled as to crop or resident. "Ladies and gentlemen, señoras and señors, look here." Dr. Carroll loudly tapped a pointing stick against the shade. "Here, above the ear, lies the sector of DESTRUCTIVENESS and, just above it, of SECRECY—observe how large these domains are. Now, here," the pointer moved to just behind the eye, "see how small the tract for ORDER and CALCULATION and LANGUAGE."

"*Este médico*, he talks more than two wives," Rojas said.

"At the base of the skull is the kingdom of AMATIVENESS—*amorousness* or *lust*—larger and in a more primary location than LOVE's principality. Would our wise and merciful God draft such sites and proportions? These so-called doctors of phrenology are agents of the devil. There is no help for the brain except as it originates in the heart, wherein resides the heavenly spark, the generative power of the soul. And what does the heart do?"

"It beats, if you're lucky," a man said.

"Pumps blood," said another.

"Breaks," said a woman.

"Yes, it beats and it pumps blood. But it no longer has to break," Dr. Carroll said. "One year ago, in a laboratory in the Sultanate of Brunei, on the Island of Borneo, the world's leading physic, Dr. J. B. Leggett, extracted from the untainted blood of the long-lived and never-ill wild Indonesian natives of Borneo, secret life-elements he combined with certain aqueous humors to produce an amazing symbiosis—a harmonious fusion, a blood purifier, tonic, and nervine that will fortify the heart and blood against *all* eradicable diseases. This miraculous curative treats the heart and its blood—strengthening the spiritual as well as the physical being."

"How much is it, Herr Doctor?" a man asked.

"How much is a healthy body and soul worth? How much would *you* give to have all nervous diseases, all diseases of the blood, all pains of the joints and bones, all diseases of the liver and bowels speedily eradicated?" Dr. Carroll brought forth a tray covered with a white cloth.

"He is like the priest bearing the Sacraments. The host and the cup," Rojas said.

Dr. Carroll uncovered a pyramid of glass bottles that reflected torchlight as fifty or a hundred tiny flames. "My friends, I hold before you the most remarkable discovery of our time: DR. J. B. LEGGETT'S BORNEO BLOOD SYRUP AND HEART FORTIFIER." The syrup in the rectangular bottle looked, in the flaming light, the color and thickness of blood. "Dr. Leggett's remarkable remedy cures even hard-to-treat diseases of the stomach. Dyspepsia cannot exist any length of time if this corrective is taken *instantly* after eating. You have never known medicine such as this. It is alterative, soporific, sudorific, and deobstruent."

Several huzzas were shouted and people pressed close, gold coins shining. Rojas bought the first bottle.

"*Para mi esposa*," Rojas said. "For me, mescal is best, I think. Always in the dark, and even in the day, I think, I prefer mescal to *alguna medicina*."

Knobby wondered if the heart medicine would cure longings for Oralia. He agreed with Rojas, mescal was better, and they spent the rest of the evening doctoring their bodies and souls.

Long after midnight, Knobby said *hasta luego* to Rojas and walked back to the barracks. Empty bottles of DR. J. B. LEGGETT'S BORNEO BLOOD SYRUP AND HEART FORTIFIER lay scattered about the plaza.

Drinking with Rudolph Hermann

For days to come there were no distractions to rival Dr. Carroll. It rained a lot in March. The nights were cold and damp, and the wind seemed always to blow from the north. With the cold wind Rudolph Hermann rode in from New Braunfels acting stranger than usual.

"*Guten Abend*, my dark amigo. May I buy you a beer? *Eine gross bier*," he said to the barkeep. "This country makes one strong, Herr Cotton, or one dies. I find myself in Texas healthy as I never was in Germany. Remarkable when you consider the irregular life I've lived here, oftentimes riding a horse all day in the wet, or in the heat breathing dust, at night sleeping on the ground out under the wide sky." Knobby thought about the slave cabins back in Mississippi, and had no sympathy for Rudolph's complaints. But the German wasn't complaining so much as he was mourning something. "What a sky, eh? Over all of Texas, God has broadcast stars and fireflies so wherever one looks one sees sparks. And the cedars—with beautiful green needles and wood red as sunset—the settlers curse and chop for fence posts. Cedar scent reminds me of our pencils back in Deutschland."

"I guess I haven't smelled enough pencils to notice."

"Nor I, Herr Cotton, for a long time. Do you know I lived a decade in Mexico in a *flechwerk* cabin to be near my *Jüngling*? Oh yes, I once had a son. There are many things you do not know about me. I am old enough, Herr Cotton, to have a past full of secrets." Rudolph nodded to the piano. "Mi amigo up in New Braunfels, Herr Claren whose sister I knew in Braunschweig—he hits the bottom, a line in a children's song—he rests now in cool damp earth." Rudolph put his head down on the wooden table and soon began to snore.

The piano player walked between tables picking up glasses. He reached over the snoring Rudolph and said, "He bought a little ape. He is a bit tipsy." Knobby shrugged, and the piano player grinned.

Knobby finished the beer and ordered a shot of rye. Warm on his tongue and in his chest, the whisky reminded him of Etienne, and he lifted his glass to the Cajun trapper. Feeling sentimental, he drank two more shots—one for Grandfather Samuel, the last for his mama, Hester.

Knobby stepped outside and something didn't seem right. It took him a minute to realize the wind had died down. The soft whine was gone. The moon was out, gray clouds moving fast in the pale light. Knobby went back to his room at the barracks and lay awake until roosters crowed. In daylight, Oralia's face did not float above him like a lovely moon. How could he be so haunted after such a short time under her spell? With the sun, he got up and moved around town. Sometime after midnight he was back on his blanket staring up at the moon again. Days and nights repeated themselves.

Leaving San Antone

The weather like everything and everybody in Texas is unpredictable,
changeable, and drastic. In the spring, if it rains it rains buckets with
thunder and lightning and you think it will never stop. Then it stops.
The desert turns green, grass grows like wildfire, and shallow brimming playa
lakes shine in the sun. By August everything is dry and yellow, dust bowls
where the lakes were. But the land so empty-looking hides survivors—all kinds
of grass and bush wait for the first sprinkle of rain. Lizards and snakes wait
under rocks, deer and elk blend in with the chaparral. At night, invisible
mountain lions scream and coyotes howl. And—deadliest, most difficult
to espy—are foraging soldiers, outlaw cutthroats, and savage Indians.

—from *Gideon Jones' Journal*

The last day of April, Reinbach's coded message finally arrived: *Reiter fliegen*— telling them to leave San Antonio. Herr Sauer at the barracks read and translated: "Like a horseman I'd go riding/ Far to the bloody fight." Even if it was a bloody fight to which they were riding, the Liberation Front was weary of the confines of the town. They met at Rojas' *jacal*, each man carrying on his horse only enough victuals for a day or two. The rest of their supplies they loaded in pack saddles on mules. Leading the mules, they rode to Hambone Hanna's, where Eye waited in the dirt yard having a smoke. Fresh-shaved and washed cleaner than Knobby had ever seen him, Eye wore a blue chambray shirt, and a red silk wipe was tied around his neck. Hanna came out barefoot in a calico dress, a pot of coffee in one hand, the fingers of her other hand curled through the handles of four or five cups. A stalk of hay had caught in her red-blonde hair. She smiled wide, revealing a chaw of tobacco and brown-stained but straight teeth. She leaned close to fill Knobby's cup. She wore no face paint. Beneath the aroma of steaming coffee, Knobby smelled lye soap. While she poured, Hanna kept her gaze on Eye.

"Where we're headed," Eye said, "cowards ain't set out for, and the weak died on the way."

They drank dry Hanna's coffeepot, and each one—Knobby, Flood, John, Irish Pat, Dwight, Rudolph Hermann, the Billingsly brothers, and the half-dozen more Knobby barely knew, thanked her kindly. Eye tipped the stump of his cut-off finger to the brim of his sweat-stained hat and mounted up. Across the plaza of San Antonio de Bexar clopped and clattered fifteen men on horseback and a short string of loaded mules. The rattles of tin cups and spoons, creaks of leather, small clouds of horse snorts, the braying of mules, and the coughing of men were answered by roosters crowing and dogs yipping. Cook smoke rose from the low roofs of *jacales*. The sun, Eye remarked, was "about horse pizzle high," and it threw their moving shadows over dew-silvered grass and the thorny ears of prickly pear.

A Mexican woman and two children knelt in the shallow San Antonio River chopping wild tule. Of a sudden, the woman screamed, "*culebra, culebra*," and splashed the water. Rojas slid from his horse, pulled a machete from a canvas sheath, and chopped off the head of a thick, black water moccasin. The severed head flew up and hit the woman in the face. Fangs sunk into her cheek. Knobby held the screaming, thrashing woman, while Rojas pulled off the snake's head. Her little girl stood ankle-deep in the water stained red with snake blood, her dark eyes flowing tears. A boy, maybe ten, grabbed the still writhing serpent, fully eight feet long, and hurled it up onto the land where it jerked and twisted, powdering itself white with dust. Rojas sent the boy to the nearest house for corn shucks. He cut off pieces of the twitching snake body and held the chopped lengths against the fang holes. The boy returned with the shucks. When none of the severed pieces of snake flesh would stick to the bloody spots on the woman's face, Rojas struck a match and set one of the shucks on fire and held the flame against the bite marks. He pulled his wipe from his neck and pressed it around the bites.

Poison ran out as if it were being poured. Rojas burned three shucks against the wound, the skin red and puckered, the bite cauterized. Señoras gathered around their neighbor petting her and mumbling, "*Maria. Maria. Se muere. Se muere.*" Her eyes fluttered, and her boy held a wet rag to her lips.

"She won't die," Rojas said to Knobby. "But this is a bad beginning for our journey."

Eye said, "Like the saying, Texas is fine for men and dogs, but it's Hell on women and horses."

On the west side of San Pedro Creek they rode through Chihuahua and passed Rojas' *jacal* without stopping. The *remudero* stared straight ahead.

"Keep your eyes peeled for Comanches and for Reb outfits," Eye said. He spurred Dolores and settled into a steady trot. All day they rode through elevated and broken country. Except for bushy mesquites, there were few trees. They passed a few *jacales*. That evening they reached Castroville on the Medina River, twenty-five miles west of San Antonio, where they made camp. Rudolph spoke German and French with colonists he said were Alsatians. Some of the French words sounded familiar to Knobby, like words he had heard in New Orleans.

"Herr Cotton, you should see Deutschland, how green and orderly."

"I don't believe in Dutch Land," Eye said. "For men like us, and all the red-skins hereabout, there's just this wild country. Only it."

Cookfire coals reflected in the lenses of Rudolph's spectacles like some wild creature's red eyes. "*Ja.* I think it is true. For me, too, only this brown country."

The next morning they crossed the Medina, knee deep and maybe thirty yards wide. Late in the afternoon, they crossed the Hondo and made camp. Knobby pulled his Texas saddle off, lighter and better padded than the Mexican rigs most of the men rode. Still, his bottom was sore, his legs stiff as posts. He spread his India rubber groundcloth, rolled up in his blanket, and slept through supper, not opening his eyes until a breakfast fire popped and snapped under a gray sky.

Their fourth day out of San Antonio, they were west of the Frio River in Uvalde Canyon and still had not encountered other riders. Nothing grew but mesquite and sparse grass. The horses and mules were weakening for lack of forage, and the men doled out corn. Eye showed Knobby prickly pear, yucca, and agave. As he learned what to look for, he saw more. Near rivers and waterholes, blue and red wildflowers turned the land purple where they grew together. The wide sky was so low Knobby felt he might reach up and touch the small white clouds bunched together at the horizon. What he sensed in the silence of all this space was akin to holiness.

Irish Pat pointed to rising dust on the western horizon.

"Indians," Eye said. "Or Comancheros come from New Mexico. No soldier boys so far out, no settlers."

They rode through dense chaparral, and Knobby was glad of his leather chaps against the thorns. The Nueces River twisted and turned, its banks spotted with dark green live oaks. The river boomed over rocks and roared through narrows. Now the land made small drop-offs, like stair steps, that the horses jumped and even the heavily laden mules had no trouble crossing. This part of Texas looked as if God had been in a hurry, had dropped His work and left it the way it landed. Lone trees grew separate and apart from any notion of forest. Solitary mountains, sharp-angled and sudden, thrust up from wide mesas. Water surprised itself, gushing from the side of a rock as if God had randomly poked His finger in or commanded a spring to form, a waterhole to exist. Knobby asked Eye how the caravan from Matamoros could cross such country, and Eye said they were still a long way north of the wagon roads.

The Nueces wound like a trick roper's lariat, and they crossed and recrossed water. The men dug up mesquite roots they burned down to sweet-smelling coals, and they grilled thick fillets of the fish Knobby and Rudolph shot with rifles from a bluff above the clear river. Another of the ways Rudolph Hermann surprised Knobby was how good a shot he was. The old German seldom missed, and he got the biggest mess of fish. One huge twisted root burned most of the night and kept the scent of smoked fish over their camp. At dawn, Knobby waked ravenous and shot and cooked more fish for breakfast.

They forded the river for the last time and entered the Nueces Strip, an unsettled outlaw land settlers feared to cross. The current was strong, and Eye's fording pole found places of quicksand to avoid. Flood let one of the pack mules he was leading get off the ford. Panicked, he ignored Eye's shouts to cut the animal loose. The mule stumbled and got tangled in the lead line the rushing water wrapped around a protruding rock. The frightened beast rolled onto its back, its legs flailing like an insect groping air. The mule thrashed and brayed, its ears back against its head, the whites of both eyes huge in the narrow face. Flood wrapped the line around his saddlehorn and backed his horse, pulling the mule under where the line had slid deep beneath the rock. By the time Eye got to Flood and cut the rope, the mule was drowned. It floated downstream, its ears and tail flapping on the surface until the floating corpse lodged in a shallow place, where it appeared to be a brown rock. Death was a natural part of this landscape.

Sandstorm and Shootout

They took refuge from a sandstorm for a day and a night within the adobe walls of a deserted ranch house, its roof long fallen in. Rojas refused to hobble the horses, saying they had to find protection from the storm. Eye insisted the mules be kept on a lead, since they carried all the supplies. Knobby pulled his wipe over his mouth and nose, pulled his sweat-stained sombrero down snug so the brim was over his eyes, but he still had to squint. His wipe was a dirt-crusted roll around his neck. Sand bit the backs of his ears, his neck, his wrists, until he rolled up in his blanket. The world was all rust. His eyes and throat burned, and warm blood ran from his nose. Sand popped and sizzled against the adobe walls. To keep sane he tried to hold Elizabeth's face in his mind's eye, but it was Oralia's face he saw. Oralia's shape moved up a staircase in soft red light, while square miles of red earth roared around him. He wondered what kind of fool let lust overtake him in the form of a sandstorm. When he should be worried about the weather he was indulging his base thoughts. One way or another he had to calm the storm that his obsession with Oralia had become.

When the howling red clouds settled, the men spent all day and half the evening rounding up their scattered horses. One mustang had broken a leg and had to be shot. They rode near ten miles to Rosita Creek and in the light of a waxing moon they washed sand from their bodies, washed their horses, unloaded the mules, washed them, and repacked all their necessaries.

The third day following the sandstorm, they made camp at a waterhole Eye said was a half-day's ride west of the village of San Diego. From here, Eye sent Rojas to scout for the Matamoros train. His fourth day of scouting, Rojas spotted the makeshift caravan.

"*Las carretas es mala, muy mala,*" Rojas said.

The train was an assortment of army ambulances, old schooner wagons, Mexican carts, dilapidated freight wagons, and carriages patched up and overloaded and protected by only a small detachment of graycoat soldiers. Eye wanted to hit them at the end of the day when men and mules would be tired and thirsty, before they had time to corral up.

"Shoot a mule in every team. That'll bog them down sufficient." Eye flung coffee from his tin cup, and they mounted up. Knobby imagined what they must look like coming out of the chaparral without any bugle blown, without any orders or war whoops yelled, just the ominous rumble of horses' hooves and the pops of rifles. Shooting from a galloping horse took a steady hand, but the second time

Knobby squeezed the trigger a Reb soldier flew backward onto the ground in the same instant the Henry rifle kicked Knobby's shoulder. Darkie charged close to the train. From the edges of Knobby's senses came the scattered pops and cracks of gunfire, nothing more than twigs snapping or leather slapping. This was the place in his mind where Grandfather Samuel had gone when the overseer lashed him. A bullet whistled by, and Knobby whirled to see who tugged at his sleeve. Warm blood ran down his arm, and in his spyglass vision a puff of powdersmoke rose from the barrel of a soldier's carbine. Knobby squeezed the trigger, and the soldier's head was a red smear against the sky.

Firing a long-barreled pistol, a soldier in a tan tunic ran toward Knobby. A muleteer jumped from a wagon, his long gray beard flattened against his chest as a bib, and came running behind the soldier. Too close to aim, Knobby let the rifle barrel drop and shot. A crimson hole opened in the soldier's chest and in the beard of the man right behind. Up and down the train muleteers and soldiers alike were screaming *cease, cease,* and *surrender.* Arms raised, the captured walked through red clouds of dust—a glimpse of Hades, these men surrendering in the red light of eternal afternoon. With the guns silenced and the horses stilled came the dying cries of mules—high whines like winds buffeting tall pines back in Mississippi. Nine soldiers were dead, one teamster, and fourteen mules. The barrel of the Henry remained warm all afternoon. Without even drawing his six-shooter, Knobby had killed four men.

A cigarette bounced on Eye's lower lip. "Looks like you and them had a little shooting and most of them lost." Knobby pulled his wipe from around his neck. He swabbed sweat from his forehead and dabbed the sweaty band of his sombrero. Eye pointed at Knobby's blood-soaked sleeve. "Let me help you." Eye ripped the sleeve all the way around the muscle. He squinted around the smoke of his cigarette. "Ain't no more than a mite."

Irish Pat wanted to shoot the captured soldiers and strip the muleteers and send them naked into the chaparral. Eye said the soldiers would be hanged in the proper military way, rope being less dear than cartridges. Rudolph suggested they give the muleteers their lives to drive the woebegone wagons. Rojas and Flood unhitched mules dead in the traces and got the rest into even harness in working teams. Knobby had resisted arguments for the mule's superior strength. Now he knew why the expression was "stubborn as a mule." The muleteers were ornerier than the beasts they drove and loyal to nobody but themselves. Knobby puzzled whether the mules made their drivers that way or the other way around. One muleteer got Flood's gun while he slept and would have killed the big Negro, but

Irish Pat cut the teamster's throat from ear to ear with a straight razor Rudolph had left on a rock by his shaving mug.

The land they had to traverse didn't make the going easier. Wheels dished, single trees gave way, poles and axles broke. Dried and shrunk in the hot sun, rawhide lashings welded broken wagon parts. When they found a creek or waterhole, they soaked dry wheels overnight, swelling the spokes and felloes tight enough for the next day's haul. They were lucky to make twelve miles a day. After a week of breakdowns and repairs everyone was ready to give up the freight business. The wagons were not laden with goods desirable for clandestine trade—arms and ammunition, whisky and tobacco—but bore less tradable blankets, brogans, bolts of wool, picket pins, panniers, saw-buck pack saddles, shovels and picks, and crates of doctoring stuff: quinine, strychnine, turpentine, castor oil, camphor, ipecacuanha, blue mass. There were foodstuffs the men were glad to have—salt, Irish potatoes, and coffee—but not enough to bring profit beyond immediate consumption.

A teamster named Charley Kinder laid out a scheme he said could benefit them all. He would guide the train up to El Cañon de las Casas de Amarillas, where the Yellow Houses trading camp was and where he'd heard the notorious Comanchero leader, Pretty, was to arrive before the end of summer. Rich after summer raids and excited about autumn buffalo hunts, the Indians would be ready to trade with Pretty, who would give good return for the Liberation Front's booty.

"With these worthless outfits, Yellow Houses is a good month's ride," Eye said.

But he couldn't come up with a better plan. And he allowed he'd long been curious to meet the Comanchero *jefe*, Pretty. So Kinder led the Union Loyal Liberation Front and their captured train north toward the Llano Estacado and a rendezvous with Los Comancheros, called by Rojas, "*los dioses bastardos de los llanos.*"

The Yellow Houses

By the time the train of captured carts and wagons squeaked and groaned to the Yellow Houses it was July, and Knobby had learned more than he wanted to know about Texas freighting—about stubborn and skittish teams, about holding carts and wagons together with rawhide, about slow travel through unbearably hot, dry, and seemingly uninhabited country. He was beginning to wonder if El Cañon de las Casas de Amarillas even existed, it seemed so remote. The teamster, Kinder, said that was the point. He said the Comancheros didn't much want anyone but the Indians to find the Yellow Houses. Kinder told Knobby the Comanchero trading camp took its name from a limestone bluff nearby. This yellowish bluff was pitted with caves, and from a distance Kinder said it looked like some ancient city. The Comanchero camp was also known as El Cañon del Rescate, because so many Indian captives were ransomed there.

Though they covered hundreds of miles, the only people they encountered were two Tonkawa scouts whose hatred for Comanches was greater than their loyalty to the Confederate troops they scouted for. The Tonks accepted sugar from Charley Kinder and confirmed they had seen the Comanchero, Pretty, on the Llano Estacado moving in the direction of the Yellow Houses.

"Pretty *es un animal tiene muy mal genio, muy bruto*," Rojas said.

"You know him, Herr Pretty, do you Rojas?" There was grit in the old German's voice.

"No, *señor*, but his cruelties are well known. He kills *a sangre frío*."

"*Verflucht´*, it's what killing is—*kaltblütig*," Rudolph said.

"This Pretty, he values nothing, not even the gold he gathers, so he cannot be predicted. He trades with anyone—*los indios, los banditos, los soldados*—he knows no cause but his purse. He throws away his gold on frivolous things," Rojas said.

"*Ja*, maybe he's learnt what we still have not, eh? Herr Rojas, do you wrangle our horses because you believe in the Liberation Front or because you like *die geld* Herr Reinbach pays you? You recall, Herr Goar, *die geld* you and I took one night in New Orleans?"

Eye nodded. "I recall, Rudolph. We were young then, and wild-blooded. The Comanchero still is. What I heard, Pretty's like some cat—got nine lives. Way it's told, he's part Comanche, and comes and goes as he pleases in Comancheria."

"Don't believe every tale you hear. I grow weary of tales that take over a life—weary when the tales become the life. As a *Jüngling* the one now called Pretty lived on a hacienda in Nuevo León, south of where the Comanche Trace crosses the Rio Grande into Mexico. Comanches and Kiowas raid Northern Mexico every summer. The Indians pass by the walled-in towns, but they make forays into villages for miles around. They take horses and women and children, kill and kidnap many Mexican peasants. *Kaltblütig*."

"Why doesn't the government send the army?" Knobby said.

"Have you speculated why so few Texans held out so long at the Alamo and won at San Jacinto against *ein grosse* well-supplied army? Mexican army commanders all want to be el presidente. They fight best one another. One summer Indians attack the hacienda in Nuevo Leon where the boy lived, kill his mother and his father," Rudolph said.

"Dutchman, how do you know so much about the Comanchero?" Eye asked.

"I live for a time in Nuevo Leon, near Montclova, on the same hacienda as the boy."

"Miguel—Miguel Ignacio Delgado," Rojas said.

"*Nein*. Miguel is his adoptive father's name. He was christened Moses Ignacio Delgado." "He was baptized? By a priest? *¿Es verdad?*" Rojas asked.

"*Ein Priester*, yes." Rojas did not look convinced. "I was there. In New Braunfels. Father Martin had just arrived on the *Phillippe* out of Dunqerque."

"What I heard is the papa, Señor Miguel, run to save his skin," Eye said. "But this Moses, just a kid, knocked a Comanche warrior out of his saddle and bit a chunk out of his leg. Impressed the Comanches. They caught the papa and give him top Comanche torture for being such a coward, but the boy they took captive."

Hermann shook his head. "Everyone was run, but there were no cowards. Indians seize Moises away." Rudolph rubbed at a pale line of flesh down his left temple. "I was there. I see it still: a brave rides down on him and snatches him up onto his racing horse. His small body, dark against the bright sun, his arms and legs move like bird's wings. I see his eyes wide and white. Right then, an innocent one was born into bloodshed."

"And that's how he became a Comanchero?"

"No, Knob, it's how he almost turned Comanche," Eye said. "Comanches show captured boys how to shoot a bow and track buffalo and how to talk Comanche. They say a year or two passed, the braves trusted the boy to watch the horses, and one night he skedaddled back to Mexico but found nobody alive he knew. Learned things he shouldn't from the local padre, like how his *mamacita* was shot so full of arrows she looked like a walking cactus before they raped her to death. The boy tried to go back to his Mexican ways—"

"He went to live in Montclova. The padres took him in, instructed him how to read and write Spanish and English, the catechism, the lives of the saints," Rudolph said.

"But after so long sleeping out on the plains he couldn't tolerate walls around him. Right, Dutchman?"

"He was still a *Jüngling*. He hated Mexico for not helping the *campesinos*, hated the Church for trying to convert the Indians instead of fighting them, hated his dead papa—and others who were there—because he thought they did not fight strong. Of course, he hated the Indians especially for killing his mother. I think he mainly hated himself for not saving his mother."

Knobby had no difficulty imagining this Moses' hatred. "Then what?"

"He changed his name, became someone who depends on no one," Rudolph said. "As if a new name wipes out the killing one has seen or done."

"He took for himself the name El Perdido. If ever there was a lost soul, it was this one," Rojas said.

"Some ignorant buffalo skinners he run off from Indian hunting lands said it 'Purdy,' and folks thought it was their way of saying 'Pretty,'" Eye said. "A man who loses everything has no cause to be scared. Pretty ain't afraid of anything. Comanches see him coming, they send up smoke words: 'Let him pass.' They figure he's crazy, like the Pookootsee—what they call the backwards Comanches—or he's got strong medicine, mighty *puha*."

"This Lost One, he is one to fear wholly," Rojas said. "El Perdido *es sin corazón*."

The following morning Rudolph Hermann had disappeared.

"Did you hear anything?" Knobby asked Rojas, who shook his head. "How did he leave without stirring up the horses or waking us somehow?"

"*¿Quién sabe?*"

"I reckon I know," Eye said. "Rudolph told me he doesn't want a meeting with Pretty, so he rode on south to wait for us in Mexico."

The horizon line undulated in the heat, and the limestone bluff had been on the horizon a while before Knobby realized what he was staring at. When they were close enough to see the dark portals of caves, the sight put Knobby in mind of biblical cities his grandfather had described in his sermons and of Grandfather's explanation of the eye of a needle being an opening made in a rock wall for a camel to squeeze in or out of. At this distance from the bluff, Eye figured they were half a day's ride from the Yellow Houses trading tents. They made camp, and he rode ahead to arrange a meeting with the Comanchero, Pretty. A long day passed before Eye returned. They were to ride to the Yellow Houses and wait there for El Perdido.

🔲

In the shade of buffalo hides stretched over four poles to make a roofed trading place without walls, they waited for the Comanchero leader and his men. Trade fairs were held under these big tents in the Comanchero camp scattered along a shallow stream that ran south into the Brazos. Knobby was glad of the stream and bathed himself in its clear water.

After two days, Pretty rode into the camp on an ordinary-looking sorrel mare. Pretty was almost as dark-skinned as Knobby. A black *poblano* hat bounced from a thong around his neck. His black, shiny hair was cropped short, and his mouth was almost hidden by the dark moustache that made his face appear to be in a constant frown. Except that he wore black, as in mourning, there was little in his appearance to distinguish him from a peasant. A carbine's stock jutted from his saddle, but the only weapon he wore on his person was a machete, a peasant's cane blade. He dropped lightly from the saddle, silver spur rowels ringing once. Off the horse, he looked shorter. Muscles in his bowed legs bulged against the tight cavalry pants, dark blue army issue. His chest was wide, his waist narrow, his arms long. He neither smiled nor frowned at anything, not even the exchange rate he made with Eye and the teamster, Kinder, for the Confederate supplies. Knobby had known of cruel slavers and overseers, but he had never seen a man who looked so far away this close up. Pretty spoke in a voice so devoid of inflection he turned common words into a strange tongue, language without nuance.

"Pretty, you need trade goods," Eye said. "I need to get shed of these wagons and get something more portable, like gold. I figure I can let you have these goods for half their cost."

"You figure wrong, señor." Pretty's eyes were dark holes in his face. "I give ten percent of value. Today. Mañana, five percent. The day after, nothing." Erect, arms at his sides, black boots polished like steel, Pretty looked like a bayonet, and his shadow came to a point at Knobby's feet. "*Importa poco.* Do we make business or no?"

Eye, Kinder, Knobby, and the rest of the Union Loyal Liberation Front rode away from the Yellow Houses with a packet of Confederate paper money and Texas treasury warrants worth maybe twenty cents to the dollar in specie, so they'd gotten less than ten percent of the trade goods' value. "At least," Eye said, "we're free of the wore-out carts, our hides are unpoked, and we're still drawing air."

Charley Kinder and the other muleteers bid the men of the Liberation Front adios and headed their carts and wagons southeast.

Pretty crisscrossed Knobby's memory as a moving shadow.

Skedaddling for Mexico

They rode south to rendezvous with Herr Reinbach in Matamoros. Knobby would see Elizabeth for the first time in months. As they neared the Rio Grande, Eye spotted a patrol of Texas state troops riding upriver on the Texas side. Eye said the troops were looking for draft dodgers or Unionists trying to get to Mexico. Eye told everyone to walk their horses and pack mules through the thick chaparral, where he showed them bits of cotton clinging to thorns. "Cotton fluff's in the air all along the border. It's selling in the bale for a dollar gold on the pound."

Near Brownsville the grass gave out completely. Nothing grew but mesquite, cactus, and salt grass the horses wouldn't eat. Knobby would have given good money for fodder for Darkie. For two days they ate a burnt flour soup and some plain mash Eye cooked up. Rojas called Matamoros "La Heroica." Here they could get anything they wanted for silver, but the paper Pretty had paid them wouldn't go far. The third day, Knobby spotted what looked like white clouds come to rest in the distance below the line of the river. These clouds were white flowering trees Rojas called *anacahuite*. "Anacahuite flowers are cooked into a syrup to still coughs, cool fevers." On the Mexican side pilings rose out of the river as from an abandoned bridge. "El Puente del Diablo," Rojas said.

"We'll cross here and hole up in the village," Eye said. "Used to be called the Hacienda del Mirador de Mil Cerros, because you see a thousand hills."

Years ago, El Patrón of the hacienda sent some of the *campesinos* from the hacienda to build his new bride a bridge so she could cross to pick the healing flowers. El Patrón had heavy timbers carted up from the interior, but when the men sunk the pilings an image of the Holy Virgin appeared in the river. One *campesino* put his hands in the brown water and when his fingers touched the Holy Virgin's robe the image became solid, though whether of gold or poor iron or plain wood none could say. This man took the image home to his *jacal*, saying he would give it to the priest when he came to say the Mass. But when the man awoke, the Virgin was gone. The men returned to work on the bridge, but the image again floated on the river. The Virgin had walked all the way from the *jacal*. The priest from La Heroica came. He said the Holy Virgin did not want the bridge built. He said a bridge from this side of the river to the other side was also a bridge from the other side to this side. The Virgen del Rio Grande, as the *campesinos* had named the image, wanted to protect the hacienda from evil that might cross over. But El Patrón was a rich man who wanted to show his bride his power. He was not going to let superstitious *campesinos* and a country priest tell him what to do. The priest took the image back to the church in La Heroica, and when the *campesinos* refused to build the bridge El Patrón sent them off the hacienda. He had to go as far as Saltillo to find men to build his bridge. When the last nail was driven, lightning flashed and rain poured down. The river rose and washed the bridge away. But El Patrón had the bridge rebuilt, and on the last day of construction brought his bride so she could immediately cross to the other side. There sun shone bright. But just before the bride reached the midpoint of the bridge its heavy ropes and planks broke apart, and she was cast into the water and her body never found. They say whoever bathes at El Puente del Diablo never strays far and always dies on this side of the Rio Grande.

The river was too deep and strong to swim the horses across. Eye paid some *muchachos* to lead the horses and pack mules four miles downriver to a cane bottom that was a shallow ford, there to lead them across and back up the Mexican side and graze them near the village called the Devil's Bridge. Rojas went with the *remuda*. Eye paid two Mexicanos to take the rest of them across in two wooden skiffs, three at a time, each boat making four crossings to get them and all the saw-bucks off the pack mules to the Mexican side, where the pilings were adorned with faded ribbons, flowers both dead and fresh, scraps of paper with writing on them. Scattered on the sand were flowers, painted wooden crosses, bits of colored cloth, strings of beads, carved and painted dolls and animals. Candles stuck up in the sand, though none was burning.

Knobby, Flood, and Eye climbed out onto a sandbar in front of a shallow pool in which women knelt washing clothes. Children in the pool washed a big sow, scrubbing her with rags. "This is sacred water," Eye said. "They wash their stock so none strays. Nary a fence in the village. Now she's washed in this water, the sow is bound to die on this side of the river."

"I hope it dies right away—I could eat a shank of roast pork," Flood said. A gust of wind blew his flop-brim hat into the river, and the current carried it away like a brown water lily. Flood's face twisted up so, Knobby thought he might bawl over the lost hat.

Soap slicks put rainbows on the river's surface and lapped suds against the sides of the low-riding skiffs. Lye stung Knobby's nose. He scratched his itchy shins through his boots and pants and determined he would make his way back here if there was no bathtub in town.

For a few pennies they rented burros from Mexicano boys. The boys walked along herding the burros with stiff leaves like palm fronds, swatting the animals' rumps and swishing the leaves against their necks to guide them. Knobby's boots

barely cleared ground. He thought of Jesus riding an ass into Jerusalem and wondered if the Lord had felt foolish, too. Probably not, with a death foretold awaiting
Him. Knobby hoped he was suffering the ride for a happier fate.

The first houses they passed were just holes dug into clay banks. Smoke rose
from cavelike openings where doorways of upright poles had been fashioned.
There were a few mud-thatched huts similar to the *jacales* outside San Antonio,
dug into the red earth with mudded stick-walls and a flat mudded stick-roof over
the cellarlike room. A hide flap hung over the open end as a door. Near what
seemed to be the center of the village, the burros halted before a low adobe building. One after another, the men stooped through the doorway into a long room
with two high window openings in which a square of sky was brighter than the
room's oil lamp. One wall was covered with gilt paper clouded with a smoke or
grease stain in the shape, Knobby thought, of a dipper about to spill whatever it
held onto several shelves and a narrow counter slapped over with red paint.

The men sat on the dirt floor and leaned back against the walls of the village
cantina. A girl collected coins while her mother filled clay cups from a demijohn
of bitters. A boy came in carrying what looked like a dead squirrel, drowned, judging from the water dripping from the boy's outstretched hands. Knobby recognized the soggy squirrel's tail as the brim of Flood's lost hat. He gave the boy a
Confederate dollar, and the woman behind the counter produced a clay pot as
big as Flood's head. She put the hat over the pot, reshaping the wet felt.

They ate corn tortillas and eggs scrambled with sausage Eye said was goat.
When they had eaten, a boy came to report the horses and mules had arrived
and, shortly, Rojas came in and had his supper. They rolled cigaritos from corn
shucks. Flood's hat drying on the pot on the counter, its wet brim hanging down
like wings at rest, looked like an inquisitive bird watching them. Flood and Irish
Pat set to picking lice out of their hair and flicking them into the fire.

Rojas overheard Knobby saying, "*¿Hable usted la cazuela por agua?*" and burst
out laughing. "You just asked for a stewpan for water." But even when Rojas asked
in Spanish for *la bañera* the woman grinned and shook her head. Knobby got a
square of soap he kept rolled in his slicker and headed to the river. The water was
warm, and the soap stung his skin. The far-off howls of coyotes were alternately
amplified and muffled by the water cupping his ears. He laved soap around his
genitals and tried to hold Elizabeth's face in his mind but, as before, Oralia's face
appeared. Knobby wondered at the strength of this mulatto woman's pull on his
passion. He knew she was following him for some reason. He splashed the moon's
floating reflection, scattering white petals over the water, sacred water in which he

was now baptized. If the shrine had real power, he hoped the part about dying on this side of the Rio Grande wasn't going to happen soon.

In the milky glow of moonlight someone walked along the river bent over like a crane searching the mud. Knobby called to the silvery shape and it answered, "*Guten Abend, Buenas noches*, Herr Cotton." Rudolph Hermann had found his way to Mexico.

Next day, they followed the Rio Grande south and east toward Matamoros, passing through identical nameless villages. Eye reminded them of patrols, Texan or Union, on both sides of the river. He also warned of quicksand along the river's edge. Near Matamoros and Bagdad boats crowded the Mexican side of the river waiting to take Confederate cotton to ships anchored in the Gulf, in Mexican waters in sight of Federal gunboats. Several *jacales* were built along the riverbank. Naked children played in old *acequias*, their shouts mixing with the barking of dogs and chirping of birds.

A city of tents appeared by the river's edge, canvas billowing up and down in the breeze like breathing. Dust turned canvas walls the color of scabs. A horde of Negroes all shades of brown poured from the tents. Not an army, but a tribe. A village out of Africa? Eye drew his sidearm, and husky whispers of steel on leather ran down the line of horsemen drawing pistols. The guns were not necessary. What flashed in the Negroes' hands were tin cups they held out begging for money, for whisky or coffee, for whatever a rider might part with. One gray-haired, gray-bearded Negro, eyes squinted against the sun, came forward. He ignored Knobby and Flood, didn't acknowledge John Johnson, but spoke to Rudolph. Knobby could not blame the Negro for assuming the leader of these horsemen would not be a Negro. Rudolph had gray in his hair, was the tallest, and he wore spectacles—a sign of book learning.

"Master, can some a you spare you bounty? We got women and children gone hungry."

"Herr Sergeant Goar?" Rudolph asked.

The old Negro turned to Eye. "Sergeant?"

Eye swung down off Dolores and walked past the old man into the confusion of tents and raggedy-looking Negroes. Knobby and the other men followed. The Negroes—mostly women and children, a few white-headed men—pressed close. Knobby smelled sweat, urine, and sour milk. Naked babies with swollen stomachs toddled as if in a daze, flies crawling over their round faces. Near the middle of the settlement was a large tent, walls rolled up, pallets in rows under the canvas. Dark bodies lay two to a pallet. Rudolph knelt and laid his palm on the brow of a little boy almost lost beneath a pile of canvas. "*Sehr krank,*" Rudolph said.

Knobby heard Grandfather Samuel's voice, the voice in which Knobby's memory always served up Scripture, intoning the verse from Matthew: *Suffer little children and forbid them not to come unto me; for of such is the kingdom of heaven.* Grandfather used Scripture to encourage the slaves, but it irritated Knobby how Negroes were always compared to children. Grandfather meant they were all God's children, but whites meant Negroes were childlike, unable to care for themselves, incapable of responsible behavior.

"We ain't got no blankets, so we pulled down some tents and covered over the fevered children with them. This here is our hospital. Our biggest place is our boneyard," the gray-bearded Negro said. Rudolph poured water from his canteen onto his kerchief and dabbed the face of the child.

"What kind of folks are you? What're you doing in Mexico?" Eye asked.

"We all runaways who hied to Mexico to be free, but they chased us out of town. There's plenty to eat in Matamoros if you can pay with gold. Some of us got jobs hauling cotton to the Gulf. Some of us don't want to sell the cotton because it's sending guns back to Reb armies."

"Where are your working-age men?" Eye asked.

"They most the onliest ones to find any job of pay in Matamoros. A goodly number is gone back with a bounty deal."

"What's a bounty deal?" Knobby asked.

"Nigger hunter comes across the river after us. Sometime he offer a deal for a slave to go peaceable back to the master. Slave has to run off again, then the nigger hunter gives half the bounty to the slave. Or the slave, he might agree to let the nigger hunter sell him to some new master, then he runs off and gets his share. Some of us does it over and over."

Rudolph told Rojas to line up all the pack mules, and then he went to Eye and said, "Herr Goar, give me your big knife." Eye's Bowie knife looked like a pirate's sword in Rudolph's hand. The old German walked down the line of mules and cut ropes where every one of the saw-buck packs were cinched and pushed and pulled each pack till it fell into the dust. There was a good deal of flour and cornmeal, dried beans, beef jerky, coffee, and sugar left in the packs. Children ran, pushing and shoving, grabbing fistfuls of flour and stuffing their mouths.

The gray-bearded Negro slapped at the wild children, called on two women to unpack the foodstuffs, got the people to make two lines. Some of the women started up singing:

> The river's bank am a very good road,
> The dead trees show the way,
> Left foot, peg foot going on,
> Follow the drinking gourd.

Rudolph handed the knife back to Eye, who nodded and pulled a pouch of tobacco from his pocket and put a pinch of loose tobacco inside his cheek.

The old Negro ran into a tent and came back with a Bible. He told all the Negroes to bow their heads, and he thanked the Lord for this miracle of manna. Then he handed the Bible to Eye. "Sergeant, sir, would you read some Scripture over the blessing you men have gave us?"

Eye held the Bible where it had fallen open. "Man you are dust to dust. Amen." The old man reached for the Bible, but Eye held it long enough to tear out half a page. Then he tapped tobacco onto the torn sheet, rolled it, and ran his tongue down the seam. He struck a wooden match against his thumbnail. "Fire and brimstone."

Waiting Out the War in Matamoros

Matamoros was all heat and dust and so crowded it made New Orleans seem empty. There were brown men, white men, black men, and yellow men. These men were Mexican, American, and European. They were Imperialistas, Juaristas, and Cortinistas. They were Confederates and Unionists, cotton merchants and adventuresses. Everyone was after something, and the unpaved streets jammed with cotton wagons echoed with noisy talk in Spanish, English, German, and French. Rebs and Yankees were fighting over the U.S. while Juaristas and Imperialistas were fighting over Mexico, and all the usual speculators were chasing gold and silver. The Brownsville and Matamoros *Daily Ranchero* was published in both Spanish and French. With enough money, a man could have anything here he wanted, and there was enough money flowing to satisfy every imaginable yearning.

Reinbach was not around, and it took them half a day to find the rooms he had let for Elizabeth, Flood's family, and other Liberation Front dependents. Knobby found Elizabeth sitting on a bench with her knees drawn up, her eyes closed, behind an adobe wall grown over with bougainvillaea and surrounded by tall date palm trees. She wore a blue Mexican-looking shift with white embroidery across her breasts. In the sun, her ebony skin looked oiled and polished. Spit dried in his mouth. Beyond the wall, a man said, "*Caray.*" A whip cracked. Cart wheels squeaked. "Elizabeth." Knobby's voice broke.

Her eyes opened wide, and she ran to him. As she slid into his arms, he thought: *she's gotten fat*—then he understood. Then a fear jumped up into his chest: *someone other than I made this baby in her.* While she said "Knobby, Knobby, Knobby," he counted months in his head: the baby was his. She pressed his hand against her belly, and the baby moved an arm or a leg. Knobby had felt foals and calves move, shifting inside the womb. She unbuttoned the dress. Her belly looked like a cannonball, and he felt as if he'd been struck by one. Runaway from Mississippi, illegal in Texas, far from any Union state, joined to a made-up army in a foreign land—what was he going to do with a wife and a child? As if answering his thoughts, Elizabeth led him inside to a bed with a corn shuck mattress and pulled him down beside her.

"Should we, can we now?" he asked. She laughed and kissed him, unfastened his trousers. Outside the wall a voice said, "*Es difícil encontrar—Este equipaje no es más que un estorbo.*" Under his fingers, her warm skin rippled. Outside a horse whinnied and horseshoes rang on paving stones, sharp tangs, blue sparks in the darkening room. Unbidden, Oralia's image floated before Knobby's eyes. He pressed his face between Elizabeth's shoulder blades, breathed her smell of sunbaked dust. His tongue licked up the crevice of her spine, savored the taste of salt, and he rid their bed of Oralia.

A few days later, Eye came round. Herr Reinbach was not in Matamoros. There was a rumor the Dutchman had run out on them, taken a ship bound for France. Eye had a different notion, couldn't shake his feeling someone had done the little patriot in. Eye rolled a cigarette. "We ought to lay low for a spell. Should suit you fine, with a baby coming." He pulled tight the string noose around the neck of his tobacco pouch. "We got all the paper from Pretty, but I can't find a man who'll give twenty cents on the dollar for it—one offered twelve cents." He scratched a match against the wall—flare of sulphur spume and smoke. "At least," Eye let out a rising cloud of smoke, "there's all kinds of work here pays in silver, so I reckon we don't have to starve."

War had driven wages, and prices, sky-high. A day's wages for any bend, lift, and tote job was eight to ten dollars paid in silver. A lighterman made forty dollars silver a day. Knobby felt a strong aversion to laboring for someone else—even for silver—because it was too much like being a slave again, but for these kingly wages he'd do it with a smile.

There were constant rumors that Federal forces were about to seize the Texas side of the river to stop the carters who traded through Matamoros and Bagdad, or that Mexico's President Juárez had been assassinated or had fled, the French army always rumored to be about to take the town and the port of Bagdad. But weeks and months passed with no threat to the cotton trade. The ferry between Brownsville and Matamoros never rested. Boys too impatient or poor to wait for the ferry swam bales of cotton across the river.

After weeks in the almost silent desert and the chaparral, Knobby was amazed by how loud Matamoros was—horses' hooves clanged, guitars strummed and singers moaned, laughter rose and fell, babies bawled and women shrieked, doors and shutters squeaked and slammed, and gunshots rang out more often than they had on the Texas side where there was a war going on. Tethered to their burdens by ropes, shirtless *barrileros* pulled heavy wooden kegs of water that left ruts in the unpaved streets. Infrequent rains turned the streets into rivers of mud. On liberty from ships at anchor in the Gulf thirty miles away, British, French, Dutch, and Russian seamen loitered. Mexican soldiers smoked cigarillos on street corners. Men rumored to be Confederate or Union, Imperialista or Juarista, agents watched one another over upraised glasses of bitters. Everyone had a proposition: peddlers and drummers had wares to show, gamblers and swindlers promised quick returns on games of chance and investment schemes. Myriad women heard the silver that jingled in Knobby's pocket. Dark-skinned and light, dark-haired and fair, they opened their long arms to him and promised time would stop in their beds. A few of these women were so beautiful they took Knobby's breath, but none was so beautiful she made him forget Oralia, and—he was grateful for this—none tempted him so much, right now, as his own ripe and swollen Elizabeth.

Knobby checked on Darkie daily, spoke to her and rubbed her neck, and he often rode the mare to the river to watch the busy ferry. The twenty-fourth of September, a Thursday, the baby was born, a big, healthy boy. Elizabeth wanted to name him Samuel after Grandfather, but Knobby wanted his father's name, William, for the man who'd died before he knew him. Baby William watched everything, his slate-colored eyes grave and wise-looking.

Two days after William was born, Eye came by with a bright-striped shawl for the infant and a proposition for Knobby. He had learned about a caravan some Reb sympathizers were taking across the border that very night. One wagon was reputed to carry new repeating rifles, rifles bought with Texas cotton intended for Reb troops. The caravan had been long delayed for want of armed escorts. Short-handed still, the muleteers were going to risk a late-night move.

"Flood and the rest are ready for a fight. We won't have trouble with the likes of these freighters. I figure you and me can liberate some of them rifles. Herr Reinbach will be proud we kept them out of Confederate hands. He won't miss one crate and a few hundred rounds."

The Liberation Front stopped the caravan without firing a shot. Flood seemed downright disappointed. Eye said he and Knobby would go back to Matamoros with the wagonload of rifles and cartridges while Flood and the others got the rest of the caravan—several wagons were already halfway across the Rio Grande—turned around and back out onto the Mexican side. When they had gotten a few miles away, Eye drove the wagon close to the chaparral and he and Knobby dragged one heavy wooden crate of guns and a box of cartridges as big as a carpet bag far into the thicket and covered them over with brush. They marked the bend in the river and paced the distance to a gnarled mesquite Eye blazed with his sheath knife. Without knowing where to look, no one would discover their stash. The rest of the guns they turned over to the Matamoros government as military contraband. There was no telling where the rifles would end up, but they had a piece of paper for Herr Reinbach documenting they'd delivered them.

The next day, news came the Confederates had won a big victory twelve days earlier at Sabine Pass. In November, Yankee vessels seized two blockade runners off the mouth of the Rio Grande. Flood heard General Banks had landed thousands of Federal troops—including a regiment of Negro soldiers—on the Brazos Santiago bar of the river. Banks occupied Point Isabella and Brownsville, stopping trade there, though goods were sneaked across above Brownsville. Banks soon took Corpus Christi, and with little news of battles in the east, Knobby dared to hope the Union might be close to ending the war.

Mexican Time

By Christmas, the men of the Union Loyal Liberation Front were running out of patience and some were ready to split up the outfit. In January, Eye sent Rudolph

Hermann up to Fredericksburg to search for Reinbach. "I'll give Reinbach one more month, then I'll disband the outfit."

A little over a month later, President Lincoln lifted the blockade, allowing trade except for military goods. There was still no word from Rudolph. "I allow time passes different down here. Mañana, everyone says. We're hid from war and the calendar, it appears," Eye said. News of fighting in Mexico was easier to come by than details about back East battles in the War between the States. In May, the French army was defeated at Puebla, and Eye disbanded the Union Loyal Liberation Front. "Go where ere you will. It's adios time."

Knobby and Flood were making plenty of money secretly fording wagonloads of cotton across the Rio Grande and bringing the wagons to the Gulf on the Mexican side. Only once did riders surprise them, bursting out of the chaparral shooting at everything in sight. Behind a cotton bale, Knobby swung the Henry rifle to lead one of the riders and winged him good. Flood shot another out of his saddle. Rifle balls tore into the bales sending wads of cotton into the sky, the heavy gunfire igniting the floating cotton. Burning bits fell back onto the bales and set them afire. Flood said, "We is in a gunfight in Hades." They abandoned the wagons and escaped across the river down the Comanche Trace into Nuevo León. It was the only caravan Knobby and Flood ever lost. Knobby tried not to think about how he was transporting cotton slaves had planted and picked, and that goods he was securing were destined to aid the Confederate cause. Flood said if it wasn't them it would be some white men making the money.

All summer there were skirmishes along the Rio Grande. In late July the Confederates reoccupied Brownsville. Knobby figured the Feds would stop the contraband trade by year's end. September came Hell-hot and dry as ashes, and Knobby and Elizabeth celebrated William's first birthday. In the fall, he and Flood escorted their last train of freight, then retired and celebrated their second Christmas in Mexico.

In January, a sailor gave Flood a yellowed copy of the New Orleans *Daily Crescent* with news of the December defeat of Hood's Army of Tennessee in Nashville. Rumors about the war's end came up with the sun every day.

The end of March, Knobby heard the Confederacy was using Negro soldiers. Freighting Confederate cotton didn't seem as bad as killing Union soldiers. In

May, Knobby heard the Federals had taken Mobile. Word came that on Palm Sunday, three days before Mobile fell, Lee had surrendered the Army of Northern Virginia to Grant. Knobby was sure they could leave for Texas by summer. Then Flood brought unbelievable news: "They shot Abe Lincoln, shot the president dead."

"No," Elizabeth said. She poured them each a cup of coffee. "I'm going to remember this moment. Going to think of Abraham Lincoln every time I drink coffee from now until I die." She got out their hoarded sugar. "See can we take any of the bitter from this cup."

Confederates and their sympathizers didn't mourn Lincoln's death so much as they worried about its effect on them. *At least Lincoln understood the South. Lincoln would've been fair after the windup. What'll Johnson do?* Federal warships remained off Texas' coast and Federal troops on the border skirmished with gangs of Rebs who didn't know about or wouldn't accept the Union victory. Reb deserters fled to the Nueces Strip, an outlaw land where to be seen was to be shot at, but where a man who knew the territory could disappear.

On arrival in Galveston in late June, the Union commander issued a proclamation declaring all slaves free in Texas. According to a three-week-old *Galveston Daily News*, Confederate companies along the Rio Grande were disbanding. Knobby figured it was safe to return to Texas, but he stayed put until July when Eye returned to Matamoros. Eye had been busy. He had hauled his and Knobby's crate of rifles and plenty of cartridges up onto the Staked Plain and buried them near the Yellow Houses trading place. "Those rifles are gold in the bank, Knob, for whenever we want to make a withdrawal." And Eye had a surefire scheme to get rich rounding up cattle. "Before all the cow-handlers get back home, all the wild cattle a man can catch are running loose. They ain't worth beans now, but they will be. I'm going to New Orleans, see can I dig up some money men to pay for Texas beeves to ship east. After all this fighting, folks are almighty hungry." Eye was going to ride overland to Galveston, then take a steamer to New Orleans. Knobby offered to go with him as far as Galveston. "Suits me fine," Eye said.

"Do what you've got to do, Knobby Cotton," Elizabeth said. "But mark this, all of us are free now. We can wait for you, or not."

Gideon Jones: A Train Divided

Indians Not Indians
(July–August 1865)

The train was over three weeks out of Westport Landing when Major Benson's scout, Rafael Flores, came riding up with news.

"We've got the Platte not far ahead, señor. Mañana noon. Wallows and Indian sign here."

"Pawnee?" the major said.

"*No estoy seguro.* Maybe Ponca."

"Pretty far south for them."

Flores shrugged.

"How many?"

"*No le se.* Too many."

The major nodded and sent word down the line to have someone with a gun watch from every wagon. That night nobody except Chief Bones slept much. Gideon sat up with his Hawken. Every coyote howl sounded like a wild Indian. But when the east grew light, the train was intact.

By noon, grass that had been high as the horses' bellies barely reached their fetlocks. Low hills of sand rose out of the rank grass. Then they came to the first of several gorges and ravines Major Benson said spread out from the Platte, still an hour's ride away. As they got even closer to the river the sand was knee-deep in places. When the Platte finally appeared it was not just one river but several narrow streams spreading like tree roots. The water was as dark brown as a bay horse, and the sandy banks were yellow.

The major parlayed with Rafael Flores and a heavyset, dark-complected man called Sweet. Rumor in the train made Sweet the half-breed son of a buffalo hunter and his Osage squaw. Different talk made him a white captive raised by the Wichita. He never spoke to anybody but Flores or the major, and when he talked to them he used a mixture of Spanish and Indian words. Gideon asked Flores what language Sweet was talking, and Flores smiled and said, "Wichita, Kiowa, Comanche, *se dice de diversos modos.*" Flores' breath reminded Gideon of the foul odors of the death ward back in the Baltimore asylum.

The major and Rafael Flores hunkered down over more Indian sign.

"Man alive," the major said. He pulled his wipe from around his neck and dabbed at his face.

Flores whistled low, "*Muchisimas indios.*"

"Can I depend on you?"

"*No vale la pena.*"

All Gideon could understand was that they were talking *about* Indians. "I don't see any Indian sign," he said.

Major Benson shook his head. He talked to Gideon as if he were a child. "You don't see these bent and broken blades of grass? Look, the flattened blades point south, same direction of the horses that trod here. We find a bare spot of earth in this grass we'll find hoofprints. Most Indian ponies are unshod. Deep prints were made in mud or when a horse was carrying a heavy load—buffalo meat, hides, more than one rider. New prints are empty, older prints hold more windblown dirt. A good tracker can blow dirt from completely hidden tracks and figure, depending on the wind and what kind of ground it is—grassy, sandy, rocky—how long it's taken to cover them."

Gideon nodded. All he saw was grass. None of it looked more bent to him than the rest. All he heard were the major's fears and words that sounded most like birds screeching and dogs barking. The major and Flores agreed a small Pawnee party had passed a few days ago, maybe a renegade band off the reservation, but more likely hunting the buffalo that had recently left their shapes in the mud. The immigrant trail followed the river west, but Major Benson decided to water up, then pull the train south several miles before continuing west, parallel to but out of sight of the river.

Gideon helped Joe and Mr. Speer get their water barrels to the river's edge. Mr. Speer had to walk eight to ten feet into the river, about half-a-mile wide here, to be in deep enough water to hold a barrel under to fill it.

"Knee-high," Speer said. "I wager it's not much deeper all the way across."

Gideon waved away mosquitoes that hung over the edge of the water. He slapped a deerfly on the side of his face and his ear rang and went hot. There was blood on his hand, the black smear of a fly big as his thumbnail. He cupped water from the river and washed his ear and neck. The water was gritty with sand.

Back at the Speer wagon, he filled a dipper from the barrel, killing time, hoping Dorsey would climb from inside their wagon. He held the water in the sun and watched sand settle on the bottom of the dipper. The water was the color of coffee and almost as warm when he sipped. Grit settled on the back of his tongue and between his teeth. He rinsed and spat, chewed the sand down.

After two days they had seen no more Indian sign, and the major headed the train back northwest to follow closer to the river. Gideon had about given up on seeing Indians. Then they topped a hill, and Major Benson gave the word to halt the wagons. Everyone got quiet except Mary Thurston's infant son, James, who cried nearly as constant as the wind. Mary set the brake and stepped back into her wagon with baby James, and he stopped wailing. The prairie wind hummed in the grass and made the wagon covers moan. Horses and oxen shifted in leather, pulled against metal hooks and buckles, against wooden rods and shafts, a constant keening song.

Gideon dismounted his wagon and walked to the crest of the hill where the major and several men crouched. A mile or more down the hillside, two naked dark-skinned men struggled to push a freighter's wagon out of a muddy depression a good two or three hundred feet wide. Major Benson had told everyone to watch for these huge buffalo wallows as a source of water. The two men stuck in the mud were not good teamsters. One of their horses was lunging, jerking hopelessly against the whip and the weight of the mired wagon. Another horse was down in the mud, unmoving, impeding any progress they might've made.

The major took a spyglass from his saddlebags and extended the brass tube, studied the men below. "Arapaho." He pushed the telescope into itself and pointed with the tube as he ordered several men, Gideon included, to saddle up to join the mounted guard in an attack.

"This far east?" Mr. Speer whistled softly, then went on, "Wouldn't Arapaho have spotted us by now?"

Major Benson's mouth tightened and his lips pouched up like he was pulling their drawstring with his tongue.

Speer said, "I've heard tell Indians along the Platte are Pawnees—reservation Indians. For all we know, we're on reservation land. And just two of them. How does it benefit us to stir up trouble? I say we go on by, quiet-like."

Major Benson looked at Mr. Speer as if he were a pitiful case, a boy playing at a man's chore. The major looked to Flores, who was over by the Speer wagon, leaned against the right front wheel with a silly smile on his face. Flores stepped to the back of the wagon where Mrs. Speer stood with her arm around Dorsey's shoulders. The man reached out and lifted Dorsey's waist-long black hair, held it up in the sunlight, and Gideon's chest went hot. His hands made fists of their own accord.

"Señor Speer," Flores said, loud enough for all to hear, "*eso se dice los indios* take the whole scalp with one slice. Once they have this pretty hair, they'll take the rest of her *más despacio.*"

Major Benson spoke in an unemotional, matter-of-fact way. "Most of you fellers got women and children. These Arapaho are savage as a meat-ax. You just put your mind on the worst things possible a red-skinned devil can do to your woman. Start with the sound of her calico being tore completely off and go on from the sight of her bōdy laid out nekkid in prairie muck. Picture a stinking, nekkid heathen stoked up meaner and hotter than his usual animal hungers." He smiled grimly.

The men stared at their boots, jaws set, eyes fixed straight ahead. Colonel Powell-Hughes had explained to Gideon that when they were confronted by Indians—Negroes, too—white men would first profess fear for the sanctity of their women. Gideon wondered if such men were afraid that their women had a natural human longing for the darker-skinned man, some primal yearning for what is mysterious or unknown that goes back to the story of forbidden fruit in the Garden. *Mostly,* Gideon thought, *these white men seek excuses for their uncertainty about anything unfamiliar and a reason to justify their mean spirits.*

"You picture what some nekkid buck is readying to do to your wives and daughters?" the major asked. The smile remained on his face until the men began to mount up. "Watch your rear. Where there's two redskins in sight, there's more hid."

Speer refused to ride against the Indians or to let the boy, Joe, ride with the rest of the men. Gideon wondered on which side of this account Dorsey would come down, and, in spite of himself, he hoped she saw him as brave and dashing in the attack he was about to join. When every rifle was powdered, primed, and cocked they charged off down the hill stirring up a world of dust. Gideon couldn't see the men in front of him. He was on a big, swaybacked plow horse off someone's farm, and she was not happy about galloping down this hill, probably the first time she'd run in years. His innards sloshed up and down, and his Hawken bounced so it was all he could do to keep from dropping it. He managed to hold on mainly out of fear Dorsey might see him let it slip. The reins of the horse slapped so loud against the rifle barrel, he thought his gun might be firing. Then louder reports sounded close, and his ears rang. With a sudden sound of hooves sucking mud, he pitched forward and landed on his back. The dust vanished, and he looked up at clear sky, brightness all air, so much air. Yet no air came into his yearning mouth, and his empty chest went cold. He wondered why he didn't feel the puncture of the arrow or the spear or whatever the Arapaho had used to kill him.

"*Qué burro eres*," said Flores from his horse high above Gideon. Then Flores was off his horse. His boot heel kicked hard into Gideon's stomach, and breath knifed into him. He sucked air so hard he got a grasshopper in his mouth. Unwounded, he'd nearly died of fright. Unfired, his rifle barrel was plugged with mud and grass. Beside him was what he first took to be a gray boulder but turned out to be a big gray American mule lying on its side still harnessed to the stuck wagon. Another mule sat like a huge dog, its rear in the mud up to its croup, its front legs locked. The sitting mule trembled, and blood flowed from a bullet hole in its neck down its shoulder and ribs to pool at its flank and from there spread a widening red stain over the mud. For longer than Gideon would have thought possible, more blood than he would have thought possible spilled from the animal's wound and covered the ground. The mule trembled, and its eyes widened, but still it made no sound. Then there came a deep rattling in its throat, the front legs crumpled, and the heavy neck and head collapsed into the mud beside its harness mate. Then Gideon saw the dead Indians—not Indians at all, but two Negroes naked as the day they were born. Their dark bodies lay beside the dead mules misidentified by the major as Indian horses.

The major pointed out blue shackle scars on the ankles and wrists of the dead men. "Runaways. Most as dangerous as Indians." He refused to halt the train to bury the bodies. "Savages and snowfall ain't gonna hold off for us to bury niggers."

Cotton trousers and feedsack tops lay folded beneath the Negroes' wagon seat. They must have figured to spare their poor clothes the mud, or the summer heat, or the joy of freedom—slaves no more, just two men beneath miles of sky, no wall or chain in sight—made them strip, though Major Benson said their nakedness was "nigger perversion."

Leaving the Train

Mr. Speer came walking slowly down the hill. Many of the women, including Dorsey, followed, craning their necks. From the trouser pocket of one of the Negroes Mr. Speer pulled a folded paper. Sunlight flared off Speer's red hair and gathered in his hands, and where the paper caught the sun, the sheet burnished gold. "Freedmen," he read out loud. He shook his head. Joe and Dorsey looked as surprised as the rest of the settlers. Gideon guessed they were surprised Speer was right and the major wrong.

"To a nigger that just means freed from labor," the major said. "I did my duty to the Union in Vicksburg, but not for the abolitionists and not for those black devils. Freed niggers slip away to suck on the teats of working whites. A nigger on the loose can't look after himself. He's a nuisance and a troublemaker prone to getting corned on cheap whisky. A nigger gets a brick in his hat, he's bound to wake snakes. Least as bad as a Indian. We likely saved some white man from thievery."

Dorsey's body shivered as if she had a chill. Speer told Major Benson he was taking his wagon out of the train.

"Those as want," Speer's voice rose, a kind of bird trill, "are welcomed to come along with us." And in spite of his singsong, the man seemed to Gideon to have grown taller and more rawboned since the first time he'd looked him over.

Major Benson said it suited him fine if ever farmer's son of them went out with Speer. The major said he'd watch for their scalps in Indian camps, look for their bodies burned black in the desert, or frozen blue in the Rockies. "Just you remember, there's no soldier boys out here to save your hides." The major's voice was so low some words got blown off in the prairie breeze. "Me and my men are all that stand between you and numberless tribes of savages. You want to follow this coot you're just crazy, crazy as a loon. When some red buck slices your scalp and peels off your skin down to the bottoms of your feet and ties your skint flesh out over a red ant hill, when he hacks off your privates and stuffs them in your mouth to muffle your screaming, when he murders your babies and rapes your wife while you lie there gagging on your bloody parts, you remember me. I want to be the last sad memory you have."

"*Hee, hee, hee.*" Flores' squeaking laugh stopped when the major flashed him a glare.

Then the major said that nobody who left got a two-cent piece back of what he'd paid. This caused an audible stir among the settlers. "Let's vamoose," the major said, and he and his men mounted up. They wheeled their horses around, backs to the wagons, and rode on, following the Platte.

Men whose guns were still warm stood over the bodies without looking at them. One and two at a time, they all but three climbed their wagons and followed in Joshua Benson's wake.

Not counting the Negroes' mud-stuck freighter, three wagons remained: Speer's, Hiram Thurston's, and Gideon's. Gideon didn't reckon he stayed behind because he loved Negroes especially, though he had a warm memory of the two black men who had delivered him from the charnel house of the Baltimore asylum. Back in Cumberland, Colonel Powell-Hughes and Win Shu had showed him how his wisest wager might be on a Scotsman or even a Chinaman. Staring down at the ebony and ruined bodies of two let-go slaves, he thought on how one day his best wager might be a Negro, or even someone who seemed as much a fool as Mr. Speer. Not that staying behind necessarily meant he was throwing in with Speer. Gideon surely did not stay because he was fearless of Indians. He guessed he stayed most because he didn't want to ride away, out of sight of Dorsey, and because he didn't trust Major Benson in the least. Even with his spyglass Benson had taken the Negroes for Indians, making him no wiser a guide than Gideon might be. Or the major had seen a way to kill two men for being colored. For such meanness Gideon counted it as dangerous to follow the major as to follow no one at all. Speer's persuasive tongue would not be any comfort against Indian war cries. Maybe Indians, hoping for greater loot, would come down on Major Benson's larger train—he now had the wagons of five families plus his two supply wagons—before they'd bother with this puny outfit of just three mutinous wagons. Of course, Indians might attack just three wagons when they would let a longer and better-armed train pass. Fact was, Gideon had never liked being preached at and threatened. Fact was, he liked his oxen and mute Chief Bones a world better than he liked Major Joshua Benson and his ilk, or Mr. Speer, either. But Speer's stepdaughter, Dorsey, was more than a temptation.

Buries Two Negroes

Gideon asked the ladies what they had in their wagons to serve for a shroud, and they shook their heads. Then Dorsey pulled from a trunk a blue-and-yellow quilt.

"Dorsey, that was the last quilt your grandmother pieced. Annie sent it from Pennsylvania, and I finished quilting it the week my mother died."

"Mama, you gave it to me."

Mrs. Speer nodded, but her face still said no. Gideon took the quilt from Dorsey, their fingers almost touching on a scrap of blue gingham cut and sewn into the shape of a star. The quilt's pattern was rows of blue stars separated by yellow stripes. When he asked did anyone have any lilac or rosewater, Mrs. Speer looked hurt enough to cry but went resolutely to the trunk and brought out a vial of amber oil that smelled to Gideon as sweet as any St. Louis fancylady. Then she left him to complete his ablutions alone, leading Dorsey away to the shade of the Thurston wagon where Mary Thurston rested on the ground beside little Lucy, who rocked her baby brother in her little arms. The Thurstons' spotted fice was stretched out asleep with his muzzle resting on Lucy's thigh.

Gideon washed the corpses in muddy water seeped up around their wagon wheel. He found five bullet holes in the chest and belly of one body that had also suffered the loss of an ear shot off. As near as Gideon could tell, the other had nine craters from bullets. He wondered how many had been fired by settlers, how many by Benson's men. With the thick brown mud, which was not far from the color of the darker man's skin, he covered wounds as well as he could. He'd had the idea to try candle wax for patching wounds, but his few beeswax candles had been costly and were honey-colored. He had read in his volume of the *Americana*, under **WAX FIGURES**, about Greek *puppet-makers, artists who worked chiefly in wax,* about the use of wax figures in sorcery, and about how life-sized wax figures *overstep the proper limit of the fine arts.* Said the *Encyclopaedia: They attempt to imitate life too closely. In the genuine work of art there is an immortal life, in idea, which speaks to our souls without attempting to deceive our senses. The wax figure is a petrified picture of our earthly part.* He read that vegetable productions, imitated in wax by more recent artists, *do not produce the same unpleasant emotions as wax images of men and animals, because they have, by nature, a more stationary character.*

It appeared to Gideon the undertaker shared some of the concerns of the artist, freed of the dictum that immortal life be caught—the undertaker's attempt being only to (briefly) deceive the senses, to petrify earthly parts for one last likeness.

He searched without success for the missing ear. In spite of the expense, had he the time he might have melted down one of his candles and tried to sculpt a more representative imitation of the missing anatomical part. Yet he knew the heat reasoned against candle wax. Such an ear would soon melt. *Man, you are mud to mud,* he thought, and he fashioned a counterfeit ear that could not have deceived the most elementary sound into entering there, but baked in the heat this brown ear should last like ancient crockery.

When he had done all he could to restore the look of life to the corpses, Gideon called Joe from where he stood with Mr. Speer and Hiram talking and digging shapes in the mud with sticks. Joe helped Gideon lift the naked bodies and lay them out on the clean quilt. He wrapped a length of leather up under one man's chin to force his gaping mouth closed and tied it tight in the furry Negro hair. Then he folded up the bodies in the one quilt, weighted their eyes with his own four silver dollars, and sprinkled Mrs. Speer's precious scent over the bright shroud. Though wrongly colored and numbered, the stars and stripes of the quilt reminded him of the nation's flag and the recent war to free men such as these unfortunates.

"No need for this heavy freight wagon to go wasting," Speer said. "What say you, Hiram?"

Hiram Thurston put a stay-chain through the loop at the end of the Negroes' wagon tongue. Mary Thurston unhitched their team, and Hiram attached the chain to his doubletree with a clevis. Mary clucked, the spotted dog barked, and Mary whistled the team off with the Negro freighter jouncing right out behind.

Gideon was surprised when Mr. Speer squatted by the bodies and tucked the freedom papers inside the quilt. Gideon read three names: *William Smith* on one paper, *Joshua* and *Amelia Jones* on the other. What had happened to Amelia? Which of the dead men was William, which Joshua?

Speer got up and without looking at Gideon said, "We best commence with the burying."

Gideon tied together broken lengths of harness off the dead mules and used the strap to truss the men tight in the quilt. He toted the bodies in the same wagon that had carried them to the prairie where they died, moving down to the far end of the buffalo wallow, far as he could get from the dead mules while remaining in the soft mud where easier digging could go deeper. Hiram and Joe started digging one wide hole. By the time they were knee-deep Hiram stopped, but Joe kept digging, so Gideon got in the grave and helped and, though the last shovels were not half full of the unyielding earth, they managed a hole more than waist deep. They stopped to rest and wipe sweat from their faces, then Joe helped Gideon lay the weighty bundle alongside the ditch.

Dorsey came and stood close. "You could bury your Indian skeleton, too. The grave looks wide enough for three."

Gideon wasn't ready to part with Chief Bones. "I've got to bury him in his home soil," he said. Dorsey nodded. But her eyes lingered on Gideon, and he wondered if she appraised him looney. He had told her he had spent time in a Baltimore asylum—maybe she took him for an escaped patient.

The Speers, the Thurstons, and Gideon stood in a mud wallow on the prairie and bowed their heads. Hiram Thurston read the part from Galatians about the bondmaid and the freewoman, ending with these two verses:

So then, Brethren, we are not children of the bondwoman, but of the free. Stand fast therefore in the liberty wherewith Christ hath made us free, and be not entangled again with the yoke of bondage.

Hiram said the words about dust to dust, and Joe and Gideon slid the bodies into the grave.

The wind slacked up for a moment, just as Mary Thurston lifted her face and sang in a voice as clear and as acute as the blue, cloudless sky so immense above them:

On Jor-dan's storm-y banks I stand,
And cast a wish-ful eye
To Ca-naan's fair and hap-py land,
Where my pos-ses-sions lie.

As she sang, her infant son cradled in her arms moved his small arms and hands as if he were directing a choir of angels singing silently above the muddy graves. Lucy joined her mother with the beginning of the second stanza, and then Dorsey started in with them. Gideon put his voice next to Dorsey's, Mrs. Speer and Hiram joined in, and, finally Mr. Speer, who sang with the voice of a young girl and, after Dorsey, was the sweetest singer of them all.

Hiram dropped his chin to his chest, and they all bowed their heads again. Gideon looked down at the blue stars of the quilt Dorsey's grandmother pieced and thought how these men were getting a kind of hero's burying, wrapped in stars and stripes, and thought how now they were freedmen. Then he peeked at Dorsey, and her eyes were on him. He hoped no one else saw the smile break across his face, though it died down some when Dorsey showed not a trace of gladness in return and he closed his eyes. After a spell Hiram hadn't said anything so Gideon looked up to see if they were still praying. Dorsey was looking up, too, and the two of them exchanged what he felt sure was a look of understanding, a look to acknowledge the forces beyond their control that had separated them from the protection of the larger wagon train. Hiram Thurston never prayed a word out loud, but after a while he lifted his head and the funeral was over, though no one commenced to shovel the dirt back. Mr. Speer, Hiram, and Joe went to the Thurston water keg and passed the dipper around. Hiram's dog begged for a drink, and when Hiram thought no one was looking he held the dipper down and let the dog lap from it.

Gideon followed Mrs. Speer and Dorsey and little Lucy and Mary Thurston carrying baby James, all of them a distance behind the men.

"Ma'am?" Gideon said, and they waited for him. When he caught up to them, Mrs. Speer turned to see what it was he had to say, and he had no idea. He just wanted a reason to stand close to Dorsey. "Ma'am, thank you for the sweet scent and for the burying-quilt."

Mrs. Speer looked at him and then looked at her daughter. He was so sure she knew how badly he wanted to get close to Dorsey he half expected her to smile or pat them both on the arm, but instead she reached up under the wagon seat and got a canvas pouch and reached in and gave him a stack of corn dodgers baked the evening before. "Here. We was taught to recompense the undertaker."

The title sounded natural enough.

Hiram Thurston Shot

There was not much daylight left. Mr. Speer and Hiram wanted to put some distance between their wagons and this killing ground. Speer thought Indians might have heard shooting or might even be watching them from somewhere in the grass. They none of them wanted to make camp in a fresh-made cemetery. Hiram and Joe would stay behind long enough to get the graves filled and packed down. They'd have put up crosses if they'd had tree limbs, markers if they'd had stones, maybe spelled out their names, Jones and Smith. But they didn't even have rocks to pile on the graves against wolves and coyotes. When Hiram and Joe finished, they would hitch the mustang Mr. Speer had bought from the Indian trader, Horse Arse, to the Negroes' freight wagon and follow the tracks until they overtook the three wagons. Mr. Speer wanted to go farther south, away from the train and Major Benson's men.

"Think on this, boys—we can drop down south and then west, keep the major between us and the river. If there are any hostile Indians, the major's train will draw them out, and we'll have a better chance."

"After a spell," Hiram said, "we can outpace the train, us with just three wagons. Angle northwest and be lying up at Fort Laramie when the major gets there. That'd be something."

"Need be, we can keep south for the Santa Fe Trail," Speer said.

So they turned south, staying down in a long crease the hollow stretched into. Speer took the lead on Joe's bay mare. Laura Etta drove their wagon, Dorsey lovely on the seat beside her. Mary Thurston drove the Thurston wagon, Lucy sleeping with baby James under the cover. Hiram's fice trotted along, keeping in the wagon's shade, and their milk cow was towed along behind. Gideon brought up the rear, his Hawken at the ready on the board seat beside him.

Out of earshot of the shovels' scrape, he looked back. One dark shovel dipped down and swung up, dipped down and swung up, a needle darning up a rent in the fabric of the prairie.

At least three hours passed—Gideon guessed them five or six miles south of the grave—before Joe and Hiram overtook them. Something was wrong. They rode double, bareback, with no outfit but a rope hackamore.

"Goddamn his soul," Joe said.

They pulled up the wagons and waited for Joe and Hiram to dismount.

"Goddamn his soul," Joe said again.

"What happened, Joe?" Dorsey's voice, in sweet contrast to her brother's fury, calmed him some. He shook his head, then went on in a voice so flat as to be more threatening than his earlier shouts.

"We got the grave mounded good and were about to hitch up the wagon when Flores and the fat half-Indian one they call Sweet rode up. They were purple with blood gore from their hands to their shoulders. The major done sent them back to butcher those dead mules. They took the Negro wagon. Said they had to cart mule steaks."

"Joe told them we had claim to the freighter," Hiram said. "Rafael Flores shot my foot."

A chunk was ripped out of the side of Hiram's leather brogan. Gideon didn't see any blood. Mary Thurston set the wagon brake and went to tend her husband's foot. Hiram sat on the ground and kept talking while Mary pulled off his boot. The sock was torn and smeared with blood, and his foot was going blue.

"Gideon?" Mary said. She held her husband's foot while Gideon cut away the sock with his knife. Out on the frontier, the undertaker and the doctor carried a common burden.

"Said they felt generous, so they let us keep our horse," Hiram said.

"Unless," Joe said, "we wanted to argue the point."

"Joe saw the hackamore in the Negro wagon and slipped it out while they weren't looking." Hiram's teeth clenched as Gideon washed his wound.

"It isn't bad," Mary said. "Just scraped off the skin, bruised the flesh." She smiled and said, "See, it's not bad. It's not real bad." Hiram patted her back. She put her head in his lap, and her body shook with crying and made his foot jiggle so that Gideon had to rewrap his bandage. The spotted dog came and poked his nose against Mary's neck and whined, poked and whined.

Tired and discouraged, they made early camp in a little bowl in the land offering some protection from the wind and, they hoped, from Indian eyes. Hiram said he was more worried about Benson and his men than Indians, but it seemed unlikely the major would go to the trouble of coming after them. So that they could catch them easily, Joe hobbled the animals. He slapped his leg and whistled for Hiram's dog. The little fice lifted his ears, then his head, looked at Joe, then put his head back down. Joe shook his head, and he and Gideon laughed at the lazy mongrel. Joe and Gideon walked up on the far side of the bowl, and there was a narrow sluice of water not fifty yards away. And where the sluice ended was something they had not seen for days. Trees. Small box elders and broom willows grew where the water stopped.

"Trees." Gideon felt a fool for naming what was right there before their eyes. It was as if he'd looked up and said, "Sky." But Joe didn't seem to think him foolish. He nodded. "Wonder why my oxen didn't smell the water?" Gideon asked.

"We come upwind of it," Joe said. "And all the animals are well watered right now."

"Want a closer look?" Gideon asked.

"In the morning. Right now all I want is to eat and sleep."

Gideon had his outfit stopped at a spot close enough to the Speer wagon he could espy Dorsey but not so close Mr. or Mrs. Speer would wonder what he was up to. He didn't know what he was up to, if anything, but he knew he wanted to be as close to Dorsey as he could manage, especially if they were to be attacked by the Pawnee. He had seen Pawnees back at Fort Leavenworth, where they were army scouts, and he didn't know enough about Indians to understand how there would be friendly Pawnees at Fort Leavenworth and hostile Pawnees out here. He had started to ask Major Benson, but the tight look he kept on his face had stopped Gideon cold.

Solaced by Love

All afternoon the wind had played with Gideon's hatbrim and shirt collar, and after they turned south from the river the late afternoon sun had slanted onto his right ear and the side of his neck not previously exposed. He was burned there, and every time he turned his head to catch sight of Dorsey his skin stung. The killing of the two Negroes, fear of Indians, and the long day's journey had worn him out. Too tired to cook, he ate some cold beans and the last few dried apples he had from Westport Landing. What he would have given for a taste of pie or cake.

He wondered if the Pawnees made things sweet to eat, and he had just about dozed off sitting up with a piece of unchewed apple between his jaws when Dorsey drew near, moving like a sleepwalker. Her eyes were closed, and she was smiling. The setting sun set her face aglow, and for a moment he turned his face away. As he turned back, Dorsey's eyelids — matched to his motion as one gear to another in a machine — lifted. For one instant their eyes shared perception. Dorsey saw Gideon and Gideon saw Dorsey and Dorsey saw Gideon see Dorsey and Gideon saw Dorsey see Gideon and, enchantment, they saw the same sight. He knew he would have that moment for years of moments yet to come, and he both treasured and pondered this touching he so keenly felt even though it was not physical. He could see that Dorsey had momentarily divested herself of the world, and that his was the first face she had ever seen, Adam to her, just as she was Eve before him. That moment had been set aside in time to wait patiently for the two of them. He recalled Win Shu's words: "We live our lives in order to know why it is we live." "Gideon, I brought you something for your sweet tooth."

As much as he had been craving a sweet taste, the sound of his name in Dorsey's voice brought Gideon more pleasure than any cake or pie. She handed him a honey hoecake wrapped in a handkerchief, and then she laughed. Her laughter was catching, and he laughed, too, and then she laughed back like an echo. They stopped laughing and just stood and smiled. Her eyes were shining, and she gave his hand a good squeeze, turned and ran through broom willow, through the shadow of a dead box elder and out into the sunset. Her dark hair lifted from its own darker blue shadow against the back of her dress, lifting and falling as she rose and dipped, running through the grass.

"Left Ox, have you ever seen a doe run? Me neither, not yet, but I know what it looks like. Right Ox, ever watch a skipping stone hop across a lake? River rapids where the water skips over the rock? That's the kind of heel and toe I'm chasing." Dorsey's hoecake was sweeter on Gideon's tongue than any candy of the confectioner's art.

Abandoned Treasures

The next day was uneventful, and the day after. Mary Thurston seemed some affected by Hiram's being shot, though his foot was healing fine and didn't slow him any. She stared off at the sea of grass and had to be spoken to two or even three times before she heard. Even when her baby wailed she seemed not to hear and had to have him placed in her arms to suck. Hiram drove the wagon and Dorsey rode with them and looked after Lucy and the baby.

The third day after burying the Negroes they were looking for a place to noon when Joe pointed to something sticking up out of the grass. It looked for all the world like a privy, but Gideon kept his hand on the stock of his Hawken all the same. When they got close Hiram stopped his wagon, and without a word Mary Thurston climbed down and went up to what Gideon now saw was a highboy made of fine dark wood—cherry or mahogany. Brass hoop drawer pulls made bright smiles in the sun, and Mrs. Thurston grabbed them two by two, opening every drawer from the top down. She lifted a white square, and the wind unfolded a long gown she held by the sleeves as it jerked in the air. She let go, and the gown drifted away, flattening against the neck of Mr. Speer's bay, which reared and pitched until the cloth flew off. Gideon watched it almost out of sight—small and frenzied as a moth—but turned away before it disappeared. Mary Thurston bent to the opened drawers and tossed linens and petticoats and camisoles into the air, and the prairie wind breathed life into them, puffed out chests and opened arms and they danced over the grass. A white shift rose, unfolded, and raced into Dorsey's arms. Jealous, Gideon took note of that shift as if it were some rival suitor.

"Look at this needlework," Mrs. Speer said. "I saw roses like these once on a christening dress a seamstress in Croydon was making for the wife of the man who owned the bank."

"Why would a banker," Mr. Speer asked, "take a wagon trail west?"

No one had an answer, but they were all imagining some story to accommodate the odd fact of a highboy and other heirlooms in the high grass. Why had such precious possessions been discarded so far along the trail? And how long ago? Gideon's guess was attacking Indians had made the need for a lighter, faster wagon.

Dorsey held the shift up against her chambray dress, and the constant wind smoothed it over the swell of her bosom and pressed it against her thighs. She smiled at Gideon.

"Pretty," he said.

"Better for me to have it than let the wind blow it all the way to the Great Desert, but finding it makes me sad, not glad."

A short distance beyond the highboy they found a long, empty pine blanket chest Gideon knew must've put the others, same as him, in mind of a coffin. They also found, hidden in the grass, a tall-case clock lying on its back. The clock was like the one he had always imagined striking the hour in "Hickory Dickory Dock."

Mr. Speer pulled the clock upright in the grass. "Can't have been here long. It's hardly dusty."

"She laid it in the grass to protect it," Mrs. Speer said.

A mother-of-pearl moon dial was displayed above an ivory face plate that had a second-hand dial above the center, from which black minute and hour hands extended, and, below center, a calendar. The time had stopped at three o'clock, and the calendar on the twenty-fifth of July. Had it stopped at three in the morning or three in the afternoon—moonlight or hot sun? Had someone stopped it so for some reason? Was July twenty-fifth the birthday of a child, a husband, a wife? Was this a grave marker that bore the day and the hour of death?

Gideon had read a long entry for **WATCH AND CLOCK MAKING** in his *Encylopaedia Americana,* so he knew something about it.

"You know how to make it go?" Hiram asked.

"I think so." Gideon steadied the clock, making sure the base was firm and as level as he could get it. He turned the key, opened the hood door, and fitted the same key into the wind hole. "It's already been wound. What day is it?"

Dorsey went into their wagon and got Mr. Spcer's hand-drawn calendar. He still sat the bay, and he walked the horse over and took the sheet of days and months. "First of August." There was surprise in his voice. They all looked at one another. They'd let a new month slip up on them. "A Tuesday."

Gideon set the clock calendar.

"Does any one of us have a working watch or clock?" He was not surprised no one said a word. In the wilderness, who wants to count the hours? Their only calendar was kept out of sight in the Speer wagon. The sun was directly overhead, so he turned the clock's hands forward from three to four to five to six to seven, round and round the hours quickly passing, eight to nine to ten to eleven and stopped just before twelve. "If this was stopped and wound when it was hidden in the grass, then someone left it here just a week ago." He opened the trunk door, straightened the chains and weights, and set the bob swinging on the pendulum rod. He removed his spectacles and stepped back from the clock to appreciate its complete character. Their little group was quiet. Near noon, gathered on the bare face of the planet, they gave their ears to the grandfather clock's voice of time. Grandfather's throat was dry and husky, breathing the minutes away. A second curved back into itself, a whirring pause, Grandfather clearing his throat, then he sang time with voices from his youth, crying twelve memories. Hiram's dog waited till Grandfather was through, then barked once—thirteen o'clock on the prairie. Hiram remarked he'd like to be here after nightfall to hear what wolves and coyotes answered to the yowling of time. Then they all climbed back on their horses and wagon seats and simply continued.

Gideon looked back over his shoulder at Grandfather, looming, and, farther behind, scattered patches of snow the blouses and camisoles had become to remind him of the mountain snow they had to beat. A mile or more and Grandfather was a dark monolith, marking where they had been. For all Gideon knew, the clock might stand there forever. He heard the mechanical voice call out one last lonely time, but as he strained to hear it again there was only the creak of axletrees and the pop of canvas in the gusting breeze.

A Heartbreaking Discovery

The attack on the two Negro freighters, their separation from the train, the run-in with the major's men over the freight wagon, the discovery of the discarded goods (especially the grandfather clock) had, in a few eventful days, interrupted the tedium of weeks of slow travel—eight to fifteen miles a day depending upon the temperament of oxen, mules, and horses, depending on the condition of wagons, depending on the availability of drinking water, depending on fords to make across streams and rivers, depending on signs and rumors of Indians, depending on weather—wind, rain, hail, lightning, mud, drouth, and duststorms. And there were still more surprises the prairie had to offer. Just two days after finding the grandfather clock, they had a disturbing encounter, especially so for Dorsey.

Gideon had taken the lead that morning, as much for novelty as any other reason. Mary Thurston had given him a warm cup of fresh milk from their cow, and he was feeling uplifted, leading the way and drinking the milk. They entered that morning a territory much the same as all the miles they had already traversed, save in the grass, shorter and of less luxuriant growth. There were wide areas of almost no grass at all, and in these places the squat, tough ears of prickly pear cactus spread out in growths thirty and forty feet across. These plants were made of bristly light green joints, round and flat, growing off of one another somewhat as the links of a chain give off other links. The earlike joints bore the little pears that gave the plant its name. The cactus made Gideon fear they'd veered too far south into the desert. Back in Kansastown, a bakery lady had told Gideon how the pears ripened a deep purplish-red in late summer. She said the red fruit held a sweetly

Chapter XX

tart pulp and once you cut away the spikes they were as tasty as any fig pie. Indians were said to remove the pear's long spikes for use as needles and then to slice and boil the meaty green flesh to eat. Major Benson said Indians sucked the juice to stave off thirst. Gideon studied one cactus ear heavy-laden with fruit, the ovoid pears still as green as the flat, round joints. He borrowed Hiram's shovel and cut off a green pear and laid it in his wagonbed hoping it might ripen there.

The spread of cacti ended in a sandy and barren flat, and Gideon wondered if they were entering the great American desert. His eyes were on this bare sand where he saw, of a sudden, as if they were formed even as he looked, deep wagon ruts and all about the wagon tracks the clear "U"s of horses' hooves and prints of bare human feet. Unlike the Indian sign Major Benson and his scouts had found a week earlier, no expert was needed to name these clear prints. Hair stood up on the back of Gideon's neck, and he recalled the instant Robinson Crusoe looked down and saw the footprint in the sand that turned out to be—he couldn't remember which—the print of his soon-to-be companion and benefactor, the one he called Friday, or of the savage cannibals who would serve him up in a broth. Gideon halted his team and called for Mr. Speer, who was driving while Mrs. Speer rested in back of their wagon. Speer got down and Joe dismounted the bay. They waited for Hiram, who was in the rear, then the three of them approached Gideon's wagon.

"Indians?" Joe asked.

"I thought Indians wore moccasins," Hiram said. He was staring down at the prints in the sand.

"These hoofprints are from a shod horse. Or horses. Indian ponies don't wear shoes," Mr. Speer said. "Out here," he walked several steps away, "where the sand is thinner and the ground harder, the prints cross over one another."

Gideon got down close to the ground, and made out the nail marks of the shoe in some of the hoofprints. Either the breeze had avoided this place or these tracks were too recent to have been blown away. The hoofprints were different sizes. The human footprints were all the same pair of feet and they circled the wagon tracks as if someone had walked around in confusion.

"At least two horses, but only one wagon," Joe said. He had a good eye.

They followed the wagon tracks for several miles. The tracks stopped where there were more of the bare footprints. And several shapes of shoes and boots.

"Look," said Lucy.

About twenty yards away from the tracks was an area, maybe ten feet across, where the grass had been cut close, the dead cuttings brushed up into a brown ring. Inside the ring was a grave, dirt mounded a good foot and a half high. And there was a marker at the end of the mound.

Everyone got down, even Mrs. Speer, whose face was as white and dry-looking as their wagon covers. They all stared at the strange-looking graveyard, toward which they walked wordlessly. The wooden marker was a wide plank, a bottom panel or seat board from a farmer's wagon. Gideon fitted his spectacles onto his sweat-slick nose and leaned close to read the marks on the wood. Carved completely through the board so the sun shone through were the letters:

BINGA

and beneath the carved-out name was this inscription, charcoaled in smaller print:

Duerfeldt
1851–1865
Des Morgens Schlangenbiss
Macht abends dir
Dieses kleinen Hugels dunkler Schatten

"Can this be my Binga?" Dorsey asked. Her cheeks were wet with tears. Mrs. Speer put her arms around her daughter. "Mama can this be Binga?"

Gideon refused to see in this encounter any sign or ill omen. It was coincidence, purely, and maybe not so hard to fathom—finding a grave not a stranger's in a land so far and wide—when you accounted how there were only two main trails west and add that this soon after the war so few settlers had made the trek.

Dorsey looked to Gideon then put her face on her mother's bosom. As much as Gideon ached for Dorsey's sadness, he ached more to own the chest against which she sobbed, for his arms and not her mother's to be the ones enveloping and comforting Dorsey.

A quart jar, the kind used in canning, was half-buried in the dirt before the marker. Inside were a silver chain and a dried once-yellow flower he guessed to be a prickly pear blossom from earlier in the year. He pulled the jar from the hardened earth and it left its deep, round shape in the grave. He unscrewed the jar, and a spicy smell he fancied to be the scent of blooming prickly pear and of spring thunderstorms came out like a genie from its lamp. The silver chain held a silver cross, and when Gideon unfolded the sheet of paper he took out of the jar a heavy gold coin fell out and landed on the toe of his boot where it reflected the sun. A message was printed in perfectly straight lines across the paper:

HERE RESTS BINGA KAROLINA DUERFELDT, OLDEST DAUGHTER OF ANNA AND ERNST DUERFELDT, SISTEROF ADELAIDE AND LOUISE, STRUCK THIS MORNING BY A SER-PENT, DEAD AFTER SUNDOWN. SHE WAS HER MOTHER'S CONSOLATION AND HER FATHER'S GREATEST LOVE, BUT GOD LOVED HER MORE AND TOOK HER TO HIMSELF. THIS TWENTY DOLLAR GOLD PIECE BELONGS TO ANY MAN WHO BRINGS TO THIS PLACE A MARKER OF STONE WITH **BINGA** CUT TO LAST. LET NO ONE ELSE BETAKE HIM OF THIS COIN. GOTT IST DIE LIEBE.

"Damn fool," Mr. Speer said. "Came out here with his whole family in just one wagon. We'll like as not find the rest of them buried along the way."

Gideon spoke before he thought better: "What kind of fools does that make us?" Nobody said a word. He folded the message and put it back in the jar with the cactus flower, the cross on a chain, the twenty-dollar piece. A lot of money just sitting in a jar placed out on the prairie.

They all stood around this grave much as they'd stood around the graves of the two Negroes. No one said any funeral words. They bowed their heads in silence. Then they went back to their wagons, all but Dorsey, who sank on her knees by the makeshift headstone. No longer weeping, she lowered her head to her knees. Her hair spilled forward covering her head and legs. She looked like some strange flora, a dream cactus, the bent stalk of her blue dress ending in the black foliage of her hair.

"I may die out here," Mrs. Speer said. "Dead and buried in this godforsaken place, and I'll never see sister Annie again in this world nor will she even see my grave. I'll be lucky to have a stone, and it will be as lonely of flowers as my poor husband's neglected grave back in Indiana."

Separated from Dorsey

Two mornings later—they had put maybe fifteen miles the day before and already five or more that morning between them and Binga's sad mound—Mr. Speer called for a rest halt. Gideon was bringing up the rear. Speer came back to Gideon's wagon on foot, a dipper of water in his hand. "Gideon," he said. "Step down a minute." Speer smiled and handed the half-full dipper to Gideon, who had been thirsting for the last hour but had been reluctant to stop and drink. The water cut the dust, and he fancied mud seeping down through his insides, cooling first his throat and then spreading out into his chest and down his arms and moving into his stomach and thence his legs. "Gift of God, Gideon, this life-giving liquid."

Even as he hoped Speer's kindness was genuine, something in the man's manner recalled to Gideon's mind Virgil's saying, "I fear the Greeks even when they offer gifts." *Perhaps*, Gideon thought, *it is my base nature that a sign of goodwill suggests to me evil intent.*

"Gideon, I haven't wanted to alarm the women, Dorsey especially, since she's been brought so low by news of Binga. We've passed more Indian sign."

"When?"

"The same day we found poor Binga, and, again, this morning."

Gideon tried to recall anything he might have missed, tried to remember when Mr. Speer stopped, staring, or was off by himself studying the ground. "You're sure?"

"Unmistakable. A big war party."

Involuntarily Gideon looked toward the wagons, seeking Dorsey. Speer's look followed Gideon's.

"I want to camp early—rest the animals. Tomorrow we'll swing north and hit the Platte again. We're ahead of Major Benson by now. He has more wagons to offer, so the Indians will let us pass in favor of attacking the longer train."

This kind of reasoning made sense if Gideon didn't weigh it carefully. He tried to figure why it sounded clear and why he knew it was mud. Hiram walked up and, close behind him, Joe and Dorsey. Speer hurried on, raising his voice now, speaking for the ears of the others.

"I have a plan to protect against hostile attack. Gideon will go ahead a ways, back north toward the river." He handed Gideon a heavy square of thickly folded red flannel. "Every couple miles, tie a red tag to the grass. You'll blaze our trail, then we'll come safe behind. When you're in sight of the Platte, hold up and wait for us."

First Hiram, then Joe, shook Gideon's hand. Overhearing this conversation, Dorsey smiled for the first time in three days. Gideon took in air, lifted his shoulders. Hiram and Joe unloaded the Thurstons' trunk from Gideon's wagonbed. Mary went through the keepsakes packed within, saving out a few baby dresses.

They left the trunk behind, open as a yawning mouth. Then Mrs. Speer handed Gideon a sealed envelope.

"My last words for my sister, Annie. You post this for me if you get through. It's all she'll have of me again in this world."

"I'll be rejoining you in a few days. Where would I post a letter?"

"Why, in any village there's a post office," Mrs. Speer said. She smiled idiotically, and Dorsey bit her lip. She was clearly keeping back tears for her mama. Mrs. Speer was more and more going far off in her mind to escape what Gideon felt must be the madness to her of all this space. He started to tell the demented woman there was no post office where he was going, but he thought maybe the self-deception would calm her mind. He nodded and stuck her letter inside the *Americana* beneath his wagon seat.

He felt as if he were leaving on a long journey of exploration. Everyone acted as if he were their guardian angel. He thought they all were somehow reassured— even he felt it—simply because they had Mr. Speer's scheme, a new idea of how they were to proceed. Even as Gideon responded to the group's enthusiasm, he puzzled over the plan, finding more questions than answers in its logic.

Mary Thurston gave him a small cotton pouch. "Sugar, for your coffee." She winked at him. She had noted his sweet tooth.

Dorsey gave him a bag of corn dodgers and—he was certain of this—she held onto the bag long enough for their hands to communicate warmth back and forth. "I cooked these myself."

"I'll think of you when I eat them," he said. He would also think of her when he was not eating them. He thought of Dorsey all the time.

Midmorning, he struck out alone, orphaned to the empty land and vacant sky. He feared for himself alone against savage Indians, of course, but pride held his tongue. He had a pang of regret for having never outright declared himself to Dorsey (though he knew she knew full well of his devotion), and he regretted leaving her behind with her solemn half-crazy mother and Mr. Speer, a man who was as hard to fix as the shadows of clouds moving on the moving sea of grass.

"Prairie," he said out loud to the endless waves of land. "Bear Dorsey safely on her way." It was a prayer he knew he would speak daily for days and days to come.

Right Ox slapped his tail, and Gideon felt better for having voiced his feelings. The immense sky tilted, and his oxen and he slid forward into the tall grass. Before long he felt reasonably peaceable. In spite of his true affection for Dorsey, the company of animals and of the silent dead, like Chief Bones, was the company with which he felt most at ease.

An Albino Prairie Dog

Without Gideon's taking notice, the sky filled with clouds—not the dark thunderheads of storms, just a muffling of gray, yet still bright, with here and there a curve of blue sky. The land had flattened out, and with no sun visible, no hill or valley to follow, he didn't know which way to go. He stopped still and the grass moved along both sides of him, an unchanging current. Afraid of making a circle, he kept the warm breeze in his face, figuring it from the south. When he couldn't feel the breeze, he found it in the parted surface of the sea of grass, and when even the grass grew still, he watched the sky until he found a drift of clouds to move against.

From time to time he tore and tied a strip of red flannel to a tall stem of grass, one solitary flower miles after another in the rampant garden of grass. He was not blazing a trail as Theseus and Hansel had to find a way back, but in the hope he might be followed by Dorsey and the others. When his stomach got so loud he feared Indians might hear from miles away, he pulled up where the grass was not too tall near a scattering of dark, dried buffalo dung. He built a fire using the buffalo chips for fuel and boiled a pinch of coffee to have with the rest of Dorsey's corn dodgers. He stirred his coffee, thick at the bottom of his tin cup with Mrs. Thurston's sugar and so hot the tip of his tongue was tender for days to come. He stood and slowly turned a full circle, staring hard at the dark distances, looking for any tiny light that might be the fire Dorsey sat near even as he stared. He longed for some cake or pie to melt in his burned mouth, but he longed even more for Dorsey's sweet presence. Before moving on, he gathered hard, dry buffalo chips and piled them alongside Chief Bones in the back of his wagon.

The chief and he traveled two more days and nights without seeing another soul. He was beginning to worry he might never find the Platte River again, might never again be reunited with the train and Dorsey's wagon. The more he worried about Dorsey, the less he worried about Indians. Then he worried he was not worrying enough about Indians to keep alert. The third day, he heard shots and saw a wagon of some kind hitched to a white horse. Behind the wagon was a solitary figure with a rifle. He got closer and the figure, a white man, waved his arm above his head. Gideon powdered up the cap, loaded the Hawken, and laid it across his lap, and then he continued.

Tall, the man held one arm up, and something dangled down the length of his arm, side, and leg to the ground. He raised his other arm, and, surrounded by rippling currents of grass, he looked like a man underwater swimming for the light above. The free arm moved again, and something flashed in the sun—the blade of a knife. The scent of water gave Gideon's oxen new strength, and they pulled faster. Now, he saw what the man held up: a blood-shiny serpent. As Gideon drew alongside, he laid the Hawken against his wagon's footboard and slid down, his oxen continuing on for the water. On the ground lay the thickly piled bodies of three giant snakes.

"Goddamn dog town rattlers." The man's words were more growls than talk. He wore a loose home-sewn woolen shirt. Dark pantaloons, wide at the bottoms, covered legs as thick as good-sized tree trunks. Moccasins, made from some hide with the fur turned in, protected the man's feet, which were small considering the rest of him. He was hatless, had long, yellow-white hair—silver in the sun and bright-smelling with lard and bergamot orange—pulled back behind meaty ears and tied with green grosgrain ribbon. His long, ribbon-decorated hair (had it not been yellow-white) and his nose long and sharp as the blade he wielded (had his skin not been the blue-white of a corpse) would have given him the appearance Gideon had imagined for a wild Indian.

"Fucking prairie dog town," the man said, and his eyes turned from the sun's brightness and pierced Gideon. They were like clear glass with small centers both blue and brown that Gideon realized were his reflected brown shirt and blue trousers. The man pointed toward the Western horizon, and his eyes went red then as tawny as the sun-tipped prairie grass. Gideon willed his eyes to leave the man's to look where the man was looking. Between where they stood and where the buffalo wallow began was an area of perhaps thirty acres of rolling land where little or no grass grew. Not twenty yards away, a furry creature raised up on hind legs barking shrilly and displaying a chest as white as this man's hair. The dark openings of holes were scattered over the area. Another of the creatures—a cross between a rat and a squirrel—stuck its head out from one of the holes.

The man glanced at the crate in Gideon's wagonbed, and Gideon wondered if the man could see Chief Bones on the far side of the box.

"Drummer?" the man asked.

Gideon described the Atkins Lightning Bolt Arrester and Protector he sometimes remembered to try to peddle. The man looked disappointed.

"Whisky, tobaccy?"

"I have a little tobacco." Gideon handed over his small pouch of tobacco. "Not to sell but to share."

"Hell yes. Hell yes. Goddamn tobaccy."

"You're welcome to what I have."

"Enoch Martin," the man rasped, and he enveloped Gideon's hand in his.

Held thus, in the pale, ghostly grip, Gideon's hand became the hand of a dark stranger, an Indian or a Negro. Inclined thus in Gideon's direction, and closer, the man's eyes grew rosy with the glow of Gideon's sun-reddened face.

"I answer to Gideon."

When the man released it, Gideon's palm was red with snake's blood. Enoch Martin soon had the skin off one snake and laid it across his low wagonbed. The snakeskin was at least nine feet long and across its widest part spread out over a foot. He cut the rattles off and handed them to Gideon.

"A goddamn rattle a year, like the rings in a goddamn tree, counts up to goddamn Methuselah snake." The rattles were dry and light as a wasp's nest. "Dogs desert a tunnel and sure as shit some damn lazy rattlesnake moves right in. Fucking damn owls, too."

When he had all four snakes skinned, Enoch Martin cut the meat into sections and packed it tight into a syrup bucket in his wagon that was not a wagon at all but a kind of sled with runners made of straight, young tree trunks bent up at either end, the bottoms left rounded. Also in the wagon were eight or ten prairie dogs, each wearing a red stain on its white bib.

He saw Gideon looking at the bucket of snakemeat, the pile of prairie dogs. "Goddamn good eating there. You come help us do a good goddamn job."

"I'm grateful," Gideon said. The longer he was separated from the other two wagons the more he despaired of ever getting back to Dorsey, so he hated to detour, but he thought he might learn things from this man to aid him in his scouting duties. "I've been headed north a good while toward the Platte River. Can you tell me where I am?"

The man looked up with one eye. The other, Gideon would swear, kept watching the snakemeat he was cutting. "Kansas," he said, matter-of-factly. "You got goddamn Kansas for a good spell in all directions. And Kansas," now both eyes looked at Gideon, "is as good a goddamn place as any to eat like a fucking king." Gideon had never met anyone quite like him—no one so pale-skinned nor so profane. Gideon wondered what prairie dog and, even, rattlesnake tasted like. He was hungry enough to find out. Enoch Martin cut off two strips of the snakeskin, its edges silvery up to where the dark brown pattern of diamonds began. "Here, Gideon. Let these fuckers dry, then stretch one length on the cantle of your saddle, when you have a damn saddle, and it'll keep away the goddamn galls. The other piece in your hatband will drive off a goddamn headache."

The snakeskin was like a fish in Gideon's hand, wet on its pale underside, its scales blinking a pattern of browns and black in the sunlight.

Enoch Martin climbed on his sled and paused. "Nothing better than fat, fucking prairie dog," he said, "except fried rattler. Ain't nothing to top rattler, except a pipe of tobaccy right on top of fat fucking prairie dog and fried rattler." Without raising his voice he said, "Horse," and the big white horse pranced wide around the mud and broke into a run, sled and heavy load racing along behind, the runners gliding over prairie grass as if it were slick snow, heading as Gideon calculated, southwest, away from where he should have been going.

Lightning, like the divine judgment it may represent, turned out to be something Enoch Martin was unconcerned about arresting, especially at the price the Atkins Lightning Bolt Arrester and Protector Company insisted on extracting, and especially since Enoch Martin and his three daughters lived in a sod house dug into the prairie. A single massive cottonwood stood sentinel between a muddy waterhole and a wooden privy behind the house. As far as eye could see, nothing rose above the prairie as high as this ancient tree that bore the black scars and amputated limbs of more than one thunderbolt from an angry god.

The soddy was the first Gideon had ever seen, much less been inside. A milk cow grazed on the roof. He stepped through the plank door Enoch Martin held open. The ceiling under the sod roof was boards with a peeled log ridgepole. Inside was just one room about twenty-five feet long and maybe half as wide. A peeled log ran the top length of each earthen wall. The only openings were a small window by the door, a small window in the east wall, and a door down into a cellar house on the west side. The windows were shuttered with planks on leather hinges and could be opened for ventilation. At the center of the roof, the room was nine to ten feet high. One end of the room was dominated by a cookstove that gave off waves of heat.

"Three goddamn women, Gideon, fills a fucking soddy with secrets," Enoch said. He jerked open a calico spread hung from a cord strung from wall to wall to separate a sleeping area from the rest of the house. Three straw mattresses done up in cotton ticking and laid out on platforms with rope supports were lined up across the end of the room, each in turn curtained off from the other by more calico. Enoch himself, he said, slept out in the cellar house even in the fiercest weather. "Hell, yes, it gets cold—cold as a witch's tit—but I won't lie the goddamn night breathing three women's stale-ass air. They damn female parts reek of foul monthly odors."

All Gideon smelled was a richness of earth and grass and something like scalded milk, for which he held accountable either the cow grazing (he heard the faint clunk-a-lunk of her copper bell) above their heads or something baking in the stove's dark oven, which warmed one side of his face as Enoch pulled aside the calico divider.

Struck by the sod house as Gideon was, he marked it hardly at all compared to Enoch Martin's daughters. Ursula, who stood behind a curtain Enoch had opened, was the eldest. "Privacy is not the same as secrets, Pa." Sharpboned at all her edges, Ursula had a gaunt, fragile beauty. Her pale arms bore bruises where her girl's body had done woman's work. Her hair was as yellow-white as Enoch's but less tended-to, pinned up tight and damp as a bundle of wash. Ursula had blue eyes with hard white lights in the pupils. Her shape was difficult to discern behind the long smock and apron she wore. Her feet, red at the heels, red at the ankles and toes, were wide and flat, her toenails stained the green-orange of prairie grass. Though she wasn't much older than nineteen or twenty, when Ursula fixed the white centers of those eyes on Gideon, an orphan all his life, he knew how it felt to be a guilty child in the eyes of a long-suffering mother.

"Effie," Enoch said. "Suella," he said. "Shitfire, where are they?"

Effie, the middle daughter, came in with an armload of buffalo chips. She teetered rather than walked. As soon as Gideon fixed his eyes on her he heard Colonel Powell-Hughes' Welsh voice reading Ovid, *Facies non omnibus una, Nec diversa tamen, qualem decet esse sororum,* and translating for Gideon, the student: "Their faces were not all alike, nor yet unlike, but such as those of sisters ought to be." Effie's hair, a deeper yellow than Enoch's and Ursula's, curled about her head. She was a pale, altered rendering of Ursula. Ursula—in an ominous way—was vaguely pretty while Effie was prettily vague. Both of them were as white as the moon. They caught the tint of firelight and it made different hues on their skin. Ursula knelt to the cookstove. Effie never spoke a word Gideon heard clearly. She moved like a breeze about the room, stirred the calico curtaining, lifted a light dust off the packed dirt floor.

Ursula took the skinned prairie dogs and the syrup can of chopped-up rattlesnakes, and with nods and glances set Effie to work rinsing and readying the meat while she stoked up the fire. "Hot as hellfire in here," Enoch said. His eyes brightened when Gideon mentioned tobacco. They went to his wagon for a bowlful. He reminded himself of his mission to learn what he could. He considered telling Enoch about the Speers and Thurstons, but decided to bide his time.

Gideon got out the pouch. "Here. Smoke your fill. I should see to my oxen."

"Smoke is goddamn better shared. After we've supped, I'll have my womenfolk unhitch your team. Them oxen can overnight in my damn shed."

Enoch filled his pipe and tamped the tobacco with a carved stick that resembled most a long-stemmed toadstool, the cap of which just fit the pipe bowl. He handed the device to Gideon, but the cap was too wide for the bowl of his pipe.

He turned it around and tamped with the handle. "There must not be any Indians in these parts," Gideon said, more a question than a statement.

Enoch moved his pipe back and forth beneath his nose and lowered his face into the smoke, squinted against the cloud and smiled widely. "Ahhh," he said. Then, "All around us. Hellfire, boy, they come and they go."

"Friendly?"

Staring at Gideon for a long moment, Enoch knitted his brow, shook his head. "Hell, no. I pay fucking tribute. Give meat, eggs, milk, goddamn cake when I can trade for sugar and get my girls to bake. Whisky and tobaccy, when I get hold of any, I hide away or they'd demand my whole store of pleasure. I was a squaw man, spent a spell among her fucking people. I try to be worth more alive than dead. So far, they leave me be."

"And you're not afraid to sleep out in the cellar house?"

"Wouldn't matter where the fuck I slept. They want to kill me, they goddamn will. Ever man passes the hour of his dying ever day. Indian whimsy or God's, what damn difference?"

Gideon had no answer, so he sent up a cloud of smoke and put on what he hoped was a wise face. His leading the way for Dorsey and the others seemed a meaningless endeavor if what Enoch said was true.

They walked behind the soddy to a woven willow crib where Enoch's white horse, milk cow, and chickens wintered. "An there's the shit house." Enoch pointed his pipestem at a plank box behind the willow crib. The sun, low behind the rough barked limbs of the cottonwood, cast such shadows that at first Gideon didn't see a shape that slipped across the ground and pressed itself against the tree's trunk. "Goddamn, Gideon, there she is, fresh from peeing, my youngest and prize filly."

This youngest one, fifteen or sixteen, moved from the shadows into a spill of sunlight where she stopped sudden and watched the two men as a wild deer might, nose up, muscles tight. Unless light and shadow played tricks on Gideon, her nostrils twitched as she read his scent. Then she did a sort of dance. Her skirt was tanned hide and swirled one way then another, the hem flouncing up to reveal a red sheen of sunlight on the skin of a bare foot, calf, or shin. Overhead, the massive trunk and limbs of the tree loomed darkly. Behind the girl rolled waves of grass. An army of white chickens marched, strutting vainly around her. In the late afternoon light her bare arms were red, and her eyes and hair were the rich dark brown of the tobacco he'd pinched between his thumb and finger and held midair halfway between pouch and pipe. Wordless, she came right up to him, her motions so sure he was surprised she didn't rattle and stomp with the weight of sword and boots. She extended her arm before her like an arrow fitted to a bow, and one pointing finger pressed his skin above the top button of his shirt. Her finger burned like a hot poker. Close now, brightness shot through her dark hair as veins of silver exposed in dark rock. The red half-sun exploded behind her. The outline of her dark hair was flaming, and only the flash of her eyes and teeth was visible inside the bright nimbus. He recalled the words of his namesake, the biblical Gideon: *Alas, O Lord God! for because I have seen an angel of the Lord face to face.* Though he couldn't speak, he saw that same face and understood why shepherds long ago were so afeared when the angel of the Lord appeared unto them.

"Whose boy are you?" the angel said.

She'd not moved her burning finger, and he wondered if she felt through her fingertip the pounding of his heart. He scarcely had time to wonder how his heart, so crowded with Dorsey, could yet be stirred and in such a different way by the creature before him.

"Suella, this young man is Gideon, and he is going to sit to supper with us."

This one was so unlike her sisters Gideon looked to Enoch without disguising his surprise.

"After my first wife died of the fucking fever, I become a damn squaw man. Suella's maw was full-blood Kiowa. Suella's got Indian-dark hair streaked white like a roan horse. Half albino and half darkness. Makes a feisty, fucking mix, don't it? See her mane and tail dance."

Only then did the girl remove her finger. "Don't worry. I won't scalp you." She reached up behind Gideon's neck and gave his hair a yank, then she ran off toward the house.

Enoch froze stock-still, pipe held in air inches from his parted pink lips. Still as the earth he stood on, he watched her run, his colorless eyes following her, measuring her with pride. His look was one Gideon had seen many times: the look of a man who has something he values greatly—a horse, say—something he intends to barter and for which he intends to exact a dear price.

Dorsey Murphy: Wind and Sky

Sandstorm
(August 1865)

The frontier is fulminate and capricious. Frontier people accept the unpredictable and sudden: sandstorm, flooded river, blizzard, overturned wagon, wildfire, runaway stock, Indian attack, deadly chills and fever. One man thrives as another dies. A man may lose his ranch in one hand of cards. I've seen a wagon train of families disappear onto the horizon never to be seen again.

—from *Gideon Jones' Journal*

The sky was blue and cloudless, and there was a gentle breeze in Dorsey's face when her brother Joe rode toward the wagon shouting, "Hurry. Down that slope ahead and set the brake."

Laura Etta pulled up on the reins, and Joe rode over close.

"Why are we stopping?" Laura Etta asked.

"Sandstorm."

"You must be crazy—the sky's as clear as a windowpane," Laura Etta said. When his mother called him "crazy," Joe closed his eyes a minute as if he were saying a short prayer. If he were calling on God, Dorsey wondered if Joe was praying for their mother's welfare or asking for patience to suffer insults from this addled woman.

"I sure may be, Mama. But you and Dorsey get the wagon down into that bowl and take what cover you can."

Laura Etta looked at Dorsey and lifted her shoulders in a shrug, but she followed the Thurston wagon. The incline was not steep and the wagon did not slide any. When her mother braked beside the Thurstons, Dorsey got down off the board. Her legs had pins and needles in them, and now she was standing she realized she had to pee. She headed up the far side of the slope, her dress catching in tall grass that pulled her back. When she crested the hill wind stung her face. Grit stung her eyes. On this side of the little hill the world was different. As if the sky were a sheet of blue steel rapidly rusting, a red-orange horizon was rising. The wind began to moan and then howl. Brown spheres that looked like wads of hair as big as wagon wheels rolled and bounced toward her. She ran back down the slope to the wagon. Mr. Speer and Hiram were tying shirts over the horses' heads while Mary Thurston and little Lucy stuffed sheets and clothes along the seams where the wagon covers met the board sides. Now the sky was blood red and the wind howled. With the sudden sound of hail on tin, sand pelted horses' backs and wagon covers.

Dorsey made it back to the wagon, sand stinging the backs of her legs. In the wagon, Laura Etta was dipping sheets and pillow covers into a bucket of water, rolling up the wet cotton, and pressing it against all the cracks of light visible from inside the wagon. The air was red grit. Dorsey's throat burned, and she coughed uncontrollably. Something cool covered her burning face—a soaked rag her mama pressed against her. She breathed through the wet cloth, her breath making sucking sounds into the cotton. Her teeth chewed the fabric, and she tasted bitter-clean bleach and sun. Wind rattled the wagon and sand roared like a railway locomotive. All Dorsey could see were red folds of the wet rag she breathed through. The wadded cloth was brown as the rows of a just-ploughed field. Each breath Dorsey felt she *must* have air without grit. Each breath she thought she was going to panic and run out into the howling wind. The end of the Osnaburg wagon cover shrieked, then collapsed into the wagon with the soft weight of piled sand.

Gideon, Dorsey thought, *where are you right now?* She wondered how far out onto the prairie the storm blew. She knew his lightning rods were well protected by their straw packing. She hoped he would not concern himself with the grisly skeleton. She pictured him grabbing his precious book and holding it to his chest, his arms around a book when they should be embracing her. *Maybe he's traveled beyond the storm's path,* she thought. She prayed, *Lord, keep Gideon safe,* and she pictured God's hand, the size of a wagon, coming from the red sky and cupping itself around Gideon so not a grain of sand stung his skin.

And then it was so suddenly bright Laura Etta must have lit the lantern. Dorsey peeked from the corner of her breathing rag. She looked out at a scene like winter in some land where snow is brown. The horses whinnied and Mr. Speer's high-pitched voice shouted something, his words drowned out by the slapping of leather and metal. The Thurston wagon was piled with dirt, the frames of its cover bare, brown shreds of Osnaburg flapping. A few of the brown spiky globes had caught beneath the two wagons and one was tangled in the Thurstons' tattered wagon cover.

"They're tumbleweeds," Mr. Speer said as he appeared out of the settling dust to stand beside Dorsey and brush sand from her shoulders, his hands darting and scratching like an animal's paws. She looked up through a giant tumbleweed at the brightening sky, the brown spines of the plant twisting and forking like the interlocked antlers of a whole herd of bucks.

Both wagons had been blown too full of sand to get them cleaned out before dark, so everyone slept in the grass, which was beaten down and torn and piled up in places with sand. They did well to wipe sand off meal bins and out of skillets so they could fry up corn dodgers for supper.

Repairing the Damage

All the next day they lost to shoveling out sand, shaking out sand, wiping and dusting away sand, and to sewing and patching Osnaburg, sewing and fitting an entire makeshift cover on the Thurston wagon. Dorsey was amazed the animals had weathered the storm as well as they had. The rag tied over one horse's eyes had blown away, and the blinded, terrified animal had run away. Joe and Hiram rubbed salve on and rigged pads for raw places on horses where the traces had to rest.

Two days after the sandstorm they saw a mound of sand that turned out to be the buried carcass of the runaway horse. After three days of shoveling, sweeping, and shaking sand from the wagon, Dorsey was still finding it—inside the extra pair of shoes she had packed away, between the planks of the side boards, in the pocket of a blouse in the bottom of a trunk. The few new green leaves Mary Thurston's apple saplings had been sprouting were wind-shredded into pointed shapes that bobbed and bounced as the wagon rolled.

Gideon Jones: An Uninvited Companion

Breaking Bread in a Soddy
(August 1865)

By the light of two tallow candles and the fire still glowing in the cookstove, Gideon sat down with Enoch Martin and his three daughters and tasted prairie dog and rattlesnake meat for the first time. Their rough-hewn plank table surprised him with bone china plates and cups.

Served with cornbread and fried apples, prairie dog tasted like chicken—only better somehow, the way a Christmas hen always tasted better than a regular Sunday-dinner hen. Snakemeat was closest to fresh fish. Fried crisp brown and peppery on the outside, the rattlesnake chunks were white and light as a cloud on the inside. Gideon wondered how a creature that slithered heavily through grass and dirt and squeezed between rocks could taste like something that swam bright water. Under a knife thin layers of meat flaked off like wood shavings, and the aroma was something like the scent of cut wood.

"This is Pawnee country, is it not?" he asked, wanting to get Enoch talking about Indians. He wanted to learn what he could to help him protect Dorsey and the others once he returned to them. Enoch kept chewing. He stared ahead as if he had not heard, so Gideon prodded. "I guess the closer to Fort Laramie, the less likely one will have Indian trouble."

Enoch stopped chewing, looked at Gideon, chewed some more. "We're going to eat like all wrath." Enoch drank down his china cup of milk. "Indians don't read the goddamn white man's maps, so they don't always know where the Hell they's supposed to be." He put another piece of snakemeat in his mouth and chewed and talked at the same time. "We way down in Kansas—a long fucking way from Fort Laramie. South of us is Indian damn territory all the way to fucking Texas. Plains Indians is horse Indians. Wanderers. Not like back-east Indians. Soldiers can't just go find they fucking home and wipe them out. They follow the buffalo. They got no home. They horse from the waist down. Horse carries all they burthens. They fold up they tipi and horse drags it along. When they can't get no buffalo to eat, no deer nor rabbits, and they tired of rats, snakes, lizards, turtles, grubs, snails, and grasshoppers, they butcher up some horse steaks. A plains Indian has got a goddamn buffalo horse and a goddamn war horse, too, saved for attacking the likes of you and me. A Kiowa, Kiowa-Apache, or Comanche can live on a fucking horse for days on end."

"Way down in Kansas," Gideon said.

"Hell goddamn yes. Not terrible far east of Colorado Territory, just a good spit from Oklahoma, and Texas not terrible bad farther if you measure just by miles."

"How do you measure, Enoch?"

"I measure by Indians. Indian territory is extra wide no matter how short the miles."

"But your wife was a Kiowa, so those must be friendly Indians?"

Enoch Martin threw back his head and laughed. "Goddamn, Gideon, you think because a squaw fucks you she's friendly?" He laughed some more. "The Kiowas do a lot of wife-stealing just to insult one another. They squaws run off, too, just to shame they husband. Suella's maw run off with me to shame her husband. I ended up paying six good horses for her. Later, she left Suella with me and run off with a high-up man in the Koisenko warrior society. Digging Bird—Suella's maw—would grin ear to ear if her warrior brought home my scalp stretched on his hoop for her to carry around on a long pole."

"Then all the Indians around here are unfriendly?" Gideon took another piece of cornbread.

"Ain't no other kind. Cheyenne is nearabout, and goddamn Kiowa, Kiowa-Apache, and even Wichita range up here. They on a hunt or a raid you might find Arapaho this far south, or your Pawnee. Most likely, most fucking likely be Comanches. When I was a squaw man with the Kiowas down on the top of Texas, in the Wichita Mountains, I learnt Indians out here—fucking wild Indians unlike those civilized Indians back in the land of steady habits—is more scared of other Indians than of us damn whites." Enoch shook his head. "This here part of Kansas is the northern part of Comancheria. I most regard the Kiowas and the Comanches, because they has no equal on a goddamn horse. You know Kiowas have ridden they ponies all the way through Mexico to the countries underneath. Brought back big green birds could talk Kiowa talk."

"Settlers at Westport Landing said Apaches are the worst to torture whites."

"They all about goddamn equal bad. Depends most on whim and how much time they have. And the Kiowa-Apache ain't the same as the Lipan Apache, or the Jicarilla, or all the western Apaches, like the Mescaleros. Most whites don't know a whit of the different tribes and it probably don't matter. I mean, who cares if the Apache whacking off your pecker is a Mescalero or a Jicarilla?" Enoch stuffed a chunk of snakemeat into his mouth and continued to talk, his words muffled by the meat. "I heard the Comanches don't torture, then I learnt different when I was a Kiowa squaw man. Comanches is the only Indians I know don't have *any* fucking white squaw men. Adopted Comanches—whites or other Indians—is always treated full goddamn Comanche, but against they enemy Comanches perfect cruelty. They always on the move, so sometimes they in too big a hurry to kill you slow. If they being chased by soldiers, say, they drag captives along, kill them as they go, leave a trail behind of body parts for they fucking pursuers to find. Worst thing is to be toted back to camp and turned over to the Comanche women."

"What chance would a wagon train have against a Comanche attack?"

"Only chance is to kill them before they kill you. Most white folks hear them braves screaming down, buffalo horns on they head, faces painted black, nekkid bodies hanging sideways off a galloping horse firing arrows or guns from under the horse's neck, white folks just hang up the fiddle. Comanches win, every white man's due to die—question is, how quick. Comanche braves have they goddamn way with white women and either torture them a lot and kill them or torture them a little bit and keep them. Babes are usually too damn much trouble, slow them down, so they kill babes unless some damn squaw's babe just died. Children a little older they most times keep."

"Have you ever seen a man scalped?" When Enoch tipped his head back drinking more milk, Gideon stared at the long yellow-white hair.

"Scalping don't kill you. Plenty of goddamn scalped women live to wear a bonnet." The cup left a moustache of milk on Enoch's upper lip. "You know why Indians scalp they enemies?"

"For a kind of trophy?"

"That's the least of it. They mix they goddamn religion up with fighting. Indian Heaven is the good hunting place down below. The fucking dead can't go to the Good Hunting Land if they don't have hair. Scalping kills the soul and turns the dead into ghosts. Ghosts hang around where they's killed, so you don't find no fucking Indians moping around at a goddamn battleground. Comanches'll sew a scalp back onto a dead warrior so he can get to the Good Damn Hunting Land. They don't want anybody in Heaven but goddamn Comanches. If they arms or legs or head or they cock and balls is cut off, the dead got to spend fucking forever like that. They spend they days and nights figuring new goddamn ways to keep a man alive whilst they torture him. They know ever goddamn body part what hurts the most and what they can kick, jab, stab, and scrape—what they can hack off, peel away, smash, or dislocate without you quite able to fucking die. Onliest time they kill fast is when they in a fucking hurry." Enoch paused long enough to stuff two chunks of prairie dog into his mouth. He shook his head again. When he resumed talking, he sprayed crumbs. "Funny." He chewed some more. "Funny how the Comanches, about the most fucking fearsome folks on earth, they love children so." Enoch smiled at his daughters. "Just like me, Gideon, just like me. I love my fucking children."

Enoch looked from Ursula to Effie to Suella—the youngest, the half-Indian wild red-skinned one—from Suella to Gideon, who met Enoch's look. Then, Gideon felt his own eyes going across to Suella, who stared right back but didn't say a word. Ursula jumped into the quiet space Enoch had left, rattled along, asking Gideon about St. Louis and what the fine ladies wear. Even Effie whispered a question or two Ursula repeated loud enough for Gideon to hear. He managed brief answers, but he was not paying the conversation his full attention. Every time he sneaked a look at Suella, she was watching him, a smile wiggling with the flickering candlelight at the corners of her dark, unblinking eyes. And every time he sneaked a look at her, he caught Enoch catching him. Enoch sort of nodded, as if Gideon were doing just what Enoch expected. Trouble was, Gideon couldn't tell whether Enoch was mad or glad. He smacked his rosy lips and clicked his teeth, chewed and swallowed. The tip of his tongue ran back and forth between his lips like the flicking tongue of the rattlesnake he was consuming.

"Mistake most white men make, they try to be friends to all the goddamn Indians. You can't have them all on one stick. You might be friends with just the Comanches. But they see you parlay with a fucking Apache—Comanches call them *esikwita*, they word for a man's ass you see when he's running away from you, running for his fucking life—the Comanches start planning new ways to kill you slow. Only other tribe the Comanches tolerate is the Kiowa. And the Kiowa is the only ones might be even better at torturing. And if you be friends with the Comanches, what you gonna do when the fucking Apaches got you at the end of a lance? Sometimes a goddamn total stranger, white or Indian, they allow to travel free. You remember that, you might get wherever you headed with you goddamn scalp. Indians has a mind to courage above all.

There's a story of a white man the Comanches caught and stripped down for torture. When a brave put a fucking knife up against his privates, he laughed in the goddamn Indian's face. Comanches figured this white had damn powerful medicine—let him go. Likely a true tale. But, Gideon, you save one loaded goddamn chamber for your ownself."

"I'll keep a close watch for Comanches."

"Hell, Gideon, you couldn't tell a Comanche from a fucking Cheyenne. They's all kinds of Comanches. Around here we got the Yap-eaters. Farther west is the Antelopes. Way south the Honey Eaters roam. But they all favor meat. Time you *see* Indians it's too fucking late. They is always a goddamn surprise. Our soldier boys say Indians don't fight fair. The U.S. Army don't understand the Indian sense of honor. To a Indian, there's no fucking honor unless he's alive and his enemy is dead." Enoch smiled and put three pieces of meat off the platter into his mouth at once. His eyes went wide, and he stopped chewing long enough to belch loudly. Smiling again, he closed his eyes and chewed on.

After Enoch, Suella ate the most. She used both hands. Her lips and chin shone with grease. She favored the snakemeat. Gideon was amazed how much he ate without feeling overfull. The platter held nothing but brown crumbs when Ursula put on water for coffee he'd contributed to the feast. Enoch broke out his pipe again, and Gideon filled it and his own with his tobacco. Enoch got a piece of kindling and lighted it off the cookstove fire, brought the flame to the table and held it first to Gideon's pipe bowl, then his own. He wheezed softly and smoke rose and drifted above the table. On the stove, the water stirred, and soon the aroma of coffee joined the burnt molasses smell of tobacco. Gideon longed for a cake or muffin but produced instead the pouch of sugar Mary Thurston had given him. He'd been hoarding it, but he was resolved to return hospitality as grandly as he was able. Suella must've had a sweet tooth powerful as his. She put sugar almost equal to the coffee in her cup. When she drank, her red cheeks sank in, and her lips pursed up like she was kissing the air. Ursula and Effie held their coffee cups in hands as white as the china they drank from. Effie lowered her eyelids and bowed over the steaming coffee as if in prayer. She lowered her mouth to the cup and sipped the coffee with the softest sound of breathing. Enoch tilted his chair back against the dirt wall. For a while no one spoke, each of them seeming content with lingering smells and tastes. Gideon reveled in these unexpected moments of small pleasures with the fond regard such small pleasures deserved, especially as he had not expected such respite from the demands of the wild and uncivilized frontier.

Enoch Martin's Accusation

Enoch pushed off from the wall with the back of his head. The front legs of his chair hit the packed dirt floor at the same moment that he brought his cup down, clunk, upon the table. He smacked his lips, dipped and turned his head. His eyes absorbed darkness from the far corners of the room, and he leveled and aimed them at Gideon like the double barrels of a shotgun.

"Gideon." Enoch's voice was just above a whisper. "You are giving off a goddamn stink."

Before Gideon could think what to say, Enoch went on in a quiet, steady voice.

"It's the stink of lust. You've been sitting here under my roof, eating my goddamn good vittles, and working up a fever of lust for my Suella, onliest half-albino Indian in captivity, my youngest and most prized daughter." Enoch's eyes were huge, the centers so pale blue in the candlelight they spread into the whites as if he had no pupils, both eyes like pockets of hot sky. The wide eyes and the way he stretched his arms against the table gave him the look of a sleepwalker. He put Gideon in mind of an Old Testament prophet stepped straight out of a desert or right off a mountain with a fiery vision burning so white-hot in his brain all Gideon saw in Enoch's eyes was the smoke from within. But what scared Gideon most was the soft, even pitch of Enoch's voice. Against his will, Gideon glanced again at Suella. At each corner of her mouth was a tooth sharply pointed as a wild animal's fangs. Ursula and Effie sat as quiet as ghosts and stared straight ahead.

"That's not true." Even as he spoke Gideon realized, in a way, it *was* true. Enoch's eyes darkened the way the sky dims when a small cloud crosses the sun. Had Gideon insulted him? "Suella *is* pretty to look at, but I—"

"You'd be blind." Enoch exhaled slowly and let go of the tabletop. Gideon let go of just a bit of his fear, but he still couldn't think of what to say. Enoch reached out and took Suella's dark hair in his white fist. He let the hair loose in thin, shining sheets that cascaded over his fingers like the fall of sun-silvered water. Her hair covered her left eye, but her right eye still stared at Gideon. "She worries *my* fucking mind. Especially now she's full developed." Enoch's hand dropped to her ribcage, just under one breast—fuller-looking above his thick fingers. "One damn reason I sleep in the cellar. Can't trust myself in my sleep."

At this, Ursula got up and began to clear the table. Effie giggled softly and reached as if to touch Suella's other breast, but her hand stopped in midair and went instead to Suella's hair, lifting it in strands off Suella's eye and letting it down gently against the side of her face. Effie's hand lingered there—a small white bird fluttering against her half-sister's red cheek—then came down on Suella's plate she silently lifted from the table. Suella did not stir to help her sisters. She had not taken her eyes off Gideon. Enoch moved his hand back to the tabletop. "Out here you have to take what you need and damn the risk, Gideon. The gray wolf spends his days and nights amongst the buffalo so he can take stragglers, the injured and the infirm, to slake his bloodlust."

Gideon nodded. He hoped he appeared detached and not guilty of any-thing.

"You go goddamn ahead. Rut with her tonight and leave with her tomorrow. But," he got up and he pointed his big, cotton-white finger down at Gideon. "I will be recompensed."

Enoch said this last in a low, soft voice, most like he was speaking to himself. Gideon wondered if Dorsey was awake by a cookfire or wrapped in a quilt think-ing of him. He tried to put Dorsey's girl's face between him and Suella's wild grown-woman eyes. Dorsey kept going into pieces, the corner of a smile, a scat-tering of freckles, a twist of wet black hair. And Suella's silver-streaked hair, her animal-sharp teeth silver against her red-brown lips, kept mixing up with Dorsey's face. Against his will his chest went hot when Suella stared at him. He knew it would be a lie to say he had no desire for what was being contracted, but the man-ner of its arrangement disturbed him. And he felt a deep concern for what Enoch would demand in return. He knew Enoch would extract more than tobacco, cof-fee, and sugar for his treasured daughter.

Not knowing what to say, Gideon said nothing, figuring it better not to risk unknowingly saying the wrong words. Enoch went outside, and Gideon stayed at the table Ursula and Effie were clearing. They moved with light grace. Suella got up and without making a sound walked to her bed at the end of the room. She reached behind her and pulled the calico partition closed. Her bare feet moved below the hem of calico, moved from side to side as if she was doing some Indian dance. Then she stood still, and there was in the quiet room a sound of sudden exhalation, and her feet stepped out of the brown surround of her deerhide dress on the floor. He drained his cup and handed it to Ursula, who did not meet his eyes. The calico curtaining Suella and her bed bowed slowly in his direction. Her body leaning into the cloth shaped a dark "S" against the curtain.

Ursula and Effie boiled water and washed plates and put away knives and cups. Without a word they dimmed the lamp and left Gideon at the table. They opened the soddy door, left the house, and closed the door behind them. He was alone in the soddy with Suella in her small calico-barred cell. He wondered where the sisters had gone—whether they nightly took the summer air, tucked in the animals, or spoke their goodnights to their father at his cellar bedside. Or was their leaving part of an arrangement? Was he now to go to Suella lying on her tick just a few steps away? Was this a prairie wedding ceremony? Was the serpent he had consumed part of a prairie spell? Did the tree of knowledge bear for him in this treeless land? Did the taste of anticipation on his tongue propel him inevitably toward a communion of evil? The snake inside him coiled and twisted, urging him toward what he desired more strongly than he would have thought possible scant days ago when Dorsey's hand first touched his.

He should rise and depart the close, low-roofed room. He should declare his love for Dorsey and openly reject this carnal offer. He wanted to feel no pull from behind Suella's curtain. But the pull he felt was strong, and Dorsey was not in any of what he felt. He was not sure why he did not part the calico and take what he desired, what was there for the taking. Even as he sat and did nothing, he was filled with regret. Regret he did not have the will to walk away from Suella, and regret that he was too conflicted to go and take what he was being offered. He pictured the gray wolf Enoch had described waiting for just one weak buffalo to lag behind the herd so the wolf could attack. Wolf Heaven must be the recollection of the tearing of throats and gnawing of flesh, a blood memory as timeless as a dream.

Gideon remained at the table in the near dark of the low lamp. Warm air from the cookstove wafted scalded milk and coal oil, and behind those odors something ripe and musky he realized was his own body's smell. He waited until he felt sure Suella's sisters were not going to return for the night. Then he rose trembling with both desire and fear of discovery, blew out the light, and made his way out of the soddy, hands extended in the cool night air feeling for obstacles in the darkness.

Departure at Dark

Neither Enoch Martin nor any of his daughters had unyoked Left Ox and Right Ox. Quietly as he could, Gideon led them away through the grass lifting his legs high and easing them back down, trying not to make running-away noises. He walked thus for a long time, afraid to disturb the relative quiet. Over the steady swish and deep rattle of his oxen and wagon, he heard an echo of parting grass. He halted the team, listening. Whatever he heard, or imagined, stopped when he stopped. The night breeze riffled through the grass, and the oxen breathed sonorously. In his wagonbed, Chief Bones slept on. Gideon mounted the plank seat, relaxing by degrees as his outfit slipped steadily down a long incline. He searched for the North Star to guide by, but clouds obscured the heavens. There was no moonlight. The breeze kept shifting. No matter, he had to get away from the soddy even if he was not gaining on the other wagons. The direction felt right. The Platte couldn't be too many miles away. Dorsey was at the edge of his thoughts, but he was not ready to let her fully in, fearful his own lustful heart had already betrayed her for Suella's feral charms. He felt the farther he got from Suella (and the closer to Dorsey) the weaker would be Suella's pull.

His mind was disturbed by his unreconciled desire for both Suella and Dorsey and by Enoch's instructions in the ways of plains Indians. Unbidden incidents unfolded in his imagination, having in common a moment when, surrounded by warpainted savages, he laughed coldly at a terrifying savage who held a huge knife between his legs. The warrior lowered his blade and the barbarians nodded in respect for the courage of this singular white man. Bestowed with buffalo robes and other gifts Gideon was released, or, in another version, led to their camp a hero, where he was given a beautiful maiden or a powerful war pony. In yet another version he was made a white chief and lived with the Indians long enough to learn their language and their customs and then worked for the end of bloodshed between his birth-people and his adopted-people.

Afraid to stop moving until he had many miles between himself and the albino sodbuster, Gideon drove and dozed, managing to keep more-or-less moving until the sky began to lighten. He was turned all about. The light was in his face—he was facing east, back the way he began. Perhaps, he mused, some homing instinct had taken over in the night. He had likely not gotten more than out of sight of Enoch Martin's sod house. He turned Right Ox and Left Ox full about, and all morning kept the sun behind them. They had labored all night long and he had to rest them soon. He searched the horizon for tree or bush, signs of water, but finally gave up and stopped where they were. He wished he'd filled his water keg before he'd slipped away from Enoch's soddy. He unhitched Right Ox and Left Ox and gave them water from the half-empty keg.

"Chief Bones, you don't hog the canteen and you don't jabber on." The skeleton was bathed in morning sunlight, and Gideon fancied a smile played at the toothy mouth. He patted the chief's crossed finger bones, then he searched the horizon once more. Nothing but grass and sky. He took some comfort in what Enoch said about Indians sometimes letting a solitary traveler pass safely.

Joined by Suella

After noon he grew so weary he dropped the reins. He set the brake and unyoked and again watered Right Ox and Left Ox. This seemed as safe a place as any to take a rest. The oxen grazed and seemed so contented he let them forage unhobbled. He took up his encyclopedia and spectacles and crawled beneath the wagon for the narrow strip of shade. He flipped the pages, **VITELLIUS, VOLCANOES, WEASEL, WEAVING, WIER'S CAVE** (See *Cave*), **WITCH HAZEL, WOLSEY, WOMAN**. The *Americana* devoted about two and a half pages to **WOMAN**, half as much information as it gave about **VOLCANOES**, but of far greater interest to him. He read: **WOMAN.** *Among savages, a slave in the harem of the luxurious, but half-civilized East, a voluptuous toy; in the more refined countries of Christendom alone is woman the equal and companion of man.* He read about the condition of woman in ancient Egypt and India, about woman in China, about Greek and Roman attitudes toward woman, about the influence of Christianity and the Teutonic nations in establishing sexual equality, and then he came to Woman's physiology. He hurried through *different sexual organs, smaller head, broader pelvis,* and *greater sensitivity* due to the *predominance of the nervous system* and discovered women are *Born to feel and to inspire the kind and tender affections, they are exempt from the gloomy and fierce passions which characterize the bilious temperament; and love, jealousy, and maternal affection are the deepest springs of emotion in the female heart.*

He stretched out and stared up at the tarred seams of the wagon bottom. He knew he should eat his remaining corn dodgers, check on the team, and spread his blanket, but he was so tired he decided to lie there just a little longer. His arm and leg jerking hard was what told him he had slept. The sun was low in the western sky, its rays slanting beneath the wagon to cover his chest like a bright blanket. He crawled out from under the wagon and got halfway to his feet when he looked of a sudden close into another pair of eyes, dark and unblinking, staring into his.

"Suella." He removed his spectacles. She squatted, poised on the balls of her feet, hunched before him, her face not a foot from his. Prairie breeze carried her scent of suet, smoke, and body sweat. "Suella," he said, an idiot hysterically discovering and stating the obvious. Unsmiling, she spread her arms as if she were swimming the prairie sea or solemnly blessing his wagon and him. She leaned toward him and brought her arms together locking him in her embrace. "Wha—" he began, but she pressed her mouth over his and cut off not only his words but also his air. Something hard pressed into his ribs and something else pinched him painfully in the groin. As he struggled for air and to escape these points of pain, he identified them as her elbow in his ribs and her knee pressing into his groin. She was at least as heavy as he and strong, too. He could not push her off, but he managed to roll from under her and get to his feet.

"You're my boy, now."

Remembering how Enoch Martin had dispatched all those rattlers, Gideon searched the horizon for Enoch's silvery head but found instead the white head of his horse. "You stole his horse?"

Suella grinned. "Now he can't come after us so goddamn fast."

Over all the swells of grass surrounding them nothing moved but his oxen, Enoch's horse, and one horsetail cloud. Gideon wasn't convinced Enoch didn't have some other conveyance to retrieve his favorite daughter, his horse, and the man he'd see as responsible for both losses.

Suella grabbed for Gideon, who backed into his wagon. "Wait. We've got to get going." He should've hobbled the animals. He waded out into the grass. "Right Ox," he said as quietly as someone praying at vespers. "Left Ox, where are you?" The wide prairie invited loud shouts, yet he dared only whisper. He topped a rise so gradual he had not realized he was climbing, and there Left Ox munched loudly. The beast leaned away, then stepped close, and stared straight ahead, his tail swishing, the embodiment of forbearance. Gideon led him back to the wagon, the animal's heavy walk a steady pulling against the length of rawhide. Right Ox stood beside his heavy yoke that lay on the ground beside the wagon, and Gideon was overcome by affection for these loyal beasts. Right Ox must've felt his owner's emotion, for he gave Gideon a lesson in forming conclusions. Just when Left Ox and Gideon were upon him, Right Ox lumbered away faster than he'd ever moved. Gideon chased him till he was out of wind and went back to the wagon for his canteen. Suella grinned as if Gideon were doing all this for her entertainment. While he stood there considering how to catch Right Ox, the animal walked placidly up and let Gideon yoke him beside his pal as if he'd just been waiting for Gideon to give up the game.

"Suella—go back."

Her eyes widened. "No go back. You're my boy. Nobody can leave Enoch man and go back. He cut me into little goddamn pieces, then you. He cook us in same goddamn pot."

Gideon recalled the bloody lengths of snake Enoch had jammed into the syrup bucket. All around them—nothing but waves of grass. "Okay. Okay. Let's just get somewhere else."

"O-kay." Suella grinned again, her teeth tobacco-stained at the corners of her wide mouth. She tied Enoch's horse to the wagon and took from the horse's neck a leather pouch, prairie luggage, and swung it into the wagonbed beside Chief Bones. She looked at the chief and cocked her head as a dog does when it hears a strange note. Gideon wasn't about to try to explain. If she was scared of an old skeleton she could ride back home, and maybe Enoch Martin would kill her and not him. But she hopped onto the board beside him, and they made straight for the sun.

When the sun sank into a narrow, twisting river, turning the water into a length of gold thread, they made cold camp. After watering and hobbling his oxen friends and Enoch's horse, Gideon offered Suella half of his last corn dodgers. Like the river, Suella's skin gave back the deep red sunset. She shook her head and offered him strips of dried meat from her pouch. While they chewed the tough, smoke-flavored strips the western horizon turned from deep red to lavender to cobalt blue.

When Gideon unrolled his blanket beside the wagon, grasshoppers flew from the grass. He pulled off his brogans, pulled his socks loose where they were stuck in damp folds to his feet. Suella spread her blanket against his. On her knees on the blanket she crossed her arms in front of her and held the hem of her deerskin blouse, lifted her arms, and pulled the blouse over her face. Dark hair fell down over her shoulders. When she reached both arms back to unfasten her skirt, her breasts thrust toward him. She dropped the skirt in the grass. Her bare brown knees pressed against his side, and her silver-streaked hair hid her face as she bent, opening his shirt and unbuckling his belt. His hands trembled when he moved his fingers over her warm flesh. Her breasts were as firm and tight as her flat belly, different from the pale, sagging breasts of the St. Louis sporting girl he had lain with weeks ago. He worked his pants down and kicked his feet free. Suella rolled over onto him. His hand touched hers where she took hold and guided him up into her. Wet lips on skin, heat and suction and clenching, ribcages and pelvis bones bumping sore, her jagged fingernails scraping his chest, the bottoms of her feet hard as boards, in his mouth her nipples covered with small bumpy knots like blackberries, and through this furious pushing away and pulling toward, arching and falling, lifting and bucking, he heaved and huffed like someone running for his life. He breathed grass smell and oily sweat smell and whiffs of Enoch Martin's chicken yard. Coyote yowlings reminded him where he was before he drowned them out with his own yowls. Suella said, "Goddamn." Her body made the notes his bones drummed against her tight skin. At length they collapsed, her weight slippery and hot on him, grass stalks poking and itching his back and bottom, and some creature not visible threaded fibrous insect feet up his shoulder to a place he could never reach to scratch. Thus entwined, they fell immediately asleep.

He woke at dawn, Suella's hair beaded with dawn-gold drops of dew decorating his arm as a jeweled sleeve. They moved arms and legs apart and stood naked. At the full daylight sight of her his body quivered from within, and Suella grinned to see the outward sign of his desire. She made a sound between the bark of a dog and the oink of a pig and reached between his thighs where he was astir. He stepped beyond her extended hand and hurried toward the river, wet grass stinging his shins. His leg was so gimpy from their night's passion, he limped. Suella did not come after him.

The water was cold and shock enough to shrink his randy pecker. He dunked his head and blew bubbles, his breath loud underwater. He came out of the river shaking water from his hair. Suella was there, already dressed and holding his clothes in her arms. They ate the dried meat she had brought, and he searched for a place to ford the river. On the other side of the river he tied one of the red cloth markers. He had to continue looking for Dorsey. He had gotten way off his intended path, and he had to find her soon. Somehow he would think of some plan to extricate himself from Suella, this half-savage new companion his mind rejected but his body embraced.

Dorsey Murphy: An Afternoon of Blood

Then Commenced the Work of Death
(August 1865)

Someone has written that the best proof of Satan's existence is how he has managed to make so many people believe he does not exist. Anyone who doubts there is an actual and unmerciful Devil with legions of demons and many ministers of death need only visit the killing grounds where Comanche warriors have savaged their victims. He will need no more convincing. I walk over the bloodstained earth where Dorsey recently trod, and my mind goes cold with thoughts of her in the sharp teeth of such cruelty.

—from *Gideon Jones' Journal*

Dorsey let the roll and shake of the wagon lull her mostly into a daze, her vision mostly unfocused, her gaze no higher than the grass. She liked being alone on the board, her mother beneath the wagon cover to escape for a while the sun and dust. Laura Etta giggled, and Dorsey looked over her shoulder. At the rear of the wagon her mama's new husband leaned in for a kiss, his face filling the round opening where the Osnaburg was drawn tight, puckered like his lips. A singular red flower swayed at the edge of Dorsey's sight, and she breathed easier on Gideon's account. She searched the endless grass for another red bloom—another of the cloth strips he was to tie marking their way to follow. Every red scrap Dorsey had cut from a new union suit meant he was somewhere ahead, still safe from Indians, Gideon and his wagonload of lightning rods and his slow but sure ox-team leading where Dorsey and the others would follow.

Mr. Speer was leading the wagons wide of Gideon's marks, turning them south, opposite the trail Gideon was blazing. By the time Dorsey spotted another red-tipped grassblade they were so far south she could barely make out the small flag.

"Mr. Speer," she said. On Joe's bay mare her mama's new husband trotted to the front of their wagon, wheeled around, and trotted back to the Thurston wagon that followed. His legs were stiff in the stirrups and stuck out at straight angles from the horse. The stump of his left arm stuck out stiffly, too, in an unintentionally horrid imitation of his legs. "Mr. Speer, we're drifting off Gideon's course." She pointed to the speck of red off to the north.

"Just never you mind, daughter. Just never you mind."

She didn't like him calling her "daughter." "What about the Indians?"

"We gonna drop down to the Santa Fe Trail whilst the Pawnees track pretty red bows."

"What about the Territory of Washington?"

"There's more than one way to get from here to there. We're going northwest by going southwest. I already figured this out, girl."

She was sure he had no idea what he was up to. Her stepfather just thought if he had a plan, especially if it included duping someone else—namely Gideon off on a fool's errand—then he could succeed. She knew Gideon would gladly serve as a decoy if he thought he could get her safely across the prairie, the plains, and the Great Desert. She resolved somehow to meet up with him later.

Daytime Nightmare

In three days, moving ever southward, they crossed four rivers, all easy crossings. Joe and Hiram kept the horses and mules watered and the water kegs filled. She spotted no more of Gideon's red rags. On the fourth day they passed, far to the east, a hill that rose into white puffy clouds like a castle out of Dorsey's dreams. They nooned in a shallow bowl Mr. Speer said offered cover, though they'd seen no Indian sign. If they'd made four miles that morning they were lucky, and Mr. Speer wanted to roll on till sunset. Their teams watered and rested, they were about to head out when a staccato screech pierced the still afternoon. The cry was close, high-pitched, and musical, a call resembling most Alexander Speer's voice of those in the wagons. For a moment Dorsey wondered what her stepfather wanted with her. A heartbeat after the cry, the ground shivered. She reckoned thunder first, then knew the earth-trembling as horse's hooves. Another screech followed closer still, eerie and frightening like nothing on earth. A chorus of shrieks. "*Yee-yee-yee. Yee-yee-yee. Aiee-yee-yee.*" Shirtless men, their skin the color of Mr. Speer's tobacco, rode white-spotted horses around and around the two wagons. *"Yee-yee-yee. Aahe."* In drawings she had seen, Indians wore long feather headdresses, war bonnets, but these Indians had horns, great horns curving out of shaggy hats of fur that hung with the Indians' shining black hair down their backs. Feathers dangled from round shields and from horses' manes. These Indians and their small spotted horses rattled and clinked with bits of bone, rock, metal, glass, and beads tied to hair and shields, manes and tails. On each man's back a square of stiff hide—armor?—bounced as he wheeled and turned. Yowling, chanting Indians circled yet moved closer, as a drawstring tightens the opening of a bag or pouch. Both wagons, each man, woman, and child and all their animals, stopped. The only motion, the only sounds, were waving, shrieking, howling horned devils and galloping, wheeling, snorting horses.

Hiram Thurston went off his head. He screamed, "aaah-gaaah," a falsetto growl, jumped on Joe's bay and charged the Indians. There's no knowing whether he was trying to escape or to attack. His only weapons were his wildly windmilling arms. Momentarily, the Indians gave way for him, then, with brutal quickness tightened their loop again, seizing Hiram in a writhing knot.

"Aa-he." A rush of brown became a jingling, rattling horse. Hanging off the animal's side was a long-armed youth. His blue leather-covered legs bulged like the horse's own flexed muscles. *"Aa-he,"* the boy-man said. He snatched Joe off his feet. For maybe forty yards the horse jerked Joe along, his boots skipping up and down against the ground. Sun flashed in Joe's hair, and he dropped like fruit from a limb, hit the ground sitting up, legs outstretched, his unfired rifle still in his hands. The Indian whirled and held up something dark. As the Indian drew close Dorsey recognized Joe's hair, his bloody scalp.

A second Indian slid off his horse and stuck a feathered pole in the ground. He raised his arms and ran to where Joe lay. *"Aa-he,"* he screamed, seizing both Joe's ears and shaking his head. Dorsey's mama jumped from their wagon. Mottled horses and dark flashing chests swirled one way and then another, each Indian making his own attack. Laura Etta ran straight for the Thurston wagon. The Indians hung by their legs and with bows no more than a yard long shot arrows from under their horses' necks. One loosed arrows so fast Dorsey couldn't see him pull them from his quiver and notch them to his string—arrows poured from his arm out of his fingers as water spews from a spring. An arrow just missed Laura Etta when she climbed onto the seat of the Thurston wagon. Mary held Hiram's long Spencer rifle, the barrel pointed straight up. Laura Etta grabbed the Spencer and swung the barrel down, aiming at the Indian who had taken Joe's scalp. An explo-

sive report was followed by a puff of smoke, and the Indian fell face forward, gobbling like a wild turkey.

Dorsey scrabbled up the grassy bowl. Red dust was the sky. Grit on her tongue,
smell of horse dung and sweat. *"Yee-yee-yee,"* a shriek male and female at once,
falsetto yet guttural, a voice out of bad dreams. And other nightmare voices: Mary
Thurston screaming "no—no, no, no," little Lucy and baby James wailing. And
a loud growl close by. Dorsey's throat burned, and she realized the growl came
through her own clenched teeth.

Grass rushed up to her, earth hit her forehead, breasts, knees. Nose and chin
and stomach slapped hard ground and heat flashed from her insides out to her
skin. Mouth full of grass and dirt. She lay on her stomach, and a heavy warmth
dropped over her like a shadow. Had she eaten dirt before? The taste put the farm
in Indiana behind her closed eyes. *Indiana*—why had she never pondered it?—
contained the word *Indian.* Her face in the grass made the world not so bright, not
so hot, not so loud. She felt like she was sleeping and this was a nightmare. Or, the
Indians were real, they had killed her, and this dream was death. Dirt thickened
the spit on her tongue. Mud cooled her gums and lips. She chewed, once, a satisfying grit against her teeth.

Firm fingers sank into her arms and pulled her from the cool earth, rolled her
over into bright sun and piercing screams. Alive, she opened her eyes, squeezed
them shut, blinked away stinging dust and bits of grass. Straddling her, his knees
pinning her arms, an Indian not much older than she was stared down at her.
She'd never been this close to an Indian. Sweat and warpaint made black rivers
through powdery shapes of dust on his skin. He said something like "Why are
peaches?" Dorsey's throat knotted. A kind of quack came out of her nose. He
thrust his flat palm at her mouth, signaling her to be quiet. Around the edges of
her eyes bright shards of bone-whiteness fell like hail from red storm clouds of
dust. Horse nostrils black and round as shotgun barrels snorted fire and smoke as
the spurning beasts lunged from the earth, but focused in the still, silent center of
her seeing was only this one dark thing—this boy.

His eyes moved over her, hers over him. Black paint striped his forehead,
and a black streak bridged his nose and angled across each cheek. From the right
side of his thick neck a scar, outlined with a tattoo of black dots and painted red,
ran down beneath his right nipple and over his ribcage toward the center of his
stomach. A rawhide strip tight around his barrel-chest held an arrow quiver across
his back. A hide belt cinched his waist holding a leather flap in front and back, the
breechclout Dorsey had been told Indian warriors wear, both flaps bunched now

against her belly. His legs were small and muscular like the legs of the wiry Indian horses. He wore skin moccasins with thick hide soles. From ankles to hips sea-shells were knotted to the fringe of his blue-painted leggings. Where had he found seashells? Dorsey fancied him gathering them out on the prairie sea of grass. His fingernails, close to her eyes, were split and jagged, stained with the black paint that marked his face and chest, red paint that outlined his scar, yellow paint that streaked the center part in his greased black hair, the top of which was hidden beneath a gruesome buffalo headdress. Tied into his hair near the yellow-painted center part, a piece of blond hair peeked from the edge of the fur headdress. Two tied queues of black hair came from under the fur and disappeared behind his back. Fixed to these long queues of bunched hair were more shells, circles of tin, knots of yellow and red cloth. Had he taken Gideon's red rags and tied them in his hair? One dust-powdered, sweat-streaked arm held his shield, a hide saucer maybe two feet across, thick and somehow stiffened. Painted on the shield, lines came out of circles, and hanging from the shield was a long bunch of horsehair held with a circlet of blue and yellow beads.

"No. No, wait," Mr. Speer said.

An Indian swung his leg and knocked Speer's feet from under him. Laura Etta sat up and Dorsey understood her stepfather's yelling. A large X of blood marked her mother's naked front, where a warrior had cut away her dress, slicing through to her skin. In his fist the Indian held the dress bunched above Laura Etta's waist, and he knelt between her thighs, the front of his breechclout poked out like a tent over a pole. Another Indian put a knife into Mr. Speer's mouth, and he screamed, spraying blood, his body bucking.

"*Nu kwuhupu*," said the Indian who'd knifed Mr. Speer. "*Nu kwuhupu*," he said into Speer's bloody face. When Dorsey's stepfather did not respond, the Indian said, "*Me hace reir*," and he laughed, air whistling through jagged gaps in his teeth.

"*Aahe*," another Indian said, and literally walked over Dorsey's stepfather, stepping on him as if he were just uneven earth, clubbing him in the face with a shield. Speer's head dropped with a thud, and he lay so still Dorsey knew he must be dead. The Indian kneeling between Laura Etta's thighs grunted and pushed against her.

An Indian threw little Lucy into the air. When she hit the grass with a soft whump, he fell onto her and tied her arms together. He tied her legs at the ankles then grabbed a fistful of her blonde hair, lifted her, and threw her like a sack of feed across a horse's back, where he lashed her to the hide pad that served as saddle. This same one went over to Mary Thurston, who had baby James smothered against her chest, both her arms encircling the baby as if she might hide him. The Indian reached for the baby. Mary rolled over and covered her child with her body, wiggling down against the grass as if she might burrow into the earth. The Indian pulled at her, but in her fury Mary was strong. She kept herself belly to the ground covering baby James, and the Indian wasn't able to roll her over. He pulled out a knife with a clay-colored blade and ripped open her dress above her hips. He jerked down her dress and petticoat, tore off her underwear and exposed brown-stained cotton rags she wore—she was in her monthlies. The Indian recoiled so, Dorsey thought he'd been shot. He screamed at Mary and yelped to the other Indians, who kicked dirt at Mary and threw at her books and cups they had scattered from the wagons, yelling, "*Ai, ai.*" Mary crawled away into the grass with baby James.

Dorsey jerked her head away, and the one on top of her slapped her across the nose so hard she no longer felt the front of her face. He stared at her, his eyes so black they had no pupils. He neither smiled nor frowned. He took hold of her dress, and Dorsey knew he was going to rip it, but, instead, he unbuttoned the dress down the front. There were no buttons down her shift beneath, and this he ripped. He put his hands, rough as boards and hot like cooking pans, against her skin. *Oh, Mama,* she thought, *let's both just die, right now.* She squeezed shut her eyes, *right now,* she thought and opened her eyes to see if she was in Heaven. But the hands still pressed her skin, hands the shining color of wet pecans. One hand moved down where he'd pulled her torn shift from between her thighs. This dark hand pulled at the curly black hair that had surprised her so often in the past year. But he only touched her, he did not attempt to violate her.

"*Taivo tiehpuer.*" He got off her, and she saw beneath his breechclout his penis, long and loose-skinned, thickly hanging with his sac like a sleeping lizard, and tied there with leather thongs wrapped tight around his thigh, a second sac, a small beaded pouch, bulged with something Dorsey somehow knew was secret, as special as the other sac. She rose on one elbow, her arms sore and tingling where his knees had pressed. Her eyes flinched: another Indian thrust against her mother's naked body. This one said, "*yee,*" then got up. "*Nea kwuuhuupuu,*" he said to yet another who lowered himself against Laura Etta and pumped and thrust like a cur. Laura Etta's eyes were open and so fixed Dorsey would've taken her for dead except for the way her fingers opened, closed into fists, opened again. Dorsey got to her feet, her legs trembling beneath her weight. The torn shift hung like stuffing out of the unbuttoned top of her chambray dress. The skirt of the dress was grass- and mud-stained and there was a jagged hole torn above the hem.

Joe and Hiram lay on their backs, wrists and ankles spread and tied to stakes. Hiram stopped screaming, and Dorsey realized she'd been hearing him and Joe together. Now, Hiram had passed out or died, and Joe screamed alone. There may have been words in Joe's shrieks, but if so, Dorsey didn't want to understand them. He screamed and screamed. He screamed longer than she would have thought a man could scream. And then he, too, stopped, sudden, and did not start up again, and Dorsey prayed the mortal agony had ceased for Joe forever.

Dorsey's captor pulled one of Mary Thurston's dresses from a trunk and threw it at Dorsey. Without thinking, she caught the dress. The Indian snorted and tugged at the hem of the stained and torn chambray. She pulled off the dress and the white shift. She stood naked in the sun and felt no shame, only weariness and the determination to kill as many of these creatures as she might and then to die her ownself. Before she could slip Mary's dress over her head, the Indian with the brown-stained broken teeth grabbed Dorsey around her bare waist and pulled her against him, but her young captor said, "*Ke, hait. Keta.*"

"*Narumuuru tiehpuer*, Wahatewi?"

"*Ke.*"

All this meant to Dorsey was, for some reason, the one who'd caught her would not let the broken-toothed one have her. Mary's blue church dress hung loose around Dorsey's waist and brushed the ground. Her captor wrapped a strip of rawhide tight around her wrists, then pushed her down and looped the other end around her ankles, cinching her feet behind her back. She held her feet in her bound hands.

The Indians herded the mules, Joe's bay, and the scrub mustang together with their many ponies. Each rider had two to three mounts, pintos except for a handful of sorrels and bays likely stolen from settlers. The Thurstons' milk cow was shot full of arrows, and one Indian, hollering and grinning, sliced off her milk bag and held it high. He greedily drank milk and blood spilled from the rent udder. The Indians ripped open ticks and pillows and laughed like children at the blizzard of feathers. They split open bags and emptied flour and seed over the ground, keeping the empty bags they stuffed inside a large feedsack. A thin, wiry Indian found a calico dress in Mary Thurston's trunk, and he held it upside down and put his feet through the arm holes and pulled it up around him. He cut a rope off the Thurston wagon and tied the skirt tight under his arms. Then he reached inside the collar of the dress, bunched up at his crotch, and pulled his penis out through the open neck. The other Indians laughed and went on pillaging.

Dorsey lay where the Indian had left her. Sweat ran down her nose, and she

457

longed to touch her face but the more she pulled at the rawhide the more it burned her wrists.

Most of what they found the Indians smashed or burned, discarding treasures the Thurstons and Speers had hoarded for months of miles. Laura Etta's stockings one man tied as streamers to his long hair. Another took Mary's china flower vase and inverted it on one horn of his buffalo-head hat. Dresses and skirts they wore over their breechclouts or pulled down over their horses' heads. A pair of ladies' gloves the broken-toothed Indian affixed to his horse's mane between its ears where the fingers stuck up like a cockscomb. Hats and bonnets they dipped into the water keg. When the hats leaked, the Indians laughed at the white man's poor pottery. Jars and tins of medicine — calomel, quinine, castor oil, Black Drought, Epsom salts, camphor, Sloan's Liniment, oil of turpentine — they smelled and tasted, making horrible faces, wiping their tongues, and shaking their heads. One broke the neck off Hiram's spirits of niter for doctoring sick horses and then guzzled the bottle dry. Another found a tin of Tube Rose snuff Mary had secreted away. He ate a mouthful and jabbered in ecstasy, spraying dark spittle, apparently exhorting his comrades to trade him something wonderful for this prize. Soon he had a cooking kettle on his head like a helmet, the wire hoop handle under his chin, and two other Indians were grinning dark, juicy grins of snuff.

Shortly, the Indians tired of these games. Broken Teeth piled dry grass against the Osnaburg cover of the Thurston wagon. He sparked together two gray rocks from a pouch tied to his pony and the grass began to smoke. When the Thurston wagon was ablaze, another Indian rolled the Speer wagon against the flames. Jars of pickles the Indians couldn't open, they tossed onto the fire. When the jars exploded, Dorsey jerked and rolled onto her stomach hiding her face in the dirt, and the Indians bent double laughing.

Dorsey became aware of quiet and realized the attack was ended. She rolled onto her back and felt the sun on her cheek. The ordeal seemed to have lasted all afternoon but had likely taken less than an hour, an hour that was a lifetime long, the world all noise — pounding, snorting horses, Mr. Speer's booming Spencer carbine, loud breath of arrows and thunk of shields and clubs, Indian shrieks and the screams of the others. Now Dorsey marked the quiet: no sounds but Laura Etta's low keening and, from the pony where she was tied, Lucy's whimpers, the barking talk of the Indians, and the huff and pop of the burning wagons. Horses stood still, sides heaving. Dust was settling, and Dorsey heard again the insistent low whine of the prairie wind.

Dorsey's Indian held up the whalebone corset her mama had bought from a drummer back in Corydon just before she'd married Alexander Speer. A small secret, Laura Etta's pride in how well she still carried her shape. The Indian tied one side of the corset to his arm and held the other side in his fist, a whalebone shield. Then he laced it around his middle. His waist was not much bigger around than Laura Etta's, and he wore the garment well. He rapped his fist against the bone stays and grinned. "*Tosabite pihi.*"

Broken Teeth rode over dripping snuff juice and smiling as if he had been born to show off his stained, jagged mouth. "*Tosabite pihi,*" Broken Teeth said. Grinning down at Dorsey, he asked, "*Un corazón blanco?*" She knew the words for Spanish, but not what they meant. "*Un corazón blanco?*" he said again. He leaned from his horse and stretched down his long arm, touched with a dark, rough finger the pale skin along the underside of her arm. "*Blanco.*" Then, he touched his chest, "*Un corazón.*" He leaned out and thumped the corseted chest of Dorsey's Indian. "*Un corazón.*" He pointed to strewn feathers. "*Blanco.*" He pointed to spilled flour. "*Blanco.*"

"White." She was surprised to hear her voice. She looked up at the Indian on the horse, their shapes dark in the bright sun. "*Blanco* is white."

Broken Teeth pounded his fist against his chest. "*Corazón.*"

"White chest?"

Broken Teeth thumped his chest like a drum. "*Corazón.*" Unless she answered in Spanish, Broken Teeth wouldn't know whether she understood or not. He pointed at the other Indians, "Numunuu." He pointed at himself and the other Indians. "Komantz."

"Co-mance. Co-man-che," Dorsey said. "Of all deadly savages, dread most the brutal Comanches, warlords from Texas"—from one of Hiram Thurston's brother's letters.

Dorsey counted eight Indians plus the one who'd been killed. They had tied the dead body onto one of their ponies. None of the men looked older than Dorsey's brother, Joe, but this one looked, in death, no more than ten or eleven. Blood from a dark wound in the dead boy's neck matted the horse's white-spotted hair and dripped onto the dry earth. The dead Indian's fixed eyes were open wide, the fascinated stare of a child who should still be playing children's games. Eight plus one killed, nine in all. Had there been only nine? While the ground trembled and dust swirled, the raiders screaming and whipping their ponies had seemed like fifty of the fiercest devils. Now just eight walked among the wagons, boys awkward on short bowed legs. They filled water bags and from small leather pouches ate with their fingers something that looked to Dorsey like brown pebbles, or tobacco streaked with yellow.

"*Tokwetikati,*" Dorsey's Indian, White Chest, said. "*Tokwetikati, haa. Haa, tsaati.*" He cut her ankles free but left her hands tied tight behind her back. "*Quimaro.*" When Dorsey didn't move, his dark eyes sparked like flint and he kicked her bottom so hard it burned up into her stomach. He jerked her up by her hair, and she was sure her skin was going to pull her eyes and nose off her face. She tried to get her feet under her, but they were numb from her tight binding and she could not make them do what she wanted. They bounced over the ground like the feet of a marionette Dorsey recalled from a drawing in one of Binga's German books. After so much bouncing both feet tingled and burned. White Chest leapt onto his pony without letting go of her hair, and with one arm, as if he were lifting an empty dress, he pulled her up behind him. Then he cut her hands free.

Lucy was still slung over the pinto horse. One Indian tied a lead to Joe's bay and put Laura Etta in the saddle. Joe and Hiram were staked out on the ground, their privates hacked off and stuffed in their mouths, the skin of their chests and stomachs flayed, their bodies shot so full of arrows they looked like Laura Etta's pincushions. *At least,* Dorsey thought, *they have gone where they will never again suffer pain.* Mr. Speer the Indians had not mutilated, except for gouging his tongue. He lay still, and Dorsey was certain he had bled to death so wide was the bloodstain beneath his head. Dorsey searched for Mary Thurston and baby James, but they were nowhere to be seen. The Indians, once they'd seen the bloodsoaked rags beneath Mary's dress and petticoat, had been terrified of her catamenia. They had wanted only to make her go away. Mary and baby James had disappeared as if the earth had swallowed them up.

Strange as it was, Dorsey had not yet shed tears. But for her mother and little Lucy, her heart had been insensible to life or to death. Her heart relentlessly beat within her, sustaining a torment too great for utterance by crying and tears. Except for the intervention of an invincible anger, the agony of her soul might have stilled her heart and become the angel of her deliverance.

"*Miar,*" White Chest said, and the ground raced by. Dorsey locked her arms around White Chest, glad of the corset so she didn't have to touch the Indian's skin. Why was she holding on? She didn't want to go with them. But if she let go she would fall, and if the fall didn't kill her it might make White Chest mad enough to stop and kill her—or worse. For some reason she had not been raped, had not been badly hurt, so she held on. As long as they were riding she was alive and not being raped. She hoped they never stopped riding.

Horse Ride through Hades

Not even a seasoned frontier scout can detect the trail of the Comanches.
They travel without roads and leave no record of their passing. Not by
skill in tracking, not by trace of hoofprint or moccasin, but only by resolute
and utter devotion will I find Dorsey and ransom or steal her back.

—from *Gideon Jones' Journal*

The sun was hotter than Dorsey had imagined the Great Desert or, even, fiery
Hades. The Indians pulled up the stiff hide squares tied to their backs, the squares
she had thought were armor plates, and now affixed them over their heads. White
Chest's umbrella was not wide enough to shade Dorsey, so her arms, face, and
ears slowly roasted. The hot air stirred by their galloping cooled her none at all.
She looked back over her bouncing shoulder. Little Lucy was tied like a corpse
over a black-and-white pony. Her hair hanging down swept through tall grass.
Four Indians rode in a line behind Lucy. Behind them Dorsey's mama rode ramrod straight, roped into the saddle of Joe's bay. Broken Teeth rode behind Laura
Etta, and strung out behind him were the Indians' extra mounts, the scrub horse
Mr. Speer had bought for Joe, and the mule teams from the two wagons. Behind
these came the dead Indian on his horse, and behind him, one solitary Indian
loped along making the mules keep up with the horses and covering their rear.
For so large a party they lifted little dust. Eight living Indians, one dead Indian,
three white captives, twenty-seven—no, she counted twenty-eight—mules and
horses, they made a good length of dark thread stitching a swatch of grass, but
Dorsey thought if she could spread her arms and fly high above them all these
thirty-nine living creatures might hardly be noticeable so wide was the endless
plain they traversed. If they were so inconspicuous a bird's eye might not discern
them, were they then out of even God's sight? If God's eye was on them, surely
He would not have let this happen. And if God had lost sight of them, how was
Gideon going to find them?

Dorsey's arms and hands ached so she didn't think she could hold on any
longer. The moment her fingers slipped apart, White Chest—as if he had been
waiting for her to let go—looped a strip of rawhide around her wrists and without slowing the pony's gait secured her arms around his waist. Muscles in his
arm were tight and corded as vines beneath her fingers. Her thighs burned raw
where they rubbed against the horse, and she longed to put her fingers there

and soothe the stinging flesh. Every gallop thudded into her and rattled her bones.

Sometime in the late afternoon she needed to pee. The bouncing horse made the need more and more urgent until it became a pulsing ache. Finally, she let go of the pain, and urine ran hotly down her legs where it both salved and hurt the raw insides of her thighs. Her skin dried and her thighs stung worse than before. The fiery air dried out her eyes and burned her nose, so she kept her eyes closed and breathed through clenched teeth. Her mouth was cottony with thirst. So numb were her feet and hands, she was sure they had fallen off miles behind. Dorsey felt only parts of her self: the numb heat that was her face, the searing of her excoriated thighs, the throbbing cut marks across her wrists where the rawhide—like some perverse umbilical cord—connected her to this death-in-life and would not let her loose. Through all the afternoon they rode without rest and even past the sun's going down, when the Indians dropped their sunshades against their backs and rode even harder. Hiram Thurston's brother's letters had said Indians never rode after dark. *So much,* Dorsey thought, *for civilized man's lore of barbarians.*

Because she knew she was opening her eyes, she realized she had slept. The ground was not rushing past. Low trees stood still. Nothing stirred. Her thighs were on fire, her wrists hurt with each beat of her heart, her head pounded from behind her eyes, and someone was sticking knives into the bottoms of her feet. She looked down and knew the reason for the stabbing in her feet—she was off the horse, standing up. A fingernail slice of moon hung low in the black sky with countless sparks of stars. A small white cloud floated above her, became her mama's corset glowing in the night, and from the corset came husky words, *"En suwaiti tihkari?"*

So it had all happened, was still happening. She'd had a second's hope she was waking from a nightmare. White Chest was eating from a small hide bag he held out to her. She smelled urine dried on Mary Thurston's dress and the sweat of men and horses and, from the hide bag, something like plums. When she did not eat, he handed her a water bag made from some animal's stomach. Her hands shook, spilling water over her cracked lips. A trickle worked its way over her chin and down her neck, tickled her skin down her chest to her belly button. Her mouth felt too full of her tongue to receive the water, but the cool wetness soaked into the crevices between her teeth and around her gums, and her tongue sank back into almost normal-feeling size and shape. Her eyes adjusted to the darkness. Horses' hooves splashed. The unmoving trees were cottonwoods around a pool of water. A few feet away someone was crying.

"Lucy? Mama?"

"Oh, Dorsey, Dorsey help me," Lucy said between sobs.

"I will, Lucy." Dorsey took another drink of water. "Don't worry, Lucy dear, everything will be all right." Dorsey was thinking of Gideon. He would find them. But she didn't want to say anything out loud to let the Indians know he would come to their rescue. When she realized Indians wouldn't understand a word she said, she grinned, stinging her cracked, scabbed lips. "Lucy, we're going to be fine. Gideon will come after us, and we'll watch these filthy heathen barbarians be killed." She spoke right at White Chest. "The first one I want to see die is this horrible, ugly, skinny, bad scoundrel. Ruffian." She clenched her teeth and fists.

"*Malo*," said Broken Teeth, who had come up beside them silently. "*Malo, tutsa. Tutsa matsohpe*," he said to White Chest.

"*Matsohpe*," White Chest said, and they both laughed. "*Tutsa matsohpe*." White Chest thumped the bone corset, and all the Indians laughed. He held out the food bag. "*Tuhkaru?*"

Inside was some kind of stringy dark meat, berries, pecans, and what looked like little pieces of bark and twigs, the whole mixture covered with yellow tallow. White Chest took a clump of the stuff in his fingers and ate. Before she had drunk the water Dorsey would have said she was not hungry. She had felt nauseous and incapable of putting anything, much less this strange-looking mixture, on her stomach that had been bounced up and down for hours. "I'm not eating any of your smelly, vomit-looking Indian food." And she meant it, so it surprised her when she took a pinch from the bag and ate. The mixture—pemmican she would learn later—waxy from the tallow, was stringy and took a lot of chewing. The taste was meaty and honey-sweet at once. She tasted walnuts and the plums she had smelled. The pemmican had a piney-resinous tang with a bitter aftertaste she didn't purely like but somehow enjoyed because of its lingering on her tongue. "Eat it, Lucy. We will need our strength."

"They won't let me. When I reach for it they knock my arm away. It's a kind of torture," the little girl said.

Dorsey found Lucy's shape in the direction of her voice. One of the Indians held the pouch out to Lucy, but when Lucy reached for it he slapped her hand. Dorsey got close to Lucy, reached in the hide bag and got a fistful of the greasy meat mixture. The Indian made no attempt to stop her when she held the food up to Lucy's mouth. In this way Dorsey fed Lucy hand to mouth while the Indian patiently held the bag open. But when Lucy reached to feed herself the Indian slapped her hand away. *This makes no sense*, Dorsey thought. But nothing in the last twenty-four hours had made sense. "Where's my mama, Lucy? Do you see my mama?"

"They took her down there." Lucy was chewing. "What happened to *my* mama and to baby James? Are they still alive?"

"I pray so, Lucy."

Dorsey's feet tingled more than before, and little shocks ran up her shins. She leaned against one of the cottonwoods, its bark thick and coarse. White Chest made no move to stop her when she stumbled down a slope toward sounds of horse hooves in water and voices murmuring. Beneath tree limbs it was even darker. Then she reached water, not much more than a mud wallow, a circle of ashen light maybe six or eight feet across around which several horses crowded. Two Indians sat filling water bags that floated beside them. Three other Indians had her mama stretched out on a flat rock the size of a wagonbed. Two held Laura Etta's arms and legs, one on each side of her, while the third hunched over her, his breechclout flapping like a towel on a clothesline as his backside rose and fell, violating her again.

Dorsey screamed, "Mama," and ran through the shallow edge of the pool to the big rock, where she grabbed the outthrust leg of the humping Indian. She held the leg low on the shin, squeezing with both her hands. The strength and force of the man's movements lifted Dorsey off the ground. Her fingers were greasy from the pemmican, and when the Indian gave her a kick her hands slipped and she fell back into the mud. The Indians holding Laura Etta laughed. One of them let go of her and grabbed Dorsey, dragged her up beside her mother. With one hand he held her arms above her head, pinned against the warm rock, while his other hand poked and pulled at her flesh. His fingers worked between her thighs, rubbed sore from the horse, and forced their way up into her. Dorsey turned to face her mama, not more than a foot away. Laura Etta stared at the stars. Her eyes were open but did not blink or move, did not appear to see anything. With his knees the Indian forced Dorsey's legs apart, and the raw burning in both her thighs came up into her as high as her stomach. She would not let this count. She would not let a savage bring ruin to her body. She would go away in her mind and not feel anything. She would not let herself feel any touch of this creature. Pure in heart was what the Scripture said, and these Indians could not reach her heart unless they cut open her chest. But just as the dark shape loomed over her, it vanished. All weight and heat lifted off of her, and cool night air lay like relief everywhere upon her, touched her as exquisitely as the delicate light of the waning moon.

"*Ke, keta. Murahcat.*" Dorsey marveled that she recognized White Chest's voice. Even saying their same growling Indian words, he sounded different from the others. He had pulled the other Indian off of her. But she refused to be grateful since he might be saving her for something equally unthinkable. Dorsey crawled across the rock to Laura Etta and looked down at her mother's fixed and uninhabited eyes before White Chest jerked her back. *"Miar."* He gave her a push. Compared to the muttering growls of the others, his voice was comforting.

"Mama," she said, but Laura Etta said nothing. *She's gone off in her head and maybe that's good. Maybe, later, after Gideon saves us, she won't remember what they did to her.* But Dorsey would remember always. And somehow, someday, she'd make these Indians suffer.

White Chest pushed her onto her side and bent her legs back, tying her wrists to her ankles. Nearby, Lucy lay on her side tied the same way. *"Ihkooi bihi,"* White Chest said.

Dorsey couldn't sleep all twisted up on the hard ground. Lucy's eyes were closed and she lay still, either asleep or dead. Quickly, all the Indians got quiet. They simply lay down where they stood, and as soon as they reclined they were asleep.

Dorsey lifted her head trying to shake bits of grass and dirt from her ear, trying to stir air against her tender skin. If she could somehow get loose while they were asleep she could get Laura Etta and Lucy and jump on horses and be gone before the Indians woke. But her rawhide bonds were so tight she could barely move her fingers. Mosquitoes hummed around her ears. They danced on her chin and cheeks, and she put her face back to the ground to keep from getting bitten on her eyes. *Our Father who art in Heaven, hallowed be Thy name, Thy kingdom come—White Chest thinks he's so—Lord, forgive me for letting my mind wander. Thy kingdom come, Thy will be done, on earth as Gideon, sense my need and hear my thoughts, find us somehow and—Oh, God, I'll never make it through this night, the mosquitoes are inside my ears they will get into my skull. Thy will—on earth—* She had not finished her prayer when White Chest shook her, and she realized he had already untied her. She must have slept, but it couldn't have been more than a few minutes. It was still dark—darker than it had been because the moon was gone. She wanted to go where the moon had gone.

White Chest and several other Indians arched streams onto the ground, relieving themselves. White Chest handed her what looked like a leather belt that had been left out in the rain, then baked hard by the sun. He and the other Indians were biting pieces off these belts. In her mouth the dried meat became chewable if not tender. She recognized the smoky flavor of deer. Dorsey pointed to the pool, and White Chest nodded. Light glowed faintly along one side of the sky.

Fully awake now, she could see better. She whispered to Lucy, who was astride a scrawny-looking pony that had walked over to stand against White Chest's horse. Lucy's eyes were closed, and she shook her head. She looked asleep. *At least,* Dorsey thought, *she's no longer thrown over the pony and tied on her stomach.* Dorsey's mama stood alone by the pool's edge. As quickly as Dorsey's stiff legs would carry her, she walked over to Laura Etta. "Mama," she said, but her mama acted deaf. "Mama, don't give up. Gideon will save us." When her mama still did not respond, Dorsey closed her eyes and prayed: *"Please,"* she said. *"Please, Please, Please."* Then she waded into the shallow pool and knelt there, relieving herself and washing herself at the same time. The water both soothed and stung her raw flesh.

The Indians all switched their small saddles to ponies from the unridden string. White Chest and one other Indian crouched in front of a rock half as big as a horse. They leaned into the rock and pushed it up, then White Chest used his foot to roll and wedge a smaller rock beneath it. In a scooped-out place under the rock were a full water bag, several stiff and twisted strips of dried venison, and at least fifty arrows, their feathered and notched ends sticking up out of a leather quiver. White Chest added to the stash a steel-bladed knife and a blanket plundered from the Thurston and Speer wagons, then eased the rock back in place. The other Indian broke off a leafy limb and swept dust over the ground near the rock until no one would have thought this was a survival cache. She wondered why they would hide a bag of water by a waterhole. Then she noted the wide circle of mud around the pool, felt the heat in her sore, burned arms, and understood. Even if the pool dried up, there was water if you knew where to look. White Chest lined up three rocks in a straight line in front of the buried treasure. If you knew where to look, the rocks were a directional arrow, or maybe even some kind of calendar—the third day or week or month, three full moons, three somethings—telling where and when the cache was hidden.

They left the pool and the cottonwoods behind and rode again over the sea of grass. White Chest's fresh horse was larger than yesterday's but bounced just as hard. This day merged with the day before: same sear sun, same sore skin, same endless roll of horse and ground. Memory and imagination failed Dorsey. There was no world beyond her senses. She opened her eyes and white steam hovered over a brown clay cauldron on yellow flames, all the world a flaming cookfire. She squeezed shut her eyes and blue stars exploded, yellow comets' tails streaked across blackness. In her ears the constant thump and clump of hooves, the swish and rasp of grass, the tink and clink of bone bits and shell and mirror shards in the hair of horse and Indian. The world smelled of suet, fire-ash, tobacco, urine, rope, and manure. Her thighs and teeth ached, grasshoppers stung her cheeks and arms. The need to pee was again a hurtful weight in her pelvis. Nausea and hunger alternately rose in her belly. Thirst swelled her throat like something yeasty baking, but the only taste on her tongue was the metallic tang of the blade she'd seen gouge Mr. Speer's mouth. Dorsey breathed when she wished she might quit breathing. The sun was angling up her sore left shoulder when low red ridges appeared on the horizon. The grass grew shorter, the ride rougher, and the ridges slowly came toward them. Hooves clattered on rock, and she jerked her head up. They had slowed climbing a rock escarpment, moving higher onto the promontories of Hell, urging their mounts up the rays of the sun, riding the red beams right into the inferno. They ascended a broad, high plain, a mesa that stretched ahead, more endless than the lengths they'd already traversed. No hills, no trees, no bushes broke the horizon. Nothing grew but thick grass so uniformly short it looked as if a giant had passed with a scythe and mowed all the visible earth. White Chest reined in the pony, and the other Indians raced past then slowed and turned back to see why he had stopped. He gave a hand signal and the other Indians rode on. He tilted his sunshade against the horizon line of a distant butte where there were a few lonely clouds. He nudged the horse with his knees, and the animal walked a tight circle, White Chest keeping his eyes on the distance all the way around. They galloped after the rest of the Indians, and Dorsey looked down and saw that all their horses passing had left no visible sign. The short, thick grass sprang back up as if nothing had traversed this high plain. She lost heart. If there was no trail to follow how would Gideon find her? Then she thought of the red rags Gideon had tied for the train to follow, and she tore a piece of her shift from beneath her dress and let it flutter to the grass behind her. *Like the Hansel and Gretel story*, she thought. The second time she dropped a scrap of cloth Broken Teeth spoke to her. "*Malo*," he said. The rest of the Indians stopped their horses. Broken Teeth jumped down and picked up the piece she had torn from her shift. He held it up and said, "*Malo*." He came over and Dorsey thought he was going to scalp her or stab her to death, but he pushed the little tear of cotton into her mouth. White Chest had turned in his saddle and laughed. He made chewing motions and laughed again. Broken Teeth nodded. Then, as if nothing had happened, the horses were moving again. Dorsey worked the material into a little ball in her mouth and sucked her saliva from it. Chewing the wad of cotton seemed to keep her mouth from being so dry, even if it meant there was no trail for Gideon to follow.

When the sun had passed overhead and was inching below her right shoulder, the Indians dismounted. They gave each captive two swallows of water and a pinch of pemmican. White Chest pressed his fingers against Dorsey's shoulder, burnt red as a scab. His fingers seared her skin and left two ghostly circles like a pair of moons that the redness of her flesh soon fogged over. Now she knew how it felt to be branded. White Chest knelt to a spiky, star-shaped cactus, sliced off one of the spiked points and slit it open. He squeezed the plant's inner flesh, thick as pudding but clear as water, onto Dorsey's sunburnt shoulder and arm. Amazed anything could feel so cool in this heat, Dorsey took the stalk he handed her and squeezed it into her hands, smoothed the coolness down both her arms and painted her face with it. Almost immediately the burning eased up. White Chest cut off another spike and gave it to her. She hurried back to the horses and put the healing balm on Lucy's pink face and arms. All of the Indians had gotten underneath their horses to rest in the shade the animals made.

Dorsey and Lucy got Laura Etta off Joe's bay. She stood stiffly in the sun, so they each took an arm and smeared the plant's juices into her skin. They doctored Laura Etta's face, then pulled her down in the shade of the horse.

"Mama, this will make you better." Laura Etta would not lie down so Dorsey let her sit—at least she was out of the sun. The Indians, and Dorsey and Lucy like them, slept until the sun slanted under the horses. Then they rode on as before. Though it was not as hot up on this great grassy plain, Dorsey's tongue began to swell again, her mouth gritty, her lips stiff. She poked White Chest in the back and pointed to the water bag jouncing along against his bare thigh. He handed her a short twig, turned and opened his mouth long enough for her to see the chewed remains of a similar twig. The twig hurt her tongue and scraped the roof of her sore mouth, then it got soft and seeped moisture and relieved her thirst. She vowed to watch, to see what tree or bush bore these water sticks.

Near sundown they came to a narrow draw. Single file the little Indian horses picked their way down the draw that opened into a deep canyon. Down the sheer rockface slanting sunlight made a gold arrow aiming them into soft shadows. It was as if they slipped through a crack in the earth to a different world. Below them the tops of trees made a dusky green line for at least a mile or more until the trees ended against a steep wall of shining-wet rock. Here and there water trickled out. Once they got to the bottom of the fissure, rivulets of water from out of the rock came together and made a stream that ran between the trees. Down here the sun had already set, but directly and high above there was still yellow sky, the same sky under which they had roasted these past days.

The trail was powdery, soft-looking dirt that muffled horses' hooves. No prairie wind whipped Dorsey's hair. No prairie grass slapped the horses' legs. From trees along the stream birdsong filled the air, and Dorsey realized it had been a long time since she'd heard their music. Down here was a place of water and trees and birds, but she might have ridden right by the opening in the earth and never seen it. *You have to know*, she thought, *what to look for.* And she began looking closer at everything.

Between green trees and pale rockface she spotted almost invisible spirals of smoke the same color as the limestone against which they rose. Yesterday she would not have noticed. Beneath the trees she made out tipis also the color of the rock walls protecting this hideaway and scattered between the tipis small fires twinkled.

Crouched and growling, their hackles and tails stiff, a half dozen or more dogs blocked the trail. Recognizing the men the dogs yipped and whined, tails up high, and careened around the horses. Out of the twilight came shrieking, laughing children, followed by silent, running women.

Mary Thurston in the Fiery Furnace

Sunstruck, half asleep, Mary Thurston dropped her hand to her breast to find what kept sliding and pushing against her there. Baby James' tiny, hot fingers gripped her thumb, and she opened her eyes. Bright blue spots outlined in yellow floated and bounced before her. Beneath the spots, in the shadow of her own head, baby James nuzzled at the torn top of her dress. She unfastened the top button, surprised the thread still held it in place, and she brought the baby to her breast. His tiny mouth chewed at her flesh, and she flinched as if bitten until he got his lips around her teat, then the steady sucking calmed her.

A gust of air breathed over the back of her sunburned neck. She shifted her eyeballs, staring to one side, and brown blur sharpened into strands of her own brown hair, sweat-darkened and twisted together. Pushing up into the tangles of hair were lighter brown stalks of grass that pricked her cheek and ear. Up close, the grass stalks, weighted and pointed at the tips by stone-colored seeds, looked like bunches of Indian arrows. *Had the Indians shot arrows all around her on the ground and yet she and baby James breathed? If she raised her head, would she see savages, naked half-grown men with the heads of buffaloes standing around her, waiting?*

Mary inhaled slowly. She smelled baby James' urine and milk odor and her own body stink of sweat and menstrual rags and something else out of the grass—a scent of scorched cotton and starch, the smells of ironing clothes. *The grass itself scorched by this roasting sun.* She was afraid to lift her head. So long as she stared down she and baby James were alone.

A grasshopper rasped and crawled up a grassblade, crossed over to a stalk of Mary's hair. Sun edged the insect's folded wings and they shone gossamer and bright as shards of ice. But *hot,* she knew, to touch. *How cursed this country is, things not the way they appear. Soft-looking as a pillow from a distance, this tall grass is stiff and cuts you when you must lie down.*

Baby James' hands, tiny red fists against her swollen and pale breast, kneaded her flesh. His face darkened and tightened into a frown and he cried out, a piercing wail, loud and steady.

"Shush, shush James, they'll hear you sure."

James screamed even louder, and Mary jerked up her head. Before her rose a long green hill spotted all over as with a light snow or—that was it—apple blossoms. Hiram had planted her hill with apples and they were all abloom. "James, we got to hurry to the house. Sakes, we been out here in the meadow so long I near forgot to start supper. Your daddy will be home from the orchards soon. Where is that sister of yours?" For a moment the baby hushed. His slate-gray eyes stared into Mary's, and he turned his head about as if he, too, wondered where his sister was.

Mary crooked one arm around baby James and stretched out her other arm like a sleepwalker. Grabbing at air, she rose unsteadily. Her dress was down off her hips in back, her petticoat and her rolled rags were bunched and wadded between her legs, and the material clung to the insides of her thighs. When she took a step the petticoat pulled at her skin. Shifting her baby up high over her shoulder, she pulled her dress waist out and looked beneath where her petticoat was peeled away, stiff and stained with blood as an old bandage. She pulled the cloth free, her skin chafed and raw. Behind her in the grass lay what looked like red-speckled eggs—the blood-splattered rolls of rags she wore during her monthlies. *What has happened to me?* "What has your mother done, James?" She stooped and gathered up the stiff balls of cloth and stuffed them into the pockets of her dress. She straightened her petticoat and smoothed the dress over it as well as she could. She raked a large grasshopper and broken stalks and brown blades of grass from her damp hair. Baby James' hair was sweat-dampened, too, and his cheeks were pink from the sun. She put her hand to his bottom—soaked. She pulled off the cloth he was diapered with and stuffed it in her pocket with her menstrual rags. She lifted James' bare bottom into the breeze to dry him. "Does that feel better?" He hiccuped once but did not resume crying. She brushed away one honey-colored seed-top stuck to his forehead. "What a sight we must be, child. We better get to the house and make ourselves presentable."

The sun beat down on Mary's head as she walked through the high, dry grass. *Have I died and gone to Hades?* she wondered. *No, if this were Hades there'd be no heavenly hill of apple blossoms just ahead.* So she guessed she was asleep. Hot bright as the sun felt it must be late and dark outside, and this was just a nightmare she was dreaming while she lay in her bed beside Hiram—little Lucy and baby James asleep nearby—in their new house beside the hillside orchard in the Territory of Washington. She bent forward so her head made a sunshade over baby James, and she kept walking, waiting to wake up.

Broken grass stalks pricked and burned like coals against the bottoms of her bare feet. Her dress rippled and snapped in the buffeting wind, the skirt flaring out into the dry grass and rasping back between her legs, cotton popping, hot and relentless as the flames of a fire. Arching up out of the grass ahead of her, endless grasshoppers caught the sun and burned like sparks. Mary recalled the Scriptures. How, in the Book of Daniel, King Nebuchadnezzar had Shadrach, Meshach, and Abednego bound and thrown into the fiery furnace. How the king peered into the mouth of the fiery furnace and said *Lo, I see four men loose, walking in the midst of the fire, and they have no hurt; and the form of the fourth is like the son of God.*

Mary cupped her hands around her eyes against the glare and stared into the mouth of the furnace. Her lovely hill of apple trees was aflame—soft white blossoms drifted on the air like ashes. Waves of heat rose, shimmied like ruined wagon wheels. She squinted her eyes shut, looked again. Red apple embers covered the ground and, in the far distance, shapes moved in the burning heat—two glowing, twisting trunks, like the last two apple trees on earth bowing in the scorching wind. Those last trees loomed, flared white-hot. Trees of fire, luminous in their own heat, each of their thousand leaves was a single curled flame blazing and hissing, yet they gave off no smoke.

The burning trees stirred. Uprooted, they moved closer, became the small fire-licked figures of two burnt-dark men who struggled through the inferno toward Mary and her babe. And she went forth to meet them, walking toward them in the midst of the burning furnace.

Gideon Jones: Beneath a Sky of Buzzards

Slakes His Thirst
(August 1865)

Gideon and Suella continued west. For three days he saw no sign of the Speer and Thurston wagons, and he found no water. For three days he looked back over his shoulder and saw Enoch Martin's white horse nodding along but no sign of Enoch coming after them. The fourth day, he gave the animals what water remained in the keg. He hoped Suella might find him a waterhole and then ride off on the white horse before he rejoined the Speers and Thurstons and needed an explanation for the half-Indian girl.

By nightfall, still no water. Gideon spent a restless night, even after he and Suella wrestled against one another again. She lay naked and slept as still and silent as Chief Bones. The animals moved constantly, dragging their hobbles, agitated by thirst. Morning, Gideon poured water from his almost empty canteen, soaked two rags and wiped their muzzles, squeezed drips of water onto their thick tongues, white with slobber. Suella refused to drink. He tipped up the canteen to his cracked lips expecting a final swallow but only got his lips damp. Suella took the reins.

"I get water." She turned the team south and east, away from the direction he expected to go in order to intersect Dorsey and the others. But without water he wouldn't last to find Dorsey.

The grass grew shorter and sparser as the sun slowly passed overhead. By midday Gideon's tongue was large in his mouth. Right Ox stopped so Left Ox had to, and both lifted their thick muzzles. The horse whinnied behind. Suella made a clucking whistle, and the oxen lumbered up and over a swell almost bare of grass. Hoofprints marked the slope down to a brown swipe of mud. The rear wheels slid around to the side, and the wagon skidded into the mud. Thus they stalled, Right Ox grown motionless as a mighty tree, Left Ox patiently pulling but only a step allowed him by the double yoke. Not bothering to set the brake, Gideon got down and released them both, untied the horse. Suella pulled off a side board from the wagon and followed the animals down the slope. Blue spots danced in Gideon's vision, and next Suella leaned over shaking his shoulder. "Drink. God-damn water."

The water was warm and muddy and at first would not stay inside his mouth but ran over his swollen tongue and out the corners of his lips the way rain on parched, hard earth runs off. With the side board Suella had dug down into the mud, and water slowly seeped up. A canteen-full at a time, they filled the keg. The oxen and horse half-buried their mouths in other holes Suella made. Gideon drank until he thought his belly was like a camel's hump, so full he would never thirst again. They rested there till afternoon, then Gideon turned them back north.

Led to a Killing Ground

Days passed and they saw no other living creatures save a distant herd of buffalo Gideon at first took for a pine forest. He tried to reckon the days traveling from Enoch Martin's soddy. But with their detour after water he could not guess the miles they had put between themselves and Suella's fearsome father. Suella slept upright on the board beside Gideon. In a trance of heat and slow movement he dozed, too. What brought him back from sleep was a sudden yip-yip, yip-yip, from nearby and a long ripple across a swale of grass to their side. Enoch or Indians, he feared, but the yipping was too tentative, too benign.

He braked, got down, and waded sluggishly toward the sound. The white tip of a tail poked up from the grass, and Gideon followed it to the spotted rump of Hiram Thurston's mongrel dog. His mouth and lips were still too dry to call the cur so he slapped his thigh and the fice wiggled toward the wagon on his belly, the yipping become mournful whines. This augured nothing good Gideon could imagine. Had the dog got left behind, run away from the wagons? Strange he would do so after so many miles at Hiram's call. Strange, too, his behavior. He would not suffer himself to be touched, yet he clearly wanted to be near. He whined and yipped alternately and nipped and snapped at both oxen until they plodded on. Gideon tried to continue westward, but the dog got in front of the wagon and whined and growled until the oxen turned north. Gideon let the reins go slack. Right Ox and Left Ox plodded slowly along, led by the yipping, whining, quivering little dog. After a while—some period of time that may have been minutes or may have been hours—Suella gripped Gideon's arm and squeezed. In the distance something like shadows jerked in the sky above two small brown shapes. As Gideon's oxen closed the distance the shapes became two sailing ships, sails struck, and the wheeling shadows above resembled a cloud of black-winged angels. He guessed what he saw was a mirage and it would soon tilt up into the wiggly sky. But they reached the sailless ships, and he knew them for wagons with their covers burned away. The dark angels overhead were a maelstrom of buzzards. The dog ran toward the wagons, tail down. It was the time of day for making camp, and someone should've been walking about, gathering wood or buffalo chips, building a fire, cooking, but there was no smoke and there were no teams, only the running, silent dog and wheeling, silent buzzards above. This was no mirage. He recognized the wagons and wished what he saw was some vision born of the heat, some trick of sun and distance and his eyes. Frightened and tired as he was, when he recognized the wagons he jumped down and ran.

Dorsey.

The Thurstons' wagon lay tipped on its side against the Speer wagon. Both wagons were just boards blackened and charred, ash stubs where the covers had been fastened to the beds. Mary Thurston's apple trees were blackened, most of the burlap burned off their balled roots. No smoke rose, yet the smell of smoke was in every breath he took. Ripped bedding and broken plates were strewn over the ground and sacks of flour spilled everywhere. The Thurstons' milk cow was a brindle mound. Arrow shafts filled its swollen side, making it appear as a giant porcupine.

Dorsey.

In this moment, "Indian attack," up until now a kind of myth of the wilderness, became for Gideon as real as the wooden shafts and bird's feathers of arrows. One of Mary Thurston's quilts was spread on the ground as if for a picnic. Two mounds of snow covered the short grass—white, white in the sun, feathers from Mary Thurston's soft tick. The breeze, lighter than usual, lifted ticking feathers that rose then sank back. There were piled feathers dull red, and he bent there and brushed away the bloodstained down, and his own blood momentarily ceased flowing.

Dorsey? Don't become such a shape.

The bodies no longer much contained what he'd known as Joe Murphy and Hiram Thurston, but enough remained to mark who they used to be. One buzzard swooped so low and close Gideon felt the warm rush of air from the spasms of its wings. He brushed away the blown, piled feathers. Both men had been stripped of their clothes, and in long strips much of their skin had been peeled away. Exposed flesh the buzzards had not yet consumed was pulpy and pink as the meat of a watermelon and pitted where the buzzards' beaks were doing their grisly work. Hiram's eyes were gone—whether by Indian torture or buzzards' beak Gideon couldn't guess—the empty sockets of dried blood a pair of dark inner eyes that stared just over his shoulder. He turned and looked behind him to see what final terror awaited them all. He was surprised to see nothing but empty land and sky. Lines of dried blood showed where Hiram's eyelids had been sliced off. Joe's visage was just as grim, though his eyeballs were not yet pecked away by the birds. The whites of his eyes had no shine and looked most like hard-boiled eggs. The flesh of both their chests and stomachs was charred, a mound of ashes on each man's trunk where coals had burned themselves out. At their crotches blood had dried black, the grass and dirt beneath them bloodstained in a pool wider than their spread legs. Both men were tied by the ankles to wooden stakes in the earth. Their arms spread wide above their heads were staked at the wrists. Each man's blood-black genitals poked partway out from between his lips. Above Hiram's absent eyes a curved gash rent his flesh, a dull red grin revealing a glimpse of white skull where his scalp had been cut away. Between Hiram's stiff, curled fingers Gideon found, one in each hand, the dead man's two ears sliced off whole. Bright spots danced before Gideon, and Hiram's mutilated form began to move, pulsing, then spinning as a wheel. Gideon put out his arms to brace himself against the earth racing up to meet him.

He opened his eyes and mouth at the same time, breathed in a feather dry and prickly on his tongue. Suella knelt beside him, canteen in one hand, her other hand stroking the back of his neck. Keeping his eyes on the ground he lifted his face where he had fainted and got to his knees and crawled on all fours away from Hiram and Joe. He had to vomit. He had to vomit, but he was unable to bring anything up. He heaved air and barked like a dog from back in his throat. Several yards away was the pink star shape of someone else spread and staked.

Dorsey?

He crawled close enough to see a gory stomach and blood-blackened thighs, a dark-stuffed mouth—Mary Thurston, he thought, or Mr. Speer. Or, please no, Dor—"Huhnnh—huhnnh." Whimpering breath. Something lived? Dorsey?

But it was Mr. Speer. Alive. For reasons Gideon felt must be unfathomable to any man not Indian, Speer had been spared his skin and his privates. His red hair was mostly gone. A curved cut across his forehead neatly sliced his scalp about halfway back his head. His eyes were closed, eyelids intact, and he rocked and shuddered with the whimpering he made, like some factory engine run on steam.

"Mr. Speer." It came out mostly a croak, the noise of some dumb beast. At the sound Speer stopped moaning then began to scrape at the ground, scissoring both legs and his one arm, scrabbling away. Gideon knelt and seized Speer's left shoulder above the stump of his missing arm. "Mr. Speer." Gideon's voice sounded to him more like his voice. "Mr. Speer, it's me, Gideon," he said. Speer opened his mouth (but not yet his eyes) and blood seeped down his chin. The noise he made Gideon could not have described, though he thought he might hear it yet in his nightmares. It was a sound akin to Speer's whimpering breath but fuller and with a fine blood spray. With his bare palm Gideon wiped Speer's face, and the wounded man opened his mouth wide and uttered a guttural cry. Hidden in his mouth was a rag he clamped with his teeth. He held his torn shirttail and pointed with the ripped end to his mouth. Gideon nodded and gently took out the blood-soaked rag. Behind the rag, the shortened, bloody stump of a tongue jerked like a dying fish. Gideon put his mouth against Speer's ear and spoke again. "You're safe, you're safe," a steady refrain, though he wondered as he spoke how safe any of them were. Dorsey was nowhere to be seen, so he still had hope she had survived. It looked as if the Indians had attacked at least a day or two ago. Neither Hiram nor Joe had begun to stink. Perhaps in such an arid climate putrefaction was delayed? The Indians—Gideon wondered if they were the Pawnees Major Benson had warned the train about—might have been silently watching even then, painted so they disappeared into the grass. Mr. Speer finally opened his eyes, squinted up at Gideon. Then Speer saw Suella and started moaning. "No, it's okay," Gideon said. He held Mr. Speer's chin and said, "She's a good Indian. A friend." He beckoned and Suella approached. "See?" Speer's eyes widened and then he passed out. *Good for him*, Gideon thought.

The water kegs on the Thurston wagon were split and drained, but on the Speer wagon one full keg had gone untouched. Suella took a clean pillowcase off the ground and soaked it in the good keg and bathed Mr. Speer's face. Gideon's hand shook so badly he spilled water all down Speer's neck but still managed to drip some into his bloody mouth. Suella tore a fresh rag and eased it inside Speer's cracked lips to press against his partial tongue. The bleeding there was slight. The blood that had been stanched by his teeth-and-rag clamp had started up when he'd tried to talk.

Gideon's mixed feelings toward the curious man came down on his side. Bad enough to lose an arm, but now his tongue was also just a stump. *Maybe*, Gideon thought, *the missing arm is why the Indians spared him, but there seems no logic in that.* Suella brought Gideon a dipper of water, and he held a swallow in his mouth and slowly let it work its way down the back of his throat, finally relaxing his muscles and drinking the rest of the dipper. He lay back on the warm earth and felt the water in his stomach. Dorsey was not here. Nor Mrs. Speer, nor Mary Thurston, nor little Lucy, nor baby James. The absence of corpses did not mean they were alive, but it offered hope they were captured and not killed. Capture might be worse than death, but he pushed those thoughts from his mind.

"Pawnees?"

Suella shrugged. She got up and walked over to the milk cow and examined the feathers and shaft of one of the arrows. "Comanche or Kiowa, Kiowa-Apache."

While Speer slept on, Gideon took water to his oxen and to Enoch Martin's horse, then he led his oxen to pull the wagon near enough it shaded Speer. Gideon unyoked and hobbled the big beasts. Then he and Suella began the necessary business of caring for the remains of Hiram and Joe. They washed the corpses as well as they could with rags torn from Mary Thurston's sheets and pillowcasings. He found a tin of some horse salve in the Thurston wagon and spread it over the flayed and burned places. Hiram's foot was dented but healed over where Rafael Flores' bullet had taken away flesh. Suella gave Gideon a dog's cocked-head look again and wordlessly watched every move he made. He stirred dirt into a bowl and mixed in spilled flour to get close to skin color. He sprinkled the mix over the sticky salve until the skinned and charred places looked nearer to normal—if one didn't look close.

To Gideon there was no shame in any particular body part once the life was gone out of it. It would show disrespect to bury a man separated from such parts as made him whole while he lived. Still, he was glad Mr. Speer was asleep and no one but Suella around to watch when he used mud and sharp splinters from the broken side of the Thurston wagon to reattach the men's privates.

The sun was low in the sky when he paused in his mortuary ministrations to tend to Speer, who had waked and was moaning loudly. He seemed in more pain than when they'd first found him. Gideon put Mrs. Thurston's salve over the raw edges of Speer's scalp, but was afraid to coat the spot where his skull was bared. Suella wrapped his scalped head with clean cloth. His complaints did not seem to be over his severed tongue. He took the rag from his mouth and showed Gideon there'd been little more bleeding. He pointed to his stomach and his mouth.

"Fucking hungry," Suella said.

Gideon found a tin of peaches and poked holes in the lid and helped Speer sip the thick juice. He nodded, his Adam's apple bobbing. When Mr. Speer was resting fairly quietly, Gideon shared the rest of the peaches with Suella.

"Mmmm, good. Fucking good." She ran her tongue over her lips to get every drop of syrup.

Her smile irritated him, and he thought only an Indian could enjoy eating in the face of such brutality. He built a fire close to the corpses so he would have its light to finish his undertaker's chores. He wanted to get the bodies in the ground before putrefaction set in. He cut from the flayed edges of each man's back flaps of skin with which to cover their eye sockets. These flaps he sewed in place with thread from Mrs. Thurston's sewing machine box—the machine itself, heavy as it was, apparently taken by the Indians. Suella squatted close, watching with open curiosity.

"Do something," Gideon said.

"What?"

"Pick up stuff. Check on Speer—the man who's alive—don't just watch me." His hands trembled and it was all he could do to keep from slapping the grin off Suella's face.

"No. I like how you make the dead pretty enough to get into the afterworld."

He ground his teeth. *Oh, Dorsey, what have I done?* He vowed he would not couple again with this heathen.

Joe had been disemboweled. Gideon put what he could find of the boy back into his body cavities and sewed up the wounds. He marked in his mind the need to buy a large store of beeswax first chance he got, then made do with mud, smoothing a thick, dark paste over the long suture. He was determined Joe and Hiram would each have his own grave, and he refused Suella's offer to help dig. Even with Hiram Thurston's good shovel he got no deeper than three feet. Speer had fallen asleep, and Gideon did not disturb him for the rites. He slid the bodies, shrouded in what remained of the strewn bedding, into their graves. Joe was too wide for the hole Gideon had dug, and he had to turn the body on its side to chop away a few more inches of earth. He found a charred leather binding—all that remained of the Thurstons' family Bible—along with a few black-edged pages from Hiram's pamphlets on apple farming, animal husbandry, and the grasses of the American arid region. He had no Bible to read over the graves. *A strange solution,* he thought, *and an even stranger selection.* He put on his spectacles and read over the graves from his *Encyclopaedia Americana* the entry on **WING**, in the hope Joe and Hiram were now souls rising on air: —*the feathers in the wings of birds is one of the instances of the mathematical exactness of the principles on which the works of creation are constructed.* And, further: *The desire of flying seems to have haunted men from the earliest times, and has given rise to many attempts to accomplish this object by means of artificial wings. The fable of Daedalus and Icarus shows how old this idea is.* He concluded his bon voyage to his fellow travelers, whose skin had been loosed by the torture of the devil and who he prayed were now become prairie angels, with this blessing from science: *Quadrupeds which fly are provided with membranes extending over the bones of the extremities, by which they are enabled to impel themselves through the air* (see Bat); *others merely have the skin so loose on the sides as to be spread out when the limbs are extended; and, being buoyed up in this manner, they are able to make surprising leaps* (see Squirrel).

Hiram's Dog Returns

When Suella put her blanket beside his, Gideon rolled over, grateful she did not reach for him. He woke well after sunup, sweat running down his face. He was off his blanket, lying beside the mounded graves where freshly shoveled dirt smelled somehow clean. His arms were sore, his legs stiff, and one hand was blistered from shoveling. He didn't feel at all rested. He was hot, itchy-dirty, and so hungry he could scarce believe he'd sat just days ago in Enoch Martin's soddy and filled himself with meat. He struggled just to sit up.

He missed Hiram Thurston's dog, the frenzied messenger who'd led him here. Occupied by his fearful search for Dorsey and then by laboring over the corpses, he had forgotten the mongrel. Now, the sad silence of sun and distance and ruin all around made him miss the yipping, whining life. He got up and whistled, but the dog did not appear. He took a close look at Mary Thurston's burnt apple trees still tied to the side of the overturned wagon. Mary's dream of apples come to dirt and ash. The tree at the back of the wagon had fared the best—it had lost a limb but two remained, and only a few holes had been burned in the burlap around the dirt and roots. He covered the ball with an empty flour sack, soaked the roots with precious water, and loaded the scorched sapling in beside Chief Bones—a sentimental gesture for which he felt no need to apologize.

Mr. Speer and Suella were both awake. In fact Speer had managed to sit up and seemed to be watching Suella forage for supplies from both burned wagons.

She had loaded into Gideon's wagon what food remained. Speer held the wagon's side rail and pointed down at Chief Bones. "I'm the undertaker," Gideon said. He didn't know if it was enough to say, but it was all he was saying. He and Suella transferred to his wagon the heavy wooden keg—all the water that remained.

Gideon felt beaten, and he knew they'd need their strength, so he risked a fire and the time it took for Suella to cook beans and corn she ground with a rock against a flat stone and mixed with meal and water and the last of Gideon's small pouch of sugar and fried in thick patties in Mary Thurston's big skillet. For a cook-fire she burned the last of the buffalo chips from the pile in the wagon.

From what sounded like a good distance out in the grass came a low cry, and Gideon rushed to his wagon for his Hawken, instantly furious with himself for not keeping the rifle in reach. A second cry, more a yelp, was followed by the brown, splotched face of Hiram's fice. The smell of beans cooking had lured him out of the grass. His tail curled high above his back, he crawled forward on his belly a few inches at a time, his forelegs pulling him in starts and stops. The dog's survival lifted Gideon's spirits.

"Here, boy. Come get something to eat." Gideon held out a corn cake. The mongrel inched closer but wouldn't take the food from his hand. He pitched the cake toward the grass and the dog snapped it out of the air, swallowed it in three lunging bites.

Suella set out a cup of water, and the fice lapped it dry. "Goddamn thirsty."

Speer's hunger, like the dog's, was greater than his pain. He ate more corn cakes than Gideon or Suella did, chewing with the front of his mouth, and, Gideon guessed, working the food somehow past his hurt tongue. He used the last cake to wipe what was left of the beans from the bottom of the pan.

"How long ago did this happen?" Gideon said.

Speer held up three fingers.

"Three days ago?"

He nodded. Gideon dreaded the answer to his next question. "What happened to the others—Dorsey, Mrs. Speer, Mary and her children?"

Speer grabbed an armful of air and moved away, came back and did it again.

"Blown away?"

"Fucking captured," Suella said.

Speer nodded, continued to stare in the direction he'd moved.

"Alive, though."

He nodded once.

"How many Indians?"

He held up his palm, five fingers spread, repeated the motion, then held up two fingers.

"Ten or twelve. Major Benson's Pawnees?" Speer made a guttural noise, "unuugha," and blood-pinkened spittle ran down his chin. *Yes* or *no*, Gideon couldn't tell—regardless of which, he'd gotten his answer in blood. He looked at Suella. "Can we trail them, maybe catch them by surprise?"

"Wasn't Pawnees. I told you, Comanches or Kiowas, Kiowa-Apaches. No one can outride a fucking Comanche. Not even Enoch Man, who is likely trailing the man who run off with his best goddamn daughter."

Mr. Speer's eyes went from Suella to Gideon and back again.

"I didn't run away with you. You came after me," Gideon said.

"To Enoch Man it's the goddamn same thing."

"You took his only horse." Suella just smiled, and without another word or sign between them she and Gideon hitched up Right Ox and Left Ox. They were overcrowded, so he nudged Chief Bones up under the board seat, crossways, against the back of the front splash board. Gideon asked Suella to help him lift the crate of lightning arresters from the wagon. He fitted a pry bar under the wooden lid and prised it off with the screech of nails. One sharp-pointed copper rod he took from the box, then unpacked from their cotton padding a blue glass globe and a wind direction arrow with red isinglass feathers. He fitted the rod into its metal tripod frame, guiding it through the openings in the glass ball, and slid the arrow into place. Suella watched him assemble the copper and glass instrument as if he were performing a miracle. It appeared Mr. Speer almost smiled. Gideon unpacked another and put it together. He sank the three metal feet of each assembled Atkins Lightning Bolt Arrester and Protector deep into the mounded dirt at the head of each grave. The sun hit both blue globes and cast purple shapes upon the ground wherein Joe and Hiram lay. Whichever way the prairie winds blew the arrows on these markers would turn, pointing always away from this place of death.

There was no word or sign between Speer and Gideon, but he knew the direction they both wanted to go. He helped Speer into the wagonbed. Hiram's dog jumped in and curled up against him. Suella sat beside Gideon on the wagon seat. The three of them took a final look at the graves and their glass and copper monuments. The wind gusted out of the north, and both wind direction arrows whirled on their axes, pointing south, aiming them right down the path behind the Indians. Pawnee, Cheyenne, Kiowa, Kiowa-Apache—Gideon ran the names through his mind—Wichita, Comanche. There might be things he could learn about a tribe's ways, things that would help get Dorsey back. Because of what Enoch had told him about Comanches and Kiowas, Gideon wished these were Major Benson's Pawnees. If they were Suella's mother's people, the Kiowas, he wondered if she would have any influence with them. Suella said the Indians who had attacked the Speer and Thurston wagons were not Pawnees, and Gideon figured they were probably not Suella's Kiowas. Somehow, he knew they were Comanches, the goddamn Horse Humans.

Knobby Cotton: A Fancyman Suit

The Mabrys' Cow-Hunt
(August–November 1865)

I mimic Shakespeare trying to describe my dark lady, how she holds my heart imprisoned. I tremble like a rabbit. When I write the word *love*, I feel lost.

—from *Gideon Jones' Journal*

The ride from Matamoros to Galveston was long and hot. Cattle gone wild during the war ranged through the countryside. August, long after the war's windup, and they saw a couple of Confederate veterans walking barefoot down a wagon trail. The Rebs stopped and watched Knobby and Eye, but when Eye asked what they were staring at they shook their heads. One said, "We is trying to make our way home."

Federal troops sent by water unloaded along the coast. Near El Sal del Rey, where the Confederates had mined rock salt, a gang of toughs chased Knobby and Eye into the chaparral before giving up and seeking easier prey. "Ain't much different from us, looking for ways to come out ahead now the war's wound up," Eye said. But the talk in village saloons was not of soldiers nor outlaws. The talk was of Indians on the rampage farther west.

Late one afternoon they crossed the San Antonio River south of Goliad and followed rising smoke to a fire surrounded by five men branding calves. Two boys—twelve, fourteen years old—rode herd on about twenty head of cattle, their wide white horns curving out like bare sycamore limbs. Knobby and Eye trotted up to one of the boys whose horse jangled with tin cups strung on a hobble around the animal's neck.

"Ho, boy, what herd is this?" Eye asked.

"We're on a cow-hunt, sir. These cattle belong all around our crowd. My pa,

William Mabry, and my Uncle Jack just come back from the Army of Tennessee, and Mr. Anderson and Mr. Dell and Mr. Davis were off fighting, too. We're putting our different brands on them and on any mavericks we find. Everone will take his home and turn them out on the range again."

A man walked over from the fire. "Jack Mabry." He reached his hand up to Eye.

"Portis Goar. Folks call me 'Eye.'"

"Well, Eye, you and your Negro are welcome to coffee." Then he shook Knobby's hand. "After they let colored men in the army, I fought beside one named Clem and knew him for a dependable shot and one who never turned tail."

Knobby dismounted to watch the branding. Two ropers on horseback picked a cow and cut it out of the herd. When one got his loop over the long horns, the other rider dismounted and grabbed the taut rope. Wary of the horns, the man on foot grabbed the tail and pulled the animal off balance. He yelled for a "hot iron." Five or six long branding irons stuck out of the fire. A couple men ran over to help hold the cow while another pressed a red-hot brand into the animal's left flank. A deep, loud bawl, the smell of burnt fur, and a drift of white smoke rose all together. One man stood with his boot on the cow's nose and leaned with a pocketknife to its ear.

"What's he doing, Mr. Mabry?" Knobby asked.

"When we brand a calf for the first time, we notch his ears. Mine get both ears cut and Roscoe's a double notch in the left ear." The man with the knife reached between the calf's hind legs. "Males get they balls whacked, too. Ever eat mountain oysters, Knobby?"

"Not ever."

The cutter slapped dust from his gloved hands, went to his horse, and drank from a canteen. The other men had their wallets off their horses and were taking out cornbread and fat bacon. Jack asked the boy, "Tally, now?"

"Twenty-nine and six mavericks."

Just then a gun fired close by, and the boy screamed. The herd ahead of him had turned, stampeding towards the river, their long horns bright in the sun. The boy's horse bolted. His reins were loose, jerking in the dust. Knobby was the first man back in his saddle. Darkie easily caught the spooked mare, and Knobby lassoed her with a hoolihan catch. Scared and embarrassed, the boy was uninjured. He'd seen a rattler and, proud of being entrusted with a six-shooter, fired at the snake. As soon as it was clear the boy was all right, the men went after the herd. In an hour the longhorns were grazing again near the branding fire.

A tall man in a sweat-stained hat brought a cup of coffee to Knobby. "William Mabry. Bill. That's my boy you helped out. I'm grateful." Knobby took the coffee and Bill Mabry went on, "Mighty nice rope work. Fine horsemanship, too."

"None better. I'm on the list of them Knob's rescued. Add your sprout."

The men invited Knobby and Eye to stay for supper. "All the beef you can eat, boys," Bill Mabry said. That evening he served Knobby the biggest pair of oysters they'd cut all day and a choice yearling steak. When the sun went down, Mr. Dell—Vernon—brought out a bottle of brandy and a deck of cards. Will Junior and his friend Jimmy took turns guarding the herd and holding up a torch for the card players. Each time the torch burned out, the men gave the holder twenty cents to fire up another. Poker stakes were the unbranded mavericks, and Vernon won four of the six. After the mavericks had been won, each man crawled under his own blanket. Eye clicked open his pistol cylinder to check his load, and a moment later was snoring. Oralia's face moved between Knobby's open eyes and stars spread across the sky thick as dust. It was still dark when Jack Mabry woke the camp pissing on a flat rock. Bill Mabry put water to boil. After coffee and grilled beef, everyone mounted up, the men to hunt more of their cattle, Knobby and Eye to head on for Galveston.

"You boys ever want cow-handling work, look me up," Bill Mabry said. "Anybody from Goliad to Victoria can direct you to our ranch."

Skyhouse without Oralia

Nine days after leaving the cow-hunters, Knobby and Eye rode onto Galveston Island over flooring laid across the railroad bridge. Most islanders were happy to haul their belongings back from Houston, happy to return to the good life on the island. Federal troops who kept arriving were economic opportunities. Knobby and Eye rode in as the hotel breakfast bells were ringing. Eye said he might just get cleaned up in time for the gentlemen's lunch laid out daily at the bar of the Tremont House. Knobby said he'd meet him later. Then he left Darkie at Major Carey's livery stable, where a boy promised to currycomb the mare and give her sweet grain. Knobby left his rifle and cartridge belt with his saddle and tack. He decided not to wear the Colt's revolver, but to carry it in the scabbard tucked under his arm. He headed straight to Skyhouse.

The same Skyhouse cook, Christine, let Knobby in the kitchen. She talked like Mississippi and reminded him of his mama, Hester. Christine heated water and filled a tub for Knobby. She stood on one side of a black-lacquered folding dressing wall and talked about how good business had been at Skyhouse since the Yankee soldiers arrived. "The mercantile gentlemen are mostly back in town, too," she said. While he was submerged in sudsy water, Christine took away his trail duds she said she'd launder. She laid out a suit of clothes that was a fairly close fit and way too fine for a cow-handler. He wondered was the stylish outfit one of Leatherwood's or had a customer left in a hurry in just his longjohns. "I'm proud a ship arrived with a load of ice. I'm going to fix you something special," Christine said.

By the time Little Bit wandered down to the kitchen, Knobby was dressed and sipping an iced mint julep Christine had served him.

"My, my," said Little Bit, smoothing her dressing gown tight over her bottom as she sank into a wooden chair. "Mr. Cotton, you look good. Where's Elizabeth?"

"In Matamoros with our baby boy."

"You here as a customer?" Little Bit asked, putting her small, warm hand on the top of his thigh just under the kitchen table. Christine opened the loading door of the stove. Heat and dancing light hit the side of Knobby's face. Leaving the stove door open, Christine stepped out onto the porch to the wood stack.

Little Bit said, "You're mighty early. Be my first of the day?" Little Bit's round black eyes shone behind the coffee steam, and her pink tongue licked at a drop of coffee on the cup's lip. Her hand remained on his leg, and she squeezed her fingers, flirting openly.

"Don't tempt me, Little Bit," he said, trying to flirt back enough to be polite. But he wasn't tempted. "How's Mr. Leatherwood?"

Christine stepped into the kitchen with an armload of stovewood. She dipped and swayed, pitching split logs onto the fire. The flame glow burnished her black face, and her silence made her seem angry. Knobby felt like she was his conscience hovering over his shoulder.

Little Bit lowered her coffee cup. "Well, business is good, so he's thriving one way, but since Miss Oralia left, he never seems satisfied with any old thing."

Knobby tried to sound indifferent. "Where did Oralia go?"

"New Orleans, honey." Little Bit took his hand. "Don't trouble yourself. She ain't for you, noway. Be happy with your Elizabeth." She squeezed his hand. "Or me. On the house."

"When did she leave?"

"Early after the surrender—first steamer that ran." Little Bit let go his hand.

"She ain't coming back, neither." Little Bit sounded tired. Then, in a voice all business she said, "Christine, honey, can I have my eggs now?"

Without asking if he was hungry, Christine served Knobby a platter of fried eggs and biscuits and a thick slice of ham and said, "Best be happy with all you have."

Christine was right. That's what he should do. But he yearned to be with Oralia. She was the kind of woman a man could be with once and be satisfied recalling her for the rest of his life. Then he could settle down with Elizabeth and the memory of a night with a woman right out of his dreams. He imagined steaming across the Gulf, passing the swamplands Etienne had guided him and Elizabeth through, chasing Oralia—or whatever he was after—all the way to New Orleans. But he could not bear the thought of going back so near to Noble Plantation and a slave's life. He had made it safe to Texas. Even if the war was over, he wasn't sure things were different in Mississippi or even New Orleans. And if he got that close to the plantation, he would feel compelled to go back to see if his mama and Grandfather Samuel were still alive. If he found them alive and free, he might have to stay and look after them. He might not ever get back to Texas. That thought made him feel a sweet longing for Elizabeth and little William. He couldn't desert them. He would take freedom over desire. "This is as far back as I go," he said.

Christine nodded and set another mint julep on the table for him.

Clothes That Fit

Later in the day, Knobby met Eye in front of the Tremont House. Eye said if he got lucky with some money men he'd hunt Knobby up. Knobby walked Eye down to the wharf and shook his hand before he boarded a steamer to New Orleans. Knobby watched the vessel out of sight on the green horizon line. The Gulf did not pull at him as strongly as he had expected. He turned from the waves and looked up at the gray sky over the bright white buildings of Galveston. He wondered if it was cloudy all the way to Matamoros. He walked to Carey's livery, saddled up Darkie, and stopped by Skyhouse to say good-bye to Christine. She had laundered his old clothes, and they felt soft and comfortable after the fashionable, close tailoring of the suit she had provided. He handed her the dressy rig.

"You keep the fancyman suit, Mr. Cotton—to remind you that what might've been might not have fit so easy or feel so good as what already is."

Knobby put the suit in his saddlebag. He remembered the fox-fur vest the swampman, Etienne, had made him and that Christine had thrown away saying it smelled of the ocean. That vest had been his first freedom clothes, and sometimes he wished he had it back. The dressy suit seemed to Knobby a white man's outfit. He guessed he fit best in a cow-handler's simple, loose duds.

Just outside the village of Brazoria, Knobby rode past a dogtrot house with a ruined patch of corn watched over by a straw scarecrow. He hallooed the house but no one answered. He tied Darkie in the shade of a live oak and walked between the rows of corn stubble. He dressed the scarecrow in the Galveston fancyman suit. Come spring, the crows who used to dine in this corn patch would take their business elsewhere.

Working for Bill Mabry

The liveryman in Victoria told Knobby how to get to the Mabry ranch. Bill Mabry's job offer still stood. Knobby asked if Elizabeth and William could come live on the ranch, and Mabry offered Knobby a toolshed behind the barn. "There's a fireplace there, used to be for firing horseshoes. Your wife could cook there, and it'd keep y'all warm." For weeks Knobby lost himself in labor. He found, roped, branded, doctored, herded, and penned strays. He repaired the horse stalls and mucked them out. He broke horses, brushed and fed them, repaired their tack. He worked harder for Bill Mabry than he had ever worked as a slave, and Mabry treated him fair and equal. He lay down at night a free man, but he lay down with plans in his head. Those plans began with Elizabeth and William joining him in Bill Mabry's toolshed and ended with them on their own Texas horse ranch.

Mexico Mail

Mabry knew a merchant in Victoria who did business in Brownsville and could take a letter to Elizabeth. Mabry gave Knobby paper and a real envelope. On the envelope Knobby wrote directions to Elizabeth's rooms in Matamoros.

A month later, Mabry returned from Goliad with five pounds of coffee, a spool of Mexican hemp rope, and a pouch from the stage office containing three letters, two addressed to Knobby Cotton at Mabry's Ranch, Goliad, Texas. The first mail Knobby had ever gotten, and he got two letters at once. The only other time he had seen his whole name written out had been on an inventory of the property of Noble Plantation. One letter was written in Spanish. Mr. Mabry got one of the Mexican hands to translate. The Mexican words said Flood would bring Elizabeth and William directly to Goliad. Flood wanted to know if Mr. Mabry would hire him, too. They would reach the Mabry ranch by summer's end.

The other letter, printed with dark pencil marks that had made holes in the heavy paper, was from Eye. He had plans for another deal with the Comanchero, Pretty—this time for <u>more money</u>. Eye would be in the town of Alhambra on the Indian frontier at the end of September and would wait a week if Knobby wanted to join him. On the back of the letter was a crude map, a star marked ALHAMBRA an inch above OLD CAMP COOPER.

The middle of September, Flood still had not shown up with Elizabeth. Mabry came late to the shed and woke Knobby. "I was in a card game tonight in Victoria. A drummer set in talking about a wagon attacked by Indians ten days past. Near old Fort Ewell. It's probably too far west to be them, but there was a dead Negro, scalped." Knobby would not wait for daybreak. Mabry packed a wallet of cornbread, jerked beef, and coffee, tied the full wallet behind Knobby's saddle, and gave him directions to Loma Alta, three days' ride west, near the abandoned fort.

Finds a Shallow Grave

Darkie got Knobby to Loma Alta in two days, horse and man lathered with sweat. Only two men in town had seen the dead Negro and neither of them could describe him except to say he was big and black.

"He looked like you. Like a nigger," one named Cleetus said.

"Excepting his face and the privates stuffed in his mouth, he didn't have no skin left," said the other, whose name Knobby never heard clearly.

"I dug a hole for him," Cleetus said. "I can tell you he was big."

Knobby offered to pay Cleetus to take him to the place.

His friend said, "You gone hire out to a nigger?"

"If he gives gold, I'll hire out to the Devil himself."

Knobby gave Cleetus a gold coin he bit down on. "Bring your shovel," Knobby said.

They rode west for two hours, Cleetus on a spavined horse so slow that Knobby had to hold back Darkie the whole long ride. A black smear on the horizon eventually became a charred schooner wagon. Arrows stuck out of what was left of a dead mule. Buzzards had worked on the mule, leaving hide, bones, and dried gore, the carcass fastened to a brown stain of bloodsoaked sand. Hacked and torn, the mule's hide slapped in gusts of wind like someone clapping his hands. Knobby searched the ashes, sunwarmed and soft as flower petals, but there was nothing he could name to look for, no ring or amulet of love or luck. Not even a tin cup remained. Whatever was left by the Indians, Cleetus or others like him had scavenged.

"Where's the deep grave you say you dug?" Knobby asked. Cleetus led him to a shallow bowl. There was no mound, just a shape of disturbed sand. "Get your shovel and dig him up."

"I ain't hired out to do no digging."

Knobby flipped another gold piece to Cleetus, who bit down on the coin as he had before, then stuffed it inside his boot. Cleetus dug about a foot and the blade sank suddenly. Knobby took the shovel. "You buried him deep, huh?" Knobby shoveled sand from a body. Above the forehead a flap of skin had been cut away leaving a small crown of wooly hair brown with sand. Knobby brushed away the sand. Swollen and rotting, Flood's face appeared. The eyelids were cut away, the clouded eyes gazed up. Beneath the broad nose, wide lips puckered around hacked-off genitals Knobby would not have known for human parts if he hadn't been told of this Comanche predilection. "You buried him without removing his privates or closing his eyes?"

Cleetus wasn't talking. Knobby looped his lasso under Flood's big arms. He whispered to Darkie what needed to be done. Darkie backed up, pulling the bloated body to a smooth place where desert breezes swayed the thick, spiky shoots of a yucca. Here Knobby dug a hole deep enough to keep out coyotes or wolves. Verses from Job came to mind:

Terrors are turned upon me: they pursue my soul as the wind: and my welfare passeth away as a cloud.
My bones are pierced in me in the night season: and my sinews take no rest.

For a marker, Knobby stuck up a blackened piece of wagon wheel, pushed the bottom spokes into the sand to the hub, the wheel's remnant as anchored as anything for miles around. Cleetus sat in shade cast by his worn-out old horse.

When Knobby mounted up, Cleetus stood and said, "Where you off to?"

Knobby faced northwest, toward Alhambra, on the edge of Comancheria.

"You going to leave me to ride back alone? My sorry horse might not make it."

"You've got your gravedigger's pay. Buy a better horse." Close as Knobby could figure, it was late September. He would have to pull foot to find the town of Alhambra and catch up with Eye, who could get Knobby to the Comanchero, Pretty. Knobby had to persuade, bribe, or force Pretty to help him find the Indians who had captured Elizabeth and William.

At Flood's resting place wheel spokes thrust into white sky.

"You can't just ride off and leave me alone," Cleetus said.

"You're lucky I didn't kill you."

My bones are pierced in me in the night season: and my sinews take no rest. Knobby gave Darkie her head and she galloped away carrying him down the lengthening shadow of the cordillera rising dark and sharp-pointed before the blood-red sun.

Gideon Jones: Tracking the Horse Humans

A Hard Ride to Bone Camp
(August–October 1865)

Suella, Mr. Speer, and Gideon left the burnt place of the Indian attack and trailed the savages a short distance into the prairie grass, but they soon lost the tracks. The Indians had headed south, so south became the direction Gideon took his wagon. Maybe he would encounter someone or something to confirm that the war party preceded him. Otherwise, he was determined to ask at forts and villages he came to where the most likely Comanche camps were. He would visit them all, if need be, to find Dorsey. Now he was glad Suella had run away from her sod house and joined him. Her knowledge of Indian ways might be worth the wrath of Enoch Martin, who was surely, Suella insisted, close on their trail. As Gideon was now chasing a band of Comanche warriors who held Dorsey's life in their hands, Enoch seemed the least of his concerns.

Mr. Speer spent most of the long days lying beside Chief Bones and the charred apple sapling in the back of the wagon. His tongue was not healing properly, and he had a fever more often than not. Growing low on food and funds, Gideon looked for a settlement where he might barter his remaining lightning arresters for supplies. But he did not espy a single house or barn into which he might sink wood screws to hold an Atkins Lightning Bolt Arrester and Protector erect so it would pierce the dark dynamo of the turbulent heavens.

They crossed a river Suella said was the Cimarron, and two days later came to the Beaver River, which she said ran along this part of the Texas border. She sniffed the air like a deer, pointed across the river. "I'm pretty goddamn sure it's Texas over yonder."

Drouth and summer heat had lowered the river's banks, and the ford was not difficult. Gideon waded ahead with a rope around Right Ox's outside horn, and Suella sat the wagon seat and held the lines. Safe on the other side they watered the animals, filled their keg and canteens, and rested. The land looked the same, but it felt different. Here was a state that, thirty years earlier, had been its own republic, a land so vast and varied no ordinary state could match it. Even back in Baltimore at the asylum Gideon had heard the names of the heroes of the Alamo. Now, he knew Texas was also the land of Comancheria, domain of the fearsome Comanches.

As they moved ever southward the air felt different—warmer, closer—and he felt the stir of heightened expectations. Beyond the Beaver, they crept all day up onto a high tableland of short grass—a limitless empty expanse Suella named the Llano Estacado, which she said meant "Staked Plain."

"Where are the stakes?"

"Goddamn Comanches know. To mark a secret trail across the plains they drove in stakes and put over them the skulls of buffaloes."

Gideon did not voice his next question: Where did they get the wood for the stakes?

"This is the fucking heart of Comancheria. Few fucking white men have ever put eyes on this country. Soldier men are afraid to ride here. Comanches let Comanchero traders come from New Mexico with their shoddy goddamn goods—bad whisky and bright damn geegaws. Sometimes Comancheros trade steel knives and repeating rifles. One rifle will bring many buffalo furs, though I've seen more than one brave jam a rifle and go back to the bow and arrow."

Whereas the prairies of Missouri and Kansas swelled and rolled and were crossed by rivers and dotted with clumps of trees near those rivers, the great mesa of the Llano Estacado was level, streams were few, trees fewer still. The grass grew thick but short. The only breaks in the relentless flatness were distant buttes and scattered high escarpments. *If this was Comancheria,* Gideon wondered, *where were its rulers?*

Their fourth day on this high plain they came of a sudden to the edge of a deep canyon, an arroyo invisible until they were at its rim. He braked the wagon for fear they might plummet into the chasm. From the edge of the grassy mesa they looked down at the tops of trees that had been hidden from the surface until they reached the brink of the precipice.

Any hoofprint left in a soft or sandy place on the rocky Staked Plain was soon blown away by the constant wind. Down in the arroyo, Suella said, there would be water and maybe sign of the warriors they pursued. She found a sandy declination, and they walked the wagon, leading the oxen down the steep passageway. The wagon slid and Gideon had to get a rope around the rear axle so he could pull back against the wheels to slow its descent. The slanting shade climbed up his shins, knees, thighs, chest. When his hatbrim no longer cast a shadow, he recalled Colonel Luellen Powell-Hughes reading out loud the musical Italian of *The Inferno* of Dante and translating the poet's account of his descent into the Underworld in search of his beloved Beatrice. Gideon vowed he would go even into Hell in search of his Dorsey. On an overhang of bare rock he pictured the words the poet saw inscribed over the portal he entered: ABANDON ALL HOPE, YE WHO ENTER HERE.

But hope was kindled in Gideon's heart when Suella found prints, shod and unshod hooves, along the sandy banks of the stream. They followed the tracks that followed the river until the arroyo widened into a kind of walled canyon. This space had recently supported a large camp. Scattered over several acres were dried piles of dung, buffalo and deer bones, the ashes of several large cookfires, shards of pottery, and depressions in the earth Suella said were from the heavy lodgepoles of tipis. Here were not only hoofprints but footprints as well.

"Big goddamn camp. Comanche. Left maybe six or seven days ago. Probably going south, warmer for wintertime. Fucking hot as it is now, sleet moon is coming."

"Can't we catch up to them? With so many, they can't move fast."

Suella shook her head. "Maybe. First, we rest, eat, salve his goddamn gizzard." She nodded to Mr. Speer, who had coughed up a mucus of blood in the wagonbed. Perhaps his exertions trying to remain in the wagon during their steep descent had exacerbated his wound. Suella took Gideon's Hawken and disappeared into trees along the riverbank. Gideon stirred the last of their salt into a cup of river water he offered Speer as a rinse.

"Maybe the salt will help. Don't swallow any if you can avoid it."

The swelling in Speer's tongue had returned. He had trouble eating and appeared so lethargic as to make Gideon think he had coughed up more blood than he let on. Gideon was concerned because of redness about Speer's throat. Rearranging Chief Bones and the burnt sapling and fashioning a pillow from his bedroll, Gideon made Speer as comfortable as possible in the wagon. Down in the canyon they were completely in shadow. Full dark would be upon them soon.

A single shot reverberated over the river. Certain as he was that Suella had fired the shot, Gideon nonetheless hunkered down beneath the wagon with Hiram Thurston's old Spencer rifle. He waited a long time that seemed even longer. Eventually Suella appeared, carrying in one hand her hide pouch smeared with blood and, over her shoulder, the skinned hindquarters of an animal.

"Sweet goddamn doe, Gideon. Fat you up some, build your strength for fucking."

He looked over at Speer, but he was sleeping. "Who taught you to hunt?"

"Kiowa taught me deer talk. Enoch Man taught me to shoot goddamn guns."

"He taught you his vocabulary, too."

"What is vocabulary?"

"The words you use, like goddamn."

Suella grinned. "I use Enoch Man's vo-cab-u-ary when I talk white words. I use Kiowa talk or hand talk with Indians. Deer talk I can't speak, just hear its meaning."

"What did the deer say?"

"Four does talking while they drank at the river said their buck had smelled humans and gone to look see. One doe was greedy. She drank so fucking long the others had to wait for her. They said, 'Hurry or the humans will find us.' She said, 'I will drink all I want.' So, I shot her, the greedy one." Suella threw back her head and laughed, and Gideon could not but laugh with her. "This greedy one drank so much we won't need water, just eat her for hunger and thirst," Suella said.

She took flintrock from her pouch and made a fire. She cut and sharpened small green limbs from willows near the river and ran them through strips of venison she cut. The skewers swayed and bobbed from her fist like the scarlet petals of some giant fleshy flower. She stuck the limbs in the ground at an angle so the meat leaned over the coals. Then she boiled water in Gideon's only iron pot and filled it with wild onions she pulled from along the river's edge. She added to the brew the liver and stomach she carried in her bloody pouch. Also in the bag was the doe's heart she offered Gideon. When he said he was happy with the steaks, she shook her head and ate the organ raw. Firelight shone on her face where fat and bits of gore were smeared. He turned away, and, after they had eaten, teased her into swimming with him so he could be sure her face and lips were washed clean. He knew he would not be able to keep his vow not to lie with her, but at least she would not smell of animal fat when she kissed him and rolled with him in their blankets.

Suella set her pot of stew in shallow water to cool so it wouldn't burn Speer's wounded mouth, and then she poured spoonfuls past his swollen tongue as water in a creek goes around a boulder. The bits of organs were so small and tender he didn't have to chew. She dug some kind of root and tied it under his nose, telling him to breathe the root's scent and it would cool his fever.

The doe's heart apparently increased Suella's vigor. After they had swum, Gideon sat awhile by the fire reading in his *Americana* a short entry on the **Whirligig**: — *a kind of circular wooden cage, turning on a pivot, and, when set in motion, whirling round with velocity that the delinquent becomes extremely sick—sometimes used in insane hospitals, to overcome the obstinacy of lunatics.*

He was wondering why there had been no whirligig at the Baltimore asylum, when Suella flung his spectacles from his face and, knocking his *Americana* perilously close to the fire, tugged his clothing off. She wrestled with him until he was beyond being spent, then she rolled on top of him and pulled and poked until he responded again. Then she rode him for the rest of the night just as they say an Indian can ride a horse that has already been ridden down. He was unable to suppress the image of himself, arms and legs spread, tied, helpless, atop a spinning whirligig. He barely had the breath to utter a prayer of penance. He loved Dorsey in spite of the acts he was committing with the savage Suella—acts he could not bring himself to cease. His devil brain voiced arguments in favor of all the transgressions he committed with Suella, warranting he needed her uncommon skills, needed her willing assistance, if he were going to find Dorsey.

Gideon wondered whether his logic would be persuasive if Dorsey ever came to know the lengths he had taken to effect her rescue. The dispute had raged within him since the first night he had lain with Suella, but all the while he quarreled with himself he continued to fornicate. His shortcoming was he was not man enough to admit he sinned primarily because it was pleasurable. And since he could not own up to his weakness and lust, his pleasure was diminished by the addition of guilt. And when he contemplated the likely fears and possible torture his beloved Dorsey was enduring at the same time that he was rutting with a half-breed savage, his guilt increased tenfold. Though had he no guilt to lessen his carnal delight, he would surely have died of delight's excess. He was stirred from these ruminations and from drifting into sleep by the loud, wet ministrations of Suella's mouth and tongue that spoke, he was persuaded, the language of just about any object in nature.

Mr. Speer Needs Doctoring

The next morning Gideon did a kind of penance on his hands and knees in the wet, searching until he found his eyeglasses, none the worse for Suella's having flung them a wagon-length into the grass. Suella's broth and the night's rest had benefited Speer, but as they retraced their way back out of the arroyo he coughed up blood. They had no choice but to get him out of the wagon to help push as they struggled back up the steep incline to the Llano Estacado, where sun and wind waited to parch all their throats. They nooned in the scant shade of the wagon, and though Suella and Gideon were hot and sweat-soaked, Speer burned with fever beyond the sun. Gideon asked Suella where the nearest town or army fort or trading post was, any place they might reach soon where there would be a doctor and water and supplies they needed.

"A goddamn white medicine doctor, I don't know. There may be an army doctor at Fort Belknap or down to Fort Phantom Hill, but probably not. There is a trading town sooner. Might be a white medicine doctor there. We hurry." She pointed in an easterly direction, and Gideon's oxen lumbered on, Enoch Martin's ghostly-looking horse patiently trailing after.

From the Arms of God to Alhambra

By nightfall they were camped near a river Suella called the Peas or Peace or, possibly, the Pees. Mr. Speer was beaded with sweat and had such violent shakes the wagonbed rattled as if it rolled yet. They covered him with all their blankets, and Suella fed him the remains of her deer organ potion. He rested through the night, but Gideon was worried on account of the swelling and redness of the man's neck. The next few days Gideon drove Left Ox and Right Ox in a race against that spreading redness, a red band spreading inexorably around the front of Speer's neck like a crimson clerical collar the Devil might wear. Watching Suella's bosoms sway and push against the front of her deerskin blouse, Gideon wondered whether Satan was inhabiting Speer's poor body just to preside over his own nightly couplings with his personal she-devil. But Suella was no devil. She had no reason, no moral code, to prevent her receiving him. He alone was responsible—or irresponsible, as he had clearly proved.

"Los Brazos de Dios." Gideon looked past Suella's bosoms to where she pointed. A dark line of trees. "Goddamn good water." *How far?* he wondered. He'd been judging time by the inexorable progress of the red ring of infection around Speer's neck. Out here, Gideon had learned, distances are deceiving. Objects seen clearly may be days distant, the horizon always receding. He smelled water and felt cooler air, or what might pass for cooler air on this arid hot tabletop. "Los Brazos de Dios," Suella said again. They were all afternoon reaching those blessed arms where they made cold camp. He still watched for Indian sign, but he doubted Enoch had trailed them this far. The next morning Speer seemed some better. They spent half the day locating a ford, then crossed with little difficulty. On the other side, maybe ten miles downriver, they came to a place called Willow Water, where natural springs made a watering hole Suella said was well known by Kiowas and Comanches.

South of the willow springs they approached a settlement of log houses and one planed-board building. There were no horses tied to the hitch rail in front of the building. Gideon docked his wagon and got down stiffly. Hiram's dog jumped from the wagon and trotted to the corner wall against which he hiked his leg, marking this new territory. Speer was awake, but looked near dead. "You all right?" Gideon asked.

Mr. Speer lifted his hands and let them fall, a gesture Gideon translated as "I've been better." Sitting up a little in the wagonbed, he craned his red and swollen neck to look at a sign hanging from the building's porch. The sign depicted a dark-haired woman in a gold dress, a gold veil over the lower half of her face, reclining beneath red-painted words: ALHAMBRA SALOON. Speer gave the representation a good going over, then he managed a gurgling whisper and pointed at the open door.

Gideon nodded.

Speer nodded back, well as he could, flat on his back in a wagonbed. He pointed at his throat, held and poured an invisible bottle, lifted his eyebrows.

"A smile of whisky might do him good," Suella said. "Help his sore throat."

Speer nodded.

"Goddamn spirits cauterize if you pour them on a wound," Suella said.

"I'll buy a bottle and bring it to you. Suella, will you stay with him?"

"Buy me my own goddamn bottle."

Mrs. Carter

A rock held the saloon door open. The dim room was barely cooler than outside. A few empty tables were scattered across a clean-swept plank floor. There were no windows, but shoulder-high openings about three inches wide and a foot high let in slants of light through the outside walls. At the far end of the room, facing the bar opposite, was an upright piano, the first piano Gideon had seen since St. Louis. He had a sudden craving to hear it played and wished he knew how to make music. Behind the bar hung a larger painting of the girl on the outside sign, only this time all she wore was the gold veil. He studied her a minute, wondering who the artist was and if he lived in this desert outpost. The style reminded Gideon of an Italian named Titian, the only painter whose name he remembered from Colonel Powell-Hughes' picture book art lessons. When the colonel told him Titian's birth and death dates, Gideon remarked he had lived for ninety-nine years, and the colonel shook his head. "Too long, then or now."

A tall, handsome woman, gray hair neatly pinned up on her head, stood behind the bar, watching Gideon stare at the painting over her head. Otherwise, in spite of the horses and the wagon and mule team outside, the saloon was empty.

"What do you want?" The woman's question seemed clairvoyant, as if she knew Gideon wanted more than just a drink. There was a bottle of Squirrel on the bar, and he pointed at it and stepped to the counter, his feet bumping a brass cuspidor that looked to have been emptied recently—that or the Alhambra Saloon had not had any customers in a good while.

The woman introduced herself as Mrs. Carter. Then she poured herself a glass of Squirrel, too, and asked Gideon where he was from.

"Baltimore, I guess. At least to start with. And, then, Cumberland, in West Virginia. And since then, just on the prairie."

"We don't get many folks in here from Baltimore." Her blue eyes were even with his, into which she stared without blinking. Like a man, she shook hands with him. Her palm was cool and smooth, her grip firm but not pinching. She told Gideon he was in a place called, depending upon who you asked, Bone Camp or Alhambra, Texas. "Mr. Jon W. Manchip—nobody knows what the "W" stands for—built and owns most of the town."

Manchip had run a number of trading posts in Arkansas and Texas. He had read Washington Irving's book, *The Alhambra*, just before he built this saloon near an underground spring that supported a grove of cottonwoods, a place buffalo hunters had called Bone Camp because of the buffalo bones they discarded there. In addition to THE ALHAMBRA, Mr. Manchip ran a mercantile store in the other half of the saloon building. His bedroom was upstairs, where Mrs. Carter said he was at that moment in the midst of his daily afternoon nap.

The town boasted a livery stable, also owned by Mr. Manchip, with a farrier he employed. There was a boardinghouse run by Mrs. Carter, from whom Gideon rented a cot for Mr. Speer. Gideon wasn't comfortable asking for a bed for himself and a half-blood Kiowa woman to whom he wasn't married. The boardinghouse offered four sleeping rooms, a room where one could buy a tub bath, and a kitchen where Mrs. Carter sometimes served up a meal. She also played the piano at the Alhambra. Few frontier saloons had a classically trained musician, and the Alhambra was surely the only one in Texas with a pianist who had studied in Vienna.

"Vienna was a while ago. And far away," Mrs. Carter said with a smile that did not keep her from looking sad.

Other permanent citizens of Alhambra included a couple of sporting girls who stayed just busy enough to eke out a living, not busy enough to move on. The girls' place of business was a tent in the cottonwood grove where buffalo bones still piled up. Out from under the cottonwoods was a cemetery with a score or more silent inhabitants. There was also a gunsmith's shack.

"You see the kinds of businesses thriving here—a burying ground but no church, not yet, anyhow, because, out here at least, killing comes before salvation. We don't have a preacher or a doctor either. We've greater need of an undertaker." Gideon mentioned he had worked in a Baltimore hospital and had some experience, if not training, in the preservation of the dead. "We can keep you in beans, then. Especially if you can cover scalped skulls and fill in holes from arrows and knives and bullets."

"I've recently had to perform just those kinds of restorative arts, and I don't mind saying the labors taxed my emotions as well as my powers of invention, especially owing as how I do not possess any of the proper chemical solutions or undertaker's instruments."

Mrs. Carter looked toward the open saloon door, and he turned to see what she saw. There sat Suella sitting up straight as a pencil on his wagon board.

"There's a man in my wagon who was attacked by Indians. Weeks ago. He got better, seemed to be healing, then got worse. His fever comes and goes. His throat is swollen and red. The Indians killed or captured everyone else in the train. I intend to pursue the Indians and locate the captives." He nodded at Suella, "She is my Indian guide."

Mrs. Carter's eyebrows went up. "I lost two husbands to the Comanches." She went out with Gideon to take a look at Mr. Speer. "Gave up your scalp, I see," she said to Speer, who nodded. She put the back of her hand against his face and frowned. She nodded at the apple sapling. "Planning on an orchard?" Gideon shrugged and walked his oxen, following her to the boardinghouse she kept, a two-story log building with the same narrow slits for windows as the saloon. They carried Mr. Speer to a second-floor room, Hiram's dog coming up right behind them. Mrs. Carter nodded at the narrow openings and explained, "Lets a gun barrel poke out but lets no Indian squeeze in."

They got Speer stretched on the narrow bed, and Mrs. Carter went back to the saloon to wake Mr. Manchip. "The best man in town for a sick horse or cow, or that mongrel dog," she said. "Of necessity, he's taken to caring for human patients, too." Since he owned the saloon, Mr. Manchip was at the scene of plenty of knife and gun fights. "He doctors horses and cattle right well—people, so-so. He gets sufficient practice on bullets and arrows. I don't know if he's good on cut-off tongues, but he can use the experience. Besides, we're days away from any other doctoring."

Another Welsh Benefactor

So tall he had to bend way over to step under the doorway, Mr. Manchip entered the room bearing a satchel that rattled and clinked. The first thing he did was tell Mrs. Carter to go boil some water. "Boiling water is a medical necessity." As soon as Mr. Manchip spoke, Gideon felt assurance in the lilt of his words. His speech echoed Colonel Luellen Powell-Hughes' speech, his voice trilled as the colonel's had.

"Are you a Welshman?"

He removed his hat that just touched the low ceiling and held out a large red hand. His grip was as warm and as firm as his smile. "Cymry." The same name the colonel had used for his homeland. "From Carnarvon. I go right back to Llewelyn the Great." All business now, he rolled up his shirtsleeves, revealing browned, meaty arms. Sun brightened the room's window slits, but they did not admit much light. He lit the oil lamp on the bedside table and turned the wick high as it would go without smoking the chimney. Gideon felt better about everything. Mr. Manchip seemed the spirit of Colonel Luellen Powell-Hughes come here to watch over him.

Mrs. Carter returned with an enamel basin of steaming water. Mr. Manchip winked at her. "Mrs. Carter makes a passable nurse. You might say she led me to this medical profession." With strong-smelling soap he washed his hands, large and scarred in several places, in the scalding water. "How long has the patient had this raging infection?"

"What month is it?"

Mr. Manchip looked to Mrs. Carter, who rolled her eyes.

"September," she said.

"Then it's been a couple of weeks, maybe longer, since the redness came back."

While he dried his hands Mr. Manchip said, "My medical calling first manifested itself at the urging of Mrs. Carter, a piano-plinking female philosopher. I answered the summons by taking up an intermediate profession as the provider of an amazing restorative elixir. I became the source of relief and hope in this relentless, hopeless place offering to those in need vital distillates of nature's healing balms." He nodded to his satchel. Gideon opened the mouth of the bag: its insides glittered with glass bottles. Mr. Manchip extracted one, held it up and read the label out loud: "DR. J. B. LEGGETT'S BORNEO BLOOD SYRUP AND HEART FORTIFIER. Of which," he lowered his voice confidentially, "I am this region's sole provider."

Mr. Manchip had Mrs. Carter leave the room and bade Gideon help him strip off Mr. Speer's clothing. Eyes squinted in concentration, Mr. Manchip pressed against Speer's joints and muscles. When Mr. Manchip lifted Speer's one arm, Gideon was overcome by nausea—a gash several inches long in the man's side was crusted black with blood. The flesh around the wound was as red and swollen as Mr. Speer's neck. "This wound may be more the problem than the tongue and throat. Where's he's been scalped all we do is keep it clean and let it heal. The hair won't grow back, of course. The roots are gone."

"How could I not have known?"

"A man wouldn't, unless he gave him a bath."

"Why didn't you tell me?" Gideon asked Speer.

Speer pulled a finger across his neck as if cutting his throat.

"Even if you can't speak, you can point."

Manchip leaned over Speer and examined the man's wounds. "I'm surprised gangrene hasn't set in. I ought to put some stitches in here so he doesn't lose this arm, too. His tongue would have done better with stitching, but now it's knitting I'll let it be." He borrowed one of Mrs. Carter's sewing needles and held it in a match flame to purify it. He rubbed the edges of the scabbed flaps of skin with whisky and, using black cotton thread, he sewed closed the rent in Speer's side as if he were repairing a shirt or a saddle blanket. During the entire operation Speer chewed on the cork from the bottle of whisky Manchip used for a disinfectant. Hiram's fice rested his little chin on Speer's twitching leg.

As near as Gideon could tell, beyond seamstressing, Manchip's only treatment of Speer's infected wounds was to wash them thoroughly, the raw scalp, beneath the arm, and inside Speer's mouth, with the same strong lye soap the Welshman had used on his hands, chased with a splash of whisky followed by a good portion of the bottle of heart fortifier he poured down his patient's throat. When "Dr." Manchip washed inside Speer's mouth the hurt man did not cry out, though he gripped the tick he lay on until his knuckles were as red as his neck. Gideon noted how gentle was Manchip's touch, surprising in a man so large. Such had been the touch of Colonel Powell-Hughes, and to the end of Gideon's life the Welsh would remain his image of angels of mercy.

"If he doesn't come around in a day or so I've got some horse pills I can give him. They don't do much good for sick horses, but maybe they'll aid your friend." That said, "Dr." Manchip held the bottle of blood fortifier to the lamp, where the line of liquid was illuminated at about halfway down the bottle. He splashed a little on the wound beneath Speer's arm, then tipped up the bottle and drained it. "A well-fortified doctor is second only to boiling water in medical importance. Remember the first Hippocratic rule, 'Physician, heal thyself.'"

When Mr. Speer got settled from the pain of having his mouth washed out with soap, he asked "the Doc," with a mix of hisses and nods and pointings, if he might have a shot of bitters. Manchip nodded to Gideon, who went back to the Alhambra to fetch a bottle of Squirrel. On his way back to the boardinghouse he handed the whisky to Suella, who still sat patiently on the wagon. She tipped the bottle that flashed in the sun and guzzled until he took the whisky and hurried up to Speer's room. Manchip held the bottle before the lamp, just as he had held the blood fortifier. Nodding, he poured off the remainder of the Squirrel into two glasses, dividing the liquor evenly. One glass he handed to Gideon, nodding toward Speer. Gideon lifted Speer's head and held the glass while the man slowly swallowed. Manchip held up the other glass and drained the whisky. "Mañana."

Gideon made arrangements with Mr. Manchip's livery man to reward Left Ox and Right Ox with some grain and to park the wagon in his lot, where Suella and Gideon might sleep. Over the next several days Mr. Speer was not noticeably better, but he was no worse. Mrs. Carter sent table scraps for the dog, which was seldom out of Speer's reach. Encouraged, Gideon went to the Alhambra Saloon to see what he could learn about where the Comanches might have taken Dorsey.

Two Strangers

He stepped onto the plank stoop of the Alhambra, and two men rose from a log that lay like a bench before the saloon and approached him. The back of his neck prickled, and he wished he had his Hawken. One of the men was a Negro. The other man was sunburnt and his right eye, glazed and milky, stared straight ahead, while his left eye pulsed and twitched. Both were dressed as cow-handlers in tooled boots with high heels, wide-brimmed hats, dusty scarves tied around their necks. Both wore handguns in leather scabbards at their sides. The one with the spasmodic left eye spoke.

"Saloon lady says you aim to track after some Comanches, says you got a squaw to lead you to the Indian camp?"

"I have a friend." Gideon wondered what Suella would think if she heard him call her a *friend.* "Her mother was Kiowa. She speaks Kiowa and knows Indian sign language."

The Negro took off his hat and slapped the brim against his thigh, sending up dust. He looked directly into Gideon's eyes and said, "Going on a month ago my partner was bringing my wife and baby boy to meet me. Indians attacked the wagon. I found his mutilated body but no sign of my wife or child. I aim to get my family back. Might be we're after the same bunch."

Gideon's heart lifted some as he went with these strangers into the Alhambra Saloon. *Optimism,* he thought, *like other kinds of foolhardiness, flares with little fuel and such flames are hard to fully douse.* With Speer off his hands Gideon determined to turn all his energies to finding Dorsey, no matter how far away the Comanches might have spirited her.

Dorsey Murphy: Captive of the Antelope

Brought to the Comanche Camp
(August–November 1865)

With reference to a concern of all others the most consecrated for any
female held captive by men whose basest animal appetites flourish without
the constraints of spiritual or moral enlightenment, (beseeching Providence
for Dorsey's protection, I record it) I pray my fears for her sanctity will
be in no part realized and an Invincible Power will husband her
and deliver her inviolate out of the hands of those devils.

—from *Gideon Jones' Journal*

The Comanche warrior walked his horse, and Dorsey let go of the corset around
his middle. Many Indians in the camp came out to greet them, laughing and slapping the backs of the warriors and the necks of the painted, decorated ponies. The
younger boys and girls were naked. The older boys wore only breechclouts. The
girls wore simple deerskin blouses and long fringed skirts, brightly beaded. Two
of the men leaned down and pulled boy children up onto the horses with them.
The women wore their shiny black hair chopped short, uneven and unkempt.
Where the men wore black warpaint, the women's faces were painted bright reds,
yellows, oranges. Wives were reunited with husbands, and faces beamed and
stretched wide with grins.

Several women ran up to the bay mare carrying Laura Etta. All the Indian
women jabbered and pointed at Dorsey's mama. Three of the women carried
whips, and one lashed Laura Etta across the back. More arms swung and whips
cracked, and the Indian women laughed. The homespun cotton across Laura
Etta's back and shoulders split open, and blood stripes oozed through. The
women pulled Laura Etta off the horse and dragged her through the dust. Dorsey

jumped from behind White Chest, but by the time her feet hit the ground he had hold of her hair and gave her a hard jerk that made her eyes water. Dorsey could no longer see her mother, though she heard the loud crack of the whip. Laura Etta did not scream or call out.

Another Indian woman moved among them, her eyes going from face to face until she spied the dead Indian on his pony. "*Kuhma,*" she said. "*Nea kuhma.*" She threw herself onto the ground and wailed and screamed. She beat her arms and legs against the earth and tore at her own clothes. She leapt up and ran to one of the Indian men and fell back with her arms up, wielding his knife, the blade mirroring the sun. She hacked at her arms leaving bloody slashes. The other Indians paid no attention. Behind laughter and welcoming shouts was the keening of this woman who sat in the middle of the narrow path and shrieked and thrashed. The Indians all went around her as if she weren't there. They didn't speak to her. They didn't interrupt her grief.

A willowy Indian girl with a blue and yellow beaded dress came up to White Chest's pony calling, "Wahatewi, Wahatewi," and White Chest slid down and put his arms around her.

"Chautavitty," he said, and the two walked arm in arm into the camp.

Dorsey saw only four tipis, but shelters made of tree limbs and brush were lined up beside the stream as far as she could see. There must have been forty or fifty lodges erected a good distance apart in two straight rows, giving the camp one long street through its center. Barking dogs, rangy and fur-matted, met the riders, snarled and snapped. The Indians ignored the mongrels. Several cookfires flamed, and a low cloud of smoke drifted down the length of the stream. Dorsey smelled meat cooking and meat rotting. Scattered over the ground were animal bones and small piles of droppings from dogs and people, larger droppings from horses. The foul-smelling piles were covered with black and shiny-green flies, their loud communal drone as relentless as the steady gusting breezes. The breezes also carried a root-dirt smell of vegetation from the streambank and, beneath that odor, a scent faintly citric.

Two men held Joe's and Hiram's scalps out to a woman who laughed and put the scalps on tall sticks in a clearing near a large tipi. Broken Teeth waved his tin of Tube Rose snuff, and several women crowded around his horse. He moved his hand over each uplifted face as if he were a fat, jovial friar giving out blessings. After he anointed them with pinches of snuff, the women giggled and grinned brown-stained grins that made them appear deranged.

The warriors and their entourage reached the tipi near the clearing where the women had displayed Joe's and Hiram's scalps, and all the riders dismounted. Beside the tipi stood two Indian men: one Dorsey figured about as old as Mr. Speer—late thirties to early forties—while the other, white-haired, looked at least sixty. In this clearing, before the appreciative crowd, the young warriors showed off the horses and mules they had taken. They ran in circles and bayed like hounds as they handed out their trophies: Mary Thurston's best linen dress, a yellow bonnet, Laura Etta's hair combs, a spool of black braid one Indian man unrolled across the clearing, Hiram Thurston's leather drinking cup, tins of Epsom salts, a bottle of chill tonic, Mary Thurston's sewing thimbles worn by several Indian men as decoration on their little fingers, and the bolt of black calico Laura Etta had grimly insisted on packing in case she had to cover a casket. The most coveted prizes—Mr. Speer's old muzzle-loading Springfield rifle Laura Etta had used against the Indians, Mary Thurston's beveled mirror, Hiram Thurston's waterproof tin of matches—were hoarded by their new owners or offered for trade for a dear number of ponies or some such outrageous price. When the celebrating raiders were through flaunting and sharing their booty, each one cuffed Broken Teeth's shoulder. Each time he was slapped Broken Teeth howled happily. Then he approached the old white-haired man, who had sat still and silent during the entire show.

The old man wore only a blue deerskin breechclout and hide moccasins. His brown legs were skinny and knotted as tree limbs. His bare chest was scarred and decorated with black tattoos. His nose was wide and long at the same time. His face was weathered, his skin cracked and deeply lined as a dry river bottom, rough as tree bark. His forehead looked higher than it was because his eyebrows had been plucked away. His lips were painted or greased so they were darker than his face and shone in the afternoon light slanting through the trees. His lips barely moved when he made the chopped-sounding Indian words. Two tied bunches of white hair hung past his waist. His hair, smeared with some kind of oil, was wildly adorned with seashells, beads, shapes of metal, small mirrors, and clumps of hair and fur. When the sun hit the greased white hair it shone like silver. A scalp lock hung down over his forehead and ended in the shriveled red foot and black claws of some kind of lizard. He wore no feather headdress and no buffalo horns—a single yellow feather decorated his head. Only the men who had raided the wagons wore the buffalo-head bonnets. Only their faces were striped with black paint. The old Indian stepped into the clearing and began to talk, a rhythmical chanting speech that lasted several minutes. He barked out short sounds Dorsey figured were the names of the raiders, because as the words were called out, the horned and black-painted men went up, each in turn, and greeted the old Indian, who stood a little straighter each time he was saluted. Dorsey understood him to be some kind of chief.

"*Tokwetikati*," the chief said.

"*Tokwetikati*," others said, and everyone crowded into the clearing to get a closer look at the stolen loot. The crowd broke into smaller groups and drifted off to various parts of the camp. The pretty Indian girl, Chautavitty, who had met White Chest and walked arm in arm with him, dipped her head, a little bow to the old chief, and then she slipped quietly away. Dorsey was up on her toes searching the crowd for her mama when White Chest shoved her and pointed to a buffalo fur on the ground. Little Lucy had been turned over to children who were leading her down to the stream, touching her pale hair, laughing and pulling at her pink cotton dress. *Now*, Dorsey thought, *what is to happen to me?* A strange quality of passivity settled over her. There were only a few Indians left in the clearing. White Chest went up to the old chief and the man beside him. Each man gave White Chest a bear hug. "*Haits*" it sounded like each one said, and then they all three spoke more throaty Indian words. White Chest moved his arms and hands as he talked. He nodded in Dorsey's direction. He hugged each of the men and they hugged him back. When these three seemed to be through talking, a woman stepped forward from behind them, grinning and saying "Wahatewi, Wahatewi." The woman held White Chest and talked on, pausing to shake his shoulders or point her finger in his face.

White Chest laughed and called her Pia, and Tatatsinuupi, and the woman held onto him as if he were a pet she feared might wander away. Then White Chest—whose Indian name seemed to be Wahatewi, unless it meant something like "hello"—pulled Dorsey up by her wrist and held her arm out to the woman who still clung to him.

"*Nea* Pia," he said, "*Nea kwuhup*."

The woman grabbed Dorsey and turned her first one way and then the other, as if to teach her some dance step. She looked Dorsey over, felt the palms of her hands, lifted her dress, and squeezed her calves. "*Tokwetikati*."

The old chief had gotten out a long bone pipe. He and the middle-aged Indian man and White Chest, or Wahatewi, sat and shared the pipe, puffing solemnly. So much pipe smoke rose it looked as if they sat around a campfire.

The woman White Chest had called Pia led Dorsey into the tipi. Dorsey was surprised how much room there was inside, how high the sides rose above her to an opening through which sunlight slanted. Furs big enough to crawl beneath and be completely hidden under were spread on the earthen floor and covered all but a dug-out place holding old ashes.

"Where's my mama?"

Pia gave Dorsey's arm a jerk, put her hand over Dorsey's mouth. The woman looked closely at Mary Thurston's homespun dress, too big for Dorsey to begin with, now frayed and torn from rubbing against the horse and lying all night on the ground. "Tue Arika," the woman said to a girl not much older than Dorsey who had followed them into the tent. Then the woman, Pia, stared into Dorsey's eyes. "*Tokwetikati?*"

Dorsey had no idea what the woman wanted. She shook her head.

Pia nodded. She barked again at the girl Dorsey's age, who slipped wordlessly out of the tipi. Then Pia worked the tattered dress off Dorsey and threw it to the ground. The Indian shook her head, fingering Dorsey's cotton shift. A short, heavyset woman tugged at the shift and Dorsey took it off and stood naked before them. The heavyset woman said something to Pia that sounded like "towel-watch-chair." She squeezed Dorsey's upper arm hard. Dorsey stepped out of the woman's grip, and she hit Dorsey in the side of the head, hit her so hard her cheek and ear burned and bells chimed in the burning-hot ear. Pia still studied Dorsey and seemed not to have even noticed the other woman's cuffing her. Then Pia squatted to one of the huge furs and rooted around beneath it. She stood and handed Dorsey a plain deerskin skirt. Dorsey pulled the skirt over her head, inhaling its strong woodsmoke smell. She was surprised how soft and cool it was against her skin. Pia pulled out a tanned hide and folded it in half. "*Tutsahkunaru,*" Pia said to the other woman, who threaded a curved piece of bone with a length of rawhide. While Pia worked a belt of hide through slits in the waist of the skirt and pulled it comfortably snug, the other woman sewed together the folded-double deerskin. With a short bladed knife, Pia made one quick vertical cut where the sewn-together hide was creased. Then she pulled the one-piece top over Dorsey's head, making the knife cut longer until Dorsey's head fit through easily, her arms coming through openings the seamstress had left below each end of the fold. Sleeveless and loose over her waist, the blouse was comfortable.

"*Miar,*" Pia said. When Dorsey did not move Pia gave her a hard shove. "*Miar.*" Dorsey stumbled through the tipi opening back outside where she almost ran into a blond-haired man who was being led toward the opening by the young girl Pia had sent away. The man was a full head taller than any Indian Dorsey had seen in camp. She looked up into eyes the pale blue of a blown glass bottle her mother sometimes put wildflowers in back on the farm. The Indian faces surrounding

Dorsey were deep shades of copper tinged darker toward bay, but this tall man's long face was dappled red, the skin of a fallen apple freckled brown. The hair of all the Indians was black as a new skillet, but this man's hair was pale yellow mixed with gray like a roan horse. *What tribe,* Dorsey thought, *is this one from?*

Yellow Rudolph

"*Ohapitu* Rudoff, *tekwari* Dutch, *taivo,* Tehano," Pia said.

"*Sprechen Sie* Deutsche? Englisch?" The man warbled like some large bird.

"My name is Dorsey Murphy. Dorsey Murphy Speer. Who are you?"

"*Me llamo* Rudolph Hermann. Komantz, they *namen* me Yellow Rudolph. *Ich hab* not so much gray—more yellow in *mein* hair when I was traded here."

"*Natsokwe,*" Pia said. She handed Dorsey a big bowl made from a hollowed-out log and a leather bag full of flat beans. "*Nahnia?*"

"*Kommen Sie.* She wants you to pound, grind up mesquite beans. And she wants to know your name." Yellow Rudolph said something quick to Pia, part of which Dorsey heard clearly— "*Se llama,* Dorr-see."

The Indian women said, "Dorr-see, Dorr-see," and they all laughed.

Yellow Rudolph led Dorsey to a flat rock, and he showed her how to split the pods and get the flat beans out and pound them with another rock into a grainy powder. While he swept the pulverized beans from the rock into the wooden bowl with a brush made from stiff grass, Yellow Rudolph haltingly answered her questions.

"Are they going to kill us?"

He snorted a laugh, shrugged his shoulders.

"How long have they held you captive?"

"Apaches captured me over a year ago—a year and a half, now—down near Fredericksburg, the Deutsche settlement north and west of San Antonio." Yellow Rudolph sat back on his haunches, splitting open mesquite pods as he talked. "I had ridden up from San Antonio to find Herr Reinbach." Rudolph gave a short laugh and shook his head at something he was remembering. Then he went on. "Komantz hate Apaches—maybe more than they hate Tehanos. A war party from the Honey Eater—also *namen* the Wasp band of Komantz—attacked Apaches who had me. The Honey Eaters sold me to a rich warrior of this Antelope band of Komantz. The warrior—the name of a dead one is never spoken again—bought me for his Frau, Hungry Woman, because he did not have a number two Frau to help Hungry Woman work." Yellow Rudolph pounded a pile of mesquite beans. "I am too old to make a Komantz warrior, so I make a Frau-helper or they kill me. I think Komantz not kill me because they say I am 'Dutchman' from Deutsche tribe, not Tehano. Also, I think, tall as me they had not seen. Maybe three weeks past, Hungry Woman's husband was killed by Texas Rangers. The Rangers are relentless, hard men and I think everyone is afraid of them. They caught Hungry Woman's man near Onion Creek, the place the Comanches call *Cuuna eted*— that means in Englisch Fire-Rock Place. Rangers, they hang the Komantz from a tree. The rope stretch, the limb bend, and his feet hit the ground before he is dead. They cut him down and make him get back on his horse, and they hang him this time from a higher, stronger limb. Then they scalp him, and they cut off his arms and legs and leave the rest of him hang there so everyone who passes by knows he has no legs to walk on in the land hereafter." Yellow Rudolph picked up another handful of beans and held them up, squeezing them and shaking them in his fist. "For Komantz, choking death is the worst. I think they are right. I saw a man choked to death years ago in New Orleans." He closed his eyes and did not speak for a long time. Then he told Dorsey strangulation means the breath, the spirit, might not escape the body to go to the Good Hunting Land. Spirits who can't get out before the body dies become ghosts and stay near the death place.

"Those who are scalped always become *der Geister*—you know, ghosts." Yellow Rudolph's eyes widened. "*Blutig* hairless creatures." Dorsey was sure Yellow Rudolph believed in Comanche ghosts, and he seemed to be haunted by ghosts of his own. *Maybe*, she thought, *he brought some German ghosts with him*.

Rudolph guided her fingers along the seam of a bean pod and it opened like a little jacket. He told her the Comanches believe the dead who are mutilated can get to the Good Hunting Land, the Land of the Dead Beyond the Setting Sun, but they remain forever mutilated in the afterlife. "*Diese Bande* will not now go by the fire rock place where *der Geist* of Hungry Woman's husband comes out with the rising moon."

After Hungry Woman's man was killed, Weak Eyes, the brother of the dead warrior, took Hungry Woman as his number two wife, but he didn't want to have to provide for Yellow Rudolph. "So," Yellow Rudolph's jawbone and his ear quivered, "in the camp I'm like orphan—I can't count on my next meal. Now, with plenty *der Fleisch* in camp, it is not difficult. I work hard so I am claimed by someone before winter." Dorsey pounded a pile of mesquite beans into white powder and Yellow Rudolph nodded. He told her he had come to Texas from Germany many years before he was captured, so he knew English and had taught himself some Spanish and Comanche. "Komantz do not know deutsch and few know englisch, but most have a few spanisch words." He told Dorsey that Lucy was young enough the Comanches would adopt her.

"Lucy won't let them." Yellow Rudolph laughed his snort-laugh again. "What about my mama?" He shook his head.

"What the men have done to her, it is not as bad as what the women will do. And after they torture her they will either kill her or make her as me, a Frau-helper."

"No." Dorsey lifted her pounding rock like a weapon. "I won't let them."

Yellow Rudolph stared at Dorsey as if she were crazy. He shook his head. "At first I think death is better. But, later, I think life is better. To die is too easy to forget one's sins, *ja?*"

Dorsey was not sure what he was talking about. He was just a strange, brooding, foreign man. But he knew things about the Comanches she needed to know. "The woman who seems to be in charge of me, Pia, is she White Chest's wife?"

"White Chest?"

"The one who brought me here. He wore Mary Thurston's corset and the one with the broken teeth told me in Spanish he was *Corazón Blanco*."

"White Heart?—*Corazón* is heart. *Nicht* White Heart. His true name is Wahatewi, Two Talks." Yellow Rudolph looked directly into her eyes. "*Außergewwohnlich* he is."

"Ausser—what?"

"Extraordinary, special. I know something about him he doesn't know himself. Maybe someday I will tell you. I am here in this band for a purpose I think. I think I was brought here to be near this special one." The strange old man's eyes brightened with tears, and Dorsey wondered if he were going to weep. "A Kiowa band visited this camp in the summer. They spoke of a Comanchero with eyes like Wahatewi. The Komantz took that as a sign of Two Talks' *puha*—that means his medicine or power—that his eyes fly as far as the eagle and see as much." Yellow Rudolph shook his head and brought the rock down on a pile of beans.

"Is Pia his wife?"

"Pia means mother. Two Talks' mother, her name is Tatatsinuupi, Morning Star, wife of Murawa, Crooked Nose. Two Talks has not yet taken a wife." Yellow Rudolph said the warrior Dorsey called Broken Teeth was Pahiwiya, Three Ropes, brother of Hungry Woman's dead husband. Three Ropes was war-leader of the men who'd attacked the wagons. When Three Ropes had tried to get a war party up, few of the older warriors believed in his medicine, but the young men had followed him because they were anxious to dance the war dance and fight their first fight. Two Talks had gone, Yellow Rudolph said, because Three Ropes' dead brother had been Two Talks' close friend. Two Talks was watching out for his dead friend's brother. "If Two Talks not join war party, Three Ropes might not persuade many men to follow him. Having brought booty back to the camp, he will have more influence. It mean he have good *puha*. I'm pretty sure most of the men follow Two Talks. Still, Three Ropes was chief of war party. Anyone who convinces others to follow him is a chief. There are plenty of civil chiefs and war chiefs so long as their *puha* is strong. All think Two Talks has strong *puha*." Yellow Rudolph scooped both hands full of ground up beans and poured the powder through his fingers into a wooden bowl.

"What makes them favor Two Talks?"

"When his band go on the reservation, Two Talks and some others joined these Antelope. For Komantz, bonds of choice mean maybe more than bonds of *die Blut*. Your Lucy, yellow hair and all, will be beloved after she becomes Komantz. Because she *choose* Our People."

There was so much Dorsey didn't understand about the Indians—red niggers, Major Benson had called them. *They are savages, and I hate every one of them*, she thought. But in spite of her terror and her grief over her mother, she was glad she was alive. The world outside this small, terrible world was dead. Dorsey had died somewhere far down inside her, and someone else moved through her days. She couldn't spend all her time thinking about her mother or Gideon or the old world. She split pods and piled up mesquite beans for Yellow Rudolph to pound, and she wondered what secret the old German knew about the warrior, Two Talks.

Learning the Ways of Our People

The first few weeks in the camp Dorsey was a somnambulist walking mesmerized through unbidden fancies. She was surprised to see her own familiar leg coming out of an animal hide skirt, her own familiar foot stepping in a hide moccasin. Her body continued to work as it always had. In the evenings she opened the buffalo robe door and stepped into Crooked Nose's tipi, where she had a place against the hide wall where one of the cedar lodgepoles rested in the hard-packed earth. She had counted the cedar poles so many times she knew each by some particularity—a light shape in the wood, a hanging flap of bark, a knot or curve. There were eighteen poles in Crooked Nose's tipi. She had counted sixteen in some tipis in camp. She had watched some women putting up a new tipi. They started with four main poles and somehow fixed the others into the frame the first four made. The poles rested against one another where they met at the top—about as high as a tall man standing on the shoulders of another tall man: twelve, maybe fourteen feet. Near the small fire in the middle of the floor a wooden stake held taut a rope that ran to the top, where it was tied across the crisscrossed poles. Smoke climbed this rope and went out a smoke flap. The rope helped hold the tipi down when strong winds blew. Dorsey counted and re-counted the poles and watched smoke or light climb the rope until she grew weary and lay down on the ground.

She woke in a tipi, in a new world. Sights, sounds, scents were hers for the first time. She squatted among trees and emptied her bladder and bowels. When Dorsey said she was hungry, Morning Star fished from a bubbling kettle a fatty hunk of bone and meat Dorsey wasn't sure she could make herself eat. But she put the half-raw meat against her lips and, of its own accord, her mouth moved— teeth and muscles chewed and swallowed. The grit of sand ground against her teeth, bone and cartilage squeaked, her cheeks and tongue smacked, sucking out marrow. She sucked so hard, pulled at the taste so strong, she closed both her eyes. Buffalo tasted like cow or deer, only sweeter, as if sprinkled with sugar. And every bite tasted of dirt and woodsmoke.

She had not forgotten how Joe and Hiram had looked when they died, Mary crawling off with baby James. Even Mr. Speer with his bleeding mouth touched her heart. But the body that carried her wounded heart did not seem to realize how bad this new life among the Indians was. Her body hungered and thirsted and ate and drank and kept on living. In fact, her body was continuing to grow, to change. Just a few days ago Morning Star had sent Dorsey to the river for water. "*Nuhkitu*," Morning Star had said. So Dorsey had run, and, for the first time, she felt her breasts jiggle up and down as she ran, and they ached with the jiggling. *Nuhkitu*, she thought, *run fast to womanhood.* And the painful bouncing pleased her.

Morning Star, Crooked Nose's number one wife, was firm with Dorsey but not cruel. Crooked Nose's second wife, Persimmon, the short burly one who had cuffed Dorsey the first day in the tipi, poked, kicked, tripped, or slapped Dorsey every chance she got. Persimmon was mean and strong, and her blows became sore, bruised places on Dorsey's body.

Two Talks slept in a brush arbor beside his father's tipi. Dorsey kept expecting Two Talks to come to her bed and force himself on her. Why else had he protected her from all the other men after he captured her? But after he ignored her for weeks, she decided he was not going to violate her. And though she did not want any man to force his way into her bed, she was disappointed Two Talks didn't seem to notice her at all. When he entered or left his lodge he looked right through her, his eyes blacker than any of the other Indians'.

Every night Persimmon tied Dorsey's hands and feet together and knocked her into bed. One chilly morning, the sky was growing light in the east but there were still a few stars out. Dorsey looked up sleepily to see Morning Star, a knife in her upraised hand over Dorsey's head. Morning Star pulled at Dorsey's hair and her arm swung down.

Half-asleep, Dorsey screamed, "Gideon, help, she's scalping me."

Morning Star laughed and cut her rawhide bonds. Dorsey put a trembling hand to her head to feel for bare scalp, blood, and gore, but found only her short-shorn hair. Yellow Rudolph explained the women cut their hair short so it wouldn't get in the way of their work. Later Dorsey saw a lock of what looked like her hair tied into the old chief's long hair.

Morning Star told Dorsey if she promised not to run away she could sleep unbound. "If you try to run," Yellow Rudolph translated, "Morning Star let Persimmon kill you slow."

Dorsey promised not to run. Some vestigial part of her—the old Dorsey—felt no obligation to such a promise given to a savage who held her captive and threatened her with death. But the Dorsey she felt she was becoming wanted to honor her word to this woman who had been kind to her. Besides, she wouldn't be able to get far on her own, and she wouldn't leave behind her mother and little Lucy. She had to be patient, to wait and watch, to learn everything she could use to make things better for herself and for Laura Etta and Lucy.

Once she was free to move about the camp on her own, she took her mama some mesquite meal cakes. Laura Etta snatched them and stuffed them whole into her mouth. She ate like an animal afraid another might take her food. She licked her fingertips, smacked her lips. Then she seemed to recognize Dorsey. Her eyes smiled like they used to, and she hugged her daughter.

"Sister, does Mama know you're playing in your Sunday dress?" The words were strange, but her mama's arms around her were so familiar and felt so good, Dorsey couldn't speak. "Don't you worry, Annie, I won't tattle." Laura Etta ran off laughing like a child. The memory of her mama's arms around her, though her mama had not known her, helped Dorsey through those early weeks in the camp. Laura Etta was ragged and mistreated. She was not herself, yet she laughed.

Dorsey could not remember her mama laughing the whole time they had been on the wagon train.

Dorsey was allowed to go to the stream to bathe as often as she liked. The Comanche women could not understand why she wanted to wash herself so often, and they giggled at her and shook their heads when she went about with her hacked-off hair pulled back and damp. When Dorsey asked for one of the bone combs the men all used for fixing their long decorated hair, Morning Star frowned and, with Yellow Rudolph translating, told Dorsey long hair, combed hair, greased and decorated hair was for warriors, not for women.

"But," Yellow Rudolph said, "I know a warrior who wears his hair short, and he is just as fierce as Two Talks." Yellow Rudolph grinned and shook his own yellow-gray hair. Sometimes the German acted so strangely Dorsey wondered if he were addled.

After lecturing her, Morning Star nonetheless dropped a short comb in Dorsey's lap. She felt better just being able to get the knots out of her hair—not to mention the gray lice and the ticks, fat and purple with her blood, she pulled out every time she bathed.

Gideon, Are You Coming?

At first she thought almost constantly about Gideon. She looked up from her Frau work hoping to see him galloping into the camp leading a whole army of rescuers. It became a kind of game, a way of making time pass and keeping her hopes alive. She kept her eyes on a deerhide she was scraping or a bowl of mesquite beans she was grinding, stared down at the short fur or the white powder and thought: *I will count to one hundred, and then I will look up, and Gideon will be here. If he's not, I'll count to five hundred before I look up again.* Many weeks passed and Gideon was never there when Dorsey looked up, and she stopped watching for him. The nights grew cooler, and the band was astir with talk of a big herd of buffalo some hunters had spotted. Now Dorsey thought less often of Gideon. When she said her nightly prayers—*Dear Lord, give me strength and please help my mama and little Lucy*—she sometimes tried to picture Gideon's face. At those times she thought, *Gideon, are you coming?* And, sometimes, she prayed, *Jesus, watch over Two Talks and Morning Star even though they are savages who do not know your name—they are nice to me and they keep Three Ropes and Persimmon from doing bad things to me. Amen.*

Charles Wesley: Chasing an Old Man's Dream

Leaves the War Behind
(May–June 1865)

For Charles Wesley Speer the war was a spiritual as well as a physical journey. He confessed to me he joined the New York Volunteers because he favored the abolition of slavery but also because he hoped to prove to his papa that Alexander was not the only courageous child in the household. And, he said, after the war he went on to Texas seeking his twin in spite of his certainty something had happened to Alexander because he also hoped to find something of his papa in Texas, since that's where the old man always resided in Charles Wesley's imagination.

—from *Gideon Jones' Journal*

Charles Wesley was directed to a dilapidated-looking steamboat that sank lower in the brown water as a handful of Rebs filed on board. They looked more exhausted than defeated. Reb and Yankee alike seemed to feel a solemn relief the war was finally over and they were still alive to quit it. A young lieutenant in a clean blue uniform was in charge of the Union patrol that seemed to have confiscated the vessel. It felt strange to be still in uniform but out of the cavalry. Charles Wesley no longer outranked anyone, but no one outranked him, either. He handed the lieutenant a pouch of silver and was nodded on board.

"An honor, Captain." The lieutenant saluted and grinned. It was all Charles Wesley could do to keep his mouth shut at this extortion. He returned the lieutenant's salute, thankful for Papa's bank drafts. He wondered what the Confederate veterans were paying for their steamboat berths. A dear price for space on the deck, yet worth every ounce of silver. Charles Wesley and the Rebs on board were fortunate to wrangle river passage. He'd heard Lee's soldiers had to foot it hundreds of miles home.

Charles Wesley found a corner where there was a dry space to lie down, and as soon as he stretched out he was overcome with bone-deep weariness, though he had slept in fits and starts on the rail car. Nashville drifted away. A Confederate wearing corporal's stripes lay down close enough Charles Wesley smelled the man's sweat—a mix of frying pork and turpentine. Soon as the Reb stilled himself he was snoring. Charles Wesley closed his eyes, and the corporal's snoring soon became the rhythmic rasp of a two-man saw buckling and jerking into green wood. In the dream he knew was a dream, Charles Wesley and Alexander faced one another from opposite sides of an enormous tree they were cutting. The sun flashed on the saw's long blade. Their motion was like rowing—lean forward then pull back—the motion of the steamboat tugging down the river. In the dream, the tree kept growing bigger and bigger around, keeping pace with their sawing. The more they cut, the more the trunk thickened. In the dream Charles Wesley thought, *This, then, is our eternity.* The long blade was the color of water and moved between them like a river. Alexander let go the saw and raised his right arm. His left arm was a stump that showed rings of wood. On the ground lay his left arm in a pile of sawdust.

Charles Wesley woke up—the lieutenant was shouting to a man on shore who shouted back. Rope groaned against wood, waves slapped, and then the river breeze stilled. A sign read: CLARKSVILLE. They were going north in order to go south. The lieutenant went ashore for about ten minutes. When he was back on board they cast off again. As they passed Fort Donelson a light rain began. By dark, they reached the mouth of the Cumberland and laid over until early morning when they took on coal and entered the Ohio River. The steady rain had not let up.

Rebs huddled under a blanket trying to keep dry while they played poker. Having spent what money they had on the boat ride, they bet their meager possessions and keepsakes and offered notes against their futures—ten percent of next year's wages, ten acres of the farmstead one hoped still waited in Texas' Brazos river bottom, and, in one case, a daughter of marriageable age who was "right comely if she ain't misdeveloped since '61."

Along both sides of the river were small towns, white houses dozing on hillsides in the steady rain, and reminders of war—deserted breastworks, splintered trees, raw places on the earth. They passed a good-sized town someone said was Paducah, Kentucky. At full dark, they reached Cairo, where they tied up again.

Not much to Cairo, a few sheds, some laid-up flats and rafts. Rumors had them taking on more veterans, but after four hours they were under way with no more passengers.

In the darkness they rode the Ohio River on into the Mississippi. Charles Wesley was wide awake, alert, feeling as if he were on the brink of a new adventure, watching both sides of the dark river's banks to see what he could see of this new country he was entering.

Well after midnight they stopped at Caruthersville, Missouri, and a sutler came aboard with his wagon and sold fresh tomatoes, ginger cakes, half-moon pies, and sweet milk, delicacies Charles Wesley felt were cheap at the doubled and tripled prices this old crook extorted. He refused Confederate money, which he called worthless. The few who complained were told they were lucky he was willing to barter for trinkets that mostly would not stand their value until he was back on shore. Charles Wesley managed to get the sutler's hairy ear long enough to inquire about whisky. Of all the manly skills Papa had sought to teach him, Charles Wesley would wager the taste for spirits had helped him the most in war's fearful business of attack and retreat.

"I can fetch pop-skull for two dollars a jigger, a jug for ten. You'll get corned on the strength of it."

The sutler took ten dollars, in advance, and the jug turned out to be just a pint bottle when he slapped it against Charles Wesley's belly.

"Take these for change." The old thief dropped two of the half-moon pies into Charles Wesley's pocket. The liquor was more yellow than whisky-brown, and he guessed it was more than likely "mean" whisky. He'd encountered similar distillations concocted out of a smidgeon of genuine alcohol—he tasted brandy, maybe—cut with water, vitriol, and something to give it color. He took a bigger swig. Some kind of wild meat had been used to give it an aged, gamy flavor. Bust-head or not, the spirits burned good going down, and he didn't regret a drop, even at so dear a price.

The rain stopped, and they cast off in a light fog rising over the shallows. Lulled by the throbbing of the boat's boilers, the slapping of water against the hull, and the warmth of the whisky in his chest, Charles Wesley dozed pleasantly until dawn. He waked to first light on the mighty river rolling red-orange and wide. His head was free of the stuffiness whisky sometimes leaves behind. He had no aches and no trembles. The minié ball in his left leg had not bothered him since he'd gotten on the boat, though his bladder ached every time he emptied it. The river's sun-glittered expanse was unbroken except for an immense dead, drifting tree, its bleached, bare limbs protruding, skeletal and weary-looking, as it was borne along. He was hungry, and he wolfed down the half-moon pies flattened in his pocket.

Pointing to the right side of the river, the lieutenant told him Missouri had given way to Arkansas. The river bisected miles of green forest, passed a few flats and woodyards, villages gouged red and raw-looking out of the green. In the rising heat, vapors rose over the wild vegetation permeating the air with odors of damp soil, rotting wood, fungus, and mold that lay like a sticky oil on the skin. At Memphis they put in for three hours, waited for a steamer ahead of them to take on more coal. Under way again, Tennessee on the left gave way to Mississippi. More forest, here and there a red clay bluff. The farther south they went the higher the river rose, bearing them closer to the burning sun. Charles Wesley opened the top of his tunic and sat on the deck. He let the sun bake him to sweat clean his pores fouled with the stench of death and decay.

That evening they passed Greenville, Mississippi, and around midnight, Vicksburg, valiant for so long under siege. When the sun rose again they were between Vicksburg and Natchez. Now, along both sides, continuous built-up earthworks—"levees"—kept the river from flooding. The steamboat rode as high or higher than the roofs of houses built on the lower ground behind the levees containing the great river. By late afternoon tall pines gave way to live oaks and cypress swamps, the trees bearded with dark curly moss—Louisiana on both sides. At dark, they put in at Baton Rouge. The State Capitol Building, high on the east bank, looked like a castle from the legend of King Arthur. Here they were given pulpy, almost juiceless, oranges and bread. They slept on deck, and the mosquitoes were terrible. All the next day Charles Wesley scratched the swollen red bites, but even his itching made him feel keenly alive.

Almost Love in New Orleans

Near evening the thirteenth of June, Charles Wesley reached New Orleans. River travel was fast. If he had gone overland by horseback, he'd still be days from Texas. The Federal blockade had been lifted, and the port was so crowded they went ashore on lighters while the boat waited for dock space. With the resumption of trade, every businessman and peddler in the world had brought his wares to New Orleans.

The Trans-Mississippi, the last real army of the Confederacy, had recently surrendered here, all officers and men to be paroled. Having seen so many die,

Charles Wesley was surprised so many could be left alive. The Reb prisoners were assigned to an area of warehouses where a Soldiers' Rest had been set up to house and feed them until transportation home could be arranged. To no avail, he asked around for a Reb named Alexander Wesley Speer. He wondered if Alexander might have used a different name. The Johnnies were given free rein, and they wandered the streets with what they had left of the near-worthless Confederate money.

Charles Wesley roamed the city too, watching for his brother's face and staring hungrily at visions of loveliness. Cream-skinned ladies in shiny dresses wearing hats with long feathers walked the streets as if they were dancing. Gaslights danced too, reflected in glass and polished brass as if someone had dropped from the balconies overhead handfuls of gold coins. High-stepping, well-fed, well-curried horses pranced past pulling behind them fast little cabriolets. And, *oh*, the food: platters of shrimp, oysters, and fish all pink and blue and silver, green and red okra gumbos, stacked melons and pineapples, bananas hanging like gold chandeliers from market stalls, and rows of amber liquors. Charles Wesley spent his papa's money freely on the delicacies everywhere around him. No matter how sweet, how tart, how rich the flavors on his tongue, no matter how much he stuffed himself, he could not assuage his appetites.

Soldiers in Confederate uniforms hobbled about the city. Like the red-headed Reb in Nashville, many had a missing arm. Charles Wesley's left arm had not pained him since Nashville, and seeing so many crippled made him feel especially blessed. Men in tattered uniforms who had just one leg, or one eye, or no arms, or no legs sat or leaned against brick walls with one good palm open for money, and Charles Wesley put at least a coin in every outstretched hand until he'd passed out all his money. He found a bank where he cashed another draft against his papa's bank in New York. Now Papa would know one son at least was alive in New Orleans, and well enough to spend money.

Charles Wesley wanted to get shed of his dirty uniform, wanted a bath and clean clothes, wanted to sit in a barber's chair cranked up high and listen to gossip while the tips of his hair and beard darkened the floor. And he wanted to go into a fine restaurant and order more delicious food—wanted a platter of oysters and a crystal glass of whisky. The uniform he had once been proud to don seemed now to hold the miasma of the war locked in its thick, damp fibers. He would wash and dry and pack away the uniform. Perhaps he could also pack away the murky vapors of war. In Texas a Union veteran might not be as well received as a tailored businessman. He walked until he came to a section where the houses and carriages had the shine and sparkle of jewels. On a corner several men loitered in dress suits. Their cigars burned red, their teeth flashed, their shoes reflected the gaslights. He waded into scents of warm wool and lilac water, good tobacco, and the sweat of strutting men. A big man, not tall but stout, well-muscled not corpulent, eyed his insignia.

"Captain," the stout one said, tilting back the brim of his hat to reveal steady blue eyes and thick gray brows. A couple of the men edged away, but the one who had spoken said to them, "Now, boys, the war's over. Might as well get used to it." He shook his head as if he were having a hard time getting used to it. The two who'd been moving stopped in their tracks. Charles Wesley speculated the stout man could have been their commander not long ago, though something about him and the men around him convinced Charles Wesley they were not, had never been, soldiers. "May we be of some service?" the stout man asked.

Charles Wesley held out his hand. "Speer." He consciously dropped the "captain" off the front of his name.

The stout man's hand glittered with a ring on every finger. His grip was soft and clammy. "D. D. Bohanan." Up close, these men did not seem as refined nor as well dressed as Charles Wesley had thought, but they would have to do. Bohanan's coat opened wide when he shook hands, revealing pink stains on his shirt front as from wine spilled there.

"I was admiring your apparel. I'm weary of these blues. Can you direct me to a good tailor, and, if you would be so kind, a comfortable hostelry where I can wash away some of the miles? Perhaps a barber, as well?"

"A. J.," Bohanan said.

"Boss?"

"You were just leaving, going to the fairgrounds or someplace weren't you?" A. J. looked surprised, then nodded. "Then you won't mind walking the captain here over to the Bienville House. And have them send Andrew's tailor over right away."

"I'm grateful, Mr. Bohanan." Bohanan saluted Charles Wesley and waited while A. J. mumbled something to one of the other men. Just then a pale blond-headed boy in a tattered shirt lurched around the corner and bumped into A. J.

"What the Hell?"

"*Entschuldigen Sie, bitte*," the boy said. A. J. jerked his arm back ready to cuff the boy, who raised his arms to protect himself and said, "*Entschuldigen Sie, bitte. Es tut mir leid, ich habe mich geirrt.*"

"Fucking immigrant shit," A. J. said. Bohanan shook his head and chuckled.

Charles Wesley spied the boy's deft movement, less than the blink of an eye, his hand in A. J.'s coat, A. J.'s wallet under the boy's waistband. Charles Wesley did not say anything. He'd let A. J. find out for himself. The man looked familiar with trouble. In a city such as this, crowded with every race, Charles Wesley knew many did worse than pick pockets. These were hard times and most merchants were profiting from the misfortunes of soldiers. He figured these flashy well-to-do idlers—they'd most probably avoided conscription by hiring others to take their places—owed someone at least a few pilfered wallets.

Both the hotel and the tailor were better than Charles Wesley expected. Measuring the pleasures of a hot bath, a ride in the barber's chair, a new suit of clothes, and a pair of soft boots cut and sewn in one day, a meal his tongue would not soon forget (of raw oysters, turtle soup, sea trout amandine, sweet glazed carrots, mince pie, and café au lait), Charles Wesley would have ranked the bath above all these delights he'd been so long denied—hot soapy water his choice if he could have but one bodily pleasure. Maybe the restorative suds even over the dark Creole women who stared openly at him. A couple of years of war got one's priorities in order.

Full of restless energy Charles Wesley roamed the city for four days, the earliest he could book passage on a steamer to Texas. All the walking agitated the minié ball still in his leg, and it burned like a thorn he couldn't reach to pull out. Hungry again, he sated his appetite with bananas off the boats from South America, Creole oranges from groves below New Orleans, and dark roast coffee spiced up with chicory. The desire for a woman was a different kind of appetite. His fellow officers in the New York Volunteers talked of nothing else, but he had kept such things to himself. He had thought only privates from remote farms or backward villages would fraternize with camp following women who set up tent cities of fornication for pay. War whores were dirty and ill kempt. Many were fat and toothless. Of the sexual myths the men passed around, one was the pleasure a toothless mouth offered. Charles Wesley would as soon poke—well, there must be many things better than some poor crone's bloody gums. There had been a couple of whores who were tempting. He recalled one evening in particular—Charles Wesley, Silas Nunner, and Jenks had stood in the flickering light of a fire before one of the women's tents where whores and soldiers passed mean whisky around and laughed at familiar bad jokes—a youngish fleshy girl had given Charles Wesley a smile behind the veil of rising smoke, and he might have gone into her tent if that ole ha'nt Silas Nunner hadn't been there. A little breeze had been blowing that made a sad whistling through the hole in Silas' head. At the time, Charles Wesley had thought how Alexander would have laughed and slapped the girl on her bottom and then gone off with her for all the world to see. Alexander could do bad things and make them appear good. Charles Wesley had known he could not lie with a whore unless he did it in secret. His pride, if pride truly named it, was stronger than his lust. Lust, it seemed to him, was a natural, unhurtful thing only preachers would name a weakness, while still others saw it as an endearing manly strength. Pride, on the other hand, was cowardly and slinking, a private and therefore doubly evil sin. Pride said, *Well, too bad, that's the way I am.* Pride made you proud of pride itself. *Well, I sure wouldn't want to be naive, unsophisticated, gullible.* So he confined his lust to his heart, mindful of the irony of the Scriptures: *But I say unto you, That whosoever looketh on a woman to lust after her hath committed adultery with her already in his heart.* He was guilty of adultery without knowing its sinful pleasures. Too proud to pay for a woman, too proud to publicly acknowledge his appetite, he remained chaste except for those few times he secretly defiled himself with his own hand—*And if thy right hand offend thee, cut it off, and cast it from thee: for it is profitable for thee that one of thy members should perish, and not that thy whole body should be cast into hell*—or times he woke with wet bedding wondering where the blame lay for unconscious sin. *That's the way I am,* he thought. *I'm not sufficiently remorseful to lie with whores, nor to cut off my hand. One day I will love a woman who will love me, and we will marry and couple in righteous pleasure.*

But on his second night in New Orleans—where it was unlikely he would be seen by anyone he knew and where there were many whores neither dirty nor unkempt, whores so pretty and young they made him feel a full-grown man—he gave in to the Devil's whispers. He entered a bordello *just to see what one is like* and was led upstairs by a dusky-skinned woman he later learned was called "octoroon" for her one-eighth Negro blood.

Like the café au lait he'd drunk after supper, this woman's skin had brown depths set off by a plain white chemise. Her scent detached itself from the house's thick swirls of lilac and gardenia and the burnt grass smell of cigar smoke. She did not smell like flowers or candy, not like tobacco or whisky, but more like the salt air he remembered from spring journeys to the Jersey shore. She sat on the bed barely sunk into the white coverlet and let the soft straps of her chemise fall over shoulders brown and smooth as the mahogany headboard. Beneath small breasts her body was narrow and hard as a packed dirt road, her belly the road's barely mounded median, her ribs the soft regular furrows down each wheel's lane. He put the heel of his hand against her belly, his spread fingertips touching ribs on both sides. She rose and the chemise slid down her body to the pine floor. She kissed his bearded cheek and the side of his nose, deftly avoided his lips. Her breath, warm and moist, was the faint citric spray of a sliced orange, sweet but with sting. She was lovelier than dream or vision—no painting, no sketch or daguerreotype had shown him such exotic beauty. He did not tell her this was his first time, but he felt she knew—though nothing in her manner was condescending or even faintly teasing. She seemed pleased by his responsiveness and held him close after he had finished. Propelled by a storm of emotions, he wanted to petition her to spend all her nights with him hereafter, to declare that whatever had brought her to this life no longer mattered. All he managed out loud was to ask her name and when he could again be with her.

"My name is Oralia. I am not a girl of this house but its business manager. I do not usually go to the rooms, but tonight I'm glad I did." Her tone became playful in a way that let him know their dalliance was ended. She laughed, and, gripping his chin whiskers, shook his head. "You may never see me again, except in your dreams."

When they were dressed, he took out his wallet. She removed all his paper money, her eyebrows raised. "Does this seem too much money for so little time?"

He answered honestly. "All there is in that wallet is not too much."

She folded the bills and put them in his palm. "Give this to Marie. She has a burn scar over her eye and cheek, and men pass by her unless she's the only girl left."

He gave the girl the money as Oralia bade him. Marie rose to take him upstairs, but he told her not tonight. When she smiled, the puckered skin of her dark pink scar almost disappeared. Up close she was prettier than any girl in the house except Oralia. He vowed he'd return and spend time with Marie.

Steamer to Galveston, Overland to Austin

Like many Easterners, Charles Wesley's papa thought all Texans were either vaqueros working cattle, Texas Rangers fighting Comanches, desperate shootists engaged in duels, or handsome gamblers with scandalous pasts. The slave question complicated a world Charles Wesley's father had imagined in simpler terms. So, of course, would the Indian question, or the Mexican question, if he had thought about those issues as questions, but he did not. What he thought about were young men going west and having proper adventures fighting noble savages and clearing the way for civilization.

—from *Gideon Jones' Journal*

The day after Charles Wesley's assignation with the woman who called herself Oralia, he received news from a messenger sent to the hotel that the steamer line had a canceled berth, and in spite of a longing to revisit the lovely octoroon he hurriedly packed his few necessaries. He headed down the stairs where he met Silas Nunner who was going up.

"Come on, Silas, we're journeying on to Texas."

Silas shook his gray head. "I'm all tuckered out. I'm going into retiracy here and now." Silas slowly climbed the stairs, and then that familiar ole ghost just kept climbing, walking air till he disappeared into a shadow along the ceiling.

"Good-bye, old ghost," Charles Wesley said, mostly to himself. He hurried to the wharf and boarded the boat. Seas were calm, and the passage took a day and a half. He reached Galveston Bay the first day of July.

A New York Volunteer, Charles Wesley had marched through barren fields in Virginia and the Carolinas and Georgia on summer afternoons so hot and muggy he was certain even Hades would have offered some respite—the shadow of the Devil's pitchfork, at least. Galveston in July gave him second thoughts. Like a Negro slave he shed his shirt, but that only exposed more flesh to sun and to mosquitoes swarming even at midday. In the city's saloons, drinking room-temperature beer, cow-handlers and former Reb soldiers (none of whom recalled a Reb of Charles Wesley's likeness named Alexander) said a man didn't know hot until he saw the Great Desert, where your rifle barrel melted closed and if you lost your hat your brains fried crisp.

After three weeks in Galveston, tired of the glare of sand and the smells of dead fish and salt air, Charles Wesley tried Houston, but found it even less to his liking. The heat was just as oppressive as Galveston's and there was no Gulf breeze. From Houston, he took the railway cars to Brenham and there caught the stage to Austin, the Wild West Papa had dreamt about.

Galveston and Houston, save the oppressive heat, had looked not much different from the Carolinas or Virginia—not too different from New York state. The trees were tall, the shrubs, grasses, and crops green. Browner Austin was where the real West began. Austin gamblers wagered anything from a dollar to an entire frontier ranch. Men who couldn't afford to eat managed to get bottles of spirits to drink away their despair. Saloon girls were always ready to take any paper or coin a man might have overlooked in his pockets. Ruffian outlaws openly carried guns and kept under heavy guard the few supplies they could get. Confederate storehouses were regularly broken into, and Governor Murrah had slipped out of the six-columned governor's mansion and run off to Mexico to escape charges of treason.

The three-story capitol building housed no government, and outlaws made off with seventeen thousand dollars in gold and silver from the state treasury. To the relief of law-abiding citizens, Union troops were encamped along Shoal Creek and on the grounds behind the capitol.

Union soldiers had been sent all over Texas for military occupation duty while Rebs, unpaid for months, hungry and angry, lolled about. Settlers from the western parts of the state who had forted up during the war were heading back to farm cabins or venturing back onto the frontier to lay claim to new land. The same folks who had prayed their Rebel sons and husbands would whip the Yankees now counted on the men in blue for protection from Indians. Most frontier ranches remained unoccupied. Buffalo had extended their range, and that, with the lack of white resistance, had brought Indians, mostly Comanches, farther south and east than they had swarmed in years. Also swarming were gangs of *white* Indians—former soldiers, deserters, and other outlaw ne'er-do-wells who masqueraded as Indians and attacked and pillaged white settlements and Indian camps alike. For Charles Wesley, talk of frontier forts and Indian dangers made for a heady atmosphere.

South and east of town lay farmland flat to barely rolling, the soil black as night. But Charles Wesley was drawn to the jagged hills west of town. He rented a lively dun gelding from a livery stable and rode west into brown buttes scattered with stunted and twisted trees, the cactus called prickly pear that bore flat ears covered with thorns, and the gray-green bushes called yucca that sent up flowering spikes as tall and white as church steeples and so uncommonly beautiful they put him in a worshipful mood. The grass here was sparse, and the greens of blades and leaves—dusty-olive shades—were less lush than around Houston and Galveston. In these western hills, said to be swarming with Indians so skillfully silent they all but disappeared, Charles Wesley found, even on the hottest days, refreshing breezes and clear streams. All through the summer, in spite of—perhaps, he admitted to himself, at least partly *because of*—warnings he might run into redskins, he took frequent short forays into these hills. In late October when leaves were turning back home in New York, Austin days were still hot as summer, though the nights were beginning to cool enough for people to move inside from their sleeping porches.

Every time the liveryman saw Charles Wesley coming, he saddled up the dun. "You ought to buy this mustang. Cheaper to pay monthly feed and storage than a day rate."

Face-to-Face with an Indian

Rugged, sun-golden hills, gnarled live oak trees, and scrub cedar bushes looked like drawings in his mother's Methodist Bible study books of the Holy Land. Those drawings of the biblical wilderness got mixed up in Charles Wesley's imagination with these rocky hills, and each time he knelt to dip his canteen in water running over a limestone ledge he expected a wild-haired prophet clothed in animal hides to step from the wilderness. That was how he had come to picture the Comanches he heard so many bloody tales about. Late one afternoon he dismounted, tied the horse to a limb, and climbed a rocky bluff to gain the distant view it promised. As he ascended the top he looked up into the brown face of an Indian. The man was much slenderer than Charles Wesley had envisioned either prophet or heathen. The Indian was also afoot and stood eating a strip of dried meat. His bare chest was tattooed with short, dark lines as if heavy thread stitched his torso together. He wore earrings and necklaces so bright in the sun Charles Wesley could not tell if they were polished stone or shards of glass. The Indian breechclout he had heard described hung between hide leggings wrapped around the man's shins above buckskin moccasins. Parted in the middle, the savage's long, dark hair was woven with animal fur and shone where it had been anointed with some kind of oil. Charles Wesley simply stared, waiting for whatever was to happen next. The tall Indian gave Charles Wesley a kind of nod, turned around, and descended the far side of the bluff. A blessing offered and received, Charles Wesley decided later, figuring the Indian—who held a lance as long as any Bible shepherd's crook— had graced him by sparing both his scalp and his life.

Back in Austin, steadying his nerves with brandy, Charles Wesley described the savage to several knowledgeable locals. After remarking how only an Eastern fool would ride into the woods with Comanches on the warpath, these former Rebs and Indian fighters assured him the creature was a friendly Tonkawa, otherwise Charles Wesley would not have lived to tell his tale. He was heartened by this, until his informants began a lengthy discussion—enlivened by a number of eyewitness accounts—of the Tonkawas' bloodthirsty predilection for cannibalism. *So much*, he thought, *for prophets subsisting on only milk and honey.*

Negroes, Veterans, and Libbie Custer

Charles Wesley saw more Negroes in Texas than he'd seen all during the war. In Austin former slave and Reb veteran alike idled the streets, a bottle in one hand, and the other out for alms. White folks in Austin feared the freedmen, but the Negroes did not seek revenge. White ruffians and robbers—penniless, hungry men who had served in the Confederate Army months earlier—did harass and rob citizens.

In November a Union detachment under General Custer arrived to maintain law and order. The General and his pretty wife were the talk of Austin. One evening Charles Wesley walked past the Blind Asylum, where the general was headquartered. An old man pointed with his cane at a woman stepping up into a buggy. "Libbie Custer, the general's wife." The lady, dark-haired and lovely in a blue caped dress, smiled at Charles Wesley. That moment became a touchstone for him, a moment of civility and grace in this rough frontier land where so many different peoples struggled to coexist.

Many freed slaves worked for the wages Federal law now required they be paid. Some were employed by their former owners. Whites who could not bring themselves to pay wages to Negroes ignored the law and got away with what they could, treating freed slaves much as they had treated them before the war had set them legally if not truly free. It seemed to Charles Wesley the only folks treated worse in Texas than Negroes were Mexicans. As one drunk opined to Charles Wesley in an Austin saloon, "Ain't nobody lower than a Meskin. At least niggers are Americans." Asked what he thought about Comanches the man said, "They not American neither, but they're about the beatingest fighters they is. I allow them red niggers is close behind us Texicans."

Dorsey Murphy: To Walk the Comanche Road

Yellow Rudolph Instructs Her
(November 1865–Winter 1866)

The sodbuster Enoch Martin knew plenty about Indians. He had been married to one and had lived for a while with her Kiowa family. While he smoked a bowl of my tobacco, he told me: "All an Indian man does is hunt animals or men and butcher both—his goddamn wives do everything else."

—from *Gideon Jones' Journal*

"Even early in the summer, before you were brought to this band," Yellow Rudolph told Dorsey, "there were many buffalo. There will be good hunting now that fall comes." Yellow Rudolph told her the buffalo molt in the fall. "When he is taking off his coat, he is easier to kill. During the last Moon of Grass Turning Brown, Two Talks had been chosen to dress in the head and fur of a bull buffalo, to wander ahead of the animals and fool them into letting down their guard. He led a whole herd to a cliff's edge, and the band came from behind on ponies beating drums and yelling. Frightened buffalo ran one after the other over the cliff. Everyone went around to the bottom of the drop-off and butchered piles of buffaloes."

Good hunting was good for Yellow Rudolph. The men were happy when there was a herd to slay, and someone like Yellow Rudolph, who had no sponsor, was more likely to be taken in and fed when there was meat to spare. Good hunting was bad only because there was much hard work to be done drying and storing meat and sewing warm robes for winter.

"We Frauen," Yellow Rudolph said, "come behind after the hunters have put their arrows in the buffalo, after they have celebrated by eating the warm liver and fresh bone marrow. If they are feeling *sehr gut*, they cut the hide down the spine and pull it down the sides for us. Most times we Frauen quarter the carcass. Then we cut up *der Fleisch*, wrap it in the hide, and drag it back to camp. There's a big party, and then we Frauen cook and smoke and dry *der Fleisch*, and tan hides, and sew buffalo robes for weeks on end."

Before the Apaches captured him, Yellow Rudolph had been in some army company or unit called the Liberation Front—Dorsey didn't know the difference in a company or brigade or regiment or any of the other names men gave military gangs. From what Yellow Rudolph told her his must have been a cavalry gang, because he seemed to have ridden all over Texas. She guessed he had been a Confederate. She knew he had land in a place called New Braunfels, so she guessed he had been a farmer, but his hands were soft for a farmer's, and he said lots of things out of books. And whenever Two Talks was nearby Yellow Rudolph went silent and just stared at the warrior. At times Rudolph seemed touched in the head, but he was gentle and kind to Dorsey, doing his chores and many of hers. He said no work was as hard as scraping and tanning buffalo hides—especially with a Comanche woman overseer.

"If no one owns you or wants you why don't you just leave?" Dorsey could not understand why he had not at least tried to escape.

"If I try to go, they kill me. *Ich habe mich verlaufen*. Besides, I am drawn to one who is here."

"You stare at Two Talks," Dorsey said.

Yellow Rudolph looked surprised, as if he didn't realize how he watched Two Talks. "Long ago, I knew *ahnlich Jüngling* much like him."

"I don't think there's anyone else like Two Talks."

"Different beans out of one pod."

"Another Comanche?"

"Only God knows."

"Do you know his name?"

"I would call him 'my best friend.' It is not polite for Komantz to call a man by his name. You call him 'friend,' or 'grandfather.'" Rudolph gave Dorsey a long stare. "Or 'son.'"

Yellow Rudolph looked so sad and lonely Dorsey said, "When Gideon comes to rescue me, he'll save you, too." She wanted it to be true, but she wondered if Gideon would ever come. She would escape on her own if she knew where to run.

Yellow Rudolph smiled a faraway kind of smile. "Yes, I know. When I was first brought here I thought my comrades in the Liberation Front would ride after me.

But nothing happened. *Ich habe mich verlaúfen.* I am lost." He shook his head. "But I have been lost before, perhaps for a long time." He laughed. "I think wherever I am I am always lost."

Yellow Rudolph seemed cowardly. But Dorsey understood his fear of running into the inhospitable land that surrounded them. After the attack the ride here had been like a ride through Hell—an endless, aching, lonely, blistering nightmare—a nightmare from which Dorsey had wondered if she would ever wake.

Making Winter Camp

Not long after they brought her to the camp, the band had packed up and moved south for the winter. Dorsey had loaded Morning Star's travois herself. The move had taken days and days, dragging the band's tipis, cooking pots, and buffalo robes. Their huge horse herd stirred a sky full of dust. Morning Star and Persimmon never let Dorsey out of their sight. The whole journey she watched for sign of a white settlement, any landmark she might remember, but everything looked new and strange. She was determined to learn where she was, to figure a way to get herself and her mama and little Lucy back to safety.

The band settled for the winter near a narrow, rushing river protected by rock bluffs close to an old summer camp. They rode over ground littered with ashes, dung, and bones to a wide area of untrammeled grass. A few poor families winterized some brush arbor lodges left here from the old summer camp, though most families would winter in the buffalo skin and cedar-pole tipis. "The band will stay here until spring, unless Blue-Bottomed *Soldaten* come looking for a fight. And that's unlikely," Yellow Rudolph said. With the war just ended the Union had other priorities. The Comanches had enjoyed four good years in Texas with so many men gone east to fight and Union troops more concerned with the coast. "Before long," Yellow Rudolph said, "the army and anxious settlers will again move against the Comanches. Then, Fraülein, you and I will be killed for Indians—or maybe set free—by the Long Knives. As it says in the Scriptures, we must watch and be ready, for our moment comes like the thief in the night at an hour we think not."

Dorsey saw little Lucy often. At first the girl met Dorsey's eyes with narrow squints, rolled eyeballs, to communicate anger at their captors. Now, Lucy refused to meet

Dorsey's gaze at all or gave her a cold stare before laughing or hugging one of the Comanche girls she played with. Dorsey's mama neither met nor avoided her eyes. Laura Etta stared at the distance. She still wore the ragged dress she'd been captured in, and Dorsey never saw her at any of the women's bathing places. Laura Etta's beautiful hair was a bramble bush. Her peeling skin was smeared with mud. But the other women no longer whipped her. Dorsey always had a piece of dried meat saved for her mama, who always ate it greedily.

Morning Star gave Yellow Rudolph his meals, so he slept near Crooked Nose's tipi and did Morning Star's bidding. He taught Dorsey to scrape fat and gristle from buffalo hide with a flat-sided limb whittled and honed down its length, to soak and stretch the hide, and to rub and knead it with buffalo brains until it grew pliant, then soft. He taught her to make buffalo robes and deerskin leggings using a stone awl to punch holes in the hide and then stitch sinew from the backbone of a deer or a buffalo through the holes with a sharp, curved rib bone. He taught her how to roast buffalo and deer meat on long, pointed sticks. Everything had to be prepared and eaten separately. "Never boil and broil meat on the same fire. Never pass by a cooking kettle, because your shadow might fall across the food and spoil it." He warned her never to eat near the men, only with women and children. "When your bleeding comes you must stay in the trees beyond the camp." Menstruation, he explained, took away all *puha*, the special medicine each man sought. Now Dorsey understood why the raiders had not stopped Mary Thurston from running off. "You even sleep out there, far from camp. When your monthlies are over, you wash in the river—wash clothes and all before you come back in camp." He shook his head. "And do not try to flee, Fraülein. Better to stay. You are *verlaüfen*, like me."

Yellow Rudolph was strange and birdlike. Skinny and tall, he walked bent over on long legs and long feet. His narrow bird-breast was covered with gray-blonde hair as fuzzy as down, and his speckled skin was as taut over his bones as the hide on an Indian drum. The struck chords of his guttural German-English-Spanish-Comanche chant made the drumbeat of an unmelodious birdsong. A Frau-man, he talked to Dorsey about the taboos of menstruation just as an older woman might have advised her. He seemed comfortable with such talk. When he did Frau-work, his deft hands moved like small birds, darting, fluttering.

When Yellow Rudolph spoke, it was as if he were talking to himself. He mentioned, only once, that when he was young he'd had a wife. Another time he said he had a son, and he said something odd. He said Dorsey would know his son if she ever saw him. When she asked how that could be, he went silent and stared away. Dorsey speculated the wife and son had been long ago, back in Germany where maybe Rudolph wasn't so different. If not a bird, he was most like a maiden aunt. *What tribe*, she wondered, *does Yellow Rudolph belong to?*

Comanche Romance

Broken Teeth, whom Dorsey now knew as Three Ropes, found her every day or two and spoke to her in a mix of Comanche and Spanish words. "*Wahipa, qué paso?*" he said, grinning fiercely. From Three Ropes and from Yellow Rudolph, Dorsey was learning Comanche talk. The more Three Ropes talked to her the more clearly she understood the steady gait of his intentions. Two Talks, on the other hand, though he smiled at her, rarely spoke to her.

Dorsey had watched night crawling girls slip into tipis and brush lodges and emerge with boys they took into the woods. One evening she watched from her sleeping place as Laughs Loud, a mirthful boy with smiling eyes who played children's games with little Lucy, was led from his sleeping place by his older sister. Feeling both bold and frightened Dorsey silently followed them to a grassy knoll beside the river where the older sister—who did not yet have a name since girls' names could wait but who was nicknamed Sugar—disrobed herself and her brother and initiated Laughs Loud to grown-up ways of love, ways Dorsey knew of only vaguely. The full moon cast a strong light. When Laughs Loud and Sugar copulated, Dorsey grew light-headed, and her hands trembled. What she saw when she watched Sugar with Laughs Loud in the moonlight was different from what she had witnessed during the attack on the wagons. The attack had linked nakedness and sex to violence—a poor splicing. The instruction Sugar was giving Laughs Loud was not at all violent—it was more like play, like dancing without music. But Sugar was Laughs Loud's older sister, and Dorsey could not imagine mixing up those kinds of love. She felt somehow wrong to look on these two naked people doing naked things. Dorsey's brain told her to turn away, to go back to her sleeping place—but her eyes and some yearning-for-what-there-is-to-know part of her held her there until Laughs Loud moaned and then did what he was named for and Sugar laughed with him and they washed, splashing and laughing more, and then returned to their separate sleeping places.

Because Yellow Rudolph was the only one Dorsey could ask and because, somehow, it seemed natural to talk about such things with him, Dorsey asked the German what she could do if Three Ropes acted on his obvious intentions.

They were crushing mesquite beans into meal, and Yellow Rudolph did not stop pounding when he answered.

"Two—tump—Talks—tump—gave you to his mother to work—tump—for her. You belong to Morning Star."

"You mean Three Ropes would have to pay Morning Star for me?"

"He would—tump—have to pay—tump—if he wanted to own you forever to work for him. Just to lie with you but not as his Frau, I think nobody would care. Afterward he would make to Morning Star some gift."

"What if Three Ropes wanted me for his wife—his Frau?"

Yellow Rudolph frowned and put down his rock pestle. "You're slave like me. Before he take you for Frau, you must become Komantz. You're probably too old, but Lucy, she be Komantz, I bet you by next summer. She become Frau to Three Ropes in three, four years."

"She won't let them make her into a Comanche."

Yellow Rudolph shook his head as if Dorsey were a hopeless student. "*Verstéhen Sie nicht.* You don't understand. Smoke Maker and Talks While Sleeping have offered Long Lance two ponies for Lucy to adopt her. Talks While Sleeping had two miscarriages. Smoke Maker aches for a son, but Lucy will be old enough to marry in a few summers. *Die* Frauen must be bought. Smoke Maker hopes some man will give more horses for Lucy than she cost." Yellow Rudolph sat back on the broad rock where they worked. He scratched his upper lip with a fingernail white with crushed mesquite beans. "A man leaves an offer, say six horses, at the tipi of *der Vater* of the girl he wants for Frau. If the father puts the six in with his horses, the wedding is announced. If not, maybe more horses are there next day. All Komantz are brothers, and most don't care if a brother borrow his Frau. He expects something in return—a good bow, a pony, or he borrows his brother's Frau." Yellow Rudolph spread the crushed beans on the rock. "Komantz man have nearly any Frau he wants to lie with. Komantz man wants for his own Frau one who is strong to bear him sons, one who can work hard at Frau-chores, one with fearlessness to match his own."

In spite of herself Dorsey pictured a Comanche man, his copper-skinned body completely naked, lying with Lucy. In Dorsey's imagination the man tore off Lucy's dress and pulled her down onto a buffalo robe. Lucy's legs locked around one dark-muscled Comanche leg as if she were climbing a young tree. The linked bodies in Dorsey's reverie rolled over so Lucy lay on top of the warrior. He had Two Talks' face. Dorsey's face flushed and her ears tingled. "What about Two Talks—you said he has no wife?"

"Two Talks had Cherokee girl, Small Nose, he won in horse race with the Blue-Bottoms, five, six winters ago. She became Komantz, then she become Two Talks' Frau, making other Komantz girls crazy sad. They all want Two Talks, the strong son of Crooked Nose, grandson of Red Dog, owner of maybe one hundred, one-hundred-fifty ponies." Yellow Rudolph looked in the direction of the camp's herd of horses out of sight on the other side of the river. Boys-who-would-be-warriors were there tending the herd. Every now and then one of them yipped or whistled. Every now and then a breeze brought scents of horse sweat and manure. Dust floated into tree limbs, but Dorsey could not see the herd itself. "Now Small Nose is with the dead, and I am sorry to speak her name. Everyone expect Two Talks to quick take new Frau, but four winters have passed since the girl died, and Two Talks stays in the father's lodge. He takes no Frau. Now he has again ridden the war trail, so maybe soon he take a new Frau."

"Who will Two Talks choose?"

Yellow Rudolph narrowed his eyes and snorted. "Probably Dressing Her Head, daughter of Good Trader, a civil chief. Dressing Her Head made her father return many horses from other men, waiting for Two Talks to leave ponies at their lodge. Maybe Two Talks does not have enough ponies to offer for her. One day I think he will have all the ponies he wants and more."

Later, when they carried a hide bag full of ground up mesquite beans back to Crooked Nose's lodge, Dorsey said, "Show her to me?"

Yellow Rudolph grinned a knowing grin. He pursed his lips, nodded to his side. "There."

Talking to Morning Star was the slender, pretty girl who had meet Two Talks the day he brought Dorsey to the other camp. Yellow Rudolph said Dressing Her Head was close to Dorsey's age, but Dressing Her Head looked and acted more like a woman than a girl. Age didn't seem the same on Indians as on whites. Dorsey tried to picture Dressing Her Head with Binga Duerfeldt and girls from church, but even in Dorsey's imagination the Comanche girl was too self-assured, too graceful to join the gaggle of giggling Sunday School girls. She looked like a storybook bride in her white doeskin dress with a white beaded bird spread across her bosoms—more developed than Dorsey's bosoms. Dressing Her Head was so lithe her feet did not seem to touch the ground. Pretty as she was, she could drag a heavy buffalo carcass for miles. She knew how to skin and dress the beasts, knew a dozen ways to cook the meat, knew how to tan the hide and sew it into a warm robe. She could take down a tipi and move an entire household on a travois. She could make medicines from any bush or tree to cure headaches or itchy skin or bind up a wound from a Tehano rifle. Dressing Her Head's knowledge of the world she lived in made Dorsey's book-learning seem paltry. Comanche girls knew more about dressing and cooking meat and sewing clothes than any girl Dorsey had known in Indiana, and Comanche boys rode horses better than grown white men. While Dorsey and Binga and other girls back in Indiana were day-dreaming and giggling about boys, Comanche girls their age were slipping into tipis at night to teach younger boys how men and women made love. Dorsey won-dered if Dressing Her Head had instructed any of the boys in the band. Dorsey pictured herself going into the lodge of a boy like Laughs Loud and leading him out to couple with her beneath a buffalo robe, and her face grew hot. One of Laura Etta's favorite sayings came to mind: *The blind leading the blind.* Who taught the girls what to teach the younger boys? Gideon had seemed older than the boys Dorsey had known back in Indiana. Out here everybody seemed older. Gideon was traveling all by himself. He drove his own wagon and had a rifle on the board beside him. Compared to a Numunuu warrior, Gideon was still a boy. While he drove his wagonload of lightning rods over the prairie with his nose in a book, Two Talks galloped amidst a herd of wild buffalo, hung off the side of a racing pony and loosed arrows into charging beasts. Two Talks had risked his life against wild animals and in raids against Numunuu enemies—not just Texan set-tlers, but also Apaches and other savages.

Conflicting Feelings

Every night of the first few weeks with the Comanches, Dorsey whispered Gide-on's name to the night sky. She prayed *Oh, Gideon, do not forsake me.* But he had forsaken her. She had been swallowed up by the earth. Weeks passed with no sign of her rescuer. She felt betrayed and lost, then angry. Gideon wasn't even trying to find her. Forsaken, she knew she would not survive in this strange world. But sooner than it seemed possible the world became not so strange. Eating Indian food and sleeping on the ground seemed not so strange. Indian games and laugh-ing, their smiles and gestures, the words they spoke and songs they sang grew familiar. At first Comanche words sounded gruff and rasping, but after Dorsey had them in her ears all day, day after day, she heard melodies in their words. Particular phrases, sounds for which she still knew no meaning, she recognized and longed to hear again. Her daily life took on new routines and weeks passed quickly. Dorsey prayed less often for Gideon to come. She didn't think Lucy wanted to be rescued, and she feared Laura Etta would suffer more if she returned to white society than if she were left with the Comanches, who, though they were responsible for her condition, did not shame her with gossip.

Since she belonged to Two Talks' mother, Dorsey saw him often. Though he was not big-boned and heavy as her brother Joe had been, Two Talks was taller than most of the Comanche men. His arms and legs were all tendon and muscle. He was like the bow Yellow Rudolph had made out of a seasoned length of bois d'arc, a wood so strong the German called it ironwood. The bow was only about three feet long, short enough to use on horseback. Yellow Rudolph had backed the ironwood with deer sinew to make it even stronger. And he had spent hours splitting, twisting together, and gluing lengths of bull buffalo sinew to make a powerful bowstring. Dorsey was surprised how little the bow weighed, yet she was unable to bend it far enough to string it. And after Yellow Rudolph strung it for her, she could barely pull back the string. Two Talks had lifted her from the ground up onto his pony with one hand. He sprang like a barn cat from the ground up into the limbs of a cottonwood by the river, then he swung and dropped into the water with barely a splash, his body slicing water like a blade. Lithe, supple, strong, the bow and its archer.

Two Talks and the other Indians frequently joked and laughed with one another—she had never imagined savages joking. In spite of her determination to hate them every day of her life, it was easier to hate *all* Indians than it was to hate each Comanche in the camp. She wanted to keep her anger kindled against every one of them, but she felt more kindly toward some than others. Two Talks had taken her captive, but he had not raped her. He had not let any other man rape her. He had put the cool healing plant on her sunburnt skin. He had not joined the other men in the violation and torment of Laura Etta. Red Dog and Crooked Nose paid Dorsey little mind. Morning Star was stern, not cruel. Persimmon, on the other hand, abused Dorsey every chance she got, and Three Ropes haunted Dorsey with slow touching looks. At these two especially, Dorsey aimed her enmity. And the men who had violated Laura Etta, against them Dorsey pledged revenge. She knew their faces and had learned the names of two, Low Forehead and Shield Painter, and every day she watched for the other two, hoping she could get Yellow Rudolph to give her their names.

"When Gideon comes," she told Yellow Rudolph, "I'll kill those four. By myself."

Yellow Rudolph nodded, but sadly, it seemed to Dorsey. "You sound like a Komantz wife whose husband has been slain by a *taivo* settler."

"Wouldn't you like to kill all the ones who have hurt you?"

The tall German laughed his short, barking laugh and shook his head. "I would have to start with those I love most and, finally, I would have to take my own life."

"I don't understand you, Rudolph."

"Nor do I understand myself. I am lost. I envy you the wrong you feel. You have a tangible hurt to redress, an anger you understand and from which you draw strength. But if you stay here long as I have, you grow less sure of who you are, as I have. If you were hurt by your family and not *dieser Indianern*, would you hate your family as you hate Komantz?"

"Anybody can see what they've done to my mother."

"Out of sympathy for the warrior who was killed in the attack on your wagons—whose name I can't speak—they give your Mutter to his widow, Red Cedar Flute, and her sister, Cooks Boiled Meat. Did you not tell me your Mutter is the one who shot and killed the man?"

The Indian had likely been killed by Laura Etta. She was the only one Dorsey had seen fire a shot, but there had been such bedlam Dorsey couldn't be sure. "Maybe. But they attacked us. She was fighting for her life. Wouldn't you kill if your life depended on it?"

"*Ich denk* we whites want permission, want justification for killing. Komantz, at the least, accept the brutality of their world." He stared so intently beyond her Dorsey turned to see what he saw—but there was nothing there but the ocean of grass and the endless blue sky. "If you are certain your Mutter was right, why must you say it so loud? Who is so hard of hearing, or so far from your voice?"

"You're saying it's all right for savages to kill because they don't know any better, but civilized Christian people can't fight back because we know right from wrong?"

"The Comanches have as many civil rules as we do, Fraülein. Theirs are just different. And they keep their rules while we change ours to suit our needs. Here, I can count on the cruelty I am promised. And, yes, Komantz are cruel, but as recently as the war dividing the nation I see just as bad between white soldiers."

"Were you a Rebel?"

"I was neither Confederate nor Yankee. I served a regiment of Union Loyalists, most of whom, it turned out, were loyal to themselves." His white knuckles trembled. Abruptly, he said good afternoon—"*Guten Tag*"—and left.

The more she learned about people the less she understood. Was every person's life a story of secrets and surprises? Did Red Cedar Flute know Laura

Etta was the one who shot her husband? Dorsey doubted it—she didn't figure any of the raiders had a clearer memory of the melee than she did. Maybe the Comanches would not blame Laura Etta for fighting back. Maybe they did know Laura Etta had killed Red Cedar Flute's husband. Maybe they had spared her life because of her courage. Red Cedar Flute's loud self-punishing grief had gone on for many sleeps after the raiders returned. She had no brother-in-law to marry her and take her in, no son to guarantee her care and protection. Her husband had provided for her and for his sister, Cooks Boiled Meat. Now both women were at the mercy of the camp. The gift of Laura Etta may have unwittingly been a cruel joke as much as an offer of help. What good was a slave to women who had no man to cook and sew for? Neither woman was of any use to the band. Now they had Laura Etta added to their burden. They made a pitiable trio, hovering around the camp, eating what meat they were given from the fires of different lodges, living mainly on wild plums, mesquite beans, and prickly pear tunas they gathered, yap roots they dug. Red Cedar Flute in her time of grieving had hacked off her hair, cut it unevenly and close to the scalp, had striped her arms with slashes that healed as thick-crusted purple welts. Cooks Boiled Meat had been abandoned by her husband years ago, after he cut off the end of her nose for committing adultery. Her nose had healed poorly, so her breath was raspy and loud, her voice hoarse-sounding. She and Red Cedar Flute and Laura Etta wandered the camp like stray dogs. Every chance, Dorsey took food to Laura Etta and tried to talk to her. "Mama, here, eat this meat. Mama, are you all right? It's Dorsey. Speak to me, Mama."

Laura Etta took and ate whatever food was offered, but she never acknowledged Dorsey, never uttered a sound except for lip-smacking and teeth-gnashing.

Morning Star worked Dorsey hard but fed her well, and Dorsey went to bed tired but without hunger. Sometimes she fell asleep before she invoked the name of the boy from the wagon train, the boy's name she had kept alive on her tongue and in her mind for all these weeks even as his face grew more difficult to keep alive in her mind's eye—*Oh Gideon, come soon.*

Little Lucy was young enough she spent her days at play. Smoke Maker had given two good ponies for her, and Talks While Sleeping doted on her as if she were a boy-child. Talks While Sleeping beaded Lucy a dazzling blue and yellow blouse from the spotted hide of a fawn—it was the softest material. Smoke Maker's brush lodge was close to the lodges of Red Dog and Crooked Nose, so Lucy often darted past while Dorsey was bent to some task. Lucy had learned many Comanche words. She answered to the pet name Talks While Sleeping had given her—Other Small One. Yellow Rudolph said a Comanche girl might have several pet names before she was ever formally named, which might not happen for years, might never happen, since a girl's name was not important. Dorsey was still hurt and angry Lucy could forget her family and friends so quickly.

"Don't, Woman"

Persimmon continued to shove, trip, whip, and slap, Dorsey—only Persimmon still treated her as a prisoner, though some of the other women poked her or tripped her when they could. Mostly, the Comanches ignored her, and that sometimes felt worse than being hit.

Persimmon's brutality came to an end one afternoon when Morning Star sent Dorsey to pick blackberries. After hours of picking, her fingers were purple-stained and sore. The chest-high vines pricked her bare legs and arms until they itched and burned. She was dirty, hot, and tired. Beneath the hill Lucy splashed and laughed in the creek with other children, and Dorsey felt jealous and lonely. She talked to Gideon in her mind. Lost in memories and daydreams, Dorsey reached far into the vines for a berry so big and purple she'd thought for a second it was a plum—*Look here, Gideon, let's pick this big one*—and she disturbed a rattlesnake, its warning a sound she knew in her blood with the certainty of history, the intuition of Eve in the Garden, and she dreaded toxin as old and as deadly as original sin. The invisible viper rattled dry as seeds-in-a-gourd but loud as teeth chattering, and it lunged in the dark tangle and twisted about Dorsey's feet and up her leg like the giant's quick, thick beanstalk, so sudden for something so heavy. Snake weight, liquid yet dry, and cold—a pulling current of cold water moving over the top of Dorsey's foot. The snake was tumescent yet firm like a muscle gone tight and hard. How she got out of the vine and why she didn't spill the hide bag of berries, she could not say. She hit her ankle against a rock, and tangled-tight vines or coil of snake or both left red rope-burns on her bare shins. She couldn't stop shaking to see if and where and how many places she'd been bit, but the snake had lunged, had struck something and maybe more than one time and, all over, her ankles and shins and calves stung and ached. She ran back to camp, *home* she thought, back to the lodges of Red Dog and Crooked Nose and Two Talks, the pouch of blackberries bouncing against her side. She reached Morning Star's cooking fire, and Persimmon loomed like a dark storm cloud, jerked the bag of berries from her and asked, "What do you have?"

Moving so deliberately Persimmon didn't understand what she was doing, Dorsey gripped a log sticking out from the cookfire, a log thick and heavy as the rattlesnake in the vines. As a warrior swings a battle-ax, Dorsey swung this log, one end red embers, and hit Persimmon full in the face. The log cracked bone, and gold sparks showered both women. Persimmon made a small sound: air trying to find a way through her crushed nostrils, broken teeth, and flattened lips. Then Persimmon made a larger sound: her substantial weight hitting the ground.

Little smokes rose from red embers scattered over Persimmon's face and down the ample front of her dress. As the story was recounted and recounted, Morning Star and Crooked Nose and the two girls, Eats Bark and Sings Softly, all agreed they'd smelled the scorch-singe odor of Persimmon's hair. Before anyone moved, Dorsey picked up her bag and emptied it onto Persimmon's smoking face, unintentionally extinguishing several embers with juicy blackberries.

"Don't. Woman, don't," Dorsey said. She did not yell—she spoke the Numunuu words clearly and firmly. She faced Morning Star and Crooked Nose, who had watched from just a few feet away. She was ready to be executed then and there. Instead, Crooked Nose broke into a big grin and his shoulders shook with chuckling as he disappeared into his tipi.

Morning Star took Dorsey by the arm. "It is well," she said. Then she helped Persimmon up and led both Persimmon and Dorsey down to the stream to wash. She put a soothing salve on Dorsey's blackberry vine scrapes and on Persimmon's burns and lacerations. Dorsey found no mark of a snake's bite on her body. From that day on Persimmon treated Dorsey with deference. From time to time Crooked Nose or Morning Star would look at Dorsey and then break out laughing.

Three Ropes would be harder to stop. She could not hit a warrior in the face with a burning log and get away with it. She wasn't sure what she would do when Three Ropes forced himself on her. Two Talks could prevent it, but she wasn't sure he would intervene.

Yellow Grass Time

One morning Dorsey woke before dawn and felt a dry chill in the air. For the first time all summer she pulled the edges of her deerskin around her. The leaves were not yet yellow, but they were curling up at the edges.

"The time of the yellow grass *kommt*," Yellow Rudolph said. "Lance Thrower, one of the best hunters in *diese* band has followed flocks of ravens and they have led him to the buffalo. The pelts grow dark, and the beasts grow fat." Yellow Rudolph showed Dorsey how sharp tips on hunting arrows were made to come easily out of the animal so they could be reused—war points were barbed so they would lodge in an enemy and could not be freed without damaging the flesh. The preferred points were metal, bought from Comanchero traders. Other points were fashioned from bone or flintrock. Shafts were mulberry and dogwood and, sometimes, ash. "One day, in forgotten time, a Komantz warrior trapped a hawk to take feathers for arrows. The hawk promised if the man released him he would give the Numunuu a secret to make their arrows better than any others. 'My feathers, and the feathers of my friend, the eagle, are better to behold than all other feathers in the heavens. But the ugly black feathers of the carrion buzzard are best for arrows because they cast off *Blut*,' said the hawk. Since then," Yellow Rudolph told her, "buzzard feathers—or turkey or owl feathers, they also shed *Blut*—guide Komantz arrows."

Dorsey had a steady hand and whittled mulberry and dogwood into straight shafts. Yellow Rudolph looked surprised. "*Sehr gut.* But," he gave her a stern look, "usually only warriors make weapons. Bows and arrows, shields, and lances can be weakened by the touch of a woman if she is unclean—still in her monthlies."

"I'm not in my time." Yellow Rudolph shook his head. "I like making arrows. Maybe if I make them good enough, Two Talks will use them. If he doesn't want them, I'll use them myself. To hunt. You have told me women can help hunt."

"*Ja,* that is so." He held the arrow close, turning it slowly. "You do a good job. *Dieser* knife will aid you." He gave her a sharp steel-bladed knife with a handle made of leather.

"Thank you."

"*Bitte schön.*"

Blood Arrow

Dorsey grew deft with the steel-bladed knife. After carving and smoothing the shafts, she used the thick end of the knife-blade to nock the butts. She liked the weight of the knife in her hand, but she dismissed it as a weapon of escape. Friction rubbed bits of leather off the knife handle, and the specks stuck to her skin like ground pepper. She liked the feel of the smooth shafts, the smell of wood on her hands. As her shadow lengthened, so did her row of completed arrows. Some men painted special marks on their arrows, designs to give the shaft more power. Dorsey didn't know much about Comanche medicine, but Yellow Rudolph had told her after Two Talks returned from his vigil he had worn a crow's beak from his scalp lock. She carved a beak's shape into the side of one of her arrows. Then, because his name was Two Talks, like an echo, she carved an identical beak beside the first one. Side by side, the beak-shapes made what looked like a "W" or an "M" or a pointy "3" or a pointy "E" or—as she thought on it—two tipis or two mountain peaks or two firm breasts or two arrowheads. The arrows were her own private hoard, and she resented it when Yellow Rudolph gathered them up, handling them carelessly, as if they were no more than fire sticks.

"Wait," she told Yellow Rudolph. "I'm not through." Not ready to give up the arrows, she took up the knife and began going over each smooth, perfect notch for the bowstring one more time. Her fingers, tired and cramped from working so long, let the sharp knife loose for a moment, like giving a horse its head. The knife's will was for cutting, and the blade made its hungry way through Dorsey's skin deep into her flesh. Her blood pooled on the blade as perfect a circle of red as any painter's palette ever held. Into her blood she dipped an unused brush—a willow stem, its end chewed into fine fiber bristles—and she ringed each arrow with a fine crimson stripe, a slender red line, the bright limb on which Two Talks' bird beaks perched.

So intent had Dorsey been in her painting, she had not noticed a shadow covering her as she worked. Two Talks had seen the dark metal slide into pale flesh, had seen how her cut hand had not flinched. He'd watched her turn blood into paint. She looked up and met Two Talks' stare. She put the arrows into his hand. Still looking her in the eyes, he said, "Puhipka." She asked Yellow Rudolph the meaning of the word.

"Puhipka, it's *Blut und Pfeil*—blood and arrow, Blood Arrow, Fräulein."

Dorsey nodded. Two Talks made no expression, but she was sure his black eyes smiled. Because Dorsey was making arrows, Morning Star put Persimmon to work making a soup of sego lilies and sumac. There were fat pearly-yellow muscadine grapes and a basket of wild plums. After they served the men, Morning Star pulled off a strip of stringy meat and handed it to Dorsey, asking her, "What name do you answer to now?"

Many weeks had passed since Dorsey had smiled. Her lips and cheeks were small aches, yet to smile felt good. She answered Morning Star with her first Comanche sentence: "*Tua sitikise* Puhipka," which she was pretty sure meant: "It is said this one is Blood Arrow."

Morning Star touched her new daughter on the shoulder. "*Tokwetikati*," she said.

There was no meat left for Yellow Rudolph. He emptied the kettle of soup and gnawed on the bones of the hare. "So, does *Blut* Arrow like her new name?"

Dorsey gave Yellow Rudolph the last of her stringy piece of meat. "What does *tokwetikati* mean?"

Yellow Rudolph smiled a greasy smile. "*Tokwetikati*—it is agreeable."

Squatting behind Yellow Rudolph to hide her curiosity, Dorsey spied on Two Talks, who stood a few feet away in front of Red Dog's tipi. Two Talks held out her hunting arrows, showed them to Crooked Nose and to the white-haired grandfather. Red Dog held an arrow up.

"*Taivo wahipa kwuuhuupuu*," Red Dog said, his voice loud.

She asked Yellow Rudolph, "What is he saying?"

"'White woman captive.' The grandfather cannot believe you made the good arrows."

Silhouetted in the orange light of the setting sun, the old chief holding the pointing arrow looked like a fanciful iron weathervane that had swung around in a breeze to aim west.

The three Comanche warriors—grandfather, father, and son—studied the hunt arrows: each shaft tipped with a sharp steel head to pierce the thickest hide, each nock carved smooth for a bowstring of bull buffalo's sinew or deer's ligament split and wrapped and rubbed with beeswax, each butt fletched with buzzard feathers to guide it through air, hide, muscle, blood, and bone.

She, Blood Arrow, had made each deadly shaft. She had put the mark of Two Talks' crow's beaks and the signature of her own life's blood on every arrow— enough arrows to fill a hunter's quiver. If Two Talks wouldn't use them because a woman made them, she would use them herself. If she could make arrows, she could shoot a bow and kill a deer or a buffalo.

Blood Arrow spoke out loud, to no one but herself, "Dor-see, Puhipka, *osahka petu?*" She said in English what she hoped she had said in Comanche: "Dorsey, Blood Arrow, whose daughter is she?"

Gideon Jones: Four Unlikely Accomplices

A Map of Comancheria
(November 1865)

"Look here a minute, Gideon." Knobby Cotton placed a folded-up paper on the Alhambra Saloon's bar. Bobbing between Gideon and the painting of the nude woman behind the bar, the Negro's round face looked like a frying pan the woman held over her breasts. Knobby spread out the paper. "Eye drew this map—he's been over most of Comancheria one time or another."

Mrs. Carter opened a fresh bottle of Squirrel and poured the Negro and Gideon each a glass. She filled a glass for herself and carried it with her over to the piano. Gideon fetched his spectacles out of his pocket and put them on. Eye's map came into focus. Drawn in black ink was a map of "Texus" and the "Injin Territory" to the north. Above that was "Kanzez," with a star drawn beside "Fort Levenworth." A wavy horizontal line was labeled "Arkansaw R." Above "Kanzez" was "Nebraskuh Territory," and another wavy line labeled "Platt R." The southern boundary line of Texas had "Rio Grand R." printed along it. "San Antone" got a star. South and west of "San Antone" was a black "X" marked "Old Fort Uell." The crease lines in the sheet were brown with dust and made squares as if the land were fenced off into sections.

Knobby's black finger traced a circle on the paper. "All this is Comancheria, land the Comanches call theirs alone—from down here in Mexico, out to New Mexico, up here near Bent's Fort, and along the Santa Fe Trail across Kansas, down through Indian Territory, back into Texas as far south and east as the buffalo graze. Miles and miles and miles—more if an Indian has a mind to chase wild mustangs or raid some settlement."

Gideon was stunned by how vast an area the Comanches ruled. Dorsey was somewhere in all that space. There were Comanche camps hidden where white men would never think to look.

Mrs. Carter began to play. The melody reminded Gideon of something Colonel Powell-Hughes used to play. The colonel had loved Mozart. Maybe this was Mozart.

"Here," Knobby put his fingertip on the "X" by "Old Fort Uell," "is where my Elizabeth and William were attacked." Tiny red rivers crisscrossed the whites of Knobby's eyes. His cheeks were rough with stubble, and his hand trembled when he lifted his glass of whisky. Stopping only to water and rest his big black horse, Knobby had ridden for many days and nights to catch up to the man, Portis "Eye" Goar, who had drawn the map and agreed to help the Negro. "Show me where your train was hit—on the map."

"West of Fort Dodge, about here, in Kansas." Gideon tapped the map. "It wasn't the whole train, just two wagons separated from the train. Back in early August. They'd crossed to the south side of the Arkansas River." Unblinking, Knobby stared into Gideon's eyes, and he felt as if the Negro stared deep into his skull and read his thoughts as easily as he read Eye's map. If that were so, Knobby would see Gideon's increasing fear that he might be incapable of traversing this Comancheria and freeing Dorsey.

Knobby shook his head. "I'll see if Eye can figure how many days' ride it is between the two places. August figures about right for a war party to have time to cover that much ground. Hard to believe the same band could range so far, but Eye says raiders range wide."

"How many war parties would the Comanches have riding at once?" Gideon tried to remember if Enoch Martin had said anything about Comanche raiders.

"I don't even know if it was Comanches who got my Elizabeth, but Eye says it's most likely Comanches or Kiowas, and Kiowas don't usually go so far south."

"Mr. Speer, the man I found alive, doesn't know a Comanche from a Pawnee, and he doesn't talk well with his tongue mostly cut off. But from what he's com-municated—by writing things out, mainly—it was Comanches who took Dorsey and her mama and little Lucy."

"Comanche or Kioway, it don't make much difference," someone said. While Knobby and Gideon had stared at the map, Mr. Goar—"Eye"—had walked up behind them. "They're all riding the blood trail, but now the war's over, they'll have the soldiers back to whip their red asses." The piano music stopped. Mrs. Carter rose partway from the bench, but Eye lifted the bottle of Squirrel high enough for her to see and held up an empty glass. She nodded and began to play again. Eye poured himself a full glass and drank it half down in one gulp. "Both these attacks were a small band, no big war party. Comanches on a raid cover a lot of territory. Could be some young brave got his pals fired up, the same gang riding all over after scalps and horses and white women to plunder raw," Eye said and drank the glass empty, his jumpy eye going back and forth.

"So you think we're after the same raiders," Gideon said.

"Like as not. Besides, unless they adopt their captives, make Comanches out of them, they're first going to take them back to camp, show off their catch, let their women torture them a spell. Then they'll trade them to Comancheros, maybe at the Yellow House trading place, Cañon del Rescate."

"You think they've hurt Elizabeth and William?"

"Aw, Knob, I don't know. Maybe not, if they plan to trade them off. But the sooner you get to their camp, the sooner you can ransom them back."

"Ransom?" Gideon hoped the quaver in his voice didn't give away the fact that he had little money left. He doubted the Comanches would want lightning rods or Chief Bones.

"Last I heard, the going figure was a hundred, hundred and fifty dollars in trade goods." Eye laughed. "Might be you can trade your half-breed gal."

"She's not mine to trade," Gideon said. Knobby gave Gideon another one of his looks, and it went clear inside his brain. He said it again. "She's not mine."

"Still, she might be a help," Eye said. "I know some Mexican talk but damn little Comanche. I ain't too tolerable with hand talk. Your squaw might help us parlay. Either her or old Pretty. Though Pretty's price is always sky-high."

"Maybe we'll have to take them, not buy them," Knobby said.

"Maybe," Eye said. "Either way, you need someone to get you into the Comanche camp. Unless you have some ruse to get in, they'll see you coming and fill you full of arrows. You've got to get to the captives before you can buy or shoot your way out."

It seemed to Gideon that Eye didn't think they'd find anyone alive.

Knobby proposed they all share their resources and go after the captives together. Gideon considered what such a union offered—two more riders, each likely a better shootist than he, and one, Eye, more experienced in the ways of the Indians. Eye knew how to find the Comanchero leader, Perdido, known as Pretty. Gideon considered what he had to offer them—Suella, half-Indian and able to read sign language and smoke words, she could help get them through Comancheria or into the Indian camp—he could contribute to the cause Suella and his poor wagon.

"I don't reckon either of you can make a fist of tracking or fighting," Eye said. "I spect that end will be mine to tote. By scant amount we might better our chances by pitching together."

"Time comes to fight, I won't flinch," Knobby said.

Gideon nodded.

"We need top horses," Eye said. "We'll cover some ground riding full chisel. Might also need Gideon's wagon to bring back the captives if they can't sit a horse. Comanches didn't use to put a mark on captives they were going to ransom off. Then they learned whites feel bad to see loved ones scarred or crippled up. Learned whites will pay more for maimed kin. One more white way Indians can't figure—why we pay high for damaged goods."

"Slavers try to heal up whip marks," Knobby said. "Those stripes are marks of defiance. Of pride. A planter figures if he buys a scarred slave he's buying trouble."

In return for lightning arresters Gideon erected at both ends of the Alhambra Saloon roof, Mr. Manchip provided a matched pair of bright-eyed horses to pull Gideon's wagon faster than Right Ox and Left Ox could manage. Gideon had not sent Phineas Atkins a payment or even any correspondence for many weeks and he wondered how he would pay for the Atkins lightning arresters he had used for grave markers or for the two he had bartered to Mr. Manchip for horses. Perhaps later he'd be able to sell the remaining arresters for sufficient profit to cover those he had appropriated. Mr. Manchip unloaded the dead-looking apple tree and said he'd plant it to see if it came back next spring. Gideon turned out his oxen in the dusty side lot of Mr. Manchip's livery stable in the care of an old hide hunter named Pete, who was deaf in one ear.

"There's no grass for them to graze, so don't forget their grain and look to the trough and keep it full of water for them." In case he was on the side of Pete's dead ear, Gideon raised his voice.

He let one of Mrs. Carter's clean, sunny rooms for Mr. Speer and left him in the hands of that exceptional lady, his medical care to be provided by Mr. Manchip, whose horse medicine had already reduced the swelling and turned the angry crimson ring around his neck to a ruddy brown. Hiram Thurston's spotted fice had permanently adopted Speer, and Mrs. Carter said she credited the cur as much as Mr. Manchip's doctoring for the improvement in Speer's health. Mrs. Carter promised to get posted Dorsey's mama's letter to her sister in Pennsylvania. Gideon did not add to the letter that Mrs. Speer was now the captive of savage Indians.

Mary Thurston and Baby James Return from the Dead

In the midst of Gideon's preparations to leave with Knobby and Eye, two strange men—though from appearance and smell Gideon would have judged them beasts—rode into town in a heavy schooner wagon loaded with buffalo hides. They pulled up in front of the Alhambra Saloon, crawled back amongst their hides, and emerged with a woman and an infant, both of whom they carried inside. When he entered behind them, Gideon was presented with a curious tableau. The two buffalo hunters, who wore hide shirts on a sunny afternoon in November—Gideon was learning how hot it could be in November in Texas—stood hunched like wild beasts at the edge of light cast by an oil lamp on the bar. Lamplight illuminated the bunched folds of Mr. Manchip's rolled-up white shirtsleeves and his bare forearms as he dipped them into the light to examine the infant on top of the plank bar. His forearms and the babe's naked body were polished with light like pink mother-of-pearl. The edges of the light gilded Mrs. Carter's hair and a row of whisky bottles while the buffalo hunters and the bedraggled-looking woman they supported between them were cast in shadow, shapes of wildness primeval surrounding the glowing infant. The scene reminded Gideon of the chiaroscuros of certain paintings he had seen reproduced in Colonel Powell-Hughes' picture books, depictions of the Christ child bathed in heavenly streams of illumination, the light-tipped wings of angels hovering close and shaggy, dumb beasts languishing just beyond the light. Moved by this panorama, Gideon vowed, once he had the briefest leisure, to secure a Holy Bible that he might carry the Scriptures atop his volume of the *Americana* and his journal of impressions and recollections, adding the spiritual to his store of knowledge and experience, the spiritual world resting upon the physical world, the firmament upon the fundament.

He and Knobby joined those buffalo hunters at the edge of the lamp's glow and watched in silence as Mr. Manchip ran his fingers along the ribcage of the silent infant whose arms and legs swam the bright air above him. The face of the woman who stared past him Gideon immediately recognized. "Mary. Mary Thurston. You're alive. And baby James, as well."

Mary gave no sign she'd heard him. He reached and touched her shoulder, and she recoiled as if he had pierced her with a knife. One of the buffalo hunters slapped Gideon's hand away and brought his scarred and whiskered face close to Gideon's. Beside this beaten and sun-browned visage even Portis Goar might seem handsome. The man's long hair curled from under his hat stiff with grease and rank with a miasma of rancid meat. A thick blue vein ran from his narrow forehead down the side of his jaw as a vine clings to a side of cordwood. His deep-set eyes were small and, except for their paleness, rodentlike. His nose twisted to one side and was covered over with a raw purple scab that yet oozed black-looking blood. The few teeth he had were broken, pointed as fangs, black where they met puffy gray gums. His neck was layered with several ringlets, necklaces of dirt and grease, and one stark white necklace, too, a puckered scar running from the bottom of one ear almost to the other.

"Leave her be," he said, his breath more putrid-smelling than his hair and body.

To emphasize the man's point, his partner stepped so close Gideon could barely draw breath for his stench, equal to or worse than the first man's, yet differently foul. This one was taller than the other and less scarred. His flat face held little expression: large, empty eyes floated aimlessly over wide lips. His appearance suggested that when he had been a child someone had hit him full in the face with a heavy plank, permanently knocking wide his eyes, flattening his nose, spreading out his lips. Gideon eased away from them both and tried to position himself where Mary might see his face in the light of the lamp, but she showed no sign of recognition.

Mr. Manchip pronounced the infant healthy save sunburned skin. Until Mrs. Carter intervened, it did not appear the buffalo hunters—whose names Gideon learned were Hines and Conger though he never got straight who was who—would let Mr. Manchip examine Mary. When Mrs. Carter promised her protection against whatever evil intentions the hunters suspected from Mr. Manchip, the ornery and foul-smelling pair relented.

Mary's feet were bruised and cut, and she had dark bruises at her wrists in the shapes of fingers. She was more sunburnt than baby James. But these wounds would heal. What Mr. Manchip feared might not heal was her mind. When asked about the Indians, she clamped shut her mouth and stared straight ahead. When Gideon spoke the name of her husband, Hiram, she smiled and said, "He's up in the orchard." Gideon hoped she was right. He hoped Hiram was up in the orchard.

Mrs. Carter persuaded Hines and Conger to let her take Mary to the boardinghouse for a bath and rest. When she said they might have baths also, at no charge, Hines and Conger both grinned for the first time since they'd entered town and shook their heads violently as a wet dog shakes off water. What they *were* interested in was the open bottle of Squirrel on the bar.

Mr. Manchip poured drinks and questioned the filthy hunters. "You gentlemen are a long way below the Arkansas River. Not shooting bison south of the Arkansas, are you?"

"No," said the taller one as both shook their heads.

"Listen," the heavyset one said, "we crossed the Arkansas not knowing what water it was. A man can get to feeling all-overish out in such wild territory."

The taller one cuffed his friend with the heel of his hand. "What do you know? You ain't no shooter." Then he addressed Mr. Manchip. "He's a skinner. He can't get on the right end of a rifle."

"What a man can get into for shooting south of the Arkansas is trouble," said Mr. Manchip, who told Gideon later that the Treaty of Medicine Lodge, to preserve the southern herd for reservation Indians, prohibited white buffalo hunters below the Arkansas.

"I don't know. I seen the army and I seen rail crews shoot into a herd way south of the Arkansas—unless, as I say, I was all-fired lost," said the taller, more talkative hide hunter.

Mr. Manchip asked him what his best guess was about where they were when they found Mrs. Thurston.

With a good deal of head shaking and head scratching the man laid out this itinerary: they'd been several days at the muddy camp that had given this place the name, Bone Camp, making forays in search of stray cows to slaughter in their grisly business. "Stray cows, now for sure them ain't ruled out below the Arkansas is they?"

Mr. Manchip nodded, and the man shook his head in apparent amazement before he continued. Two long days' ride northwest they had come upon the woman and baby. They had put Mary and baby James in their wagon and back-tracked her path through the grass for three more days before they'd found two burned wagons and two graves.

"The graves I made for Hiram and Joe," Gideon said.

They'd found the Indian ponies' prints, eight or nine mounts they figured. At least two ponies were carrying double their prints were so deep. The tracks ended close to the wagons, where they could tell the Indians had swept them away with tree branches and leaves.

"Which way were they going?" Knobby asked.

The heavyset man shrugged, rolling his round shoulders as if they itched. His partner grinned. "Home," he said. "Up the Staked Plain."

This new intelligence located the raiders far south of where they'd attacked the wagons in Kansas and suggested they could have attacked and killed Knobby's friend near the Nueces and captured Elizabeth and baby William. It wasn't much, but it made Gideon ready to ride.

Mrs. Carter appeared in the saloon's open front door. "You are a pair of animals," she said evenly. The flat-faced one's eyes opened even wider. His pal bared his teeth at Mrs. Carter, then laughed a squeaky, falsetto laugh. Mrs. Carter exhaled loudly. "She's been violated. By these two most likely, maybe by the Comanches first. Though I don't know why the Comanches would do that and then let her go. We can't let these two get to her again."

"She's our woman. We found her," the tall one said.

"But the child wasn't ever feeling too chirk. We done what we could to chirk it up, but it wouldn't give up wailing," the heavy one said.

Mr. Manchip took Gideon aside and said, "I'll keep the bastards liquored up and in a fog till we can get Mrs. Thurston off to someplace she can get some help."

A Long Ride to the Yellow Houses

Mr. Manchip completed Gideon's outfit with a good store of beans, bacon, cornmeal, and coffee Gideon paid for with almost the last of his gold coins. He added to the supplies a pouch of tobacco for Suella and a small bag of sugar for himself, enough for coffee if not for baking. Then Eye loaded into Gideon's wagon a pick and shovel that made Gideon anticipate grave digging.

"Might come in handy," Eye said. He was nearly as rough-hewn as the buffalo hunters but appeared mostly good-hearted. He was clearly experienced in frontier ways. But the Negro, Knobby Cotton, was the one in whom Gideon placed the most faith, though he had no reason to expect Knobby had reciprocal feelings. Who could blame a Negro for doubting anyone of white skin? *Perhaps*, Gideon thought, *I will have an opportunity to prove to Knobby that not all whites are hateful.* Until such opportunity, Gideon determined to honor the Negro by showing no pious, false deference, neither any condescension. Suella was glad to be out of the bouncing wagon and on her own mount, but that was where her happiness ended. She ignored both Knobby and Eye and made it clear she rode along only for her interest in Gideon.

So they were four who rode together, but, save whatever allegiance Eye and Knobby held for one another, and save the curious fidelity Suella and Gideon shared, they were four who rode apart, separated by mistrust and self-interest. Their goal was the same, but their motives were different. Gideon judged Knobby and he had the purest motive—the recovery from enslavement of those they loved. Suella rode with them to be close to Gideon and, not quite the same, to escape her own bondage to Enoch Martin. Gideon knew Eye thought he had obscured the mercenary nature of *his* motives. But he had mentioned the Comanchero, Pretty, and his trade wagons too many times. Gideon had no doubt that Eye wanted in on Pretty's profit from the Indians.

Eye lifted his hat, scooped it full of air, put it back on his head, and they were off. At the pace Eye set, Gideon's wagon rattled, so he doubted mile by mile it could hold together a moment longer. The few remaining Atkins lightning arresters, in spite of their straw packing, clinked glass against brass inside the wood crate, and poor Chief Bones clicked like dice. They stopped twice to eat Mrs. Carter's biscuits and to water the horses. It was dark before Eye reined in by a waterhole. Even if they were able to maintain this pace, he said they were some days yet from the Yellow Houses where the Comanchero leader was supposed to be encamped. Gideon wondered what intelligence brought Eye knowledge of Pretty's movements.

They made a cold camp, supping on the last of the good biscuits, strips of dried venison, and the warm water from the pool beside them. Gideon's back was stiff, his hands were sore from hours of driving the spirited horses Mr. Manchip had loaned him, and his head pounded as if he still bounced on the wagon board. He unrolled his blanket beside Chief Bones and the pick and shovel, hoping Suella would see there was scant room for her in the wagonbed. All day she had ridden last, behind Gideon in the wagon, and the two of them had scarcely had time or opportunity to speak. Now she surprised him by bedding down apart from the rest of the camp without even passing by his wagon for a goodnight word. Though he was mostly relieved, he felt also a curious hurt, a tinge of jealousy, though he had no one to be jealous of unless he begrudged the hobbled pony she slept near to. To assuage the need he felt for absolution, Gideon put his near-sleep thoughts on Dorsey and beseeched the Heavenly Father and the uninterested stars to intercede in her behalf and spare her from suffering, from fear, from loneliness. And Gideon prayed God's blessings on poor Mary Thurston and her infant child. Then Knobby's hand was on Gideon's shoulder waking him in the yet-dark, midday-hot early morning.

The others, Suella too, were already saddled and mounted. There was no tree to stand behind, so—embarrassed that he felt so embarrassed—he walked a ways out onto the grass to relieve himself, fancying the whole time Suella was watching and that his modesty was amusing everyone. From his drinking gourd he splashed water on his face, cupped a handful to his dry morning mouth, and, still chewing on a venison strip, lifted the reins to Mr. Manchip's horses someone had already hitched back to the wagon. By the time the sun yellowed the eastern rim of the mesa Gideon was back in the continuous dream of the day before, the reins fit along red creases permanently added to his palm. He bounced so his teeth ached, and his eyes jiggled in their sockets.

No matter the direction he looked, nothing marked the horizon. Nothing lay before them but the short grass of all the hours of yesterday. He wondered what internal compass guided men like Eye, frontiersmen who seemed as at home in the wilderness as wild beasts.

Repeating Rifles

Mid-morning Eye pulled up, and Gideon reined in Mr. Manchip's matched pair. Squeaking loudly, the wagon came to a stop beside Knobby's black mare, which did not shy even one sidestep. Eye was off his mount, and at his feet lay the skull of a buffalo, one horn aimed at the sky, the other missing. Gideon thought of the foul-smelling buffalo hunters they'd left behind. Momentarily, he speculated they'd escaped Mr. Manchip, possibly done him and Mrs. Carter bodily harm. But this skull was too decayed to be their doing, and Mr. Manchip, who was mixed up in Gideon's mind with memories of Colonel Powell-Hughes, did not seem a man easy to escape from.

Eye walked a circle around the beast's skull and bent to the grass. He worked free two round rocks almost covered over with sand. Knobby dismounted and got the pick and shovel from the wagonbed. Eye stood with a boot in each of the holes left by the rocks, then he paced off steps, eight, if Gideon counted true. There Knobby stacked the rocks atop one another and pitched the shovel down beside Eye, where it hit the short grass and bounced with a tang that reverberated in the wide emptiness around them. By the time Eye bent to the shovel, Knobby was breaking the packed earth with the pick. Shortly, the iron point crunched something solid. Knobby dropped the pick and stood back while Eye's shovel unearthed a plank box the length of a child's coffin, black-stenciled: U. S. Army.

"What are you two digging up?"

"Rifles," Knobby said.

"U.S. Army?" Gideon asked.

Eye squinted up. "Where do you figure we got 'em?"

"Doesn't matter," Knobby said. "They're going to pay for our women back. We held back one crate from a caravan of rifles we stopped when we were riding in the Liberation Front. Herr Reinbach paid for them, but the U.S. government would say they're stolen military property. Better us than the Reb army they were headed to." Knobby knelt to the dirt and with his bare hands dug around the corners of the box.

"They're worth more than just Indian ransoms," Eye said. "And I hate to say it, Knob, but you best set your teeth to it—your woman and child may have gone to their Maker. The red devils have a terrible way with a white woman. She ain't likely the same. No telling what they'd do to a black one."

Knobby froze for just a heartbeat, then he stood and slapped the dirt off his hands against his thighs.

"Knob, you know what I mean. White woman or black. They violate and kill captive Indian squaws, too. Anybody not Comanche. Maybe they haven't, but it's usual they do."

Gideon couldn't help but wonder if Eye was counting on the Comanches having killed Elizabeth and William, and—Gideon could scarcely bear to think it—Dorsey. Then Eye could trade for the entire crate of rifles, get more from the Comancheros.

Eye grunted as he wrestled the crate up out of the hole. "Being as these are repeating rifles, heaps better than the Model 1873 single-shot army carbines, this box is a treasure chest."

"We are not after riches," Knobby said.

"We've got enough ammo to load all them rifles several times over. Out here, these cartridges is cheap at ten-cent a round. Indians, they'll pay double that or more in hides or horses."

Suella looked at Gideon as if maybe he knew what this was all about. He started to ask what the Liberation Front was but thought better of it. He had little to say about what these men did, and, besides, his sole purpose was finding Dorsey. If Eye and Knobby had stolen U.S. Army guns, what business was it of his?

Eye used the shovel edge to pry up the lid of the wooden box. He got his fingers under the lid and pulled it up several inches, nails screeching. He reached beneath a row of nails that looked like some beast's fangs and withdrew a rifle. "We'll carry one in with us to show the braves what we've got to trade."

The barrel was covered with some kind of grease. Eye handed the carbine to Knobby, who took the kerchief from around his neck and wiped off the grease.

"Keeps rust away," Eye said. "As if anything would rust in this bone-dry place."

Eye pushed the board top back down, and with his boot heel tamped the nails into place. He wrapped the rope from his saddle around the end of the crate, then dragged it to the edge of the grave-sized hole. He leaned down and with both hands pulled up a heavy box. "Ammo," he said. "Key to the lock."

Knobby played out the rope, lowering the crate back into the earth. While Eye swung the pick in another spot, Knobby shoveled dirt back over the rifles. Suella had closed her eyes and gave all appearances of taking a nap where she sat in her saddle.

Eye put the pick and shovel back beside Chief Bones in the wagonbed. With the blade of his sheath knife he opened the long ammo box, took out a fistful of cartridges, then wedged the box up under Gideon's board seat.

Knobby clucked Darkie to him and tied his rifle to the rope strap on his saddle. Gideon got back on the wagon and put his foot against his Hawken, which rested across the bottom of the wagon board. Eye mounted up. He pulled his single-shot from the rifle scabbard on his saddle and tossed the old gun out onto the bare ground. Knobby retrieved Eye's old rifle and put it in the wagon.

"Can't you get over being a slave?" Eye asked.

Knobby said nothing. He brought the new repeating rifle to his shoulder and sighted down the barrel out across the empty plain. Then he swung the barrel until it pointed at Eye. He worked the lever, and the mechanism—oiled metal against oiled metal—barked once. Knobby lowered the rifle and held out his hand. Eye walked his horse over to Knobby and handed down several cartridges, their brass jackets golden in the sun. One at a time, Eye pitched Gideon cartridges. Knobby filled the magazine of the rifle, then they resumed their original westerly direction. Gideon caught himself looking back at the raw mound of dirt to assure himself the digging episode had taken place. From a distance the disturbed earth looked like a fresh-made grave.

Early afternoon, Suella pointed at the horizon. "Smoke talk say four come."

"Anything else?" Eye said.

"They think me Komantz." Suella grinned. "Let you pass safe with me."

Eye nodded and slid off his horse. He found a few buffalo chips scattered in the wagonbed. "No reason to hide. They're already watching every move we make." He made a small fire, boiled up some coffee, and they nooned in bright sun on the wide, empty space.

They ate the last of their venison strips, guzzled hot coffee, and wished for more of Mrs. Carter's biscuits. Eye relieved himself, his stream loud on the packed earth. Before he mounted his horse Knobby spread his blanket roll over Chief Bones. "No need to give the Comanches a notion to skin us down." Knobby poured a handful of water for Darkie and mounted up. Back on his wagon board Gideon listened to leather creaking, horses stamping and snorting against cinches. He knew the animals felt their collective restlessness.

The Comanchero Trade Camp

Ever since he'd left the eastern treeline in Missouri and entered the vast expanse of the West, Gideon had been surprised by the country—by its vastness and by the secrets it revealed—but nothing had prepared him for the Yellow Houses. The Staked Plain stretched flat and empty as some giant's tabletop. Nothing moved save a few cottony clouds. For hours he saw nothing but the distant horizon-line. Then, he could not have named the moment he first perceived it, where there had been nothing appeared a dark shape like some bizarre centerpiece on that table-top, a shape that slowly approached, and what could have been cloud shadow or imagination or mirage defined itself as a brown rectangle. It drew nearer—a high limestone cliff dotted with caves. And beyond, a lower rectangle also yellowish in the late afternoon sun. This second shape was almost hidden on the far side of the bluff and It was a farther distance to ride over than he would have guessed. The second shape was some kind of Indian lodge. No tipi, it was an open pavilion with a flat roof of buffalo hides sewn together and stretched over a frame supported by several vertical posts eight, maybe ten feet high. This big trading tent was sur-rounded by wagons of all description—freighter, oxcart, schooner, and Cones-toga. Beyond the wagons, the Staked Plain was dark and moving with horses.

Because, at least from a distance, they had taken Suella for a Comanche, the Comancheros were letting the party ride right into their camp. Gideon wondered if he had thought the words out loud when Eye said, "They can kill us whenever they want. They're waiting to see our trade goods."

"Why trade for what they can take for free?" Knobby asked.

"Kindly goes against the grain at the trade places to just outright steal. Of course, there ain't no law," Eye said.

"There's a Chinese saying my old friend Win Shu was fond of: 'Honor the spirits, but keep your distance from them,'" Gideon said.

"We've got to have eyes all over our heads," Knobby said.

Cookfires burned and the smell of singed hair and animal fat filled the air. Feral-looking dogs barked and growled, hiking their legs against the wheels of wagons circled into scattered camps. Dark piles of dung dotted the bare earth. Eye veered over to an empty grassy bowl and slid down off his horse. Gideon braked his wagon and climbed off the board, glad of the chance to walk out the kinks in his legs. Knobby unhitched and watered Mr. Manchip's team, hobbled the fine horses that were already pulling at the grass. The ammunition box just fit beneath the wagon seat, out of sight. Gideon secured his most precious possessions, his encyclopedia and journal, his bottle of ink and pen, tucking them under Eye's blanket on which lay Chief Bones—the only critic Gideon would suffer of his written musings. Eye and Knobby swung back into their saddles. Knobby held out a pale palm, offering Gideon a ride behind him on Darkie, but Gideon shook his head and climbed up behind Suella on Enoch Martin's white horse, which dropped steaming green dung as it walked. Knobby's black mare snorted and nodded. Eye led them single-file on a twisting route into a mélange of display and barter.

Various wagons Gideon guessed were Comanchero outfits were loaded with pots and pans, boxes of matches, tins of peaches, bags of sugar and coffee and tobacco, umbrellas, hair brushes and combs, mirrors, bead necklaces, bolts of brightly dyed cotton, bottles of spirits diluted with who-knew-what concoctions, bottles and tins (elixirs, tonics, liniments and salves), children's dolls, their blue glass eyes open wide in round faces white as ghosts in the brutal sun. On planks beneath the roofed area more such goods were spread. A pair of brown-skinned men in breechclouts held between them a two-man tree saw (in this treeless expanse) and moved the handles up and down to make the metal blade buck and pop. They looked like two railroad men Gideon had seen back in Cumberland pumping the handles of a handcar, moving it down the tracks, but the saw sent a mournful music whining and twanging across the plains.

Indian women with short-cropped hair stared at themselves in mirrors, sending small bright suns against the sides of wagons and the backs of men's heads. Flashing like the mirrors were knifeblades and whisky bottles. Men staggered drunkenly between the wagons. Two naked Indian boys fought over a doll. One pulled the doll's porcelain feet, stark white beside his bare, dark penis that bounced and jerked with his struggles, and the other pulled its yellow painted head as if he might take the little scalp. A Mexican in a red shirt juggled oranges bright as balls of gold to the tune of guitars and gourd rattles played by three of his comrades. Giving up bagpipes for these Mexican guitar strummers, the scene was what Gideon had pictured when Colonel Powell-Hughes had described country fairs back in Wales. Beyond the wagonloads of Comanchero goods were buffalo hides in tall stacks like small brown houses, a village on the plain. These hides, stolen cattle, and horses were the Indians' trade currency. Back East the furs brought a dear price. Beyond the piled hides was a huge herd of horses watched over by surly looking Indian boys who appeared too old to play with dolls, not old enough to trade for knives or guns.

El Perdido

Even at a distance, and though he had never before seen the man, Gideon recognized Pretty, the one who had named himself El Perdido—a lost soul. Alone, self-contained in the midst of all these people, he leaned against one of the roof supports of the trading pavilion with his arms folded across his chest. Plain black boots came almost to his knees, and he wore tight cavalry trousers with the reinforced seat, a black twill shirt, a wide-brimmed hat that might have been black or blue but was so dust-covered it appeared as a gray storm cloud over his head. He wore no sidearm, just a wide-bladed machete in a canvas scabbard. Eye, Knobby, Suella, and Gideon moved close to him. Pretty did not move, yet, subtly—a tilt of his head, a dip of his shoulder—he acknowledged their arrival. His black brows and eyes and thick black moustache looked burned like a brand into his hide-brown face.

A hatless man who wore his hair in one long braid kept himself a few steps behind Pretty. He constantly glanced around but his eyes were never off of Pretty for long. Gideon guessed the hatless man to be some kind of bodyguard.

An Indian in blue leggings wearing a woman's faded blue chambray dress lurched toward the Comanchero leader. Gideon's breath caught—the dress looked just like the one Dorsey had worn the afternoon he had followed her to the pond. He yearned to hold the material between his fingers. He had the curious notion his touch would recognize cloth that had lain over Dorsey's skin, as if her body would have left its essence in the weave as a body leaves heat behind in a bed. The Indian in the dress carried a nearly empty bottle of spirits and made his way in tilting angles. When he saw he was about to walk right into Pretty, the Indian, drunk as he was, managed to steer wide of the unmoving Comanchero. There must be many chambray dresses, Gideon told himself. A rip in the back of the dress bore a brown stain as from mud, or—he did not want to consider it—blood.

"*Qué pasa*, Pretty?" asked Eye.

"*De nada*, gringo." Barely visible beneath the thick moustache, Pretty's upper lip did not move when he spoke. His eyes passed over each of them, narrowing and darkening. When Knobby nodded at him, he touched a finger to his moustache.

Eye spoke to the man Gideon had taken for a bodyguard. "*Buenos tardes*, Brown Fred." The man nodded. Eye went on, "Ain't as many Indians as last time I come to Yellow Houses."

"*Asi parece*. Many Comanches, Kiowas, and Kiowa Apaches ride up the Little Arkansas for a council meeting with the gringo agent, Leavenworth."

"Rest of the Indians go peaceable to a reservation it'd kindly kill your business," Eye said.

Gideon did not recall ever having seen so cold and dispassionate a look as the one the Comanchero gave Eye. There was a hint of a smile at the corners of the man's mouth, and his body gave an imperceptible shrug—like a tremor in the ground one might disregard until an earthquake leveled mountains and opened up chasms in the earth. Brown Fred, the Comanchero bodyguard, shifted his weight, making a creaking of leather like a saddle shifting on a horse.

"Señor Goar—the *Eye* who does not miss a thing." The Comanchero's sarcasm was as sharp and straight as a razor. "You have surely seen many Numunuu of the Buffalo Eaters band and even more of the Antelope here. These Antelope buy more guns, more iron for arrowheads and lance points, than all the other bands now on reservations. *Sí no estoy mal informado*, there is a warrior who joined the Antelope from the Honey Eaters, a leader of much appeal, a magnetic force. This warrior, Two Talks, is rumored to be gathering a great army to overthrow all the *taivos*." The Comanchero leaned close to Eye. "*Intentaré explicárselo*. A magnet has a force, a pull. Do you see, Señor Portis 'Eye' Goar, a magnet should attract iron, mi amigo. Especially any shooting iron El Perdido has to trade for buffalo hides, cattle, horses. Every hide brings Pretty plenty of gringo gold. But this Two Talks does not come to the Yellow Houses or any trading place. He tells his band not to trade Comanche hides and horses for *taivo* trinkets. He says we Comancheros trade blankets that carry sickness, and our whisky makes warriors crazy like the backwards ones. He says we Comancheros are as bad as Tehanos. He tells his band to leave Pretty's trade goods to rot on the plains." Pretty shook his head and pursed his lips. "Such talk is bad for my business." The Comanchero boss shook his head as if he were suddenly sad, or weary. "During the long war between themselves the gringos sent all the guns to the fight in the East. The supply has not built back up, so guns are better even than gold. Two Talks needs the rifles-that-speak-many-times."

"Is he the big Comanche war chief now?" Eye said.

Pretty shrugged. "I have never seen him. I just hear stories. But I believe his *puha* is not so strong as all these stories. Pronto some other Indian savior will push Two Talks from the feeding trough, and we will hear *de la triste noticia de su muerte*. Soon, the knives are covered with rust. Another with strong *puha* will want the rifles. Oil the parts. Every rifle is gold in my safe. Sooner or later someone pays my price."

"Take a look at this," Eye said. He handed Pretty the repeating rifle he had taken from the buried crate.

Pretty worked the bolt, opened the magazine, squinted into the works. "*Bueno. ¿Cuantos?*"

"All you need," Eye said.

Gideon was surprised to hear Knobby speak. "El Perdido, Eye is always out for gold, but Gideon and I are searchers after captured women."

"The ugliest man in any camp has a lover," Pretty said. "I buy guns. You must see another to buy back *los prisioneros*."

"If you broker an exchange, we will pay you in these repeating rifles," Knobby said, looking directly at Eye, who said nothing.

"I always get paid," Pretty said. "I'll come by your wagon mañana."

After a meal of roasted hare—Suella brought the meat, skinned pink, to their fire—they stretched out on blankets in their grassy bowl. Gideon was glad of the distance between them and the next group of wagons. Though that half-mile or so offered no protection it afforded a sense of privacy. After she delivered their supper, Suella wandered off. Gideon hoped she might remain on the prowl and leave him in the solitude of his bedroll. So near to numberless savages he was surely too anxious for sleep, but he lay down beneath a canopy of stars to commune with his thoughts, fancies that someone in this camp had knowledge of Dorsey, that Pretty wanted the rifles badly enough to help find her. Gideon felt he was drawing closer to Dorsey day by day.

A *Parlay with Sleeping Wolf*

Gideon awoke to the smell of coffee and the insistent voice of the Comanchero called Brown Fred. "*Andale, andale,*" he said. Knobby handed Gideon a hot tin cup of coffee. The sun had not yet cleared the eastern horizon, the morning air still cool. Knobby carried one of the repeating rifles and Gideon's small pouch of sugar. Only a few women, either Comanche or half-breed squaws of the Comancheros, were moving about tending smoky cookfires, bending to clay pots over these fires. Gideon gulped coffee as he walked and burned his tongue, but the bitter brew warmed his chest and invigorated him as if it were medicinal tonic. Brown Fred led Knobby and Gideon beyond the cluster of trade wagons and tents to a shallow arroyo worn into a shining, wet rockface. Water seeped out of the rock and pooled in a rough depression around which grew several twisted cedars. Beyond the scrubby trees a few tipis rose.

"Is this an Indian camp?" Knobby asked.

"No, señor, these are trade tipis, out of the sun, places to talk private." Brown Fred bent to the opening of one of the tipis and said something Gideon could not understand. The Comanchero leader, Pretty, appeared, holding open the hide door flap. They entered single-file, bending low as if they were bowing at the altar as they entered a chapel, which is what the tipi seemed like inside. The curved ceiling vaulted high to an open smoke flap that admitted rays of the sun that spilled down the hide walls as melted gold. The packed dirt floor shone as polished slate or tile. Cedar smoke rose from a small fire in the center of the earthen floor, an aroma as holy-smelling as incense. Rough-hewn cedar poles framing the structure reminded Gideon of the wooden cross on which the Savior died. Behind the fire an Indian sat with his legs crossed beneath him, his hands in his lap, his eyes closed behind small, round spectacles much like Gideon's own. Gideon somehow knew the Indian was not sleeping, yet his eyes did not flutter. His graying hair curled down before and behind his ears, and his face was lined and wrinkled. He was older than any of the Indians Gideon had seen, and he wondered if this was a Comanche priest or medicine man, a chief at least.

"*Con permiso,*" Pretty said. Eyes still closed, the Indian nodded, his spectacles catching the firelight. Gideon had never imagined an Indian wearing eyeglasses. Pretty sat, and they all followed. "*Haa, tsaati i, haitsi'i?*" Pretty said.

Gideon put on his own spectacles that had been in his pocket since he'd lain down the evening before. *What is one to think*, he wondered, *of a people who every one sleeps inside his personal cathedral?* Sunlit dust motes met rising sparks from the fire to form constellations of red and gold against the smoke-darkened walls. His impulse was to close his eyes and join the old Indian in prayer.

The Indian's eyes opened black and magnified by the lenses. "*Tokwetikati.*"

"*Por favor.*" Pretty held a palm out toward the Indian, then swung back his arm to include all of them, and raised his voice in a formal manner. The Comanchero spoke a mixture of Comanche and Spanish, translating words into English as he talked. "Esahabby, Sleeping Wolf, of the Penateka band of the Komantz."

"*Haits. Hina ini?*" asked Sleeping Wolf.

"*Buenas días*, mi amigo. I want *nada*," said Pretty. He smiled at them all around the circle around the fire. "*No me falta nada.*"

"He's a Honey Eater chief?" Eye asked.

"*Sí*, the Penateka are the Honey Eaters. Sleeping Wolf has been a war chief, but he has not ridden the warpath for a long time," Pretty said.

From behind his glasses Sleeping Wolf's eyes touched each of them one by one, then came to rest on Knobby's rifle, which Pretty took and handed to the Comanche. The blued barrel looked like a charred stick lifted from the fire. Sleeping Wolf was round and weighty like his namesake, and the gun seemed small in his dark, muscled arms. He aimed the rifle around the circle, finally stopping with the gunsight at rest on Knobby, who did not flinch or blink. When the Indian dropped the gun and rested it bridging his crossed legs, Gideon let out air, realizing he had been holding his breath.

"*Con permiso*, the new repeating carbine. Won't get hot and jam like your single-shot army carbines. I can provide many," Pretty said. He nodded at the gun. "*Este es para usted.*"

Sleeping Wolf rested his palm atop the rifle's magazine. He held his fingers to his nose—gun oil and sweat (Gideon, too, inhaled the scents)—and stared at them with open curiosity. He wore only a flap in front and back of the Indian breechclout, a leather apron that covered his privates and behind. His lower legs were covered by hide so soft it wrinkled like skin when he moved. These leggings were the high tops of bootlike moccasins with thick hide soles. Painted pale blue, the leggings had silver medallions like coins tied down both sides by rawhide strips. He stared at Knobby so steadily, Gideon wondered if Sleeping Wolf had ever seen a Negro.

In the Comanche's bare side, where his copper-brown skin stretched smooth as a drum's hide, was an oblong scar, a raw and angry red shape where a lance or blade must have pierced him in battle. The scar was surrounded by pale flesh puckered as if from a burn, where someone had cauterized the wound with a hot firebrand. The red scar was surrounded by blue triangles, the tattooed tips of knifeblades or arrow points. His muscular arms were streaked with long scabs, the flesh dry and flaking. His wrinkled fingers ended in split and uneven nails stained the color of prairie grass. He extended a hand toward Knobby, the little finger missing. "*Tutaivo.*"

"Black white-man," Pretty said.

"I'm not any kind of white man," Knobby said. "Tell him."

"*Importa poco.*"

The Comanche swayed with laughter, holding himself with his arms. Two long bunches of his hair tied with leather thongs fastened with silver buttons shone with grease and decorative silver medallions. A part in the center of his head was painted vermillion, as were his ears, from one of which dangled an iron frizzen from the firing mechanism of a flintlock.

Eye nudged Gideon and, as if the two of them were alone somewhere and not in a tipi with a Comanche warrior, said, "I could eat like all wrath. Wonder what time it is?"

Without thinking, Gideon pulled out the silver watch Colonel Powell-Hughes had given him and read the hour: 3:00. The silver watch ran on its own schedule, separate from the earth's spinning, but judging from the afternoon sun outside Gideon thought this might be the first time the watch had known the true hour. "Three," he said.

The nostrils of Sleeping Wolf's wide, flat nose flared, twitching as if he were taking in each separate scent on the air. So creased was the skin about the round lenses of his spectacles, he appeared to have two or three sets of eyelids deep behind which his pitch-black eyes waited, lying in ambush of whatever he might aim them.

An Indian woman silently entered the tipi. Sleeping Wolf took from her a long rod of orange clay Gideon took to be a flute, then saw by its bowl it was a smoking pipe.

"*To'i.*" Sleeping Wolf held up the long wood stem. "*Punche.*"

"*Gracias. Con mucho gusto,*" Pretty said. To Eye, Knobby, and Gideon, he said, "He offers to smoke with us. We accept with pleasure."

"Does he talk Mexican?" Eye asked.

"*Sí, señor, me hable español—poco,*" Sleeping Wolf said. "*Numunuu, soy-aque.*" Then he talked more Comanche, words running together like water gurgling over rocks.

"He says the Comanche are like the mockingbird—they speak many tongues though it is their own song they sing best," Pretty said.

"*Punche,*" Sleeping Wolf said. He filled the pipe bowl with tobacco dark and stringy between his fingers, then lit it with a twig from the fire. A flame glowed in his glasses' lenses. Holding the pipe with both hands, he drew deeply, and smoke (it smelled—Gideon counted this strange—like dead fish) escaped his nose and mouth. He passed the pipe to Pretty, whose mouth moved under his moustache revealing brown teeth ground short and uneven. Pretty inhaled and a few heartbeats later let out a cloud of smoke before he handed Gideon the warm pipe. The wooden pipestem went all the way through the bowl, and Gideon took that end with his left hand and held the bowl with his right. The stem was loose and he realized he needed both hands or the stem might slip out of the bowl. The mouthpiece was moist with Pretty's saliva, and for fear that the Comanchero's cruel bodily humors might make him weak as Samson after Delilah cut his hair, Gideon gripped the stem between his teeth so it would not touch his lips. The hot smoke was tart like a green apple and sent a stinging into his ear and neck the way a first taste of persimmon or apricot sometimes does.

Ten Bears spoke to Pretty in Comanche. The Comanchero translated: "He says for us to speak of what we want and of what we will give his people in return. He says, let these things we offer be bright like gold and sweet like sugar."

"*Me gustan joyas—anillos, artes y pulseras de oro, collares de plata,*" Sleeping Wolf said, tapping the gold frames of his glasses.

"I like jewels—rings, earrings, and bracelets of gold, necklaces of silver," Eye translated. "He talks damn good Mexican."

"Mockingbird teaches me also Tehano songs," Sleeping Wolf said.

"American, too." Eye shook his head, and the Comanche smiled slyly.

"I am here, as always, to trade," Pretty said. "Buffalo furs for these new rifles. But two of these seek those they love captured by Antelope raiders."

Knobby handed Sleeping Wolf Gideon's pouch of sugar. It had been so long since Gideon had tasted cake or pie he'd have given his outfit for more sugar and some eggs and flour. Sleeping Wolf stuck his finger in the sack and sucked his fingertip. He nodded and spoke again. Everything he said, Pretty translated:

"What gold tastes as good as sugar?"

"I can bring more sugar," Knobby said. Pretty translated, and Sleeping Wolf grinned.

"Hills of sugar rise on the Comanchero trade wagons. Does the *tutaivo* seek captives?"

"*Ya lo creo*," Pretty said, nodding.

Sleeping Wolf spoke in Comanche, and Pretty said, "He asks if it is true the *taivo* paints his servants black to see if they run away? He wonders if the black white-men are in the Tehano tribe or a different black tribe."

"Tell him no white man painted me, and I ran away at night when I could see the whites who chased me but they could not see me."

Sleeping Wolf nodded solemnly, looking Knobby up and down. The old chief grinned and said, "*Ke*-Tehano."

"Not Texan," Pretty translated.

The chief talked some more Comanche and Pretty translated: "Maybe, in some darkness life, the white man was servant to the black—maybe, in that life, the black man paints his servants white so he can see them in the night. Has the white man put a spell on *tutaivo* hair so it does not grow straight?"

Knobby removed his wide-brimmed hat and coils of black hair spilled out. "In Africa, the land of my people, black men let their hair grow and braid it and decorate it with bones, beads, feathers, much as the Numunuu do." Knobby said the guttural word, Numunuu, as if he had spoken Comanche all his life. Gideon perceived a smile on Sleeping Wolf's lips. The old man reached and touched Knobby's hair. With his palm on Knobby's head Sleeping Wolf looked like a priest giving a blessing.

"Yours is softer than other *tutaivo* scalps I have touched," Sleeping Wolf spoke and Pretty translated slowly, word by word. "Those ones were dry like short grass, stiff like horsetail hair the Rope Heads plait into their braids to make them longer." The Indian stared straight ahead as he spoke: "A band of Antelope has your woman and boy-child," Pretty translated.

Knobby's fingers dug into the dirt floor. "Where?"

Sleeping Wolf removed his spectacles and rubbed his eyes. He stared as if he might see the captives through the wall of the tipi. "Wears Out Moccasins, a Numunuu of the Liver Eaters band, took them. His band now follows Wahatewi and his raiders."

"That's Two Talks," Pretty said.

"Where is Wears Out Moccasins?" Knobby asked so slowly and quietly it made the hair on the back of Gideon's neck stand up.

"Wears Out Moccasins wants the *tutaivo*'s woman for wife, the boy-child for son."

"I said, 'Where is Wears Out Moccasins?'" Knobby said again. Sweat ran down Gideon's forehead, but he dared not wipe his face.

"*¿Quién sabe?*" Sleeping Wolf asked.

Then he went on in Comanche, and Pretty translated: "It is spoken that Two Talks has strong *puha*. It is said he has waked up the spirits to join again with Our People. It is said Crow flies ahead to warn Two Talks of dangers on his road and even the spirit of the rocks moves boulders to offer him protection. Two Talks' band of the Honey Eaters refused to go on the reservation to live like the white man's cattle. They joined the Antelope. Smoke words say many bands will come together to number more than all the white guns from Washington Land. Comanche warriors will darken the earth for as far as the hawk can see. More Comanches will move through the grass than all the buffalo of all the herds that ever grazed in the good hunting times of dark fur. Wears Out Moccasins and the black-white woman and boy-child are in the Antelope camp of Two Talks even this day."

Sleeping Wolf lifted the rife and pointed it in Gideon's direction. His mouth felt full of cotton. When the Comanche sighted down the rifle, his spectacles flashed light like fire out of the barrel. Gideon could not keep from flinching, and the old warrior grinned.

Pretty spoke into the silence, "What has Sleeping Wolf, who sees as far as the eagle, seen of three whites—a girl, a young woman, an older woman—who were taken from a pair of wagons north of the Llano Estacado?"

Sleeping Wolf spoke and Pretty translated, "Who seeks after these ones?"

"I do." Gideon's words sounded in his ears as brittle as autumn leaves.

Sleeping Wolf leaned close to him. "*Ekahpuh hihwee?*"

"You have sufficient gold—ransom?" the Comanchero translated.

"Yes," Gideon said, thinking of Knobby's and Eye's buried rifles.

Sleeping Wolf spoke in a faraway voice. "White ones fired the first shots at the Numunuu and made sorrow in our camps. Our women hacked their hair and fingers for their dead ones, and our warriors danced the war dance. We Numunuu blocked your road. We took your women and children. Now, our warriors take captives to ransom—gold to buy the fast-speaking guns. Since the Blue-Bottoms smoked the peace pipe with the Gray-Bottoms, more Tehanos have come. The white father in Washington Land sends as many *taivos* as stars in the night sky. Maybe the guns that speak without resting will help the Numunuu take back the grass and the rivers, the sun and the breeze. Maybe this new leader, Two Talks, will join all Numunuu bands into one, as a warrior binds melted iron and buzzard feathers to mulberry shafts to make a killing arrow. Maybe it is too late for the Numunuu. If that is so, then it is a good day for dying."

Gideon tasted a salty drop of sweat and recalled the story Jesus tells the Pharisees as recorded by St. Luke: a rich man cries out from Hell begging Father Abraham to send Lazarus from Abraham's bosom to dip just the tip of his finger in water to cool the rich man's tongue.

"Sleeping Wolf," Gideon said, desperation giving him words, "take this gift that marks the time, whether it is a day for dying or a day for living."

Firelight danced on the watch face. Sleeping Wolf brought it close to his ear. He grinned, then he said, "Its heart beats as a man's. Its hands turn with the sun." With the watch still at his ear, Sleeping Wolf spoke, and Pretty translated: "The ones you seek are also in the camp of Two Talks. They say bullets pass through Two Talks as raindrops through a cloud. Some say Crow showed Two Talks the hole in the sky that leads from this world to the next."

In Jesus' story, Abraham refuses to let Lazarus cool the rich man's tongue, saying that between the two realms of the dead there is a great gulf fixed and no man may pass from one realm to the other. In Colonel Powell-Hughes' Presbyterian Bible lessons, the judgment of those who had perished was final. Jesus and those He raised from death passed between the world of the quick and the dead. It seemed to Gideon unlikely a wild Indian could make such a journey.

Pretty translated right behind Sleeping Wolf's words: "An Antelope visitor speaks of a dark-haired white woman in Two Talks' camp—a young and strong *mujer*, a woman like a wildcat. The others you seek, the white wildcat's mother and the girl-child who runs and plays with the children of the Antelope band, are in the same camp. Our visitor Two Talks took these ones who now answer to Comanche names, talk and eat and kiss with Comanche lips, listen with Comanche ears."

"Where's Two Talks' camp?" Knobby asked.

Pretty translated Sleeping Wolfe's words: "It is said Two Talks looks beyond riches. He gives his men every *taivo* blanket and spoon he takes. Strong ponies he gives away. He keeps not even sugar or tobacco." Sleeping Wolf held up the watch. "Even this silver eye with a heartbeat, I think Two Talks would give up. A man who does not desire to possess things is a man difficult to predict. For these gifts of sugar, the gun that speaks without resting, and the beating spirit in the metal eye, Sleeping Wolf will take his new friends to try to bargain for their dear ones."

Sleeping Wolf folded his arms and stared straight ahead. Gideon guessed what that meant. "That's it, that's all, talk ended."

Knobby got up to follow Pretty out of the tipi.

"*Kiss*," Sleeping Wolf said. It meant "wait," or "stop," or some such. The Indian woman behind him handed Sleeping Wolf a small gourd, and he handed it to Knobby.

"To make your *tutaivo* hair soft as a Numunuu warrior's," Pretty translated.

Then and there Knobby dipped his fingers into the gourd and brought out a dark gob of dung-smelling grease he stroked over his long, coiling ringlets. Though Gideon had never set foot in Africa, he recognized Knobby as a fierce African warrior.

"*Tokwetikati*," Sleeping Wolf said.

"It is agreeable," Knobby translated.

They all stepped out into bright sunlight. Gideon removed his spectacles and blinked blue spots. Knobby walked away alone. Pretty and Eye went with Sleeping Wolf to fire the new repeating carbine. Pretty and Eye were both calculating the value of the rifles. Gideon knew neither would give up all the repeating rifles to trade for a few captives.

Surprised by a Wagonbed Tryst

Gideon looked for Suella to see if she might have heard where Two Talks' camp was. An Indian woman passed carrying a carved pole from which dangled a long silver-white length of hair, and Gideon's breath caught. He'd seen but one such head of hair. Though it surely meant he was safe from Enoch Martin's retribution, the long albino scalp brought Gideon no pleasure. He wondered if Suella had seen the scalp and guessed it for her father's and whether the scalp meant Enoch Martin was captured and possibly somewhere nearby or, more likely, had been tortured to death. Gideon remembered the albino's advice if you were captured by Indians: "You hold back a cartridge for yourself."

Among all the dark Indian heads he sought Suella's silver-streaked red hair, looked for her shape beneath deerhide dresses from one end of the camp to the other. Men stood in knots, drinking coffee from tin cups or smoking pipes or cigarettes rolled from Comanchero makings. Their frequent laughter was unsettling. Gideon expected them to mutter or scream war cries. He stopped in the middle of the path, and someone walked into him from behind. He turned to see who he'd collided with. A Comanche child grinned and shook his head, and Gideon shook his head, too. He started laughing and the little boy joined in. For a minute neither of them could stop. The boy touched Gideon's arm and went on his way. Gideon's skin held the heat of the child's hand. Perhaps the Comanches who captured Dorsey smiled and laughed and touched her arm, too. Gideon remembered Alexander Speer's severed tongue, his swollen red throat, and Enoch Martin's white scalp. Gideon had buried the mutilated bodies of Hiram Thurston and Dorsey's brother, Joe. Surely, Dorsey wouldn't forget. The Comanche boy was too young to have mutilated anyone. But he'd surely witnessed brutality. Indians fighting whites, different tribes fighting one another. It was easy for Gideon to feel Indians were savage, but it was hard to look a Comanche boy in the face and hate him.

Reading the looping letters a gusty breeze wrote on the tall grass, Gideon descended the long slope to the place Knobby, Eye, Suella, and he had made camp. Back at his wagon he took out his *Encyclopaedia.* The struggle between conqueror and conquered has been going on since the beginning of time. He read from the *Americana* the final volume's first entry, **VISIGOTHS**—*but they became hostile whenever the promises made them were violated; and scarcely was Theodosius dead, and the empire divided, when the Visigoths, under Alaric, broke forth upon Italy, and Rome fell, in 410, into the power of the Visigoths.*

His comparison worked so long as he was certain whites were the Romans and Indians were the Goths. If so, the warning of history was: "Keep your promises." What would Suella have said—half-Indian, half-white, where did her true loyalties lie? Why had he never talked to her about anything that mattered? They had lain together, but they did not know one another.

The deserted camp filled him with loneliness, and, still carrying the *Encyclopaedia,* he walked a ways beyond the edge of the camp. Mr. Manchip's horses grazed in their hobbles. From where Gideon stood the cookfire looked like a smudge of ashes. Blankets lay like dark patches stitched to the ground. Even the memory of his stolid oxen left behind in Alhambra stirred his sense of isolation, and his emotions followed the compass needle of his heart straight to Dorsey.

Of a sudden a high-pitched unearthly yowl came from the direction of his wagon. Had he and his companions not been in the Yellow Houses peaceably, he would have taken the cry for a war whoop. The yowl came again—a coyote? in broad daylight?—and a dark shape arched up in his wagonbed. Was Chief Bones come to life? Just as Gideon was about to call out, the shape reappeared above the rim of the wagonbed long enough for him to recognize Suella's roan hair, its silver streaks catching sun like knifeblades, her chestnut red and completely bare backside humped like a bucking horse. She gave out a squeal he'd heard only when she'd rolled with him in his bedding. Now he reasoned why she had shed her buckskins, and he dropped to all fours. There were no nearby trees to hide behind, but he did not want to witness Suella's carnality with someone else. As fast as he could crawl he went for the only cover available—the bouncing shadow of the wagon rocked by Suella's lunging and thrashing. Beneath the wagon, he was more trapped than hidden. Dust and grit rained on his head. Phineas Atkins' lightning arresters shifted back and forth above him, the glass balls clinking against the rods in their straw nests. The pick clanged the shovel blade, and Chief Bones rattled and clicked, his teeth chattering like a squirrel after nuts. Gideon heard more than he wanted to.

"Don't you dare stop, goddamn you. Don't stop now," Suella said, her words rising and falling with her body that was bucking like an unbroken mare. Once more came the ghostly, coyote howl. "Goddamn you, you fat weak rabbit. Hold stiff for me, milkweed."

"*Kekunabenitu,*" a voice said.

"Don't tell me to quit biting. I'll really show you biting if you stop fucking before I'm done. Keep poking, goddamn you." The wagon shook as if the Devil's own demons were fighting there. Suella's breathing grew faster and louder, and the wagon bottom bowed down. Gideon lay flat on his back, certain the bottom was going to split open and empty its load on him. Once more Suella gave out her high squeal, ending this time in a heavy series of bumps and, then, such silence he was afraid she and her accomplice would hear his heart thumping. His eye stung, then a drop of liquid hit his upper lip. He ran his tongue over his skin and tasted salt. Tears? Sweat? Suella's or the person with her? Gideon's fingers cramped, both his hands gripping the rear axle, his arms spread. He pictured himself like Samson pushing apart the temple pillars, pushing apart the two rear wagon wheels and the wagon's heavy load crashing down on top of him.

How long he sat there with the axle seized in his fists he had no idea. The shadows of the wagon wheels lengthened into egg shapes, his shape between them like a thick tree trunk with outspread limbs. He lay flat to make his shadow disappear. From above him came loud snoring he knew as Suella's heavy sleep after the brawling she called fucking.

Two brown feet dropped down near Gideon's face. The heels were grass-stained, the bottoms blackened as many a corpse he had tended back in the Baltimore asylum. Above the feet two knotty calves were cut in half by the frame of the wagonbed. A network of pale scars forked like a river into many tributaries down one dark leg. The other leg bore a green bruise outlined in purple, and both legs were speckled with red scabs from clawed insect bites.

A Comanche man, pot-bellied and bandy-legged, slid from the bed and stood beside the wagon. He wore a white woman's dress unbuttoned down the back, the long skirt hanging between his legs in a vulgar, suggestive way. Gideon was glad he could see nothing else hanging down. The Comanche leaned his wide bare bottom against one rear wheel, the spokes making red stripes against the backs of his thighs as if somebody had whipped him. Gideon wondered why he had not at least tried to whip the man. He pulled moccasins on over his bare feet, his leggings and breechclout wadded in his fist—an arrogant gesture that said he didn't care who saw him, naked from the waist down, walking away from Gideon's wagon wherein lay an even more naked half-Kiowa squaw. When the man barked at Suella what must have been "good-bye," he revealed a mouthful of broken and stained teeth. The weasel was in Gideon's henhouse, but all he cared about was remaining undiscovered. This fat Comanche was the way for Gideon to extricate himself from Suella. But he did not feel happy. He felt weak and unmanly. He wanted to dispatch the arrogant Indian with the kind of roundhouse punch he'd heard described in saloon fracases. It is not too late, he told himself, as the Comanche wobbled through the grass, his bare bottom flashing from behind the swinging skirt. But Gideon held his tongue and lay still until the man was out of sight.

If he had been led there so he might discover Suella's base nature, thus to turn his heart more steadfastly on Dorsey's purer love (though such reasoning gave the God of Scripture the nasty sense of humor of a practical joker), the example had its intended effect. Gideon pledged himself anew to Dorsey and climbed upon his wagon board to wait for Suella to wake and find him sitting there in silent judgment. He was not sure how strong his faith was in the God Colonel Luellen Powell-Hughes had envisioned for him. The colonel's was a Methodist vision that made Satan seem just as real and almost as powerful as God. Gideon's journeys had convinced him that the best proof of the Devil was how he managed to convince so many people he didn't exist. As if proving his persuasive powers, Satan soon had Gideon gazing with growing lust on Suella's naked form stretched boldly on her back. She had thrashed like someone possessed—maybe demons inhabited her body even now, resting for the next contest. Her copper arms lay above her roan hair. Her legs, spread apart on the boards of the wagonbed, twitched in her sleep. She shifted in her dreaming, and her snoring became a soft murmur matching the breeze in the grass all around them. When she shifted thus her upthrust breasts stood above the shadow of the wagon wall, two bare islands rosy with the heat of life and of her Indian blood, and he felt a growing response in his groin. Chief Bones had been rattled around so he lay back-to-back against her and would have faced away from her voluptuous shape, but his sunbright skull was twisted around backwards to afford him a good view of the loveliness against him. Gideon imagined the chief's turned skull an act of ghostly will.

Gideon reasoned that if halcyon sleep were indication of a guiltless conscience, then Suella had no concern for her soul. She lay naked beneath God's wide sky, the breeze fanning away insects and drying the sweat of lust until she did not look like someone possessed of the Devil. She looked as innocent and brand-new as any of God's angels. She slept so peacefully and long he was unable to maintain his self-righteous anger. When she woke and spied him, she held out her arms. "Shed off those damn homespuns and fuck with me while we have the sunset light." Suella's words were as husky as the rattle of the wind in the dry grass. What prevented him, truth be told, was not his minutes earlier pledge to Dorsey but his revulsion for the man who'd just lain with her. Unwilling to sully himself by going where the fat Comanche had so recently been, Gideon took his bedroll out into the grass.

Performs a Miracle

Early the next morning a Comanche girl came for him. "*Vamanos,*" she said.

Eye was shaking coffee grounds from their pot into the edge of their cookfire. The grounds fell in hissing clumps of steam. "She's talking Mexican. Sleeping Wolf wants you. I'll come along."

Against the morning chill Sleeping Wolf wore a thick fur robe and appeared as a bear with a human head. When he moved the robe swayed open to reveal a pouch bright yellow and blue, tied around his thigh against his dark and wrinkled scrotum, partly hidden by his thickly hanging penis. He squatted and the robe closed him in heavy folds. Gideon knelt opposite. Never before had he seen a face that, with no frown, no outward sign, so radiated anger. Sleeping Wolf's voice was barely louder than a whisper. "*Sua-su-makati. Muerto.*"

"He says the watch breathes no more. It is dead." Eye said.

Without taking his eyes from Sleeping Wolf's eyes, Gideon shook his head. He told Eye, "Tell him the watch spirit is in a deep sleep, but I can restore its beating heart. Tell him I must minister to the watch every day, each time after the sun passes overhead."

Eye spoke a mixture of Spanish and Comanche, and Sleeping Wolf nodded. Gideon held out his hand solemnly, and the Comanche put the silver watch in Gideon's palm. The metal was warm from Sleeping Wolf's hand, as if it held life. Gideon heard himself saying lines close to those in a Psalm (he didn't remember the number) favored by Colonel Luellen Powell-Hughes, one of David's prayers for a time of trial, "Remember me, how short my time is: Wherefore has thou made all men? For what vanity?" As he spoke thus Gideon stared up at the sun and twisted the watch stem back and forth, hiding this winding by passing his other hand over the watch. When the second hand twitched, he brought the instrument to his lips and exhaled, fogging the glass face. He said to Eye, "Tell Sleeping Wolf I have restored life to the Spirit of Time. Tell him the watch is a silver ember that can be stirred to flames by my breath alone."

As Eye spoke, Sleeping Wolf grabbed the watch and held it to his ear. He nodded in time to the ticking and hugged Gideon to him with his free hand. Life had been restored to the silver stone.

Each morning thereafter Gideon was received at Sleeping Wolf's tipi, where he repeated the ritual, spoke each time the prayer from the Psalms, and silently added his own request for the watch to start up again. One morning after he had restored the watch with much nodding and talk, Gideon was introduced to the Antelope visitor who had brought news of white captives in Two Talks' camp.

Imagine his emotions when he recognized the Antelope, fat and gap-toothed, as Suella's new paramour. This visitor, Three Ropes, confirmed the Antelope had three white females taken together from a couple of wagons eight or nine moons ago: an old woman who was a backwards one—loco, Pretty said—a girl-child now adopted into the band, and a skinny but strong dark-haired woman of marrying age. Most of the Comanches in the camp seemed to Gideon happy. He had been surprised how much they laughed, especially when they played with the children, which they did a good deal of the time. But this fat Antelope seemed sullen and insolent. He said something that sounded like "cow pistol your hate," and he and Sleeping Wolf both nodded. Sleeping Wolf tapped his forehead with his finger, repeating the word that now sounded like "crow pissed on your plate."

Sleeping Wolf again tapped his head with a finger. He said something in Comanche and grinned at Gideon.

"Smart, savvy," Pretty said. Three Ropes said Two Talks had a big brain to capture whites. He says they are more valuable to trade than buffalo furs.

Sleeping Wolf asked Three Ropes something, and the gap-toothed man solemnly shook his head. Pretty translated: "Two Talks won't come to Yellow Houses. He won't trade with Comancheros." Pretty shrugged. "For the guns-that-speak-without-resting he will trade with Perdido."

What dark comedy was God directing that this unsavory savage, Three Ropes, should be Gideon's source of information about Dorsey even as the fat Antelope leered at Suella, slapped her bottom as one slaps the rump of a favorite horse, spoke Comanche to her in an undisguised tone of lust. Suella seemed happy to have his attention and unfazed by his brazenness. When he leered, she leered back. When he slapped her rump, she stuck it out again. If she missed coupling with Gideon, she gave no sign. She was now with Three Ropes. When she said his name in Comanche, Pahiwiya, it sounded like "Pay Sty Why You." In Gideon's mind, he was Pig Sty. Suella brought Pig Sty plates of boiled meat, wooden bowls of wild onion soup, and pouches of dried plums she got from women in the Comanchero camp. She had never waited on Gideon so.

He would not sleep in the wagon that smelled of Suella's and Pig Sty's trysting. He lay in his blankets under the bright pricks of stars and on the itchy pricks of grassblades and reminded his stirring groin he was well shed of the heathen girl. When he wasn't suffering the pangs of lust or the sting of jealousy, he *was* glad. He told himself he was going through a ritual of purification before he completed his crusade for Dorsey, his one true love, whom he would soon free from the Devil's legions.

Charles Wesley: To Alhambra after His Shadow

Buffalo Skinners' Tale
(December 1865)

Nearly everything the Comanches owned came from the buffalo.
Their tipis, their clothes and moccasins, their reins and saddles, their
shields and arrow quivers were made of buffalo hide. They ate buffalo meat.
But Easterners craved the furs for lap robes in their carriages. According
to the Austin *Daily State Journal* most buffalo hunters killed thirty to
forty a day. Using a Sharps .50 caliber rifle one famous hunter,
Frank Holcomb, killed two hundred and fifty beasts a day.

—from *Gideon Jones' Journal*

Austin seemed to Charles Wesley the beginning of the West. Here, flat, black
farmland turned abruptly into the bleached-looking limestone hill country that
stretched westward for miles and miles. The trees suddenly grew shorter and more
wind-twisted. In Austin no one cared who your people were or where you came
from. This was the most "here-and-now" place Charles Wesley had ever been. He
had felt immediately at home, and he wondered if he had somehow inherited his
papa's romanticized yearnings for this place. He imbibed a smile, as Austin gents
called a drink of whisky, to his own health and to Papa's as well.

The bright December sunlight dimmed, and a long shadow slanted through
the saloon doors into the smoke-filled room. Charles Wesley looked up at three
men in buffalo robes too large to pass three at once through the doorway. One
hung back, but neither of the other two would step aside for his companion. They
squeezed at once through the entry, looking together like one of the fat, wooly
grizzly bears that roamed the Texas hill country. The third, smaller man followed
them to the bar. Their scent was worse than the stench of dead and rotting fish

at the Galveston wharf. "Air's one more category." The drunk lowered his voice. "A close match to a Meskin—a goddamn buffalo hunter—a ignorant, filthy, foul-mouth hide-skinner." The drunk ran his tongue around the lip of his empty glass, then staggered out, headed no doubt to another saloon.

The only bar girl not occupied with a customer left the room, ascending the stairs, her heels clicking wood. A man in a cow-handler's outfit, wide-brimmed hat and leather chaps, moved down the bar away from the buffalo hunters. The biggest of the three banged a gold piece on the bar as if he were driving in a nail. The bartender wiped his hands with a towel, taking his time. The buffalo hunter banged again, then he leaned over the bar and reached for a bottle of Squirrel. The barkeep stepped over and grabbed the bottle, his other hand out for the gold piece. The hunter pulled back the coin. "Glasses."

The barkeep stared long into the man's deepset, tiny eyes that stared back over a bent and scabbed nose. The barkeep picked up three glasses from a shelf, his thumb and fingers inside the glasses held together so their three openings made the shape of an ace of clubs. When the glasses clinked down, the gold piece dropped into the barkeep's hand. The tall buffalo hunter filled two of the glasses. He and his companion tossed back the whisky, and he refilled their glasses. The smallest man reached for the third glass, only to have his companion slap his hand away. Denied a drink, this third man sat at the table the saloon girl had vacated and dropped his chin to his chest. His hat hid his face.

"We need us some grub," the tall one said in a high-pitched child's voice.

"Steaks," the heavy, bearlike one said.

"Two dollars apiece," the barkeep said.

The bear reached into his layers of fur, pulled out another gold piece and slapped it onto the bar. He and his pal lowered themselves into chairs beside the third buffalo hunter, whose head still rested on his chest as if he were napping or praying. A tinker who had been buying drinks for a saloon girl got up and left. The tall buffalo hunter called the abandoned girl over. When she sat in the lap of the smallest man the other two broke out in snorting laughter spraying mouthfuls of whisky onto the dusty tabletop. The barkeep returned from the kitchen. Charles Wesley nodded for a refill. It was cold outside, and this was getting interesting. A group playing cards had gone back to the game, and two men with a saloon girl between them were whispering in her ears, but everyone else was quietly watching the three buffalo hunters.

"You don't stink bad as they do," the saloon girl told the small man who raised his head.

"Give our friend a kiss, girlie," the bear said.

"Give me something, first," said the saloon girl.

The bear produced a coin the girl dropped down between her ample bosoms. She pushed the small man's hat from his long, greasy hair and pressed her lips over his. The other two snorted and giggled and beat one another on the back. "Look here, girlie." His shoulders still shaking, the bear pulled off layers of fur down to the small man's dark wool shirt. This shirt the bear ripped open, popping buttons onto the floor, to expose a gray union suit, probably once white. He yanked the neck down to reveal a woman's pale breast.

"She's our *other* girlie," the tall one said, throwing his arms around the saloon girl's neck and pulling her to him. She turned her face, and he kissed the side of her nose. He laughed again and filled the third glass. The saloon girl guzzled the drink. The tall one cuffed the buffalo hunter he'd revealed to be a woman. He reached and squeezed her bared breast, her flesh pale between his dirty fingers. "We brung her out off the prairie. Up to Alhambra they tried to take her away. We slipped off with her, but they kept her babe. She's a huckleberry above a persimmon. Right fair knobs on her, boys." Some of the men in the saloon chuckled, encouraging the man. He put his mouth over the woman's breast, and she whimpered like a hurt puppy. He left a red curve beneath her nipple, his ruined teeth marking her skin. "Boys, I might give you a chaw or two of this here." He pulled on the woman's breast and drew a little more laughter.

One of the card players said, "You chew on her, but more important is will she chew on you?" The rest of the card players laughed with their buddy, and he said, "Better still, will she chew on me?"

"Watch here." The bear stood facing the female skinner and reached beneath his layers of fur. The rope-belted waist of his trousers dropped, revealing, fat-pitted, milk-white, and darkly hairy, the backs of his thighs. He held the woman's bared breasts, one hand on each, as a man takes both ends of a plow handle. "Now missy, *now*," he said. The woman reached one hand beneath the hanging fur layers between the pale legs. Her arm moved, bumping the table where she sat. With her other arm she gripped the bear's glass of whisky. The card players whooped and the cow-handler at the far end of the bar whinnied and giggled. The woman's hand moving steadily between his legs, his words quavering as leaves on a shaken tree, the man said, "Anyone know them folks up to Alhambra? They's a funny-talking big man, a woman piany player, and a one-armed fellow what hisses and frowns like a preacher."

A mouthful of bitters burned Charles Wesley's throat. A *one-armed fellow*—

he had not forgotten the face in the crowd of Johnnys in Nashville, a second's recognition and indecision, the face of a Reb with one arm. Charles Wesley's left arm had pained him over the last year, and he'd chalked it up to rheumatism, all those nights lying on hard, damp earth, leaning against mud battlements. He swallowed the rest of his drink, cleared his throat, and croaked, "A one-armed man, you say?"

"Who wants to know?" asked the tall one in his high voice.

Charles Wesley held up an unopened bottle of Squirrel, and when the tall man stood to take it the saloon girl got up and scooted away. The other woman still stroked her hand back and forth between the legs of the bear, whose lips pulled back exposing teeth that made a serrated line across his face similar to a jagged scar across his neck where someone—a woman, perhaps—had sliced his throat unsuccessfully. He squealed, more like a hog now than a bear, squeezed the woman's breasts so hard that when he released her flesh his fingers left red prints. The man bent over suddenly, bowing several times at the waist as a musician whose song is over. During his squeaking song everyone in the room leaned close, and when he collapsed into his chair a scattering of applause rose and quickly died. Her shirt and union suit still unbuttoned, the buffalo fur woman drained the bear's glass of whisky. Charles Wesley held tight to the bottle and nodded at her. She stared ahead as if she were asleep with her eyes open.

"Do you mind?" Charles Wesley nodded again at the woman.

"We don't," said the bear.

Charles Wesley pulled the woman's union suit up to cover her breast. The two skinners shrugged. Charles Wesley poured whisky into the glass the woman still held. She drank greedily, spilling whisky down her chin and onto her dirt-streaked neck. This close, the stench of the men was almost overwhelming—a mix of sweat, urine, suet, and something rank like decomposing flesh. He kept his glass close to his nose, the stinging scent of the whisky cutting the foul, curdling odors of the skinners.

It cost him two more bottles—the barkeep was out of Squirrel, and Charles Wesley had to buy a more expensive brand, McAllen's—to learn the one-armed man, the survivor of an Indian attack, was in the town of Alhambra, north of Fort Griffin out from the Mountain Pass mail station. The buffalo hunters had left Alhambra just weeks past. The tall skinner said the one-armed man was a preacher, but the bear said, no, he was a mustered out Reb. A war hero, the tall hunter said. He said he recollected the one-armed man's name *was* Speer. "Might be Alexander—Alex?"

The bear shook his head. He said he recalled the Reb's name. "Wasn't the other name Speer? Or was it Greer, maybe Deer? Could have been Fear," said the bear, whose name turned out to be Hines.

The tall one, Conger, said the one-armed man was called Reverend Spare.

Charles Wesley put his hand to his face. "Does he look like me?" He put his hands over his cheeks. "Without my beard."

Hines gave his head a shake and held out his empty glass.

"Can't rightly say," Conger said.

Hines gulped whisky. "Reckon he might, without that beard."

Conger squinted at Charles Wesley. "Your spitting image, now I shave you off in my thinking."

"Nope," said Hines. "He were a whole lot taller."

Charles Wesley stood up.

"Oh, well, now you're near tall as he was."

Charles Wesley turned to the woman who had guzzled three glasses of whisky. He'd get no confirmation from her—she was asleep, elbows on the table, empty glass held between her hands. Her low snoring was audible just above the drumming of Charles Wesley's heart.

From Austin to Alhambra

Early the next morning, his breath in the cold air making small clouds as if he were puffing a cigar, the liveryman hallooed Charles Wesley. "Getting a early start?" He led the dun gelding, a Mexican mustang, already saddled, into the yard beside the barn and tied him to the corral post.

"How much for the dun, outfit and all?" Charles Wesley's words made clouds, too. And so did the gelding's breath as it stood patiently by the post.

"The dun is my only Meskin saddle horse. He's in high demand."

"Then how have I been able to rent him any day I wanted?"

The liveryman, a skinny coot with a grizzled gray beard, didn't smile in the least when he said, "I been saving him special like for you."

"How much?"

"This is a fine Meskin saddle. Built solid."

The corral held several mustangs so skittish they didn't seem even green-broke. After two years in the cavalry Charles Wesley could ride just about any horse alive, but he had no experience breaking wild mustangs. And he had no time. He wanted to leave this morning for Alhambra to see if the one-armed man was his brother. In the barn was an American horse closer to the thoroughbreds he'd learned to ride in New York, but she'd bring a dear price and require grain. He wanted an animal used to Texas grass and Texas weather.

"I see you seen thet mare in the stall. Ain't she something? Brung out by one of Custer's officers. Expensive, but worth it every bit."

"Why did the officer sell her?"

"Can't say. I reckon she's too much hoss for him. He wasn't no rider such as yourself."

"How much?"

This time there was no hesitation.

"Fifty dollars, saddle and bridle extra."

Charles Wesley had expected the man to ask at least a hundred. There must be something wrong with her. But the old man had made a mistake going so low. Now Charles Wesley could argue a lower price for the dun gelding. If the livery-man asked higher, he'd have to admit there was a flaw in the mare. "Let me see your saddles." Charles Wesley would let the liveryman think he was considering the American mare. There wasn't much in tack. The double-rigged heavy Mexican saddle he had ridden on the dun every day he'd rented him was as good as the old man had, though Charles Wesley was still not used to a saddlehorn. "The saddle on the dun is the best of the lot, but that's not saying much."

"They's a saddlery down the street. Go buy new, if you want."

"If I wanted to pay for new. Not until I get used to these Western saddles, the horn in my way. The Mexican saddle won't let me forget, the horn's so big."

"Thirty dollars for the saddle. Five extra for a thick blanket."

"Eighty-five for the American mare, the blanket, and the Mexican saddle I rode before?"

The liveryman nodded and bent to uncinch the saddle from the dun.

Charles Wesley took out his wallet and removed several new-looking bills he'd gotten from the bank the day before. "Leave him be. I don't want the mare." What the dun mustang lacked in size and confirmation, it made up for in sturdiness and pluck.

When the liveryman saw the cash, he took seventy dollars for the dun, saddle, bridle, and blanket. Except for the liveryman's grin that said he had bested this Yankee, Charles Wesley didn't mind paying high—he had the money, he wanted the horse, and he was in a hurry.

The three buffalo hunters were passed out in the saloon and snoring as strongly as they smelled. Even if he could have waked them, Charles Wesley wasn't sure they would know how far they had come from Alhambra. They had mentioned Phantom Hill, and the clerk at the stage depot gave Charles Wesley fair directions. He took the stage road north. His third night on the road he slept in Burleson's Keystone Hotel, the stage stop. The proprietor tried to persuade Charles Wesley to bathe in mineral springs outside the town. Riding the next day in a cold drizzle, his left leg throbbing where the minié ball resided, he pictured himself in those warm restorative springs. He was four more nights getting to Brownwood, maybe seventy miles from Burleson. In a stone board-inghouse he waited out an all-day ice storm, not much warmer in his room than he would have been on the road. His horse had better lodgings. A barkeep in Brownwood claimed to have ridden all over the territory before the war, and he drew Charles Wesley a map. "I don't recollect Alhambry, but if it's near Willow Springs I can direct you there."

Charles Wesley checked the calendar the day he left Brownwood—the tenth of December, and he notched a stick of sweet-smelling cedar and carried it in his saddlebag to cut a mark for each day and judge his progress toward this Alhambra, if it even existed. In spite of the map, he took the wrong road from Brownwood and didn't discover his mistake until dark, when he reached the town of Comanche, named after the Indians because they raided the settlement so frequently. He couldn't imagine what attracted the Comanches. There was little to the village save a couple of sandstone buildings and a grove of enormous oak trees. He was able to buy beans and cornmeal but no coffee and no meat.

From Comanche, he had to ride cross-country through pioneer ranches abandoned during the war. The going was slow, and once he thought he passed the same board house twice. They all looked alike so he could only make another notch on his stick and press on. Except for Fort Griffin and a detachment at Phantom Hill, he would be easy prey out here for Comanches or Kiowas. He rode without seeing another traveler or passing any habited place until he counted fourteen cuts on his cedar stick: Christmas Eve. He was having his doubts about the bartender's map. A light snow had fallen on and off the past few days covering over what cow trails there were to follow. Deep twilight, and the snow spread over the prairie purple as a bruise. Charles Wesley's feet were so numb he wasn't sure they were in the stirrups. The reins were frozen around his fingers, which were as stiff as antlers. The only part of his body he could feel were the insides of his thighs where the horse's body warmed him. He peered through frozen eyelashes as through the icy needles of a pine tree and, in spite of the kerchief across his lower face, he felt no ears, no nose, no lips. Now and then he stuck his tongue against a slick spot on the kerchief where his breath had frozen.

In New York, Mama and Papa and the girls were getting ready for Christmas. Charles Wesley was tempted to break down and write home. Papa would not venture after him in the middle of winter. They'd have baked goose and wild rice and sweets of all kinds—maid Anna's rum omelettes, mince pie, brandied peaches, and plum pudding. Christmas morning Papa would make eggnog with rum, and the girls would drink champagne cider. Christmas Day would be spent before the parlor fire with the girls playing the piano. The little crystal glasses would be golden with Mama's nutty-tasting sherry while Papa would drink red ale and brown porter. They'd have a cold supper of smoked fish and afterwards coffee and a Madeira or old port. His Christmas fare this year would be corn cakes and beans, melted snow to drink. Unless he found a deserted ranch house or shack, he'd sleep in the snow.

Was he traipsing all over Texas after an apparition, the memory of a face that like as not had been a trick of his imagination? There were plenty of one-armed men in Texas now, veterans home from the carnage. Like as not Alexander had neither lost his arm nor come to Texas. Wouldn't the joke be on Charles Wesley if his twin were right now warm and cozy before the fire telling Papa about his exploits for the Rebs and lifting mugs of hot buttered rum and plates of pound cake with both his good arms and hands?

A Backwards Comanche

Charles Wesley, look up. Alexander's voice, an urgent whisper. Charles Wesley looked up. In the purple distance dark shapes rose along the horizon. He blinked his frozen eyes and looked again. The shapes moved yet stayed in place bent to the ground like animals drinking. Wind blew their tails—or long hair? Indians? He should stop, dismount, get out his Spencer rifle and approach on foot using the horse for cover. But if it cost him his life he was not moving his frozen hands and feet. The gelding had not caught the scent of horses or men. The horse walked steadily through the snow making sucking sounds each time he lifted a hoof. Charles Wesley got close before he saw the shapes were trees bent over by wind and the weight of snow. They looked like women bent in prayer, their long hair hanging down sorrowfully. The gelding stiffened. Bobbed his head, whinnied and balked, stepped sideways. Charles Wesley squeezed his knees, and the horse moved forward, then sideways. *Charles Wesley, go cautiously.* He kept the reins tight but gave the horse his head step by step. They circled the trees around to the west. What daylight was left now came from behind them. One of the trees moved. Not just swaying in the wind—it came toward him. Charles Wesley made his frozen arms pull the Spencer from its canvas case beneath his right leg. The tree, more like a bush, wide as it was tall, raised two limbs and laughed. Then it spoke.

"Tehano? Norteamericano? Numunuu?" The tree's voice was as loud and clear as a stage actor's. When Charles Wesley said nothing, the tree laughed again and said, "Hunter hide."

The tree came close, and Charles Wesley saw its leaves were fur and hair and feathers, all sticking out stiff as the quills of a porcupine. The broad shape was human, walking backwards, draped in the furs, and decorated with feathers of different colors. The voice sounded male, though Charles Wesley could not be sure. The upraised limbs were bare and dark. Ten fingers moved as if the figure were picking snowflakes from the sky like cotton from a field. "Hunter hide?" The still backwards-walking figure's resonant voice cut through the wind.

Charles Wesley held the nervous horse still and made a noise of greeting as well as he could, something like "yeah" and "hello" that came out "Yea-low."

The figure walked a backwards circle around Charles Wesley and his horse until it was walking backwards back toward the trees from which it had come. Now Charles Wesley could make out a wide, dark face within layers of fur. The face—Indian was all Charles Wesley could tell—turned toward the sky, and its big wedged nose sniffed loudly.

"Stink don't you, hunter hide no you're."

"What are you saying? I'm a weary traveler trying to find a place called Willow Springs near another place called Alhambra that I'm beginning to think doesn't exist."

The uncovered face gathered to itself the dying light, and when the wide lips curled up two rows of large yellow teeth glowed amidst the falling snow. "Destination your reached have you," the man said. "Springs Willow to welcome."

"Springs Willow? You mean Willow Springs?"

The man nodded. "Drink and food take—fire my by sit." With fur-covered hands he patted his fur-covered belly, just like the fat and furred character in the amusing poem by the Episcopal theologian Clement Clark Moore, the one Mama read them the past few Christmases, "A Visit from Saint Nicholas," patted his belly and had a pouch full of gifts.

All the way into the grove of frozen trees and alongside a mud-wallow glazed with ice the squat Indian walked backward, arms still upheld, his grin wide and unflinching. Closer to the frozen mud, oaks gave way to river willows. Charles Wesley dismounted. His feet numb, he walked the gelding. He held the Spencer in one hand, the barrel pointed skyward resting across the horse's neck, the reins in his other hand. Above the barely sour smell of his own frozen breath on his kerchief and the odor of wet wool and wet horse, he smelled roasting meat. He followed his nose and the backward-walking Indian to a low lean-to fashioned out of woven willow limbs illuminated by a fire. Five or six small skinned animals were leaned over the flames, skewered on sticks stuck into the ground. The meat popped and sizzled. The Indian backed around the fire and sank down on his haunches. He spread on the ground beside him an oval of fur. "Meat of plenty."

What kind of Indian was this? He spoke mixed-up English and walked backwards. Though he wondered if he were about to be murdered for a fool, Charles Wesley could not bring himself to so publicly mistrust the Indian's hospitality as to carry the rifle into the lean-to. He tied his horse to the side of the lean-to out of the wind. He saw no other horse. For now, he decided not to unsaddle. The fur on the ground was warm from the fire and soft after the hard saddle. As he sat, the dull throbbing of the minié ball in his leg eased up, and an aroma came to him more heavenly even than that of the roasting meat. Coffee. Apparently capable of knowing another's mind, the Indian took a tin pot from the edge of the fire and poured. When Charles Wesley took the cup his frozen fingertips sent up little wisps of steam. He drank, watching the Indian over the warm, dark circle of the cup into which he lowered his frozen nose. The Indian grinned as if he had this night invented coffee and were sharing it with only the second person to taste it in the history of mankind. And it tasted that new and wondrously good. The Indian's smile died down with the fire's flames.

"Sugar no." He shook his head.

"Doesn't matter. Nothing could taste better than this particular cup of coffee." Charles Wesley put out his hand. "I'm grateful. My name is Charles Wesley Speer."

The Indian cocked his head sideways. "Name my is Titsiwaii Paua Hakani." The Indian sipped his coffee. "Spear That Is Long How—English in means it."

"Spear That Is Long How—How Long—Spear That—oh, How Long Is That Spear?" Charles Wesley asked.

The Indian nodded. "Name my is that."

With a steel knife from his pouch How Long Is That Spear sawed off a slice of smoking meat, held the meat out hanging from the knife's point. Charles Wesley stole another look at the man's pouch and thought again of the bag full of gifts brought by Saint Nicholas. Papa would love hearing about this Christmas Eve, if Charles Wesley survived to recount it.

"Dog prairie."

"Prairie dog?" Charles Wesley asked. The meat was hot and slippery between his icy fingers. Papa's roast goose could not have tasted better. It was all Charles Wesley could do to slow his chewing enough to say, "Good, thanks." How Long Is That Spear chewed, too. Neither spoke again until three of the roasting prairie dogs were just bones picked clean.

"More want you?"

"No more meat. Some coffee, if you can spare it."

"Plenty have I, sure."

"Pig Latin," Charles Wesley said without thinking. The Indian cocked his head again. "The way you talk, reminds me of a secret way my brother and I talked when we were young."

"Backwards talk I. Backwards go I. Indian backwards am I."

"How did you learn it?"

"Backwards born."

"How did you learn English?"

"Quakers—school friends. East me sent missionaries."

The more he listened to How Long Is That Spear, the easier it was to understand him. Charles Wesley had to catch himself from imitating the reversed words. He didn't want to sound like he was making a joke of the backwards talk. How Long Is That Spear might be sensitive, was surely deeply crazy. After he had eaten and thawed out, Charles Wesley unsaddled the gelding. How Long Is That Spear led him to the far side of the wallow, where two paint horses were hobbled. The gelding pawed ice along the pool's edge, and How Long Is That Spear picked up a heavy log and broke a hole in the ice for the gelding to drink from. Then, from within the copious layers of furs he wore, the Indian withdrew a big fistful of hay. "The final straw," Charles Wesley amused himself by thinking. He could not imagine a man who looked like a poet's Saint Nicholas who carried hay for his reindeer—his horses—could not imagine such a jolly fellow murdering a traveler. Before the two of them crawled between buffalo furs to sleep, the Indian built up the fire and told Charles Wesley they were not far from Alhambra. "Tomorrow, there you take will I."

Charles Wesley's notions about Indians, how stealthy and quick they are, were tested the next morning. How Long Is That Spear crashed about in the lean-to and in the woods and by the time he was ready to head out for Alhambra—"Camp Bone," he called it—the sun was midway up the cold Christmas sky. · When the backwards Indian finally mounted the larger of his two spotted horses, he amazed Charles Wesley once more. He got on the horse backwards and rode leaned against the horse's neck. By this arrangement, so long as Charles Wesley remained somewhat behind the paint horse, they rode face-to-face.

"Was I where see to like I."

"But how do you see where you're headed?"

The Indian reached back and stroked the paint's head. "Eyes has horse."

The Citizens of Alhambra

Christmas morning was cold, but the snow and the howling wind had moved on. The sun melted the snow enough for grass to stick up in dark patches, making the barely rolling land look like the hide of a mangy dog. Mid-afternoon they rode into Alhambra. How Long Is That Spear pulled up before a two-story building of raw wood. A sign hanging off the porch advertised the ALHAMBRA SALOON, the sign complete with a hand-painted harem girl wearing a gold veil and dress. The Indian pointed to a small, plainly lettered sign across the way, LIVERY, where they went first. Behind the livery stable was a bizarre scene. Before the rough trunks of a grove of cottonwood trees were piled mounds of bones gleaming in the cold sun. Rocks and white-painted boards stuck up haphazardly inside a fenced area—a crude cemetery—and, beyond the cemetery, a wall tent swelled and sank slowly on a sudden gust of wind. The picture reminded Charles Wesley of a battlefield general's headquarters. No wonder this place was called Bone Camp, but did the name celebrate the exposed bones of buffaloes or the dirt-mounded bones of men?

Once the horses were stalled and their feed arranged, How Long Is That Spear walked—backward of course—toward the cemetery. Charles Wesley followed. As they drew near the graves a high-pitched voice said, "Long Pizzle." A plain-looking woman ran out of the tent wearing only a white shift. The woman threw her arms as far she could reach around How Long Is That Spear's considerable girth. As Charles Wesley drew close another woman emerged from the tent, wearing as little clothing as her companion. If the first woman was plain, this one was downright homely. Her hair might once have been blonde but was now an ashy brown streaked with gray. She rivaled How Long Is That Spear in size, but the Indian had better teeth. She, too, embraced the big Indian. Charles Wesley was about to take his leave when a long-haired boy darker than the women but not as dark as the Indian emerged, walking backwards from the tent.

"Brother, hello," said How Long Is That Spear.

"Brother, whisky bring you?" the other Indian asked.

Charles Wesley wondered if they were brothers, though they did not resemble one another. How Long Is That Spear embraced the younger Indian, lifting him off his feet. The two talked in the barking guttural Indian words. The big woman grabbed Charles Wesley's crotch.

"Come on, honey."

The other woman, younger and not so heavy, hurried over and held him by the elbow. "Choose me. My cot is warm."

How Long Is That Spear and the other Indian man disappeared, backwards, into the wall tent, their Indian talk audible but muffled.

"Have us both?" asked the younger woman. "For the price of one?"

"Thank you, no." Charles Wesley hurried back past the livery, where he read now a sign he had earlier missed:

ALHAMBRA LIVERY FEED & STABLE.
WILL TRADE AND RACE HORSES WITH ANY MAN.

There was no one else on the frozen mud street, but smoke rose from pipes above the saloon and from a log house across the street. From within, a piano played. Mozart, he realized, the Turkish Ronda Papa loved, from one of the sonatas—tum-tum-ta-dum. The full chord played and rolled like the drums. He followed the lively music into the Alhambra Saloon doing his best not to strut in a march step.

Going from bright sun into the dim room temporarily blinded him, and he stood just inside the door while his eyes adjusted. In the sudden darkness the piano notes filled him up like rapid heartbeats. The music stopped, and a lovely face surrounded by a halo of gray hair approached.

"Well, come on in." The woman's smile was natural and open, but he still took the precaution of introducing himself only as "Charles." She took his hand the way a man might, but her hand was smooth and cool. "I'm Mrs. Carter." Her hair, up in a silky-looking bun, was the gray of a grandmother and her face showed the lines of years of smiles, but her eyes were youthful and her skin was smooth. "This is baby James." She pointed to a cabinet behind the bar where an infant slept soundly in a drawer padded with blankets. She uncorked a bottle and said, "Christmas Greeting, Charles." She poured him a glass of brandy, looking not at the glass but into his eyes. "Rode in with the backwards Comanche, did you?"

"Why does he move, talk, and even ride backwards? He acts crazy."

"Not crazy, just different. Ole Long One got sent east by missionaries and came back too civilized for Texas. He couldn't go back to the Honey Eaters and live on a reservation so he camps in these parts where there are a few others like him."

"Like the boy who came out of the tent?"

"Oh, you've met Pahdaqua."

"Pahdaqua?"

"Means Wet and Tired. Comanches are usually named after something that happened to the warrior who is giving the name. Pahdaqua was named by a Comanche man who fell in the water down at Willow Springs. His pony took lame and he walked the horse miles back to the Indian camp."

"Is Wet and Tired a backwards Comanche, too?"

"The backwards Indians, don't you see, they tend to their own kind," said a deeper voice as a man entered the saloon through a door behind the bar. Charles looked into the unblinking eyes of a gray-haired man in a white shirt, both sleeves rolled up. "Manchip, here," the man said.

"Just because he talks pretty, don't believe everything he says." Mrs. Carter smiled again, topped off Charles Wesley's glass with the bottle of brandy, and went back to the piano.

Mr. Manchip grinned at her and poured and lifted a glass of the brandy. "Welcome to Alhambra, Welsh capital of Texas." He took a good pull on his drink. "Where'd you meet ole Long Thing?"

"Up by Willow Springs, last night. He shared his fire and food, led me here today."

Mr. Manchip laughed. "How Long Is That Spear—that what he told you his name is?" Charles Wesley nodded, and the man laughed more. "His name is damned near unpronounceable by a white tongue. It means 'How Long Is That Penis?'—seems he's suggesting it's as long as a spear." He lowered his voice. "The backward Comanches, among other things, prefer men. Over gals. To take to bed, I mean."

"The Indian boy at the tent?"

"Precisely. Long One went into the tent with Wet and Tired I assume?"

"That's why you asked where I'd met him?" Charles Wesley asked. Mr. Manchip straightened bottles on the shelf behind him though they were orderly to begin with. Charles Wesley spoke to the Welshman's broad back. "He didn't, we didn't. I mean, I didn't—"

"Of course you didn't, lad. That you would not is as clear as the sky out there. I meant no offense. Long Dick—a polite Welsh translation—is harmless enough. He's our Nancy-boy. A kindly soul. Rare out here, among savage or civilized. Have another drink and think no more of it."

Mrs. Carter rescued the moment by resuming her playing, the notes drifting like the motes of dust in the narrow shafts of light that slanted in from gun ports in three walls of the saloon. Plaintive, melancholy, the notes clung together and Charles Wesley recognized Franz Liszt, the popular Hungarian whose music Mama loved so, *Liebestraum*, the Love Dream.

Right now in a tent across the way the Comanche and the half-Comanche, two men, were—were doing whatever two backwards Indian men do—and the two whores, sad, weary-looking women—he wondered if they were also in the tent. Had he chosen to he might be there now, coupling and uncoupling like cars in a railyard, linking up for the same destination. He wondered if he would ever again listen to *Liebestraum* and not think of the tent—a circus tent, a carnival freak-show of unimagined possibilities.

"Mr. Manchip—" Charles Wesley's voice failed him, and he cleared his throat. "Mr. Manchip, I have come here on a faint hope following the only trail I had, a scant and unlikely scent left by a most unlikely, most untrustworthy pair of buffalo hunters named Conger and Hines, no friends of mine, I hasten to add." Mr. Manchip held his glass with its last drop of brandy halfway to his lips. Charles Wesley had his attention.

"These skinners, you say there were two?"

"There was also a woman with them. She was dressed all in furs. I first took her for a man."

"Damn me to Hell, Mrs. Carter. I let them carry her off."

Mrs. Carter did not pause her piano playing. "You can't take blame for underestimating the Devil." She shook her head and played on.

"They mentioned a man they had seen here," Charles Wesley said. "A man who has but one arm and is recuperating from injuries suffered at the hands of the Comanches. This man, these hide-hunters reported, goes by the name of Speer."

"If such a man had passed this way," Mr. Manchip asked, "what's your business with him?"

"My last name is Speer. Charles Wesley Speer. I seek my brother, my identical twin, Alexander Wesley Speer."

The piano notes ceased.

"Something does not reason true, here. Our Mr. Speer has but one arm, but I'm bloody sure on appearances he's no kin of yours."

"Only one way to know." Mrs. Carter rose from the piano and lifted the sleeping baby James from his cabinet drawer bed. With the baby on her shoulder she came around to Charles Wesley's side of the bar.

Mr. Manchip now brought his glass the rest of the way to his lips and emptied it. "Right you are, as usual, Mrs. Carter. Let's visit our patient."

Orten Trainer as Alexander Wesley Speer

Orten-as-Alexander had lain in bed in Mrs. Carter's boardinghouse so long he'd lost his sense of time passing. The swelling in his tongue had gone down with regular doses of DR. J. B. LEGGETT'S BORNEO BLOOD SYRUP AND HEART FORTIFIER. As his tongue had healed, so had his throat, though he could still not speak, might not ever. The more he healed the more difficult the masquerade became. Could he talk, he would given away his true identity. He still thought in his old name. When the time was right, he would confess his taking of Alexander's name, and he would credit that rebirth with his survival of the Nashville penitentiary.

Where he'd been scalped had healed completely, leaving him with a high forehead that looked like both eyebrows were arched in a permanent look of surprise. The wound under his arm was cantankerous. Every time he felt nearly decent, he moved his arm too far and pulled loose the stitches. Twice, Mr. Manchip sewed up the rent place again. The third time, Manchip decided enough stitches remained for the flesh to hold. By then the wound had begun to itch and sting. Mrs. Carter dabbed the itching flesh with a warm washrag then rubbed coal oil in. But at night he woke with such terrible itching he missed his left arm more than ever. He even got Alex's arm from its case to see if he could use it as a back scratcher to get up under the good arm, but the best he managed was to slap at the itch with the stiff fingers of the cut-off arm. Warm water helped mollify the itching. Ort-as-Alexander took more baths under Mrs. Carter's care than he'd had in all his life before.

Mrs. Carter was a saint. She washed what the Comanche knife had left of his red hair and trimmed it short in back so it didn't tickle his ailing neck, and she shaved him almost daily. The warm lather on his mending neck was next in pleasure only to having his side rubbed with coal oil. And she brought him food the likes of which he hadn't eaten since his stay in Richmond in his second-story room over Mrs. Worsham's place. Those meals Mrs. Worsham had cooked offered greater variety, but no one could outdo Mrs. Carter for rearranging the taste of buffalo meat. He was sure she had a carpetbag full of spices, and she knew all the ways there could be to roast, bake, fry, boil, steam, jerk, dry, and smoke buffalo meat. She brought it to him cut up in stews, hidden in breading, wrapped in bacon fat, between layers of dumplings and pie crust, beneath gravies of all colors and tastes. She entertained him with tales about musicians, how Mozart played for royalty when he was a child, how Beethoven was born with a clubfoot and hard of hearing. She brought him a stack of paper, a good quill pen, and a bottle of India's ink she put in the drawer of a table by his bed. Now he scratched messages on the sheets, the other sides of which were lined and covered with the marks of music—little flags with solid black or open white circles for feet. Mrs. Carter said these were songs she had tried to write.

She brought him books from Mr. Manchip's library: a hilarious one, *Don Quixote*, by a man named Miguel de Cervantes—a Mexican, Ort figured from the name. There was a true story written down by an Englishman, Defoe, about a girl named Moll Flanders. Part of it Mrs. Carter read out to him. This made him uneasy on account of his hidden identity, especially because she peered at him over the top of the page suspicious-like when she read the beginning, a confession:

> My true name is so well known in the records or registers at Newgate, and in the Old Bailey, and there are some things of such consequence still depending there, relating to my particular conduct, that it is not to be expected I should set my name or the account of my family to this work; perhaps after my death, it may be better known; at present it would not be proper, no, not though a general pardon should be issued, even without exceptions and reserve of persons or crimes.

When Mrs. Carter read this, his mind wandered off speculating on who could offer a pardon for the crimes of his conduct. Avoiding honest work all his life he had run away from the chores his father gave him, and he had run from battles all through the war until the fighting at Franklin, Tennessee. He had taken without permission the name of his only friend, then he'd slipped off and lied about which army he'd fought for. He'd lost count of the lives he'd invented for himself over the years—the different selves he'd been. For two wrong reasons he'd married Laura Etta—she had a farm he could sell, and she had a comely shape and presented herself boldly. Because of him, she and Dorsey were surely dead from unspeakable tortures. For some unfathomable reason the Indians spared him. On savage impulse they had let his life continue. The book he should read was the Holy Scriptures. Mrs. Carter had no Bible, but said she would ask around town for one. Mr. Manchip did not own a Bible either, and he doubted there was a book of Scriptures in Alhambra. One evening Mrs. Carter brought in a girl she introduced as Mattie, who was toting a big Bible.

With his eyebrows and shoulders he made a question.

"Mattie lives with another girl, across the way. Mattie had this Bible and said she'd be glad to share. You're welcome to keep it in your room as long as you like."

Ort-as-Alexander nodded. He did not recall seeing any girls in Alhambra when Gideon brought him in on the wagonbed. Of course, he had been feeling poorly, not looking closely about him. Mrs. Carter was her usual generous self when she introduced Mattie as a "girl." Middle-aged woman was more like it. She wore a dress of unbleached domestic the color of her pale skin. Thin and long-faced, she possessed a fragility, an ethereal quality the exact source of which he could not yet determine. Her brown hair was woven up on her head like a bird's nest, several strands escaping to hang in wisps against her cheeks.

"Mattie, this is Mr. Speer whom the Indians wounded." Mrs. Carter took from the table a tray that held his empty cup and bowl. "I'll leave you two to get acquainted."

Mattie smiled and handed him the Bible. He brought the heavy book close to his face, breathed leather and ink and a strong scent of lilac, a scent he had smelled only once before, on the doily on Laura Etta's dresser she sprinkled with the flower-smelling powder. "I don't read too good, Mr. Speer," Mattie said. "But I learnt most of that book by memory. I can tell some of it aloud so you don't wear out your eyes."

Ort-as-Alexander took pen and ink and wrote out, *Thank you. Maybe another time when I'm stronger.*

Mattie said, "I'll visit back directly."

Determined to find the penalty for the crimes he had done, Ort began with the beginning and read steadily through the Old Testament. He read blood aplenty and crimes and punishment enough to satisfy him that he might earn redemption for his conduct, perhaps a general pardon. Biblical heroes did not inspire him. They filled him with despair. When he read of Job's trials, Ort wept, but not for Job's steadfast loyalty to God—no, he wept for how far short he came of such strength. He would have given in to the first sufferings God let Satan send Job. It was the miserable failures Ort-as-Alexander found, especially when he got to the New Testament, that inspirited him. The disciple Peter became a likely model as depicted in both Matthew and Mark. If one as close to Christ as Peter, one of the twelve, could deny his Lord thrice in one night Ort reasoned there might be redemption for one as far as he was from Christ. Ort knew well the cry of the man who brings his demon-inhabited son and asks, as recorded in Mark's gospel, what Christ can do for his child. Jesus says, "If thou canst believe, all things are possible to him that believeth." The man's response became Ort's daily prayer: "Lord, I believe. Help thou mine unbelief."

It comforted Ort that nowhere in the Scriptures did he find a limit to the number of times a sinner might be forgiven. He had heard preachers say a sinner must be born again to find salvation, but he decided he would have to be born again and again and again. He might preach such a message, though his tongue would have to heal better for a crowd to hear him. He could write clear enough to share this message, but many who needed to be redeemed were unable to read. He might learn to use Indian hand talk. He had to be a disciple of this unconditional love. Though he was not on his knees he figured thoughts such as these were prayer—he could not keep them from God's all-hearing ears—so he hastened to think: *Don't get me wrong, Lord, I'm not praying to be given back speech, not making a deal for my old clever way of talking. If You want me to be dumb forever it's fine with me. My silver tongue has got me in enough trouble for one lifetime. Might be good if I can't talk smooth anymore.*

Under the care of Mrs. Carter, his wounds were mending. Under his own self-examination, his spiritual wounds were healing. He had gotten through Revelation and was starting over in the New Testament when the woman, Mattie, knocked on his door one evening.

"Mr. Speer, I come back like I promised." She wore the same muslin dress, or one just like it, and her hair was pinned up as before. So much the same did she look as when he first met her, he felt as if he were living that day over. She took the straight chair nearest the bed. "We can commence with the woman at the well."

He nodded. Weren't there several women at wells? He seemed to remember so.

"Jesus come to Jacob's well," Mattie said, leveling her eyes on him. "And the

Samaritan woman come to get a bucket of water and Jesus says to get him a dipper. She says why would Jesus, Him a Jew, ask her to fetch Him a drink? In them days Samaritans and Jews didn't have truck with one another. Kindly like the Yankees and Rebs only I don't think they had them a war. Or maybe like Comanches and Texicans or niggers and whites—one a them natural hatreds? That's when Jesus says if she knew who He was she'd ask Him for a dipper and He'd give her living waters." When Mattie told this part, her eyes shone and her voice got full of her breath. He had to listen closely to hear her. "So she says for Him to give her this water to quench her thirst permanent. Jesus sends her to get her husband, and she says she's got no husband. Jesus says she spoke true, and He tells her how she's had five husbands and was right then housed up with a man she wasn't married to." The Bible was opened on Mattie's spread skirt, and she gripped each side with a fist. She had not read a word. He looked where the lamp fell on the page and saw she was in the Psalms. "This here's my favorite part." Mattie closed her eyes. "The woman knew He was the Savior and she said, 'You told me all the things I ever done.'" Mattie put the Bible in Ort's lap. "I wanted to read you this part first because I've been a strumpet like the woman at the well. I've known lots of men not my husband." He nodded and smiled to show he understood, but she didn't understand. "I mean I have made my way doing bad."

He reached for the pen and paper and wrote, "Me too."

Mattie started coming to his room most every night. Sometimes she read to him in a halting childlike way, but, mostly, she talked and he listened, or they just sat together quiet. Sometimes he read to himself, and she watched him. Mattie took over from Mrs. Carter bringing him his meals and bathing the wound under his arm. She sang to him when he had trouble getting to sleep. Having bared her soul to him, Mattie became the voice of his conscience, someone he couldn't deceive. His bodily recuperation had become a spiritual retreat, an occasion for meditation leaving him open to influence.

Such was his state of mind on Christmas night. He and Mattie had eaten the midday meal with Mr. Manchip and Mrs. Carter at the saloon and had returned in the late afternoon to rest. Mattie went to the Alhambra and brought back a light supper for Ort-as-Alexander. She sang him to sleep with Christmas hymns. He lay sleeping and waking, in and out of dreams as he had been for weeks of nights. Mattie slept quietly in the chair beside him. Mrs. Carter appeared in the doorway holding a lighted lamp. It was well into the night, and he wondered how close it was to morning and listened for the rooster that the other whore, Lizzie, kept with some hens for eggs at the whores' tent where Mattie used to live and sometimes still slept. In the flame light of the oil lamp, Mrs. Carter's face shone golden. She looked—there was no other way to say it—like an angel.

"Alexander Wesley Speer?" Her voice rang as if she were a lawyer announcing Orten Trainer's illegal name in a court of law. Behind her came the heavy tread of Mr. Manchip and the steps of another. Mattie's eyes opened wide. From inside the light Mrs. Carter gave off, stepped a vision. Before Ort-the-imposter stood Alexander, back from the grave, his arm returned to him.

Ort stood and the Bible fell from his lap. He reached to feel Alex's left arm, and it flexed firm and warm. The cut-off arm in its hide case still leaned against the wall. Wherever he'd been in heavenly Limbo, Alex had grown a beard. Orten put his hand over Alex's beard—to picture clear the face unshaved as he had it in his memory.

"What is it, man? You look as if you've seen a ghost," Mr. Manchip said.

God was letting Satan test him like Job. How else explain Alex back from the grave?

"Do you know my brother?" the bearded Alex asked, pulling his arm free. "Where'd you get his name?" he asked, his voice rising.

"Is this your brother?" Mrs. Carter asked the imposter. Alex-with-a-beard looked up. "He's not Alexander," he said in a voice just a note deeper than the voice that Orten would never forget of his dead comrade.

You're not Alex, Ort thought.

"Alexander is my twin brother. My identical twin," the bearded Alex said.

Alex had never mentioned an identical twin. Never mentioned any brothers or sisters. Orten sank down on the bed and closed his eyes. *Alex reached for his arm. A shot rang and echoed.* Orten shook his head. He wished he could change so many things.

Alexander-with-a-beard came close. "Why do you use my brother's name?"

Ort wrote on the back of Mrs. Carter's music: *Never. Unless it was fever talking.*

"You've answered to 'Alexander' clear-headed many a time," Mrs. Carter said.

He shook his head and pointed to the paper.

Mr. Manchip stepped into the light. "Mr. Speer, when Gideon Jones brought you to us he called you Alexander Speer, stepfather of the girl, Dorsey, he sought among the Comanches."

Ort shook his head. The pen scratching the paper was somehow louder so late at night: *I do not know the man.* Lizzie's rooster crowed the day, the same rooster that woke Orten every morning. He looked to the window, the sash bars holding the four panes making a dark cross in a square of pale light. Alex's bearded ghost and Mr. Manchip and Mrs. Carter all stood as still as statues. Orten reached out, perhaps to touch one of them, but the touch he found was Mattie's warm hand. He held her fingers to his throat and began to speak. The noises he made burned in his throat but hurt even more in his heart.

Communes with His Past and Envisions His Future

Charles Wesley had come in vain. The man got up, dropping a Bible from his lap, and lurched forward, eyes and mouth open wide, a dark stump of a tongue pumping up and down, the end pink and stretched tight much the same as the stump of the man's left shoulder, where skin was drawn over the wound and sewn in a circle like the hide over a drum. Both skin flaps were, above all else, vacant-looking, like sheets of blank paper. The man's mouth moved as a fish's mouth after air, and a kind of mewling escaped his throat. A dark-haired woman who sat beside the mute's bed sank to her knees and held her hand pressed beneath his moving chin. Her fingers moved up and down his neck as one feels the frets of a stringed instrument. She held her eyes closed and, shaking her head, held the first finger of her free hand against her pursed lips, begging for quiet. Like a telegraph operator listening to the jumping key and jotting down dots and dashes, listening in Morse code, she transmogrified into words the vibrations her fingertips received from the mute's neck. The pace and volume of the man's lallations increased, and the woman seemed seized in a trance. She spoke louder, her body stiff and her words clear but distant, as if she were a sorceress or medium in communication with spirits from the afterlife, her lips moving with the speech of the dead.

Mr. Manchip, Mrs. Carter, and Charles Wesley stood like communicants at a séance. Rapt supplicants, they leaned close to the talking woman and the gurgling wordless man to hear the transmutation of sounds into speech—the testimony of this fiery-haired, one-armed witness. Through the lips of the entranced woman, Orten Trainer confessed that his brutalization at the hands of the Indians had led him to a fervent experience of religious conversion. If one believed Orten's story, Alexander Speer more than Comanches had brought about the change. A coward and a ne'er-do-well who shirked responsibility and trust all his life (his evasions having often cost him energy and intelligence in excess of the demands of honest labor), Orten had astounded himself by his heroism in the Confederate Army in the battle of Franklin, Tennessee. He was convinced his bravery was in response to the constant allegiance of Alex Speer, an innocent of whom Orten had taken advantage financially and personally. Orten rested his eyes on Charles Wesley, and the girl said, "I hope your brother looks down from Heaven and forgives me." Orten related Alexander's accidental death at the hands of a Yankee lieutenant and Orten's subsequent masquerading his way into marriage and onto a wagon train that never reached its destination. Here he recounted the Comanche attack and the loss of his silver tongue. Since the theophany he had experienced (Orten's word as translated by his amanuensis, Mattie, late of Alhambra's tent of prostitution)—since the theophany, in which the Comanches had been God's instruments—since the loss of the better part of his tongue he'd done more listening than talking, more reading than scheming. His library contained but one book, the Holy Scriptures. Orten opened the Bible to the Book of Matthew and pointed with a trembling, hairy finger to the words of Christ Himself:

—if thy right eye offend thee, pluck it out, and cast it from thee: for it is profitable for thee that one of thy members should perish, and not that thy whole body should be cast into hell.

"What more than my tongue," Mattie voice spoke, "had offended me with its deceitful persuasions? I wrestled with Alex's indefatigable amity just as Jacob wrestled all night with an angel. Jacob demanded a blessing from his wounding, and the angel gave him a new name: Israel, Prince of God." Just so, Orten took Alex's name. At the time he did so for self-protection. The Comanche attack he compared to the blinding light that announced God's appearance to Paul on the road to Damascus. Paul was told to go unto the city to be told what he was to do, just as Orten had been brought to Alhambra where he had received from God a commission to preach Christ's grace first revealed to Orten through his namesake, Alexander Speer. "Alex never mentioned a brother. Nor sisters, either," Mattie said for Orten.

Charles Wesley was not surprised his twin had not claimed him. Alexander had long fled their connection. "How can a man with half-a-tongue be a preacher?" Charles Wesley asked.

"Best kind," Mr. Manchip said without a trace of irony.

"Mattie will be my tongue," Mattie translated. "I *am* his tongue." She blinked tears.

Having delivered his first sermon, Orten Trainer rose, clearly exhausted, and crossed the room to retrieve from where it leaned against the wall a long leather case he handed to Charles Wesley, who wondered why this strange man was giving him a rifle.

"I carry part of him with me always," Mattie said, translating Ort's gagging speech.

It distressed Charles Wesley to write Mama and Papa that Alexander was dead. Papa would be proud Alexander had fought for the Texan Cavalry, dismounted. In his letter Charles Wesley suggested they consider a journey to Texas to visit Alexander's grave and to see their other son, more mature he hoped than when he left home. *Texas is a wondrous place,* he wrote, *as Papa always said. Though the wonders are not those Papa anticipated.* Charles Wesley pondered his own loss, all the losses and gains since the war had begun, a ledger he could not tally. He did not think his left arm would pain him anymore. It was a gain that measured a loss.

He gave Mrs. Carter the envelope in which he sealed his letter, and she propped it up behind the bar to wait for a traveler who might post it to pass through Alhambra headed to Weatherford, or Fort Worth, or down to Waco.

Blood Arrow: Antelope Daughter, Antelope Bride

Rescues Spitting Grasshopper
(The Moon of Recently Green Leaves 1866)

The Comanchero Brown Fred was Mexican, but he'd lived for a time
with some Comanches called the Burnt Meat band. I recorded some funny tales
Brown Fred told about these Indians: "A Burnt Meat warrior once saw a white
trapper in a canoe. First boat he ever saw. He thought the boat was the trapper's
legs, so he called him 'one-who-can-sit-on-rivers.' The same warrior brought
some tin cups and a five-shooter he had stole, and he put them outside his tipi.
I asked him why he put them on the ground, and he said he was going
to wait for them cups to grow to kettles, the pistol to a rifle."

—from *Gideon Jones' Journal*

"Dorsey, Blood Arrow, *hilfe*," said Yellow Rudolph. Dorsey hurried toward the
sound of his voice. "*Mir bitte helfen.*" He stood in the middle of the creek where
water rushed white and loud around big rocks. On his back rode Spitting Grasshopper and Looks Down, the young sons of Smoke Hair and of River Walker.
Spitting Grasshopper held on with one arm. Looks Down had a grim expression
on his face. "*Mein* foot is caught. I cannot move," Yellow Rudolph said.
Spitting Grasshopper teetered, and Looks Down pitched forward, then climbed
back onto the German's bony shoulders.

"*Bitte bringen Sie mir ein* rope," Yellow Rudolph said. "We have to get the
children safe to shore. Then I can work loose my foot."

Dorsey hurried back to Crooked Nose's tipi and grabbed a horsehair rope.
She wrapped one end around a cottonwood and threw the other to Yellow
Rudolph who grabbed the line and held it tight. He bent and lowered Looks
Down to the rope. The boy pulled himself hand over hand to the bank, where

Dorsey caught him. Spitting Grasshopper dropped into the strong current, but he missed the rope.

Without a word, Dorsey plunged in after the child. The underwater roar was organ music back in church in Indiana. All was murky green with angled planes of brown and brightness. Her legs beneath the skirt of the sodden heavy deerskin dress could not kick hard enough. She worked the dress over her head and swam out from under it. She stretched her toes for the bottom hoping for purchase to propel herself forward, but the water was too deep. Naked, she sliced through the water downstream toward Spitting Grasshopper. She stroked and stroked and kicked and kicked. She reached for the boy, but her hand bumped him away. She lunged, and her fingers found wet hair. Spitting Grasshopper's little body was as cold as the melted snow water. She swam against the current, struggling with the child's weight. She heard calls from shore and just as she got flat rocks underfoot the boy's father, Smoke Hair, met her in the shallow water. On the shore Her Blanket Is Beautiful, the boy's mother, covered her face with her hands, then raised both hands to the sky, then covered her face again. River Walker came carrying Looks Down safe in his arms. Beside him came Yellow Rudolph, still dragging the wet rope. Ten Buffalo waited with the medicine bag. He squeezed Spitting Grasshopper around the middle, and the boy spat water. Ten Buffalo rolled the boy onto his belly and beat with his hand on the boy's back as on a drum. With his other hand, the shaman stroked the boy's neck with a blessed eagle feather, that the great bird's spirit might beat its wings and bring back breath.

Water dripped from Dorsey's hair, darkening the dirt where she stood. She realized she was naked. Numunuu faces the color of clay, faces innocent yet wise, did not look on her nakedness but on the child struggling for life. Hands gripped other hands, the members of the band locked in love for the boy who barked with hiccoughs, his body twitching, Numunuu faces opening with light, eyes widening with relief, lips spreading into smiles. *I'm naked and nobody cares, least of all me*, she thought. *Dorsey would be embarrassed, Blood Arrow is not.* Two Talks appeared at her side and touched her elbow. Her face shone in each of his eyes. Warmth settled over her—a buffalo robe wrapping her and with it the arms of Smoke Hair.

"Very, very happy," Smoke Hair said.

Her Blanket Is Beautiful had their boy in her arms. She stroked dirt from his cheek, wiped away saliva and phlegm. She kissed his head and his ears and his neck and his nose. Then she held out her son to Dorsey. *"Tubitsi hait,"* she said.

Dorsey looked at Yellow Rudolph, who grinned and said, "It means 'real friend.'"

That afternoon Her Blanket Is Beautiful came to the tipi of Crooked Nose with a dress of the softest deerhide, hemmed with rawhide stitching dyed red, and sewn all over with red and black beads. "I cannot imagine a celebration grand enough for such a dress," Dorsey said.

"How about marriage?" Yellow Rudolph said. "Two Talks looks on you as he once looked on Dressing Her Head."

"I haven't noticed." But she had noticed. She felt a strong wind through her heart blowing away any lingering feelings she had for Gideon. For months she had wanted him to rescue her, but now she felt a kind of dread of his coming. He was a stranger, a boy-not-yet-a-warrior whom she had known when she was not-yet-a-woman. He'd never been her beau. He'd been the first likely boy to come along—the only unmarried boy her age on the wagon train. That was before she learned the Western plains would feel so familiar, like home. That was before she could make Numunuu arrows, before she knew Blood Arrow lived inside her.

"Fraülein, you no longer hate the People with your eyes."

"I feel like I've been here a long time. Sometimes at night I lie on my buffalo fur and smell all the Indian smells of fur and smoke and wild onion soup, and I try to recall just one entire day, from sunup to sundown, when we were in the wagons, and I can't. I can't even hold still in my memory the faces or voices of white people I knew before. I try to see their faces and I almost can, and then Two Talks' face or your voice gets in the way. Part of me thinks I should want to go back, but a new part of me asks why. I want to stay close to Mama and to Other Small One, who used to be little Lucy. And close to you, too."

"And to Two Talks." Yellow Rudolph winked at her. Then he touched her arm. "But what of Low Forehead and Shield Painter and the others who violate *Sie* Mutter?"

"I can't forgive them. But, now, the Antelope accept Mama. If she went back to live with whites, she'd never survive the gossip."

"This life may be no worse than what *Sie* Mutter would have found with her new husband in the Northwest Territories."

True Friend

Dorsey's first occasion to wear the beautiful ceremonial dress bestowed by Her Blanket Is Beautiful was not marriage, but adoption. Smoke Hair's first wife, Little Turtle, had borne him no children so he had taken Her Blanket Is Beautiful as wife number two, and she brought him Spitting Grasshopper. He loved his son with the love of a father who had feared he would never be a father. Blood Arrow had risked her life to return the boy to him. After the near drowning, Smoke Hair came to Crooked Nose's tipi and smoked the long, straight pipe. He had a son. Now Smoke Hair longed for a daughter, an older sister to instruct the boy in important ways.

"*Tokwetikati*," Crooked Nose told Dorsey. Morning Star acted happy. Only Persimmon seemed less than joyful, but she was always sullen. When Dorsey woke the next morning, a new beaded bag sat by her head. Inside, she found her personal possessions: her deerskin dress someone had pulled from the river and dried and cleaned, her bone comb and a scraping knife Morning Star had given her, two buzzard feathers Yellow Rudolph had given her for fletching arrows, the bone cup she had made herself, and Binga Duerfeldt's book: *Josh Billings, His Sayings* by Henry Wheeler Shaw. Her new red and black beaded dress was folded beside the new bag, and there, too, were new moccasins that fit perfectly. She thought of the Cinderella tale Mama had told her long ago. Morning Star came in and pointed to the moccasins.

"*Tokwetikati?*" Morning Star said. "I made them for you to walk home in."

"*Tibitzi tokwetikati*," Dorsey said. What did she mean, walk home? Dust and dung smell burned her nose. Outside, horses' hooves stamped and dug at the earth. It sounded like many horses. Had Gideon persisted against her will? Dorsey's heart beat fast. Had he brought the army? *They can't make me leave*, she thought. She put on the beautiful dress, ran her hand through her hair. When she faced the army she wanted to look like a Numunuu woman. When she was little she had wished for long golden hair like Cinderella in the tale her mama told her. All along, her black hair had known her destiny.

When she stepped out of the tipi into the bright spring morning there was no *taivo* army, only a herd of paint ponies nodding and snorting and dancing sideways in the dust. There were Smoke Hair and Her Blanket Is Beautiful and Little Turtle and Spitting Grasshopper—all dressed in ceremonial finery. Wearing leggings fastened with Mexican silver, Smoke Hair carried a quarter of buffalo meat. Her Blanket Is Beautiful and Little Turtle wore fringed buckskin dresses. Smoke Hair handed to Crooked Nose a vermillion horsehair lead connected to the halter of the first horse. Smoke Hair was the finest tracker in the band and had the most horses. Lest anyone doubt how highly he valued his son, or his confidence he could rebuild his herd, he had brought to the tipi all one-hundred-forty of his horses. Crooked Nose's son, Two Talks, took the horsehair lead. Crooked Nose gave Morning Star the quarter of meat. She handed it to Persimmon, who gave

Dorsey a nasty look. Men and women alike gathered before the tipi to watch.

Crooked Nose spoke: "To the Antelope band is added this one, Puhipka, who henceforth walks the path of Our People and dwells in the lodge of her father, Smoke Hair, who this day has a beautiful new daughter."

Now it all finally made sense. She was being made Numunuu. Dorsey Murphy was now Blood Arrow, one of Our People. Smoke Hair and Her Blanket Is Beautiful were adopting her. Spitting Grasshopper ran forward dressed in rabbit furs. He carried one last gift. As her fingers closed on the cool, hard disc, Dorsey remembered it. A large mother-of-pearl button from one of Mary Thurston's Sunday go-to-church dresses. Mary had lifted quilts and aprons from her trunk to show Dorsey the dress, a calico that danced in the breeze like the black-and-white-spotted horses now stepping from one leg to another. She squeezed the button and it left a red ring on her skin. The button, an ancient artifact from long-ago days, a relic from another time. A hide thong ran through one of the buttonholes. Dorsey tied it around her neck, and as if it had always been a part of her, the button rested in the soft place where her collarbone made a "V."

Spitting Grasshopper called her "older sister" and took her hand. Little Turtle took the new bag and carried it. Her Blanket Is Beautiful embraced Blood Arrow. Finally, Smoke Hair held her by the shoulders and said, "My beautiful, new daughter, Puhipka, brave woman of Our People, our lodge is your lodge."

Now Dorsey was Puhipka, daughter of Smoke Hair, and she was treated as the favored child of a rich man. Little Turtle built a brush arbor for Blood Arrow's *taivo* mama and the two old crones who went about with her. The women had wandered the camp for so long they weren't happy sleeping in the willow lodge. Dorsey could put to rest her fears for Laura Etta. So long as Smoke Hair lived, Laura Etta—whom Her Blanket Is Beautiful had started calling Looks Far Away—would be provided for. Persimmon had looked for ways to make Dorsey miserable, but Her Blanket Is Beautiful and Little Turtle looked for ways to make Blood Arrow happy. Her Blanket Is Beautiful made her pet name for Blood Arrow, Dawn. Yellow Rudolph said that was because Her Blanket Is Beautiful said her new daughter brought light and warmth into their lodge ahead of Father Sun. Remembering her *taivo* mama, Laura Etta, Blood Arrow touched the mother-of-pearl button resting beneath her neck. She asked Yellow Rudolph how to say "Other Mother" and then she repeated after him the pet name she chose for Her Blanket Is Beautiful: Other Mother.

🏵

Blood Arrow tried reading Josh Billings, His Sayings again, but the English words on the page mixed with Numunuu words in her mind and the things Josh Billings said not only were no longer funny, they didn't make much sense to her.

Yellow Rudolph told her Gideon had been spotted tacking his wagon back and forth across the plains as a sailor veers across a sea. The Comanches kept their distance from the skeleton in his wagon. They reported Gideon acted crazy as a backwards one. He had even been seen with one of the black white-men wandering after dark out on the Llano Estacado, moonlight making his eyes as big as the eyes of the cannibal owl that sweeps down at night to eat Our People. Blood Arrow no longer clearly remembered the *taivo* Gideon's face. She confused his look with the face of her new brother, Spitting Grasshopper.

A Marriage Proposal

One day Blood Arrow was playing with Spitting Grasshopper in the green grass when he gave her a solemn look and said, "Two Talks called me 'younger brother.'" A few sleeps later, she returned from bathing in the river and a herd of horses stood stamping and neighing before the tipi of Smoke Hair. The horses made her heart beat fast. She entered the tipi and Her Blanket Is Beautiful hugged her.

"Other Mother," Blood Arrow said, "Why do tears stain your cheeks?"

"My more-than-two tears show joy that my daughter will be the wife of such a mighty warrior and my more-than-two tears show sadness that my daughter dwelt in our tipi for so few sleeps."

Smoke Hair entered the tipi, and Her Blanket Is Beautiful and Little Turtle left so Blood Arrow could speak in private about the marriage offer. Smoke Hair could read the faintest sign. If he recognized the curve of a hoof where other men saw only dust, if he espied in a world of grass one broken blade where a buffalo or a deer or a horse or a man had trod, if he saw in dung or ashes or scraped rock the nature of a beast or a man who had passed, couldn't he tell from her face Blood Arrow's thoughts? Having no thoughts to hide, she opened her face so Smoke Hair might easily read her heart and mind. "All of these fine horses but one knew their way to our tipi," he said. "Two Talks has returned to my lodge every horse I gave for you, my new and only daughter. He added one beautiful mare, a strong pinto." Smoke Hair's smile revealed a dark space where some Tonkawa or Apache or Texan had knocked out two of his teeth. "This is the most ponies ever paid for a wife in my memory of the Antelope band. Two Talks' father and grandfather are respected among Numunuu—even beyond this band—for their bravery, *puha*, and wealth. I would choose Two Talks over all warriors to be my son-in-law, but the choice is not mine, it is yours. If you make him a rejected one you will put smiles on the faces of more than two young women who would offer themselves in your place."

"Smoke Hair will ride the pinto," Blood Arrow said. "I have held Two Talks in my *pihi* for many moons. Soon my *pihi* will beat with his. I will go and put the horse into Smoke Hair's herd."

"This pinto will become my favorite *puku*, and each time I ride my personal horse I will remember my daughter Blood Arrow," Smoke Hair said.

The camp seemed empty because everyone was staying out of sight. It would be bad manners to make Blood Arrow accept or reject a marriage offer in front of others. But many eyes peeped from inside lodges and from behind cotton-wood trees. The mare's coat shone in the sun. Two Talks must have washed her many times. The bright-eyed pony pulled on the lead dancing backwards and whinnying before she nodded and followed Blood Arrow. Smoke Hair, Spitting Grasshopper, and Sure Enough Hungry would bring the rest of the herd after Blood Arrow's symbolic public acceptance of Two Talks' proposal. Watchers had probably already told Two Talks that Blood Arrow had accepted. Two Talks, his father Crooked Nose, and Smoke Hair would work out the rest of the trade and seal with the bone pipe the marriage agreement. Then Blood Arrow would pack her beaded bag and put on her beautiful dress and walk to a new tipi Morning Star and Persimmon had built. Blood Arrow grinned at the thought of Persimmon having to sew hides for a tipi for Blood Arrow. Now they were to be sisters-in-law.

When Blood Arrow released her, the pinto mare did not run into Smoke Hair's herd. She twitched her ears and stared with knowing eyes. Blood Arrow's adoption had been part of a larger scheme. Two Talks could not have married her unless she was Numunuu. If Crooked Nose and Morning Star had adopted her she would have been Two Talks' sister, and he could not have left horses at his father's tipi—that would be like giving and taking from yourself. There was much she had to learn, but she knew her birth origins—her blood and the color of her skin—did not matter. Only her heart mattered. In her heart she was the Numunuu woman Blood Arrow.

Numunuu Wedding

Blood Arrow was in the middle of a menstrual period when Two Talks left the horses at Smoke Hair's tipi, so the wedding had to be delayed until she was through her cycle. Yellow Rudolph had told her what a strong taboo menstrual blood was. A wife left her husband's tipi and returned to the lodge of her family during each monthly period. When Blood Arrow was over this time of bleeding, Her Blanket Is Beautiful and Little Turtle took her to the river and helped her bathe. Her Blanket Is Beautiful asked if Blood Arrow had yet bled from the opening of her woman's path. Had she yet been lanced in the small shield she carried between her thighs?

Blood Arrow said, "Yes, on the farm after riding a pony."

When Dorsey had bled from riding bareback, Laura Etta had fussed at her. A taivo man wanted blood in his marriage bed. A Numunuu warrior wanted only the blood of enemies on his hands. Other Numunuu women teased Blood Arrow because she washed so often, but each of them washed after a monthly cycle before she returned to her husband's tipi.

Her Blanket Is Beautiful rubbed sheep's oil into her daughter's skin, and Little Turtle gave her sweet-smelling leaves and berries ground into a damp mash. She wiped the scent into her creases and crevices—behind her ears, under her arms, between her thighs, and between each toe. She put on the soft, beaded doeskin dress, and her sister painted her ears and forehead with vermillion, darkened the lids of her eyes with berry stain, and brightened her cheeks with orange rouge. Little Turtle painted ocher stars pierced by arrows on Blood Arrow's cheeks and forehead. Finally, she painted vermillion and ocher rings around Blood Arrow's pale breasts. The willow brush weighted with paint sent goosebumps down her arms. Morning Star sent a necklace of Comanchero silver pieces, and Her Blanket Is Beautiful offered a necklace of bleached white shells. Beneath the silver and the shells Blood Arrow wore the mother-of-pearl button-amulet Spitting Grasshopper had given her.

Since she had become the daughter of Smoke Hair, she had gained some nice new things: a red fox fur hat to keep her ears warm when the brown grass time came, an iron skillet from the cabin of a *taivo* settler, a good blade for scraping hides, a curved bone sewing needle with sewing sinews, a pouch of blue beads Smoke Hair had traded away from a man in the Those Who Stay Downstream band.

Smoke Hair tracked and killed a doe to roast to celebrate his daughter's marriage. While family and friends ate and told tales and sang songs, Blood Arrow, in all her finery, carried her bags to the new tipi. Late afternoon sun on the tipi's dirt floor, packed with warm buffalo blood to harden and waterproof it, was deep purple. She waited until her husband's shadow fell upon that purple earth. She looked up as he stepped inside. He had bunched and tied his hair into long queues shiny with grease that smelled like oranges. He'd tied white shells, silver buttons, and strips of blue cloth into his hair. The part along the center of his head he'd painted ocher and tied there a yellow scalp lock. He had painted one side of his face blue and the other side white as a cloud. He had plucked out his facial hairs and eyebrows. "Puhipka," he said deep in his throat. "*Kima habiki.*"

Blood Arrow translated, "Blood Arrow. Come. Come and lie down."

Vermillion paint on her husband's lips was a remembered taste Blood Arrow could not quite name and powdery-soft as flour. His teeth were stained red from his lips. A wisp of wild onion in his breath, his tongue touched the roof of her mouth, bumped over her teeth, twined as a warm vine around the length of her idle tongue. Their two tongues slid one against the other as two people slide against each another inside a warm buffalo robe, the feeling languorous and lazy-delicious. Dust scent mixed with pungent cedar sap that glistened where it oozed from freshly cut lodgepoles. Closer smells were orange bergamot in Two Talks' hair, mint leaves and berries rubbed beneath his arm, and his sweat smell like a grain bin of moldy oats beneath a faint scent of skunk. Mixed with tobacco and horse, his oaty, sour-skunk smell was sweet to Blood Arrow.

She stepped out of the soft blanket her skirt made over her feet. She held Two Talks' arm and stood on first one foot, then the other, stepping out of each moccasin. Naked, she lay back on buffalo fur. Except where Little Turtle had ringed her small white breasts red, yellow, red, yellow, Blood Arrow's skin was pale as moonlight. Each of her painted breasts looked to her like a wooden top she remembered from her first life.

Two Talks untied his breechclout and tossed it against the tipi wall. He lowered himself on one knee, that knee between her legs. "*Kwuhu.*" He kissed her again, and his knee pressed against her pubic hair and the arch of bone beneath. Her mouth against his mouth made wet sounds—nursing noises. His mouth left hers, cold space where it had been warm, her chest cold as he raised up. She opened her eyes. He sat on top of her, manlike and boylike at once, one knee on either side of her thigh, much as he had sat on her during the attack on the *taivo* wagons. Now, as then, he put his hands on her bare skin, hands warm as cooking pans and rough, dark as wet pecans, dark as her stiffened nipples. Back then, she had feared he would push apart her legs and rend her, split her from crotch to throat. Now, she groped for him as in a dream, reached to pull him inside her. Her fingers closed around his cock, a curved length firm yet yielding when she squeezed. When she held him there his skin moved over the firmness beneath almost as clothes slide over arms and legs.

"*Kuhma*," she said. "Husband."

He grinned. "*Kwuhu*," he said.

"Wife," she translated.

She held and guided him, learning the length and breadth and weight of him—of bones and muscles: shins, calves, knees, thighs. His smooth chest, the hoarse song of his breath. She was Blood Arrow, the bow, arched against her husband, Two Talks. She was Puhipka held by Wahatewi. He fit his arrow to her bowstring and both let loose.

Dark now the hide wall and beyond. Faint slant of firelight through the tipi's opening danced over their skin. She lifted his arm, one of her hands cupping the bone heaviness of his elbow, the other holding his earth-stained sleep-curled fingers. His skin purple-gray as a ripe plum, firelight flecked with red and brown.

He touched her breast. "*Pitsi*," he said. "*Pitsi*." He touched her damp armpit. His finger tickled, and she smiled. "*Ahna*," he said.

"Armpit. Wahatewi, you'll teach me Numunuu words this way."

He held the fingers of her right hand against his neck and said, "*Pia kuits*." His Adam's apple pulsed, and his voice's vibration against her fingers seemed to Blood Arrow as intimate and knowing as lovemaking. She lay awake all night long. Why sleep, when awake she felt her happiness? In her heart she became fully Blood Arrow, and she pledged herself to Two Talks and to Our People.

Visitors from the Buffalo Eaters Band

Just two sleeps after Blood Arrow became the wife of Two Talks, a rider from the camp of the Buffalo Eaters band of the Numunuu brought to the Antelope camp news that the *taivos*' Great Father in Washington Land was calling together all the plains tribes for a great council to be held during the Moon of Grass Turning Brown at the Little Arkansas River in the hunting ground the *taivo* named Kanzas Territory. The Great Father in Washington Land wanted all the chiefs of all the plains tribes and bands to smoke the long pipe with his chiefs and listen to them tell about the blankets and tobacco and other gifts he would give if they would put their marks with his marking stick on his words without pictures. Blood Arrow's husband and other Antelope men spoke together of this council at the Little Arkansas River. She stayed near the cookfire and brought her husband and the other men horn cups of sassafras tea and bowls of singed wild onions. She told herself she was perfecting her ear for the Numunuu words these warriors spoke, but she knew she was proud of how everyone listened close to her husband's words. She wanted to hear if any *taivos* might still be coming after her and her mama and Other Small One, and she was anxious to know when her husband might lead a war party. Two Talks and his Antelope brothers saw no reason to journey so far north to smoke the long pipe with the *taivos*.

"The fur is thick on the backs of the buffaloes. We Antelope will hunt instead of listening to more *taivo* lies," Two Talks said. "Why do we want *taivo* blankets that sting when we have the soft robes of the buffalo?"

"Wahatewi's words are as clear and sweet to me as the dove's song," River Walker said. He was one of the most successful war chiefs in the Antelope band. He had the respect of all the warriors. Red Dog and Crooked Nose had great respect, also, but they were Two Talks' grandfather and father so their support was expected. Blood Arrow felt great pride when River Walker spoke so highly about her husband. None of the Antelope was interested in *taivo* blankets.

"If these *taivos* had strong medicine they would give away more than blankets. If they gave me a repeating rifle I would go to hear their words." Dog Eating, who had recently returned from his first raiding party, spoke for the first time.

"I would let the *taivo* rifle talk back for me," Two Talks said. Numunuu from other bands stopped to enjoy Antelope hospitality on their way to Medicine Lodge Creek. The Antelope was the only band of Comanches that had declined to send anyone to the council, though only a few of the Buffalo Eaters band were going. All other Comanche bands were sending many representatives, as were the Kiowas, Cheyennes, Kiowa-Apaches, and Arapahos. The Antelope band did not trust Arapahos or Cheyennes, though they would ride with them against the Seminoles, Delawares, Shawnees, and, especially, Kickapoos, who had been trespassing on Comanche hunting grounds of late.

Emboldened by his own voice, Dog Eating spoke again. "Just as Our People killed all of the Lipan, we will kill all these ones who ride from the lodge doorway direction."

Dog Eating's words still rang in Blood Arrow's ears when ten sticks of warriors riding from the camp of a Those Who Stay Downstream band of Numunuu on their way to the council meeting with the Indian agent, Leavenworth, at the Little Arkansas River rode into the Antelope camp. Their civil chief, Hears the Clouds Talk, asked if this was the band of the warrior Two Talks, whose name had been carried far on the wind.

Blood Arrow's husband said, "Rest in the tipi of Wahatewi. It is your lodge. Eat and rest with us before you continue on your journey."

Blood Arrow broiled buffalo strips and seasoned them with muscadine grapes in honor of their Tenewa visitors. Hears the Clouds Talk asked Two Talks to go with him to Medicine Lodge, but not to put his mark on the *taivo* promise paper. Hears the Clouds Talk wanted Two Talks to speak to the other civil chiefs who would be at the council meeting. Instead of journeying to the camps of different Numunuu bands and plains tribes he had only to ride to Medicine Lodge to talk to them all at one time.

Having given their tipi to their guests, Blood Arrow and her husband slept in the brush arbor under a heavy fur. Before sleep came to them Two Talks asked her if she thought he should ride to Medicine Lodge Creek.

"You must, so the chiefs of so many tribes can hear your words."

"In the morning you will pack a travois."

Blood Arrow's heart beat fast—she was to accompany her husband.

Council Meeting at Medicine Lodge Creek

Happy that Two Talks had agreed to journey with him, Hears the Clouds Talk made a gift to Two Talks of a fine horse, a mustang named Frost, which was all white except for a bonnet of black that covered its head and one ear. That night Blood Arrow followed the North Star with a small party of Antelope and several of the band of Those Who Stay Downstream to Medicine Lodge Creek. In the dark the white horse her husband rode looked like a cloud or fog.

Light streaked the grass, purple blades tipped with vermillion. Mother Earth loved most the Numunuu, her chosen ones. Blood Arrow felt recently new. She had been born one time as a *taivo* farm girl, and now she was born again as the Numunuu wife of one who would be a great war chief.

By the time they arrived at the Little Arkansas River the Blue-Bottom soldiers and the men in black clothes from the *taivos'* Great Father in Washington Land had taken down their big tents. A long row of burned-out cookfires made black sores on the land surrounded by the holes where tent pegs had been pulled up. Yellow piles of cornmeal lay between charred logs.

"Our ponies eat the corn the *taivos* would have us eat," said a Kiowa-Apache chief named Crossed Eyes. "The words of the *taivo* men in black robes are bitter like gourds."

"Did you put your mark to the peace paper?" Two Talks asked.

The Kiowa-Apache shrugged. "We all did so we might get presents from the *taivos'* Great Father. Good presents make me feel good as a warm day under a Big Cold Moon. But the best presents had been given away before we smoked the pipe. Next time, I will come early."

Though many of the Cheyennes and Arapahos had already gone home, Crossed Eyes helped Hears the Clouds Talk gather many of the chiefs who remained at Medicine Lodge to hear Wahatewi. Many of the chiefs wore ceremonial headdresses and some painted their faces. They sat in a circle and passed the pipe. The wives and children who had come to the council meeting talked and played together while the men met, but Blood Arrow took a deerhide she was beading and sat near enough to hear the talk.

The Kiowa-Apache, Crossed Eyes, spoke first, using Kiowa talk and Mexican talk and hand-talk, so that all the chiefs understood. He told how even the Kiowa-Apache knew the name Wahatewi and had heard how the Numunuu war chief had belched out ammunition for his raiders to kill many Tehanos. Then Hears the Clouds Talk told how Two Talks had been chosen by Crow to unite the tribes against the *taivos*. "If each of you ride with us, each of you doubled by a brother—Comanche, Kiowa, Kiowa-Apache, Cheyenne, Arapaho—our guns will speak more times than even the Great Father in Washington Land has warriors to die."

Finally, Blood Arrow's husband rose to speak. She listened for the words he had practiced for her ears in their sleeping robes.

"For all the winters I can remember the Numunuu rode only with Numunuu. When other-than-Numunuu came into our hunting land and killed the buffalo, we killed all the other-than-Numunuu. The Tonkawas came, and we killed most of them and drove the rest from our land. When I was a boy, the Lipan came and became the enemy of the Numunuu, even worse than the Tehanos. The Rope Heads also hated the Apaches and sometimes we Numunuu rode with the Kiowas. We chased away all of the Apache and as they ran from us they became known as *esikwita*. Warriors who count the same coup will walk together one day in the Land Beyond the Living. Though the eagle does not fly with the hawk, the eagle is more like the hawk than like the sparrow. The eagle and the hawk are mightier than the sparrow, but the sparrow lays more eggs. I will lead our tribes of eagles and hawks against the many sparrows, the *taivos* who want our land and our buffalo, who want us to put down our bows and our guns and walk into their pens like cattle and sheep. They would feed us seeds we must bury and wait until they are big enough to eat. Such seeds do not satisfy our hunger. White hunters kill the buffalo for his coat and let the buzzards eat his meat. The spirit of the buffalo must be sad to be trapped in the stomach of a nervous buzzard. The Blue-Bottoms' chief says we cannot stop the white tribe any more than we can stop the sun or the moon. My grandfather Red Dog is in the fourth age group. He has told me of a long ago time when Father Sun was hidden by a black sun like a piece of night, when a same piece of night covered over Mother Moon. Perhaps such a time is coming again. Perhaps we will be given the medicine to stop the sun or moon. The Episcopalian and the Quaker bands have sent talkers to the Honey Eaters' reservation. All the *taivo* tribes wait for the warrior named He's Us to unite them and take them straight to the Land Beyond the Living. The missionary men at the reservation say He's Us watches over our tribes also, and that He's Us will lead Comanches and Kiowas and Kiowa-Apaches and Cheyennes and Arapahos to the Good Hunting Land Beyond the Living. Grandfather Red Dog asked one of these missionary men, 'If He's Us is our savior, too, why has he never entered a tipi of the Numunuu?' The Moon of the Most Blood comes soon. We must steal *taivo* cattle we can trade for rifles that speak ten times. Crow flies high enough to watch all of our camps. He will send a sign. Then we will make the whites cry. We will strangle them so their spirits will wander the land they tried to steal. We will scalp them so they cannot enter the Life after Death. We will cut off their noses and ears, and if they follow us to the Good Hunting Land our women and children will laugh at them."

Blood Arrow's knuckles were white with the heat of her husband's words. She felt sad for the settlers, though. People like Gideon and Mr. Speer, like her mama, like she herself used to be when she was Dorsey. People such as these did not realize they were stealing Numunuu land. But she felt no sorrow for the army generals and the soldiers, nor for the men back in Washington who wanted to kill not just the Numunuu but all Indians.

Many warriors at the Little Arkansas had great respect for the words of Two Talks. Some said they would still take blankets from the Great Father in Washington Land for the cold nights to come, but when the warmer moons came they would follow Wahatewi all the way to the Land Beyond the Living.

Says Good-bye to a Close Friend

When Blood Arrow and her husband returned to the camp of their band sad news awaited her. Yellow Rudolph had disappeared. She asked Two Talks to help her search for the strange but sweet old German. Her husband did not understand why she would look for one who was old and had probably gone away to sing his deathsong in private.

"He had his eye always on you, husband. I don't know why, but he once told me you reminded him of a boy he had known. He would never leave on purpose. He was not Numunuu. In his German tribe they do not sing the deathsong when they grow old."

"The German tribe must be slow and weak," Two Talks said. But he picked two fresh ponies and took Blood Arrow to search the Staked Plain around the camp for the lost one. They crossed the shallow stream and followed it south. They did not have to ride far. Beside a dead cottonwood tree the old German lay on his back staring up at the gray sky. He held a small book full of the German words Blood Arrow had seen before when she lived as Dorsey and her girlfriend, Binga Duerfeldt, read to her the throaty German talk from one of her parents' books. Yellow Rudolph's body still held warmth but did not pulse at the neck when Blood Arrow put her hand there to feel for life. There was no wound, no mark on the German's skin.

"I think his heart just stopped," Blood Arrow said. "He always said he was *ver laúfen*, the word his tribe uses for 'lost.'" She put her fingers on Yellow Rudolph's eyelids and held them closed, her palm on the gray face as in a benediction.

"He was old when he came here," Two Talks said. He laid the long, skinny body across Blood Arrow's pony and pulled her up behind him for the short ride back home. She would greatly miss Rudolph, whom she had come to think of as a sad uncle. A cold wind blew off the stream, blew them back to camp, the wind softly moaning, *verlaúfen, verlaúfen.*

Gideon Jones: Yellow House Winter

Among the Comancheros
(Late November 1865–March 1866)

At the Yellow Houses trading camp Gideon learned Comanche time was different from white man's time. Whether to count it gain that civilization hurried his days he couldn't decide. Sleeping Wolf was in no hurry to take them to meet Two Talks. The Indians were settled in for winter. Gideon passed the slow hours amending entries in his journal, adding his impressions of the Indians and the Comancheros he observed, and reading his *Americana*. He made himself not count the days that were growing shorter. The grass was turning from summer green to autumn yellow, and after sunset there was a chill in the prairie breezes. The blue-violet sky gave way to gray-brown clouds that marked the heavens like bruises. Some of Pretty's men, those with wives and children, returned to New Mexico for the winter, but most of the Comancheros settled in to drink and gamble until spring. Reputed to care about nothing, Pretty seemed to be at least curious about Two Talks, the Honey Eater turned Antelope warrior. The Comanchero leader seemed to have become curious about Gideon, too. The colder winter got, the more Pretty seemed to warm up to Gideon, and the Comanchero spent many an evening at Gideon's and Knobby's campfire.

Gideon and Knobby fashioned a wood frame and covered it over with buffalo robes. Every child at the Yellow Houses came to giggle at the square tipi. They got it in their heads this was the kind of lodge the black white-man tribe built, and they asked Knobby how the smoke from his fire would get out with no hole, and how would snow and ice slide off the flat roof.

It turned out Colonel Luellen Powell-Hughes' pocket watch the Indians called *tosawi*, which Pretty told Gideon meant "white metal," did help Gideon out, though not in any way he'd anticipated. The Comanches were convinced bullets from *taivo* guns could not hurt the Antelope warrior Two Talks. Some said he wore a blessed blouse that warded off bullets. Others said he was able to make himself invisible to his enemies. Still others said Two Talks was close friends with the bald mountain that rested one sun's ride below the River of Wild Hogs the Tehanos call the Llano. Two Talks whispered to the metals in the bald mountain and told them when the *taivos* dug them and made them into bullets they must always fly around Two Talks.

One morning after Gideon made a show of praying over the watch while he secretly wound it, Sleeping Wolf said he would tell Two Talks that Gideon was a medicine man with great *puha* who spoke the language of metals. He said he would tell Two Talks how Gideon whispered to the silver metal and made the heart beat inside. And the war chief gave Gideon a Comanche name which Pretty translated as Talks with Silver. Sleeping Wolf said he would tell Two Talks to meet the white shaman who tracks the skinny-but-strong white woman, Blood Arrow. That was how Gideon learned the Comanche had given Dorsey an Indian name. He took it as a good omen that, now, he too had an Indian name. Perhaps it augured well for his being reunited with Dorsey. What would she think when she heard she was not the only white to carry a red person's name?

Sleeping Wolf spoke to Knobby and Pretty translated: "Our visitor from the Antelope band, Three Ropes, says he believes the ugly one, Wears Out Moccasins, of the Liver Eaters band, will come to the Antelope camp to hear the war words of Two Talks. He may bring the *tutaivo's* woman and the boy baby."

"*Tutaivo*, that means black white-man. That's my Elizabeth and William," Knobby said. "Where is the Liver Eaters' camp?" he asked.

"*¿Quién sabe?*" Pretty said. "The Liver Eaters is a small band that roams south and east of here, but Wears Out Moccasins cannot easily hide his ugly face and figure."

Tales of Two Talks' Strong Medicine

Gideon was not surprised Pretty and Sleeping Wolf wanted to meet Two Talks. Three Ropes said the Antelope warrior had performed four miracles, one for each direction of the earth. In the Comanchero camp, Gideon heard many different miracles ascribed to Two Talks. He was said to have raided a ranch down below the Brazos where Major Van Dorn out of Fort Belknap had gotten fresh mounts.

Overnight the best horses, including the mounts of Van Dorn and his officers, disappeared from strong new stalls in which they'd been chain locked. According to the Comancheros, Two Talks led the horses through solid wood posts and boards. Another story credited the warrior with rescuing a Kiowa war party on the Blanco River. The Kiowas had been raiding the hives of a beekeeper when a detachment of Texas Rangers showed up. Though the Kiowas outnumbered the Rangers the Indians were out of cartridges and were holding off the Rangers and their repeating carbines with bows and arrows. Just as the Rangers were about to turn the skirmish into a rout, Two Talks showed up with a raiding party. When the Kiowas told him they were out of ammunition, Two Talks belched up enough cartridges to supply a small army. The Rangers had to retreat, and the Kiowas chased them all the way back to San Antonio. Many of the Honey Eaters band believed Two Talks was responsible for their misfortune after they went on the reservation. They believed he had the spirits punish them for going on the white man's road he had spoken against. In the seasons since Two Talks had left the Honey Eaters band to join the Antelope, death had visited the Honey Eaters band many times. A woman of the Yap Root Eaters band who spoke fairly good Spanish told Pretty that Two Talks did not do killing miracles, he only did healing miracles of mercy and goodness. She had seen him breathe life back into a dead horse. She said he cured many of the Honey Eaters band on the Clear Fork Reservation when the killing spirits got on them from the white man's blankets. Two Talks had such strong *puha* some believed he had passed without dying from this world into the Good Hunting Land and come back to bring together different bands of Numunuu and other tribes to lead their last war party against all *taivos*. Once again the Numunuu would be the lords of the plains and rule Comancheria—all the land for as far as the eye could see.

Pretty told Gideon the warrior's name "Two Talks" was the name of the Echo Mountains—the mountains the Tehanos call the Chisos Mountains that lie down on both sides of Stinking Buffalo Water. "An echo," Pretty said. "Talk that goes away to be heard and comes back again. Two Talks. But not like the Two Spirit people, those men who take other men as their lovers."

Long Days and Cold Nights

Eye seemed to spend most of the short, gray days drinking rotgut whisky with the Comanchero Brown Fred. One afternoon when the sun came out Eye appeared at the square tipi looking for company. Gideon put some coffee on to boil, and Eye stretched out beside the small cookfire. He used his hat to wave the smoke away through the tied-back tipi flap.

"I wish to God the Comanches weren't so strong against white squaw men. I'm so hard up I'd stick my pecker in a knothole." Eye laughed. "Makes me a ole woodpecker."

"There seem to be women enough for the Comancheros," Gideon said.

"That's a fact. Meskin and all kind of breeds from New Mexico tribes. They just like them camp following whores during the war. Not that I'd kick one from my bedroll."

Gideon poured them each a tin cup of the boiling coffee. Eye must have known his thoughts.

"Too bad that breed gal of yours run off on you. You could have rented her out to me by the hour."

"You know I only have room in my thoughts for my Dorsey they stole away."

"Ain't your thoughts I was feeling sorry for. Besides, Pretty's going to help you out with them captives, you and Knob. I told him you two was kindly orphans, just like him. I made that place you was back in Baltimore sound just like the monastery he was mostly reared in. And I paired Knob's being a slave with the time the Comanches had hold of Pretty."

"Your enterprising ways on our behalf surprise me, Eye. Not that I'm ungrateful."

"Save up on grateful. I got a mind for selling the rifles. Figure it can't hurt to bend El Perdido in our general direction. Pretty has been friendlier since we settled in here. Likely, you deserve the credit. But the colder it gets the more you're going to wish you'd held onto that she-devil you let go. She's sure as Hell warming the blankets of one fat Comanche."

Three Ropes moved in with Suella in a tipi she erected. They consumed large quantities of Comanchero whisky and stayed in their *kahni* all day long. Comanche women would not walk close to this tipi, and they turned away from Suella whenever she showed herself. Gideon wondered about the exact nature of this ostracism. He figured it had more to do with the couple's open slovenliness than anything else. He, too, avoided their tipi. When Gideon did encounter Suella she gave him the stony stare of one who holds a great grudge for some unpardonable wrongdoing. How she managed to cast him as villain and herself as victim in the short drama they had acted out together, Gideon had no idea. Though it made him sad their final scene was such a sorry one, he was glad to exit the stage when the curtain fell.

Marking Time

The nights were getting downright cold. By the time Sleeping Wolf's wives began to pack a travois with buffalo robes and beaded deerskin blouses and Comanchero trinkets to give away and trade with the Antelope, the gray skies were spitting snowflakes. Gideon figured they were way into December, but when he told Eye he hoped to sit before a Christmas fire and feast with Dorsey back in Alhambra with Mr. Manchip pouring glasses of Squirrel and Mrs. Carter playing Christmas songs on her piano, Eye surprised him.

"I done forgot to pass the word on Christmas," he said. "Forgot the New Year, too. We gone on into January, might be as far as February. It's eighteen and sixty-six. Likely be spring before you get to the Antelope camp."

Even when he had lived in the asylum they had noted Christmas and the New Year. How far had he come and into what land where no one marked these days? For the Comanche, Gideon knew, one day was as another. A good day was when they had plenty of buffalo meat in their tipis or, even better, Texan scalps on their poles. But being so far from what day or month or, even, year it was made him, an orphan, feel lonely and homesick, though he could not say just exactly what or where he was lonely and homesick for. Dorsey, he decided. Though the gray skies above made it seem unlikely, he knew springtime would nigh be upon them, and he prayed he might usher in the season of renewal and rebirth with Dorsey by his side. He scarcely allowed himself to fret over how she might be marked by all this time she'd spent at the mercy of her captors.

Preparing to Leave Camp

One afternoon—Gideon had all but given up hope they would ever leave—Pretty told him that Sleeping Wolf's wives had all his gear packed and ready to depart. *Finally*, Gideon thought, *we're going*. Then the Indians started building up big fires.

"What's going on?" he asked Eye.

"Comanche war parties always leave a camp at night. Some way-past, long ago raiders left in daylight and got everone of them killed. Ever after they eat and dance and leave in the dark."

"But this is no war party."

"Might be the start of a mighty big war party. Sleeping Wolf can't take the chance of bringing Two Talks bad medicine. You think these bucks are stirred up now, wait till they parlay with the Antelope. Pretty's going to trade Comanchero crazy water for buffalo fur, and a whole mess of red devils is going to get drunker than a coot and pass the bone pipe and cut up didoes ever which way—you ain't never seen such dancing. You boys lay back patient-like. Concentrate on spotting your gals. Whilst all the Indians cavort whole hog, you grab the gals and babes and light out."

A Conversation with Pretty

Late that night Sleeping Wolf and his band were still feasting and telling Comanche stories about warriors like Wolf's Anus, called Wolf's Tail by the whites, because, Pretty said, "Whites hate to admit they have assholes. You know, Señor Gideon, I once asked a padre of the monastery at Monterrey if Jesus walked this earth wholly a man didn't He have to shit the same as I? The padre said God made Jesus as man, but that men, of course, are imperfect and God made Jesus a 'perfect man.' Jesus, the padre told me, ate and drank, this we know from the Scriptures—but He did not shit. Shit is never mentioned in the Scriptures. The priest, of course, did not say *shit*, he used the word *defecar*, 'to defecate.'"

"I've never thought about it," Gideon said.

"I have wondered many things since I was a child being taught the Catechism and the Sacraments. I have many questions. If Cain and Abel are the sons of Adam and Eve, I want to know about fucking in the Garden of Eden. And shitting there, too. And I want to know whether Jesus had a woman. If not, how can He know what it is to be man? But I did not ask these questions of the padres."

Not knowing what to say, Gideon nodded.

"Civilized people like you and me, Señor Gideon, we would never name someone Wolf's Anus, or Barking Buttocks, or Makes Intercourse in the Water—all Comanche names. Los Indios do not mind shit as much as *taivos* do. The People shit on the ground like the wolf and coyote and buffalo do, and they don't cover their shit piles over with dirt. When their camp starts to stink they move their tipis somewhere else."

"Why did you leave the monastery and become a Comanchero?"

He shrugged and looked up at the night sky. "When I was young I lived as the child of a *campesino*, a peasant farmer on a big hacienda. One day, los Indios attacked. People I loved were killed, and I was filled with anger. The Honey Eaters war party took me back to the Honey Eater camp. After I learned Comanche ways, they let me roam the camp freely. After they trusted me more and more, I was able to slip away for good. I rode back to the hacienda. Everyone was gone. The monastery was where I hid from my anger. While I grew to be a man, I studied the words of dead men. I took pleasure in the Greek and the Latin. After a while the old words stopped bringing pleasure. The words were all the same, and they had little to do with a man's life in Texas."

"Did you get over your anger?"

"I could talk Mexican, Texan, Indian, but I did not know which I was. Comancheros are half-breeds or worse. They do not belong to anyone but themselves, so I rode with them. I did what pleased me. What I wanted, I took. Taking pleased me. I took money. Having money pleased me. People tried to stop me. I killed them. Killing pleased me. Now I take pleasure in nothing. I ride where I want and trade with anyone I want. I succeed because nothing brings me pleasure. It is hard to outtrade or outfight a man who takes pleasure in nothing."

"Maybe we have one thing in common." Pretty raised an eyebrow, and Gideon said, "I think Eye has told you that while you were in the Mexican monastery I was in a Baltimore orphanage and asylum. We neither of us has a home. We don't know where we came from, so we don't know where we want to go."

Pretty laughed. "You think too much, amigo. I take no pleasure in such thinking. Maybe I am waiting for something."

"For what?"

"To get even," Pretty said quietly.

"With the Indians, or someone else?"

"*¿Quién sabe?*" He smiled for a moment, just a heartbeat. "*Debo dormir algo.*"

The smile vanished instantly and so completely Gideon wondered if he had only imagined it. The man's face made no expression when he talked. Pretty's visage was what Gideon imagined in the face of the wax figures he had read about in his encyclopedia: *The wax figure is a petrified picture of our earthly part.* He had seen such a picture before only in the faces of dead men he had undertaken for their final journey. This Pretty, El Perdido, did not have the face of a man. He had the face of a corpse. If he were mortal man, he was surely on the precipice of immortal Hades.

Shoots Straight and Kills a Thief

As Gideon neared their square tipi that amused the Indians so, Knobby's snores greeted him. His lantern wick burned low, casting dim light on Knobby's dark face and on his tin cup on the ground beside him. The low-ceilinged room smelled of Comanchero whisky. Next to Knobby's cup lay the *Encyclopaedia Americana.* Gideon retrieved his spectacles. His volume was opened to page 143 under the heading, **WHALE.** Why would Knobby read about a big fish this far from any sea? Gideon read a passage describing a whale's tail cracking as loudly as a whip and how a whale struck with a harpoon may flee to the ocean's bottom with sufficient force to break his jawbone. That put him in mind of slavers' whips that likely had struck Knobby. Gideon pulled Knobby's covers up. In lantern light his arms were as smooth and purple-black as eggplants Win Shu had grown in his garden for the colonel's suppers. Gideon crawled under his own blanket. Wrapped in buffalo fur, the *Encyclopaedia* made a good pillow, and Gideon fancied knowledge might migrate from its pages and cross the border of his skull to settle in the mostly uninhabited territory of his brain.

He lay his head on the makeshift pillow, and he was on the slick purple-black back of a giant eggplant surging out of the prairie sea of grass suddenly become ocean, cold and gray. Below him a shadow swam—the forked shape of an enormous serpent's tongue or a giant's dowsing rod—but when it cracked loud as Satan's meanest whip, he knew his mount for Leviathan from the pages of his pillow and out of Knobby's mind. A second crack he knew was no whale's tail nor any whip. Rolling onto his stomach he lifted his head and parted the fur doorway.

On his wagon board sat Three Ropes, the one Gideon had named Pig Sty, his face as dark as mahogany. Mr. Manchip's team was in the traces, their breath rising like steam from an engine. Beside the fat Comanche, wrapped in a blanket deep red as the sunrise suddenly lining the eastern rim of the world, swelled Gideon's unfaithful half-breed Kiowa whore, her face stretched wide in joyful betrayal. Buffalo hides were mounded so high in the wagonbed it appeared Pig Sty and Suella were carrying a shaggy brown mountain off to fix it on the horizon. The potbellied Comanche cradled Gideon's Hawken rifle in his uplifted arms as if he were some wood-carved marionette, *The Assassin*, in a puppet-stage morality play.

"What are you doing?" Stupid question. What they were doing was obvious.

Three Ropes said to Suella something sounding like, "Butcher this boy."

"Talk to me, not her." Gideon's voice was someone or something growling.
"*Hay que estar sobre aviso.*"

Now Gideon was yelling. "No Indian talk." He crawled halfway out of the tipi.

"He talks Mexican talk," Suella said.

Gideon still lay on his stomach, looking up at them. A shadow cast by the rising sun behind the mound of furs in his wagon fell on grass silver with frost between his square tipi and his wagon. The shadow touched him, lengthened, and touched Knobby's arm, which appeared from behind the tent flap as in a dream holding out to Gideon a six-shooter.

"Doesn't seem, you know, fair," Knobby said. "Gideon's having no gun, I mean, and you borrowing his rifle along with his wagon and Mr. Manchip's horses."

The pistol's grip was damp, the gun weighting Gideon's arm so it rested on the thick *Encyclopaedia Americana*, now against his chest.

Where the Comanche's heart beat beneath his hide blouse, a small red fire flared, a bright eye opening then closing, followed by a tiny cloud. The whale cracked his tail, and the *Encyclopaedia* slammed against Gideon's chest. His wrists pressed against the book's hard edge. He tried to hold steady Knobby's heavy Colt's Army revolver. The whale cracked his tail again and again. Gideon's face burned and his ears rang to aching.

"Gideon," Knobby said as from a distance. "Gideon." His shoulder burned with Knobby's hand's squeezing. He shook Gideon as to wake him. "Whoa. Whoa-up," Knobby clucked at him as at a skittish pony. Smoke stung Gideon's eyes. On the wagon seat Suella bent over then raised up. Too late he saw the barrel of his Hawken rifle she had taken from the Comanche. Iron rang against iron inside his head. Suella pitched backward into the tall grass. From where Gideon lay tangled yet in his covers, Suella's red blanket was a clump of wildflowers curiously blooming above the killing frost. He got to his knees, his arms and thighs shaking as from the cold though his chest smoldered and his face felt sunburnt. A good thirty paces from the wagon Pretty lowered his repeating rifle, a wisp of smoke drifting indolently up from the barrel.

"Those are my pelts," Pretty said. Knobby looked surprised, and Gideon figured the Negro could not believe Gideon had hit anything at all, much less a Comanche warrior shooting at him. He was surprised. And he was fearful the Comanches would kill him for killing one of their own. But Pretty said Three Ropes had shamed himself and died without honor. "Killing such a one will not hurt your cause. Your thick book may rival the medicine of the blouse they say protects Two Talks." A hole in the cover of the *Encyclopaedia* showed where Three Ropes' shot had gone. The paper was burnt brown around the hole deep into the pages.

There being no one else to undertake the bodies, it fell to Gideon to do his final duty for a man he had slain and a woman he had coupled with. He wondered if a Comanche ever felt weak of stomach after his killings. He thought not and reasoned he was ill-fitted to be a warrior.

Once he lifted the bodies and got a bucket of water and rags to work with, his shakiness and nausea passed. Gideon felt a proprietary solemnity toward the body of Enoch Martin's half-breed daughter. He washed both corpses clean of dirt and blood. These ablutions and the fixing of the final masquerade makeup and costume were more intimate than what Suella and he had shared in his wagonbed. He felt sure he and Three Ropes were not the only men to have wrestled carnally with this body, but he knew that he alone would give these limbs their final human touch. He asked Pretty could he get some of the paints the Comanches used to decorate their faces and the hides of their horses for warfare and other rituals. Such dyes, Pretty said, cost dearly. When Gideon refused Pretty's suggestion the corpses would make a fitting sacrifice to the coyote and the buzzard, he grudgingly provided the cheapest shades from the Comanches' palette of cosmetics.

Three Ropes' corpse, for all his bulk, was poorly developed. His belly was distended. He was small-boned with skinny arms and legs, and he suffered from various skin maladies. From his rotten and missing teeth to his scaly, insect-bitten skin, his flesh reminded Gideon of the malnourished, wasted bodies of infirm children he had prepared for the burial wagon at the Baltimore asylum. He had no clear memory of it, but Knobby and Eye both affirmed Gideon had fired five times emptying Knobby's revolver. Two of his shots hit the Comanche. One bullet passed through the shoulder—not more than a flesh wound and not, Eye said, a hit to stop a man. The other entered at his right temple and took off the back of his head. Gideon found a few small pieces of his skull. The entry hole he filled with mud, sealed with sap he scraped from a green board beneath his wagonbed, and dusted over with a flour the Indians made by pounding mesquite beans. This powder he stained with dirt to match the man's dark color. He wanted vermillion, but Pretty said it was too precious for burying. To pull back Three Ropes' lips Gideon sewed deer sinews from behind the ears to green willow sticks he fastened inside the dead Indian's cheeks, but he couldn't alter the sardonic smile fixed on Three Ropes' face.

Suella's flesh, ample without being excessive, responded to Gideon's touch as if she were still alive. Pretty's shot had passed through her heart and, once she was bled out, she needed little packing. Her copper-red skin held its glow, fading only slightly as she stiffened. The Comanches' sandy red-ochre pigment mixed to a smooth paste and gave the half-breed girl a rosy glow in her cheeks and sufficient flush across her forehead and over her generous lips to suggest the fire that kept her angry way of attacking life kindled from within. After he returned to both corpses the look of life, he dressed them in the clothes they'd died in. A long knife still hung like a lizard's tail from the back of Three Ropes' belt.

The Comanches would have nothing to do with either body, and Pretty cited their fear of ghosts, especially of those who do not die bravely. Pretty said burying such as these was a waste of effort. He did spare one of his Comancheros, who got the pick and shovel from Gideon's wagon and helped him dig the graves. The ground was frozen, but only the first few inches. In about four hours, they had two decent holes. Eye and Pretty helped slide the corpses down. Knowing Pretty to be an educated man, Gideon beseeched him to say some words over the bodies. "This one could make a blade outspeak a gun. I don't know why he shot at you instead of throwing his knife." Pretty bent and pulled out Three Ropes' scabbard knife. "This will make a fitting marker. He forgot he lived by the sword, so he died by the gun."

Gideon couldn't bring himself to speak over Suella, so he gave Knobby a look he hoped was pleading. Knobby frowned, then said, "As unlikely as it seems, the Bible says we are all God's children. This daughter has gone home to be with her Father."

The shooting had been at dawn. By late afternoon, Three Ropes and Suella were mounded over. Gideon kept waiting to feel remorse or shame, but mainly he just felt tired. That evening he surprised himself with his appetite and ate an elk steak and drank two full cups of whisky. The whisky relaxed him, but he was not sleepy. He sat with Knobby by a small fire outside their square tipi and drank and fed the fire and watched stars shoot across the wide, black sky. Gideon figured Knobby was thinking about his wife and son, and Gideon was trying to affix Dorsey's face before him on the starry sky. He wondered why he was not haunted by images of the fat Comanche and of Suella.

Eye came out of the dark, squatted by the fire, and rolled a smoke. "They're going to head out tonight. Got your outfits packed?"

Knobby and Gideon nodded. Eye finished his smoke and helped himself to the demijohn of whisky. Sleeping Wolf and several men were talking loudly around a fire not far from theirs. Around midnight Sleeping Wolf held up the silver watch Gideon had given him and gave the signal to depart. The old chief slipped so drunkenly onto his pony it did not appear he'd be able to stay on horseback. He was taking one wife who led a packhorse pulling a loaded travois. Brown Fred rode up and waited. Pretty and Knobby mounted up. Gideon climbed onto his wagon seat.

Pretty leaned forward, his saddle creaking. "Señor Eye, are you coming with us after los Indios?"

"Why should I? I ain't lost nobody."

Knobby Cotton: A Comanche Welcome

Two Talks' Camp
(January–March 1866)

At the Yellow House trading tent white men laughed at Indian ignorance when a Comanche gave ten steers for a hand mirror, a common trinket. But the Comanchero, Pretty, said the Comanche had made the better bargain. Hundreds of Tehano steers grazed the range there for the taking. For ten stolen beeves—that did not taste as good as buffalo, antelope, elk, or even deer—the man had gotten something that gave him back himself—a small smooth pond in his hand—a thing that captured the sun and put it on a hillside or flashed it into a bush like a small fire.

—from *Gideon Jones' Journal*

A big low cloud appeared as a scroll unrolled from Heaven down to earth. The crossed tops of many tipi poles made a line of dark "X"s, as if a tribe of unlettered men, red-skinned or black, had penned their marks across the bottom of the scroll, a document of freedom, a covenant between God and the unlearned, the pure in heart. Since entering the tipi of Sleeping Wolf, Knobby had felt a partial kinship with the Comanches. Like most slaves, the Indians could not or would not write the white man's words. But the Indians did take captives and treat them as slaves. Grandfather Samuel had told Knobby there were tribes of black men in Africa who bought and sold other black men. *In such a world*, Knobby wondered, *who can I trust?*

They had followed Sleeping Wolf out of the Comanchero camp sometime after midnight, but the drunk old chief had ridden only a few miles before he stopped and leaned over asleep on his pony. His wives made camp, but left him on the horse. The next morning Sleeping Wolf held his head and shouted a lot.

The women took all morning making him some kind of poultice they wrapped around his head. He drank a broth they made and went back to sleep. Some time after midday Sleeping Wolf stirred. He ate several handfuls of pemmican and drank a full bag of water. Then he finally mounted up again and they'd ridden southeast all afternoon.

Now they walked their horses, Knobby close behind Sleeping Wolf and Pretty. Behind Knobby came Gideon's rattling wagon, and behind the wagon walked two of Sleeping Wolf's wives, leading a horse that dragged a heavily loaded travois. Pretty's Comanchero captain, Brown Fred, brought up the rear of the procession and kept an eye on their backside. They had brought the repeating rifle to demonstrate what they had to trade for the captives.

Sleeping Wolf had told Knobby and Gideon to leave their other guns at the Yellow Houses, but Knobby carried his Colt's Army six-shooter hidden in a muslin shirt inside his saddlebag.

The tipis still far ahead of them, they rode downhill. From the distance came the steady rushing of water over rock. On the other side of the river rose red rock walls. The rocky, bare trail widened spreading away from cottonwood trees growing along the river's edge. Knobby nudged Darkie closer to Sleeping Wolf, and the understanding horse came abreast of the Indian's pinto. Between their procession and the tipis ahead a blackened field of ashes seemed to lift and billow like a dark blanket. Then the field broke into pieces like dead leaves scattering, rising on a breeze, and circling until Knobby knew the black shapes for buzzards.

Their horses carried them over flattened dead grass here and there stained with blood. Blue-black flies and white maggots covered piles of excrement—dog, horse, and human—and crawled over purple mounds of buffalo innards buzzards had pecked and clawed from sun-bleached bones that lay everywhere upon the grass. Knobby breathed the stench of rotten meat and dung and heard in his mind the voice of his Grandfather Samuel reciting Scripture from the first book of Samuel, exhorting the slaves on Noble Plantation:

The Lord maketh poor, and maketh rich: he bringeth low and lifteth up.
He raiseth up the poor out of the dust, and lifteth up the beggar from the
dunghill—

Beyond the fly-covered piles of dung and rotting meat and the scattered ghostly bones, they entered the edge of the Antelope camp. Saddle creaking and outfit jingling, Pretty's wiry Mexican horse pranced. The Comanchero reined in, and Darkie brought Knobby close.

"*¿Qué paso?*" Pretty asked.

"*Nada,*" Knobby said, and the Comanchero grinned.

"*Se hablo español.*"

"*Yo hablo un poco de español,* Pretty. What was that field of bones and rot?"

"The Antelopes' old camp. The People think they own the Llano Estacado, everything for hundreds of miles. When their camp begins to stink they move to where the air smells sweet. They always leave something for *el buitre* who circles high above carrion and for the many vermin who make their miserable lives out here. Little feet and teeth and stingers sunk in shit or gore are little feet and teeth and stingers not sunk in Comanche flesh. *¿Comprende usted?*"

"*Sí,*" Knobby said. "But what I mainly want to *comprende* is getting my family back. How many rifles you think that's going to cost us?"

Pretty smiled and shook his head. "*Da nada.*" He gave Knobby a look Knobby had seen before on the faces of men who bought and sold. The look told anybody with eyes to see that the Comanchero already considered the rifles his.

Snarling dogs, tails curled over their backs, came out to greet them. Antelope children so bundled in fur they looked like dogs themselves ran, dodging scattered cookfires between rows of tall tipis and little houses made of woven willow limbs. Not since he had slept in the stalls on Noble Plantation back in Mississippi had Knobby smelled so strongly the scent of horse: a mix of dung, dirt, hay, sweet grains, and salt-sweat.

Gideon stood up on his wagon board the whole slow ride into the center of the camp looking, Knobby knew, for the girl, Dorsey, just as Knobby had been scanning the camp for Elizabeth. Sleeping Wolf had said Elizabeth and baby William belonged to Wears Out Moccasins of the Liver Eaters band camped nearby. No reason to figure Elizabeth and William would be right here. Grandfather Samuel said God freely gives His Grace, but He just as often hides His gift for us to find. If giving is free and easy, learning how to accept can take a lifetime.

Pretty reined up before a large tipi, Sleeping Wolf close behind him. Knobby counted the ends of twenty-one poles. This one had taken many more hides and was about twice as big around as tipis nearby. Darker than the buffalo hide walls, a big hide with the fur on the outside covered the tipi's entrance, before which stood a group of Indians.

Pretty and Sleeping Wolf dismounted, and Sleeping Wolf spoke to one of the men, who embraced him. They seemed to know one another. After a few minutes Pretty disappeared into the tipi.

"Rest your bones, Señor Cotton," Brown Fred said. "While El Perdido parlays with Wahatewi to make trade terms we will enjoy the generous welcome of los Indios."

Feasting

The sun was low in the wide sky, casting the shadows of tipis like dark arrow points on the bare earth. Comanche women knelt at the white-hot coals of big cookfires all about the camp. Wrapped in dark blankets, the women looked like the nuns Knobby had seen in New Orleans kneeling at cemetery tombs. A young woman handed him a gourd bowl warm with broth. For a moment she looked like Oralia, her copper skin a close match for Oralia's dusky complexion. She was the prettiest Comanche woman he had seen. She was prettier than Elizabeth, but she was not as pretty as Oralia. He drank the soup, chewed bits of meat and onions. The Antelope woman was not near as good a cook as Elizabeth.

Deerhides were spread on the ground for them to sit on. Brown Fred dismounted and Gideon braked the wagon and climbed down. When Knobby slid off of Darkie an Indian boy took the reins and nodded. Knobby nodded back, and the boy led the mare away.

From a pen of tall posts encircled with flat, dried strips of hide a woman took from one of several does a suckling fawn and brought it to an old Comanche man who slit the fawn's throat, opened up the gut, pulled out the smoking liver, sliced open the gall bladder, and dripped its salts over the liver he handed up to Sleeping Wolf. He took a bite and handed the dark meat to Gideon, who chewed it slowly. The Comanche butcher pulled out the end of an intestine and gave it to Brown Fred, who stripped it through his teeth sucking out the innards. Children begged for bites. The butcher sliced off the fawn's head and cracked open the skull the Indians then passed around like a bowl, dipping fingers in and sucking off gobs of raw brains. Women dipped horn cups into the fawn's stomach and passed around the curdled blood-pinkened milk. Sleeping Wolf brought a horn full of the milk and offered it to Gideon, who shook his head and passed the cup to Knobby, who brought it to his mouth.

A scent most like urine burned Knobby's nostrils, and on his tongue he tasted metal, as if the knifeblade had left its flavor behind. Still-warm, the bloody milk coated his tongue, so sour as to be almost sweet. Grass—he tasted grass. And he knew this grass from other grass, knew it from different-tasting grass. In its taste was knowledge of a stag who had walked over this grass and marked it as his territory.

Another stag's scent carried his lack of courage. Knobby held to the earth with four hooves and stared between the hide strips that enclosed him, held captive with others of his kind. Knobby was sheltered under warm fur. In a safe shadow he suckled at a teat and tasted the grass in warm doe's milk and understood what the grass told. Knobby looked through rawhide bars at grass, trees, and sky all gray as a dream, and then his eyes met Sleeping Wolf's eyes. Knobby stood upright on two human legs again.

Sleeping Wolf spoke and Brown Fred translated: "Does the one of the black white-man tribe taste the deer's way in its milk?"

"Tell him in my tribe's homeland we drink the organ liquors of lions and tigers, beasts stronger than bears, faster than horses, and we take into ourselves the power of these creatures."

"I don't think I can say all that in Comanche. I'll come passable close." Whatever words Brown Fred used, Sleeping Wolf grinned as if he did not believe a word but liked the tale anyway.

When he had dipped from the stomach all the bloody, curdled fawn's milk, the Comanche butcher pulled out the stomach and tossed it to some women who barely wiped across the grass the thickest of the brown and yellow filth coating the lining before they devoured the tripe. The men moved on to buffalo and antelope steaks and to cups of Comanchero whisky. From the fawn and from its mother they also slaughtered, the women cut organs and viands they shared amongst themselves and the children.

In a Tipi with Blood Arrow

Comanchero whisky was oily and bitter, flakes of bark or ash floated on the surface, and a residue like sand slid thickly against Knobby's teeth with the final cup-emptying gulp, but he liked the weightless feeling it made in the back of his neck. Beside him on another deerhide quilt Gideon sipped his whisky the way white women sip Sunday afternoon tea. He worked on the same cup all evening. The pretty woman who had given Knobby the bowl of soup handed him a wood spike speared through a thick strip of singed meat. As Knobby bit into the near-raw meat, Gideon tapped his shoulder and pointed out a pair of old women walking around the edges of the camp. Now and then an older child tossed them a bone or piece of meat they caught and ate. A woman kicked the older-looking one in the seat of her homespun cotton dress.

Gideon leaned close and said, "The crone looks like Dorsey's mother, captured with her."

The woman had mostly gray hair smeared with dirt. Her skin was dark, but it was impossible to tell by firelight if she had the dark, coppery skin of a Comanche or was just brown from sun and dirt. "Her nose is kind of puny, like white folks' noses."

Gideon spoke to the woman, but she ran off like a scared dog. Knobby spotted Brown Fred leaned back against a wagon wheel drawing on a cigar. In the near dark the tip glowed red, then dimmed. "Why do the Indians ignore those two old women?" Knobby asked.

Brown Fred took the cigar from his lips and let out a long, slow stream of smoke. "They are loco. They have no husband to plunder for them. They beg food and run with the children and dogs. Summertime they sleep out in the open. When winter comes and los Indios move into the warmer tipis, the widows and orphans of the band who can't sweet-talk some rich man to look after them take shelter in abandoned summer lodges." Brown Fred nodded at Knobby's spear of steaming meat. "You can catch a *mujer* with the right bait."

Knobby held the meat out to the crazy-acting woman. She grabbed the stick, but Knobby held tight. He gripped her wrist. She put the meat into her mouth and chewed while Gideon asked about Dorsey. She gave no recognition of the name, but the woman with her, who looked to be an Indian, nodded and held out her hand. Knobby tore off some meat she grabbed and swallowed whole. Then the Indian-looking woman said the name, "Dor-see, Dor-see." She laughed and ran into the shadows. Knobby was close behind Gideon, chasing her. Knobby lost sight of the woman, and he could not hear her steps or even Gideon's for the laughter and singing of groups of Indians all around them. They passed tipis and willow lodges glowing with firelight from within. Gideon stopped so suddenly Knobby ran into him from behind. The hag they had followed held out her hand, and when Knobby gave her the last of the meat she ran away.

"There," Gideon said. A woman crouched by a fire stirring something in a round iron pot. "There she is."

The woman looked up. Her chopped short hair was black, but firelight on her face revealed a narrower face than a Comanche woman's. Her nose was longer, her lips straighter.

"Dorsey?" Gideon spoke barely louder than a whisper.

The woman took a long stick from the fire and held up its burning end. Dirt around the fire turned soft gold. Holding the torch high, the woman came closer. Her eyes were even darker than a Comanche's, but they didn't slant like Comanche eyes. Her arms and face were browned from sun, making the scattering of freckles over her nose barely visible. "*En coehqui.*" The words were Comanche, but the voice was a white girl's.

Gideon reached for her, his arm pale in the torch glow, his fingers outstretched, but the girl stepped aside as if she were swaying her body to a slow reel. "Dorsey, this is my friend Knobby Cotton. Knobby, this is Dorsey Murphy Speer." Gideon's voice was tremulous and slow. "We've come for you, your mama, and little Lucy. And for Knobby's family, too."

"Naseka, *miar*," Dorsey said.

"Puhipka, *tokwetikati?*" asked a Comanche woman who stepped into the torchlight.

"*Haa. Haa. Miar*, Naseka," Dorsey said, and the other woman went away. "Come." Dorsey led Gideon and Knobby to a small tipi. She bent low and dipped inside, Gideon and Knobby right behind her. "Mr. Cotton," Dorsey gave Knobby her hand as if he were a white man being introduced to her at a fancy dance party back on Noble Plantation. Her took her hand, not nearly as white nor as smooth as the hand of a plantation lady.

Flames illuminated Dorsey's white-girl's face as she lay her burning stick in the coals of a small fire in the tipi floor. She stared at Gideon. "For so long I thought you would come. Then, no. When I heard Sleeping Wolf was bringing a Comanchero and men with rifles, I thought, could it be Gideon? I thought I would never see you again."

"Are you all right? They cut your beautiful hair."

"The wagon train was some other life. I stand on one side of a river and see that earlier me far across on the other side."

"We'll get you back to your true life."

The girl shook her head. "I can't leave Mama or Other Small One. That's Lucy's Numunuu name. She has been adopted by this band of Our People."

"Adopted? I didn't know heathens bothered with such niceties."

"Numunuu ways are different from *taivo* ways, Gideon, but Numunuu follow their path better than most *taivos* follow theirs."

Gideon reached for the girl, but she made her hands into fists and his hands stopped and hovered over the fire. "They've tried to turn your head, don't you see? It's only natural you'd be confused. When we get you and your mama back you'll come around just fine."

"They'd lock Mama away. She has no memory of being a white farmer's wife. Sometimes she doesn't know me. But things are going to be better for her, soon."

"Have you seen my wife and son?" Knobby asked.

"The Negroes, yes. They are in the camp of Wears Out Moccasins, whose wives have borne him no children."

Knobby did not want to let any of that sink in. "My son?"

"The Numunuu love children."

"Mary Thurston might say different. She barely escaped with her baby," Gideon said.

"Baby James?"

"Buffalo hunters found them. Baby James is fine. Mary's alive, but her mind's suffered."

"She could come live here with Mama."

"Comanches have done all they can to her. Took her daughter and killed her husband."

"The whites take Numunuu land, kill Numunuu women and children. Mr. Speer told me stories of what white men did to one another in the great war. Our People are at war," Dorsey said.

"Speer won't be telling any more stories," Gideon said. "Your People cut out his tongue."

"He's alive?"

"When I left him, he was. But neither talking nor eating are going to be much of a pleasure the rest of his life."

Dorsey seemed not to hear Gideon. She spoke to Knobby. "Wears Out Moccasins will want many rifles."

"Where's his camp?"

"Show us, Dorsey," Gideon said. "Let's ride there, now."

"You don't want to leave at night like a war party. Wears Out Moccasins would think you were attacking. The Liver Eaters' camp is small and poor. Wears Out Moccasins would not want you to see the ribs of his mongrels and horses and, even, the children in his camp."

"He doesn't want me to know he needs rifles more than he needs a Negro wife and child. He doesn't want me to have a trading advantage," Knobby said.

"He wants to suffer his band's poor fortune in private. He would not want others in his band to see his face when he gives up his new family."

"Last time my Elizabeth got sold off the master didn't have any tears to hide, and nobody worried about her face or her mama's or mine, faces separated maybe forever. Comanches aren't so different from slavers in Mississippi."

"Did your master invite slaves into his family?" Dorsey said.

"A slave is not the same as a real wife. Wears Out Moccasins doesn't mind having his way with a slave gal, but repeating rifles are the same to him as money is to a Mississippi slaver."

"If a Numunuu wants something another Numunuu has, all he has to do is ask for it. They believe things belong to those who want them most."

"That goes for wives, too, I've been told," Knobby said.

Dorsey's voice got softer. "For many Numunuu men, that is true. Though some do not share their wives. And the Numunuu never share their women with anyone not Numunuu." She looked Gideon in the eyes, then she stood as if to go.

"Dorsey, wait."

The girl faced Gideon. Torchflames turned her face deep red.

"You need time to get over what you've suffered. Come back to civilization and get help for your mother."

"At first," Dorsey said, "every night, I prayed for you to find me and rescue me. How we would rejoice. But you took too long. I can't explain, but I have changed. After what has happened to her, Mama can never go back. Here, she is without shame, like a child. I don't think she knows Joe is dead. I don't think she remembers Mr. Speer. She is in a different world here, without those losses."

"How can you stay with people who killed your brother and hurt you and your mother?"

Dorsey searched Gideon's face as if for an answer to his question. She looked around the tipi. "Now, this feels like where I belong, here is *nu sokobi*." Her hand pressed against her chest, the fingernails torn and dirty. "You understand? *Nu sokobi*—that is 'my land,' and *numukahni*—that is 'the people who live together in this lodge'—my family."

"I thought you cared for me."

"I have walked a long way since then."

"If we take you back you'll come to your senses. People will say it's my obligation."

"*Ke.* You'd have my body only. My spirit lives with *numukahni*."

"Dorsey, I love you. Don't I mean anything to you anymore?"

She closed her eyes and took a slow breath. "All my life—*nuhkitu*. That means 'I ran.' Ran from. When you joined our train I was running from farm life and from Mr. Speer's dreams and schemes. Now I run toward. You love Dorsey, but I left her behind many sleeps ago."

"Somehow I have to get you out of here."

"I come and go as I want. But I won't go with you."

"We can get Knobby's family, then we'll leave together."

The girl lowered her eyes as if praying. One of her hands reached out as if to take Gideon's hand, but, instead, took her own other hand. Her knuckles went white. Her voice quavered. Her eyes collected all the light the fire gave.

Knobby imagined his eyes had likely gleamed like this girl's the first time he'd gazed on Oralia back in Galveston. This once-white woman's eyes radiated unbridled—maybe crazy—joy. He had to resist the urge to put his hand over her face to shield Gideon from the blaze. "I'm adopted and married. My name is Blood Arrow. My name is Puhipka."

"Can you help me get my wife and son back?" Knobby asked.

"Wait and trade the guns."

Knobby touched Gideon's shoulder and left the tipi, walking away from any private words Gideon had to say to Blood Arrow, a Comanche who used to be a white girl named Dorsey.

Whisky Talk

Alone in a tipi an Antelope family had vacated for their guests, Knobby tipped a demijohn of Comanchero whisky over his tin cup. He wondered if Etienne, the short, wily trapper snug in his cabin on legs in the tree-shadowed, moss-draped Louisiana swamp might be lifting a cup at the same moment. He wondered if Grandfather Samuel was still alive. He thought of his mama, Hester, and tried to imagine what had happened to her after the war ended. Once he got Elizabeth and William back, maybe he could locate his mama and bring her to Texas to live. The Comanchero brew was strong and bitter, the corn flavor barely detectable beneath the oily burn on his tongue.

Two full cups of the harsh whisky later, Knobby heard heavy breathing and Gideon slipped wordlessly into the tipi. Knobby poured Gideon a cupful, refilled his own, and they sat on buffalo robes and silently drank.

When Gideon's breathing finally slowed down, he said, "She's a little off her head—all that talk about Our People. But she'll be fine, once she's back with her own kind." His voice raced up and down, and he poured more spirits for himself. "A heathen adoption—like taking in a stray cur. No judge, no document—in the civilized world it's got no legality. You might say it never happened." Gideon's eyes were wet, the whites shining. "Who would change sides this soon? She's like a storybook maiden who's had a spell cast over her, a bad charm or evil curse.

She'll be fine. Your wife and son will be fine, too." Gideon drained his cup and filled it again.

Knobby had been keeping that question and others about Elizabeth and William at bay. It would do them no good for him to get merry-tailed as a hound after a bitch in season. One thing a slave learned well was patience. He'd had to bide his time every day of his life. Now he was learning freedom, at least a kind of freedom, and he was perfecting patience. He brought the cup to his lips. The tin was cold but the whisky gave off warmth like it was alive. He tipped the cup until his mouth was full of the harsh plains-brew, and he held it there. How long would the whisky burn if he didn't swallow? After several minutes he got to where he was not just tolerating it. He got to like the heat on his tongue and against the back of his throat.

"We ought to leave tonight. Take Dorsey and go get your family," Gideon said. "By God, let's." He leaned and refilled his cup.

Knobby swallowed the mouthful. The whisky burned all the way down his throat, heated his chest and then his belly. "How far is the Liver Eaters' camp?"

"I don't know."

"How big a camp? Just Wears Out Moccasins and his family, or a big band?"

Gideon shrugged.

"Unless I show up with plenty of rifles or ponies, or something else Indians like better than wives and children, the only way I'll get Elizabeth and William will be to go in shooting."

"We can get the repeating rifles, use them."

Knobby took another swig. "Bullets start flying, Elizabeth and William are as likely as any Comanche to get killed."

"What can we do?"

"I don't know about you. I'm going to get something Wears Out Moccasins wants."

"This Antelope band has a huge horse herd. We can steal them and trade them."

"I'm going to get something easier to transport, something I can take without alerting the whole Indian camp."

"Repeating rifles."

Knobby nodded. "A crate full."

"They're half Eye's." Gideon's eyes were closed, his mouth remained open.

"Reinbach paid us to steal them from the army. If a man has stolen goods does he own them? I'm a runaway—I stole myself from my master. Before the South lost the war, Mississippi law said I still belonged to my master who paid for me. Possession and ownership, Gideon, are not the same. Eye and I possess the rifles we buried. The Reb teamsters we took them from and the U.S. Army they took them from could claim they own them."

"We trade them to the Comanches, they'll kill whites, women and children, too. How could Dorsey live with such savages?"

"They're going to get the rifles. Only question is whether Pretty and Eye trade them for furs and horses or I trade them for Elizabeth and William."

"Or we use them to kill Comanches and take back all the captives and set them loose."

Knobby drained his cup and set it on the ground beside him. *We*, he thought, *aren't going to do anything. From now on, I'm on my own again looking after my own.* If Gideon would quit being so blind he'd see that he was on his own, too. Dorsey hadn't been forced to say she wanted to stay with the Indians. She talked pretty good Comanche, and she answered quick to her Indian name that sounded like someone talking with his mouth full.

"We need a plan, Knobby." Gideon made a fist. His cheeks shone with tears.

Knobby lay his head on his saddle and against his side felt the hard shape of the six-shooter in the saddlebag he'd hidden beneath the buffalo fur the Indians had provided.

"Knobby?"

He had no idea how he was going to get Elizabeth and William back. "I'm going to sleep on it, Gideon." He closed his eyes and waited for whisky and sleep to carry him off.

El Perdido: Seeing Double

Recognizes Someone He's Never Seen Before
(Big Cold Moon 1866)

Brown Fred, second in command of Pretty's Comancheros, said Indians—
Comanches, Apaches, Kiowas, and Wichitas—raid and kill and take more
captives south of the Rio Grande than in all of Texas. "In Mexico," he said,
"whole villages dress in black, and all the eyes are filled with tears."

—from *Gideon Jones' Journal*

Pretty stepped into the tall tipi, a lodge fit for a war chief. When the fur flap closed
behind him cold air and the murmur of the camp died away as a wind suddenly
stops. The floor was layered thick with buffalo robes around the center clearing,
where a fire lighted and warmed the tipi and sent smoke high up to the smoke
flap.

"Wahatewi." Pretty spoke the name that was on so many lips, the name of
the former Honey Eater who was now the much talked about war chief of the
Antelope band—Two Talks—a warrior with strong medicine, one who dared take
Crow as his totem, one many Numunuu believed would unite the bands with
other plains tribes and drive out all *taivos*, all Tehanos, all Norteamericanos, from
all of Comancheria. Pretty respected Two Talks, but Pretty knew there was no end
to the whites.

"*Kimaru*. Sit down," Two Talks said.

Most Comanche men were barrel-chested, heavy through the middle. They
had short, bowed legs and were natural horsemen. But Two Talks was lean like
Pretty, his ribs as flat and hard as the laths of a chair back. Standing, the man was
not quite as tall as Pretty. But the Comanche was barefoot, and Pretty wore leather
boots with high stirrup heels. Firelight danced up and down the Comanche's bare

skin. A scar ran from below one ear all the way across his chest and down to his belly and was tattooed and outlined with vermillion and ocher paint. Decorating the two long queues of Two Talks' bunched and tied hair, little pieces of mirror flashed small shapes of the fire and threw the tiny flames against the hide ceiling of the tipi filling the inside sky with stars.

Pretty stepped close and stared into the face of the Antelope warrior. The rising heat between them made the Comanche's face wavy and wiggly the way Pretty's own face looked when it was reflected in a basin of water. Two Talks' face had been plucked clean of hair. Without brows his eyes were like dark stones deep in a pool of clear water. Pretty's eyebrows were thin but dark, and his upper lip bore a moustache to mask his expressions. His own short hair was hidden beneath his hat and the shadow of its stiff brim. But when Pretty looked beyond Two Talks' gaudily decorated hair, looked beyond the face that had been plucked hairless and stared deep into the warrior's eyes, Pretty's own eyes stared back at him.

He reached out and almost touched Two Talks' jawbone, but when he realized what he was doing he stopped, his hand stilled in the space between them. He imagined the Comanche's cheek warm against his fingers like the fireheat rising between them. Looking into Two Talks' face as into a mirror, he ran his fingers over his own jaw.

Does Two Talks see it, too? Pretty wondered. If he looked at the Comanche in the right way Pretty saw himself. His hat, his short hair, his eyebrows and moustache, the dark shirt and cavalry britches and high-heeled boots camouflaged what he saw in Two Talks' eyes. Pretty had learned people see what they expect or want to see. With his long hair and painted face and wearing only a hide breechclout, Two Talks was a Comanche, and that was all people saw. Under his sombrero with his short hair and moustache and wearing cavalry pants and high boots Pretty was a Comanchero—*eso es todo.* If Two Talks saw his face in Pretty's face, he made no sign.

"*Kimaru* and sit down." Two Talks sat, legs crossed, opposite Pretty. "*Tuhkaru.*" He nodded to bowls and platters spread out on the hides around them.

The band had had a good hunt in the fall, and the mild winter had kept plenty of deer and antelope in the hills. The Antelope lodges hung heavy with meat. Besides roasted buffalo strips, Two Talks' wife had set out huge halved gourds filled with dried currants, mulberries, juniper berries, tunas of the prickly pear, acorns, pecans, wild onions, the crunchy root Pretty knew as jicima, and pinole, cornmeal roasted on rocks in a cookfire. There was also a pouch as big as a horse's feed bag full of pemmican.

Chewing a green onion, Two Talks said, "Get your guns ready."

The Godmother

When he was still a small boy, before he renamed himself, after the Honey Eaters band had attacked Pretty's hacienda they took him back to their camp and taught him how to walk the Comanche path. For the first time in his life he'd almost felt at home. But each night when he lay down to sleep in a Comanche tipi he thought of La Madrina. She told him God had brought him to her, so he called her La Madrina. His adoptive father he just called Manuel. La Madrina said a Deutschlander, Rudolph Hermann, was God's angel who had found her lost babe. The German angel man that when he had been a child Pretty had called Uncle Rudolph. The Comanchero felt sure the old German was long dead.

In the dark tipi, after he said his prayers, La Madrina came to him. Her words whistled with air from arrow holes in her cheeks. Her words were wet with blood from arrow holes in her heart. *"Mi muerte tiene pena de muerte,"* she told him. He had waited all these years for the chance to avenge her slaying as she had wanted.

After he had lived awhile with the Honey Eaters, he began to talk Numunuu talk. He could not kill the entire band, so before he started thinking Numunuu thoughts and feeling Numunuu feelings he ran away and returned to the hacienda. The *jacal* in which he had lived with La Madrina and her husband Manuel was gone, not even its ashes remained. The raiders had dragged his godmother into the timbers. Only Manuel's mound of dirt and a wooden cross marked the place where his godmother had been violated and murdered. The wise Deutschlander had disappeared, maybe murdered, maybe captured. The padres at Montclova said his godmother's body was not found.

He named himself El Perdido and went to live with the black robes. The padres taught him to read the ancient words of Greek and Latin. In the monastery he considered thoughts written down long, long ago. And, of course, he studied the Scriptures the padres said were written by God but Pretty knew were written by men. The Old Testament was not spoken by the same voice as the New Testament. The Old Testament was a man's story of war and punishment. The New Testament was a woman's story of forgiveness and love. Pretty thought Yahweh had a man's heart while Jesus had a woman's heart. Maybe the Holy Spirit had the heart of a child.

A New Brother

In Genesis, Pretty studied the first stories about brothers: how Cain slew his brother Abel and was marked forever, how Jacob betrayed his brother Esau, how Joseph's brothers hated him and cast him into a pit and sold him into slavery. These brothers and more marked the paths brothers have walked since God made the world.

Now, in the tipi of the Antelope war leader Two Talks, Pretty finally understood why he had always felt an empty space where his heart should be. For years he had felt incomplete, but he had blamed it on the murder of his godmother and on his strange childhood—first with Indians and then with hermetic priests. This warrior, Two Talks, had his own face. After she birthed them, their blood mother must have wanted only Two Talks. Los Indios had discarded Pretty. Two Talks stood where Pretty should stand. Like Jacob taking Esau's birthright and blessing, Two Talks had supplanted Pretty. In the Scriptures when Esau's father realized he'd been tricked he told Esau one day he would have dominion and would break the yoke of his brother from off his neck.

That day has finally come, Pretty thought.

Negotiating the Trade

"*Haits,*" Pretty said, addressing Two Talks in the polite, formal way, as "my friend." A Comanche warrior did not directly address another warrior by his name. Pretty wondered what would happen if he used a kinship term, called Two Talks the true brother he knew he must be. "I will take you to a place where the rifles-that-speak-without-resting will grow out of the soil as corn grows during the Moon of Green Leaves."

"Sleeping Wolf spoke of only one crate of rifles," Two Talks said. "I need many crates. I need many boxes of cartridges."

"The gringos have many of the guns-that-speak-without-resting and many cartridges."

"For these rifles and cartridges I will give good horses, good hides," Wahatewi said.

"For my part I will gladly take Numunuu horses and hides," Pretty said. "But the *tutaivo* seeks neither horses nor buffalo hides. The black white-man seeks his wife and son who are in the Liver Eaters' camp of Wears Out Moccasins."

Two Talks nodded. "I know of these ones. Wears Out Moccasins will trade, but he must have many guns for the woman who brings with her a boy who could be a Numunuu warrior."

"These gringos are like children, *Haits*. They will do what you say they must to get what they want."

"No one spanks his own child any more than he whips a horse. There are uncles and grandfathers to instruct children."

"These two will not believe the People are giving up the captives they seek unless you bring the black-white ones and the others."

"Who else do they seek?"

"An old hag who is like the backwards ones, a girl-child named Lucy, and a young woman named Dorsey. There are five. These three and the two black ones."

Two Talks shook his head. "These three are Numunuu now. The old one is under my protection. The other two are adopted daughters. One is the bride of an Antelope. The Numunuu remain with the Numunuu."

Pretty nodded. There was no reason to argue. Of all the plains tribes only the Comanche refused to sell or offer women to outsiders. Many Comancheros took Indian wives, but they could not take Comanche women. And if these captives had been adopted—one even married—then they were treated exactly the same as a full-blood Comanche. The only way Gideon would get the three white women back would be by force. But Pretty would tell Gideon whatever it pleased Pretty to tell him.

"Tell the *taivos* to get their guns. I will send for the medicine bag. When I decide to make this trade, then I will send for Wears Out Moccasins and the *tutaivo* woman and child he owns. Then we will bring horses and hides for the guns of the one who seeks the three who are now Numunuu."

"*Haits*, it is said you have strong *puha*. It is said the Kiowa and other tribes will join you to drive the Tehanos and the Norteamericanos from Comancheria."

"I did not think Comanchero traders put their ears to the wind for the songs of excited little birds, the gossip of the enemies of Our People."

"I know many mighty warriors with strong *puha*. Sleeping Wolf and the Kiowa, Sitting Bear, have both spoken of Wahatewi's powerful medicine and his wisdom."

"Sleeping Wolf's band, the Honey Eaters, has gone on the reservation to live in pens like cattle. But Sitting Bear is one of the greatest of all warriors."

"My men and the gringos who seek these captives have all asked whether Two Talks' *puha* is so strong he has the courage to come alone with the captives to trade for the-guns-that-speak-without-resting. I think the gringos are afraid to meet with Two Talks' many warriors. They have great fear of Numunuu with the repeating rifles. They may be afraid to make the trade in the shadow of many Numunuu warriors. I told them Two Talks is not a nervous deer. I told them Two Talks and Wears Out Moccasins would come alone with the captives."

"How will Wears Out Moccasins and I alone carry away the many guns and cartridges?"

"My men will put the guns onto a *taivo* wagon so Two Talks can cart the heavy load back to his camp."

"I will seek the counsel of Ten Buffalo who carries the medicine bag."

"*Haits*, I think these gringos are the frightened deer, the little jackrabbits who run. Unless Two Talks and Wears Out Moccasins come alone, these who bring the guns may run away south into the timber."

"And what of you, Comanchero? What do you seek from me?"

"The gringos pay me from horses and hides you bring. If you come, I get what I want."

Two Talks looked long into Pretty's eyes. "For so many of the fast-talking guns, I will bring a string of fine ponies and a travois of soft furs. We will meet at Ebituesi Toyabi, half a sun's ride from my camp or yours."

"I know the way to Blue Horse Mountain." Pretty stared at who he might have been—a naked, unlettered savage but one who believed he was more, much more. *Poco importante*, Pretty thought. *I am stronger because todo es nada.*

"I know Two Talks' word is true."

"I will hear Sleeping Wolf, then I will send my answer in smoke words."

"*Bueno*," Pretty said. *Todo es nada.*

Gideon Jones: A Trade Gone Wrong

Ruminates about Dorsey's Transformation
(March 1866)

Gideon had gone over it in his mind again and again. The Comanches must have attacked the wagons and captured Dorsey about the time he was first laying eyes on Enoch Martin's three daughters in their sod house. That had been a little over nine months ago, which did not seem long, though in that time a seed can grow into a birthed baby—new eyes to see the world, new ears for first sounds, a new nose for fresh scents, new lips and tongue to utter new cries, a new brain to gather impressions. What civilized person could know the effects of months of slow days in the hands of savages? Nine or ten months of such captivity might seem much longer to the victim. What free man can reckon the captive's calendar? Gideon was determined to be patient, to give Dorsey however much time she would need to find her old self, to return to her senses and to him.

Now that he had finally found her, gazed upon her face for the first time in all those months of worrying about her and longing for her, what he noticed first was what was *not* Dorsey—what was missing. To begin with, her long, beautiful hair. Hacked off uneven as rough-hewn stair steps. But the greater loss shined, or did not shine, from her eyes—eyes that had once touched him and moved over his flesh as fingertips, eyes that had kissed his skin as lips. That night in the Antelope camp, nothing in Dorsey's gaze touched him when he stepped, as off a precipice, into the tipi where Dorsey led him. *How long,* he wondered, *had she known he was there in the camp aching to find her?*

Besides what was missing—Dorsey's long hair and her eyes' flint spark against the stony look he must have given her—he saw all she had added to herself. Deerhide clothes clung to her body. Moccasins wrapped her small feet. Buffalo grease gilded her face. Her once-smooth fingernails were split and uneven, stained with grass and clay, and her palms looked shiny-hard. He had held those fingers in his own when they had been still soft, where only wagon reins had rubbed. In that dimly lit tipi, he finally gazed on those familiar hands for the first time in months—*Dorsey's same hands,* he told himself. Her scents that he had carried in his memory of lye soap and rose of glycerin were covered over now by the cold, waxy stink of suet, the rust smell of blood and marrow. In the twitching light of her torch, Dorsey's skin glowed as from a fire inside, shone red as any Indian's.

In spite of his couplings with Suella—behavior he still could not account for and about which he still felt guilty and bewildered—for many months of lonely nights he'd imagined his name on Dorsey's lips. Her remembered voice was the melodious song of a night bird testing the wide and empty fields, her song the only call he heard, just as his namesake in the biblical tale heard the voice of God's angel. That ancient Gideon had slain with only three hundred warriors the multitudinous tribes of Midianites and Amalekites. Surely he could find a way to defeat one band of Comanches. But in the Antelope camp his name on Dorsey's lips did not sound like any bird's call. It was just the weary salute of one who recognizes an acquaintance from the distant past. Only when she spoke her new Comanche name did her voice trill. "My name is Blood Arrow," she sang, but Gideon would not let himself hear what she was telling him. Dorsey was no captive caged.

When she bade him go away without her, he pledged he would not leave her in the hands of savages. She looked at him, lowered her lids, and shook her head. They stared through rising smoke as across a thickly fogged gulf. Their feet again stood on the same soil, but they were on different roads.

Terms of the Trade

Later that night Pretty emerged from the tipi of Two Talks and told Brown Fred they were leaving at dawn to return to the Yellow Houses. They were to wait at the Comanchero trade camp until Two Talks sent up smoke words confirming the trade of the repeating rifles for Knobby's wife and son. Reluctantly, Gideon departed the camp. He longed to see Dorsey just one more time to tell her he was not giving up on her and that he would be back as soon as possible. He fought against the impulse to begrudge Knobby the trade he had made.

When they got back to the Yellow Houses, Eye was waiting.

"Two Talks wants all of the rifles in return for the captives," Pretty said.

"Hell no," said Eye. "Half them guns belong to me, and it's a mighty bad lay he's offering."

Pretty shrugged and said, "Bad or not, that is Two Talks' only offer."

"What're you getting out of this trade, Pretty?"

"Some ponies and a few hides for my trouble, Señor Eye."

Gideon did not think Eye would challenge the Comanchero for a share of the horses and buffalo hides, but Eye could not disguise his displeasure. "El Perdido, what about the white women in Two Talks' camp—Dorsey Speer, her mother, and the Thurston girl, Lucy?"

"*Sí*, them too. Two Talks agreed to bring them, all five: *dos Negres* for Señor Knobby and your three. For so many captives, many rifles."

Gideon did not know what to believe. "Dorsey told me she had been adopted and had married a Comanche. She said she's not leaving the Indians."

"She may change her tune, no? Such adoption and marriage means nothing under your laws, is that not so?" Pretty said.

Gideon shook his head. Surely, once he got Dorsey away from the Comanches and back to civilization she would return to her old self. He would stay by her side for years if necessary.

Eye was more determined than Gideon would have expected. He went straight to Gideon's wagon and came back with the heavy box of cartridges from under the board seat. "See here, Pretty." Eye held the box of ammunition cradled in his arms. "Put the wrong cartridge in, these fancy new guns might just jam up."

Pretty shrugged again. He looked at Knobby, who was watching Eye carry off the cartridges. Knobby wiped sweat from his forehead with his shirtsleeve. "How long before Two Talks sends those smoke signals?"

"Soon, Señor. Soon," Pretty said.

"We'll be ready to ride. With the rifles *and* the cartridges," Knobby said.

"Even that many cartridges will not kill enough Tehanos," Pretty said. "Two Talks will want many more."

"Yeah, but it'll get him started. I knew plenty of slaves would have been willing to begin by killing that many whites."

Hard Thoughts and a Bad Dream

Gideon could not believe he had finally found Dorsey only to lose her. He alternated from deep sympathy for her—for all he imagined she had suffered—to anger and self-pity—how could she reject him? He had loved her since he first saw her, and for the last several months he had lain down at night and risen at morning with her on his mind and in his heart—even those times Suella had been tangled in his arms. Dorsey's choice seemed to him so unjust he was not able to grant the waiver society allowed the female of the species from the laws of reason and logic. He recalled Colonel Luellen Powell-Hughes' favorite Scripture, from the Book of Matthew: "Our Heavenly Father maketh His sun to rise on the evil and on the good, and sendeth rain on the just and on the unjust." Why was God so unjust? How could He let Dorsey lose her love for him? Gideon's pride was sufficiently in submission to allow the question he dared not answer: How could Dorsey choose life with savage Indians over life with her own kind, life with him? The thought led to comparisons in which he had the advantages of civilization, but those advantages did not do him much good in Texas—a wilderness state of society. The image troubling Gideon's sleep was the wide-eyed and puffy face of the Comanche Three Ropes, surrounded by a perversely white funeral wreath of smoke from Gideon's Hawken rifle. Colonel Luellen Powell-Hughes was responsible for all Gideon's formal instruction, and the colonel had painstakingly cultivated in his student a prohibition against deeds of violence. If the killing of Three Ropes was a necessary and pardonable action in self-defense—an all-too-common event on the frontier—how could Gideon excuse himself the violence if he also yielded to the temptation to count himself more manly, somehow more courageous, because he had been forced to shoot to death another person? His mind configured shapes of thought against his will: perhaps God was not the New Testament God of love. Perhaps God was the Old Testament Yahweh of judgment—an eye for an eye and a tooth for a tooth—and He had influenced Dorsey's heart against Gideon in retribution for his sin of fornicating with Suella. Having lain with an Indian—half-Indian—he now could be forced to witness his beloved take herself off from society to live with wild Indians and be the bride of a heathen savage.

Disturbed by such reasoning—as primitive, he had to grant, as the reasoning of any Indian—he procured a bottle of Comanchero whisky and retired with it to the square tipi, where Knobby lay sleeping. Gideon sat wrapped in the oily odor of the buffalo robe and drank until sleep finally drew him into the nether reaches of the dream world where he was back in the death ward of the Baltimore asylum.

He trod between rows of asylum beds, a long aisle his dream transmuted into a long path between rows of tipis. As if one tribe were trying to exceed the other in hatred and blood lust, the gauze-wrapped and shrouded corpses of lunatic prisoners screamed and spat and threw at him bedpans and foul bandages and then tore off chunks of their own dead flesh and bones to pummel him with. Decorated with feathers and claws, the hide-wrapped bodies of malevolent Comanches cried out and hurled lances and knives and then pierced their own dark flesh with arrows so they might shoot at Gideon the blood-tipped missiles.

His own muffled moans woke him, and he tasted blood where he had bitten his tongue. In his dream struggles he had cast off the heavy fur, and he was cold and stiff from lying uncovered all night. He squinted in the gray morning light of the low-ceilinged square-rigged tipi. On his knees, Knobby was strapping on his holster. He seemed not to have heard Gideon's waking noises. Knobby pulled the six-shooter from the scabbard a time or two. Satisfied, he tugged his hat down and crawled outside. Gideon got up, pulled on his brogans, and followed Knobby toward the tipis in the main camp of the Yellow Houses.

Takes the Cartridges

A few women and children and several bony curs walked about the camp. Loud snores came from most of the tipis. Brown Fred lay outside one sleeping where he had passed out, cold dew silvering his long hair. Beside him lay an empty Comanchero whisky bottle and gnawed bones abuzz with shining blue-black flies. Knobby walked past Brown Fred, then bent before a tipi and looked inside. Just before he entered the tipi he looked back, right into Gideon's eyes. Knobby had known all along Gideon was following. Silent as his held breath, Gideon went into the tipi behind Knobby.

Eye lay naked and snoring on top of a sleeping Comanchero girl, one of the squaws who traveled with the New Mexico traders. The girl's lips were puckered tight, and Gideon wondered who she was kissing in her dreams. The dark thatch of hair between her thighs was bisected by Eye's skull-like knee. Her eyes opened, and she looked at Gideon, looked about as if she might call out when Knobby pointed his six-shooter at her. He waved the barrel toward the entrance, and she rolled from under Eye and slipped naked from the tipi. Eye snorted and clutched close to his chest the fur the squaw had been lying on. Eye snored on. His bad eye was open almost as wide as his gap-toothed mouth. Sleeping with one eye open. His sun-browned face and neck, hands and wrists, made the lines of collar and cuffs where his flesh turned white as a union suit. The cotton-colored skin was peppered with dark hair and all-over puckered and dented, welted with pink and purple seams—scars from battles, honorable or dishonorable, with men and beasts. Near his fingers that twitched each time he exhaled were a bottle of whisky containing one last swallow and his unholstered military revolver—its wooden handle sweat-stained and worn, its blue-black cylinder and barrel shiny and new-looking rested against the box of cartridges for the repeating rifles.

Knobby nodded to the box Gideon picked up and carried outside while Knobby kept his pistol trained on the sleeping man. After Gideon, Knobby stepped backwards from the tipi, his gun still aimed toward Eye.

Brown Fred had stirred and was walking crookedly, shaking himself as a mongrel after a soaking. Gideon saw no dogs, no children, no one else awake in the camp but one woman Brown Fred kicked for being too slow to remove herself from his path. He reached a trade wagon where he dropped his pants and squatted. Holding to the wheel spokes he saluted Gideon and Knobby with one hand—the other hand held his belt while he emptied his bowels.

Undertakes and Buries Another Corpse

Before their square tipi Gideon faced the smoke of a small fire he made, preferring the scent of burning mesquite to the bodily odors that rode the morning air. While Knobby secured the cartridges inside the tipi, Gideon added to the smoke the invigorating smell of coffee—most precious, save sugar, of all Comanchero goods. But persistent thoughts of Dorsey living amidst foul-smelling savages dulled his taste even for coffee.

Knobby's black face shone with beads of sweat. He brought a cup of boiling coffee to his purple lips, steam obscuring his expression. Gideon turned to see what Knobby stared at.

Shirtless, suspenders swinging from his waist, Eye lurched headlong toward them. His fixed smile stretched the scar above his upper lip white as if a length of thread stitched his mouth onto his face. He had not shaved in days, and his beard made a dark cloud beneath his eyes, one eye jumping, watching all around him at once, the other as still and false as the frozen grin he gave. His eyebrows arched up as two dark thunderheads below the gray heavens of his wild, unkempt hair. He stared with a crazed, cornered look Gideon knew from patients back in the Baltimore hospital, though not even the insane under guard in the asylum sent a greater jolt of fear through him than Eye's cursed-looking face that morning.

"Partners, I'm mighty sorry I was adrift when you come calling."

Gideon's throat closed. Knobby's Adam's apple moved up and down as he drank his coffee. Eye turned to Knobby.

"Boy, years back you saved my hide in New Orleans. I pulled your fat from the fire a few times whilst we fought for Reinbach in the Liberation Army, and I figure we've settled the hash—our yards are swept clean, now." Knobby set his cup on the ground beside his left boot. His face held no expression except, perhaps, a look of patience. He hunkered down, waiting for something to happen. "Where's my cartridge box?" Knobby nodded toward the square tipi, and Eye jerked up his head. Knobby raised one shoulder, an indifferent shrug. Gideon stood and eased away. "This ends here and now," Eye said. He pulled his long-barreled pistol from the scabbard on his right thigh. This was no quick draw but a studied move that seem intended to be sufficient unto itself as if just bringing forth the pistol would be all that was required. Knobby drew his Colt's six-shooter just as deliberately, as if he were only practicing. Next, Eye's hammer snapped, metal striking metal. Knobby extended his Colt's, his left hand beneath the pistol butt steadying his aim. Eye looked down at his weapon he'd dry-fired.

"You should say *morning* prayers, too, Eye," Knobby said. "I check *my* load first thing every morning. But I know you fill your cylinder every night at bedtime."

Eye swung open his pistol's cylinder. "Empty as a church on Saturday. You pulled out my cartridges." Eye shook his head. "Took a mighty big chance."

"Not with a man as faithful to a habit as you are with your gun. Most slaves risk more, every ordinary day."

"You best get it done whilst you can." Eye began removing loads from his cartridge belt. Knobby stood and took four long strides toward Eye. Knobby pulled back the hammer on his pistol and put the barrel against Eye's bare chest. The gun rested just below his neck where his sun-browned skin made an arrowhead point aimed down his white front. Eye dropped his handful of cartridges, scattering them over the ground like big seeds.

"I'm saving your life again, Sergeant Goar." Knobby eased down the firing hammer. "You owe me, again. I'll take the rifles and cartridges in payment. I need them to buy my family back. All they'll bring you are hides or horses."

What happened next surprised Gideon so, that, even though he was standing right there, he could scarcely follow how everything took place. Knobby turned and walked away. Eye seemed to jump of his own effort, both feet up, and leap backward. Knobby whirled back around. A small cloud puffed before Knobby's chest, and two explosions reverberated, loud and louder. Gunpowder burned high in Gideon's nose, and both his ears rang. Eye lay on his back, blood pooling above his shoulders. His blue shirtpocket looked sucked into a thumb-sized black hole high on his chest. His right boot scrabbled sideways on the ground leaving two parallel stripes of blood in the dirt. Gideon knelt and felt Eye's throat for life. His jumpy eye opened.

"Well, Hell," Eye said. "I misjudged and have to pay the fiddler. Gideon, fix me good as you can and plant me deep beyond any coyotes' digging." He held up his left hand where he had long before lost the first finger at the first knuckle. He squinted up. "I wish you could fix me on a good trigger finger — might need it where I'm headed." Blood ran from the corner of his mouth. "Damned if my foot don't ache," was the last thing he said. He gurgled, his chest rattled, and he settled as if drifting into sleep.

Knobby walked close and stared down. Eye's gun barrel sent up a wisp of gray as from a rolled smoke. There was a black hole in his right boot just above the toe.

"How did you know?" Gideon said.

"Counted. Look." He nodded to the brass on the ground. Four cartridges. "He only dropped four, and he always loaded five. When his cylinder clicked I fired away." Gideon shook his head and Knobby said — more to himself or to Eye — "I don't owe anything to any white man."

"Whooee, shot twice." Brown Fred leaned close, his lips pursed as if he were going to kiss someone. "A kill shot in the heart, but he shoot himself in the foot." Brown Fred examined Eye's boot. "These boots, *bueno*, they have many miles of walking left." He looked up sheepishly. "I need boots. *¿Con su permiso*, Señor Eye?" He started going through Eye's pockets. A couple of half-breed women and a Comanchero named Ernesto wandered over to see what the commotion was, but when they saw it was just a shootout between whites they went on about their business. Brown Fred sat beside Eye's body and rolled himself a smoke with the pouch of tobacco and papers from Eye's shirtpocket. "Lucky you didn't shoot these excellent makings." Brown Fred let out a breath of smoke, grinned, and said, "*Gracias.*" Knobby looked through the man as if he were empty space.

Knobby gave Gideon until the next morning to get Eye undertaken and buried. Since the foot was ruined beyond what Gideon had material and means to repair, he took off the first toe and affixed it to the stump of Eye's long lost finger, the toe a close match in size to the stump of the finger. One of Brown Fred's men helped Gideon dig a fairly deep hole. When they went back to get Eye's corpse, his boots were gone.

The girl who'd lain with Eye the night before and two crazy-acting half-breed women she jabbered with appeared at Eye's open grave. The women were dirty and unkempt. They reminded Gideon of the three witches stirring up foreboding prophecies in Mr. Shakespeare's *Macbeth*, Colonel Luellen Powell-Hughes' favorite tragedy.

Eye's missing boots walked up to the edge of his grave on Brown Fred's feet. The Comanchero removed his hat and made the sign of the cross, but he did not bow his head.

The Comanchero women having put Gideon's mind on it, he read a few favorite lines he'd saved in his journal from *Macbeth*:

Ah, good father,
Thou seest, the heavens, as troubled with man's act.
Threaten his bloody stage: by the clock, 'tis day,
And yet dark night strangles the traveling lamp:
Is't night's predominance, or the day's shame,
That darkness does the face of earth entomb,
When living light should kiss it?

And then he ended up with chapter one of John, verses he knew by heart about the light and how the darkness has not overcome it. Though, often, Gideon had his doubts.

Two Talks: Another Deathsong

Red Dog Paints His Face for the Last Time
(The Moon of Hot or Cold 1866)

When a Comanche warrior has the misfortune not to die in battle,
he sings out his last words, a kind of life poem known as the deathsong, before
he takes himself away to die. As one long acquainted with the dying and dead,
I believe the specters that remain behind to haunt us after the soul departs and
the body corrupts are living cries and whispers that echo yet. Some say all our
spoken thoughts live after and at the Judgment we must sit amidst the angels
and hear each and every one of the human utterances we made in our earthly
life. Even now—out on the wide Staked Plain—one can hear the parting
testimonies of those who came before. That cold keening whine, the
endless low moan that stirs dust is not the wind.

—from *Gideon Jones' Journal*

Before Two Talks had decided whether to trade with the Comanchero chief
for the rifles-that-speak-without-resting, Grandfather Red Dog appeared in Two
Talks' tipi bringing inside with him a fine dusting of snow. Two Talks' heart leapt.
The old man had painted his face black—the color for war, the color of death. If
Red Dog had come to say good-bye, if he were strong enough to die in battle, Two
Talks would not just shave the old man's horses' tails as a stingy relative would. He
would give away all Red Dog's horses and his weapons. The old warrior had a few
good black paints and Appaloosas in the herd, though his war *puku*, White Rump,
was ancient. The cold moons were hard on Grandfather, who said he made big
fires not so much for heat but to see in his dark vision the red flames. The old man
walked with one arm held out to see for him since his eyes had filled with gray

clouds. When one can no longer see others, others do not see him, but they see how much food such an old one eats—food that might go to someone stronger.

Blood Arrow served the sarsaparilla tea to show Red Dog she had respect for him even though he was beyond the fourth age group. His hands shook the bone cup of tea. He spat out tree fungus he chewed for toothache, though he had few teeth left.

Red Dog's lips were white with spittle when he spoke. "*Aho.* First speak your thoughts alone to the persimmon tree, so you can pick them as ripe persimmons when you need their sweetness to persuade warriors."

"I train my public words as one trains a horse before riding into battle, my grandfather."

"Remember these words, too: 'From behind talk, come bullets.' I named you, sharing my medicine, and I have shown you the path to walk."

"You have long been my close friend."

"This metal blade still has sharp teeth." Red Dog held out his best possession, the knife with the elkhorn handle.

"Sharp to take Tehano scalps." Two Talks accepted the knife.

Red Dog Takes Himself Away to Die

Ignoring the hand Two Talks offered, the old man struggled to his feet. Two Talks followed his grandfather outside where White Rump stood saddled, barely visible in swirling snow. The scarred old war pony was painted and decorated with feathers and bright rags. Blood Arrow stood beside the lodge. From the tops of tipis smoke made the sky gray over the camp. Doorways were covered. Only Two Talks and his wife would witness the old man's departure. Red Dog clapped, catching snowflakes between his palms, and the horse came to his moving hands.

On his pony Grandfather did not look so old. He spoke over Two Talks' head, "The *taivos* must be kin to the hare. We kill ten sticks of them and two escape to burrow away and soon ten sticks more of them come running over our land. If we could count them all, maybe we could make enough arrows to kill them. But that would take more wood and flint than there are trees and rock, more feathers than the buzzard and the owl could grow." Then the old warrior leaned down and said to his grandson, "My grandson, let me hear my name spoken for the last time."

"Take many scalps, Red Dog. Tehanos still tremble all over when they hear the warrior Ekasari rides the warpath."

Grandfather Sings His Deathsong

The wind carried off Two Talks' words and with them went White Rump, trotting like a young stallion, his longtime rider crying, *"Yee, yee, yee, yee."* Then Red Dog began to wail his deathsong—

> O Moon of Sleet,
> you always come back again and again,
> but we come back no more again—
> That is all. That is all.

—until sight and sound of horse and rider were covered over by blowing snow. The same day Two Talks gave away his grandfather's ponies. Never again would his given name be spoken.

Gideon Jones: An Unposted Letter

To Dorsey

21 March 1866

Dear Dorsey,

Even as I put down these words I fear you will never read them. Worse, I know you do not wish to read them. I rue the day I let your stepfather persuade me to leave you and your wagon behind. The day I rode away I felt sure you kept me safe in your heart as I kept you. But while I was away I lost you. Not to the savages, I now believe, but to something savage that was always in you. It was in your eyes each time we walked the prairie together. Oh, I was there in your eyes, also, but they seemed most hungry for the horizon and the wide sky. When I saw you in the Indian tipi, your hair shorn and your skin greasy with animal fat, your eyes had grown darker, filled up with Indian secrets. Your lips that once pressed against mine now shape guttural Comanche words I can never decipher. Preachers say we must be born again to the light. Now, I know we can be born again to darkness, too. I will never love any other. And I would have loved you even knowing I would lose you. Better silent memories of you than another woman's sibilant breath on my pillow.

I will ride with Knobby and the Comanchero to Blue Horse Mountain for the exchange of stolen rifles for our stolen women and children, but I know there is something false in this trade, and I suspect most El Perdido as I cannot reason his motive in helping Knobby and me ransom back our loved and lost ones. Knobby may get back his family, but I am doubtful my beloved Dorsey will appear. If you do, then may we and our children look back and read this letter in years of gratefulness to come.

You once told me that after our wagons left behind the treeline your heart came to rest on the wide plains. The great distances that make most civilized women mad comforted you. You said you felt as if you had been promised to these high plains. You said the uninhabited space had inhabited you since before you were born. Dorsey, you are as unreasoning as any feral creature. You run wild, ignoring my calls.

Does the wind carry my scent of betrayal to you? I am as guilty as Adam for eating of forbidden fruit. Were there any chance you might read these words, I wonder would I even confess my faithlessness. An eye for an eye, a measure of the unbearable loss of you against the mortal sin of knowledge. In the flesh of the half-Indian, half-albino creature bred of a sodbuster and a Kiowa squaw, I tasted both light and darkness. It may speak worse of me that even as my flesh yielded to hers I never surrendered my heart that still belonged to you. You are incapable of such a half measure. When your Comanche husband holds your flesh he holds your heart.

I have long disguised the dead, dressing them for their final journey, so I am at home with the artistry of the counterfeit. If I return from Blue Horse Mountain without you, I will undertake to conceal the pallor and stiffness of my heart that has not beat once since you held it against your bosom. I will cease my wanderings. I will spend the rest of my days building pine caskets. The constant drumming of my hammer will fill the absence of my heartbeat, and like the corpses to which I restore the appearance of life, I will pass for one of the living.

Eternally yours,

Gideon

Two Talks: A Sign of Good or Evil

Seals the Trade
(The Moon of Hot or Cold 1866)

Before Two Talks met us to trade for the repeating rifles, he had made a sort of speech at a council meeting up on the Little Arkansas River. The Indian agent recorded the words of several chiefs that day, and I later copied Two Talks' words from the Austin *Daily State Journal* that Mr. Manchip got by stagecoach in Alhambra: "We will never walk the white man's road. The white man's heavy clothes and blankets make our blood run slow and make our muscles soft. The near-dead ones on the reservation eat with the white man's iron sticks and their teeth get loose. They drink the hot black waters and their words smell sour. The white man measures out everything so he can make Our People pay for things the spirits have made. The white man even measures Father Sun into pieces he calls hours." That was before, as Knobby put it, "all Hell broke loose."

—from Gideon Jones' Journal

Now that the Moon of Hot or Cold had begun, Wahatewi was eager to gather many warriors from many tribes to fight the *taivos* and Tehanos. He was as full of life and energy as the green tree buds, as brazen as green blades of grass poking up above the frost covering the Llano Estacado. All through the cold moons, Two Talks had bided his time. He had fasted and sought to understand his *puha*. He had practiced speaking to the persimmon tree words he would pick like fruits to persuade others to join his war party. "From behind talk, come bullets," his once-close-friend had said. Now that he knew what the Comanchero chief wanted, Two Talks would ask the counsel of Ten Buffalo. The medicine bag he carried would help Two Talks know if he should go and get Wears Out Moccasins so they could trade the black captives and some ponies and hides for a wagon heavy with the repeating rifles. Then they would have the rifles to help them drive the whites from all of Comancheria.

The Comanchero chief, El Perdido, still waited for the smoke that would speak Two Talks' willingness to make the trade for the rifles. For many suns Two Talks had listened again and again to the words the Comanchero had left in the quiet tipi.

Crow had lighted in a cedar tree in Two Talks' camp, but the trickster had nothing to say. Two Talks wanted the repeating rifles, but he knew he would eventually run out of the cartridges that fed the rifles. He could go to the Blue-Bottoms to trade or lead a raiding party to capture a wagonload of their cartridges. Still silent, Crow flew away. Two Talks wondered if the visit by the trickster bird was a good sign or a bad sign. He returned to his tipi where his wife sat by a small fire. She had made wild onion soup they shared as they shared the silence. After Mother Moon had lain down behind the horizon to sleep and only the stars were awake, he took Blood Arrow's hand.

"My wife, when Father Sun gets up I will build a smoke fire to send my words to El Perdido that I will make the trade he offers of the repeating rifles for the two black white ones in the Liver Eaters camp. Wears Out Moccasins does not want to give up his *tutaivos*, but he wants to ride the war trail again. This trade may bring him strong *puha*."

"Husband, rest with me, now."

His Near-Same Face

Two Talks let Blood Arrow lead him to their piled high buffalo robes, and they lay against one another. "Crow may be tricking me. The leader of the Comanchero traders wears *taivo* clothing, but he has a Numunuu face."

"I did not see him up close," she said. "His hair is short like a Numunuu woman's." She ran her hand over Two Talks' head and pulled at a red rag tied in his long hair. "Yellow Rudolph told me some Kiowas had seen a Comanchero whose eyes were like yours."

"He does not pluck the hairs from his face. But we have much the same appearance."

"Did he see your face in his?"

"He gave no sign, but I believe he saw what I saw. When I was born my father had a dream-vision in which Brother Coyote carried a pup into the tipi. Even though it was night the pup had a shadow pup, and the shadow pup moved even when the pup was still. Maybe the shadow pup became the Comanchero."

"Maybe the Comanchero has Numunuu blood. Were any boy children lost or stolen from the band when you were young?"

"Grandfather watched every small head. The eyes of this one called Pretty stared at me as I stare back at myself from still water. I fear Crow is up to something, but he will not speak of it to me. Ten Buffalo did not find an answer with the medicine bag."

Blood Arrow nodded, but he was not sure she understood his words. Resting her head against his chest she spoke in the *taivo* talk she could not yet throw away even though she was now Numunuu. Her *taivo* words were as drifting and slow as leaves as they fall from limb to earth and Two Talks' eyelids came down with them.

His Wife's Counsel

Two Talks woke and it was still dark, but his wife had left their sleeping robes. He stepped from his tipi into the cold. Blood Arrow's cookfire had gone to coals. Our Father in Heaven sent vermillion streaks across the forehead of the sky, as if He were painting the sky's face for a celebration. Two Talks was careful not to let his weak morning shadow fall across the black iron bowl-with-a-handle Blood Arrow was so proud of. Two Talks mouthed the *taivo* word his wife had taught him— *skill-it*. In the *skill-it* one of the *taivo* flat-breads—he called them "looks-like-a-small-sun"—sizzled. Blood Arrow knew he liked these foods of hers, especially when she smeared them with honey or blackberries. A clay pot at the edge of the fire was stacked full of "looks-like-a-small-sun," a meal to show he was a warrior with so much *puha* he could afford to eat feast food for any morning.

A horse whickered, and Blood Arrow came toward her husband between the long rows of tipis. She carried water, and she smiled at him.

While he ate the small suns his wife had poured honey over, she spoke like a mockingbird, using Numunuu words she had heard except for one word—"twin." She said, "I do not know Numunuu talk for this. Do you ever remember two just-alike babes being birthed in the Honey Eaters band or here with the Antelope?"

"Such a birth is a bad sign. Once, long ago, the buffalo spirit deserted us for many moons. We ate deer and even horses. This happened when Blue Heron gave birth to two daughters in one birthing, and they were the same daughter twice. Even though Blue Heron left both daughters to sleep in the snow and the band moved from that place, the buffalo stayed away all spring."

"Do the People always kill such identical babies?"

"Ten Buffalo may know if such a birth ever happened before Blue Heron."

"When a *taivo* woman delivers at once two babies alike the joy is doubled."

Two Talks shook his head. Nothing about the white tribe made sense. He took the last small cake of sun, wiped the honey from the bowl, and filled his mouth with the chewy sweetness.

"Just because babies look alike, they are not the same. They may act differently. When the Comanchero leader and the two who ride with him came to our camp I looked long into El Perdido's face. Without the moustache he would look like you. Morning Star must have delivered two sons, and she, or someone, gave one of you away. Or she left one baby to sleep in the snow, and someone found him," Blood Arrow said.

"I must speak of this to Ten Buffalo."

"That is what Crow expects you to do. But if you do not speak of this the Comanchero will go away. Maybe no one will notice the similarity. My husband, you are going to join together all the bands of Numunuu as well as the Kiowa and the Kiowa-Apache. But if they learn there is another who appears just as Two Talks, they may believe El Perdido is Coyote's Shadow from your father's dream-vision when you were born. They may think your *puha* is weak. I think Ten Buffalo covets your power. A medicine man may see what he wants to see."

"Maybe El Perdido is the coyote pup's shadow come back like the evil ghosts of strangled ones. Maybe my *puha* is not strong."

"The Comanchero chief is a man like any other. He must be your brother somehow separated from you at birth or at least a close cousin."

"If I have a brother with the same blood maybe I should welcome him home."

"What would other Numunuu think if there were four of your eyes? Crow may be testing you to see if he can make you doubt your power."

"Perhaps Crow brought you to be my wife and to give me your wisdom. I know of no other woman who could guess the ways of Crow. Your hair is darker and shinier than the hair of any Numunuu woman. Perhaps you are Crow come to counsel me as my wife but unable to hide your darker-than-night feathers."

Blood Arrow smiled. "Do I seem like a blackbird under your covers?"

"If Crow *has* taken the shape of a woman, I am the only Numunuu to have coupled with a spirit." Two Talks would take his wife's, or Crow's, advice and speak to no one of the shadow self who had come to him as a Comanchero trader. He would go to the Liver Eaters' camp and persuade Wears Out Moccasins to trade the black woman and baby for rifles. Then they would send up smoke words to El Perdido, and they would ride to meet the Comanchero at Blue Horse Mountain and get the rifles-that-speak-many-times.

Gideon Jones: Gunfight at Blue Horse Mountain

Readying to Rendezvous with Two Talks
(Late March 1866)

Gideon had just boiled their morning coffee when Pretty brought Knobby and him news of Two Talks' signal. Pretty pointed northwest, but the smoke talk had already disappeared. Since they had returned from the Comanche camp Gideon had stared constantly at the horizon, but he could see nothing but red earth and blue sky. Suella, were she still among the living, would have seen the smoke and alerted him before the Comanchero saw it. Lest guilt dull his senses he forced his thoughts from Suella.

In two days they were to meet the Comanche warrior at the place called Ebituesi Toyabi. Pretty told Gideon that *ebituesi* was the Comanche word for a blue horse and *toyabi* meant hill or mountain. Before they could meet Two Talks to make the exchange for the captives, they had to ride to where the rifles were buried, unearth them, and load them in Gideon's wagon. To make room and so as not to spook any of the Indians, Gideon gathered Chief Bones up into his arms and carried him into the square tipi. He could not prevent the macabre thought that instead of Dorsey, the bride he lifted across the threshold and lay on his bed was this skeletal and indifferent specter.

Knobby was saddled and ready to ride. Before Gideon could get Mr. Manchip's team hitched, Pretty walked his horse up beside Knobby. He would ride with them to retrieve the crate of rifles, he said, and then he could lead them directly from where the guns were buried to Blue Horse Mountain.

Knobby laughed. "Those rifles and that big box of ammunition under Gideon's wagon seat have more friends than anybody I've ever known."

Knobby got lost a couple of times, and it took all day to ride back to where Eye had hidden the rifles. They finished digging up the crate and loaded it in the wagon by the light of a buffalo chip fire. Pretty made coffee, and they supped on dried buffalo, chewy and smoky-sweet.

The fire burned down to ashes and the air turned cold. Pretty rolled a smoke. Eye's face appeared above the struck match, and Gideon realized he would never watch a man shake tobacco onto paper or a corn shuck without remembering Eye, who had seemed to always have a cigarette bobbing from his lips.

Knobby had unrolled his blankets and was already lying down. Gideon's mind was so astir he doubted sleep would come easily. Pretty smiled and offered Gideon the bag of tobacco. He shook his head.

"Señor, you should prepare your heart for disappointment. I know of no women *prisoneros* of the Comanches who ever returned to the life they lived before."

"Weren't you captured once?"

"*Los muchachos,* if they are not killed or adopted and if they are not too long with the Comanches, can go back. But a *mujer,* no. A while back, Texas Rangers took from a Comanche camp a white woman with the infant daughter she carried. They learned she was Cynthia Ann Parker. Maybe you have heard this name?" When Gideon shook his head, Pretty shrugged. "Parker is a well-known *taivo* name. *Rico.* Like me." Pretty laughed. "When the Rangers said the name Cynthia Ann Parker, the woman wept, but she said she did not remember one English word. She begged to return to her Numunuu husband and sons. She ran away, and they brought her back. They had to put her under guard to keep her from escaping to the high plains. Her baby caught some white sickness and died. Then Cynthia Ann Parker cut her arms and howled and cried for days. She sank into despair and would not eat or talk. Before long, she died of a broken heart."

"But Dorsey has been with the Indians just nine or ten months—less than a year. She will cast off any spell they may have put her under."

"*¿Quién sabe?*" Pretty said. He shrugged again and smiled. "Comanche days are not kept by the white man's calendar." He touched Gideon's hand with cold fingers. "*Lo siento.*"

You're a cold-blooded rattlesnake, Gideon thought. He nodded and said, "Dorsey will be fine." He unrolled his blankets and lay down. Knobby was snoring softly. Gideon lay awake a long while watching the Comanchero who sat by the fire smoking and staring out at the empty darkness all around them.

A Cold Ride

They rode all morning without seeing another living creature. Lulled by the steady rattle of his wagon and by the featureless landscape, Gideon didn't see Blue Horse Mountain until they were almost to it. More a butte than a mountain, it appeared almost as a mirage rather than a part of the natural landscape. Longer than it was high, the butte was about the size of the squat two-story, red brick dormitory building at the orphanage asylum in Baltimore. What he first took for shadow turned into a wide waterhole along the base of the butte. It was too near midday for anything to cast a shadow. They reined in to make the horses walk and cool down before they drank from the waterhole. When they got close, Gideon saw ice all around the edge of the water and realized how cold it had been overnight. The spring thaw was taking its time.

"Now what?" Knobby said.

"We wait," Pretty said.

Where Is Dorsey?

The Indians appeared on the horizon as unexpectedly as Blue Horse Mountain had. One minute Gideon stared at the empty plains, and the next minute riders approached from behind the butte. He estimated they were about three hundred yards beyond the waterhole when he was able to distinguish and count riders. He counted only three. They slowed from a lope to a walk. One of the riders led a herd of six or eight horses, but no one rode those horses. Gideon looked at Pretty, who stared back at him. Pretty was not watching the Indians.

"*El valor es necesario*," Pretty said.

"There are five captives," Gideon said. "There should be more than three riders. I count just three."

"They're stirring a lot of dust," Knobby said. "The string of mustangs, and they're dragging something."

"A travois." As Pretty said the word Gideon made out the shape. Behind one of the riders was the pair of long poles lashed together where they met fifteen or twenty feet behind the horse. This travois was heavily loaded, stacked high with thickly furred buffalo hides.

"Elizabeth," Knobby said.

Walking behind the travois was a woman whose face was so dust-clouded Gideon couldn't see where skin ended and hair began. She carried a bundle against her chest. The bundle had to be Knobby's baby son. Now they were close enough for Gideon to make out a fat Comanche woman wrapped in brown blankets astride the horse that pulled the travois of hides. Tied to her wrist was a long leather tether that dragged the ground all the way back to the Negro woman.

Wears Out Moccasins' dark face was wider than it was long, and he had no chin, just folds of fat. His broad nose bore a pink scar, and his teeth were yellow kernels of corn. The Liver Eater civil chief wore a buckskin blouse, a breechclout, and leggings up over his knees. He wore a full feather headdress—something Gideon had yet to see on a Comanche. His clothes were decorated with so many trinkets of tin and iron he clinked like a man in shackles. He stared down from atop a big black and white paint. Just behind him the fat woman sat the horse dragging the travois and Elizabeth. It was a splaybacked roan with an army brand, the letters U S, on its hip.

A gust of breeze made a cloud of dust Elizabeth stepped from as if she were a dark angel carrying in a pouch tied to her chest the scowling baby, William, his dark head just visible above the leather cocoon. Knobby's wife and son were both alive.

But where was Dorsey? Her mama and little Lucy?

The other rider rode a mostly white horse with a black shape over the top of his head and one black ear. This had to be the warrior Two Talks. He was not as large as Gideon expected, given his mighty-warrior reputation, but he looked— Gideon searched for the right word—*formidable*. At the same time, there was something strangely familiar in Two Talks' aspect. His black-eared white horse stopped effortlessly and stood as still as the land around them.

When Two Talks reined up he dropped the lead he held and the string of ponies—there were eight—went to the far side of the waterhole, pawed the ice with their hooves, and nodded their noses in and out of the pool flinging silver water and ice.

Pretty walked his horse several feet from Gideon's wagon toward the Comanche. Knobby sat his black mare on the other side of Gideon.

"Where's Dorsey?" he asked no one in particular, to everyone in earshot.

"*Tranquilicese,*" Pretty said quietly.

"Not excited?" Gideon said. Pretty had lied to him. That's why Pretty had told the story about Cynthia Ann Parker and told Gideon to be brave. "You bastard Comanchero."

Wears Out Moccasins pulled from his mouth a bone knotted with fat and gristle and flung it down dark and foul-looking in the dust. "*Haa,*" the dark Indian said. The fat woman beside him tugged at the lead and jerked Elizabeth's arms tied together before her.

Elizabeth pulled back hard and gave her head a fierce shake. "You old sow."

"*Pit-see, sat,*" it sounded like Wears Out Moccasins said.

This was a slave auction. The Indian was showing off the goods. Knobby bared his teeth. "Damn you to Hell."

"Where's Dorsey?" Gideon heard himself say again. The one called Two Talks raised a rifle, his black eyes unblinking.

Then Elizabeth spoke, her words carrying clear and calm through the dust that settled, coating her red. "I saw the white girls and the old white woman in the Indian camp. They're all Comanche now. The older girl, the one they call Blood Arrow, is the bride of Two Talks himself. Ain't none of them for sale."

At the name "Blood Arrow," even in English, Two Talks stiffened in his saddle.

"You knew all along," Gideon said to Pretty.

"Don't be upset," he said, and he slowly swung his rifle in Gideon's direction. "They brought *los negros,* many hides, and eight ponies."

"Whoa up, you two," Knobby said, a tremor in his voice.

Behind Words Come Bullets

When Pretty moved, Wears Out Moccasins pulled a rifle from beneath a blanket unfurled over his horse's neck. For Gideon, that moment stopped, frozen like the edges of the waterhole beside him. He suffered in that instant the fulfillment of all his worst apprehensions. He knew then Dorsey was never coming back to him. Muscles down his arms and legs knotted and burned and his fingers clenched and unclenched around the firm new rifle, hard wood and cold steel, that jumped of its own will to his shoulder. Tears blurred his sight. The rifle jerked up. His ears rang with the explosion. *Dorsey is never coming back.*

When he looked back later to record in his journal what happened that day—a chain of events that probably began and ended within only one minute, one sweep of the second hand around the face of the colonel's silver watch— Gideon was amazed how slowly so few seconds could pass. Looking back in memory was like looking down on the tragic little drama with the eye of an eagle. From what seemed a great distance, he saw everything clearly, just as it had happened:

Gideon's shot struck Pretty in the shoulder, knocking him sideways from his saddle but not, surely, a grave wound. Gideon's ears were still full of his rifle's blast, but at the edges of his hearing Knobby yelled for Elizabeth to *get down.* Wears Out Moccasins' rifle flashed from beneath the blanket. Beside Gideon, Knobby's rifle fired and—when the fat Comanche woman slid from her horse and lunged with a knife toward Elizabeth—fired again. In these two heartbeats Two Talks' white mustang had reached Pretty. The warrior leaned low as if to pull Pretty to safety onto the white horse with him.

Two Talks said something in Comanche to Pretty, and Pretty answered, "I'm not your shadow."

Then Pretty grabbed Two Talks' outstretched arm, and it appeared the Comanche warrior would ride away with Pretty. But, quick as a breath, Pretty's free hand came from behind him wielding the long knife off the back of his belt. The blade flashed and opened up a tattooed scar along the Comanche warrior's neck. Blood stained the white mane and neck of the horse that whirled and raced away with its wounded burden. Gideon squeezed the trigger. His rifle exploded again. This time his aim was true and a dark hole opened in Pretty's chest.

The Quick and the Dead

They didn't know how direly Two Talks was wounded, whether he was alive or dead, whether he would soon return with more Comanches or send others back for revenge. Gideon wondered if Two Talks had conscious sense of Gideon's shooting his attacker. Knobby was rightfully concerned for his wife and child. Gideon bade him take the wagon and return immediately with his family to the Yellow Houses. Knobby called up the string of ponies that had run far around the waterhole. They came to him like dogs to their master and Gideon thought of the name of this place, Blue Horse Mountain. Elizabeth tied to Gideon's wagon the army horse that was pulling the load of hides.

Fearing retribution, Knobby voiced his resolve to convince the Comancheros their leader had been killed by the Comanches. As it turned out, Brown Fred said, "All life is uncertain," thanked Knobby for the share of the mustangs and hides he gave him, and assumed command of Pretty's outfit.

Though Knobby said he counted it beyond foolish, Gideon insisted on remaining awhile at Blue Horse Mountain to fulfill the undertaker's obligation to the bodies left behind when the souls departed. Gideon told Knobby, "All men are equaled by death and even savages deserve preparation for the journey on Charon's ferry to the far side of the river."

Not for fear of Two Talks' return but for lack of his undertaker's kit of tools and preparations left behind at the Yellow Houses, Gideon's ministrations to the corpses were brief. Beside the icy waterhole, he washed dust from the corpses and got their eyes closed under heavy coin, their mouths shut with thorns from a lonely mesquite he discovered on the far side of Blue Horse Mountain. He made a little deeper the three shallow graves Knobby had insisted on helping him dig before he and Elizabeth left ahead of Gideon in his wagon.

Wears Out Moccasins, the fat woman who Elizabeth said was Mr. Moccasins' number one wife, and El Perdido, the lost soul who was the second soul Gideon had personally dispatched to the nether regions—each he lay in a different grave. He spoke from memory a verse from the fourth chapter of James:

Whereas ye know not what *shall be* on the morrow. For what *is* your life?
It is even a vapor, that appeareth for a little time, and then vanisheth away.

Then he shoveled dirt over them sufficient he hoped to discourage coyotes and wolves.

When he had all but Pretty covered over, Gideon stared for the last time into a face from which not even death could remove the twist of anger. A sprinkle of dust had blown over Pretty's face obscuring his dark moustache, and Gideon saw what all of them had missed. The Comanchero had the face of Two Talks. And Pretty's last words came back to Gideon: "I'm not your shadow." He supposed he would wonder for the rest of his sad and solitary years what brothers' tale had transpired that Pretty had slain his own likeness. So, when he buried El Perdido Gideon buried the secret of the man's birth.

Knobby Cotton: Baptized Again

Reunited
(The Last of March 1866)

Not even the Comanchero, Pretty, as heartless as man as I ever saw,
had the resolve of Knobby Cotton. If Pretty's cold heart came from his
having been abandoned, Knobby's indomitable will came from his having
been another man's property. Knobby never yielded his spirit to
the corruption that enslaved him.

—from *Gideon Jones' Journal*

"Knobby, is it you?" Elizabeth's voice, a forgotten melody, lifted his heart.

"Real as can be." He approached her slowly, as he would a skittish horse. He
put his arm around her, and she lifted baby William out of the carrying pouch.
Moss clung to the naked boy's small penis. His arms and legs swam air. The ridges
of his son's ribs immersed Knobby in guilt, followed by anger. He was glad he'd
killed Wears Out Moccasins. Growing up a slave, Knobby had known any woman
he came to love, wife or daughter, would never be his alone. All slaves belonged
to the master. The master of Noble Plantation never lay with any of his slaves.
Contradictory as it seemed, the master had been a Godfearing man devoted to his
family. Other masters were less circumspect. Slave men had to share their women
without complaint. When the war had come and the master of Noble Plantation
had sold off Elizabeth to the New Orleans slave auction, the fear a slaver could
have his way with her had hovered in the back of Knobby's mind. The back of the
mind was where slave men had to keep such fears. Those who couldn't suppress
their anger suffered the lash, or death. Some slave men bore their jealousy by
blaming their beloved—a wife or a daughter became culprit rather than victim.
She carried the master's scent ever after, and nothing could wash away that odor.

It had taken Knobby a while to believe the Cajun trader, Etienne, was not after lying with Elizabeth. When Elizabeth's Comanche master, Wears Out Moccasins, stood before him, slave-man jealousy had ignited in Knobby's heart. Jealous anger still lay on him like a weight he had to put down.

As soon as he rounded up the string of Comanche ponies and helped Gideon dig the three graves, he and Elizabeth took the wagon and trailed behind them the string of horses and the travois of hides and headed back to the Yellow Houses. Elizabeth was exhausted and leaned against him on the wagon seat sleeping off and on. The baby mostly watched Knobby, who felt almost hypnotized by his son's wide, dark eyes staring at him as if they could see into his soul. At once, baby William appeared innocent and wise.

Safe at the Yellow Houses

When they reached the Comanchero camp, Knobby told Brown Fred that Wears Out Moccasins had pulled out his rifle and the trade quickly went bad.

"Pretty took his cane knife to Two Talks. From all the blood, I wager Two Talks didn't make it far alive." The new leader of the Comancheros did not seem too worried.

"Comanches have not made war in our camps in Nuevo Mexico for *setenta y cinco años*. The Antelope band is the only band that was never part of the peace between us and the other Comanche bands. The Antelope have mostly respected it, though. They come to our trade fairs, especially for guns. Wears Out Moccasins was poor, and his band is small."

"What if Two Talks does make it back to his camp alive?"

"*¿Quién sabe?* If they think his medicine has gone bad they will follow him no more." Brown Fred took the hides and let Knobby pick out four of the Comanche mustangs. He wanted to pack up and ride right away, but Elizabeth said he'd go alone if he left now.

"Knobby, I'm worn out and so is our child. He doesn't even know you. Why throw us on some bumpity horses when we can light here a spell and let the boy get over his scared of you? An' if the Comanches come after us, it's safer here with these other men and their guns. We spent forever running from white folks, and now you're in a rush to get back."

"We're free now. I'm ready to be on our own."

"Your ready can wait on my tired out."

Down to the River

The square tipi Knobby and Gideon had erected was not large enough for all of them. Brown Fred moved into Pretty's tipi and told Knobby he and Elizabeth could stay in the army tent he had vacated. There on a soft buffalo robe Knobby knew he would have to confront his jealousy, and he wasn't ready. He needed to get over Elizabeth's having been with a Comanche warrior—an *ugly* warrior. In some ways, Knobby was glad Wears Out Moccasins was ugly—he didn't want her remembering some chief like Two Talks.

Elizabeth did not rush Knobby into the tipi. First she led him to the river.

"The Liver Eaters don't wash often. I may never get my fill of bathing. You plan on sleeping in the tent with me and William, you better get yourself in some water, too."

They walked the edge of the stream until they were far enough from the Comanchero camp, the horses and stolen cattle, that they no longer smelled dung or rancid meat. William grew still in Knobby's arms. Elizabeth pulled off her deerskin top. Two red streaks crossed her shoulders. Knobby wondered why they had warpainted her, then realized she'd been whipped.

"It wasn't anything. It's for looks."

"For looks?"

"Yeah. Taw-are-we—close as I can say his name–wanted me to look mistreated because when white folks think they're saving captives from Indian tortures they get weepy and pull out more gold. I told Taw-are-we, you're not white folks, but he said he had to get plenty of guns for me and William. He only let her whip me twice, just hard enough to show."

Knobby wished he had salve for Elizabeth's back. She unfastened her skirt, spread the blouse and skirt in the sun, and pulled off her moccasins. She swayed and bobbed as naturally as the tall grass, picking her way down to the stream. Holding his silent son, Knobby pulled off boots and socks, dropped his trousers and, shifting the boy from one arm to the other, pulled free of his shirt. He could not bear to set the boy on the grass, could not bear to let go of him. The air was cold but the sun shone and there was a promise of spring to come, though no birds sang yet.

"Whooo." Cold water took his breath. William turned his head to see what creature made such a silly sound. The boy accepted the water's cold and floated like a dark leaf just beyond Knobby's fingers. Elizabeth was far out into the pool, stroking without kicking, quietly swimming toward the other side. "William, I am your father, Knobby Cotton."

The baby showed no fear of the water.

"He gets around in water almost like a fish." Elizabeth's words carried over the water. "Maybe from the weeks his mama waded the swamplands before Etienne took us in. He's almost like an Indian, too. Darker people, even ole Taw-arewe, have warmer hearts than white folks do." Her wet hair clung close to her head and made her look smaller, more vulnerable. "Indian children play all day long. William laughed when they laughed."

Knobby was about to ask if the boy was learning Comanche talk, when Elizabeth dipped underwater. William floated and paddled back toward Knobby, moving like a baby duck. Knobby felt the sudden pressure of Elizabeth's hands pressing him down. He stared into silver balls of foam. His nose and throat burned, eyes stung. She squeezed her knees against his ribs.

"Do you remember our first baptism together, Knobby Cotton? Saltwater stinging our bitten and cut places and putting a healing balm on us when we jumped over the little swamp man's cane knife and pledged ourselves to each other before God and them few seagulls?"

Knobby nodded. He remembered.

"I baptize you again, Knobby Cotton, out of your old life and into your new life with your wild, black Texan family. Let go of old dead ways. Forget whips and chains, sucking bayous, Galveston whores, the Liberation Army, warpainted Indians—get shed of all those old masters."

They splashed just for the silver sheets of water, yelled just for the high, animal loudness they could make, for the breath pushing out against their chests. They swam and tussled with the water and with one another until Knobby's tired muscles ached gloriously. He followed his wife and carried their son up out of the river. Water let go of Elizabeth reluctantly. Falling-back sheets peeled down her arms and legs, stretched to silver ropes, untwined like a lover after coupling.

Coupling. Cold as he was, his balls tight against him as two pecans, his cock stiffened and bobbed ahead of him. Coupling. Elizabeth's smooth and rock-firm buttocks in his hands, her mouth finding his as she rose against him. Coupling. William, blanketed in Elizabeth's buckskin skirt, nestled in the grass, babbling to the sky untranslated words of innocence. Coupling—nothing before or since. On her spread skirt on the grass, both of them wild to be grass greening, they held tight and coupled as for the first time in their lives.

After coupling—almost as good—lazy and timeless uncoupling, separating yet still linked by warm dampness, strands of body liquors, touches, breaths, words into phrases.

"Knobby, can you tell me the month it is? And what year?"

"The year of our Lord, eighteen hundred and sixty-six. End of March, first of April. Close to spring."

"In like a lion, out like a lamb." She petted the head of his shrunken cock when she said "lamb," both of them giggling. "The Comanches I was with call March, 'the Moon of Hot or Cold.'"

"It may be April. What do they call April?"

"'The Moon of Recently Green Leaves.'"

Things Said and Left Unsaid

He had let Oralia go, had not thought of her for weeks, but he wanted Elizabeth to know. At times, he was sure she already did know, though they had never spoken openly of his lust for Oralia. Lust was all it was, but it had been fierce in its grip on him. Now, he wanted to confess he had wanted another, though he never coupled with her. He wanted forgiveness for his lust even as he wanted credit, praise for not consummating it. Yet, he knew he would have done so if he could have. But if Elizabeth thought he had, it seemed unfair for him to suffer any hardening of her heart for something he had not gotten to enjoy. He would test her. He would see if she took the bait. He hinted at it, the way songbirds seem to chirp questions before they really sing: "All these nights apart. You on the ground in a Indian tipi, while back in Skyhouse they were lying up on those high beds and fancy sheets." He waited, to see if she would say something to let him know how to go on. But she gave nothing but silence, and then she rolled away, her back to him. The two stripes from a Comanche woman's switch washed clean by the cold water were barely visible now, as if the mysterious healing had already begun. "I'll get William." Knobby lifted his son from Elizabeth's buckskin skirt, wrapped the boy in his daddy's big flannel shirt, and tied the arms together over William's waist. The baby stared up at Knobby without blinking, his eyes dark and wise-looking. Knobby stood to hand the skirt to Elizabeth, but his foot was on the hem, and he ripped the rawhide cinch from around the waist. "I'm sorry."

Elizabeth looked at him hard and, without softening her look, said, "I can fix it."

"Can I do anything?" He was at once aware of the larger apology in his words.

She held his chin and kissed his lips, not a long kiss, yet more than a peck.

"Ole Taw-are-we wasn't so bad as he looks. In all the time I was in his tipi he only came to my bed once, and I think because he thought he was supposed to. He lay with me but stayed far away in his head—didn't even kiss me. I put my faith in the Lord and thought how men have looked at me worse than the way old Taw-are-we laid with me." Elizabeth squeezed his hand and looked at him hard but soft at the same time. "I wouldn't have told you if you had asked. I wouldn't have told you, except you loved me up the way you did just now, without having first to know answers to stuff that doesn't matter. It's a fallen tree limb you've got to go over or go around. Taw-are-we most fancied Terrible Singer. She was passed over, I guess for being fat and homely, but she's strong for hauling stuff. Old Indian loved William terrible big. You think on that part."

Now Knobby knew he must not assuage his guilt by confessing his passion for Oralia. Whatever Elizabeth had guessed or knew about Oralia was more stuff that didn't matter. Now he understood they had found grace together, had achieved a kind of equilibrium, and Elizabeth's unflinching stare said neither of them was going to risk losing that. "We better feed our child and rig him up some clothes to wear in front of white folks," Knobby said. He laughed tentatively, and Elizabeth nodded. "We're going round together, from now on."

Elizabeth fastened her skirt with a sharp stick. She carried William, who batted at her chin with both hands. Knobby marveled at these two people he now had time to get to know.

"I'm thinking I'll do some freighting. I know horses, and I've been learning wagons. I can sell Darkie and the rest of my outfit for a good freight wagon, save up for a team. Meanwhile, I'll keep rounding up stray cattle. By the time William's old enough to ride, we'll have a small herd and I can teach him to be a first-rate cow-handler." He paused and listened to their bodies moving through the grass, the river moving along behind them. Elizabeth nodded, and he went on talking. "I could try the army. They're taking on soldiers, anybody they can get. Most all the Fourth and Tenth Cavalry are Negroes. All but the commanding officers. It would be bad enough taking orders from a black commander—like an overseer on a plantation—but it would be nearly impossible to take orders from a white man." Elizabeth didn't slow or look back. "I worked for a rancher named Mabry down near Goliad. He'd hire me back, I expect. He's kind and fair, but I'd rather not work for a white man." Knobby thought he heard a bird, maybe the first robin of spring, if robins were allowed to fly into Comanche land. But it wasn't any bird. It was Elizabeth humming, and so Knobby went on talking, enjoying how her humming and his daydream talk mixed together like the words and tune for a brand-new song.

Blood Arrow: The Dead Do Not Lie Still

A Good Day to Die
(The Moon of Recently Green Leaves 1866)

In Independence, Missouri, a missionary on his way to save Indian souls shares his views on the crusade to reclaim these sons of the plains from their savage course. Says he: "Like all aborigines in the path of civilization, their destiny is annihilation. Obdurately tenacious of their barbaric and pagan ignorance and without the capacity for unified and skillful resistance, they must mile-by-mile and death-by-death yield to their superior enemies. Soon their destruction will be history, their ways and places no longer known. Dark of aspect and dark of rational or spiritual vision, darker still is their destiny." What then of Dorsey? When she joined the redskins, did her soul also change its aspect?

—from *Gideon Jones' Journal*

Though Our Father in Heaven was already high in the sky, Blood Arrow still lay beneath her buffalo robe. She was slick with sweat and her stomach beat back and forth like a moth's wings. The bottoms of the tipi walls had been rolled up for cool breezes since the Moon of Recently Green Leaves, but today nothing stirred but her stomach. Whenever Two Talks was away her nights were long. She was always lonely for his body against hers. Feeling ill, she missed his touch even more.

Unable to find the open space close to the ground where the sides were rolled up, a fly buzzed and beat against the tipi wall high overhead. Blood Arrow heard a distant wailing, a whining chorus to the fly's angry song. Had she slipped into a nightmare, or was her fever filling her ears with noise? The wailing song was Morning Star's. Her cries and moans made Blood Arrow tremble. Two Talks had been gone nine sleeps. This *was* a nightmare. She growled like a dog, growled loud like a grizzly bear and ran from the tipi of her husband. She ran toward the screeches and barks of her mother-in-law, ran past the turned away faces of Numunuu who would not look on her. Wahatewi, Wahatewi, she prayed.

It took forever to find Morning Star. It took no time at all. Blood Arrow's mother-in-law was down on her knees and elbows beating earth with her fists, moaning without pause, staring up at Frost, the mostly white mustang turned into a nightmare horse that bore the body of Blood Arrow's husband. Ghost-white except for the dark cloud of black on its head, the beast stood heaving, muscles trembling, legs splayed. Its white coat was streaked with dirt and dried rivulets of blood. Its black lips stretched wide in a frozen grimace—its big horse-teeth bared. From both its nostrils froth foamed, and bubbles floated like gray flower petals to the brown grass. The animal's chest and sides were lathered with sweat. No one had yet touched the rider.

Two Talks sat the horse, his arms locked around a spiky tumbleweed. His hands met in front of the tumbleweed, his fingers knotted together in the horse's bloodstained mane. Blood dried dark as his black warpaint had poured out of a wound in Two Talks' neck, a wound as wide as Blood Arrow's spread fingers. Flies hovered before the deep gash, and one landed on Two Talks' neck, crawled into the opening and disappeared. Her husband's head was thrown forward so his chin rested in the top of the tumbleweed. Blood painted a line as wide as a warrior's fingertip down his chest and through the tumbleweed, darkening the twisting, forking spines. Persimmon appeared in the nightmare and added her mewling to the keening song that filled the sky. At the base of the stiff tumbleweed, blood pooled in Two Talks' fingers and the long hair of the horse's mane he gripped. Blood Arrow pried free her husband's fingers and Two Talks fell sideways but would not entirely give up the horse. He could not let go until Blood Arrow sliced away spikes of tumbleweed and thick strands of horse mane fused by dried blood. Her husband's body was still warm. She put her ear to his chest and heard the distant and slow drumbeat of his heart.

"He lives yet," she said, and Morning Star and Persimmon stopped keening for the dead and helped her carry the barely living warrior into his tipi. The scar on Two Talks' neck had been rent and had spilled blood like a sewn bag would spill water. The blood had crusted and stopped, but began to seep when they moved him. Blood Arrow and Persimmon washed the wound and Morning Star sewed back the flaps of skin with a thorn needle and deer sinews. Two Talks' body burned and Blood Arrow sat with him through the afternoon and night keeping wet hides on his flesh.

Near dawn Two Talks opened his eyes, and she knew he recognized his wife.

She dripped buffalo meat broth on his lips, hoping to give him strength to fight the fever. She leaned close to kiss his cheek and felt his breath escape his lips.

"My shadow bore the knife." His words were as low as the murmur of a far-away river. "My *puha* was not strong. Crow tricked me with my own shadow." The wound at his neck oozed dark blood and the fever raged.

Morning Star sent for Ten Buffalo to bring the medicine bag. The *puhakut*, Ten Buffalo, sent everyone out of the tipi. From outside, Blood Arrow smelled the spice leaves the medicine man burned and heard his soft chants. He came out shaking his head.

"Your husband has not yet passed into the Good Hunting Land, but he won't come back to this land," Ten Buffalo said. "He rides somewhere between the two lands. I have used all the power in the medicine bag to persuade him to turn around and ride back, but not even the strong *puha* of the skunk has turned what-ever horse your husband now rides."

Ten Buffalo had done all he could. Word soon passed to every tipi. Two Talks had come back without the guns-that-speak-twice. He had lost eight ponies and many hides. His *puha* had failed to protect him or those who had ridden with him. Everyone in the band, the raiders especially, was dejected. Everyone stayed away from the tipi of Two Talks and slunk around the edges of the camp staring at the ground. Broken again was the dream of an invincible warrior with mighty *puha* who would lead them into a great battle against the *taivos* and Tehanos and drive the enemies of the People out of Comancheria forever.

Strong Medicine Gone Bad

Blood Arrow sat alone in the dust and buzzing flies that had found their way into the tipi. She stared down at the man she loved, dying before her eyes. In just a few sleeps, her husband had gone from being a figure of faith to being one of despair. The warriors who had believed the most strongly in Two Talks' magic were the most dispirited. No one appeared to take up weapons against the enemy. Men who had united under Two Talks' influence now bickered and split into different groups. Some talked about going on the reservation lands.

Two Talks never returned to the Antelope. In the middle of the night he made a Numunuu war cry, *yee-yee-yee*, and rode into the Land Beyond the Living.

Blood Arrow held her husband's body like a child's straw doll. A long moan came through her clenched teeth and grew louder and faster as she rocked back and forth. Spittle sprayed from her teeth, and her chin, slick with drool, slid back and forth against her husband's cheek. She stopped rocking only long enough to take up the knife and slash her arms, each red gash satisfying in some small way her great anger, hurting her hurt, striking back as hard as she knew how. Her wet chin was black with her husband's warpaint.

While Father Sun climbed high and then crept away down the blue sky, Blood Arrow still held her husband's body. She moaned and wailed and screamed until only husky breaths and barks croaked out of her throat. She slashed all down both arms and hacked the flesh of her thighs, drawing the blade against her skirt until blood oozed up through the buckskin. She pressed the blade down on the third finger of her left hand until she severed bone. She would keep this finger on which a *taivo* wedding ring might have declared she belonged to a *taivo* husband.

Other Numunuu walked wide of the tipi, respecting her need for grief. Only her mother-in-law, Morning Star, intruded, weeping and moaning, her body's shaking pulling her son's leg and moving his body up and down in Blood Arrow's embrace. She was aware of Morning Star in the way someone in the dark senses another nearby. When Mother Moon lighted the sky and came in through the smoke flap, the ground shone wet, and Blood Arrow vaguely felt the heat under her thighs of urine pooling from under her mother-in-law.

After two more sleeps, when Our Father in Heaven sent his vermillion- and ocher-painted scouts onto the horizon, Persimmon brought a pemmican bag and a clay pot full of warm wild onion soup. Blood Arrow felt Persimmon's hands. Her sister-in-law, who had always treated Blood Arrow badly, pulled her back from the body and guided her to her feet. Blood Arrow's legs tingled and buckled under her. Persimmon held her until she got steady. Then Persimmon unclasped her mother's hands from her brother's leg. The three women carried the warrior's body down to the stream. Crusted blood flaked like red ashes from the corpse and from the wounds Blood Arrow and her mother-in-law had inflicted upon themselves. Blood Arrow soaked strips of soft deerhide and bound up her mother-in-law's flesh.

Where Spirits Live

Blood Arrow sewed a beautiful buckskin breechclout for her husband to wear in the Land Beyond the Living. She did not touch the small beaded medicine pouch still tied tight around his thigh against the pouch of his testicles. Crooked Nose painted his son's face. Blood Arrow thought of Gideon for the first time in many moons—how he had prepared the bodies of the two Negroes the men on the wagon train had murdered for Indians. Gideon had smoothed over wounds to make the dead look not dead but asleep. The Numunuu would not understand such a counterfeit. They believed dead ones had to carry any mark or mutilation with them to the next life.

"Morning Star," Blood Arrow spoke to her mother-in-law, "in my old *taivo* life I was taught, if you believe in Jesus, your spirit goes to Heaven and you will get your body back when Jesus comes to His people again."

"If you are scalped your spirit dies. If you are strangled your spirit cannot escape, and it is trapped inside the corpse. If you die at night your spirit may get lost and not find its way to the Good Hunting Land beyond the setting sun," Morning Star said. "Life is happy always in the Land Beyond the Living. The winters are mild there, the buffalo plentiful. But you need your body to walk and ride, to eat and sleep, to couple with your wife when she comes there. If this He's Us is a good spirit who cares about His people, why would He keep their bodies from them? Why would He not let them enjoy the hunting path while He was gone away from them? *Taivo* 'Heaven' must be a sad place of waiting, a place of longing-to-hunt."

"The *taivo* say unless you believe in Jesus you go to Hell where you burn always but can never die," Blood Arrow said.

"Some of Our People believe there is a bad land where the Evil Spirit lives. I do not think so. I cannot see why He's Us would give bodies to the spirits of some of His people and send them to a land where the bodies He gave them would burn."

"Jesus is the son of the *taivos*' Great Spirit, 'God,' who punishes all of His bad children."

Her mother-in-law shook her head. "The Great Spirit made the thunder and the mountains and all the animals to protect Our People. The Great Spirit has many sons and daughters: the thunderbird spirit who makes weather, the eagle spirit who gives warriors strength, the wise wolf spirit, the buffalo spirit who feeds his people, the deer spirit who sends quickness, the healing bear spirit, the even stronger healing skunk spirit, the fierce bear spirit, the mischievous spirit of Coyote who is a brother to Our People, the malicious spirit Crow, and many more. These spirits live amongst Our People, but the Great Spirit lives far away—as distant as Father Sun and Mother Moon. They walk their own faraway paths and do not gaze often on Our People. If He's Us is a son of the Great Spirit, why does he never show himself to Our People? What good medicine can He's Us give to Our People?"

Blood Arrow tried to remember the words from sermons she had heard, but she could not bring them back. "I think Jesus is like the lizard who turns green when he walks in green grass, brown when he crawls up a brown tree trunk, yellow when he rests on a yellow leaf, white when he suns on a rock. He's there, but you have to look close to find Him, and usually He is where you least expect Him to be."

"When you find He's Us, does He then jump away like a flea?"

"I'm not sure I ever found Him. But they say if you find Him, He's with you always."

"If you find a stray dog he stays always," said Persimmon, who had been listening.

Blood Arrow took from a hide carrying bag the rolled-up picture of Jesus her husband had brought back from his vision quest journey many moons past. "Jesus is this one who looks like yet another identical self to my husband but with hair on His cheeks."

Morning Star nodded. "If what the *taivos* taught you is true, then maybe this He's Us put hair over His face to hide from Our People."

"If I have seen Jesus ever it has been in the face of my husband."

"It may be so," Blood Arrow's mother-in-law said. "In his time of good *puha* my son was guided by different spirits. I don't know why my son would have called on a *taivo* spirit, but it may be this He's Us, the hard-to-see spirit, was one of those who watched over my son."

A Name Spoken No More Forever

After Blood Arrow and her mother-in-law and sister-in-law had bathed Two Talks' corpse and scented it with spicewood leaves, after Crooked Nose bunched and tied the hair of the corpse and adorned it with his son's favorite ornaments, after he painted the face of his son's corpse, he put by his son's side his sharp knife, a warrior's lance, a strong bow, and a full quiver of arrows. Then they wrapped the body in a doeskin hide covering all but the face and buffalo-head headdress. They lay the body on the back of the mostly white war horse who had been washed in the river and painted with warpaint and decorated with mirrors and bright cloths and amulets carved of wood and bone. Because the dead warrior had lost his medicine many of the men who had ridden with him when he was strong stayed away from his burial. Crooked Nose carried his son's body to a steep crevice on the far side of the stream and wedged the body in and covered the opening with a boulder. Then, as the People had done in long-ago times, Crooked Nose and Blood Arrow and Morning Star knocked the horse to the ground and Crooked Nose cut the horse's throat and rubbed his black ear and between his eyes and sang to him until all life bled from him:

White horse, white horse,
overtake the wind, outrun the river,
go far from this land, far from here,
to the land where Father Sun sleeps.

White horse, white horse,
the spirit of our close friend
will ride you there,
will ride you there, white horse.

When the horse was dead, the buried warrior's father and mother and sister went from the burying place, all but the one who had been his wife. She stayed behind and tried to think of words to speak over the grave of her beloved. In her old life as a *taivo* one book of their Scriptures had been her favorite because it was a story about a woman who found her true love. Blood Arrow remembered the story Dorsey had read many times—how Ruth, a Moabite, had married one of two sons of Naomi, who had come to Moab from Bethlehem with her husband, who soon died. Then both of Naomi's sons died, and she told her daughters-in-law to return to their people. One daughter-in-law, Orpah, kissed Naomi and went back to her old life. But Ruth begged to remain with her mother-in-law, saying words Dorsey had memorized, words Blood Arrow spoke over the grave of her dead husband:

Entreat me not to leave thee, or to return from
following after thee: for whither thou goest,
I will go; and whither thou lodgest, I will lodge:
thy people shall be my people, and thy Gods my Gods:
Where thou diest, will I die, and there will I be buried—

And then Blood Arrow turned and followed her mother-in-law home. She and her mother-in-law would grieve publicly for weeks, but she knew her private grieving would never end. She looked back only once. Black buzzards slowly circled high, above where the dead horse lay.

A Blessing

Every morning now Blood Arrow woke sick in her stomach. Morning Star asked why her daughter-in-law no longer ate the meat the Buffalo spirit granted them. Blood Arrow asked for the leaves to chew to make your stomach rest. Morning Star looked Blood Arrow over slowly. "Has your time of bleeding come this moon?"

Blood Arrow couldn't recall. The time before her grieving seemed long ago.

Morning Star smiled. "Do not chew the leaves or take any herbs." She put her hand on Blood Arrow's stomach. "If the strong son of a once-great warrior grows in you he might not like the taste of stomach cures."

Blood Arrow's heart lifted. If there were a child there was a reason not to die.

After she knew for certain she carried the warrior's child, she visited her husband's grave. His spirit was gone on, but she wanted to speak her news where his body rested. Father Sun had risen just six times since the burial, yet the white horse had disappeared. Buzzards, coyotes, and other eaters of carrion had picked clean the bones left to bleach in the dry heat. Bloodstained dirt around the horse's skeleton showed claw prints, sharp-pointed shapes, side-by-side, that resembled most the beaks of two birds.

By the bones of her husband's war horse Blood Arrow stared at the totem she had painted onto her husband's arrows and that had given her the Numunuu name Puhipka, and she told the earth that a great warrior would soon be born to lead Our People on the war trail against the *taivos* and Tehanos, who were stealing all the hunting lands of the Numunuu.

When she left the grave of her husband and climbed down the hill to cross the river, two crows called from the limb of a cottonwood then flew away together on wings that made no sound. *I know what moves*, Blood Arrow thought, *in sky I love*.

Charles Wesley:
The Likeness of a Cow-boy

Staying in Texas
(April–September 1866)

Two cattle trails to Kansas passed near Alhambra, and I had occasion to observe several drives. Most drovers hire eight to ten cow-boys for twenty-five to thirty dollars a month to drive a couple thousand head of unruly Texas longhorns ten to twelve miles a day—when they're lucky—for two to three months through blistering sun and blowing rain, dust and mud, lightning and hail. They must get the longhorns across swollen rivers and around deep ravines. Cow-boys sleep on the ground mindful of deadly scorpions, venomous snakes, and marauding Indians. But the cow-boy's biggest fear is a stampeding herd trampling and goring everything in its path. At night, to keep the cattle calm, they serenade them with voices that mix Rebel war shout, Indian chant, and coyote howl. Here are the last lines of "The Cow-boy's Dream":

> They say there's to be a great round-up,
> When cow-boys, like dogies, must stand,
> To be marked by the Riders of Judgment
> Who are posted and know every brand.

—from *Gideon Jones' Journal*

Charles Wesley spent the winter in Alhambra. He had not heard from Mama and Papa, but he couldn't be sure his letter had reached them. He had no enthusiasm for returning to New York. Since the war he'd felt like he had no home to return to. Almost daily he visited with Mattie and Orten, who had gone back to using his own name. "First time in years I haven't been afraid to be who I am," Orten wrote on the paper by his chair. Charles Wesley enjoyed Mrs. Carter's piano playing, listening to Mr. Manchip's storytelling, and idling in his room with books borrowed from Mr. Manchip's library. Charles Wesley reread Malory's *Le Morte d'Arthur*, because he felt much like a knight-errant now the war was over. He read part of William Hickling Prescott's *The Conquest of Mexico*, which he disagreed with though he admired Prescott's style. He tried *Nature and the Supernatural* by Horace Bushnell, but the Congregational clergyman's views on the Trinity, which had caused a stir before the war, seemed to have little to do with life in Alhambra, Texas. He opened John Greenleaf Whittier's latest collection, *The Panorama and Other Poems*, to "The Barefoot Boy" and was disappointed. The details were colorful but overly familiar. He preferred Whittier's tougher abolitionist verse. He started *Tempest and Sunshine, or, Life in Kentucky*, the first of Mary Jane Holmes' popular novels, but Mrs. Holmes, whom Mama had liked, was too inspirational for him.

Saloon Surgery

When the minié ball in his leg throbbed, even the South Seas adventures of Melville's *Typee* could not distract him, and he limped over to the Alhambra Saloon to dull the ache with whisky. One night he hit a bottle of Squirrel so hard Mrs. Carter asked what was ailing him. She pressed until he told her about the shot still in his leg. An hour later he lay atop the Alhambra's bar surrounded by lamps turned so high their chimneys glowed. Owing to the intensity of his pain, owing even more to the amount of whisky he'd drunk, he had agreed to surgery for the removal of the ball. Mr. Manchip's large hands shone pink from a good scrubbing. Near Charles Wesley's head stood a nearly full bottle of Squirrel—to serve as both local antiseptic and general anesthesia—and several tools for the doctoring of cows and horses. While Charles Wesley squeezed Mrs. Carter's hand so hard he feared he might break her bones, Mr. Manchip cut open the leg and probed with some blacksmith's tool. Had Mrs. Carter's presence not stoked Charles Wesley's pride, he would surely have yelled like a banshee. The lamps floated above him and black spots danced in his eyes when Mrs. Carter said, as if he weren't there to hear, "Stop, Jon, he's going to bleed to death."

"I can feel the blasted thing with the tip of the poke, but it keeps rolling off."

"Well you're going to have to sew him up. His hand's gone cold as a blue norther."

"Straighten his leg then, so I can stitch proper."

From a distance, Charles Wesley heard metal clink against metal and then a soft drumroll.

"God bless the queen."

Baby James laughed and uttered singsong lallations.

"I don't believe it. You've got Merlin's magic or more luck than you deserve," Mrs. Carter said. Wind rattled the front door, and the lamps dimmed.

Charles Wesley woke with a throbbing leg, a throbbing head, and a mouth so dry he couldn't move his tongue. Mrs. Carter dabbed his mouth with a wet rag and shook her head. She rolled a black ball between her thumb and forefinger. "When I moved your leg for Jon to stitch you up the shot fell out." She dropped the metal ball into Charles Wesley's palm. "Just like that."

He suffered more from all the anesthesia he'd drunk than from the incision in his leg. In a few days he was up and about. "*Doctor* Manchip," Charles Wesley said, "what do you charge for such a successful surgery?"

"I'd gladly take all the market would bear, except your guardian angel gets the credit. The ball of shot jumped out on its own."

Charles Wesley wished he could poke and prod and get the war out of him like a ball of shot. The ball in his leg at least proved he had been in the war. Now that it was gone, he could not be sure. He knew Alexander was still in it, missing in action forever. Now, Charles Wesley needed a mirror to see his reflection. Every time he shaved he stared at what he had lost: his best side, Alexander's profile.

Charles Wesley believed life to be a balance book of gains and losses. That spring, after his leg healed up, he toted up one more gain that made him smile. Mary Thurston's pitiful apple sapling Mr. Manchip had planted out behind the saloon was full of new green leaves, and the Welshman pointed out the tiny buds he said would soon be white flowers. Though some would count it small gain, Charles Wesley measured it near a miracle that a little sapling that had suffered heat, lack of water, sandstorm, Indian attack, and fire could put down roots in such tough soil and grow and blossom and maybe yet bear fruit. He only wished Mary could see the blooms when they came.

Becoming a Cattleman

Most Saturdays a stage passed through with a copy of the Waco *Register* or the Austin *Daily State Journal* that was only a week old. Mr. Manchip and Charles Wesley fashioned a ritual around the newspaper that included bitters, full pipes,

and lively discussion. The paper usually carried stories about Comanche depre-
dations and listed the prices of beef. Sirloin steaks were selling in New York for
twenty-five to thirty-five cents a pound. Charles Wesley wondered if even Papa
could afford to pay prices so high. He asked Mr. Manchip if he knew anything
about the cattle business.

"There's fifteen to twenty cattlemen and their families forted up north of
us, between Fort Phantom Hill and Old Camp Cooper. They live in drop-log
houses—pickets mudded over—close together for protection against Indian
attack. The men serve frontier service—patrol the border and watch over their
cattle at the same time. Comanches steal them when they can."

"These cattlemen make a living?"

"During the war they just got by, hung on to their herds. But last fall a couple
of families drove a herd to New Mexico. I heard they made seventy-five dollars a
head profit."

"I'd like to go talk to those folks."

"Not a bad idea. With the war ended, I've considered cattle myself. It's not
safe to ride alone, but you could go with the next army patrol."

When Charles Wesley mentioned to Mattie and Orten he was going to visit the
Clear Fork country to see what he could learn about the cattle business, Orten scribbled on a sheet of paper a list of the ferrotype artist's equipment he wanted, including
a multiplying camera with at least four tubes, nine if he had sufficient funds, a plentiful supply of chemicals: collodion, nitric and sulphuric acids, ether, and alcohol. He
also bade Charles Wesley see whether he could secure spools of magnesium wire
to burn for flash lighting when the sun was dim. Ort clunked onto the bar a small
cotton ducking bag—by shape and sound the pouch held gold or silver coin—and
asked Charles Wesley to consign the order to a freighter in Weatherford.

Just twelve days later an army patrol arrived in Alhambra from Fort Phantom
Hill. When this patrol, under Lieutenant Franklin Bergon, headed southeast,
Charles Wesley rode with them. Lieutenant Bergon was from New Paltz and had
served in the Ninth New York Regiment in Virginia. He was a well-read man,
he knew and loved the West, and he proved a more than able guide for Charles
Wesley's journey.

For miles the country was barren, the expanse of coarse grass and sharp-
needled cacti broken only by sudden rocky arroyos or by silver-gray buttes that
rose suddenly and looked in the distance like ancient ruins abandoned by some
prehistoric civilization. Lieutenant Bergon was obviously an educated man, and
he had taken the trouble to learn what he could about the wild place he found
himself assigned to. With the patience and self-deprecating humor of a natural-

born teacher, the lieutenant instructed Charles Wesley about the landscape they rode through.

"This is the southern edge of the Llano Estacado," Lieutenant Bergon told Charles Wesley. "If you don't like it, keep riding and it will change, but not as fast as the weather."

Before sundown they crossed an old road and soon entered a valley thick with green grass. Grassland stretched for miles, and the hills all around were covered with mesquite, oaks, and pecans. The lieutenant had the patrol sergeant pick up the pace. Before full dark they crossed the Clear Fork to the east bank where Fort Davis rose in shadow.

Charles Wesley was well received in Fort Davis. Just two days earlier a wagon train gone for almost a month had returned with a supply of meal, salt, coffee, beans, wool, and, someone said, *whisky*. Everyone in the settlement was giddy with anticipation of what they called an "infare"—an all-night dance and feast to celebrate the wedding of a local cattleman to the daughter of another cattleman. There were beef and venison and wild turkey and quail and fish and buffalo tongue. Hats were passed and filled with coins for the fiddlers. Between dances Charles Wesley ate roasted pecans and heavy yellow cake. Over coffee laced with a bittersweet brandy he learned all he could about cattle drives—the profits were not as good as Mr. Manchip had heard, closer to fifty dollars a head than seventy-five. But if a man put together a big enough herd he wouldn't have to make many drives before he was wealthy. Charles Wesley speculated whether the Indian threat would be less if you drove your herd north to railheads in Kansas Territory for the Eastern market, rather than across the Llano Estacado, the heart of Comancheria, to New Mexico. There were plenty of sharpshooting Rebs out of work who could guard a herd. If he could get Papa involved he might put some pressure on Congress to send enough Federal troops out here to solve this Indian problem once and for all.

After a fortnight's stay he went with a wagon train from Fort Davis to Weatherford, where he placed an order with a freight company for Orten's tintype equipment, which the freight clerk said might have to come from up north.

By August Charles Wesley had talked with most of the cattlemen in and around Fort Davis, Picketsville, Old Camp Cooper, Owl's Head, and Lynch's Ranch. He learned you could buy cattle in the Clear Fork country for six to ten dollars a head, gold or silver—no specie. "Figure pack mules," a grizzled man named Uncle Garrett told Charles Wesley. "A thousand-dollars' silver weighs sixty-seven-and-a-half pounds. There's plenty of grassland. We just need more cattlemen in the war against the Indians." Charles Wesley asked if the Indians stole cattle. "No, they ain't rustlers. But they're death on horses. More than horses, they favor Texan scalps." Uncle Garrett seemed as wise as he was rough-edged. "Most Indian rustlers turn out to be white-redmen—depredators, outlaws who paint themselves up and wear feathers and wigs to veil their thievery. Don't trust appearances. The ones in charge are always villains. That's true of redskin armies or white and any kind of government."

Riding back to Alhambra Charles Wesley and a detachment of troopers traversed the Clear Fork country in hot summer sunshine. The grass was thick, and, beneath the low green mesquite trees, sunflowers in full bloom turned the long valley bright gold. Good rains back in the spring meant even small streams were still flowing.

Lizzie's Going Away Party

Near noon on a day in the middle of September Charles Wesley rode back into town. The blue shirts of the soldiers riding with him were black with sweat. Like a mirage his memory of the dim, cool interior of the saloon and a long biting smile of McBryan whisky danced in his vision. They passed the livery stable and the raw yellow planks of a new building shone in the bright sun. From each corner of the new roof rose a copper lightning rod, each rod sporting a small globe of blue glass and a wind-direction arrow with red isinglass feathers. The blue globes—Charles Wesley fancied them four small planets—cast circles of blue light on the ground, on the wall of the Alhambra Saloon, on Charles Wesley's dusty shirt front. The wind arrows were shifting in the gusty breeze, and each of them indicated a different direction. A freshly painted sign on the building announced:

ALHAMBRA MORTUARY
est. 1866

In the new building's already dusty window stood a skeleton, the skull adorned with a feather. A small sign was affixed between the first finger and thumb of the skeleton's right hand:

CHIEF BONES

OUR ADVISOR AND CONSULTANT

"Town's growing," said a corporal.

Almost as eager for news and gossip as for a drink, Charles Wesley trotted his tired mount to the Alhambra, but for the first time in his memory the saloon was closed—locked tight. He tapped on the door, then knocked hard calling out for Mr. Manchip, Mrs. Carter. No response.

Mrs. Carter's rooming house was unlocked, but no one was home. His room was as he had left it, except the tops of table and dresser shone where they'd been dusted. From the second-story window, he looked down on the street. The soldiers and their horses stood where he'd left them in front of the saloon, as still as a painting. The new funeral home and the livery looked deserted. But at the edge of town in the other direction a crowd of people stood outside the whores' tent. Had Lizzie found a new girl to take Mattie's place? Were the whores giving themselves away for free? Had some sudden influx of buffalo-hide hunters filled the tent?

He hurried downstairs, ran down the dirt street, walked up behind Mrs. Carter calling her name. She turned and squinted against the sun. Her lovely face was streaked with tears, her eyes red and swollen. "Oh, Charles, you're back." She smiled and embraced him, her hair brushing his ear, a floral scent—roses?—lifting off of her.

"What's happened?"

"It's Lizzie. She's dead I'm afraid."

"Whooof," a soft breathy explosion came from inside, and the end of the tent opened out like a double door. Mattie stood between the canvas flaps. In one arm she held baby James, and with the other arm she looped rope around the tent flaps. Orten aimed at the corpse a wooden box that looked like Mr. Gatling's multibarreled machine gun. Charles Wesley counted nine barrels sticking out of the box. Ort's multiplying camera had arrived.

Sun through canvas made a deep yellow light inside, and the warm canvas gave off a yeasty smell like starch under an iron. Lizzie lay on her cot decked out in gaudy finery. She wore a shiny plum-colored dress with pink and lacy collar and cuffs. Her mousey brown hair had been combed and fluffed, then, mercifully, mostly hidden beneath a wide-brimmed pink velvet hat topped with overlarge strawberries that sprouted long multicolored feathers—plumage to make an Indian war chief proud. Lizzie's wide cheeks were red with rouge, her small mouth made larger with lip paint. A maroon velvet ribbon was partly hidden by a circular fold of fat where a small cameo brooch held it fastened around the woman's pale neck.

Ort struck a match and lighted what looked like a fuse on a tin tray he held aloft. The magnesium wire he had asked Charles Wesley to order momentarily lighted up the tent like a hundred oil lanterns. Soon Orten was unscrewing, dusting, folding up, and packing away his photographic gear. On the empty cot opposite Lizzie a scholarly-looking man in spectacles was also packing, filling a box—a kind of suitcase—with some of the necessities of his trade: cosmetics, brushes, emery boards, a long narrow-bladed knife, a steel file, spools of twine and wire. Mrs. Carter introduced Charles Wesley to the town's new mortician. "Gideon, you've done wonderfully. She looks just asleep."

Long Pizzle had found Lizzie at dawn. Taking her a cup of coffee he had sunk down at the foot of her cot. "Gal ole up wake," he'd said to her, setting down the hot coffee. She hadn't been snoring, so he'd known she wasn't sleeping. Her bare shoulder was as cold as a north wind.

Mr. Manchip invited all the mourners to take a break from the midday sun, have a smile of whisky on the house before forming the funeral procession from Lizzie's tent to the cemetery. Even inside the Alhambra Saloon the heat pressed down.

"No sign of foul play," Mr. Manchip said, pouring whisky all around. The soldiers lined the bar silently out of respect for the dead woman. "Looks as though her heart just gave up."

Before Charles Wesley had finished his first glass of whisky a tingling warmth moved from his mouth into his chest, then he felt it in his arms and legs, the amber liquor working its magic, unloosing him from all the miles of his travels. Mrs. Carter appeared with pitchers of milk and platters of venison steak, wild turkey, biscuits and jellies, and preserved peaches. Before they returned to the tent to bear Lizzie to her grave, Charles Wesley had to unfasten a few buttons and move back his belt a notch. He had barely known Lizzie. They had nothing in common but geography—the small space this saloon, the rooming house, livery, and whores' tent shared. Geography and proximity—the afternoons he'd passed near enough to the tent to nod and speak to Lizzie, who was usually just rising after doing her nocturnal chores with buffalo-hide hunters, soldiers, freighters, or drummers off the main roads. Maybe proximity was all anyone shared. In the wilderness, on the frontier, acknowledging and greeting one another might pass for friendship, if not love. So he grieved for the whore as for a friend. At least she had passed peacefully, and she would have been proud of the turnout. The whole army patrol followed her pine coffin to the graveyard beside the buffalo hunters' bone camp, and, long into the night, more than one toast was lifted in Lizzie's name by soldiers who had known her well.

Rest in Peace, Alexander

Four days after the funeral Charles Wesley walked to the new Alhambra Mortuary carrying the hide case containing Alexander's lost arm. A teamster's wagon was docked at the new building, and Charles Wesley joined Mr. Manchip and Mrs. Carter, who were watching a Negro unload half a dozen gravestones. Directing the placement of the markers in the side yard of the establishment was the mortician, Gideon Jones, who introduced Charles Wesley to the Negro freighter.

"Meet Knobby Cotton, who once journeyed into a Comanche camp and ransomed back his wife and son." Mr. Cotton's black face shone with sweat, and his hair hung down in ringlets like the mane of a dark lion. "Knobby's working for Nigger Britt Johnson's freight company out of Weatherford, but he's a first-rate cow-handler, and one day he'll have a ranch of his own."

The Negro shook Charles Wesley's hand and headed to the saloon for a well-deserved drink. Gideon Jones invited Charles Wesley inside the new mortuary. In the front room, a small white stone with a carved lamb lying across its smooth top sat beside a horsehair chair. On the floor, beside several different-sized chisels lay a huge half-eaten wedge of yellow cake being attacked by a raiding party of flies. A row of pine coffins exactly like the one Lizzie had been buried in leaned vertically against the back wall. Gideon Jones perched on the edge of a wooden stool and offered Charles Wesley the horsehair chair layered with the fine white dust of chiseled stone.

"You've a store brimful of coffins and markers for a town this small." Charles Wesley smiled to show he was being facetious. But the undertaker nodded seriously.

"My inventory may appear overlarge," Gideon Jones said. "But many travelers pass this way, and there's the military presence nearby. With the war over, the cattle trade will expand. Drovers will camp near the springs and frequent our saloon. My stones are imperishable. I have nowhere else to roam."

Charles Wesley drew the stiff, shriveled arm from the deerskin case, and Gideon Jones leaned close. He was interested in what methods had been used to keep the arm preserved. He admitted to being more engaged by the mortician's artistry than by the cabinetmaker's craft, but he was confident he could fashion a sound casket for the arm. Charles Wesley selected one of the newly delivered stones, a simple slate with an arched top. He neatly printed: ALEXANDER WESLEY SPEER and added Alexander's years of birth and death to be chiseled. From the mortician's printed list of suggested epitaphs, Charles Wesley selected number 51:

Soldier from the night of sorrow
You awake to the light of morrow.

A Wedding and Departure

Late September the Alhambra Saloon was festive with ribbon down the length of the bar and a bow resting beneath a circle of wax candles on Mrs. Carter's piano. Before noon a Methodist preacher rode in from Waco by way of Weatherford. Orten had written the new governor, Throckmorton, begging his assistance in locating an ordained clergyman of any denomination who could come to Alhambra to officiate at the wedding of a fellow clergyman and, in this case, a Texian hero who had survived Comanche attack and mutilation.

The Reverend Duncan Hunter was seventy years old but had the energy of a man half his age. He drove into town in time for breakfast and unloaded from the back of his wagon an overstuffed leather chair. Wherever Reverend Hunter went in Alhambra he had the chair toted, and only in that chair would he sit. Charles Wesley pictured the white-headed, quick-witted minister waving from his chair as from a throne borne about town like a foreign potentate on the shoulders of four strong bearers. When he recited Orten and Mattie's marriage vows and then pronounced them husband and wife, his rich baritone rang out in the Alhambra Saloon like the voice of God Himself. After the ceremony the visiting preacher surprised everyone by taking a glass of whisky for his rheumatism and asking Mrs. Carter to play dancing music.

"It is a known fact," Reverend Hunter said, "brown bears dance in the wild. If our Lord gave wild bears rhythm I don't see why men and women can't at least do a modest jig." The preacher scooped up baby James and circled the floor gently swinging him in tune to Mrs. Carter's merry piano. The whole happy celebration was preserved on sheet iron by the groom himself. Mrs. Carter stood several of the little tintypes against the back of the bar so that in the days to come anyone who wanted could gaze into the face of the bride and relive the happy event.

A Durable Portrait

A couple of months after the wedding Knobby Cotton brought a shipment of spirits to Mr. Manchip, along with salt, coffee and sugar, and mercantile goods. The drummer who'd received the order had asked Knobby to deliver to Mr. Manchip a pair of tooled leather chaps decorated with conchos made of nickel—chaps so fancy no cow-handler would enter the chaparral wearing them. The enterprising drummer also sent a pair of button spurs with rowels as big around as coffee cups and a wide-brimmed snow-white hat with a gilt cord around its high crown and a chin strap with an ivory slide and gilt tassel. The hat was too small for Mr. Manchip, who bade Charles Wesley give it a try. The hat rode Charles Wesley's head so perfectly Mr. Manchip gave it to him along with the chaps and the spurs.

Orten offered to make a likeness of Charles Wesley in the cow-handler's outfit. Charles Wesley purchased from Mr. Manchip's new stock a linsey-woolsey shirt and a pair of leather pants. The spurs were too big to fit the heels of the boots Charles Wesley had bought in New Orleans so, for the tintype pose, he wore boots Gideon had taken from a cow-handler's corpse as payment for services rendered. High-heeled, they were of red-dyed leather, full shinbone length, with crescent moons tooled on the tops. Charles Wesley reverently unpacked the Harper's Ferry Dragoon pistol his papa had given him, the mate to one Alexander had, rest his soul. He would hold up the dragoon pistol as if he were a shootist, an assassin for hire. Mrs. Carter contributed a gold brooch to complete the costume. The shape of a star, it made a sheriff's badge pinned to Charles Wesley's shirt.

Behind his camera Orten got carried away and had Charles Wesley lie down atop the bar with his head on a saddle. Before Ort inserted the glass plate, Mattie knotted around Charles Wesley's neck a red silk kerchief. When Orten lighted his magnesium wire the saloon flared so bright Charles Wesley was momentarily back on Slaughter Mountain, Virginia, where he had seen the elephant. Just before Charles Wesley's likeness made its impression on the light-sensitive plate, Mrs. Carter lifted the scarf over his mouth. Thus the tintype presented him as both a lawman bearing a sheriff's star and an outlaw wearing a highwayman's mask.

Whether with early daguerreotypes or with tintypes or paper photographs, the photographic artist preserved, possibly redeemed, his subjects. On the shelf behind the bar, beside an angelic-looking Lizzie recumbent on her deathbed and several frozen faces from Mattie and Ort's wedding, the portrayal of Charles Wesley reclined on the bar might also have been taken as a death cast except for the luminosity the magnesium had sparked in his eyes. The keen-eyed lawman or outlaw in fancy chaps and shining spurs was given a variety of handles—New York Charley, Yankee Charley, Charley Sharpshooter, Deadeye Charles, Killer Wes. As often as not Charles Wesley leaned against the bar during public viewings of his portrait, but strangers never recognized him.

Had anyone asked, Charles Wesley Speer could not have said what brought him from New York City, having shed the uniform of a Union soldier, to recline on a plank bar built over Texas soil wearing the habiliments of a hero, a costume fashioned from disparate dreams: hat and spurs the gifts of a Welshman, an old-world badge from Vienna, the silk mask of a used-to-be sporting gal, the cartridge belt and scabbard and six-shooter of a runaway slave, and high boots off of a cow-handler buried in his socks. Custom-made, the boots might outlast this wearer, too. They might last long enough to ride over Texas for years yet to come.

Epilogue

Ghosts of the Plains

The Tale and the Journey End Together

News of Two Talks' death in the spring of 1866 raced over the plains like a grass-fire, incinerating the recurring Indian dream of a great war party that would strike a fatal blow to the whites—a dream that flared again when Coyote Droppings preached he was a prophet with strong enough *puha* to exterminate the whites. His medicine failed, too, when he and close to a thousand warriors—Comanches, Kiowas, Kiowa-Apaches, Cheyennes, and Arapahos—were stopped by a handful of hide hunters with long-range Sharps rifles at the old Bent's Trading Post at Adobe Walls on the morning of June 27, 1874. After the Indians' defeat at Adobe Walls only the Antelope band of the Comanches continued to resist the whites.

Led by Quanah Parker—the half-breed son of Nocona and of the *taivo* set-tler Cynthia Ann Parker, who had been captured at Parker's Fort in 1836—the Antelopes, with whom Dorsey remained, vanished far up the Llano Estacado. Heavy rains in the winter of 1874 washed away their tracks. Full moons that spring were blood-red Comanche moons, as Quanah and the Antelopes tried for the last time to defeat the Tehanos and Norteamericanos. Quanah was Comanche for "Sweet Odor," but the Tehanos and Norteamericanos he fought did not think there was anything sweet about the warrior. Years later, his former enemies would brag that Quanah Parker was such a courageous and wily fighter because he was part Texan. He and his Antelope band did not surrender easily, but by now there was more cavalry than buffalo on the plains. The Antelope war chief had only two choices for his people—fight the United States Army to the death, or give up the wild range of Comancheria and submit to the white man's road. Finally, in June of 1875, Quanah gathered all the Comanches he could find and took them with him onto the reservation.

As soon as Gideon Jones heard the last of the Comanches had surrendered, the mortician and journalist journeyed to the reservation at Fort Sill in Oklahoma

Territory in hopes of seeing Dorsey again. It was a trip of some hundred and fifty miles and took Gideon over a week by wagon. And for what? When Gideon asked to see her, Blood Arrow gave the Indian agent (who acted as Gideon's intermediary) a blackened finger and said she had no words for the white man. Gideon put on his spectacles and brought the finger close. The mortician's art, in Gideon's view, absolved of grotesqueness any part of the human body. Dorsey's finger that he had once thought would wear his ring and that she herself had hacked off grieving her husband's death, was precious to behold, though it filled Gideon with a funereal sense of loss.

Before he left the reservation to return to Alhambra, Gideon bribed an army corporal to take him to a commissary storage room from where he might espy his one true love. The soldier and Gideon watched through dust-dimmed panes, their boots grinding cornmeal on the plank floor when one or the other of them shifted his weight. Crossing the fenced reservation yard Comanches looked smaller, less bright-shining than they had out on the sun-drenched high plains where long, bunched hair and feather decorations danced on shifting winds.

A Comanche boy, maybe eight or nine, passed the commissary window, leading by the hand a woman who wore a plain hide dress with no adornments. A decade had passed since Gideon had first seen Dorsey Murphy Speer on the wagon seat and fallen forever in love with the girl from Indiana. She was still young, but she had the stooped gait of the aged or defeated. Her gaze, however, was fierce and unbroken. Gideon gripped his fingers into fists.

"That's her," the corporal said. "And her half-breed kid with her."

Scars striped the woman's arms, and her hair was cropped short. She appeared a Comanche woman, but beneath the disguise Dorsey abided yet, just as a living visage will linger beneath the mask of death. Gideon had restored the look of life to many a face after the veil of change had cast itself over familiar features. Where freckles had once been sprinkled cinnamon, Dorsey's skin was now creased and browned by a decade of wind and sun. The Comanche boy said something and grinned, swatting playfully at Dorsey, this Comanche woman clearly the boy's mother. He looked about the right age to be Two Talks' son. Gideon had the curious sense he was related to the boy, and he felt strangely proprietary towards him, as if he were Gideon's stepson. When the Comanche woman gazed on the boy her face filled with light, and momentarily, Gideon glimpsed a grinning girl on a settler's wagon seat with the sun and the wide Western sky in her eyes. The Comanche boy feinted and, laughing, ran ahead, then slowed so his mother could catch him. Arm in arm they walked on.

The glass pane was cold against Gideon's cheek. Feed smells and dust burned his nose. The corporal beside him stirred, but Gideon's feet were nailed to the floor. Dorsey and her son grew small. Just before they disappeared, Gideon turned away. He could not bear to watch them out of sight.

Writer and mortician alike craft illusion. Gideon Jones spent his life trying to preserve the resemblances of characters who had walked the same landscape and who had greeted him and one another over time. As journalist and as undertaker Gideon had had the same mission: the preservation of life-likeness, a memorable image of the past presented to the present, the composition of something true out of gestures that seemed random.

For over three decades Gideon Jones was the only mortician in Alhambra. Before he relinquished his earthly life he watched the calendar turn from 1899 to 1900. By that new millennium the cloud of witnesses that had surrounded him had drifted away.

Samuel Speer never saw his twin sons after they went off to fight on opposite sides of the great conflagration. On a sunny morning in April not long after President Johnson was sworn in to complete Lincoln's term, the elder Mr. Speer had left his house to visit his downtown office. Stroking his beard where it had gone gray at both corners of his mouth, lost in a reverie of Alexander and Charles Wesley galloping together over the Texas plains, Samuel stepped into the path of a horse-drawn streetcar and was killed instantly.

Scant months after Samuel's appointment with the streetcar, Mary Speer died in her sleep. In the parlor of the brick house in Murray Hill, she lay in repose in a mahogany casket lined with Chinese silk-satin. Her minister was struck by the wry smile fixed on her face. The undertaker, taking his artistry more seriously than he should have, claimed the credit. But Mary's final earthly smile was a gift given by Samuel, who had, at the moment of her passing, met her in the ether and confessed he had always (covertly) liked Mr. Lincoln, and, as she had long suspected, Samuel admitted he had voted for the president twice. Samuel said he'd be pleased to introduce his beloved wife to Honest Abe, whom, Mary just then realized, her tall dark-bearded Samuel favored.

In January of 1871 below Flat Top Mountain, Knobby Cotton and three other carters driving with the Negro Britt Johnson, were ambushed by Kiowa raiders who scalped all five men. Knobby alone escaped with his life. His scarred head and missing hair earned him his final sobriquet, "Skinned Alive." For a time frontier businessmen would trust their goods with no other freighter. "Ole Skinned Alive will get your goods through come Hell or high water." Out on the Llano Estacado high water was not likely, but Hell seemed a probable risk. After a few more years most of the tribes had been forced onto the reservation, and Knobby Cotton gave up freighting and moved to a ranch he'd bought on Lost Creek near the town of Jacksboro. He soon became much respected for the fine quarterhorses he raised and sold.

Orten Trainer and Mattie adopted the infant, baby James, and left Alhambra for Waco, where a flock of Baptists needed a shepherd. Gideon often wondered what those Baptists, used to hellfire from the pulpit, thought when God sent them a mute who spoke through the soft and lilting voice of an angel who used to be a soiled dove. When Orten and Mattie left Alhambra, the little fice rode the wagon seat standing up, its merry little tail pointed skyward like the lightning rods atop each end of the Alhambra Saloon. Charles Wesley knew Mrs. Carter hated to see Orten and Mattie go, but the one she was really going to miss was the cur dog.

One soul Preacher Orten saved was that of Mary Thurston, brought to Orten's church in Waco by an outfit of Texas Rangers who had dispatched a couple of buffalo skinners turned horse thieves. One of the Rangers wrote his mother (who sang in Orten's church every Sunday) about the white woman they found kept almost a slave by the men they later hanged. *Bring that lost lamb home*, the Ranger's mama wrote back. Mary Thurston's mind would probably never be quite right, but in the hands of kindly ladies in Ort's fold she was well cared for and safe from predators. Orten wrote that Mary didn't seem to recognize her husband's dog, but the little fice remembered her and the mongrel kept her company many an afternoon. Mary lived a good while under Orten's protective wing and died sweet-smelling between clean sheets in a room built just for her attached to the church she swept and dusted every day for the remaining years of her life.

Charles Wesley Speer and Mr. Manchip formed a successful cattle partnership and annually drove herds of longhorns north. Barbed wire, touted for being "light as air, stronger than whisky, and cheap as dirt," arrived in Texas in 1875. By the early 1880's fence-cutting wars raged between cattle outfits. Fenced-in herds led to controlled breeding and the demand for longhorns fell off. When Charles Wesley was killed in 1883 in a stampede outside of Caldwell, Kansas, Mr. Manchip sold his cattle holdings and retired to Alhambra. By then the reservation had been broken up. With an allotment of a hundred sixty acres set aside for each Comanche, most of the high plains was opened to white settlers.

Mr. Manchip and Mrs. Carter never married but remained close until the Welshman passed in his sleep on Christmas Eve 1887. His will provided for drinks on the house and everyone in Alhambra turned out for his funeral. Mrs. Carter left town under escort of the next army patrol. Weeks later Gideon received a note from her written on a program from the San Francisco Opera House. He never heard from her again, but every time Gideon rode alone onto the Llano Estacado Mrs. Carter's music gusted through the grama grass.

Shortly before his death, Gideon Jones left his mortuary in Alhambra and drove a wagon far out onto the Staked Plain listening for war cries and watching for the dust cloud of a Comanche war party, but the Indians were all dead, or struggling to be dirt farmers, or lost in the euphoric visions of peyote or the fog of too much whisky. Yet they haunted Comancheria, the land they had ruled with blood.

Gideon crossed and recrossed his own path, so confusing the trail he left not even a Comanche could have tracked him. Wind tugged his hair, lifted his shirt collar, and whispered the songs of ghosts. Clouds scattered across the sky were remembered faces: Colonel Luellen Powell-Hughes, Win Shu, Phineas Atkins, the two Negro freedmen he had buried on the prairie, Hiram and Mary Thurston, Suella, Knobby Cotton and Elizabeth, Portis "Eye" Goar, Pretty, the Indian warrior Two Talks, Charles Wesley, Mr. Manchip, Mrs. Carter, and, of course, Dorsey. Always Dorsey. The only woman he had ever loved and most of those who had traversed the Texas frontier with him had disappeared. He had buried many of them himself. Witnesses who had surrounded him were gone away or gone to dust, blown over the plains on the constant wind.

There on the high and endless-seeming Llano Estacado, Gideon pulled up and set the brake. Ghost-haunted, he opened his tattered final volume of the *Encyclopaedia Americana* and read: **VISIONS**, *Ghosts, phantoms, apparitions, spectres, spirits — the vocabulary of superstition is rich in terms — or, in philosophical language, spectral illusions.* Wind rippled the page.

He tore from his shirt the pocket covering his heart and wrapped in the cloth Dorsey's petrified finger he had kept for years in a small iron safe in his bedroom above the undertaking and coffin shop. With a spade from his wagonbed, he dug a small but deep grave and nestled the finger down in the dry dirt of the plains. Instead of mumbling over the mounded earth words out of a Bible, Gideon read one last excerpt from the *Americana* in his lap: *The illusions of the superstitious consist of demons or angels, and all sorts of fantastic shapes, benign or malignant.*

The sights seen bear a strict relation to the character of the seer, and of the superstitions of the age and country in which he lived.

Memories of uncivilized years and frontier places swirled like dust devils on the wide plain. Gideon let the heavy volume fall open in his hands. The wind riffled page after page of knowledge and meanings outdated or forgotten. Words fluttered and rattled like small, dark birds he was releasing into the wide sky, signals he was sending from a faraway time.

—The End—

Acknowledgments

I am grateful to the Texas Institute of Letters and the University of Texas for a Dobie-Paisano Fellowship and to the University of Tennessee for a semester's research leave. Steve Chastain generously helped me with computer file conversions. Keith Gregory and George Ann Ratchford at SMU Press have been wonderful, and I cannot imagine a better editor than Kathryn Lang, whose wisdom and insight have saved me more than once. Finally, I thank family members and friends who supported and inspirited me during the long while I took to research, write, and revise this novel. —Allen Wier

Tehano is a work of the imagination, but a list of sources I consulted to learn more about the time and the place runs several pages. Among those I relied on most are Frederick Law Olmstead's *A Journey through Texas*, David Dary's *Cowboy Culture*, Carl Coke Rister's *Fort Griffin*, E. C. Abbott's *We Pointed Them North*, numerous slave narratives published by the WPA writers' project, Wallace and Hoebel's *The Comanches Lords of the South Plains*, T. R. Fehrenbach's *Comanches*, and Thomas Kavanagh's *The Comanches: A History 1706–1875*. Kavanagh provided additional help with the Comanche language, supplementing Manuel Garcia Rejon's *Comanche Vocabulary*, translated and edited by Daniel J. Gelo, and *Comanche Dictionary and Grammar*, by Lila Wistrand Robinson and James Armagost. In Chris Segura's *Marshland Brace* I found Acadian names and expressions and the plants and animals of South Louisiana. Edward Henry Durrell's *New Orleans as I Found It* (published in 1835 under the pseudonym H. Didimus) describes the city at that time. I first encountered the Gnostic Valentinus' claim that Jesus "ate and drank but did not defecate" in Milan Kundera's *The Unbearable Lightness of Being*. In the University of Texas' Eugene C. Barker Texas History Center, I read Civil War letters, soldiers' papers, settlers' diaries, immigrant memoirs, and various other records of early Texas life.

Acknowledgments

Excerpts of this novel have been aired by, or published in, the following: National Public Radio's *The Sound of Fiction, A Pocketful of Prose: Contemporary Fiction, The Wedding Cake in the Middle of the Road, Black Warrior Review, New Millennium Writings, Texas Review, Idaho Review, The Southerner* (online), *The Distillery, The Vanderbilt Review, Metro Pulse, Five Points, Appalachian Life, Literary Lunch, Yalobusha Review,* and *The Cry of an Occasion.*

ALLEN WIER has published three other novels, *Blanco*, *Departing as Air*, and *A Place for Outlaws*, and a story collection, *Things About to Disappear*. A former Guggenheim, NEA, and Dobie-Paisano Fellow, Wier has had fiction, essays, and reviews appear in such venues as *Southern Review*, *Georgia Review*, *Shenandoah*, and *The New York Times*. A Texas native, Wier currently teaches writing at the University of Tennessee in Knoxville.